D1554855

Jim Morrison's Adventures in the Afterlife

Jim Morrison's Adventures in the Afterlife

A Novel

MICK FARREN

ST. MARTIN'S PRESS ⋈ New York

FIC
FARREN
M

Design by Jane Adele Regina

Farren, Mick.
    Jim Morrison's adventures in the afterlife : a novel / Mick Farren. —
1st ed.
        p. cm.
    ISBN 0-312-20654-2
    1. Morrison, Jim, 1943–1971 Fiction.   2. McPherson, Aimee Semple,
1890–1944 Fiction.   3. Holliday, John Henry, 1851–1887 Fiction.
I. Title.
PS3556.A7727J56   1999
813'.54—dc21   99-33279
                                                                      CIP

First Edition: November 1999

10 9 8 7 6 5 4 3 2 1

This book and its completion is dedicated to Felix Dennis,
Captain of the Hispaniola, who, more than once,
sailed to the rescue in the nick of time.

The only completely consistent people are the dead.

—ALDOUS HUXLEY

Jim Morrison's Adventures in the Afterlife

1

Say what you like, folks always make a big deal over death.

Aimee McPherson stood on the terrace and stared balefully across the landscape of Heaven. For perhaps the two millionth time since her death, her rage at the manner in which God had betrayed her boiled to one of its cyclical peaks. How dare He, if indeed He existed at all, treat her with such unconscionable treachery? She had done so much on His behalf. She had avoided temptations, bypassed indulgences, forgone the pleasures of the flesh. She had sacrificed to the maximum in His name and, from her perspective, He had cynically betrayed her. Her entire life had hinged on a single belief in which she had placed absolute trust. He had promised a Heaven when she died. That He then so totally reneged on the deal transcended the criminal and took the burden of guilt to a new level of divine iniquity. Aimee McPherson had arrived in the Afterlife only to discover that, if she wanted a Heaven, she was expected to build it herself. God Himself had failed to put in even the most cursory manifestation, and she had begun to doubt that He actually existed at all.

If there was a God, He appeared to believe that this psychic erector set would be ample reward for a lifetime of love and devotion, of prayer, praise, and supplication. He had presented her with a blank celestial slate and left her to make it up for herself. After all the promises, the only Heaven she had received or perceived had come directly out of her own imagination, without help, without encouragement, without even the benefit of an instruction manual.

Aimee McPherson stood on the terrace and stared balefully across the landscape of Heaven and knew that it was entirely her own creation. This should have pleased her, if for no other reason than that of pride in accomplishment. Pride in accomplishment, however, counted for little beside abandonment by God. This Heaven had been torn, at a great cost of emotion and energy, piece by piece and construct by construct, from the deepest soul core of her imagination, and the effort of its manufacture had not been easy. Back on Earth, from the moment that she had devoted herself to God and His works, she'd had little call to use her imagination, and now she found it a weakened and atrophied thing. Creating Heaven from the ground up had been a struggle and chore, imposed on her at exactly the time she was expecting only relief. Heaven should have been ready and waiting for her when she arrived, spick-and-span, fluffed and folded, like some metaphysical five-star hotel with Saint Peter to greet her at the reception desk, angelic bellhops to assist her, a deputation of long-deceased pets waiting for her with soulful eyes and wagging tails, and a metaphoric complimentary mint on the pillow.

Even coming up with an overall design concept had been no easy thing. At first she had leaned heavily on what she remembered of the work of the artist Maxfield Parrish, coupled with no slight touch of Disney's *Fantasia*. This early borrowing, and her admittedly flawed memory, tended to account for the overly vibrant cartoon colors, the wine-dark indigo of the water in the lake, the dazzling ultramarine of the cloudless sky, the deep somber green of the cypresses and Scotch pines on the headland on the far side of the water. The heliotrope of the ice-cream mountains in the far distance and the velvet unreality of the immaculate daisy-flecked grass that ran down to the water's edge, drawn directly from the Disney school, was, if anything, less plausible. She had to admit that the way the outcropping of raw, gold-veined marble tended to resemble some strange, overripe, processed cheese food was actually her own fault. She seemed to be incapable of producing authentic-looking minerals, much in the way that some people can't draw hands. The Maxfield Parrish memory also accounted for the presence of the small neoclassic temple over on the promontory that projected into the lake some two hundred yards from where she was standing. Parrish had inspired the half dozen diaphanously clad virgins who danced, hand in hand, perky and unflagging sprites, endlessly circling in a dance with basic choreography in the interpretive tradition of Isadora Duncan. Disney, on the other hand, had provided the fawns, bunnies, and happy little bluebirds that cavorted in the air above, whistling and cheeping the melodies of saccharine pop ballads of the thirties, forties, and fifties, as Aimee stood on the terrace regarding her Creation.

As though sensing, if not her actual thoughts, certainly her general mood, a lone bluebird darted to within eighteen inches of her face and hung hovering, smiling blandly and whistling disjointed snatches of "Over the Rainbow." Suddenly furious, Aimee snarled and swatted at the bird. "Get away from me, you inane figment! Get the hell away from me!"

The bird deftly dodged her slapping hand, but then only retreated some six inches and continued to hover. It started to whistle the chorus from "Swinging on a Star." This time she swung at the bluebird with a clenched and unexpectedly accurate fist. The blow connected, taking the bluebird completely by surprise. It staggered back, cartoon-style on empty air, with small stars, suns, and planets circling its head. Aimee allowed herself a grim smile. "That'll teach you to screw around with me, you flying rodent."

The bluebird shook itself in midair, shedding three feathers that drifted lazily down to the terrace. The bird looked at her reproachfully and then zigzagged away to join its companions. Aimee glared after it. "I ought to erase the whole bunch of you and start all over again."

In moments of self-doubt, anxiety, and depression, Aimee would castigate herself for concocting a Heaven that resembled nothing more than a very bad animated painting on black velvet, set to a soundtrack of *Snow White and the Seven Dwarfs* blended with New Age elevator music. In the depths of this emotional trough, she found it all too easy to believe that even her own creations, the bluebird included, were turning against her and secretly laughing at her presumptuous ambition. Fortunately, after she discovered that both Prozac and Valium could be conjured out of the air merely by thinking about them, she was able to ensure that the frequency of such moods was strictly limited, and she began to find both the construction of Heaven and the contemplation of the finished product a great deal less stressful.

For a time, she had half believed that God might come to her, like some crowning glory or ceremonial prize, when Heaven was finally completed to both His and her satisfaction. This belief had finally wilted and died, however, when God failed to put in His much-anticipated appearance. After no manifest rainbow, no pillar of fire, not so much as a lousy dove, her attitude had changed and her resolution hardened. If God was going to forsake her so casually, she, doing as she had been done by, would likewise forsake Him. She would continue to extend her Heaven, and it would be open to all who came. It would be exactly what every Christian soul needed and expected after the trauma of death and its immediate aftermath, right down to the very last golden sunbeam, faithful collie, and cascading waterfall. The only difference was that she would provide the godhead herself. She would make herself the focus of the cumulative praise and adoration; she would be the happy recipient of the lauding and magnifying. She knew that it might take a certain degree of adjustment, particularly on the part of the males, before they could accept her as the legitimate deity. On the other side of the coin, she would have the instant loyalty of all those feminists who maintained that God was a woman. She was aware that there might be a number of unwavering fundamentalists who, even in death, would refuse to accept a fait accompli as to the legitimacy of her divinity. For them, of course, there was always Golgotha and the Pit.

In life, the idea of beating God at His own game would have been the ultimate blasphemy. Here in the Afterlife, it felt more as though she and God were on a level footing, and the concept of blasphemy demanded a noticeable inequality between blasphemer and blasphemed. Blasphemy was a mortal sin, after all, and she was no longer mortal. Of course, should God finally notice and take exception to her efforts, she would be glad to fall down and worship Him. If He chose to cast her to the fire or otherwise chastise her for her presumption, so be it. At least she would have His attention.

At first her plans had not been too grandiose. Heaven would be a modest, fairly exclusive place, a Club Paradise, with just room enough for her and a few million faithful who might choose to follow and dwell with her. Unfortunately, Aimee McPherson, possessed of that megalomaniac drive and absolute certainty of ambition that is almost unique to evangelical preachers, found it difficult to retain a modest attitude toward anything for very long. As a concept, her Paradise grew and grew until she knew the only logical conclusion was to engage in a Holy Mission, perhaps an actual Crusade, to forcibly reconfigure the entire Plane of the Afterlife to her image of Heaven. Only then would the newly dead know for certain that the biblical promises and predictions were true, that

4

covenants had been kept, even if she was filling in for the absentee Almighty. Unfortunately, her powers of creation were unable to match the scope of the concept. For a while, she and Semple had still been a part of the same single entity; warring factions, perhaps, but at least united under quasi-flesh. They had managed to work together. Aimee had done the expansion; Semple had filled in the details. Increasingly, though, Semple had used the construction of Heaven as a vent for her perverse sensuality, her willful pride, and her invert's delight in the sick and abominable. Aimee's Heaven became littered with small pockets of the irrational and the warped, many too disgusting even to cite in passing, and the split between the two of them had shown itself as manifestly inevitable.

In the end, the conflicted sisters, Aimee and Semple, had faced reality and divided, by a unique binary fission of their own inventing that made them two instead of one. Aimee had compensated for the loss of what amounted to half of her personality by becoming even more obsessive about the transformation of her personal Paradise into what she increasingly thought of as the Omniheaven. Without the Omniheaven, she was nothing but another previous human living in a world concocted from delusions and fantasy gratifications. If she couldn't bend others to her perspective, she was no different from the fool who pretended he was Moses and staged quasi-Cinemascope, biblical spectacles so he could spend eternity righteously smiting sinners of his own creating, forever and ever, world without end, amen. Although Aimee didn't care to admit it, even to herself, the removal of her sister from the original and essentially schizoid personality had taken with it many of the previous checks and constraints. Aimee discovered that her manic enthusiasms and headlong obsessions tended to run faster since Semple's departure, always more reckless and always at full flood. Likewise the depressions tended to mire her even more deeply. In divorce from her apparently dangerous dark half, Aimee had herself become darker and more dangerous.

Once split, the sisters had maintained little contact, although they were constantly aware one of the other, and were capable of a frightening empathy. Semple kept mostly to herself, indulging in her dubious amusements and pastimes in the environment that she had created since the one had become two. Aimee had never visited the place, but she had the impression that it was a replication of Semple's idea of Hell. In many respects, this fit serendipitously well with Aimee's master plan. Her Heaven, counterbalanced by her sister's equal and opposite Hell; a positively Newtonian theology. This didn't mean, on the other hand, that she had any plans to visit the place.

Separation also didn't keep Semple from deliberately devising ways to irritate her from afar. At all-too-regular intervals, her sister would play some minor prank, causing a black and sinister helicopter to clatter across Aimee's azure sky, disturbing the fleecy clouds with its violent prop wash, or sending a flock of malicious and predatory birds to set le in the cypress trees and stare at her with bleak, beady, Alfred Hitchcock eyes until they abruptly left and flapped away to the other side of the sunset. Semple also had a habit of removing the odd cherub or angel for her own nasty amusement. Although Aimee could hardly approve, these abductions were of little importance. Angels could always be replaced.

At that moment, however, Aimee had more pressing matters on her mind than Semple and her games. The master plan was hardly coming to fast fruition, and Aimee had to admit that she lacked the imagination required to conjure a suitably infinite Celestial Vault. What she needed was a helper. A Michelangelo who would labor in her Sistine Chapel. What she needed was a visionary whom she could bend to her will and inculcate with her vision, and who would help her make Heaven the place that it really ought to be. For a while she had considered making overtures to the phony Moses; the size and elaboration of some of his spectacles certainly bespoke a measure of power and directorial talent. They also indicated, if by nothing other than their bizarre repetition, that the Moses guy was barking crazy. Despite, in theory, having all eternity in which to work on it, Aimee knew she would never bend him to her will. His insanity was too inflexible. What she really needed was an artist, a painter or a poet, one who was fresh from death or otherwise clean-slated, without preconceptions and totally vulnerable to suggestion and manipulation.

As with so many of her recent trains of thought, the railroad eventually led back to Semple. Aimee knew she would need Semple in on this capture of a creative hireling. The artist would have to be located. He would have to be kept ignorant and off balance, and then be brought to her quickly before he could develop any inclinations or preferences of his own. Aimee knew she wasn't the half with the capacity to accomplish this. It was Semple who had the necessary cunning and seductive charm. It was Semple who would have to find and snare the poet or painter for her, and persuading her sister to accept the assignment would not be easy, unless Aimee could somehow appeal to her innate perversity.

As Aimee turned away from her less-than-satisfactory landscape and walked back along the terrace, an uninvited vision wandered aimlessly into her mind. A young man, wild dark curls, a sensual pout, and thumbs in the conchoed belt of a pair of narcissistically tight leather pants strolled idly down a dusty road, roughing the dirt with the heels of his worn engineer boots, dragging on a cigarette. He clearly had no place in Aimee's design and she consigned a thunderbolt to the vision, garbaging it before it could grow or develop. The young man staggered, stunned, and left her mind. The obvious first reaction was to blame Semple, and Aimee would certainly quiz her on the intrusion, but she knew instinctively that the apparition of the strange young man was something other than one of Semple's annoyances. She also hoped he wasn't a portent of future problems.

Jim Morrison shook his head, trying to clear it. Had he been mauled? Mindfucked? Struck by lightning? Large parts of his consciousness were wastelands of fractured shards, data retrieval had become history. Sometime, someplace, someone had royally flamed his memory, though he couldn't recall where or when. He had a flash of sun, dust, and a back road, idly dreaming of an ice-cold beer, but it was such a brief sparkling fragment it could provide not even a pointer to the thread of a real story. So it went with most of his mind. All he knew about himself was that he had once been a poet and that, at least for the time being, he would be forced to live absolutely in a highly specialized moment where even the mundane appeared strange and unexplored, and reality checks could only come via the benevolence of the passing crowd.

One of the few things about which Jim Morrison was certain was that his true death had not occurred on that dusty back road. All thoughts of his true death conjured fragmented but repeated impressions of lukewarm water, a womblike tub, and the city of Paris. Beyond that, all he could retrieve was a useless combination of details, motor skills, and unrelated images. One major problem was that, for

the time being, his own name was one of the things that determinedly eluded him. He could read and write, he could remember
the names of songs and the titles of books. He knew enough to put
his pants on one leg at a time and zip the fly when he was done. The
rest was a destructed jigsaw of fear, rage, and unhappiness, both his
own and others'. A woman ran with her hair on fire, smoke drifting
across a bleak concrete freeway lined with withered palms and
choked with frightened cars, while a threatening red sun on the
hazy horizon struggled to shine through that same smoke. Blind
horses drowned in slate-gray ocean and Indians died on the sands of
a sterile desert.

He sincerely hoped the apparent garbaging of his memory was
purely temporary. Painful as it might prove, it was his and he wanted
it back. He was fairly optimistic that it would one day return. Something, possibly a perceived familiarity with advanced and multiple
intoxication, told him that his life on Earth had been replete with
blackouts and memory lapses, and suggested that this could well be a
cosmic version of the same condition. If it was, he had only himself
to blame. One of his most profound desires, when he had found
himself discorporated at such an unexpectedly early age, was that he
could somehow avoid the thereafter being merely a rerun of the
same drugged, drunk, chaotic shambles. As far as he could tell, and
to his eternal shame, his resolve wasn't holding up too well.

The immediate concrete fact before Jim was that he had suddenly
found himself at a party, and he knew enough to realize that it was
no ordinary party. Jim had no clear idea of how or why he had arrived there, but it was plain that this Cecil B. DeMille production of
howling, dancing, undulating vice was full of others who had rendered themselves as mindless as he was. He could see the unmistakable vacancy in the eyes of a high percentage of the revelers. They,
too, had sacrificed mind and memory to the specific moment; for
them, it was a moment of vibrance and abandon, a gratifying instant
of tongues and hair, sweat and flesh, lips and liquidity. All set
against the backdrop of a towering, slowly erupting volcano that
spewed majestic flows of bright, sulfurous, hellfire lava and sent
them slithering and easing their way sinuously down the upper
slopes in ponderous slow motion. All around him, faces gleamed
with flame reflections of red-orange heat, and demon-black shadows
crouched among the crush of groaning, howling participants.

The thousand or more human beings who made up this plunging

mass, plus the hundred or so other entities who couldn't quite be classified, were crowded into a natural amphitheater at the base of the mountain. The set for this epic surrender to hedonism and sexual abandon was a flat-bottomed basin surrounded on three sides by high black basalt walls that looked to have been carved out of prehistory by some vast, violent geological scoop. Within its confines, men and women, intoxicated to the borderline of psychosis, clawed and pawed at each other's greased, painted, and perfumed bodies. Some lay sprawled in spread-eagled abandon on the now damp and stained cushions that had been strewn across the floor of polished stone, while others groped, staggered, and stumbled, bent on staying on their feet come what might. Such clothing as had been worn back when the festivities had started was, for the most part, long since shredded or ripped away, and, along with it, any sense of individual identity, even on the most minimal level. The crowd had all but merged into a single, moving, but apparently unthinking, entity. This lust-driven composite was a constant flux of wave motions that, at regular intervals, would erupt into screaming pockets of mass hysteria or moaning cluster orgasm.

On a rock ledge above the seething crowd, Ethiopian drummers, their shining, oiled forms festooned with gold jewelry inlaid with turquoise and ivory, and their faces hidden by the fall of their dripping dreadlocks, pounded furiously on the hard hide heads of leopardskin-draped kettledrums, rhythmically urging the already furious crowd to even greater frenzy. The drummers seemed all but oblivious to the women and men who crouched at their feet, seemingly worshiping what they saw as the driving force of the orgiastic confusion. Intrusive, urgent hands stroked the players' legs and shamelessly cupped their genitals and buttocks, but the ritual drummers missed not so much as an inflection or accent. Even when bold, eager tongues licked the very sweat from them, the beat went on, relentlessly maintained, unwavering and unchallengeable.

On a second ledge, immediately below the drummers, relays of young men and women, all but naked in sheer drapes of near-transparent Hunan silk, poured dark, aromatic, psychedelic wine from a seeming endless supply of stone jars into the upheld goblets and even directly into the open mouths of the *Mad* magazine mass that milled below them. The hair of these serving youths was garlanded with twines of white flowers and some wore luxurious orchids behind their ears. Every one of these exquisite servants swayed in time

9

to the throb of the drums as they slaked the mob's obvious thirst, and they broke frequently from their appointed tasks to allow themselves to be kissed and fondled by absolute strangers and even carried down, unresisting, into the squirming carnality. When these dalliances interrupted the wineflow, celebrants would climb up and help themselves. Entire jars would be passed down and borne away, their contents slopping and staining what remained of the surrounding crowd's disarrayed clothing, and adding to the profusion of fluids that drenched and lubricated the desperate celebration.

The Golden Calf itself squatted balefully at the center of the entire sensual maelstrom, presiding over the sinuous chaos. Over fifteen feet high from its cloven hooves to the tips of its branching Texas horns, and constructed entirely from beaten gold and crusted with precious gems, it provided the ultimate focus and singular provocation of all that happened around it. Ultimately pagan in its sculptured ferocity, the tall idol's nostrils flared, and the huge rubies that formed its eyes glared down with implacable bovine contempt at those who prostrated or disported themselves before it. The Golden Calf had been festooned with more white flowers, splashed with wine, and columns of smoke rose on either side of its massive head from braziers of burning incense, all but creating the impression that the beast was breathing fire. Two women, bodies bare from the waist down, straddled the wet ridge of its metallic spine, rocking their hips backward and forward, riding the towering effigy with eyes closed, faces ecstatic, locking in lewd oblivion. The idol even came with its own sacrificial maiden, who hung in chains suspended from its mighty horns and, in the tatters of her blue silk ball gown, bore an uncanny resemblance to Debra Paget in the Vista Vision, wide-screen version of *The Ten Commandments*, although in the movie Debra Paget had not been used with such repeated depravity by such a representative cross section of the massed celebrants. In historical and mortal fact, that kind of thing had been the prerogative of Howard Hughes.

That Jim had no idea of how exactly he had come to be under this particular volcano at the time in question had, after repeated draughts of the purple wine, pretty much ceased to bother him, in part because, as the crowd swayed around him, he was hallucinating to the point of near-blindness. At one point the effects of the wine had prompted the vaguest of recollections of being in the middle of a pitched battle in a high mountain pass between the Dionysians and the Apollonians. The Apollonians had come in with automatic weapons and air support, while the Dionysians had only coup sticks and ghost shirts. Needless to say, he had been on the side of the Dionysians in this unequal conflict, and his memory may have been the price that he paid for his ill-advised participation.

About the only thing of which he was sure was that he hadn't created the orgy himself. His recall might be down, but he still knew his own personality, and he was confident that his tastes, although certainly of a Bacchanalian bent, didn't run to such old-Hollywood, pornographic grandiosity. When he found himself at the base of the Golden Calf, caressing the exceptionally full and well-formed breasts of a naked and nameless young woman who resembled a very young Mamie Van Doren, he knew it was the work of some mysterious other. If he had been in control, he would never have allowed himself to be dragged from off her so early in the encounter.

Initially the young woman had been energetically eager, and in the mere space of their first minute together she had entirely ripped away his white linen shirt. Jim hadn't been too concerned about the shirt, and when the woman had started unbuckling the belt of his ancient leather jeans, he had been quite prepared to swim with the prevailing sensual tide. The only thing that bothered him was that, when she spoke, he found himself unable to understand a word she was saying. At first he was alarmed that he had been deprived of language as well as memory. This theory hardly seemed to fly, though; he not only thought in English, but when he attempted to say anything, he formed English words and sentences despite the drunkenness of his condition.

The woman's speech also seemed to lack the form and natural repetition of language; it was little more than a sequence of unstructured grunts and glottal cries. Jim's next assumption was that she had consumed so much of the psychedelic wine that she was actually talking in tongues, but then he noticed that a similar glossolalia was being mouthed and uttered by most of those around him. Could it be that whoever had fashioned this lavish and ultimately impressive event, and possibly even brought Jim there from wherever he'd been, had problems with giving speech to his creations? Either that or he wanted to keep his celebrants in mindless noncommunication in his lush pit of Babel. It was while Jim pondered this question that he discovered that he who ponders can also lose. Two men, a bull-dyke lesbian, and a creature who could easily have been a Sasquatch

11

had picked up the Van Doren replicant by her arms and legs and physically removed her, while the surrounding crowd brayed with laughter. Jim considered the action neither friendly nor sexually ethical, but he was too loaded to make an issue of it.

After that, he had wandered aimlessly through the chaos of the orgy, shirtless in his jeans and scuffed engineer boots, finding himself repeatedly splashed with wine and fondled by total strangers of both sexes and none. This licentious buffeting soon grew tiresome, and he looked around for some detached vantage point where he could observe the epic debauch without any compulsion to become part of the action. He noticed a hollow niche some twelve feet up on the rock wall, opposite the ledges occupied by the Ethiopian drummers and the youths serving the wine. A usable if rudimentary path led up to the niche and it seemed to be exactly the kind of spot to which he could happily withdraw. The only snag was another individual already had the same idea. A fully clothed man was sitting there, knees drawn up, shoulders against the rock face, and a wide-brimmed black hat pulled down so it concealed his face. He was the only fully clothed, not to say elaborately dressed, character in sight, which, in context, made him appear singularly perverse.

As Morrison observed the man who had beat him to the sanctuary, his rival pulled a silver one-pint flask from his coat and took a long drink. He then returned the flask to his pocket and almost immediately fell into a spasm of uncontrolled coughing. He struggled to extract a white lace handkerchief from another pocket and bring it to his mouth. When he finally withdrew the uncharacteristically dainty piece of linen, Jim could see, even from a distance, that it was stained with fresh red blood.

The man looked strangely familiar to Jim, although he was of course unable to put a name to him or locate him in any context. That someone in the Afterlife should be suffering from what appeared to be not only a terminal earthly disease but one that was classically Victorian was remarkable enough, and the man's style was certainly in profound contrast to any of the other guests at the orgy. Where the rest were primitive or Old Testament, he was clearly a son of the nineteenth century. The cut of his black velvet frock coat and ornamental brocade vest could only be described as rakish, and the same applied to the long, old-fashioned cavalry boots that extended well above his knees. His soft floppy hat was turned down at one side in a decidedly dandified manner, and in Morrison's estimation he had struck an almost-balance between western gunfighter and dissolute pre-Raphaelite aesthete. Jim wasn't quite sure how he recognized these origins, but he was relieved to find that at least his cultural reference bank hadn't completely gone off line.

While he was entertaining these thoughts, Jim also found himself being pawed at by a naked and grossly obese hermaphrodite who not only talked in tongues but did so with a repulsively sibilant lisp and a spray of drool. Jim quickly decided that enough was enough. He ducked away from the creature's damply eager clutches and unappetizing, fish-belly flesh and began to negotiate the series of hand- and footholds that led up to the niche now occupied by the familiar stranger in the frock coat and soft hat. The hollow in the rock was large enough to accommodate three or four grown men; the worst the stranger could do, Jim reasoned, was scream at him to go away. As he approached the man, Jim called out, extending what he saw as a minimal social courtesy even if it wouldn't be understood.

"Do you mind if I join you up there?"

The frock-coated stranger pushed back his hat, revealing a sickly pallid face with a dark drooping mustache, hard blue eyes, and the expression of one who is easily irritated. To Jim's surprise, he answered not only in English but in a deceptively indolent drawl that might have had its origins in the old, and largely fictional, antebellum south. "May I assume that you're looking for some peace and quiet and not some kind of homosexual liaison?"

Jim halted halfway between orgy and niche. Despite the lazy speech, the stranger's overall demeanor was quite enough to warn him that this was not a character with whom to trifle. "I'm definitely looking for some peace and quiet."

The stranger shrugged. "Then come ahead, young man. Come right ahead."

As Jim reached the hollow in the rock, the stranger looked at him questioningly. "You seem, sir, not to be remembering me?"

Jim instantly adopted an improvised approximation of the stranger's fanciful speech patterns. "I fear, sir, I have no memory at all."

The man's eyes narrowed dangerously. "Considering the nature

13

of our last encounter, I'm surprised that you would have forgotten it in such a hurry."

Jim was quick to explain. "I mean I have no memory of anything. I appear to have materialized here with no recall beyond a sorry and confused blur."

The man seemed content with the explanation, at least for the present. "That's unfortunate."

Jim sat down, allowing a civilized distance of almost two paces between them. The man seemed to accept this as a mark of well-mannered respect. "At least you and I are not the wanton creations of whoever started this thing."

"What makes you say that?"

"If you and I were mere fantasy figments, we would not be up here, playing the part of nonparticipant watchers. We'd be down there, wallowing with the rest of the recently invented swine. To mangle Descartes a little, we observe, therefore we are."

This statement was so far from anything that Jim might have expected that he was temporarily at a loss for a response. The stranger, for his part, seemed to have nothing to add, and the two of them sat quiet for a time while the bacchanal continued to howl and throb below them. Finally, Jim could contain his curiosity no longer regarding the familiar stranger's identity. "I fear, sir, you have the advantage of me."

This time the stranger didn't bother to raise the brim of his hat. "You think so?"

"I do indeed. You would appear to know who I am, while I have no recollection of either your name or where we might have met. In fact, I'd be more than happy if you could tell me who I am. My own identity also appears to have escaped me somewhere in the mysterious transit that brought me here."

The man chuckled and then coughed as a result of the unguarded laugh. "Are you saying that you want me to introduce you to yourself?"

"I suppose I am."

"That's some singular request, my friend."

"But one that I need to make."

The familiar stranger paused for a very long time, toying with Jim, perhaps, or pondering the ethics of reuniting an individual with his mislaid identity. Below them the orgy showed no signs of abating. The Debra Paget look-alike chained to the golden calf was now being forced to pull a train for a gang of burly Cro-Magnons with thick red hair all over their bodies. Finally the stranger made up his mind. "In that case, my friend, your name is Morrison . . . James Morrison."

"James Morrison?"

"James Douglas Morrison, commonly known as Jim."

"You're telling me that I'm Jim Morrison?"

"That's what you were calling yourself last time I saw you."

"You're putting me on."

"Indeed I am not."

"*The* Jim Morrison?"

"So you said. You claimed you were the Lizard King, whatever that might mean. You went on to boast that you could do anything."

"I suppose I was drunk."

"As a skunk. Indeed, a good deal drunker than you would appear to be right now."

Jim nodded slowly and thoughtfully. This took some digesting. "No shit."

"As I recall, you were inordinately proud that you had made something of a nuisance of yourself for a short while in the twentieth century."

Jim was beginning to get the distinct impression that the stranger was making fun of both him and his disability. "I'm beginning to remember."

In fact, a whole block of memory had abruptly tumbled back into place, memories of crowds and lights, fame and fortune and a myriad of women, of hashish and heroin and massive quantities of alcohol. Of flash and flamboyance offset by monstrous hungover depression and a constant dicing with the death that had ultimately become inevitable.

The familiar stranger took another pull on his flask. He also coughed again, but only a couple of times and without the previous painful violence. "Of course, you may not really be Morrison."

Jim frowned. "What do you mean?"

"You know how it is."

"No, I don't."

The stranger pushed back his hat. "That's right. I was forgetting. You don't have a memory."

"I'm getting some memory back and it's all Morrison."

15

"Well, it would be, wouldn't it?"

"It would?"

"We all indulge our fantasies, my friend. We strive for seamlessness."

Jim was now totally confused. "We do?"

"It rather goes with the territory. In fact, it quickly becomes all the territory we've got."

"I don't understand."

"Of course you don't. You lost your memory on the way to the orgy. You don't remember the death trauma. You may have left it in the cab."

"Left it in the cab?"

"A figure of speech."

"Oh."

"You really don't remember, do you?"

"I'm afraid I don't."

"And you certainly don't remember the next stage, hanging cursed and discorporate, one of the million tiny, anonymous pods in the Great Double Helix."

Jim shook his head. "Are you kidding me?"

The stranger scowled. "Why should I do that?"

Jim shrugged. "I don't know."

The stranger turned his head and looked directly at Jim for the first time. His eyes had changed from merely hard to downright dangerous. "You wouldn't be about to suggest that I'm a damned liar, would you, sir? You wouldn't think of suggesting some slanderous thing like that?"

Jim half-smiled. "Oh no. I've done some dumb shit, but nothing that dumb."

The stranger nodded. "I'm glad to see that at least your animal cunning and instincts for self-preservation haven't deserted you."

For a while neither man spoke. The stranger tapped his right foot gently in time to the relentless drumming. Finally Jim decided that he should prompt the stranger to go on with his story. "You were saying . . . "

The tapping foot stopped. "I was saying what?"

"I was a discorporate pod hanging in the Great Double Helix."

The stranger nodded. "Indeed you were. We all are directly after death. And some of us like it so much we pay repeated visits, just to start again."

"So then what happened?"

"You began to find that you had the capacity to make this stage of the Afterlife practically anything you wanted it to be."

"I did?"

"Damn right you did. The pods dream."

"The pods dream?" The drumming or the wine sloshing in his stomach, or maybe the ongoing confusion, was starting to give Jim a headache.

"The pods dream and find that their dreams might become their reality. The pods think and thoughts become things. A few, the really unadaptable, go the disembodied route, hanging around waiting for a séance to happen or spooking out and haunting some of their lifeside mortal hangouts. Those of a more Hindu mind-set take the Canal and get busy reincarnating themselves as kings or cockroaches, entirely according to their level of earthly self-esteem."

"And the rest of us?"

The stranger unscrewed the cap on his flask. "The rest of us? Indeed, Jim Morrison, what of the rest of us? The rest of us create an environment out of our previous realities and fantasies."

"You mean that, after death, there are people who take on the identities of the famous and notorious?"

"Why the hell not? Maybe on Earth you were some sorry, no-class, turd-shoveling creature of insignificance, but you don't want to go damned from here to eternity like that. Oh dear me, no. What happens is, after a couple of incalculable timeless aeons hanging in the Helix, you realize that you can be Alexander the Great or Catherine de Médicis or the Old Whore of Babylon if you so wish. And so you wish and, presto, that's exactly what you become. That's what you are until maybe you think better of it and transcend."

Jim frowned. "But surely you must retain some turd-shoveling memories?"

"Believe me, friend, they fade like a dream with morning in this wonderful new postmortem reality." The stranger suddenly grinned. "Hell, I'm not even sure that I'm really who I claim to be."

"And who might that be?"

Again the stranger turned and stared at Jim. "My name, sir, is John Henry Holliday, although many people call me Doc."

He slowly extended a thin, rather feminine hand. Jim grasped it, noting that it was as cold as that of corpse, which, of course, technically it was. "So you're Doc Holliday."

"Indeed I am. To the best of my knowledge and belief."

"I'm proud to meet you."

"And so you should be, boy."

"I used to watch movies about you."

"They liked me in Hollywood. I was the perfect foil for the insufferable Wyatt Earp."

Jim eased in a question before Doc Holliday could embark on a tangent of recollection. "There is one thing I don't understand."

"And what might that be?"

"I didn't create you out of my fantasy. I'm certain I didn't create any of this."

"Of course you didn't."

"So what am I doing here?"

"That's a good question."

"Is there an answer?"

Doc took a pull on his flask. "Even in death, no man is an island."

Doc Holliday seemingly took a delight in elliptical conversations, and Jim figured that, for the moment, the best policy was just to wait out his loops. Eventually he would come across with something approaching an explanation.

"The first thing you learn when you start building an existence here in the Afterlife is that a billion other sons of bitches are doing exactly the same thing. In my father's house there are many mansions. Unfortunately, they all have walls as thin as a cold-water walk-up, interconnecting doors and unending corridors. You start colliding, overlapping, banging into each other, and setting up a general interlocking confusion."

Jim framed his next words cautiously. Now he knew that the stranger was, at the very least, an analog of Doc Holliday, his survival instincts still told him it was probably unwise to piss him off, real or not. "That doesn't quite tell me how I got here."

"I can tell you why I'm here."

Jim figured that this was better than nothing. "So why are you here?"

"The truth is I was already here."

"You were?"

Doc gestured airily to the eruption behind them. "I was up on the volcano disposing of a power ring that had turned out to be singularly destructive. It's the only way to get rid of those damn things. You bring them to life and after a while you find they're not only taking on a life of their own but also taking over yours. You have to burn them up in either an active volcano or the breath of a dragon. I imagine that, in your case, you were probably wished here by whoever's throwing this al fresco wingding."

"Me?"

"You may not know it, but you've got something of a rep around the hereafter."

Jim groaned. It seemed that history had been repeating itself. "And my memory got scrambled in the process?"

"You got it. Unless you've been hitting the absinthe or ingesting alien fungoids."

"I'm afraid I'm still confused."

Doc chuckled. "You'll be even more confused when you find out about the other problems."

"Other problems?"

"Like how the bit players in the fantasy also take on a life of their own."

"Would you care to explain that?"

"I'm not sure there's going to be time right now." Doc gestured to a point above them, a rocky promontory higher on the slopes of the volcano. "I fear Moses is come upon us to smite the fornicators."

Jim turned and looked where Doc was pointing. A tall bearded figure, angular and bony in a tattered and dirty woolen robe, and with a mass of gray hair that hung well past his shoulders, was standing on the rocks, glaring down at the orgy around the Golden Calf with the disapproving stare of patriarchal wrath. Jim glanced at Doc. "That's really Moses?"

Doc shook his head. "I very much doubt it. Just some turd-shoveler putting on the style. In point of fact, Moses was bicameral and he couldn't make a move without his right brain telling his left brain that it was the Voice of God. He probably transcended millennia ago, and now he's sitting on what he fondly believes is the right hand of Jehovah."

Jim saw that the Moses figure was actually carrying a pair of stone tablets like miniature headstones. "He seems to have the Ten Commandments with him."

"Of course he does. They go with the costume."

"So what does this turd-shoveler want?"

"Like I said, he's most likely here to smite the fornicators."

"Can he do that?"

"Sure, that's probably the reason he set up this rat-shit drunk, buck-naked hoedown in the first place. Nothing these Bible-thumping retards like better than smiting a mess of sinners in flagrante. Doubtless that's why you were dragged here at the unfortunate cost of your memory."

"Moses set this thing up?"

Doc was getting to his feet. "Sure he did. A pristine piece of ego tripping. His mission is to punish sinners, so he has to create a few sinners to punish. He also buses in outside talent like you to give the proceeding a measure of heft."

Some of the celebrants below had broken off from their fun and games and were staring up at the figure on the mountain with its stone tablets. The drums faltered and stopped together. Jim also scrambled to his feet. "Are you saying we're going to get smitten?"

Doc pushed back his coat, revealing a nickel-plated Colt .45-caliber automatic with a mother-of-pearl handle inlaid with a gold lightning flash. "Not if I can help it."

As Doc spoke, the Moses figure braced his legs, drew himself up to his full height, and raised the stone tablets above his head. His voice, monstrously amplified and heavy with unnatural and highly electronic reverb, roared out and echoed around the mountains, "I SAY TO YOU, OH ISRAEL, YOU HAVE CORRUPTED YOURSELVES!"

The impact of the sound was like a thunderclap, and, even inured as he was from his days on Earth to super-amplified noises, Jim flinched momentarily. The roar of Moses was certainly enough to bring the orgy to an abrupt stop. Drunks halted in their tracks and copulating couples froze in midthrust. Individual revelers broke away from each other, retreating for supposed protection in the shadow of the Golden Calf.

Moses advanced down the mountain, bearing the tablets of stone above his head. "YOU HAVE ERECTED A GRAVEN IMAGE AND MADE YOURSELVES AN ABOMINATION IN THE EYES OF GOD."

Jim glanced at Doc. "I don't even believe in God."

Doc smiled grimly. "I don't recall that ever giving one moment's pause to any Bible-thumper."

"THOSE WHO REFUSE TO LIVE BY THE LAW MUST THEN DIE BY IT!"

Threateningly bright and powerful streams of plasma energy undulated from the stone tablets and circled Moses, ducking and weaving but growing in strength. One suddenly darted out, swooped down into the amphitheater, and struck the Golden Calf, burning off one of its horns, and a large chunk of the idol's golden head. It also totally vaporized the Debra Paget look-alike. This seemed scarcely fair or just to Jim. Bound and restrained as she had been, she was about the only one at the party whose participation in the depravity hadn't been obviously willing. He could only assume that prophets and patriarchs still operated on the principle of guilt by association. If you're there, you're guilty, and damn the extenuating circumstances.

Doc growled angrily in his throat as a second plasma stream struck the Calf on its haunches, vaporized a dozen or more sinners in a single dazzling explosion, and scattered a fine rain of molten gold over the terrified crowd. Now the guests at the orgy were scurrying in every direction, looking for any way out or any available cover but finding none. A third plasma bolt struck home and the amphitheater began to resemble a battlefield more than a party.

"I think it's time I did something about this." And so saying, Doc Holliday drew the Colt automatic from under his coat and pointed it at Moses.

Jim looked at him as though he were crazy. "Surely you can't kill anyone in the Afterlife? I mean, we're all already dead."

Doc grinned unpleasantly. "I can still fuck him up some. This piece was made for Elvis and the bullets are gold. It should have some effect." He gestured with the gun in the direction of Moses. "Depending on that son of a bitch's belief structure, a gold bullet going through him could trigger a bunch of possible responses. The Elvis connection should also make its contribution."

"You've really got that thing loaded with gold bullets?"

The look in Doc's eyes was starting to verge on insanity. "To be strictly accurate, the shell casings are only gold-plated, but the slugs themselves are pure twenty-four-karat. Soft-metal hollow points, guaranteed to make one hell of a mess of both bone and tissue. Now shut the fuck up, I need to concentrate."

Steadying his right hand with his left, fingers extended in a way that was almost delicate, Doc took slow and careful aim at the figure of Moses. More plasma crashed down on the sinners in the amphitheater, but Doc didn't duck or flinch. His focus was such that he seemed unaware of anything but his target. This being might not be the genuine and original Doc Holliday, but he certainly had a cold killer's calculated detachment down pat and Jim had to admire him for that. When it came, the report of the pistol was unnaturally loud with an artificial echo similar to the intensified Moses voice. Doc allowed the recoil of the weapon to carry it up to a two-handed, high port with the gun beside his head. His gaze, however, was still locked on Moses. The simulated patriarch reeled backward for three faltering paces. His spine arched unnaturally, as though cringing somehow to accommodate the impact of the gold .45 slug, but almost immediately he appeared to recover. His body straightened, and it was clear, even from a distance, that his sinews were stiffening with righteous fury.

Moses slowly turned, as though searching for the heretic behind this blasphemous assault. "WHO DARES TO SMITE THE PROPHET OF THE LORD THY GOD?"

A silence so profound that it could have come directly from the gulf between galaxies fell over the amphitheater. The ex-revelers froze in their panicking tracks. As far as Jim could objectively tell, the silence lasted for five, maybe six seconds before it was shattered by the soft tubercular wheeze of Doc Holliday's hollow laugh as he answered the irate Moses. "I guess I'm your boy, pilgrim. Are we going to make an issue of this?"

Jim could only suppose that, at this point, Moses' rage had simply boiled all the way out of character. He looked the same, he sounded the same, but the content was hardly from the Book of Exodus. "FUCKING-A RIGHT WE'RE GOING TO MAKE AN ISSUE OF IT."

And with that, he hurled one of the stone tablets directly at Doc. Doc, however, gracefully sidestepped, and five of the Ten Commandments, streaming a rainbow plasma contrail, spun past Jim, just scant inches from his left shoulder. The stone burst on the rocks behind him like a divine hand grenade, with a blinding, phosphorus-white flash and a shock wave that all but blew Jim clear off the ledge. From that point on, all hell broke loose. Firing from the hip, Doc proceeded to empty the entire clip of the automatic into the figure of Moses, but this seemed to have little effect except to make him even more furious and cause him to hurl the other tablet at them—the one containing commandments six through ten—and then, when this second explosion failed to dislodge Doc and Jim, to call down the full-blown Energy Storm of God.

In fact, the Energy Storm of God was borrowed intact from *Raiders of the Lost Ark*, but Jim didn't know this. Thus the plasma, howling past and threatening to engulf him with its screaming skulls, came at Jim like hallucination horrors. Moses, the amphitheater, even Doc, none of them were any longer visible. All Jim could see was a funnel cloud of vague disjointed forms spinning around him in the blaze. They all seemed to be flying. Or possibly falling.

Blood-ruby light streamed through the narrow, irregular slits in the high-domed ceiling of the chamber. They formed long unwavering beams that cut through the smoke haze and shafted down to the black marble floor below, creating a geometric design in three dimensions. When viewed from most possible angles, it resembled nothing more than an elongated, cat's-cradle cage of brightness. A slightly larger, circular aperture at the apex of the dome produced a single and absolutely vertical column of illumination, somewhat wider and more intense than the other pencil-thin rays.

The obvious stylistic influence and overall effect of the chamber was decidedly Islamic, akin in some ways to an anteroom in a huge and magnificent mosque. This had been Semple McPherson's original intention when she had conceived the chamber and all of the other rooms in her extensive domain. She had been striving for an obvious counterbalance to her sibling's overbearing, open-air Christianity. Where mosques, however, were places of cool holiness, the smoky red light and the abstract, vaguely flamelike mosaics, in black, scarlet, and gold, that adorned the walls and snaked up all the way to the apex of the dome whispered of damnation and punishment. The ever-burn chromium spheres floating in the convex space, moving about their randomly combustible sphere business, hinted at a cruel surrealism. The runic inscriptions and cabalistic symbols etched in gold on the black marble of the floor provided a louder literary confirmation that this was a place where sweetness and mercy had been banished, right along with faith, hope, and charity. If Semple's creation was a mosque, it was seemingly a mosque in Hell where, rather than prayer and devotion and the worship of Allah, the primary focus was the practice of torture and subjugation. If any further amplification was needed, the way the central beam of light fell directly on a chained and kneeling winged figure crouched on the marble floor said it all.

That the light came from above tended to suggest that, somewhere beyond the dome, a larger world existed, perhaps even some semblance of a sun and a sky. In fact, that was not the case. Semple had never bothered to devise any greater reality to give context to the invented Hell in which she dwelled, amused herself, and whiled away a perfectly satisfactory Afterlife. Semple disliked the outdoors. Such niceties like earth and sky were the province of her sibling. If Aimee had her way, all of everywhere would be reconfigured in the image of her narrow, conservative, and boringly orthodox concept of a pastoral Heaven.

As with much in the Afterlife, the relationship between the opposing kingdoms of the two sisters was complicated. To think that Aimee's Maxfield Parrish Paradise was somewhere above, and that Semple's Arabian Hell was somehow below, was convenient but sadly nonsensical. Such relativities were merely handed on from the mortal coil, handy luggage from the earthly life. They had no factual basis in postmortem complexity.

A wingless second figure stood over the first, unbound and dressed in a costume of military cut that seemed to have been tailored out of either plastic or highly polished leather. This second figure waited just back from the central beam of light, but sufficiently close for highlights to glint on its reflective costume. The standing figure was Semple McPherson herself, arrayed for oppression, eyes hidden behind huge, insect-eye sunglasses. She tapped a slender, wandlike device lightly against the flat palm of her gloved hand and regarded the chained figure on the floor in front of her with a combination of contempt and amusement. After a number of thoughtful taps, she began to walk slowly around him. "You know that you have seriously disappointed me, don't you? It was a simple, if intimate task, but you managed to prove yourself entirely inadequate. Are you aware of the extent of my disappointment? I gave you every chance, but you failed me abjectly."

The voice that came from the winged figure was scarcely more than a whisper. "I'm sorry." The prisoner's voice had a pleading melodic quality that contrasted with Semple McPherson's chill interrogation.

Semple halted in her circling. "Speak a little louder, will you?"

"I'm sorry."

Semple resumed walking around the prisoner. It took five paces to trace a circle around the kneeling figure in the pool of light. As Semple moved, the cruel rap of her ultra-high heels on the mirror-polished stone echoed around the walls of the chamber and produced delayed resonances from the curves of the dome. The leather of her costume creaked and its decorative chains rattled softly, but these faint sounds were hardly loud enough to produce echoes as precise and defined as those of her footfalls. They simply added their own micro-reverberations to the general background sigh that drifted like a sad and recurrent atonal theme through the chamber. Semple was dressed in what she liked to call her "Gestapo" costume, her usual attire for the questioning, abuse, and torture of prisoners and abductees from Aimee's Heaven. As with most of her outfits, she had designed it herself.

When she and Aimee had separated, Aimee had retained the major part of their original physical appearance, although, with Semple's contribution to the composite personality removed, she seemed to fade somewhat, into a vapid, ineffectual blonde with large, moist doe eyes that contrasted with her small, judgmental, and almost lipless mouth. Semple, on the other hand, had found herself free to make up a whole new outward persona for herself, absolutely from scratch. With Aimee resembling such a washed-out, constrained, and self-satisfied little prig, Semple had gone for the voluptuous and exotic. She had chosen to become a six-foot-tall, raven-haired Amazon superheroine who combined the best features of Jane Russell and Elizabeth Taylor, writ large and with a few added extra flourishes of her own invention. Combinations of mix and match were the key to much of Semple's creativity. It was certainly a technique that had been applied to her Gestapo outfit. She was arrayed in what looked to be an amalgamation of the standard sexual dominatrix garb and the dress uniform of some fanciful Nazi Space Patrol, consisting of black leather jodhpurs with a red stripe down the outside seam, high black boots with stiletto spikes, a severely tailored tunic with red inset panels and flashes, and heavy with decorative medals, chains, and epaulets. Her jet-black hair was piled high on her head, her emerald eyes invisible behind the oversized glasses.

After one circle of the figure, she stopped and slowly extended her arm into the column of light so a shadow fell on her kneeling subject. As it passed over him, he shuddered slightly. Semple didn't know if the response was one of ecstasy or fear, and she didn't particularly care. She removed her hand from the light and spoke again. "I think I can safely say, without the slightest fear of contradiction, that your understanding of my needs and their gratification was completely unsatisfactory."

"I'm sorry, my lady."

Semple ignored him. She could feel a tirade coming on and she saw no reason not to indulge herself. "I made allowances for the fact that my idiot sister saw fit, in an insane outburst of prudery and sexual repression, to create you and your kind without even the slightest hint of genitalia. Having made these concessions, however, I would feel it should be incumbent upon you to spend as much thought, time, and effort as possible perfecting your expertise in other areas of the same endeavor. Do you understand me so far?"

The subject nodded silently and a rustle ran down his wing feathers from shoulder to tip. Semple noted the response with open contempt. The kneeling figure was one of her sibling's ludicrous angels, and Semple had always found their physical construction decidedly implausible. Their luxuriant, swanlike wings were simply attached to their backs, close to the shoulder blades, as though they had been glued or cemented there with little or no thought as to how the actual function of flight was to be achieved. It was a result, of course, of Aimee's willful ignorance of human anatomy and her deeply inhibited distaste for any study of the subject, no matter how it might have improved the authenticity of the Heavenly Host that she claimed to care so much about. Of course, the angels, when they flew, were hardly required to overcome an actual terrestrial gravity, but Semple still believed they ought to look as though they were.

Or perhaps it wasn't altogether justifiable to blame the unreality of the angels entirely on Aimee's prudery and ignorance. Back when they had still been joined as one, Semple had attempted to work out a mechanically coherent muscular structure for the wings of angels.

Unfortunately, the task had proved all but impossible without tolerating a level of deformity that was close to monstrous. Dynamically correct angels came doubled-over and hunchbacked, not unakin to an avian version of the servant Igor in the old black and white Frankenstein movies. Such a thing would have been completely unacceptable to Aimee, and Semple had abandoned her efforts. She continued to believe, however, that the traditional image of the angel, essentially an idealized human with wings sprouting from his or her back, endowed with the capability of flight, was both anathema to physics and a technical impossibility.

Her final fallback had been to make it clear to Aimee that, in her opinion, the angels looked stupid at best and even stupider when they were in flight. She had suggested that they should be left out of the heavenly inventory altogether, but her opinion had cut no ice. Aimee, unbending traditionalist that she was, had insisted that Heaven could never be complete without not only angels but cherubim, seraphim, and all of the other whimsical features of the popular Victorian sacred picture-postcard image of the choir celestial. This was probably why Semple now took such a lasting delight in involving Aimee's less rational creations in her experimental studies regarding the limits of spiritual endurance. If she couldn't make angels logical, she felt fully justified in abducting and torturing such pathetic half measures.

She continued her interrogation of the angel at hand. "I asked you if you understood me."

Again the angel mutely nodded, but this wasn't good enough for Semple. "Out loud, please."

The angel's voice choked slightly as though he were doing his best to hold back tears or terror. "Yes, I understand you." Again, his wing feathers rustled.

The prisoner angel's wings were, at that moment, secured by a pair of polished steel alligator clips some eight inches long, attached by short chains to anchor rings set in the floor. The angel's wings might defy scientific logic, but they could also be one hell of a nuisance if the damn thing started to panic and thrash about. The wings of angels in this tailored Heaven had a strength that was more than equal to those of terrestrial swans or eagles.

"So what do you intend to do about it?"

"Do about what, Lady Semple?"

When the angel had first been brought to Semple's domain, he had been informed that he should afford his captor due courtesy by addressing her as Lady Semple. If he should refer to her by name to a third party, it should be as *the* Lady Semple.

"About your inability."

The angel didn't answer. He strained against the bonds that held him, but no words came.

"Speak up. I can't hear you."

The angel partially found his voice. "I . . . "

"I still can't hear you."

"I don't . . . "

"You don't what?"

"I don't . . . "

"I'm beginning to lose patience." Semple touched the angel lightly with the tip of her wand. He grimaced in sudden pain and recoiled from the contact with a desperate gasp. His answer came out in a single rush of breath as though some block had suddenly been released. "I don't have any experience. Nothing of that kind ever comes to pass in Heaven."

Semple's lip curled. "Well, it wouldn't, would it?"

"I did the best I could."

Semple held the wand in front of the angel's downcast eyes. "You creatures are such weaklings."

"Perhaps if I was allowed to practice a little more, I might . . . "

"You want to practice?"

The angel raised his head so he was looking at Semple. "That's if you don't destroy me first."

"Are you attempting to make a play for my sympathy?"

"I don't want to be destroyed."

"I hardly overflow with divine forgiveness."

As though to indicate her lack of basic compassion, Semple glanced over at her three rubber guards who stood a little way off, watching impassively from behind the eyepieces of their grim and featureless suits. The rubber guards were completely identical, and, as though demonstrating their role in Semple's realm, each one clutched a heavy-duty electric mace in its stubby fingers. These three rubber guards had been the ones that Semple had summoned to drag the terrified but unresisting angel from the luxury of the lady's nouveau purple bedroom to the Moorish horror of the torture chamber.

The rubber guards were one of Semple's more original creations and she used them extensively to spread terror and alarm among her fabricated subjects. Although bipedal and humanoid in shape, that was pretty much where any human resemblance ended. The loose suits of inch-thick black rubber with their anonymous circular goggles and air filter snout, not unlike a built-in World War I gas mask, endowed the rubber guards with a shapeless and ultimately sinister uniformity. They were slack but dangerous, heavy balloons with arms, legs, and absolute obedience to their designer. They stood over seven feet tall, and the suits hung loosely like the skin of an elephant, but lacked the amiable pachyderm's reassuring arrangements of folds and wrinkles.

When originally designing the guards and retainers for her personal Hell, Semple had first toyed with the idea of using traditional medieval demons, but had rejected that as being far too much like what her sister might do if she had been cast as the dark half. In the case of the rubber guards, she had confined herself to a ballpark of the imagination bounded by George Orwell on one side and Jean Cocteau on the other, seeking a monstrous paramilitary figure that was midway between a dehumanized warrior and a bioengineered robot. She had forgotten the exact details of the structure that she had devised to provide the functioning machinery beneath the enigmatic rubber. That was the way with the Lady Semple. She might labor long and hard over an element of her manufactured environment, but the moment the task was complete, she involuntarily and irrevocably downloaded it from her mind. Data crashed and was no more.

The rubber guards breathed, or at least made a regular asthmatic hissing through their filter snouts. The bodies also made a faint liquid sloshing sound when they moved, suggesting the presence of internal bodily fluids. Since they were able to stand and move and exert considerable physical strength when so instructed, they obviously had a supporting skeletal structure. They obeyed orders, and thus were possessed of at least a rudimentary brain. All Semple knew was that, in formulating the blueprint of the rubber guards, she had taken the concept of man and debased it to nothing more than a bladder of contained and controlled aggression. It seemed an adequate degree of payback for what she had suffered on Earth at the hands of men.

The thought of debasement again turned Semple's attention back to the unfortunate angel. "I suppose, if I wanted to take on your education, I could put you in with some of my women. My retainers may look girlish, but they can be wickedly ingenious and might be able to do something with you. You could probably keep them amused for a while."

"I'm sure I'd learn extremely fast."

"Unless, as you say, I destroy you first."

"I beg you not to do that."

"You enjoy your existence?"

"It's the only one I have."

Semple looked curiously at the angel. This one seemed to be exhibiting an exceptionally well-developed sense of individual identity. Had Aimee somehow altered the way she made them? Had she modified the cosmic cookie cutter to give the things more sense of self? It hardly seemed like Aimee. "My sister created you?"

"That's what I was told."

"Then it's perfectly simple for her to create a replacement for you."

The angel hesitated. "Yes, but . . . "

"But what?"

"It wouldn't be me, would it? If you destroy me, I will no longer exist."

Semple looked at the angel with some renewed interest. The creature may have had no balls on the physical level, but it was demonstrating a certain psychological masculinity. "Are you trying to tell me that you consider yourself a unique and irreplaceable being?"

"I am . . . from my point of view."

Semple thought about this, but before she could come to any conclusion, something happened that radically diverted her attention from anything so mundane as the perceptions of an angel. A rotary Princess phone, apparently made out of solid gold, materialized out of nowhere, right on the marble floor, slightly less than three feet from her left foot. No sooner had it appeared than it began to ring with a bright, melodious soprano trill. Semple looked down at the thing with distaste. "That can't be anybody but my sibling."

Jim Morrison awoke, if indeed "awoke" was the correct word, with a headache of such catastrophic proportions that his head felt about to shatter and fragment into a hundred pieces. Despite the pain, though, a part of him was aware that the headache was of his own creating. In that part of his mind where all things are certain, and pretense or self-deception is not tolerated, he knew it was nothing more than a reflex retreat. The hangover was a defense mechanism rooted in his mortal debaucheries, which in the latter days had inevitably ended in similar monumental suffering. He was defending himself against the experience from which he had just made his exit. By re-creating the symptoms of an epic mother and father of mornings after, he was seeking to relegate the way he had been forcibly thrust all the way back to the Great Double Helix to a more manageable level. He was attempting to pretend it was no more than a psychotic nightmare, a psychedelic hallucination, or an alcohol-induced delirium, rather than face the truth. The truth was that such self-deception was all but impossible. In the Afterlife, one saw too clearly. His plunge back to the central majesty of the Great Double Helix was too strong in his immediate memory to be disguised or held at bay until some later time.

After the first shock of Moses hurling the stone tablets and the resulting chaos and plasma storm, Jim had found himself subjectively falling, discorporate and almost mindless, hurtling down a spiral energy stream, surrounded by violent, vibrant color and a screaming roar of horror that hardwired itself directly to what remained of his nerve endings. In every way, it was all but identical to the first fearful onslaught of the death trauma itself. It had resembled the phase of confusion before the light took over and protective tranquillity kicked in, except that, in the death trauma, one always rose, and Jim had been descending, fast and furious, all the way until he bottomed out in the cloud envelope.

In the cloud envelope, out on the far margins of the Great Double Helix, he discovered to his relief that he had partially stabilized. He was not going back to the vacantly dreaming pod form. Instead, he floated with a ghost gauze remnant of the Jim Morrison body still draped in tenuous wisps across his consciousness. Before him, but at a merciful distance, seemingly too far away for it to draw him in, the Great Double Helix revolved in its awesome vastness, cloaked in attendant vortices of impossible, unbearable brightness, and with the parallels of forcibly curved space arching around it like concentric parabola. If he turned his perception through some ninety degrees, he could also see the Canal of Reincarnation tangentially dropping away to the Edge and the mortal Earth beyond. For a while, he was sorely tempted to maneuver himself so he would be pulled in by its quasi-gravity and take its path to a second mortal go-around. A deep-seated belief in karma, however, dissuaded him. He had hardly excelled in his last life, and the idea of returning as an insect, a virus, or maybe even yeast, in no way appealed to him. On the other hand, he had absolutely no desire to spend an undefined eternity in indistinct Limbo, the null zone that was the worst fear of all in the Afterlife.

It took him a seemingly long, although obviously immeasurable time to realize how the way out was in fact ridiculously simple and completely in his own hands. If he concentrated all of his energy on perceiving and reconstituting the details of the slowly fading Morrison body, he would ultimately recorporate. Essentially he was replicating the pod process, except that, unlike a pod, he had conscious control and didn't have to wait out the randomness of a pod's haphazard dreaming. He didn't even need to make the effort to move. The more the body gathered substance, the more it was repelled by the ectoplasmic wind of the Great Double Helix. If he simply hung in and didn't struggle, its celestial backwash would ultimately toss him back into the fantasy of the Afterlife like some fisherman's rejected catch. He'd "wake," with the exact blinding headache from which he was now suffering.

Jim groaned. "Oh fuck, I think I'm going to throw up."

In truth, Jim was actually feeling somewhat better. As he confronted the fullness of what had recently happened to him, the pain noticeably mitigated, although it was still a matter of better as opposed to worse, rather than better moving through to good. He still didn't feel absolutely ready to open his eyes and face the light, but then the voice cut in on his thoughts. "At least you're back. For a while, we thought Moses had tossed you to the end of nowhere."

The voice took Jim completely by surprise. It was, however, young and female, and it sounded friendly, with a faint trace of a Latina accent. Jim took a deep breath and very gingerly opened his eyes. At first he thought that the light would blind him, but after a few seconds he grew accustomed to it and was able to make out a woman's face looking down at him with obvious amusement. The amusement increased as Jim struggled to sit up, and he altogether failed to share the joke. "I wish you'd tell me what you find so goddamned funny."

"I guess this is what you have to expect if you go out honky-tonking with Doc Holliday."

"I didn't go out honky-tonking."

The woman plainly didn't believe him. "I heard the two of you were attending an orgy."

Jim avoided her eyes. "Yeah, well, there was an orgy and we were there, but it wasn't from choice, I can assure you."

"That's what they all say."

Jim wearily started to protest. "It's the truth."

"I suppose the devil made you do it?"

"I think Moses made me do it."

"That's a new one."

The woman was slim and pretty in a tough, no-nonsense way, with olive skin and straight glossy black hair that hung almost to her waist. She was dressed in a low-cut white cotton peasant dress trimmed with lace, but in total contrast she also wore a bandolier of cartridges, slung bandit-style across her shoulder. Her blue and white Cuban-heeled cowboy boots gave her a sexy, confident stance, and Jim started to pay more careful attention. Even in the Afterlife, an ex-human's erotic radar still continued to function. "So what's your name?"

"Donna Anna Maria Isabella Conchita Theresa Garcia, but you can call me Lola."

"Lola?"

"That's what Doc calls me. He has a very bad memory for names. I think it's a side effect of the opium."

Jim propped himself up on one elbow. "I'm Jim."

"I know all about you, Jim Morrison."

"You do?"

"You were famous long ago."

"For playing the electric violin, Donna Anna Maria?"

She looked at him impassively. "Lola."

Lola was carrying an engraved silver tray. Jim gestured to it. "What's that?"

"Your breakfast."

"It's been a long time since I was offered a breakfast."

Lola set the tray on the bed and Jim noticed that she wore a silver identity bracelet on her left wrist, but the name tag was blank. He leaned forward and inspected the tray's contents. What part did food play in the Afterlife? Nostalgia for mortality? Part of a ritual? A hedonistic indulgence? A simple prop for an invented lifestyle? Eating was a piece of comfortable holdover behavior that had absolutely nothing to do with nourishment or survival, and Jim rarely bothered with it. His first look revealed, however, that this breakfast was a highly individual one. The bone china coffee set, the glass of orange juice, and the two slices of wheat toast were reasonably conventional. The collection of multicolored pills and capsules, the ornate flask of laudanum, the loaded opium pipe, the thin black cigar, and the four fingers of whiskey in a crystal shot glass that were also carefully arranged on the tray came, on the other hand, squarely out of left field. Jim looked at Lola questioningly and Lola shrugged. "We didn't know what you wanted, so we gave you the same as Doc."

Jim blinked at the spread that was now set before him. "Doc has all this for *breakfast?*"

Lola nodded as though it were really no big thing. "Every day when he's in town."

Jim picked up the glass and sniffed the whiskey. It was bourbon and, if his nose didn't deceive him, at least twelve years old. "What are the pills?"

Again Lola shrugged. "Don't ask me. I think Doc invents them. As long as he gets a jolt, he don't care to sweat the pharmacological details."

"Is Doc here?"

"He's around."

"And did Doc create you?"

Lola's eyes flashed angrily. "What you say?"

"I asked if you were one of Doc's creations."

"You think that somebody made me? You think that I'm some irrelevant piece of set dressing?"

Jim knew that he had said the wrong thing. "I just asked. I wasn't trying to be disrespectful."

Lola leaned toward him and her expression was dangerous. "You listen to me, Mr. Jim Morrison, and you listen good. I ain't nobody's creation. I'm here because I want to be. You know what I'm saying, ese?"

Jim eased back in the bed. "I'm sorry. I didn't mean to offend you."

"Just don't do it again, okay?"

Jim nodded, looking as contrite as possible even with a headache, without compromising his devil-may-care charm and allure. "I surely won't."

Lola turned and walked out of the room, and Jim watched the sway of her retreating hips with singular appreciation. It would have been an understatement to say that she interested him. It might have been a side effect of his recent brush with what had been painfully close to a second death, but right at that moment she seemed about the best-looking woman he'd seen in a long time. Once she was gone, he pushed back the sheets and swung his legs over the side of the bed and tried sitting up. For a moment, he felt dizzy and disoriented, as though mind hadn't quite locked into body and the two were operating out of phase. With an effort of concentration, he eased the two halves of himself together until he felt as though they were properly meshed, then he waited a moment and the dizziness passed. Deciding that he was now about as fully integrated as he was going to get, Jim slowly looked around the room.

The best word to describe the place was "incomplete." It was obviously a bedroom, since it was dominated by the huge canopied bed on which Jim had been lately lying, and the stairs down which Lola had made her exit suggested that it was on an upper floor of some larger structure. What was less clear was why the place had no roof and only two and a half of what should have been four walls. In many respects, it resembled a film or stage set. It also hinted Dali, although no soft clocks flowed. Since he'd risen to a sitting position, Jim could see a blue and cloudless Technicolor sky beyond the canopy of the bed. One wall had been completely finished, right down to red velvet wallpaper, and even an ornate gilt mirror hung at approximately eye level. Another wall was missing entirely, and beyond the wooden framework that should have held the wall in place, Jim was treated to a view of flat, rust-colored desert, with mesas and hazy mountains in the distance. Instead of a third wall, a bannerlike bolt of what looked to be saffron-dyed silk had been hung in its place, and it undulated gently in a slight breeze. The silk extended beyond the level of the floor, and, for all Jim knew, might have reached all the way to the ground, wherever that was. Aside from the bed, the room contained little in the way of furniture. A pile of clothing rested on a plain, straight-backed chair, and an ornate Victorian washstand stood in front of the wall that wasn't there.

Since Jim was quite accustomed to anomalies in the Afterlife, he didn't spend too much time puzzling over either the nature or origins of the place in which he found himself. Instead, concentrating on the practical possibilities of the moment, he turned his attention to the contents of the tray. He poured himself a cup of coffee, wondered about smoking the cigar, but decided he wasn't ready. Even in the Afterlife he had never mastered the knack of not inhaling, and cigars inevitably made him cough. What really interested him was the drugs. The array of medication was formidable. A total of seven pills and capsules were arranged on a blue and white Wedgwood plate, two large white pills, two smaller yellow pills, two red and black capsules, and one more in turquoise and orange. "Sweet Jesus, Doc, who do you think you are? Jerry Lee Lewis?"

Jim pushed the pills around on the plate with his index finger, arranging them into different patterns of colors. Finally he selected one yellow pill, a red and black capsule, and both white pills. He had no idea what they might be, but how much harm could they do? He was already dead, after all. He put all four in his mouth at once, and, before he could think about it any further and reconsider, he washed them with a gulp of coffee, followed by a fast shot of bourbon and a chaser of orange juice. The old reckless Jim was back in the saddle again, going with the impulse and damn the torpedoes. Maybe, if he kept it up, his coherent creativity might actually return. Having escaped the Great Double Helix, he felt he was taking the first steps in a new phase of being. And these steps would not be cautious or faltering: better a lurch than a whimper. The best of times had always come when he'd pushed self-destruction to the fate-to-the-wind limit, and that was where he was headed now. There's danger at the edge of town. By the way of compromise, though, he ate a single slice of toast, if only to indicate to the world, and maybe Lola, if she was the one who cleared away the tray, that his repast hadn't been purely chemical. Then he sat back to wait and see where the pills might be taking him.

Jim didn't have long to wait. A loud bang, and a vibrant flash like an exploding TV screen, heralded the onset of at least one of the drugs. The entire room, and the world and sky beyond it, began to spin violently. Jim's vision shattered into fractal chaos. From the intensity of the rush he estimated that, had he still been mortal, his heart would probably have exploded. The effect lasted for only a few seconds, though, and then he returned to normal. A second later, a small army of six-inch-tall, anthropomorphic cartoon rodents in tiny military uniforms appeared, quite literally out of the woodwork, and proceeded to march across the floor in formation. They halted in front of Jim, saluted, and then vanished. Even Jim found himself a little stunned, and had to remind himself that, like so many other things, drug abuse in the Afterlife was exempt from the restrictions of cause and effect.

Before anything else could happen, Jim reached quickly for the opium pipe. He didn't bother to search for a match with which to light it; he wished it alight and it was lit. He inhaled deeply, happy that spontaneous combustion was one of the perks of being dead. Opium, along with alcohol, was a drug that could, for the most part, be relied on to have a similar effect to that which it had on Earth. A couple of long pulls on the pipe were enough to mellow the environment to the point where further explosions or rodent animations would hardly daunt him. The smoke didn't exactly take him all the way to the Palace of Mirrors, but he found himself in a far more amiable state of mind than he'd enjoyed in a long time. Maybe Doc Holliday had the right idea. Jim's headache had completely gone; when he inadvertently dropped a red-hot coal from the pipe on his bare thigh, he was only marginally aware of the pain.

Putting the pipe down, he attempted to stand. To his mild surprise, he neither reeled nor staggered. He simply floated with an easy naked euphoria in the direction of the mirror on the red velvet wall. He smiled at his own reflection. In death, he had miraculously shed the weight gain that had dogged him through the final years of life. He could see the bone structure in his face, his stomach was flat as a board, and he was once again the sullen prince who had taken rock and roll by rebel storm. He laughed out loud. "You're one handsome devil, Jimbo. Don't you ever die again, you hear?"

He realized the absurdity of what he had just said, but he was too opiated for it to bother him. He turned away from the mirror, suddenly gripped by an urge to get out of the room and do something. He realized he was probably expected to dress. From his brief encounter with the man, Jim couldn't imagine the immaculate Doc Holliday setting up his home someplace where everyone went buck naked. A thought stopped Jim momentarily in his tracks. Hadn't Doc said that they'd met before? Jim still had no recollection of such an encounter, so plainly not all of his memory had been returned to him. Unless, of course, more than one Jim Morrison was running around the Afterlife. It was the first time he'd considered such a possibility; maybe the pills and the opium were giving heightened powers of perception. Did any mechanism exist within the Great Double Helix to prevent two people from taking on the same persona? Somehow Jim doubted it. The Great Double Helix manifested little respect for individualism. He would have liked to ponder the problem, but the drugs were doing nothing for his attention span.

Dressed. That was what he had to be. Concentrate on the practical now, leave the applied metaphysics for later, when he was no longer quite so airborne.

He looked at the clothes on the chair and wondered if they were intended for him. Then he saw his old scuffed engineer boots standing side by side at the foot of the bed, as if awaiting instructions. If his boots were there, the clothes also had to be for him.

Jim picked up the top garment. It was a loose Mexican shirt made from rough cotton. Beneath it were his familiar scarred and battered leather jeans. He quickly dressed, took one final look in the mirror, and started for the stairs.

"I need your help."

Semple McPherson raised an eyebrow and half-smiled. Aimee needed something, thus the sudden materialization of the golden Princess phone. Semple saw no reason to be helpful. "I'm kind of busy right now."

"What are you doing?"

Semple was tempted to tell her sister that it was none of her fucking business. It was so typical of Aimee to want to know what she was doing. As though she had the right to evaluate whose priorities should be the ones to take precedence. Instead, Semple made her voice sweetly innocent. "Actually, sibling, dear, I was busy torturing one of your angels."

Aimee sighed. "I wish you wouldn't keep doing that."

Semple glanced at the angel, who steadfastly refused to look at her. "Why? There are plenty more where he came from."

"Isn't it all a little childish?"

Semple could just imagine her sister, standing on her goddamned marble terrace looking out over her ludicrous Heaven, a sad patient smile on her miserable face and bluebirds fluttering all around her. It would make a welcome change if one of the wretched bluebirds took a shit on her. Except, of course, Aimee's bluebirds didn't shit. "The word you're grasping for is 'childlike.' "

Aimee's voice took on an edge that foreshadowed full-blown exasperation. "The word I'm grasping for is 'pointless.' "

"This particular angel had failed to accomplish a very rudimentary sex act."

"They're not designed for sex."

"You don't have to remind me. Besides, I was bored."

The moment she admitted to being bored, Semple realized that she had made a bad tactical error. Aimee immediately pounced on it. "If you're so bored, you clearly have the time to help me with what I'm doing."

"Extending your damned Heaven?"

"What else?"

"I don't think so."

"Why not?"

"I'm not that bored."

"We would be doing the work of God."

Although she'd been through this routine countless times before, Semple started to lose her temper. "The fuck we'd be doing the work of God."

Semple was predictably scandalized. "How can you say that?"

"Because there is no God. There is no God, Aimee. When the fuck are you going to grasp that? Since you died, God hasn't sent you so much as a fucking postcard, let alone clasped you to his bosom like a little lost lamb. Accept the obvious, woman. God is a no-show. God has stood you up."

Her outburst was greeted by a long silence. Semple knew she'd wounded her sister, but she wasn't about to feel any guilt. Aimee would not only get over it, she'd exact payback sometime in the future. "You could do it for *me*."

"Like, *you're* God?" Semple adopted a Valley girl intonation. She had discovered it during one of the irregular browsings through mortal culture she had made since her death. It was custom-tailored to irritate Aimee.

Aimee, however, came right back at her. "I suppose you could look at it like that."

"But you're not God."

"I'm doing my best."

Aimee was actually sounding a little frayed; for a moment Semple took pity on her. "What exactly do you want me to do?"

"I want you to find someone for me."

"Find someone?" This actually had more promise than Semple had expected. She momentarily savored a vision of herself as Semple McPherson, girl detective. She saw herself in a trenchcoat and an exceedingly cool hat, prowling dark and dangerous streets.

Aimee continued, "I need you to find someone to help me with what I'm doing."

"Who in their right mind would want to help you enlarge that ridiculous Heaven of yours?"

"They don't have to be in their right mind. In fact, I'd like them to have as little mind as possible. All I need is someone with enough creative panache."

"A clean slate?"

"Exactly."

"A man or a woman?"

"A man would depend entirely on my mood at the time."

"Either way, you'd get to use your not-inconsiderable powers of seduction."

"Are you saying you want me to set you up with a man? You want me to procure for you?"

Aimee sounded shocked to the bone. "It would be nothing like that. How could you ever think it?" Semple didn't find the shock in Aimee's voice altogether authentic. To her ear, Aimee was protesting too much.

Grinning nastily, Semple continued as though Aimee hadn't spoken. "It'd be just like old times, wouldn't it? I reel them into bed, I fuck them, you enjoy the experience from afar, but by never actually emerging until there was a hard-won orgasm to be had, you always left room to pretend it never happened, that you were still God's own sainted, deep-frozen virgin."

"It wasn't like that all."

"Wasn't it?"

"It certainly wasn't. I really don't know where you get your ideas."

Semple's lip curled and her voice turned B-girl tough. "Same place you do, honey. Don't forget, once we were one."

Aimee said nothing, and neither did her sister. Semple was aware of the entrance of Igor, her diminutive butler with the popping amphibian eyes and high Germanic voice of Peter Lorre. Igor was one of the few denizens of Semple's domain whom she hadn't constructed herself. He had arrived out of the blue, driven there by his own twisted, vice-laden fantasies, and since he served her with groveling devotion, she turned a blind eye to his voyeuristic skulking around in furtive observation of her tortures and abuses. He probably wished *he* were in the place of the angel. Semple let the silence run itself out, just to see what Aimee would come up with next. When Aimee spoke again, her voice had totally changed. Suddenly, as though a dam had burst, she was in tears. "Please help me, Semple, I have no one else to turn to. I know I'm obsessive, but I can't do this on my own. I really can't."

Semple silently cursed her sibling. If Aimee started crying, Semple knew she couldn't turn her down. It was her great weakness: she was a sucker for the crudely pathetic. It was all she could do to shut Aimee off with a fast provisional agreement. "Okay, okay, I'll think about it."

Aimee's voice disintegrated into a suppressed sob. "You will? Then, we need to talk about it."

Aimee recovered with amazing rapidity. "I thought we *were* talking about it."

"Face-to-face."

"Is that a good idea?"

"I'll meet you in Golgotha."

"Does it have to be Golgotha?"

"You made the place, not me."

Semple could feel Aimee take a deep breath before she answered. Golgotha, the Place of Skulls, the one sector that didn't fit in the rest of her cutesy-poo Heaven. "Very well."

"Then Golgotha it is."

Semple had assumed the conversation was finished, but Aimee had another thought. "You're always telling me how you need to get out more. This will be the perfect opportunity."

This last remark was a low blow. Both of them only left their created environments on the rarest of occasions. Semple liked to pretend that she was ready for anything, but, deep in her being, she feared the territories beyond quite as much as Aimee did. She was unsure of herself in those environments that apparently stretched to infinity all around her cozy Hell and Aimee's Heaven. Aimee, well aware of this, used it against her whenever she could, but Semple didn't parry the blow. She wasn't quite ready for another round of sibling conflict, and she just snapped at Aimee. "Like, just meet me in Golgotha, okay?"

No sooner had Semple hung up the golden phone than it vanished. She stood lost in thought. After a long lapse of quasi-time, one of the rubber guards began wheezing loudly. Semple turned and looked at him, then down at the angel. Aimee's unexpected call had caused her to forget the matter at hand altogether. Semple found she'd lost all previous enthusiasm for continued abuse. She gestured impatiently to the rubber guards, pointing to the bound angel. "Just get rid of him."

The angel struggled against his bonds. "Please . . . "

"Or give him to Igor if he wants him."

"No . . . " The angel continued to struggle, but Semple had no time for his entreaties. "Do shut up. I need to think."

An idea was already spawning in the blackest layers of Semple's intricately devious mind. Oh yes, she'd find Aimee her creative force. She'd find her a genius, but he wouldn't be the kind to put Aimee's precious Heaven to rights. She'd find her sister some utter bastard, and see how she liked them apples.

2

When the music stops, watch out!

White horses moving through the fog
White horses moving through the fog
Tall white horses moving through the fog
Pale horsemen following a red-eyed dog

The old man in the blue-green watered silk suit who called himself Long Time Robert Moore was playing the blues with an inspiration that far surpassed anything mortal. Moore sat in the musicians' corner of Doc Holliday's cantina, right beside the upright piano. Ruby, the resident piano player, remained on her stool, but merely watched him, her big-knuckled hands never so much as straying near the nicotine-stained keys. Robert Moore sat bent forward in a hard wood chair, his pearl-gray fedora pulled down so it cast a black-hole shadow where his eyes were supposed to be. Gold flashed on his right hand as he claw-picked with unerring precision. Silver flashed in his left as the stainless steel bottleneck rode the strings. More gold and a lone diamond flashed in his mouth as he sang. Moore had long since hit his stride, and every now and again he registered the fact by allowing himself a faint but knowing smile. He was now into that zone where voice and instrument dovetailed as one, interwoven twin factors of a single intent. The urgent slide guitar figure hummed and spun, chimed like a funeral toll, and then coiled back on itself with the surety of a striking snake. The sound resonated from the instrument's metal body and commenced a journey that took it, rolling and tumbling, beyond the boundaries of the room, out through the doors and windows and missing walls of Doc's half-completed cantina, to run echoing down the street and across the surrounding desert's wild sounding board, finally to return as eerie, delayed reverberation.

Jim Morrison sat on the wooden sidewalk of another unfinished building across the street from Doc's skeletal cantina, willing to idle for the while, sprawled against an upright; with a half-full whiskey bottle dangling loosely from his left hand, he listened with something close to awe to the music that Long Time Robert Moore was creating. Back on Earth, such purity of tone and sheer intensity of volume would have been impossible without major amplification. Here in the Afterlife, the majestic sound simply flowed from Moore's acoustic National steel with no visible assistance. Music in the Afterlife could approach the magically sublime, as pickers, unencumbered by physical limitations, were free to indulge total audio fantasy. But the sound of Long Time Robert Moore still remained profoundly exceptional. Jim was glad he had Robert Moore to keep him entertained, as he settled into comfortable drunkenness. He was drunk enough not to want to negotiate the crowd that had now gathered in the cantina, but sufficiently comfortable that he was content to do nothing but slouch on the sidewalk and listen, eyes closed, his mind riding the chords.

Jim had noticed that it was almost impossibly easy to get drunk in Doc Holliday's environment, and he wondered if that, and the magnificence of the music, had something to do with the unique quality of the air. The air in this land of Doc's seemed unnaturally pure. Jim had noted this immediately when he'd emerged from the cantina. Although it still vibrated with the aftermath of the daytime desert heat, the atmosphere had an alpine crispness. It tasted as though it had been filtered, liquefied, distilled, and then reconstituted with an extra shot of oxygen. This was Antarctic air, Center for Disease Control, laboratory-conditioned air. Jim was surprised and a little amused by the care Doc took over his air. It hardly seemed in character for a man who smoked both opium and black, rank, rum-soaked Cuban cheroots; who deliberately maintained his near-terminal, blood-hacking tuberculosis as a signature of personal style. Or did it? Maybe virgin-pure air was Doc's one concession to the physical.

> *How hard is that next page to turn?*
> *How hard is that next page to turn?*
> *How hard is that next page to turn?*
> *How hard is the lesson to learn?*

A purple night had fallen over Doc Holliday's environment and the lazy indolence of the day had given way to a promise of dreaming urgency. As the light had dwindled and even the crimson and burning gold beyond the mesas at the horizon had eventually faded to black, the cantina and the whole tiny town had started to stir with expectations of the night to come. Lola had vanished for a while and then reappeared in a scarlet flamenco dress, matching shoes, and lipstick, with her hair in a mantilla. Lola's red dress seemed to be the sign that the night's festivities were open for business. Long Time Robert Moore had pushed back his hat and, with a sparkle of the diamond tooth that matched the wicked glint in his bloodshot eyes, opened the beat-up black case that contained the National steel. People Jim had never seen before converged on the cantina, hard-drinking men and women of the wild side who transformed the place from a sleepy afternoon refuge for wastrels to a juke joint so determinedly jumping that the eventual crescendo of what promised to be a cannonball night would bring either violent paranormal saturnalia or equally violent fistfights and gunplay.

Jim had been as determined as anyone else to go the dark distance and embrace anything that came his way. It was thus something of a surprise that he found himself flagging, taking himself out of the race to seek the sanctuary of a private bottle and a support to lean against. It might have been the air; it might have been a kind of delayed, second-time-around death lag, an aftereffect of his recent brush with the Great Double Helix. It might also have been the quantity of unidentified but effective drugs he had consumed for breakfast. Whatever the cause, Jim languished until the china-eyed black dog came up and spoke to him.

"Did you know that the electric chair at Parchman Penitentiary is painted bright banana yellow?"

Jim shook his head. "No, I didn't know that."

The black dog nodded, its tongue lolling out. "Not many people do. It's not something they publicize."

Jim wasn't at all surprised by the talking dog. He knew that people entered the Afterlife as dogs, horses, mules, and kittens, almost all of them able to talk. One guy had come through as a giant sea turtle the size of a Volkswagen; devoted Kafka enthusiasts sometimes faced life after death as giant bugs. The dog, however, had an odd look in its mismatched eyes. Jim decided his safest bet was to humor the animal. "I'd imagine it'd be something they'd want to keep quiet."

The dog looked at him suspiciously. "Why should they want to do that?"

Jim hazily pondered this. "I don't know. I guess I always figured that the electric chair ought to be a nice, dignified, judicial mahogany . . . mahogany with copper fittings, kinda like a coffin or the judge's bench in the courtroom."

The dog all but snapped. "Well, it ain't. Least not at Parchman. You can take my word. It's banana yellow. Layer upon layer of cheap banana yellow gloss enamel."

"Weird."

"Yeah." The dog changed the subject. "You waiting for Doc?"

Jim shook his head. "No, just waiting. Hardly even doing that."

"Doc's down at the opium den. He don't usually come out until things have started hotting up in town."

Jim looked up with interest. "An opium den?"

The dog showed its canine fangs; Jim took the grimace to be one of friendship rather than hostility. The dog pointed its nose to the other end of the town's single main street. "Sure, down there, behind the laundry. Beside where the whorehouse used to be."

Jim pushed himself away from the post. All through his mortal life he'd dreamed of going to a real old-fashioned opium den. He had almost made it to one in Paris, but his death had ruined that plan. "Are you kidding me? An opium den? A real, all-the-way, Chinese opium den with bunks and fans, and guys with pigtails cooking the pipes?"

The dog nodded. "The whole fortune cookie, plus John Coltrane and Miles Davis on the sound system. It's run by a guy called Sun Yat."

"No shit."

The dog looked at Jim intently. "Before you ask any more questions, you could offer me a drink."

Jim looked down his bottle. "I'm sorry. I didn't think dogs drank."

"This one does."

Jim frowned. "I never fed whiskey to a dog before. How exactly do I do it?"

"It's easy. Just put the neck of the bottle in my mouth and start pouring. Just don't pour too fast or I drool."

The timing of the pouring process required more skill than Jim had imagined, and buying a dog a drink proved a messy and wasteful transaction. A considerable quantity of liquor ran out of the side of the dog's mouth, dripping on the ground and on Jim's leather pants. This in itself didn't worry Jim overmuch. Plenty of booze had been spilled on that pair of pants. He just didn't like to be thought of as a sloppy drunk, especially when he wasn't the one doing the slopping. When he finally took the bottle from the dog's mouth and wiped the booze and dog spit from his leathers, he saw the liquor level had gone down considerably. The dog braced its legs and shook itself, producing a fresh spray of saliva. Finally the dog swayed slightly and growled contentedly. "Damn, but I needed that."

Jim had never seen a dog sway on its feet before. At the same moment, a lone rider moved slowly down the street, a strangely insubstantial figure wearing a ragged Civil War uniform, bowed over in the saddle of a pale and exhausted horse. Jim glanced quickly at the horse and rider and decided that he didn't even want to speculate on their story. He turned back to the dog and gestured toward the opium den. "If I wanted to go to that place, what would I have to do?"

The dog was noticeably slurring now. "Well, you don't just go walking in the front door. That's for sure."

"I need to be introduced to Sun Yat?"

"It's not even as easy as that."

"It isn't?"

"The truth is that it's all down to Doc's whim. And you better believe me, Doc has his whims."

Jim sighed. "I'd sure like to get me some of that opium time. I could handle laying in the rack and just drifting and dreaming."

The dog grinned. "I heard that Doc drifts all the way back to Earth in his opium dreams."

Jim nodded thoughtfully. "Indeed? I really could handle some of that."

The dog wasn't exactly encouraging. "I wouldn't worry about it too much. If Doc likes you, you'll get an invite. If he don't, you won't be around long enough to need one."

Jim didn't want to hear what happened to people to whom Doc took a dislike, so he turned the direction of the conversation a couple of points sideways. "You said Sun Yat's place was next to where the whorehouse used to be?"

"That's right."

"So what happened to the whorehouse?"

The dog laughed. "Oh, the house is still there. It's the whores that are gone. They all got religion and moved on. You know what whores are like when they get religion. Some say it's because they spend too much of their working life staring up at Heaven."

Jim didn't know what whores were like when they got religion. All the whores he could remember had pretty much remained whores, except the ones who switched careers to become junkies, but he let it pass. "So where did they go?"

The dog shook his head. "I don't know for sure. Rumor was that they split to some holier-than-thou ectosector run by this broad calling herself Sister Aimee."

"Sister Aimee?"

"That's what I heard. Seems she's got a place set up way down yonder, like some Sunday school heaven."

Jim thought about this. "Didn't Doc kinda take it amiss?"

The dog frowned. "Why should Doc worry?"

"Didn't he create the whores in the first place?"

The dog looked at Jim as though he were an idiot. "Hell, no. Doc didn't create too much of this."

Jim was surprised. "He didn't?"

"Well, I mean, he made the buildings and stuff, but you can see how much trouble he took with those. Dr. Caligari lavished more care on his cabinet."

Jim looked around. Most of the buildings were unfinished in some way, leaning on each other at disconcerted angles.

"Goddamned things are held together with nothing more than faith and baling wire," the dog continued. "I gotta tell you, I don't even feel safe pissing on them when Doc's not paying attention. It's a miracle they make it from one day to the next, but Doc doesn't exactly cotton to making things too solid."

"But what about the people?"

"Doc didn't make the people."

Jim was having trouble getting a handle on what the dog was saying. "No?"

"He didn't make you, did he?"

Jim was still confused. "No, but I assumed—"

The dog cut him off. "Don't come around here assuming, boy. This is not a place to be making assumptions. Doc strongly disapproves of dreaming up people just to act as extras in the fantasy. It's like he always says, 'If you can't attract a population of real folk, then fuck you.' Doc thinks cookie-cutter populations tempt the psychos and sadists."

"So how did all these people get here?"

The dog looked at him impatiently. "Listen, if I gotta be the goddamned talking guidebook, you could at least give me another drink."

Jim held up the bottle. Little more than an inch and a half of whiskey left in it. He looked at the dog. "If I give you a drink, it'll kill the bottle. You fucking spill half of it."

"So you get up and go over to the cantina and get another one. What's the problem?"

"The problem is I'm not sure I can walk."

The dog regarded him bleakly. "Of course you can walk. You just don't want to make the effort."

The dog's attitude was starting to piss Jim off. "So why don't you go and get your own bottle? You've got four fucking legs."

It seemed that Jim was beginning to piss the dog off, too. Its voice took on an aggrieved snarl. "It's hard to carry a fucking bottle when all you've got is paws."

Jim didn't need to be snarled at by a damned alcoholic dog. "Maybe you should hang a barrel of cognac around your neck like a fucking St. Bernard."

The dog bared its teeth at Jim in what amounted to a snarl. "Fuck you. I'll go someplace where the drunks are a bit more hospitable."

For a moment, Jim thought the dog was about to bite him and he wondered how the hell he should deal with that. Could you actually punch out a dog? Then the dog started to walk away. Jim realized he'd probably made an error in good manners. He called after the dog. "Hey, wait up. You can have the last of the booze."

The dog turned and looked at him with an expression of utter canine contempt. "Keep your fucking booze. I got friends, if you know what I mean." And with that ambiguous parting shot, it trotted off in the direction of the cantina.

Jim watched as the dog vanished inside the cantina. He half expected it to reemerge a few moments later, followed by an entire pack of talking dogs intent on ripping him to shreds in canine retribution for the disrespect that he had afforded one of their number. Although Jim had never actually witnessed or even heard a firsthand account of such an occurrence, a rumor did exist in the Afterlife that, should you be torn apart by dogs, blown up, or otherwise have your quasi-corporate body fragmented into multiple pieces, you were in a lot of trouble. The essential core of one's being, the part that some called the soul, would almost certainly return to the pod; that wasn't the problem. The real problem was that the other bits might actually attempt to reconstitute themselves with often grotesque and monstrous results, and even come looking for you.

He struggled to his feet and stood waiting, but when, after a reasonable passage of time, no vengeful dog crew snarled from the cantina, Jim sat back down again and resumed his previous indolence. Long Time Robert Moore had started in on another tune, and Jim simply relaxed, closed his eyes, and let the sound wash over him.

If I wake tomorrow
I ain't guessing where I'll be
Maybe in some other time
Maybe in misery

Jim's eyes remained closed, until a second voice roused him. Someone else seemed bent on breaking in on his precious internal privacy. He looked up and discovered a bulky man wearing a dashiki, a riot of red gold and green, with his hair puffballed out in a vast Afro. The man was standing over him, grinning down with a mouthful of jewel-encrusted teeth that put Long Time Robert Moore's lone diamond to diminutive shame. "I'm Saladeen."

Jim nodded. "Saladeen?"

"Right?"

Jim found it hard to drag his eyes away from the gem-filled bridgework, but he extended a tentative hand. "I'm pleased to make your acquaintance."

Saladeen grasped the offered hand, fortunately with no fancy ritual handshake. "You Jim Morrison, ain't you?"

Jim tensed and slowly drew his legs up protectively, in readiness to flee or fight as circumstances might dictate. "I was last time I looked."

"I saw you one time."

Jim relaxed slightly. Apparently he didn't owe Saladeen money and he hadn't done anything terrible to his sister. He raised a neutral eyebrow. "You did?"

"I did. It was in Oakland in 1968. Of course, you didn't see me. You was up on the bandstand posing in the spotlight, I was down in the crowd selling loose joints and nickel bags."

"I hope you enjoyed the show."

"I thought you were a crazy motherfucker."

Jim decided to accept that as a compliment. He eased himself out of fight-or-flight mode and raised his bottle. "Well, thanks. I'd offer you a drink, but this bottle's all but dead."

Saladeen shook his head. "I'm okay for the moment. Besides, I've got my own euthanasia." So saying, he pulled a fat, double-corona, three-paper reefer from the folds of his dashiki, and gestured to the sidewalk next to Jim. "You mind if I take the weight off? I ain't invading your space or nothing, am I?"

Jim raised an invitational arm. "Help yourself, man. I got all the space I need."

Saladeen lowered his bulk to the wooden sidewalk. "I see that crazy fucking Euclid was hustling you for drinks."

Jim was puzzled. Had he missed something? "Euclid?"

"The dog you were talking to."

"That's Euclid?"

"That's what he calls himself."

"Euclid the mathematician?"

Saladeen lit the imposing joint by simply igniting his index finger. For a moment his Afro was so wreathed in smoke that the two were almost a single cloud. "Fuck no, Euclid the dog, man. Euclid the mathematician has to be out somewhere with Einstein and Stephen Hawking by now, helping run the universe."

"He seemed kind of put out when the bottle started to run dry."

"Euclid's kinda short on good manners. Mostly folks let him slide, though, on account of he was executed and all."

The conversation seemed to be making odd jumps and Jim attempted to slow things down enough for them to make at least minimal sense. "The dog was executed?"

"You think he was a dog in his mortal life?"

"No, but . . . "

Saladeen passed Jim the joint. "He told you the electric chair in Parchman was banana-colored, am I right?"

Jim inhaled deeply and immediately felt a little solarized at the edges. "Yeah, that's right. It was his opening line."

"So how do you think he knew that?"

"I don't question it. I was talking to a drunken, crazy-looking dog."

Saladeen's smile faded. "You got some kinda prejudice against dogs? You maybe think you're better than a dog?"

Jim wasn't going to go along with this one. He did his best to avoid conflicts, but the guy was going too far. He passed back the joint. "You may not believe this, but there are times when I really do think I'm better than a dog. I mean, you won't ever see me catching Frisbees in my teeth."

Again Jim tensed slightly in anticipation of a possible negative reaction. To his surprise, Saladeen merely laughed. "So you ain't buying my line of bullshit, huh?"

Jim shook his head. "Not tonight."

The gems in Saladeen's teeth flashed in the lights from the cantina. "Just checking, if you know what I mean."

Inside, Long Time Robert Moore was still rocking the joint.

> If I wake tomorrow
> I ain't guessing where I'll be

Saladeen glanced at Jim. "Cat sings like a motherfucker, don't he?"

Jim nodded. "He surely does."

"I don't figure that his real name's no Robert Moore."

"No?"

"You just think about who he sounds like."

Jim thought about this, but he didn't feel that any answer was required right there and then. Particularly as Saladeen had already turned the discussion back to the subject of the black dog. "If you'd met Euclid back in the world, back when he was a human, it's likely you'd still have thought you were better than him."

"Yeah?"

Saladeen nodded solemnly. "Oh yeah."

"Low?"

"Real low."

"How low?"

"Low motherfucker. A piece of sorry-assed white trash that went by the name of Wayne Stanley Caxton. Shot three folks dead in a fucked-up, thirty-five-dollar armed robbery at a corner grocery in Tunica, Mississippi. I figure it was no loss to the world when they fried him. Some of the shit must've gotten through to him, though. If he come out of the pod as a dog, motherfucker must have developed some sense of shame."

"You think so?"

"Lot of folks here got themselves executed. Doc's real good

about letting them settle in his area. Figure it's because he came close enough to getting hung himself a couple of times. When you get yourself executed, man, you hit the pod feeling about as low-down and abject as it's possible to get. A lot of the worst of them just wraith out and become haunts and night creepers. Particularly the serial killers and sex butchers. By the time you make it to the priest and governor and the thirteen steps to the Great Divide, you're thinking that you don't got any other option. The man got the system set up so you be feeling like an all-time fucking wretch when they strap you in the chair or the gas chamber or onto the gurney for the lethal jolt. Think about it. You spend years on death row. Eight, nine, ten years, man. Twisting and turning, appealing and petitioning, with everyone telling you that you've sunk so low you no longer deserve to live. So, when you land in the Great Double Helix and all them dreams come to you in the pod, they ain't about you going into the Afterlife as King of the fucking World, I can tell you."

"You'd know about that, bro?"

"Is that a discreet way of asking me if I was fried myself?"

Jim kept a perfectly straight face. "About as discreet as I could put it."

"Well, the answer is no. I didn't go to the chair or the gas chamber or the lethal injection, or even a Utah firing squad or a French guillotine. Me, I was shot by a fucking cop. A small-town, red-necked, Coors-beer, pig son of a bitch who thought he'd pulled over Eldridge Cleaver or some shit. November tenth, 1972, Barstow, California at nine-seventeen in the evening. Just trying to get myself the fuck away from L.A."

"I guess that didn't make you feel so good, either."

"I'm telling you, man. I came out of that pod as mean as hell. After a while, though, when I saw how things were, I started figuring that I was probably lucky."

"How did you figure that?"

"I never had to trip on no death row contemplation, bro. Or no terminal cancer ward, for that matter. And for those mercies I was profoundly grateful, you know what I'm saying? If you gotta go at the hands of the man, you best make it fast and furious."

The joint was now down to a roach; Saladeen nipped off the hot coal with a callused thumbnail and ate what remained. "That's maybe why Doc lets them hole up here. He didn't go no fast and furious. He did his own share of twisting and turning on them TB blues before he passed over. Fast and furious be the only route."

Jim nodded. "I can see that."

"Lee Oswald, man. That's the only way to go. You're walking through the door into that parking garage, man. Nothing on your mind except how the fuck are you going to get out of this deep shit and then BAM! Jack Ruby with his hat on and you gone before you even know it, homes. No ten years of lawyers and thinking about it."

After that, Jim found himself at a stoned loss for words. There was really nothing to say, and for long minutes the two men sat in silence until Saladeen spoke again. "He was here for a while, you know?"

"Who was?"

"Lee Oswald."

"You're putting me on."

"I swear. A wandering soul wandering through. He was calling himself Harvey Hydell, and he'd taken on the physical form of Leon Trotsky, but most everyone knew. And those that didn't figured it out in time."

"Leon Trotsky? Are you jerking me around?"

Saladeen looked angry. "Leon fucking Trotsky. Leader of the motherfucker Red Army, purged by Stalin, assassinated 1940, Mexico City. What's the matter, jerkoff? You think I don't know what Leon Trotsky look like? You think I'm stupid or something?"

Jim held up a hand. "Just slow down here, okay? Don't get so fucking hair-trigger on me. I was just thinking what a weird choice it was to look like Leon Trotsky. I mean, those fucking glasses and the beard and the sticking-up hair. Jesus Christ."

Saladeen shrugged. "I guess the motherfucker wasn't aiming for handsome. You know what I mean? Being a paradox wrapped in an enigma got to be some burden to bear. Can't leave you too much time to be doing handsome, yo?"

After Saladeen's sudden flash of temper, Jim thoroughly expected him to get up and take his leave after this statement, but the big man surprised Jim by remaining exactly where he was. He didn't speak for a while and then he grinned sheepishly. "Listen, I—"

Jim shook his head. "No big thing."

Saladeen turned away, staring off down the street and across the desert. "I guess I still ain't gotten over being mad at—" He abruptly stopped and his back stiffened. "Uh-oh."

Jim quickly turned. "What?"

"Uh-oh."

This second uh-oh was one of the least encouraging uh-ohs that Jim ever remembered hearing. Saladeen continued to peer out into the desert. "I think we may have a problem yonder."

Jim looked where he was looking. A bright blue-white light was zigzagging across the desert, laid low to the ground but, as far as Jim could tell, making for the town. Jim glanced at Saladeen. "What is that?"

Saladeen ignored him as he watched the light. It seemed to be coming nearer. He cursed slowly under his breath. "Shee-it."

Jim was starting to become a little alarmed. "So what is it?"

Saladeen scowled. "It could be anything. There's always lights buzzing about in the desert. Could just be random leak-through. Or it could be a harbinger."

"A harbinger of what?"

Saladeen's scowled deepened. "That's always the tricky part with harbingers."

The hard, rocky, and already uneven ground of Golgotha was now so littered with human skulls and bones that it was all but impossible to walk without crunching them underfoot. Semple's high heels constantly threatened to twist out from under her, and she was beginning to profoundly regret that she had insisted that the meeting be held in this accursed place. To deliberately irritate Aimee, Semple had chosen a suit in guardsman red, an eighties-style *Dynasty*-retro number with a short and very tight skirt and a flounced jacket with enormous shoulders. The ensemble was completed by matching pillbox hat and veil, and the already-mentioned shoes with their impractical heels. Aimee, on the other hand, had dressed in blue for their meeting, pumping her image of innocence and purity on this occasion with shades of the Virgin Mary. She even had a faint rainbow halo hovering above her head. Aimee definitely seemed to be in the process of making the transition from the loyally devout to the independently divine; plus the simple fact of having been organized enough to arrive first allowed her to establish her high ground and spare herself the need to stumble over the strewn bones in front of an audience. In this respect, Semple had definitely been aced out in the current round of the struggle.

Prior to the complete separation of herself and Aimee, the fiction had always been that the horror landscape of Golgotha was a creation of Semple's. She was the dark half. Who else could bring into being such a vivid tableau of desolation, suffering, and mortal misery? Semple, however, had repeatedly denied this. She had no memory of doing any such thing. Certainly, the necessary evil lurked in her heart, but the grisly brutality of Golgotha, with its multiple crucifixions and its stark, wind-scorched terrain, just wasn't Semple's style. Golgotha was primitive, stinking, and foul, and her signature wasn't on any part of it.

After a long time, Aimee had all but managed to convince her that she must have brought the ghastly location into being quite unconsciously, in a dream or when she was occupied with something else. Aimee had reasoned that it must be the product of a deeply buried nastiness from the lower murk of Semple's tainted psyche. It was only after the separation had become absolute, and Golgotha had not only remained but also extended itself, that the truth had finally to be faced. Golgotha had nothing to do with Semple. It had grown and continued to grow from some flaw of corruption in Aimee's soul. Semple might be the dark half, but Aimee wasn't without her own secret reservoirs of shadow. From Semple's perspective, the only disturbing factor in the revelation was that, if Aimee wasn't as pristine and perfect as she pretended, it might also indicate that Semple herself wasn't all bad. At some point in the future, an unanticipated inner virtue might rise up and betray her at the worst possible moment.

Once the truth was out, Semple had taken every opportunity to remind Aimee of the embarrassing fact that Golgotha was entirely hers. That was why Semple had insisted that they meet there, but now it looked as if instead of Semple rubbing Aimee's nose in the wart on her psyche, she was about to twist, distastrously, one or both of her own ankles. Semple's scarlet alligator spike crunched down on a partial human rib cage and she stumbled badly. She had to take three quick steps sideways to avoid falling, while, to her total chagrin, Aimee watched with an amused smile and the crew of nuns that flanked her hid their faces in the wimples of their white habits and tittered behind their hands.

"Are you drunk, sibling dear?"

Semple regained her balance and glared at her sister. "No, I'm not drunk. It's becoming impossible to walk in this place. Couldn't you have someone clean it up? Or at least clear some paths through the bones?"

"Perhaps it's the extreme impracticality of your footwear?"

This remark drew a fresh burst of smothered sniggering from the nuns, and Semple wished that she had the time to create a dozen or so Mongol tribesmen or Russian soldiers from World War II. They would make short work of those bitches. "If you have to have this accursed place, you could at least make some effort to maintain it. If they aren't cleared out soon, the damned bones will start piling up in drifts. Where do you think you are? Pol Pot's Cambodia?"

Aimee glanced at one of the nuns. "Make a note, my dear. The Place of Skulls needs to be tidied up."

The nun nodded and produced a small notebook and silver pencil to take down the memo. Semple had heard that both the retinue of nuns and also the gaggle of women dressed in torn and filthy sackcloth, the ones with the wild hair and mad staring eyes, who clustered at the foot of the crosses watching the agonies of the gasping, groaning victims with ugly relish, had previously worked as prostitutes in the notorious ectosector of the degenerate ex-dentist and hired killer called John Holliday. They were, however, a recent addition to Aimee's human menagerie, arriving well after Semple had gone her own way, so she could not be completely sure of the story's veracity.

Aimee turned her attention back to Semple. "Why don't you come closer, my dear?"

Semple shook her head. "I think I'll stay right here." Another attempt to stumble across the field of dry bones would only risk further humiliation and even injury.

Aimee smiled indulgently. "So have you decided to find me my poet?"

Semple nodded. "Yes, I have."

Aimee looked surprised. "Just like that? No conditions? No discussion? No negotiating points?"

"I said I'd do it, didn't I?"

Now the two sisters faced each other across a space of about fifteen feet. All around them, a forest of crosses, some empty, some bearing a roped and nailed occupant, reared against the angry red sky and the roiling purple clouds like diseased and leafless trees. Since they were already dead, the victims of Golgotha never actually died, but at some point in their torture, often after a number of days of excruciating pain, they simply vanished. The suffering became too much for them and they vibrated out and took the wind route back to the pod. The strange part of it all was that no real reason existed for these individuals to suffer at all. In theory, they could have made their exit before they even reached the cross, or the first nail was driven into their feet or hands. The obvious inference was that those who went along with their own quasi-executions were either advanced masochists, guilt-racked religious fanatics, or insanely locked into the fantasy.

Another peculiar consideration was that the majority of those who underwent crucifixion were genuine entities and not Aimee's tame creations. The unfortunates were drawn from the numbers of odd spirits who had trouble assuming an identity and personality of their own in the Afterlife and gravitated to the constructs of others, in this case Aimee's personal Heaven. By far the greater percentage of these sad arrivals caused no problems in Heaven, blending easily with the manufactured angels and cherubs. The victims on the crosses—all but a couple of exceptions of the male gender—must have transgressed in some way and were paying the price. Semple understood that the malefactors and heretics were usually fingered by one or another of the ex-prostitute nuns, who had the dual function of acting as Aimee's spy net and ideological secret police. As the saying went, there was nothing more righteously vindictive than a reformed whore. The only thing that remained a total mystery to Semple was where the constantly increasing numbers of bones were coming from.

Aimee, having arranged to be slightly farther up the sere, central hill of Golgotha, was able to talk down to her sister with a far-from-warranted superiority. "So when do you intend starting out on your quest?"

"I thought I'd go right now."

Aimee looked surprised. "Right now?"

Semple nodded. "That's right. Unless you can think of any reason to delay."

"I can think of none. Where are you intending to commence your search?"

"I was going to travel directly to Necropolis."

Aimee frowned. "Necropolis? Is that wise?"

"It's the closest confluence."

"Necropolis is an evil place. Old and evil and made worse by the passage of time. I heard there were over a million souls there, all subject to the will of one being who claims to be the god Anubis and is reputed to be the personification of iniquity."

Semple smiled annoyingly. "I thought it would be my kind of place."

"You could encounter many strange things in Necropolis."

A troop of small black monkeys with bald white faces like little old men was rooting through the litter of bones and tossing them around as though attempting a miniature re-creation of the prologue of Stanley Kubrick's 2001. At the mention of the word "Necropolis," however, they stopped what they were doing and appeared to settle down to listen to the conversation. Semple noted that animals and birds were a new addition, and wondered what fresh weirdness might be eating at the underside of her sister's mind. Along with the monkeys, a flock of vultures flapped and squabbled between the crosses, rats scurried through the lower levels of the bone piles, and skinny yellow dogs snarled and scavenged. "Like it's so totally normal around here?"

"Don't take Anubis too lightly. I understand he runs a brutally sophisticated police state."

Semple glanced at Aimee's gang of nuns but didn't comment on their homegrown secret-police tactics. "I have quite a rep as a funster myself. I don't see why I should be afraid of any jackal-headed Egyptian death god. Besides, he's almost certain to be a phony."

"Phony or not, I've also heard he encourages cannibalism."

Semple looked hard at her sister. The monkeys continued to watch intently. "Does something about my leaving worry you? Are you trying to put me off?"

"Of course not. Why should it?" Once again Aimee's answer wasn't ringing true. "Are you concerned that putting distance between us will create some kind of problem?"

"That's ridiculous."

"Is it?"

"I hadn't even considered it."

"You hadn't?"

"No, I hadn't."

Semple shrugged. "It did occur to me that a separation might have an effect on us."

"What kind of effect?"

Semple suddenly realized that her observation had been more accurate than she had imagined. "I don't know. A stretching of the bonds and connections between us might in some way weaken or diminish us."

Aimee was starting to look a little frightened. "Do you think it will?"

"I don't know. It might."

"But you'll take that chance?"

"You want your poet, don't you?"

"Yes, but . . . "

"Then I have to leave. It had to happen sooner or later. We can't remain joined by an invisible umbilical for all eternity."

"I know that."

"Particularly if you have plans to replace God."

Aimee took a step back and looked around quickly at her entourage of nuns. "I don't have plans to replace God. That's a terrible thing to say."

"It's true, though."

"It's blasphemous."

"That doesn't mean that it's not true."

"But it's *not* true."

Semple gestured to the nuns surrounding her sister. "You want to watch out for those bitches, Aimee. Like Winston Churchill used to say about the Germans, they're either at your feet or at your throat." She glanced up at the nearest cross in clear warning. "Don't make any wrong moves, sister, or they'll have you nailed to the wood."

Semple gave Aimee points for speed of recovery. She gathered her attitude, and was once again sweet and superior. "Is that your parting thought?"

"I suppose so."

"And you intend to leave from here?"

Semple forced a grin. She was a little scared, too, but the nonchalant swashbuckler in her would never allow her to admit it. "Here's as good a place as any to vibe away. No point in waiting around."

"You'll wind-walk directly to Necropolis?"

"It's big enough. I doubt I can miss it. Will you and your crew of nuns help energize me?"

Aimee nodded. "Of course."

Semple indicated that Aimee and her nuns should form a circle around her, with Aimee directly facing her. As the nuns started to comply, the victim on one of the nearby crosses suddenly spoke. He was a swarthy man, only recently nailed in place, with fresh blood still running from his feet and palms. He addressed himself to Semple. "She's right, you know. There are cannibals in Necropolis. I should know. I was one. That's why I came here. To find salvation. It was—"

"You will remain silent!" He was cut off by one of the nuns breaking from the forming circle and rushing, screaming, at the unfortunate man. "No one asked you to speak! How dare you speak?" She reached the foot of the cross and flailed unmercifully at him with a heavy wooden rosary. Fortunately for him, the nun was comparatively short and even with the rosary she was able to land blows only on his legs and feet. Aimee quickly beckoned her back to the circle, and then glanced at Semple. "Are you ready?"

"I suppose so." The truth was she was having a little difficulty maintaining appearances. The crucified man's testimony had unnerved her more than she cared to admit. She might have had a renegade imagination and been fascinated by advanced vice, but Semple was well aware that eating people was fundamentally wrong.

The nuns raised their arms and pointed at Semple. Energy flowed from their fingertips directly to her, increasing in strength as Aimee and the nuns locked and focused their concentration. Semple's exterior began to vibrate. The landscape started to waver. She took a final look at Aimee. "I shall return with your poet."

Semple McPherson filled her mind with an image of Necropolis and vanished from her sister's Heaven.

The light was so intense that Jim felt as though hard radiation were coursing through his very being. The crisp air crackled and hummed and Jim could smell sudden whiffs of highly charged ozone. The walls of the incomplete buildings in Doc Holliday's tiny township vibrated with eerie, sympathetic resonances, and tremors shook the ground under his feet. Jim all but staggered under the assault on his senses. Even his taste buds were registering something bizarre and metallic. The roughly spherical maelstrom of light had made three fast passes, about four feet off the ground, up and down the street, from the desert approaches all the way to Sun Yat's opium den and back again. Then it had come to an abrupt stop right by the cantina, and right by where Jim and Saladeen, now on their feet and, in Jim's case, suddenly sober, were wondering what the hell was going to happen next. When the light halted, Long Time Robert Moore also stopped playing, and to Jim that was nothing but an ill omen.

The light was both a single entity and a composite of billions of tiny brilliant points, pulsing, revolving, and dancing, like the concentration of stars at the core of some violent galactic spiral. The overall effect was of blinding white, but if one dared to look for more than a moment, all the colors of the spectrum were present within it. Jim and Saladeen stood side by side, arms raised to cover their already tightly shut eyes. After a moment Jim sneaked a quick peek, but even that was enough to risk a retinal burn.

The light remained stationary for maybe a minute, although to Jim it seemed one hell of a lot longer. He began to fear, even though he felt no actual heat, that his clothes would start smoldering, that his exposed skin would be fried to a purple crisp. To Jim this looked like the kind of light that could put a bend in the universe and that might be equally capable of vaporizing his soul. Then, as he was on the verge of cutting and running, the awful light began to fade. Jim slowly lowered his arm as it dimmed, and the first thing he saw, among the lingering confusion of afterimages, was a group of three indistinct but apparently human figures at the heart of the glow.

Jim glanced at Saladeen. "What the fuck?"

But Saladeen had turned away, his eyes still shut. "No!"

"What?"

"NO!"

Saladeen's explosive response took Jim completely by surprise. The man was plainly terrified, something so out of character that it left Jim at a total loss. He looked back at the light and at the three figures. The light was little more than a dying ripple of pale stars, all but gone, and now he could see the figures as they really were. And that immediately posed the question of what they really were. Humanoid, but this clearer inspection raised major doubts that they were strictly human, more like characters from a tropical nightmare. All three stood close to nine feet tall, carrying with them an air of the unnatural. The central one was a statuesque female with ebony skin, wearing a floor-length robe that, as far as Jim could tell, was tailored from sheets of frozen flame. Her head was crowned by a massive headdress of spun gold and ostrich plumes.

To her right stood an impossibly skinny male, emaciated to the point of being scarcely more than a stick figure, dressed in formal evening wear, white tie and tails and a stovepipe hat so elongated and extended that it brought his overall height to well over eleven feet. The pale face below the hat was a naked skull, molded from some virgin-white material akin to fine porcelain. The third figure was also male, but more robust, decked out like the Fourth of July in a grandiose military uniform somewhere on the scale between Hermann Goering and Michael Jackson. The primary motif among his massed insignia was a jagged lightning bolt not unlike the flash on the uniform of Captain Marvel, Jr., or Elvis Presley's self-designed TCB logo. Jim might easily have judged this third figure as nothing more than an overdressed clown, right up to the moment that he saw the face. It was about as clownish as the face of Idi Amin, a face quite capable of talking to the severed heads of its victims for hours at a stretch, a face that looked able to sustain an immortal fury well beyond any reasonable limit.

As Jim wondered about the nature and purpose of this triple apparition, a voice inside his head, possibly some dislocated memory from the right brain, surprised him with at least half the answer. "The woman is Danbhalah La Flambeau, Queen of the Persisting Fire. The thin one is Guede Docteur Piqures, that's Dr. Hypodermic in English. He is the ruling spirit of narcotics and those addicted to them. You've had dealings with him before, although you won't remember. The one in the uniform is Baron Tonnerre, the Baron Thunder, the incarnate wrath of the gods. They are all middle-echelon Mystères from the Voodoo pantheon. They are very old and very cold and they are absolutely real, not a part of some ambitious stiff's fantasy. They're also very dangerous and you'd be well advised not to fuck with them."

Almost as though he could hear the message in Jim's brain, Saladeen urgently grabbed him by the arm. "Don't be looking at them, man! Just don't be looking at them!" Saladeen's eyes were still tightly shut, his head turned away even while he pleaded with Jim. "They can mount you and ride you. They can use you up until there's nothing left. Don't let them catch you looking at them, man. They carry the keys to the Masterlock."

But it was too late for Jim. He had looked and the three Mystères had seen him looking. As one, they turned and faced him. The light had now completely dissipated to the point that not a single tiny star remained. Now the Mystères were solid figures, glowing with a dead-fish shimmer. Their feet did set off tiny flashes of static, though, when they moved, as if they still carried a residual charge left by the radiation. Saladeen dropped to his knees, muttering incoherently. By far the worst feature of the three Mystères, though, was their eyes. Even from a distance, Jim could see those eyes far more clearly than he would ever have desired. The three pairs of eyes, even by the standards of the Afterlife, had no place in any human quadrant of either space or time. They were terrible windows to somewhere else, a place that Jim would never want to visit, let alone inhabit.

Dr. Hypodermic suddenly moved in a flurry of pale blue static. He was coming toward Jim, and Jim's insides turned to a very mortal ice water. In the normal course of events, the worst that could happen to one in the Afterlife was to be sent back to a pod on the Great Double Helix without passing Go. Who knew what a Voodoo Mystère could do to you, if he caught you looking at him and took a mind to mess you up? Mercifully, Danbhalah La Flambeau gestured to Dr. Hypodermic and he halted and turned away.

At the same time, the sound of a door slamming echoed from somewhere near Sun Yat's, and Doc Holliday came slowly but determinedly around the side of the building and down the street. The Voodoo gods shifted to face him. Distracted from Jim, they stood waiting for Doc while Jim breathed a sigh of temporary relief. It was Doc's town; let him deal with this terrifying trio. Maybe he was prepared for tourists from the Sinister Beyond. Certainly Doc didn't seem fazed by them. He showed no signs of hurry. His ruffled shirt, partially unbuttoned, seemed to have been hastily tucked in his black pants. A certain unsteadiness in his step suggested he was at least half in the opium bag.

The arrival of Doc also appeared to reassure Saladeen. He got slowly to his feet, but kept his eyes firmly fixed on the ground as he muttered a little shamefacedly to Jim, "I guess I just lost it."

Jim nodded. "I was close myself."

"This shit goes deep, if you know what I mean."

"I know what you mean, but Doc seems to be handling them."

"Doc's seen it all. Either here or in his dreams. Of course, Doc's True Bad himself."

Jim wasn't quite ready to believe that Doc was on a par with Voodoo gods. "Not like those things."

"No, not like those things, but he got his depths."

Indeed, Doc was now in conversation with the queen, the doctor, and the baron, seeming not even slightly intimidated by their size or demeanor. Doc's voice was soft and a little slurred and Jim couldn't make out what he was saying. The Mystères spoke in Haitian French patois, which Jim was absolutely unable to understand. What he didn't like, however, was the way Doc and the Mystères kept glancing in his direction as they conferred.

Saladeen shifted uncomfortably. "I hate to say this, homes, but I think you've been noticed."

Jim nodded worriedly. "I fear you're right."

Doc now appeared to be indicating to La Flambeau, Hypodermic, and Tonnerre that it might be a good idea to continue their conversation inside the cantina rather than out on the street. The doctor and the baron seemed to think otherwise, but Danbhalah La Flambeau took control and set off with Doc toward the entrance of the cantina. After a moment's hesitation, the two gods reluctantly followed. An intriguing logistics problem immediately presented itself. The doorway of the cantina afforded no more than seven feet of clearance, and Jim wondered how La Flambeau would negotiate it. Would she stoop down or what? Jim didn't think so, and, in confirmation, a section of the wall above the door dematerialized to permit her a suitably dignified entrance. As soon as she passed through, the piece of wall reappeared.

Hypodermic and Tonnerre had also mounted the steps, but instead of going straight inside, the two of them stopped and turned. They treated Jim to a long look before continuing into the cantina, and in the core of Jim's soul, the ice water rushed back with a vengeance.

As her sister glowed briefly, distorted, and vanished, Aimee McPherson felt a sudden wave of weariness and misgiving sweep over her. Semple was gone and there was no knowing when she might return and with what. She had asked her sister to seek out a poet, a creative force to help her expand and complete her Heaven, but it was anyone's guess what adaptations Semple might make along the way, what complications she might add the basic plan. A degree of malicious intent had to be figured into any equation of which Semple was a part, and possibly a measure of capricious improvisation. Aimee also felt suddenly very lonely. Semple might be difficult, even dangerous, but she had always been there, all through their life on Earth and clear into this very unsatisfactory Afterlife. She truly wondered how, now that Semple was no longer close at hand, she would fare without her. She knew all the stories about twins, Siamese or otherwise, and how, following the death or removal of one, the other would also terminally languish. She and Semple weren't exactly twins. In fact, they were closer than that. They were two separated halves of a single whole, and that posed a different set of problems.

She looked around Golgotha. Sweet Jesus, how she hated it. If it was at all possible, she never wanted to set foot in the Place of Skulls again. She turned to the entourage of nuns with a sigh. "Let's get out of here and go about our righteous business."

Semple McPherson arrived in Necropolis as a beam-me-down shimmer of transitional atoms, bounced across the curve by the collective telekinesis of Aimee and her nuns. As Semple emerged into comparative real-space, she discovered that she had arrived in an exact volumetric area already being occupied by an itinerant street boy, a cut-price, bicameral James Dean wearing two-tone eye makeup and metallic faux Egyptian clothing. Under other circumstances, the collision might have produced a serious conflict, perhaps even a low-yield plasmic detonation. The boy, however, who could have set new records in contrived vacancy, was absolutely no match for Semple's honed steel will and the collective energy still flowing through her. Her mind swarmed his, stunning all functions and rolling it helplessly over. At the same time, her molecules made an end run around his material structure and collapsed its base integrity, swiftly forcing him out toward Limbo.

"Back to the pod, kid. That'll teach you to get in my way."

She felt little more than a faint protesting whisper of his departing presence as she displaced him. The whisper, however, was enough to communicate the boy's gender, and for a single nanosecond she was tempted by the idea that it might be fun to retain it. She might enjoy being a boy, but she immediately rejected the thought as wild but impractical. She was on a mission in strange and maybe dangerous territory, and the novelty of being male might offer fatal distractions. The mere thought proved enough to raise a splinter on the banister of smooth transition, and Semple found herself snagged by a shard of the previous occupant.

The boy's soul may have gone easily, but the glitched body was harder to lose. Her momentary lapse had turned her into a burly hermaphrodite with full female breasts, both a vagina and a penis, a dishwater-blond pompadour and sideburns, and a bad case of acne. Worst of all, she also discovered that there was a great yawning divide between the two halves of his/her brain. Only a final and supreme effort of will restored the familiarity and comfort of her accustomed form, erased the superfluous male organs, and returned functional synchromesh to her frontal cortex. Even when all that had been achieved, though, she realized that her troubles had only just started.

Her body might be back, but she was now dressed in inherited clothing, albeit mercifully gender-corrected. In some respects, this was just as well. The scarlet *Dynasty* outfit would have been hideously out of place in this environment. On the other hand, the new costume that clung to her now presented its own challenge. She looked down at herself and saw that, apart from a wide collar of gilt and lapis that concealed nothing but part of her shoulders and her collarbone, she was naked from the waist up. The only consolation was that she was not the only woman so exposed. Toplessness, it seemed, was high fashion in the city of Necropolis.

Further observation quickly revealed that the creator of Necropolis was obsessed by the question of what ancient Egypt might have been like had its religion, aesthetics, and culture survived all the way to the end of the twentieth century. The creator, presumably the individual now posing as the god Anubis, had incorporated many of the fanciful projections of this obsession into the design of his postmortem world. One of these was that the women of Necropolis went around bare-breasted in public, much in the style of the thirteenth century B.C. Semple had never been anyplace where convention dictated naked breasts, and the experience took a little getting used to. It wasn't that Semple was a prude, or had any philosophical objection to flaunting her tits. When she and Aimee had divided, she had made sure that all of those inhibitions and hang-ups had been deposited with her sister. As if to prove her cultural flexibility, she swiftly reshaped herself so that the now-exposed and unsupported parts of her body showed themselves to their best advantage.

She then took stock of the rest of the ensemble that she would apparently be expected to wear for the duration of her visit. It consisted of a wraparound skirt with a long, narrow, decorative apron that extended from her waist to below her knees. Primary accessories proved to be the aforementioned gilt collar and a narrow cobra chaplet, also gilt, that circled her head, holding her now exceedingly curly black hair in place. On her feet, she discovered a pair of gold open-work thong sandals. Though she had no mirror, she suspected that, had she been able to see herself, her makeup would have been very like that of Elizabeth Taylor in *Cleopatra*. All in all, the effect was a futuristic version of a fresco from the era of Ramses II. She wasn't sure if she liked it, but it had a definite coherence. For something that had been quite literally thrust on her, the new look could have been a great deal worse.

Her next move was to take stock of the place where she found herself. She appeared to have materialized in a public plaza or atrium that ran the length of a huge, tunnellike structure of glass and cast iron that greatly resembled a Victorian railroad terminal from the golden age of steam, although, of course, it came without trains or tracks. The edges of this paved pedestrian area were lined with merchant stalls and booths, while its center was taken up by a long avenue of geometrically planted palm trees and massive marble statues of the gods of ancient Egypt. The tallest of these reared to a height of forty or fifty feet, almost to the curved glass roof of the structure. The place seemed reasonably busy. All around her, citizens, looking a lot like her, hurried and bustled about their business. Indeed, business appeared to be the key in this world. She had entered Necropolis in the middle of some mercantile center. As Semple absorbed all this, she scowled and took a deep breath. "I appear to have landed topless in a mall."

Shopping malls had, of course, developed well after Semple's and Aimee's death, but she had made an ample study of them during her investigation of Californian Valley girl culture. This example in Necropolis appeared to be a mall in decline. The overall look was one of dirt and neglect. The air was rank and polluted, and Semple's eyes were soon watering. Depressing gray light filtered through the filthy panes of the once-magnificent roof, more directly where they were actually missing. The precise lines of palms were either dead or dying; some had gone altogether, their planters standing empty like the sockets of decayed teeth. Drifts of ignored and uncollected garbage were heaped up in nooks and corners. Unhealthy, mal-formed pigeons flapped, fluttered, and scuttled between the feet of pedestrians, and Semple thought she saw rats moving among the piles of garbage.

As if in harmony with the dirt and decay, the people of Necropolis looked worried and stressed, as though the burdens of Afterlife lay heavy on them. Semple wondered how many of them had come there of their own accord, and how many were, like Aimee's angels, created by Anubis for his own amusement and gratification. They showed a distinct uniformity. They all wore the same clothes and similar makeup. They were all dark-haired and dark-skinned, and approximately the same height. No children were in evidence. All this led Semple to believe that the majority were created creatures of Anubis rather than formerly mortal souls. One sign of uniformity gravely disturbed Semple. As far as she could see, each and every one of the population had a computer barcode, black, rectilinear, and slightly larger than a postage stamp, printed squarely in the middle of his or her forehead, about three-quarters of an inch above the bridge of the nose, like a high-tech version of a Hindu caste mark.

Semple's immediate conclusion was that coming to Necropolis had been nothing less than a terrible mistake. No way was she going to find the poet of Aimee's schemes and dreams in this place. Poets couldn't flourish among a people so locked down that they let them-selves be computer coded. The manner of her arrival had also left a lot to be desired, and looked to have all the makings of embarrass-ment, or worse. Her brief but furious struggle to achieve a suitable bodily form had been observed by a large number of passersby, many of whom had stopped to stare as the body of the street boy had dis-solved into a vague column of shapeless ectoplasm and then recon-figured itself, first as the grotesque hermaphrodite and then as a tall, good-looking woman. Obviously this was no regular occurrence, and gawkers continued to gawk for some time after the fact, making it hard for her to blend with the surroundings.

As Aimee had predicted, Necropolis looked to be an iron-grip police state. From where she stood, Semple could see no less than three pairs of heavily armed and armored men, with the unmistak-able arrogant amble of law enforcement on patrol. In Necropolis, the faces of the cops were grimly anonymous, fully hidden behind the full-face visors of sinister egg-shaped helmets, wholly smooth apart from a decorative pair of stylized vestigial wings where the ears should have been. The officers' bulky, dark blue body armor gave them a weight of bully-boy power that caused the rest of the populace to allow them the widest possible berth. The armor was constructed from flat flexible bricks of Kevlar, arranged in the manner of an insect carapace, perhaps as some kind of scarab homage. The complex large-bore weapon that each officer carried in the crook of his arm was the ultimate demonstration of potential force. Semple had never seen guns like these before, but she could guess at their destructive power.

Semple's first impression, that coming to Necropolis had been a fundamental error, was now being confirmed by every fresh detail. She decided that her only chance was to get away from this too-public area. She needed to hole up in some secluded place and think through her next move. Without a team circle like Aimee's nuns to provide her with the necessary telekinetic energy boost, she couldn't simply vibe out the way she'd come, wind walking to the great wide open. She would have to blow town under her own power, but without the slightest knowledge of the geography or relative dimensions of the place, she knew this might require a modicum of planning.

Even in finding temporary refuge, Semple was beset by obstacles. The first rank of merchants and vendors along the edge of the plaza were just casual traders with small removable stalls. Behind them was a line of permanent structures that Semple had to assume were the Necropolis equivalent of stores and cafés. The problem was that all the signs were written in the hieroglyphics of the nineteenth dynasty and Semple was totally unable to read them. She could, of course, follow her nose. She had been around the block enough times to be confident that she could locate a bar or even a coffee shop by sense of smell. What worried her more was that she knew nothing of the manners and protocols of the city. What, for instance, was the status of women? Could a woman just walk into a bar and order a drink, or was that some kind of social taboo? And how would she pay for it? Did they have currency in this place? She remembered from her time on Earth that in certain bars ladies drank for free. If such a place existed here, how would she know? Damned hieroglyphics.

Semple was starting to realize how much she had forgotten about her and her sister's tent-show hustling days. The first two rules of going into a strange town were a girl had to know how to read the signs, and had to have a cash stake to get rolling. The Afterlife, with its easy fantasy fulfillments, had made her careless. If she didn't get back on the ball with some alacrity, she could well be paying for her isolation the hard way.

Head down, avoiding all eye contact and keeping as far as possible from the patrolling pairs of law officers, she quickly put some distance between herself and her arrival point, and the handful of witnesses who had seen what had gone down with the boy and the transitory hermaphrodite. Despite all her efforts to melt into the crowds, however, people kept on looking at her. No matter what evasive tactics she might employ, she continued to receive batteries of constant and curious stares. Even the stallholders at the edge of the square, who couldn't possibly have seen her strange arrival, glanced at her with expressions that might be reserved for some outlandish mutant.

Semple started to feel spooked and desperate. "What the hell is wrong with me?"

As far as she could tell, nothing was particularly unusual about the way she looked. She should have been at one with the crowd. It couldn't be her clothes. Both men and women wore some variation on the wraparound skirt. The colors and patterns might be a matter of individual choice, but no one deviated too far from the basic design. Everyone wore eye shadow and lipstick. Both genders were basically bare to the waist, although some of the men sported sleeveless jackets with jutting, science-fiction shoulders. Most wore decorative collars similar to the one that was around her own neck, and these only really differed in size and in the lavishness of their decoration, possibly serving as an indication of the wearer's status or wealth. Semple's collar was large and heavily inlaid with lapis; if the status theory held good, the goddamned proles ought to be treating her with a measure of respect, not eyeballing her like she had two heads.

"It has to be my face." She could see nothing wrong with the parts of her that were visible; the only logical conclusion was that the fault lay in an area that she was unable to see. She doubted that anyone had managed to affix the Necropolis equivalent of a KICK ME sign to her back. Had she come through somehow deformed, an elephant woman with three eyes or two noses? She had an easy and immediate way of finding out. She hurried to the glass display window of the nearest store and peered at her own reflection. She saw no disfigurement. In fact, her face looked pretty much as it always had, apart from a frame of new curls. As she had guessed, she was wearing a Cleopatra paint job. Her eyes were ringed with black kohl, drawn to elongated points at the outer corners and shadowed with imperial purple. What she hadn't expected was the white pearlized lip gloss, but she'd seen a number of other women sporting a similar innovation, so that could hardly be what was making everyone look. So what was the problem?

And then the weight of realization dropped on her. No barcode. No fucking barcode! She froze with her face close to the glass of the store window. Her heart sank. Everyone she'd seen, without exception, carried one on their forehead. She all but cursed out loud. "I'm in a fucking Egyptian police state with no fucking papers!" The clothes and makeup came with the goddamned territory. How come no barcode?"

The ramifications hardly bore thinking about, and questions crowded in so hard and fast that they all but pushed Semple to panic. How bad was the omission? Well, seemingly bad, if everyone goggled as though she were a freak. And what exactly did the barcode signify? Was it just a permanent ID, or did it go further? Maybe it was a money substitute, a tattooed credit card that was the basis of the city's entire economy. If that was the case, her pooch was screwed. Not only would she be regarded as some weird mutant, but she'd also be left to beg or starve. "Like, what do you intend doing about it, okay? You're in a mall with no money, girl."

The short-term answer seemed fairly simple. Everyone in town wore makeup, so there ought to be cosmetics stores in abundance. Beg, borrow, or steal. Get hold of an eyebrow pencil. Draw in a barcode of her own. It might not buy her a cup of coffee, but at least it would stop the stares. She scanned the line of stores on either side of her, and saw nothing that approached a beauty parlor or drugstore that might provide what she needed. The window she was using to examine her reflection belonged to some kind of fabric supply and displayed various colored bolts of the popular metallic cloth. The two stores on either side were disused and boarded up. This Necropolis mall was a haven for failure.

Semple began walking slowly along the row, turning her face away when anyone approached, trying to attract as little attention as possible. She passed a store that appeared to sell assorted stuff in earthenware jars that she assumed were some kind of foodstuffs, and another that had a window display of elaborate, harnesslike devices fashioned from leather and chains that she neither understood nor wanted to think about. No sign of cosmetics presented itself, but for all she knew, a sign saying FREE MASCARA HERE could have been staring her in the face and she wouldn't have been any the wiser. The next place she came to had no display window, but its stucco frontage was covered by a mass of hieroglyphics in garish multicolored neon. Although Semple had no idea of the literal content, the nature of the place was plain. A bar was a bar was a bar, anywhere in infinity.

Semple had a great deal more experience of bars and how to work and operate in them than many would have expected. Back when she and Aimee had inhabited the same mortal body, it had been Semple who, late at night, while Aimee withdrew from consciousness, dolled herself up, ultimately whore-trashy, all the way from lingerie to lipstick. It was Semple who slipped out of the hotel and went saloon cruising for sailors, studs, and salesmen, so in the morning Aimee could pretend that she hadn't enjoyed them.

This bar in Necropolis had a smell that, although unmistakable, was a little sweeter than the usual shot, beer, and cigarette aroma of a regular twentieth century joint. Semple didn't know what this might portend, but she figured she absolutely had to make a move. She walked past the neon hieroglyphics, turned into the alcohol warmth of the dark doorway, hesitated for a moment, and, hoping for the best, went inside.

Two deep sonorous booms, like slowed-down thunderclaps, echoed from the cantina. They were followed, a couple of seconds later, by rapid fire-bursts of blue-white light like the popping of photographers' flashbulbs. The thirty feet of hanging silk that covered one of the missing sections of wall suddenly billowed outward as though blown by an exhalation of giant breath. In the middle of the street, Jim glanced at Saladeen. "Looks like the Haitians are having themselves a high time in the old saloon."

Saladeen shuddered. "Don't even talk about them."

By this point, all but a handful of the human and animal clientele had left the cantina. Long Time Robert Moore had been among the first, hurrying out with his guitar case in one hand and the other clamped hard to his hat, holding it in place like a storm was threatening. Euclid the dog was hiding under the same section of sidewalk where Jim and Saladeen had previously been sitting, invisible except for a pair of wary, mismatched eyes. Both Doc and Lola, however, had elected to remain inside. Jim was tempted to go inside and take a look. He was curious to see how a trio of honky-tonking Voodoo demigods disported themselves. More important, he could feel the booze calling out to him through the traumatic night, just the way it had done one million times before, booze being no respecter of either place or situation. He was over the shock of the blinding light and the Mystères' arrival, but now he was a little put out that his benignly comfortable high had been so rudely demolished. He wanted to get to work rebuilding its warm protective euphoria as soon as he could. About the only thing that stopped him from boldly going up the steps and in the door was the fact that Saladeen would undoubtedly freak out. Afro-boy seemed positively terrified of the Queen, the Baron, and the Doctor. The chance existed, of course, that Saladeen knew something he didn't, and for the moment Jim bided his time.

It didn't take long, however, before Jim's cravings overtook him. He started walking, but faltered when another of the rumbling booms rolled from inside. This hesitation gave Saladeen a chance to catch up with him. "Are you out of your fucking mind, man? You can't go in there."

Jim turned angrily on his short-time companion. "Who the fuck says I can't? I've got a killer thirst coming on and no bunch of shantytown spooks is going to eighty-six me out of the bar."

Saladeen all but turned green. "You're fucking crazy, Morrison. You don't know what the fuck you're messing with."

"And I suppose you're going to tell me?"

Saladeen was staring wide-eyed at a new popping flurry of blue brilliance. "I ain't telling you nothing."

Jim was losing patience. "What's with you? You sound like a fucking Tarzan movie. 'Don't go in there, bwana. Many evil spirits.'"

This was too much for Saladeen and anger finally overrode his fear. "You wanna watch what you're saying, motherfucker. No one talks to Saladeen Al Jabar like that."

Jim stared hard in Saladeen's face. "Oh yeah?"

They were virtually toe to toe. "Fucking right, motherfucker! Nobody."

The two men might have fallen to brawling right then and there if Doc Holliday hadn't come walking out of the cantina at the same moment. He looked around, spotted Jim and Saladeen, and started in their direction. "Morrison, a moment, sir. I need to have a word with you."

Jim stepped away from Saladeen and took a breath. "We'll get back to this later."

Saladeen glared. "I'll be waiting on you."

Doc took in the way the two men were bristling at each other. For a moment, it looked as though he were going to comment, but then he seemed to think better of it and addressed himself directly to Jim. "You had better relax yourself, my friend. I have a request to make of you that I don't think you're going to like."

Jim sighed. "I usually have to be in town at least a full day before they start giving me the bad news." He glanced at Saladeen. "I mean, I haven't even gotten in a fight yet."

Doc ignored the glance. "I regret I'm going to have to ask you to leave town."

Jim couldn't believe Doc was saying it. "Leave town?"

"You got it."

"You're running me out of town?"

"That's about the size of it."

"But I didn't do anything."

"I didn't say you did."

"You've got multiple-murdering dogs drinking themselves stupid on the street and you want to run my inoffensive ass out of town?"

"It isn't any negative reflection on your character, believe me."

"It isn't?"

"You've got to realize that it's nothing personal."

Doc half glanced in the direction of the cantina and Jim immediately fixed on this. "This is some Voodoo-instigated bullshit, right?"

"It is, but don't ask because I can't tell."

"They told you to toss me out of town?"

Doc treated Jim to a hard, warning look. "Keep your damned voice down."

Saladeen threw in his ten cents' worth. "You tell him, Doc. Lame won't listen to me. Motherfucker hasn't got the brains to be scared of them."

Doc regarded Jim bleakly. "A man's best friend can be a measure of healthy fear."

"I thought a man's best friend was his dog."

"Not the way dogs are here."

Saladeen upped his bet to a full quarter. "If someone told me to get out of town and was good enough to let me know it was Queen Danbhalah motherfucker La Flambeau and her crew behind it, I'd be long gone; no questions. You know what I mean? Lawdy mama, feets do your stuff; *all* the minstrel bullshit, and this nigger wouldn't give a damn. You better believe me, Morrison. I'd be history, and willingly."

Jim looked from Saladeen to Doc, and a glint of the old devil was kindled in his eye. "And what if I just stayed put?"

Doc half turned so the light glinted on the gold lightning flash and the mother-of-pearl grip of Elvis's deluxe Colt. The gun rested heavy in the shoulder holster on the left side of Doc's chest. Jim's eye was immediately drawn to it. Doc observed where he was looking and he cracked a dry smile. "Persuasive?"

Jim slowly nodded. "It's the Gun That Belonged to Elvis, isn't it?"

Doc's expression was uncompromising. "Wholly correct, my unfortunate friend."

Weapons in the Afterlife, particularly firearms, were mainly props to image or vanity, or leftover habits. In the normal run of things, they presented little more than a momentary threat to anyone but the created creatures of fantasy. The Gun That Belonged to Elvis was a little different, however. Like the Flaming Sword of the Red Angel, the Slingshot of David, Hitler's Revolver, the Knife Prince Yussupov Used to Kill and Castrate Rasputin, or the Great Siege Cannon of Don Carlos O'Neal, the Gun That Belonged to Elvis was a significant figment of celestial mythology and postmortem folklore. As such, its effect was totally unpredictable. A gold bullet from its barrel might well blast Jim all the way back to the Great Double Helix, or even rearrange him into some totally new, unknown, and probably unacceptable form. Jim had seen the very same pistol used against Moses, and the self-designed prophet had appeared to suffer nothing more than brief pain, but Jim Morrison wasn't going to take any chances. Now that his memory was slowly returning, he recalled too many of the legends concerning the Colt of Elvis. That Doc Holliday should even threaten him with it meant the situation was grave; no negotiation or debate.

Jim deflated with a shrug. "So I guess that's it. Come with the dust and be gone with the wind."

Without anyone noticing his approach, Long Time Robert Moore was standing beside the three men. The lone diamond in the gold tooth twinkled as he spoke. "I'll give you a ride as far as the Crossroads, if you want it, boy."

Jim frowned. "A ride?"

The old bluesman grinned. "In my Cadillac."

"You got a Cadillac?"

"Sure do. Long and black and fully loaded."

"As far as the Crossroads?"

"All the way to the Crossroads."

"What happens at the Crossroads?"

"You go your way and I go mine."

Jim hesitated. The other three looked at him intently. Finally Jim laughed. "Sure, I'll take a ride to the Crossroads in your Cadillac."

Robert Moore nodded. "Then I'll go and get the car. You all just wait right here."

As Moore walked away, a pair of more staccato, higher-pitched bangs cracked from the cantina. Jim, Doc, and Saladeen half ducked, but Long Time Robert Moore just kept on walking.

When he returned with his Cadillac a few minutes later, the first thing Jim knew was that Robert Moore's car couldn't be faulted for magnificence. It was a black Coupe de Ville, probably a '56 or '57, but so majestically customized that its true origins were obscured. It sported six headlights and four military spots. It had been lengthened to forty feet long, and the oversized fins looked designed for a V2 rocket. The black gloss of the Cadillac's paintwork was so perfect, so opulent and deep, that it threatened to drown anyone looking too closely. Instead of the standard lavish chrome bumpers, the ones on Long Time Robert's car were in the form of two relief figures of naked women, sculpted in the style of Erté.

The huge juggernaut of a car pulled up beside Jim. The passenger door swung open and Long Time Robert Moore waved for him to get in. Jim looked at Doc. "So I guess I'm out of here?"

"Like I said, it isn't personal."

"I never did get to visit Sun Yat."

"Maybe next time."

"Next time?"

"Infinity is a very long time, my friend."

Jim sighed. "Ain't it just."

He lowered himself into the leopardskin interior of Robert

Moore's Cadillac. It smelled of incense, old leather, Chanel No. 5, and high-test marijuana. Robert Moore sat behind the wheel; to Jim's surprise, a Marilyn Monroe blonde, complete with white dress, was sitting in back. She smiled at him as he got in, but said nothing. Long Time Robert Moore put the car in gear and glanced at Jim. "Ready to go, rock and roll boy?"

Jim nodded. "Ready to go."

Although the outside light could hardly be described as bright, it took Semple's eyes a few moments to adjust to the red gloom inside. As soon as she was able to see, she was pleased to discover that her supposition had been correct. The decor might be Egyptienne, but it was a saloon as she knew and recognized one, complete with bar, stools, and booths to one side. All it lacked was a jukebox playing Patsy Cline or Frank Sinatra, but they probably didn't have such things in Necropolis. The dim interior made it hard to see every detail, but the place reminded her of a run-down version of some up-market deco joints she had seen on Earth.

She had half expected something weird and exotic, like reclining couches and a sunken bar, or perhaps oiled slaves wielding peacock fans and pouring odd-colored wine from stone jars, but what she'd found was all disconcertingly normal. Maybe the standard barroom setup from the twentieth century was simply the most practical design for serving alcohol, or maybe Anubis's imagination had failed on this detail. About the only radically different element was a flat, triangular, wall-mounted screen behind the bar. Semple had to assume it was a Necropolis television set, but, coming as she did from the age of radio, she had little experience of TV. All she gathered was that, at least at the moment, Necropolis TV wasn't showing any actual programs. Just the jackal head of Anubis, slowly and regally revolving against a dramatic sky filled with threatening storm clouds.

Semple selected a barstool and seated herself. She experienced a certain dismay when she saw no other women customers; she'd been hoping to borrow a makeup kit in the ladies' room with which to fake a makeshift barcode. On the other hand, she hadn't been instantly ejected, so she seemed to have made it this far without violating any local custom. The only other customer was an overweight man, his unattractive stomach sagging over his skirt. He and the bartender, a slimmer but balder individual, were at the far end of the bar, discussing the up-and-coming public punishment of runaway slaves. Apparently such events were a popular spectator sport. But the revelation that Necropolis was a slave culture could hardly be good news for anyone who was unable, as she was, to prove her free citizen status.

The bartender broke off his conversation and moved toward her. As he sidled the length of the bar, he made a long and undisguised appraisal of her bare breasts. If the bartender was representative, and bartenders usually were, regular exposure to naked tits apparently did nothing to diminish or reduce the average male fascination with them. "So what's it to be, lady?"

Semple rejoiced. At least she understood the local language. Either the bartender was speaking English or her brain was now rigged for instant translation. She looked around quickly and then indicated the drink the overweight customer had in front of him. "Give me one of those."

"I ain't so sure that I should serve you."

Semple inwardly groaned but readied herself to bluff it out. "Why not?"

The bartender gestured to her forehead as though it were self-evident. "You know why not. No mark. You're an outlander."

"Is that a crime?"

Semple immediately realized that she had said the wrong thing. The bartender laughed nastily and called out to the overweight customer, "Little lady here wants to know if it's a crime to be an outlander."

As Semple's heart was sinking without trace, the overweight customer climbed down from his stool and wheezed toward her. "So let's have a look what we've got here."

Seeing the man standing, Semple had to revise her first impression. He was more than overweight, he was downright fat. He waddled up to her and peered into her face. A chubby thumb and forefinger grasped her chin and he turned her head first one way and then the other. For the moment, Semple didn't resist, even though, when he spoke, his breath was rank with garlic and something that smelled like cheap gin. "No mark."

The bartender nodded. "No mark."

"So give her a drink anyway."

"How's she gonna pay for it?"

The fat customer grinned. "I'll pay for it."

The bartender looked doubtful. "You could get me into trouble."

The fat customer was dismissive. "Who's to know?"

"You could get yourself into trouble."

"Don't be so chickenshit. It's a perfect opportunity."

The bartender. "It is?"

The fat customer's eyes were beady and unpleasant. "Sure it is. Have some fun with her before we turn her in."

As far as Semple was concerned, this had gone far enough. "Hey, boys, don't I have a say in any of this?"

Both men looked at her in surprise. "You?"

Semple was not only frightened but angry. "Yes, me."

"You don't have nothing to say, bitch. You're an outlander. You better be nice to us."

"And if I'm not?"

"You think we care? I mean, who you gonna complain to, huh? You can't exactly go running to the guards, now, can you? You just make nice, and maybe we'll let you slip away when we get finished."

Semple tried playing for pity. "I know I'm an outlander, but it was all just a mistake. It was a total accident that I wound up here. You don't have to turn me in, do you?"

The fatso's face was wreathed in an oily smile. "That depends on you."

Now she played dumb. "I don't understand."

The fat man waved a finger at the bartender. "Give her a drink."

"It's your funeral."

The bartender set a shallow blue glass bowl on the bar and filled it from a bottle with a hieroglyphic label and a metal pourer. He added a dash of something from another, smaller bottle and finally dropped in two things that looked like dried peppers. For a moment, Semple wondered if he was finally going to set fire to the whole concoction, but he didn't. He simply scanned the fat man's forehead with something resembling a flashlight. Something else under the bar whistled asthmatically as the data downloaded. Semple recognized the sound of a pneumatic computer. Something was usually amiss with Afterlife cultures that included pneumatic or steam-driven computers.

With the drink concocted and charged, the bartender moved back to a neutral position. The fat man smiled nastily and slid Semple's dish along the bar so it was closer to her. "Here, girlie, drink up."

Semple hesitated, if for no other reason than that she wasn't exactly sure how she was supposed to handle the odd, shallow container. Most of Semple's experience had been with drinks in tall glasses that came with ice. For all she knew, in Necropolis they lapped their drinks from the saucer like pussycats. She decided, however, that this was a little unlikely. With as much gentility as she could muster, and using both hands, she lifted the dish with her fingertips.

The fat man hissed in her ear, "Down in one, now. Show us you're a big girl."

Semple tilted the dish. The stuff tasted like curried creosote, but she didn't show her distaste and went right on tilting until the liquid was all gone. Anything to defer the inevitable flashpoint. She replaced the dish on the bar. The dried peppers still lay in the bottom. She didn't know if she was supposed to eat them, like the worm in the bottle of mescal, but she thought probably not. If that had been the case, the fat man would certainly have insisted that she do it right then. He was the kind that wouldn't miss any chance to humiliate the supposedly helpless. He again gestured to the bartender. "Do her one more time."

It was about then that the drink hit her. Her throat burned, her stomach cramped, and she gasped for breath as the room made a couple of fast three-sixty circuits. Semple's eyes watered, her vision blurred, and her head spun. She felt like throwing up and she didn't quite understand why. In the Afterlife, one didn't have to automatically respond to stimulants. One was supposed to have a choice. She would have liked to control and even abort the swimming, queasy feeling that currently gripped her, but she couldn't. Had the rules been somehow changed in Necropolis? All she could do was look quickly at the bartender. "No, not yet. Give me a minute to get over the last one."

The fat man ignored her. He glared at the bartender. "I said give her another."

The bartender started the pouring routine, but with an attitude that made it clear the fat man was on his own. When it was done, the fat man leaned close to Semple. "Drink it up, girlie."

Semple shook her head. "I told you already. I need a moment."

A fat hand was on her thigh. The fingers were digging into the muscle, tightening their grip until it was hard enough to bruise. "I said drink it, bitch."

Semple let out a short, angry breath. "Okay, okay."

The fat fingers relaxed slightly. Again she picked up the dish with both hands and raised it to her lips. Suddenly the fat man's arm was in the way. His hand clamped roughly on her breast. Semple slowly and patiently lowered the dish, exhibiting every ounce of jaded weariness that she could summon. "Either I drink or you feel my tits. You're going to have to make up your mind, because to do both is physically impossible."

The fat man's face turned beet-red. He came half off the stool, hauled off and slapped Semple hard across the face. Semple was knocked all the way off her stool and the blue glass dish went flying. It spun like a Frisbee and shattered on the far wall. The fat man was breathing hard. "Sewer-mouthed outland whore!"

As the bartender protested, the fat man stood up to hit her again, but he was flabby and out of shape and Semple wasn't. Her knee snapped up and, despite her blurred vision, it connected with his groin. She must have gotten his testicles, too, because the fat man doubled over with an almost girlish scream. Semple didn't wait around to see what the bartender would do. She was going for the door with all the speed of self-preservation. Her single instinct was to run, into the dirty daylight and away. Except that, right outside the door, unable to check her headlong flight, she collided with something large and hard and blue. Her outstretched hands encountered what felt like the plates of a giant insect. She looked up and found she was staring directly into a blank, unforgiving visor. Blue gloved hands gripped her wrists. "So what seems to be the problem here?"

A second blank mask joined the first. Apparently the cops in Necropolis were at least a head taller than the rest of the population. This one repeated the question. "So what seems to be the problem here?"

Semple wanted to point to the bar, but she couldn't. The cop still had hold of her wrists. "In there . . . this man . . . "

The second cop peered into her face and turned to his companion, the one holding her. "No mark."

The first cop also looked and nodded. "No mark."

The cops' voices came from their helmets muffled and metallic. The first cop looked at the second cop. It was like a conversation between two not particularly bright robots.

"Going to have to take her in."

"Yes. Going to have to take her in."

Before she could resist in any way, Semple was spun around by the officers; a framelike device of stainless steel clamped over her wrists. The next cop-voice statement was even more robotic, intoned as a legal ritual. "I arrest you as an unregistered female wandering at large as defined under Section Ninety-three, Subsection Forty of the Code of Anubis. All future conduct will become a matter of record in this case. I say again, I am arresting you. Do not resist or you will be immobilized."

It had all happened so fast that Semple was too stunned to resist. She allowed herself to be led away. Somewhere behind her, other officers had arrived, and the fat man also seemed to be under arrest. It was a fact that offered her little comfort.

Long Time Robert Moore handed Jim a fat joint of the finest Hawaiian herb rolled in wheatstraw paper. "Figure we did the right thing back there, Rock and Roll."

"You mean getting out of town?"

Moore nodded. "I surely do. When them Caribbean Mystères get to jooking, I always believe it be time to duck and cover, if it ain't time to plain duck and run."

Jim took the joint with a certain resignation. Here he was, taking drugs in yet another car, on one more road to who the hell knew where. The story of his life also seemed to be becoming the story of his death. The truth was that he was less than happy about being ordered out of Doc Holliday's little town. He had hoped the place might have provided him a refuge for a while, a place to chill and maybe get a handle, to reconstruct his memory as far as he could after the destructive craziness of the Moses orgy. He had even been hoping to get to know Lola. He'd thought he might be able to avoid having to run through the darkness yet again, but here he was doing exactly that.

"I thought you were pulling out anyway. Like going to the Crossroads."

"We're going to the Crossroads now. That's for sure."

"You want to tell me about the Crossroads?"

Long Time Robert shook his head. "No."

"No? Just like that?"

Long Time Robert Moore's gravel voice exhibited a definite trace of irritation. The old man might have chops close to divine, but he was one closemouthed son of a bitch. "Listen, Rock and Roll, you gonna find out about the Crossroads soon enough. In fact, if I have you figured, you already know plenty about the Crossroads."

"I do? I hadn't noticed."

"You *been* to the Crossroads."

"You could have fooled me."

"Sure you have. You just ain't recalling it right now."

Jim drew hard on the joint, deciding that his best policy was probably to shut up and try to avoid annoying Robert Moore. What-ever was coming next would be on him soon enough; there was no point in talking about it. As he passed the spliff back, he glanced into the vast rear of the Caddy and smiled at the Marilyn blonde. She returned his smile with a sexy pout and a recrossing of her legs. That seemed to be her entire repertoire of social communication; Jim began to wonder if she could talk at all. It was hardly his prob-lem, though, and he eased back into the soft leather of the lavish front seat, a virtual in-car armchair, as large as a first-class seat on an airliner. Maybe later Marilyn would serve cocktails. He stretched his legs and did his best not to think. The interior of the car was an easy place to do this, cozy and womblike, an enclosed capsule of safety, reefer, soft darkness, and moving luxury. The only light was the muted green glow from the dashboard, giving it a sense of almost submerged submarine protection in which all possible futures could be held at bay.

Jim narrowed his attention to staring idly out of the window. At that particular, subjective moment, the car hardly seemed to be moving through anything like regular space-time, traveling on a twisting ribbon of unsupported highway that ran through a three-dimensional forest of tall, slender, crystalline pyramids, each of which radiated its own internal blue-green light. Small spheres, Day-Glo red and vibrant acid yellow, drifted overhead in untidy clusters of a dozen or more, just above the peaks of the pyramids, like strange flocks of animated bubbles. Jim wondered if, somehow, the car had switched to traveling on the molecular level. This was, after all, the far country where just about anything was possible.

As soon as he had started to take the pyramids for granted, Jim was surprised to find himself staring at a radically altered landscape.

He didn't remember dozing, but he could hardly recall a transition. "I guess it's just one of those missing holes in time again."

Robert Moore glanced sharply at him. "What you say?"

Jim shook his head. "It was nothing. Just talking to myself."

"Sometimes that's the only way to get an intelligent conversation."

The spheres and pyramids had been left behind, and now the Cadillac was rolling on a perfectly normal two-lane country blacktop, under a pitch-black night sky filled with bright, unwinking stars. A huge orange moon hung close to the horizon, and cornfields, flat as a billiard table, without a tree, building, or even a grain elevator to break the monotony, stretched as far as the eye could see. "How did we get to Kansas?"

Long Time Robert Moore looked at Jim as though he were crazy. "This ain't no motherfucker Kansas."

"It sure looks like Kansas."

"I'm telling you, Rock and Roll, this ain't Kansas. And you ain't Dorothy and I ain't Toto."

As they continued deeper into what Jim was now thinking of as the corn belt, he started to see huge geometric shapes, hundreds of feet long, stamped in the standing crops, circles within circles, joined by the straight lines of extended radii, so they formed complex and enigmatic patterns.

"Crop markings?"

Robert Moore nodded. "Get a lot of them 'round these parts."

"You ever meet anyone who could read them? Anyone who knew what they meant?"

Robert Moore shook his head. "I did try playing them a couple of times."

"Playing them? You mean like musical notation?"

"I tried it, but the tunes sounded like shit. All these Neil Diamond chord progressions."

"You still think they're some kind of giant song chart?"

Moore turned and looked at Jim. "You know something, Rock and Roll?"

Jim sighed. "You don't like me asking questions."

"I got a question for you."

"What's that?"

"How come you gave up singing?"

"Who said I gave up singing?"

"I've heard it all over. You ain't sung a goddamned note since you fucked up on dope in Paris."

Jim couldn't believe what he was hearing. "That's bullshit."

Long Time Robert shot him a sidelong glance. "Yeah? So when did you last sing, Rock and Roll?"

"I don't know. I have this problem with my memory."

"So how do you know what I'm saying is bullshit?"

Jim shook his head in bewilderment. Maybe it was true and Long Time Robert Moore was right. He didn't know anything for sure. That's why he'd wanted to hang around Doc's town for a while and sort out a few of these problems. "I need to think about that."

"Well, don't take too long, boy. We're coming up to the Cross-roads."

Jim peered through the windshield. It was just as Robert Moore said. Up ahead, a second country road intersected the one they were on. As far as he could see, the two made a perfect right angle, slap in the middle of unsignposted nowhere. As they came to the place where the two roads met, Long Time Robert Moore slowed the car to a halt. "So I guess this is far as we go."

Jim was tempted to ask Moore what he was expected to do now, but he knew that he was unlikely to receive anything but some down-home bit of Zen by way of an answer. Either that or the question would be countered with another question. The bluesman shut off the Cadillac's engine. "Think I'll take me a look around."

Before he got out of the car, Long Time Robert Moore reached around behind his seat and pulled out his guitar case. He took it with him when he climbed out. This puzzled Jim. Was the old man intending to serenade the deserted Crossroads, or maybe try to play the music of the crop circles again? Jim couldn't believe that he didn't intend coming back to the car. After he made his exit, Long Time Robert Moore didn't seem to be in any hurry. He walked a short distance from the Cadillac and then stopped and looked up at the sky. Jim turned to the blonde in the back. "You have any idea what's going on?"

Marilyn merely shrugged. Her face formed into the familiar, extended upper lip pout. Still Jim couldn't fathom what she was. Some oddity who had taken Monroe's form along with a vow of submissive silence? A sex toy that Long Time Robert took on the road with him? Jim knew this was another puzzle to which he would probably never have a solution, and he decided the best thing he could do was get out of the car himself. He walked slowly to a spot near the old man, but maintained sufficient distance so he would not be accused of crowding or following him. Without Jim having to say anything, Long Time Robert turned and looked at him. "You're wondering what I'm doing, ain't you, Rock and Roll?"

Jim half smiled and nodded. "Yeah, I'm wondering, but I didn't want to ask."

"I'm just waiting for my next ride."

"What next ride?"

Long Time Robert Moore pointed to a spot on the distant horizon. "Look there, Rock and Roll, it's coming now."

A small orange light had appeared at the horizon. It performed a swift, jittering dance and then came directly toward where they were standing. After experiencing the arrival of the Haitian Mystères in their blaze of static, Jim watched the fast-moving light with a certain apprehension. The object halted directly over them, silently hovering. Jim looked up at it in baffled amazement. "This is a joke, right?"

Above the two of them, some forty feet in the air, nothing less than a flying saucer floated in total silence. Long Time Robert Moore's face was expressionless. "I don't see no joke. All I see is that there UFO."

Still Jim couldn't believe it. The saucer was the classic design, the kind that was supposed to have crashed at Roswell in 1947, a large disc like an inverted soup dish with a kind of upper turret mounted at its center. The orange light was just the glowing domed top of that turret. On the underside were three large hemispheres that were supposed to have something to do with its means of propulsion. Jim could feel his hair starting to stand on end, just as it was supposed to around flying saucers. "That's an Adamski saucer."

Robert Moore looked blank. "I don't know too much about the makes and models. Just looks like a saucer to me."

"George Adamski. Back in the early fifties, he was the first guy to claim he was contacted by aliens."

"He wasn't the first guy."

"He claimed to have taken pictures of saucers just like that one. They were all discredited as fakes."

Long Time Robert seemed unconcerned. "Looks pretty real to me."

"But what would real aliens be doing here in the human Afterlife?"

Robert Moore grinned. "Them aliens get everywhere. Here, life-side, everywhere."

"You're going off in that thing?"

"Sure am."

"Jim could hardly believe this. "You gonna be singing the blues on Zeta Reticuli?"

"I got friends in high places."

"Can I come, too?"

Robert Moore shook his head. "I don't think so. Them alien guys are kinda choosy about who they pick up."

No sooner had the bluesman spoken than a beam of white light stabbed down from the underside of the spacecraft. Long Time Robert Moore was in the exact center of the beam, but Jim was also caught in its periphery. The saucer started to descend, and Jim, now definitely awed, backed quickly away. Robert Moore also took a couple of steps back. The beam of light was shut off and the saucer dropped to just a few feet from the ground, creating tiny dust devils on the surface of the road. For almost a minute, it remained perfectly stationary, and then a hatch slowly opened. Blue light streamed from its interior, and a narrow ramp extended until it was touching the ground. Long Time Robert Moore turned and looked back at Jim. "So I'm gone, Rock and Roll. I'll be seeing you."

Carrying his guitar case, the bluesman walked quickly up the ramp. At the precise moment that Robert Moore set foot on the ramp, the Cadillac simply vanished, as though it had ceased to exist now that the bluesman had no more use for it. Jim could only assume Marilyn had gone with it. As Jim watched Robert Moore disappear into the interior of the saucer, a sudden angry impulse took over. Screw the bunch of choosy aliens. He'd had enough of aliens during his life on Earth. They'd always been out there somewhere, lurking in the shadows, materializing and vanishing, bothering pilots, annoying the government, kidnapping travelers on lonely roads, scaring Vern and Bubba while they were fishing in the swamp. The guppy-eyed, gray-skinned, three-fingered little bastards had never deigned to reveal themselves. They never landed on the White House lawn and said, *Take me to your leader*. (Although, in Jim's lifetime, the leader would have been Richard Nixon, so who could blame them?) They'd teased him enough. Finally a saucer had appeared and Jim Morrison was damned if he was going to be left behind wondering. He'd find out the truth once and for all. Either he'd see the aliens as they really were or, if the whole thing was sham, he'd know who was behind it.

Without weighing the possible consequences, he darted forward. The ramp was beginning to retract, but Jim jumped, gaining a footing on the moving metal. He swayed for a second like a surfer, struggling to get his balance, and then he dived after Long Time Robert Moore, straight through the entrance and into the craft.

3

Say what you like, aliens can be a goddamned pain in the ass.

All of Semple's instincts told her that the jail had been deliberately designed the way it was, ludicrous inefficiencies and all, and that its creator had done his work with an abrasive attention to viciously absurdist detail. Confirmation was all around her. It was born on the tepid air, thick with the reek of ammonia and dirty plastic mattresses. It was swallowed morning and evening with the gray cardboard slop that passed as food. It came with the mass of contradictory regulations that regularly ground everything to a bureaucratic halt for hours at a time. The very walls vibrated with it, along with the waveforms of sighing misery, and the constant undertow of confined penitentiary echoes. It was even underlined by the way all color had been washed out of the equation. In many respects, the perfect summation of the entire oppressive ambience could be compacted into the form of the four-hundred-pound female guard in the reinforced glass booth who was currently staring at Semple as though she were a logical impossibility. "You have no paperwork. How can I process you through when you have no paperwork?"

Semple stared back at the guard from her side of the glass. Revulsion and slow-burning anger were a given, but she was all too well aware of the pointlessness of any demonstration. Confrontation with a system as convoluted and tangled as the Necropolis City Jail would amount to issuing an open invitation to institutional violence. Semple, once she was past the first shock of arrest and incarceration, had resolved to roll with the absurdities of the program until she had a handle on her new surroundings. After all, didn't she preside over a place not dissimilar to this back home in her own environment? And wasn't the primary operating rule that prisoners never be allowed to win a point?

It wasn't as though she'd invented the concept for herself, either. She had discovered it during her mortal time on Earth. She had been arrested twice during her earthly sojourn; once in Bakersfield, California, for disturbing the peace, and once in Louisville, Kentucky, for lewd vagrancy. Each incarceration had been the unfortunate climax of a protracted debauch with the local Victrola cowboys. Whenever she managed to dislodge Aimee from the body for a few days, the sheer relief was more than enough to send her on a full-bore, gin-on-the-rocks razzle, and on this pair of occasions the razzle had waxed rowdy enough to attract the heat. The prisoner never wins, she learned that in those jails, and Semple could only conclude that all prisons operated in much the same manner on either side of the veil.

She had, however, observed that nothing operated very well in the Necropolis City Jail, and this gave her hope that she'd eventually be able to organize her way out. She had organized her way out before, in both Bakersfield and Louisville. The first time, in Bakersfield, she had initially thrown conscious control back to Aimee, but Aimee had proved totally useless. Her sibling had become so horrified by the experience of waking in a filthy drunk tank surrounded by prostitutes, shoplifters, and madwomen that she'd been effectively paralyzed. Semple had been forced to resume control and deal with it. In Kentucky, she hadn't bothered to rouse Aimee, she'd simply gone ahead and coped. Of course, she'd had the not insubstantial cash resource of the Aimee Semple McPherson Ministry, Inc., at her disposal and found that cash made freedom reasonably accessible. All she had in Necropolis was wit, sex, and intelligence. On the other hand, in Bakersfield and Louisville she had to worry about keeping the entire incident hushed up. All she wanted here was out. They could write her up in the fucking Necropolis tabloid press and she wouldn't care. She wouldn't even be able to read it.

On each of the two occasions she'd been busted on Earth, she'd had the advantage of being emotionally buffered by a considerable quantity of alcohol. In Necropolis, she was without any such comfort cushion. When she was first brought in by the two helmet-head cops, she had been in a state of nervous disorientation. She had tried to calm herself, but her surroundings had rushed by her like an unreal and threatening blur, moving too fast for reflection or even a deep breath. As time passed, however, human adaptability kicked in, and when she was neither murdered nor gang-raped she began to regain her objectivity. Now, as she faced the guard behind the protective glass of the booth, she was able to look at the situation with almost dispassionate detachment.

She lifted up her cuffed wrist with the slow zombie resignation that was considered appropriate inmate behavior. A steel ID tag, stamped with a row of unreadable hieroglyphics, dangled from the narrow canvas strap that had been locked around her right wrist when she'd first been brought in. This tag was the key to her existence in the system. In many respects, it counted for more than her physical body. A second, similar band had also been locked around her left wrist, but that one carried no tag. All of the prisoners wore these wristbands. They seemed to serve a double purpose. They dog-tagged the inmates' identity and they could be hooked together by their metal clasps, like instant manacles, whenever the guards decided that hands and arms needed to be immobilized. Right at that moment her hands were free, though, and she moved her wrist slightly so the ID tag swung like a hypnotist's pendulum in front of the guard in the booth.

"This is all they gave me."

The guard creaked around in her swivel chair and peered balefully at the postcard-sized monochrome screen of her pneumatic computer. "The tag has to be cross-indexed with your personal barcode before I can allow you to pass. That's regulations."

Semple sighed. She had been through this seemingly insurmountable paradox some six or seven times already. The jailhouse computers had no provision in their programming for an inmate with no barcode, and the human guards that tended them were apparently incapable of improvisation or intelligent flexibility. Each time the matter came up, the exchange quickly turned into a seemingly infinite loop. It would begin with Semple stating the obvious. "I already told you, I don't have a barcode. I wouldn't be here if I had a barcode. That was why I was arrested in the first place. Because I didn't have a barcode."

The guard would then take the position that the obvious was impossible. "You have to have a barcode. If your inmate ID can't be cross-indexed with a barcode, the computer won't issue the paperwork, and if I don't have the paperwork, I can't clear your transfer."

"So don't clear my transfer. I don't care. Send me back to the lockup. It's all the same to me." Semple might have been biding her time, and handling the absurdities of the Necropolis bureaucracy with absolute passivity, but every now and then she allowed herself a slight exasperated edge. Small rebellions were vital to the retention of sanity.

The guard shook her head. "I can't readmit you to population. Your transfer's on the computer."

"So what do we do? Am I supposed to stand here, holding up the line for the rest of time? Maybe you should just let me go, then I won't be fouling up the system."

Semple realized that this time she might have gone a little too far. The guard's eyes narrowed dangerously, enough for hairline cracks to appear in her makeup. The woman wore the same daubed-on cosmetics as everyone else in Necropolis, except, of course, the inmates of its prisons, who were deprived of everything save the pair of wristbands and a short cotton kilt, stamped with the winged ankh symbol of Anubis. This particular guard was by far the ugliest that Semple had encountered since the start of her incarceration. Her Cleopatra paint job was so thick and clumsily applied that it turned her already near-bestial features into the face of a malignant and threatening clown. "Porcine" was not a word that Semple used too frequently, but in this woman's case it was too apt to pass over.

The guard weighed easily four hundred pounds, and Semple judged that she couldn't have stood more than five feet two in her sandaled feet. She had also, for some reason Semple didn't care to imagine, completely shaved her head. The naked skull added an edge of perverse brutality to the mountainous flab, but in Semple's estimation the most charmless features were the woman's vast and pendulous breasts. For someone so grossly overweight, the universal Necropolis fashion of going topless was grotesquely unsuitable, and her tits hung well past the waistband of her uniform skirt. Where most of the inhabitants of Necropolis had smooth olive skin, the guard's was pig-pink and blotchy, mottled with pimples and areas of chicken flesh. Semple could only assume that she was either some obese and unhappy construct or the result of an unfortunate misfire in the re-creation process.

The guard turned back to the computer, clearly blaming Semple for the screwup. "Wait."

And Semple, having positively no other choice in the matter, waited, as did the eleven other women in her transfer batch. The huge guard pecked slowly at the keyboard with two uncertain index fingers. With a computer that ran on hieroglyphics, the keyboard was massive, with a hundred or more keys, like some strange, multi-tiered Johann Sebastian Bach organ.

While the guard tried to come up with a workable solution, Semple looked up and down the long corridor in which she now seemed to be trapped. The corridor was dead straight and appeared to go on forever. It was somewhat wider at the floor than at the ceiling, and its walls were constructed from huge blocks of precision-hewn sandstone. The overall impression was one of being deep in the heart of a great stone pyramid. Every fifty feet or so, the corridor was sectioned off by steel-barred gates, presumably to present an obstacle to a fermenting riot or an attempt at mass breakout. The gates, like all the other metal surfaces in the jail, were painted a dull sandy beige, the color of Rommel's tanks in the World War II desert. The gates were also automatic, controlled by guards in glassed-in booths positioned at every third set of gates, identical to the one at which Semple was currently receiving bureaucratic grief. On either side of the corridor were lines of sliding grids, the entrances to the tanks, the big gloomy rooms, each with its two dozen triple-tiered bunk beds, that housed all of the overcapacity inmate population, except for the incorrigible in solitary, the demented in the padded rooms, and the ultraprivileged who, having fallen foul of the Code of Anubis, were rumored to be held in luxurious private detention suites somewhere on the upper levels.

The guards who had come to fetch Semple and the others from their tank had blanked all questions regarding their destination or the purpose of the excursion. They had simply summoned them to the sliding door and ordered them out. Initially, Semple had been terrified. The fear that she'd experienced in the immediate aftermath of her arrest had returned with a vengeance. The possibility of summary execution without trial and a dozen other kindred horrors and atrocities shrieked through her imagination. Then, in the moment of confusion as the women were being filtered from the tank, a whisper had gone around that they were being sent to Fat Ari.

Semple had no idea who or what Fat Ari might be, but since none of the other women had showed any marked dismay at the prospect, Semple had joined the line with only a measured trepidation. Also, every one of the women selected was both young and attractive, and that gave Semple some kind of idea about the nature of Fat Ari and why they were being brought to him. If the fate of this batch of twelve was to be some kind of sexual exploitation, perhaps it would offer the window of opportunity for which she was so patiently waiting. Semple knew well how sexual desire, even among those in authority, could derail both sense and sensibility.

After leaving the holding tank, the twelve women had moved in single file along the punctuated corridor, with one guard leading them and a second bringing up the rear. Both were considerably thinner and more limber than the fat guard in the glass booth, and both carried a short cylinder of transparent Lucite that delivered a painful, nonlethal shock much in the manner of a cattle prod. These were the guards' only weapon, and if the twelve women had attempted a sudden rush on their escorts, they would have had little trouble overpowering them.

No such thing happened, though, and Semple could only wonder at the docility of her fellow inmates. Without exception they passively accepted their penitent status and submitted to everything they were told without rebellion and rancor and, most surprising of all, with a minimum of complaint. Semple was starting to wonder if the prison population in Necropolis were not real criminals at all, nothing more than animated set dressing like Aimee's cherubs and angels.

Her developing theory was that the majority of the city's inhabitants were fabricated beings with little or no will of their own, created for the amusement of Anubis or one of his underlings. It was possible that the whole prison system, and perhaps even the oppressive police force, had been established, not in response to any real problem of crime and punishment, but simply because someone on the planning level thought a city wasn't complete without such things, and installed them much in the same way that a small boy with an obsessive hobby might add a new section to his model train layout.

Had Semple been more diligent in keeping up with the trends in popular mortal, she would have known that the environment she now occupied was little more than a local modification to the genre of low-budget women's prison movies with titles like *Caged Rage* and *Chained Heat*. The ever-present Egyptian motif and the heavy overlay of unworkable totalitarian baroque might have thrown her off track, but all the required details were in place, right down to the glandular guard and the coteries of butch and burly lesbians who ogled her body with a masculine candor.

Even though she'd missed the cultural origins of her situation, Semple was beginning to realize that, although Anubis may have been responsible for the overall concept of Necropolis, a lot of the details must have been delegated to subsidiary minds, allowing them to indulge their own fantasies and fixations. He had, in fact, done what Aimee was hoping to do: recruited the newly deceased to help construct his hereafter. The more she thought about it, the more she was convinced that Necropolis was a conspiracy of the deformed. Anubis might have been its guiding force, but this all must have been the produce of a legion of warped minds.

The line of twelve women and two guards had moved smoothly down the corridor until Semple had attempted to check through the gate at the first glass booth, when the fat guard had brought it to a shuffling halt. The prisoners looked on with boredom as Semple paralyzed the process with her lack of a barcode. The guard bringing up the rear was less patient. "So what's the goddamned holdup?"

The fat guard didn't answer, but she did seem ready to enlist some outside help. She resentfully tapped out a sequence on the oversized keyboard, and a pinched irritated face appeared on the tiny computer screen. Semple assumed it was the obese guard's immediate superior, some harried, middle-echelon administrator. A tinny voice crackled from a speaker. "Can we make this fast? I really don't have the time to be dealing with complications at every damned section gate."

"I have a female unit here with no barcode."

The man's mouth became a small, sour line. "You bothered me with that?"

The guard didn't seem too impressed by the man's exasperation. "The box wouldn't pass the paperwork. What was I supposed to do?"

"You couldn't run up the help manual?"

"I haven't been able to access help since before Lotus Day."

"You called maintenance?"

"Sure I called pigging maintenance. I'm still waiting."

The administrator frowned. "Isn't this batch for Fat Ari?"

The guard was becoming decidedly peevish. "Of course this batch is for Fat Ari. That's why I've got to have the pigging paperwork straight."

"It could bollix up the entire term-end profit-share bonus."

The fat guard's peevishness sharpened. "You think I don't know that?"

"So run it on a Gazelle/Leopard ten seventy."

"Why didn't you say that in first place?"

A weary scowl twisted the man's face. "I still cling to the archaic notion that people should know how to do their own pigging jobs."

The face vanished and the tiny screen snowed out. The guard hit more keys, the terminal wheezed, and about nine inches of punched paper tape extruded from a slot in the computer. The guard ripped off the tape and dropped it into a file basket, then glared at Semple. "Get on through, unit. You keep Fat Ari waiting and you'll find out what pigging trouble's really about."

The twelve women were now on the move again. Either the fat guard or the administrator had instructed the booths ahead how to process the woman with no barcode, or maybe the guards in these booths were more on the ball than their overweight colleague. Whatever the reason, the line passed three more checkpoints without any further trouble. After the third, things began to change. The rumble of deeply buried machinery was clearly audible and a smell of ozone overwhelmed the ammonia in the air. A couple of the women looked a little anxious, but Semple had an idea what was coming next. The corridor came to an end in an open space that led in turn to a much larger circular tunnel, the floor of which was a motorized walkway, a conveyor band that could move large numbers of people at something like twice the speed of a fast walk. Anubis was just the kind for Heinlein rolling roads. They were big favorites in the environments of many a control-obsessed paranoid megalo. The herding gene turned techno. Semple had seen other examples in the tangential communication that passed for *Better Homes & Gardens* in the Afterlife.

The women prisoners were temporarily halted in the open space while their escort produced a long length of light steel chain and shackled them to it by the straps on their left wrists, spacing them at intervals of about two feet. When the string was complete, they were moved toward the walkway itself. The area where riders actually stepped onto the moving walkway was dotted with signs, presumably the kind of regulations and instructions to passengers that the managers of transit systems everywhere are unable to resist. She noticed that the hieroglyphics on the signs had been defaced by amateur and universally obscene embellishments that paid particular regard to the genitalia of the various gods, humans, animals, and birds that made up the alphabet.

Actually stepping onto the moving walkway required a certain degree of skill and judgment, but Semple, by visualizing the effects in advance, accomplished the trick with ease and grace. The woman behind her, on the other hand, misjudged the necessary matching of pace and stumbled. Semple quickly grasped her arm to prevent her from falling and bringing down the whole string. The woman nervously smiled her thanks. She glanced around to see if the guards were looking in their direction and, discovering them otherwise occupied, whispered quickly to Semple. "I guess this pretty much settles it."

Semple didn't understand. "What settles what?"

"It's Fat Ari's for us."

"Is that good or bad?"

Now the woman looked as though she didn't understand. "It is what it is. It's Fat Ari's."

"I don't know what Fat Ari's is. I'm an outlander."

"You mean you've never seen it on the telly?"

"Never seen what on the telly?"

The other prisoner spoke as though she were stating the obvious. *"Fat Ari's Slave Shopping Club."*

The hatch closed, the lights went out, and Jim was falling. What he thought was going to be his first alien encounter had suddenly turned into a dirty sucker punch. The rug had been literally jerked from under his feet, and someone or something was screaming at pain-threshold volume. He hoped the screaming was only the rush of air past his ears, but remembered that same extended scream a little too well, as well as falling through absolute blackness. It all said Paris, as though somehow his passing had been recorded on the magstrip of time. If he was dying all over again, it hardly seemed fair. Although he knew it was both naive and illogical, he had pretty much expected the aliens to be pleased to see him. After all the LSD he had taken during his life, all the Erich VonDaeniken books and magazine articles on the paranormal that he'd consumed, after all the times that he'd seen *The Day the Earth Stood Still*, all the episodes of *Star Trek* he'd soaked up in idle beer-drunk hotel afternoons, he felt he was definitely ready for the ETs, and he had imagined that, even if they didn't greet him with open arms, they'd at least be ready for him. The last thing he'd expected was that they'd drop him into a goddamned black hole, and maybe even kill him all over again. To go back to the pods at this juncture was a thoroughly disgusting and depressing prospect.

When he continued to fall for what felt like a major slice of time without hitting anything, Jim started to rethink his situation. Perhaps he was in free fall. Perhaps the UFO was switching him between external and internal gravity. As if as a reward, or punishment for his deduction, a searing flash of static blinded him, leaving him in a kaleidoscope of dazzling afterimages. He fell heavily, maybe a foot or more, to a metal floor. The impact was bone-jarring, but did no damage. Jim groaned and rolled over. His shoulder hurt, his elbow was throbbing, his ego was bruised, and he was angry at the inhospitable reception. Slowly he climbed to his feet, wondering what the next indignity might be.

The air was breathable and warm, although it was a little too humid and smelled of something industrial. He slowly turned, half crouching in the stance of a circling wrestler, arms slightly in front of him, ready for anything. He spoke tentatively, more to observe what might happen than to actually communicate with anyone. "You know something? This is really not my idea of being piped aboard."

As he spoke, the lights came up and the air changed. The atmosphere turned clammy, and the unidentified industrial smell was replaced by something more like battery acid. The light was, in every sense, unearthly. The blue glow looked like the interior of a iceberg. It seemed to have no direct source but somehow suffused the entire chamber with a soft luminescence. The nature of the light made it hard to judge distances; had Jim not been well versed in hallucination, he might have thought something was wrong with his eyes.

He seemed to be standing on the curved bottom of a ribbed metal cylinder, like the inside of some large storage tank, perhaps about twelve feet in diameter. The arching ribs of the cylinder and sections of the wall plates were engraved with lines of unreadable ideograms. Aside from the extraterrestrial script, it all seemed a little mundane, but Jim reserved judgment. Although the script meant nothing to him, the individual characters bore a distinct resemblance to the crop markings he had seen on the way to the Crossroads. He shook his head. "If you want to leave us notes in the cornfields, you really ought to learn to write English. Or send us a dictionary."

Immediately the final phrase came back at him, loud and squeakily metallic, something between a mimic and an instant replay: "If you want to leave us notes in the cornfield, you really ought to learn to write English. Or leave us a dictionary."

This mimicking voice had a Mickey Mouse pitch, like his own voice on helium. Jim blinked. A second level of alien bullshit? His mood was turning surly. He needed a drink. "What did you say?"

"What did I say?"

Jim sighed. "Don't give me fucking Ray Charles."

The disembodied squeak also sighed. "Fucking Ray Charles."

Jim knew he was being mindfucked. "Yeah, I get it."

"Yeah, you get it."

"How long do we have to play this game?"

"Until you feel ready to step through the membrane."

This actual reply to a question took Jim by surprise. "The membrane?"

"The membrane."

Jim wasn't sure if the parrot routine had started again. Without his saying a word, the voice answered him. "No, this isn't the parrot routine. If you don't like it where you are, pass through the membrane."

"What membrane?"

"Look to the end of the chamber, schmuck."

Raising an eyebrow at the jibe, Jim looked to the far end of the chamber. What could only be described as a circular translucent membrane, some four feet across, had appeared in the center of the circular end wall. Its outer surround was a beveled ring of shiny, copper-colored metal. The membrane itself was filmy and insubstantial, a pulsing, mother-of-pearl gauze. Tiny sparkles of bright energy danced up from it and vanished, like bubbles from a fresh glass of champagne; Jim couldn't tell whether the thing was solid, liquid, a heavy vapor, or something else entirely.

"You want me to go through that?"

"Unless you intend to remain here in the lock. If you do that, you will probably become exceedingly uncomfortable. Hungry, thirsty, claustrophobic, resentful—all the things that afflict humans when they think they're not getting enough attention."

"Okay, okay, I get the picture."

"Okay, okay, you get the picture."

Jim knew he had no chance of beating the helium parrot, so, taking carefully measured steps, he gingerly crossed the chamber until he was standing in front of the membrane. He leaned forward and peered closely at it. It seemed vaguely moist. "I'm supposed to climb through this?"

"You're supposed to climb through that."

"It's all a bit Freudian, isn't it?"

"This is all a bit Freudian, isn't it?"

Jim tried another tack. He shouted as loud as he could. "Hey, Long Time Robert, are you in there?"

The membrane vibrated and a large pair of lips, more than a foot across, appeared in three-dimensional relief on its surface. The lips formed words and shouted back at him. "Hey, Jim Morrison, are you out there?"

The air temperature was dropping, the smell of battery acid growing stronger. Jim had no choice. He wondered what the aliens might bring into play next if he continued to resist. He was feeling distinctly like a B. F. Skinner lab rat, without the benefit of any jolts to the pleasure centers. For all he knew, the next item on their menu might be direct cortical shock, or something even more unpleasant. It was becoming clear that, no matter how he might twist and turn, the ETs were going to have their way with him.

The lips of the membrane pouted sexily. "That's right, Jimbo. We're going to have our way with you."

The chill in the chamber was deepening. Jim knew that aside from staying where he was and being freeze-dried, he was out of options. "Okay, you win. I'm coming through."

The lips' pout turned into a happy smile. "Okay, we win. You're coming through."

Jim hesitated. "Only . . . "

"Only what?"

"You'll have to lose the lips."

"You don't like the lips."

"I'm not climbing into a mouth. Not even the illusion of a mouth."

"Does it make you feel too much like a human blow job?"

"You read my thoughts, damn it."

"Of course we did."

The lips vanished. Jim placed the palm of his hand flat against the membrane, but then quickly pulled it away as a sharp jolt of static twitched painfully up his arm. "Damn!"

The Mickey Mouse voice was back, and with a definite contempt in its tone. "You're not going to let a little shock stop you, are you?"

Jim snapped back. "To hell with this." He didn't bother to feel his way. Suddenly angry, he violently punched his entire forearm clear through the membrane, and fuck the aliens if they didn't like his attitude. The membrane resisted slightly, but he continued pushing until his arm had penetrated right up to the shoulder. At that point, the resistance seemed to reverse itself and the rest of him was jerked through by a sudden, wet kiss suction. He experienced a moment of panic as the stuff of the membrane closed around his face, but then he was through and into another moment of complete disorientation and darkness.

Jim was outraged. "Wait a fucking minute, will you?"

A bright white overhead spotlight snapped on. This light wasn't at all diffused or hazy and its source was clear and obvious. Jim, though, didn't have time to waste considering light sources. An alien—Jim Morrison's very first—was standing in the exact center of the beam. Jim's alien was barely three feet tall. Its skin was gray. Its body was slight, fragile, and resembled that of a long-armed fetus. It had only three fingers on each hand. Its head was huge, hairless, with no ears and only the slightest approximation of a mouth and nose. Its eyes, in total contrast, were huge and ancient, without iris or pupil, like the eyes of some vast, distant, super-intelligent megaguppy. It was the classic extraterrestrial of abduction paranoia, dubious amateur video, autopsy hoaxes, and tabloid reportage, the gray alien that was the bad guy of UFO folklore. At least Jim now knew what he was dealing with. Unless, of course, the familiar form was simply a new level of deception.

The alien was holding a small vial filled with blue-green liquid in one of its three-fingered hands. "Wanna drink, pal?"

Mercifully, the alien's voice was a far cry from the helium squeak. In fact, its tonal tailoring was coming from entirely the other end of the spectrum. The incongruity of a pint-sized alien using a voice from the staccato school of Mickey Spillane/Humphrey Bogart wasn't lost on Jim, but he reserved comment. "Do I what?"

"I'm offering you a drink, kid. Don't you want it? Isn't that what's been gnawing at your guts since you took it on the lam from Doc Holliday's?"

"I'd say gnawing at my guts was something of an overstatement. I'd like a drink, but . . . "

"We understood you were a world-class alkie, kid."

Jim was starting to have trouble with this tough-guy voice coming out of the slight spindly frame. "That was then, this is now."

"You telling me you weren't as drunk as a skunk back at Doc Holliday's? Or at the orgy before that?"

Jim really didn't like the direction the conversation was taking. "What the fuck are you running here? Some interplanetary twelve-step inquisition?"

The alien's face didn't alter, but the voice took on an aggrieved tone. "Listen, pal, all I was trying to do was offer you a drink." It held out the vial again. "You want it or not? It's good stuff. I kid you not. Make you see stars."

Jim suddenly laughed. "Ah, what the hell." The alien was only offering him a drink. The gesture was culturally fundamental. Why not take it on face value, even if the face in question was an unreadable ovoid the color of a button mushroom, with a texture to match? He took the vial and threw the contents back in one gulp, like a lumberjack downing his first shot after a hard day's logging. The instant the booze hit his metabolism, Jim saw not only stars but also suns and ringed planets. For a moment, it seemed as though the top of his head had lifted off of its own accord, flipping up like the lid of a pedal bin, to relieve the intolerable pressure in his brain. He doubled over, his throat burning and his stomach contemplating convulsion. As a confirmed shot-and-beer motherfucker, Jim had always found cocktails a little too Dorothy Parker. He'd been around the block enough times, however, to know that what he'd just consumed could qualify as the transcendentally perfect gin martini. The only mistake was that the stuff had the impact intensity of drag strip accelerant. When he finally straightened up again, his voice was a rasping wheeze and he had tears in his eyes. "Sweet God Almighty! That was intense."

"Kinda strong for you?"

"Maybe the recipe needs a bit of rethinking."

"But you feel better?"

Jim took a couple of deep breaths. The battery-acid smell seemed to have stayed on the other side of the membrane. "Yes, I definitely feel better."

The alien nodded. "That's good. We like to make you humans feel at home."

Jim looked at the empty vial. "You certainly do." The alcohol burn had given way to a warm and not unpleasant glow. "Yes, you certainly do."

He handed the vial back to the alien, who took it and placed it in thin air beside him, as though he had set it on an invisible shelf. The vial remained standing for a few seconds and then vanished. Jim maintained his cool, refusing to look surprised. "That's a pretty neat trick."

"We gotta million of them."

"So what happens next?"

"Well it's been nice meeting you, Jimbo, but we gotta get you on to the medical examination."

Jim's glow crashed and burned like a vampire in the sun. "Medical examination?"

"The medical examination. Everyone gets the medical examination. I mean, we're aliens, ain't we? That's part of what we do."

Jim dug in like a recalcitrant mule. He'd heard too many anecdotal reports regarding the role of body cavities in alien medical work. "No way."

The alien raised a hand. "Hey, pal, don't be telling me 'no way.' I just do the meeting and greeting. If you got a problem, take it up with the croakers. Don't be busting my balls, okay?"

"So where are these croakers? The sooner I put them straight, the better."

"You want to talk to a sawbones about this?"

Jim nodded. "Yeah. That's exactly what I want."

No sooner had he spoken than a second alien appeared beside the first one. In every respect, the two of them were identical, and Jim looked curiously from one to the other. Finally he focused on the new arrival. "Your friend here tells me that you're the one I need to talk to about the medical exam. If it's all the same with you, I really think I prefer to pass, particularly as I'm already dead."

The huge black alien eyes looked straight into Jim's; the voice was that of a robot with just the faintest trace of an Austrian accent. "The medical examination is nonnegotiable."

Semple found herself in the calm center of frenzied chaos, the eye of a uniquely disorganized show-business hurricane. Even though she had died well before television had locked its grip on planet Earth, she knew enough from her irregular observation of the lifeside to recognize that she was inside a TV studio. In addition, her intricate familiarity with human nature at its worst told her that it was controlled by a megalomaniac, some kind of panic-prone neurotic who believed that any problem could be solved by inflicting screaming, hysterical abuse on his underlings. The name Fat Ari hardly did the man justice. He was huge in every direction. He stood well over six feet tall and was twice that around. The full horror of his stacked tires of flesh was fortunately swathed in a flowing, lavishly embroidered red-and-gold caftan that could have been the bell tent of God. He even seemed exempt from the ancient Egypt look. Perhaps, as the King of the TV Slave Salesmen, he actually had the juice to override the fixations of Anubis and dress as he pleased.

Semple and the other women from the jail stood in a roped-off area to one side of the set waiting for their call. Aside from a couple of walk-through rehearsals, and then actually being paraded for sale on the show itself, their part was, by this time, all but done. Until *Fat Ari's Slave Shopping Club* went on the air, their primary tasks were not to get in the way and not smudge their makeup. The latter was not, in fact, as easy as it sounded. Even standing was made difficult by the spindly five-inch clear-plastic heels on which they were forced to balance. Here was another small factor where Fat Ari seemed to feel free to buck the mandated Egyptology. Fat Ari's merchandise all seemed to conform to a more twentieth century, Times Square hooker authenticity, screw the trappings of the nineteenth dynasty. Unfortunately, Semple was about the only one in the batch who actually knew how to walk on high heels; the rest tended to reel and teeter unless they kept perfectly still.

Since they were to appear on the show naked but for shoes, the exteriors of Semple and her companions had been layered with cosmetics from head to toe, from glitter nail varnish to a special color-blended rouge that had been liberally applied to their nipples. They could neither sit nor lean. Although crowded together, they could not touch each other, and if they so much as sweated under the studio lights, a bad-tempered makeup boy would rush to powder them down.

The boy was something of an ordeal all on his own. He had the knack of maintaining himself in a state of perpetual snit. While he powdered, he mercilessly berated the woman on whom he was working, and even those around her, in a low querulous voice. He was also armed with a flashlight-sized version of the prison guards' Lucite shock prods, and if Semple or one of her companions especially aggravated him, he would administer a waspish, stinging jolt to a part of her anatomy where the resulting red mark would not be visible on camera. The entire production of *Fat Ari's Slave Shopping Club* seemed to be run on the dynamic of intimidation and spite.

That Semple and the others were merchandise had been made abundantly clear from the moment their prison escort had accepted a receipt for them from a harried associate producer and they had become the property of Fat Ari. After being stripped of even their prison kilts, run through a fast shower and blow-dry, they lined up for a perfunctory camera test. Three times, they were made to walk past a static camera, nude and unadorned. After that, Fat Ari and his director went into a two-minute huddle over the results, looking from the screen to the real woman and back again. Finally Fat Ari made an angry, disparaging gesture and stalked toward the women as if, whatever the current problem might be, it was definitely their fault.

"For my sins, you are all going to appear on tonight's show. Personally, I would rather have hot needles jabbed into my eyes than let a substandard collection like yourselves loose on an unsuspecting public, but since the incompetence of my staff leaves me no other alternative, there are some things you need to hear before the worst happens."

Fat Ari turned and, with a dramatic flourish, pointed in the direction of the long catwalk that was the centerpiece of the show's set. "Behold the runway, the place that makes or breaks you. The place where you will be sold or remain unsold. That is where the great viewing audience will decide if you are prime merchandise or merely damaged goods."

He gave a theatrical shudder as if to say he himself would be horrified by the spectacle. "During our short time together, there's really just one thing I expect you women to grasp. I don't know where you came from and I don't know by what accident of circumstance you got here. You can also rest assured that I absolutely don't give a fuck. As far I'm concerned, you have no history, no background, and no sad stories. You are my product. That's all you have to know."

Fat Ari looked at the women to make sure they were paying complete attention. Not one of them, Semple included, would have had the courage to do otherwise. When satisfied, he continued, "You are merchandise. The 'For Sale' sign is upon you. You are stickered and listed, and my job is to sell you. It is also your job to sell yourself. You sell yourself by doing exactly what you are told, and by making the maximum possible effort when your turn on camera comes. Your goal is to persuade the great unwashed to lust after you, to persuade them that they can't live another day without you. You have to convince them to bid their hard-earned credits like there's no tomorrow, just to get their greasy hands on your illusionary flesh. We have no artistic standards here. Be sensual, be erotic, be downright lewd and dirty. Just be sold. There's no second chance for unsold merchandise on *Fat Ari's Slave Shopping Club*."

If anything, Fat Ari was more Mediterranean than Egyptian. He wore his hair and beard so long and unkempt that it was hard to tell where one set of greasy ringlets stopped and the other began. It was all too possible to imagine him cheating crusaders out of their gold, somewhere in Constantinople in the twelfth century, or selling whores and hashish to GIs in the twentieth. Fat Ari was the universal merchant/pimp/hustler. As his dark, infinitely calculating eyes moved from one woman to the next, Semple decided that he'd probably been exactly the same in every life he'd ever known.

"Some people in this business will tell you that rejection is something to be faced philosophically. That rejection is something that shouldn't be taken personally. You will not find that attitude on this show. On this show, rejection by the viewers is strictly personal, very personal. I take it personally, and I can assure you that you will do the same. Those who fail on my show, those who remain unsold, receive no condolences. They are not told, 'Better luck next time.' Rejection on this show is followed by recrimination, humiliation, misery, and pain. I hope that you all fully understand that."

The women all stood transfixed, but this wasn't the response that Fat Ari was looking for. He singled out one woman, just beside Semple, and he and his caftan bore down on her like an angry galleon in full sail. "Well? Do you understand?"

The woman's eyes widened as though she were about to die on the spot. "Ye-yes."

Fat Ari rolled his eyes heavenward. "I don't know why I waste my time." He gestured to the entourage around him. "Get this worthless trash into makeup. Tonight is going to be a disaster. I know that for a fact. We are beyond help. Just get them to makeup and pray for a miracle."

Makeup was by far the most elaborate phase of the preparations. Out on the studio floor, the black-cowled techno-priests might sweat over the positioning of lights and struggle with their bulky cameras, but for Semple and the other women the long narrow makeup room—with its bright lights and greasepaint smells, lines of mirrors and milling bodies—was the hub of the universe. Inside that hub, they were both the core and the focus. They were greased and teased, oiled and manicured, painted, powdered, and latexed, with ultimate attention to detail, all the way to the trimming and shaping of their pubic hair. All blemishes were eradicated, anything unsightly disguised. At regular intervals Fat Ari's immediate underlings would storm through, checking the work and demanding that some particular woman be done over.

Semple wondered if this was how it had felt to be a Las Vegas showgirl, or a top-line Paris stripper, like one of the girls at the Crazy Horse, waiting backstage to go on, anxious amid all the bustle and excitement. She found that she could almost stop thinking of herself as naked and helpless and take a weird pride in becoming an object, a product, something to be desired, to have her true worth actually measured out in hard currency.

At least in the TV studio, unlike the jail, they were allowed to talk, although it seemed as though the makeup people did most of the talking. An effeminate and motherly man called Remu even went to some pains to explain that it wouldn't be half as bad as they imagined. "Actually a girl can do very well for herself if she puts her mind to it. Get bought by some horny old idiot and you'll have him bent around your little finger in no time. Next thing you know, he'll be springing for your freedom and a pardon and you can go your own sweet way."

One of the women from the prison was less than convinced. "Yeah, but what happens if you get bought by some psycho who wants to do all kinds of terrible stuff to you?"

Remu plainly didn't think the girl was taking a sufficiently positive attitude. "Well, my dear, accidents do happen. I mean, if you didn't want a few problems and uncertainties, you should never have got yourself put in prison in the first place, should you? Nobody said there were any guarantees. You're lucky this isn't the old days, when it was really rough and ready. Back in the Dark Ages, before we even had color, the Fat One sold anything. Domestic servants, big strapping quarry slaves, huge Nubian overseers with whips, you name it and he had it up on the runway. The entire place smelled of sweat, toil, semen, and the gods only knew what else. At least, since he discovered that the big score was in sex toy auctions, most everyone who comes in here is reasonably decorative and unthreatening." He rolled his eyes. "Unless, of course, you count the specialist oddities."

The woman with the negative attitude, far from being reassured, was becoming increasingly agitated by what Remu was saying. "I don't want to be a sex toy."

Remu's eyebrows arched. "Don't knock it until you've tried it, darling."

"But it's all a mistake. All I did was cheat on a devotional audit."

"With that attitude, girl, you'll wind up not getting sold at all. And then Heaven help you. You heard Fatso's little speech of welcome. He wasn't flapping his gums to be nasty, you know? He gets very disappointed with the unsold." He looked at his chronometer, which hung from a collar fob. "But I can't stay here all day chatting. I have to go to the other side and see that they're not making too much of a mess of the boys."

According to the gossip in the makeup room, a dozen young men had been brought to the show at approximately the same time as the women. It may have been that the young men were being processed and prepared for sale separately, but at no time had the women been allowed to set eyes on them, any more than the men were allowed a glimpse of the women. Semple could hardly believe that, in a sink of ethical and moral degeneracy like Necropolis, slaves of different sexes were segregated, but different places did have their different quirks.

Since the makeup crew working on Semple and the others was composed almost entirely of women or gay men, the conversation frequently strayed back to the subject of what might be going on in that other makeup room. One of the women on the crew who specialized in doing eyes had winked at Semple while she was carefully tracing the contours of her right upper lid with a fine brush. "Of course, doing the boys is a lot more fun, if you know what I mean. There's always the bit about the size of their cocks just before they go on camera."

"You're kidding me."

"Keep still, dear, or you'll fuck up all my good work." The eye expert tilted Semple's head back. "Fat Ari's got this thing about how the boy merch has to be well hung. So we have this little exercise just to slightly enlarge the size. Not a full erection, you realize, nothing . . . how can I put it? Nothing overt. Just a little manual enhancement at the last moment. That's not to say that every so often somebody doesn't take it a tad too far, or one of the boys doesn't get a bit overexcited, and then the obvious happens and the boss has a shit fit."

As showtime grew closer, the level of tension escalated. For a while, as long as the merchandise kept themselves still and quiet, they were exempt from most of the last-minute yelling and vitriol. When, however, the time came for their first walk-through on the runway, they were irrevocably drawn into Fat Ari's orbit of fury. For Semple, this fury reached its crescendo when the twelve naked but lavishly packaged ex-prisoners were paraded for final inspection. Fat Ari advanced down the line with the grim determination of Napoleon before Austerlitz. As he glared at each woman in turn, each did her best to look desirable. To Semple's horror, Fat Ari chose to stop dead in front of her. He leaned forward and peered into her face, then he rounded angrily on his nearest assistant. "And what the holy fuck is this supposed to be?"

The assistant looked blank. "She's number five on the roster."

Fat Ari's expression turned corrosive. "I can count that far on my fingers." He seized the assistant by the back of his head and thrust his face right into Semple's. While Semple wished that the studio floor would open up and swallow her, Fat Ari quizzed his assistant like a retarded child. "And what's wrong with this picture?"

Semple wasn't sure if she or the assistant was more terrified. The pitch of the assistant's voice climbed in direct proportion to his desperation. "She doesn't have a barcode."

"Very good. She doesn't have a barcode."

"But we already knew that."

"We did?"

"I thought we did."

Fat Ari let go of the assistant. "It's the first I heard about it."

The assistant looked betrayed. "But at the meeting this morning—"

Semple would not have thought that Fat Ari's face could grow any darker, but somehow it managed to when the assistant mentioned the meeting. Even Semple had realized by now that one would only be courting disaster by contradicting Fat Ari. His voice turned chill and absolute. "I said it's the first I heard of it. You understand me?"

"Yes, I'm sorry."

"So why doesn't this bitch have a barcode?"

"She's an outlander. She has no barcode."

"So why wasn't she branded?"

"We thought she'd be exotic the way she was."

"You thought?"

"Yes."

"You shouldn't think. You don't have the capacity."

"I'm sorry."

"You thought it might be exotic to have this outlander running up and down without a barcode? You thought a piece of unregistered cooze would get the rubes all hot and bothered?"

"It wasn't put quite like that, but yes, that was the general drift."

"Then perhaps you'd like to tell me, when they reach this state of carnal dementia and want to make a purchase, what happens when they zoom in to bid on her by barcode?"

"They'll find no barcode."

"And what would happen then?"

The assistant knew he was cornered and his responses turned into a guilty rote. "The rubes will get confused."

"And what happens when the rubes get confused?"

"The rubes stop bidding."

"And if they stop bidding?"

"We stop selling."

"And if we stop selling?"

"We die in agony."

"Now do you see why you shouldn't attempt to think?"

The assistant stared at his sandals. He seemed to be praying that Fat Ari had finished upbraiding him, but the gods of his choice had betrayed him. Fat Ari still glared down. Semple had noticed that all of Fat Ari's entourage seemed to be shorter than he was. "So what are you going to do now?"

The assistant didn't fall into this trap. "I don't know, boss. What am I going to do now?"

"You're going to take this piece of worthless protein up to Dr. M's as fast as you can, and you're going to get her branded."

The assistant nodded eagerly. "I am. Right away."

"Once she's branded and she has a price tag, she can legitimately call herself merchandise and we can start all over again. By their prices shall ye know them."

The assistant continued to nod. "I'll have her branded right away."

At the first use of the word "branded," Semple's every instinct of self-preservation jangled for her to do something. The third time it was repeated, she spoke without thinking. "I can't be branded. I'd have to get a whole new body."

Fat Ari didn't even look at her. "Keep quiet."

The assistant frowned. "Even if we get it done right now, she'll still be groggy from the anesthetic when she hits the runway."

"So do it without anesthetic."

Semple's horror couldn't stay silent. "No!"

Fat Ari looked at her this time. "You be quiet. You have nothing to say in the matter."

"I'm not being branded!"

Even the assistant seemed to be on her side. "That would be a punitive branding."

Fat Ari swung back on him. "So?"

"It's beyond the bounds of our authority."

Fat Ari's eyes were dangerous. "There are no bounds to my authority when it's two hours to air."

"She still might not be able to handle the runway."

"She'd be conscious, wouldn't she? Run her as a submissive in bondage."

Unable to think of anything else but to play the hysterical slave, Semple fell to her knees, grabbed hold of Fat Ari's robe, and began to scream. "You can't brand me! It's impossible! You can't brand me like a steer!"

Fat Ari curtly shook himself loose. The act was an utter failure. "Get security. Gag her if you have to."

"But we'd need paperwork for a punitive branding. The doctor could get difficult if we just march her in there."

"Then you will simply remind Doc Mengele of what he owes me for the last two sets of twins."

"The medical examination is nonnegotiable. It is required of all life-forms who board our vessels."

Jim squared his shoulders and drew himself up to his full height. So far, the aliens had been having things too much their own way. The time was more than right for Jim to start asserting himself. He didn't know if two skinny, yard-high aliens could be intimidated by his greater height and mass, but it was worth a shot and also about the only thing he had left. "I've learned that most things are negotiable, given sufficient motivation."

The Bogart alien and the robot doctor alien stood in the single spotlight, making no attempt to approach or back away. Their huge, enigmatic eyes were directly on Jim, and they didn't look intimidated in the slightest. "That is exactly the kind of remark we have come to expect from Earthlings."

"It is?"

The Bogart alien took a drag on a cigarette that wasn't there. "He's right, pal, you're a bunch of natural-born troublemakers."

"We are?"

"Your statement had all the properties of the prelude to a threat."

Although Jim would hardly admit it, the doctor alien was absolutely correct. He was certainly weighing the odds. The creatures looked frail and feeble, and it was hard to imagine what kind of a fight they could put up if Jim went in swinging like a barroom brawler. The UFO crash at Roswell indicated that they could be hurt. Hadn't that left dead and broken aliens scattered all over the chaparral? A simple frontal assault, though, took no account of science fiction trickery like invisible force fields or concealed death rays. Obviously any being who could stand a glass in thin air and have it vanish at will certainly knew some more tricks. He decided to switch to another line of persuasion, putting a two-fisted John Wayne eruption on hold for a while. "Strictly speaking, I'm not actually a life-form. I'm dead, dig? More like a metaphysical entity."

"You're here, therefore you are. And if you are, the medical examination is mandatory."

Jim wished that the damned aliens would blink or twitch or something. Anything but paraphrasing Descartes. He knew it was one of Doc Holliday's favorite tricks and he wondered if they'd pulled the idea out of his own mind. He couldn't shake the thought that, behind the blank masks, the sons of bitches were doing the telepath and having a good extraterrestrial laugh on his dime. "Yeah, that's right, I'm here, but that still doesn't make it right to be sticking probes in me. I mean, anything could happen."

"That's what makes it all the more interesting. We probe and then we see what happens. That's the fundamental nature of a probe, now, isn't it?"

"I suppose so, except . . . "

"Except what?"

Jim was wondering if the UFO and it occupants were strictly a part of the Afterlife, or if they'd invaded this space with the same lack of by-your-leave as they did Earth. Jim decided he might as well ask. "I guess you guys are dead too, right?"

Jim couldn't read any expression in either of their faces, but something told him that the creatures weren't impressed. "No, we are not dead."

The Bogart alien added its confirmation. "You better believe it, Jim. Alive and ready to probe ass."

Jim could have sworn that the doctor alien's face registered a twinge. "So to speak."

"So what are you doing running around in our human Afterlife?"

"Our mission is the seek out new life-forms and new civilizations."

"Don't try and con me. That's fucking *Star Trek.*"

"You noticed?"

"I'm no idiot."

The doctor alien spread its hands as though it had long ago given up on humans. "It's hard to tell. Sometimes your kind can be so fiendishly clever; on other occasions, you're mind-boggling in your stupidity."

Jim frowned. "Is that why you never just set down one of your ships on the White House lawn and said, *Take us to your leader?*"

Bogart leaned into the exchange. "Listen, buster, that wasn't our idea. All the lies and deception came strictly from your end. You think we wanted to be dismissed as marsh gas, flocks of birds, and weather balloons? We were quite ready to go live on *Ed Sullivan* or *Face the Nation* and reveal ourselves to the world. We even had a guy at William Morris, but Hoover had a shitfit and Truman vetoed it. It was those sons of bitches that wanted us to do the whole Area Fifty-one covert ops bit, in and out of the back doors of the Pentagon all the time, the interplanetary fifth column selling ray guns to the natives. They claimed that irrefutable proof of life elsewhere in the universe would freak the living shit out of the Arabs, the Bible Belters, and the Hasidic Jews; for all they knew, the Pope might resign unless he could come up with a good reason God had never warned him we were out there. Kennedy was okay with it, but look what happened to *him.* You know some of them even tried to blame us for that shit in Dealey Plaza?"

114

Jim held up a hand. "Hold it a minute. Are you seriously telling me that the William Morris Agency knew all about you?"

Bogart nodded. "At least a month before the FBI."

"You were going to go on *Ed Sullivan?*"

"It worked for Elvis and the Beatles."

Jim shook his head ruefully. "It never worked for me."

The doctor alien made a dismissive gesture. "That's because you had to be the petulant rebel and keep in the drug reference. I mean, they warned you, didn't they?"

Jim saw he was making no headway. "I'm not one of your abductees, you know?"

"We are well aware of that. You came aboard uninvited and of your own free will."

"So just drop me off at the nearest accessible spot and we'll forget the whole thing."

The alien doctor shook his head. "I'm afraid it's a little too late for that."

"I could incapacitate your warp drive with ectoplasm."

Although the doctor alien had no mouth, Jim could have sworn that he sneered. "We don't have a warp drive. That's also *Star Trek.* Now who's conning whom?"

Because they had no iris or pupils, it was impossible for Jim to tell exactly where the big alien eyes were looking, but he had the distinct impression that they had left his face and were now staring past him into the darkness. A moment later, as if in confirmation, he heard the patter of tiny feet coming toward him, the patter of dozens of tiny feet.

Semple was more helpless than she could ever remember. The chair in which she sat could have been in any dentist's office except for the padded restraints; no dentist would have secured her body with a tightly cinched belt around her waist and an equally tight crisscross of webbing across her chest that kept her from moving her shoulders and upper body. No dentist would have fastened her ankles to the footrest of the chair to prevent her from kicking out, or locked her skull in a steel clamp, or placed a rubber gag in her mouth so she was unable to utter a sound. Semple's fear was off the scale. The outward trappings of this were definitely medical. The small lab was bright and scrupulously· clear, all white surfaces, gleaming stainless steel, and glass cabinets. The individual in charge was even referred to as the doctor, though the intention of the operation that this so-called doctor was about to perform was nothing but gratuitous and agonizing torture.

Had Semple been a different person, had she retained some of Aimee's guilt when the siblings split, she might have made use of the time while she waited for the worst to happen regretting all the pain that she had just as gratuitously inflicted on others. In some ways, her own torturings were less morally excusable than that which she was about to receive. At least Necropolis had a system, no matter how diseased; Fat Ari was just trying to make the equivalent of a buck. The suffering she had inflicted on the unfortunate angels, cherubs, and wandering spirits who had fallen into her clutches had been strictly for her own bored and private amusement. In that, she was equally as culpable as Mengele, maybe more so.

Semple, however, was made of sterner and much less repentant stuff. Even with no gag in her mouth, she would never have considered making any promises of atonement. Her only words would have been vitriolic, obscene, and abusive, directed at the doctor and his assistant, at Fat Ari, at the cops who had arrested her and all the others who had conspired to bring her to this place of degradation and promised pain. Helpless as she was, Semple still flexed her muscles against the restraints and bit down angrily into the hard rubber of the gag, determined that, when the awful moment came, she would give no one the satisfaction of seeing her cower.

The awful moment turned out to be a long time coming. Soon even the doctor began to grow impatient. He frowned vexedly at his assistant, who was bent over a wheezing computer that leaked wisps of vapor from bad seals in its microplumbing. "What the hell is the problem? This is a straightforward branding. It's not supposed to take all day."

"It's the morons at Public Records. They're making a whole performance about assigning me a number blank."

"Fat Ari wants this unit back before his ridiculous show goes on the air."

The assistant hit a sequence of keys. "Believe me, I'm well aware of that."

"And we have a cheek-and-jowl job booked in twenty minutes."

"I'm aware of that too, Doctor."

"Then damn well get on with it."

Semple swiveled her eyes and tried to turn her head to see exactly what was happening, but the steel plates clamping her skull made movement impossible. The eternally springing hope of the condemned suggested that maybe, if the delay was long enough, Fat Ari would give up on her and the branding would be canceled. She was enough of a realist, though, to know in her heart that this would never happen. If she missed the show, they'd brand her out of pure spite and hold her for the next one. On the way in, she had taken a good long look at this character everyone called the doctor and recognized on sight that his personal glacier of sadism ran cold and deep. He did even the most rudimentary things with a precise, perfectionist attention to detail, and Semple suspected that he had enjoyed maybe more than one lifetime honing his sinister act.

She had also observed that the doctor, like Fat Ari, was not required to dress up for a night on the Nile. His white lab coat covered and protected the neatly creased pants and fully buttoned vest of a trim, ultraconservative, 1930s-style three-piece pinstripe suit. His hair was pomaded and brushed straight back, his fingernails immaculately manicured, his black oxfords buffed to a mirrored sheen, and his wing collar rigidly starched. The doctor's dapper and almost obsessive cleanliness made the horror of her situation somehow worse, even if Semple couldn't pinpoint exactly why.

After a further five minutes, the assistant turned from the computer in discreetly weary triumph. "I have a number, Doctor."

"And about time. Is the matrix heated?"

The assistant nodded. "It's white-hot."

"Then conform the bars and let's get this nonsense over with."

Semple could smell hot metal, and her stomach convulsed against the webbing. Despite her try for iron control, she was going to throw up.

"The brand is ready, Doctor. I'm removing it from the heater."

The doctor entered Semple's limited area of vision. He leaned over her, exuding a ghost-odor of cologne and breath mints. He lightly pinched the skin of Semple's forehead between a pale, antiseptic thumb and index finger, and when he spoke, Semple knew he wasn't talking to her. "It should take a good impression. I foresee no problems here."

No sooner had he spoken than the computer on which the assistant had previously been laboring hissed, belched, then let out a mechanical Klaxon howl. Semple couldn't see the assistant, but his voice sounded awed. "That's the call of the Lord Anubis himself."

The doctor was merely irritated. "It's been a while since the Führer saw fit to interrupt me."

Now the assistant sounded frightened. "Please, Doctor, we could all be in trouble if you were heard calling him that."

But the doctor cut him off. "Don't worry. There are no listening devices here. I made sure of that when I allowed the dog-headed simpleton to set me up in his ridiculous city. I also have the place swept regularly for bugs. And not only for ones installed by him. I also have to be watchful for those who would steal my research." The doctor moved quickly to the computer and hit a key. His voice took on a jovial respect. "My Lord Anubis. How nice. It's been a long time since we spoke."

The voice of Anubis was both huge and unreal. It gave the claustrophobic impression that it was not only filling the entire room, but using up all the air. "Has the outlander been branded yet?"

Semple swallowed hard. Now Anubis himself was getting in on her humiliation. The doctor replied briskly, "Not yet, my Lord. We have had some trouble with the records office. I'll be through very shortly."

The voice of Anubis again boomed around the surgery. "Don't do it."

The doctor blinked. "Don't do it?"

"That's what I said. Do we have a bad connection? Am I failing to make myself clear?"

"No, my Lord. You are abundantly clear."

Semple couldn't believe what she was hearing. She was off the hook by a miracle. Never again would she ignore the eternally springing hope of the condemned.

"I want the outlander brought to me."

The doctor sounded almost disappointed. "Unmarked?"

"Unmarked and unbranded."

"I'll have it done immediately."

"Do that."

"It's been wonderful talking to you, my Lord. You must come here sometimes and inspect my work."

But Anubis was already gone. Seemingly, Semple would soon be confronting him. Was this a rescue or merely a stay of execution reserving her for a worse horror in the future? She knew her wisest option would be to take refuge in the moment, and not even think about what the future might hold. Just rejoice that hot metal wasn't at that moment searing her brow. Unfortunately, the dog god was all too central to the thematic operation of the city and she couldn't help but speculate about him. Until now, she'd only seen pictures and statues of this figure who had taken the image and personality of the jackal-headed Egyptian god. Now she had heard his voice for the first time. Did the man always talk like that? Even when you were in the same room with him? Semple could only think that the voice was some kind of audio construct, like Tarzan's bellow in the old Johnny Weissmuller movies. The Tarzan cry was reputed to have been a primitive overdubbing of an African bull elephant, a roaring lion, and a well-known yodeling cowboy. Working on the same principle, the voice of Anubis could have been digitally sampled from equal parts of Benito Mussolini, James Earl Jones, and late Elvis Presley at the full-stretch crescendo of "Bridge Over Troubled Water."

The assistant was unstrapping Semple from the chair. After Anubis terminated the conversation, the doctor had stalked out of the room, plainly livid at the snub and miffed at the lost opportunity to inflict pain. As the assistant worked, he glanced around the room, as if unconvinced by the doctor's assurances that no listening devices were planted in the surgery. He removed the gag and smiled a patently phony smile. "It's a great honor to be summoned to Anubis."

Semple massaged her jaw. She was in no mood for small talk. "Kissing up to the Big Boss, just to be on the safe side?"

The assistant looked at her plaintively. "Do be careful. They listen in much more than anyone thinks."

Semple was in no mood for conversation. "Screw you, boy. You were just going to brand me."

"I was only doing my job. It was nothing personal."

"That's what your kind all say. And don't start telling me your fucking troubles, okay? Right now, I don't give a fuck who's listening. I was almost branded with a hot iron on my forehead. What the fuck else can they do to me?"

Despite her show of bravado, Semple was actually asking herself the same question. What the fuck else could they do to her? So far, this adventure had amounted to an unpalatable cocktail of Voltaire and De Sade. She knew what Anubis looked and sounded like, and she had seen some of the worst that the city he created had to offer. All inputs indicated that here was some mess of deep insecurities, overcompensating on a monumental scale. It did not bode well for their coming encounter.

As she finally stood up from the chair, Mengele returned to the surgery. He scowled at her. The doctor was also a bad loser. "So you've managed to elude my clutches?"

Semple flashed him a dazzling smile. "Better luck next time, Doc."

The doctor didn't smile back. His eyes hardened. It was as though a window had opened in some Arctic fortress of solitude. "Oh, there'll be a next time. You can count on that."

The lights dimmed to the blue glow, and Jim found himself surrounded by twelve or fifteen little gray aliens, two and a half feet tall, shorter than the doctor and the alien with the Bogart voice. They teemed around his legs like a bunch of eager, friendly children, as his mind was being inundated with cloyingly good vibes. Some were trying to take hold of his arms, others were feeling the rough texture of his cotton shirt, and running their little gray three-fingered hands over his leather jeans. Jim tried to move them back, shooing them away from him. "Hey, careful of the jeans, they've come so far with me they're a symbol of my character."

The little aliens refused to be shooed and didn't appear to care about symbols of Jim's character. They just twittered and chattered happily, making a sound between the wuffle of puppies and cheeping of baby birds, and the good vibes became even more saccharine. They treated everything he did as part of a marvelous children's game. Jim found, however, that they were slowly and subtly propelling him in the direction that they wanted him to go. He was also aware that something else, something different, was in the room, along with him and the little aliens, something much bigger, cold, old, and malign, that observed without apparently wanting to be seen. Each time he tried to look directly at it, the little aliens ran interference, and the something-else moved out of sight, making use of the hallucinatory, inexact quality of the blue light to conceal itself. Jim's only impression was of an elongated, equine, nonhuman head, long angular arms, and sinister arachnid motion. The word "mantis" came into his mind, but he didn't know quite why, although the right side of his brain was definitely getting nervous. "Don't trust these things. I'm telling you. You can't trust them. Just think about it. If you were some ugly, unscrupulous space thing with tentacles and a see-through brain, and you wanted to create a false sense of security in another species, what would you do?"

The left brain considered this. "I'd disguise myself."

"And how would you disguise yourself?"

Again the left brain considered. "I'd take on all the attributes of the young of the species I had targeted to screw over."

The right brain was positively congratulatory. "Exactly, the big eyes, the frail bodies, the overlarge heads. They're all calculated to make you feel protective and unthreatened. They're all fetal decoys."

The left brain had a question. "And what about the mantis thing?"

The right brain didn't like the answer it was giving. "I fear that thing may be the real deal."

The two halves of Jim's brain reconnected, agreeing that he would no longer be buying the alien bullshit. Unfortunately, all the bicameral brainwork quickly proved wasted as Jim saw the table. It wasn't like any operating table he'd ever seen, but there was no mistaking its purpose. The table was white and circular and had weird side trays holding laid-out instruments. Odd cantilevered devices were poised over it, ready to be swung into use like miniature cranes. The tools of the ET croakers were all fashioned from a highly polished, sapphire-blue metal, with odd, fluid configurations like some Henry Moore nightmare, but no mistake could be made about their function. Down to the smallest clamp, they were designed for probing, penetrating, and implanting—the whole abductee workup. He'd been taken for a sucker. He stopped in his tracks.

"Okay, this is where I get off."

He looked around for the Bogart alien but saw no sign of it. The nearest of the small ones took hold of his hand, but Jim slapped it away. "Listen, you little fuckers. My name is James Douglas Morrison and the shit stops here. No way are you getting me on that table. The closest I like to be to the medical profession is on the receiving end of a prescription for narcotics. Take my word for it, kids. Mr. Mojo's rising."

The little aliens started to back away. So far, hostility seemed to be having the required effect. Then he spotted one of the taller ones, and it wasn't backing away. It was coming toward him, holding what looked uncomfortably like a weapon, pointed directly at him. When it spoke, he knew it was Bogart. "I don't feel good about doing this, sweetheart, but you asked for it. You could have just rolled over and made it easy on yourself, but it seems we have to do it the hard way."

Shortly after she had split with her sibling, Semple had developed the unconscious and annoying habit of compulsively judging her actions against those of the characters in old Joan Collins movies. Obviously she was looking for a way to distinguish herself as the antithesis of Aimee's milksop blond purity. The problem stemmed from the time, before the split, when she was still working on her new physical persona. In the course of building her image, she had done an extensive study of Collins, starting with *Dynasty* and working backward all the way to the actress's low-budget, British errant-teen roles in movies like *The Good Die Young*. Right after the split, her studies had meshed with the insecurity of being on her own for the first time, and she found herself hardly able to make a move unless she could relate it to a Joan Collins movie. It was almost as though she were using the actress as a sibling surrogate or an invisible friend. Semple had, of course, rigorously trained herself out of the habit, and kept the lapse a close secret ever after. When it suddenly resumed its grip on her as she entered the Throne Room of Anubis, she half concluded that it was due to the stress to which she had been subjected since her arrival in Necropolis. Whatever the reason, from the moment she entered the Throne Room, she couldn't help but think of herself as being on the Cinemascope set of *Land of the Pharaohs*.

The rest of Necropolis may have been threadbare and stain-encrusted, but the Palace of Anubis verged on the preposterous in its ancient Egyptian splendor. The color scheme in the Throne Room was turquoise and gold, and the spatial proportions were indisputably epic. As far as Semple could tell, the Throne Room was used by Anubis only for the receiving and overwhelming of guests and deputations from his subject population, but it was the size of at least two basketball courts, divided by twin rows of massive fluted pillars that held up a forty-foot-high ceiling. The walls were decorated with towering murals of gods and demons, all clearly designed to demonstrate Anubis's dominant role, mentally, physically, and sexually, in the pantheon.

Semple had been instructed to enter the Throne Room through the massive gold double doors that stood at the opposite end of the vast space from the throne itself. As a new arrival, she would come out onto a raised platform and walk down a wide flight of stairs to the main floor. She had been told to wait on the platform, and not descend until Anubis indicated that he wished her to approach. When the signal came, she should go down the stairs and commence the trek of fifty yards or more to the throne. Had Semple not long since convinced herself of her own fabulousness, she might have been overawed by it all.

The preparation for her encounter with Anubis had been even more elaborate than her trials on the Fat Ari show. Under different circumstances, she might have been exhausted by such pampering twice in one day, but the perfection of the finished product made it tolerable if not actually enjoyable. The jackal head might have the direst plans for her, but at least they would be executed in luxury. By this point, Semple was also feeling lucky. Anubis might be steamrollering the Afterlife in the trappings of the god, but she knew that, somewhere, buried deep within him, lurked a stunted and highly insecure human male. For Semple, the manipulation of human males had never presented a problem. Given time, she would have him doing exactly what she wanted.

The prepping for the audience had started with a second fullbody scrub and cosmetic makeover. Apparently what had been good enough for Fat Ari's camera's hardly made it at the court of the godking. It wouldn't have been fair to describe the handmaidens who performed the task as more skilled than Fat Ari's crew. It was like the difference between Belgian lacemakers and New York garment workers. The handmaidens of Anubis worked in total reverent silence, as though they were embroidering the Bayeaux Tapestry or illuminating holy manuscripts. Given a choice, she would rather have had the constant coarse and caustic dialogue at Fat Ari's, but she had no complaints with the work of the handmaidens. Fat Ari's crew had made her lewd and salable, but the handmaidens were making her exquisite.

The makeup artists were followed by the dressers. The costume chosen for Semple was hardly elaborate, a very up-market variation on the standard wraparound skirt, though it came with a highly Egyptienne hawk-wing cape, with wide, built-up shoulders and a pinion motif. It was the precision of its tailoring and the quality of the fabric that truly impressed her. The metallic red, green, and gold shot-silk mixture shimmered and undulated as she moved, like the hot skin of some fantastic molten reptile.

Before she was let loose on Anubis, Zipporah, the primary concubine, a midperiod Catherine Deneuve who ruled the god-king's seraglio with the iron will of an Afterlife Margaret Thatcher, had instructed her in the correct manner in which to approach their glorious leader for the first time. The short lecture was delivered as a formal, almost theological speech, which seemed only fitting if dealing with a god. At the end, however, as the woman put particular emphasis on how Semple should never, under any circumstances, contradict or disagree with their lord, Semple made a mental note that, as soon as she resolved the questions of her own status and survival, she'd find a way to cut this fool deity down to size.

The gold doors that led to the Throne Room were flanked by a pair of muscular and heavily oiled Nubian guards. Semple had been escorted that far by a retinue of handmaidens, but as they approached the guarded doors the handmaidens halted and Semple was allowed to go on alone. The guards were identical in every respect, as though they had been assembled on the same production line. They stood over seven feet tall, with shaved and shined heads, clad in brief military kilts that left nothing to the imagination. Armed with long gold scimitars, they stared straight ahead, unwavering and not acknowledging Semple in any way as she walked toward them. Zipporah had said nothing about the guards, but Semple, although sorely tempted, refrained from ogling them. Without so much as a lingering sideways glance, she walked through the gold doors and out onto the platform at the head of the stairs, and was treated to her first glimpse of Anubis.

What confronted her, in fact, was not one but two versions of the god, Anubis in the flesh and also a giant sculpted likeness. Anubis himself sat in the Mighty Throne of the God, and the Mighty Throne of the God stood on an elevated dais between the massive feet of a ceiling-high statue of himself hewn from polished black volcanic rock and highlighted with flourishes of gold and precious stones. Lit from below by recessed banks of constantly moving spotlights, the glowering statue sat four-square and formal in its own sculpted throne, arms crossed across its chest, stone hands gripping the traditional power symbols of the reaping hook and flail. In total contrast, the real Anubis sprawled in his throne, studiedly decadent, with one long bronzed leg cocked over the armrest. Like the statue above him, the live Anubis was arrayed in gold. A short gold kilt was wrapped around his hips; a massive, beaten-gold collar was draped around his neck and extended clear to his navel.

To say that Anubis was well built was an almost ridiculous understatement. The human body of Anubis was the buffed peak of iron-pumping perfection, although Semple seriously doubted that the god ever did anything as gauche as actually pump iron. Even seen from a distance, his divine muscle definition was clear beneath a skin that was the color of oil-dark antique leather. Semple couldn't exactly estimate his height while he sat, but she imagined that, like his Nubians, he was well in excess of seven feet tall. What surprised Semple, even as accustomed as she was to bizarre Afterlife fantasy fulfillments, was the way his jackal head was married to the human body. The only slightly ambiguous feature was the god's rather odd conical neck, but his advanced physique seemed more than adequate to support it.

As Semple might have expected, the god was not alone in his Throne Room. Two more Nubian guards stood on either side of him with grim expressions and scimitars across their chests. Three near-naked handmaidens sat at his feet, pouring his wine, caressing his legs, and offering him gold platters of exotic finger foods. The guards and the girls conformed exactly to formula. The final figure in the tableau at the far end of the Throne Room was a lot less predictable. It looked like a Carthusian monk in its full-length robe. The cowl was pulled forward so the face was hidden, and the figure filled Semple with a sudden unease. The shadowy being remained out of the halo of light around Anubis, keeping him- or herself half in the shadows behind the throne. Semple could only assume that this was the classic gray eminence, the all-powerful, whispering advisor who had the ear of the despot, and the capacity to make or break rivals and lesser mortals. Semple knew from both experience and history that such individuals could be deeply and fundamentally dangerous.

Even as these thoughts were going through her mind, the figure in gray leaned forward and spoke into the god's ear. Anubis's head turned sharply and he looked in Semple's direction with the suddenness of a predatory bird. As the self-created god stared at her, a spring of healthy subversion bubbled up inside her, in the form of an urgent and almost overwhelming need to giggle. Something about Anubis had suggested the kind of absurdist, devastatingly funny idea that comes with prolonged anxiety and fear. From certain angles, Anubis, with his pointed, erect ears, looked like Batman with a grafted-on canine muzzle. Semple had suddenly seen Anubis as nothing more than a composite of the Caped Crusader and a cartoon dog. Then Anubis gestured in her direction, and the comic vision fled. The voice was, if anything, even more overpowering in the flesh than it had been when she had heard it over the speakers of the computer in the doctor's office. "Semple McPherson, you will now approach us."

Semple took a deep breath, straightened her back, and started down the steps, doing her best to look as impressive and dignified as possible. Joan Collins would have been proud of her. It was only as she was halfway across the vast expanse of pristine marble that she remembered how, in *Land of the Pharaohs*, Joan Collins had been tied to a pillar and flogged—then buried alive at the end of the movie.

Without thinking, Jim grabbed the arm of the nearest little creature and swung it as hard as he could at the Bogart alien. From that first moment of action everything seemed to run in slow motion. Jim was amazed at how light the alien was. He was able to pick it up as easily as a Styrofoam doll, something he would never have been able to do with a human child of comparable size. "That's right, you little gray sons of bitches! Run away! Get the hell away, you big-eyed cock-suckers! You've got a fighting-mad human on your hands now. I'm not one of your shell-shocked abductees! I'm a real representative specimen. One of the badass monkey tribe. All we had to do was invent fire and the fulcrum and there was no holding us. We pretty much fucked up our entire planet, so it shouldn't be so hard to fuck up a few of you!"

Jim turned. What he needed was a weapon. All rational moderation had left him. He didn't care that he'd come aboard the spacecraft of his own accord. He didn't see how that gave the aliens any reason to assume they could interfere with him in any way they wanted. The fact that doing random damage in a UFO in flight might have been a suicidal act also didn't bother him. Hadn't he, when drunk, bored, and self-destructive, tried to open the emergency door of a Pan Am DC9 somewhere over the Rockies, in flight between Los Angeles and Chicago? For the satisfaction he'd gain from devastating the saucer, he was, at that moment, quite prepared to go back to the pods of the Great Double Helix.

The Bogart alien was down, pinned under the arms and legs of the creature that Jim had used as a missile. Jim started toward the operating table. Somewhere amid the trays of surgical instruments, he ought to be able to find a decent weapon. He spotted an object about ten inches long that looked like a bone saw, seized it, and turned, ready to fight to the finish. The bad news was that, as far as Jim was concerned, the finish had come. Bogart had disentangled himself from the other two and was crouched on his knees, holding the strange cylindrical weapon in a very businesslike, two-handed grip.

Only rage prevented Jim from realizing that he didn't have a chance. If he'd had any sense he would have dropped the saw and given up. Instead, he rushed straight at the alien with the weapon. The flash of its discharge totally blinded him. He could feel nothing, so he didn't know if he was still on his feet or not. All he could see was an unrelieved vibrant blue, and that was all Jim Morrison wrote.

The purple tongue of Anubis darted out and licked surplus horseradish dip from his dog muzzle. The tongue was long and spatulate and reached all the way to his dog whiskers. With the sole exception of his larynx and voice box, the workings of the head of the god-king of Necropolis were so entirely canine that Semple wondered if his tongue tended to loll in hot weather. She actually found it hard to gauge where man ended and dog started. Some other more intimate questions regarding the purple tongue of Anubis also posed themselves at the periphery of her curiosity, but, as Anubis was in the process of subjecting her to an intense visual scrutiny and seemed about to speak, she put all speculation on hold.

Looking her up and down, Anubis portentously cleared his throat. "If you're considering lying to us or weaving some long and fanciful story to explain your arrival in our reality, I really wouldn't bother. We know all about you, Semple McPherson."

Leaning forward in his throne, he picked a strip of raw sirloin from the silver platter. It was hard to tell if Anubis ate all the time, or whether he was using this initial encounter between them as an excuse for a protracted snack. The platter of sirloin treats was supported by one of the handmaidens, acting as a human side table. The young woman was all but naked, wearing only body paint, thonged sandals, a gold and turquoise necklace, and a matching gold chain around her waist. Anubis dipped the sliver of meat into a bowl containing a mixture of mayonnaise, sweet mustard, and creamed horseradish proffered by a second handmaiden in a blue silk turban, a giant opal in her navel. Having liberally coated the morsel with dip, the god-King raised it above his black button nose, lifted his head slightly, and dropped it into his mouth. He closed his eyes and stared to chew, relishing the experience with a gratuitous and noisy display of enjoyment that Semple considered indecent. When he had finally finished and run his tongue around his mouth for a second time, he returned to his inspection of Semple.

"We also know all about your sister Aimee and her quest for the perfect Heaven."

Semple, who had not spoken up to this point, decided that it was worth risking a comment. "You appear to be remarkably well informed, my Lord."

Anubis's eyes narrowed slightly. "Of course we're well informed. We're a god, aren't we?"

Semple looked down at the floor in what she hoped was a suitably demure indication of submission to the creature's divinity. It was too soon even to try exerting her own will; for the moment, she might as well play along with the charade of his omnipotence. She would really have liked to look at the figure in the shadows in the gray robe. Like Fat Ari and Dr. Mengele, the figure in the robe clearly had enough clout to maintain its own, thematically incorrect fantasy image, but this was hardly the time to be caught staring.

"You arrived here uninvited."

"I'm sorry, my lord. I was unaware there were protocols governing such things."

"It would appear that there is much of which you're unaware. For one who previously commanded a modest domain of her own, you seem uncommonly ignorant."

It had been a long time since anyone had called Semple ignorant and biting back her anger took an effort. She knew her safest course was to go with the flow and ladle on the fawning diplomacy, but it wasn't easy. Anubis raised her hackles. "My journey to your domain was made in all innocence, my lord. I had heard great things about the wonders of your city and merely wanted to see its glory for myself."

Semple thought that she'd done tolerably well until a growl rumbled in Anubis's throat. "We warned you not to lie to us, Semple McPherson."

Semple raised her head and looked Anubis straight in the eye. "I assure you that I'm not lying to you, my lord."

"You're hardly telling us the whole unvarnished truth."

"My lord?"

"We can appreciate that you might want to see the glories of our realm, but we're also aware that you're engaged in a poaching mission on behalf of your sister. Do you deny that you came here looking to recruit a fantasy artist to assist her in enlarging and improving her wretched little Heaven?"

After he delivered this bombshell, Anubis's eyes remained locked on Semple's for a four- or five-second eternity before he looked away and reached for another piece of sirloin. Semple had to use unnatural restraint not to let the shock register in her face. How the hell did this megalomaniac know so much about her and Aimee's plans? Was it possible that he actually had informers inside Aimee's Heaven? Or, worse still, inside her own Hell? Someone or something had to be feeding him information. She had seriously underestimated the dog-headed boy. He probably had an evil network of out-of-control intelligence agencies tearing all over the Afterlife and getting into everybody's business, doubtless manned by a deranged cadre of misfits, sadists, and malcontents eager to spend their hereafter playing James Bond or J. Edgar Hoover. But hindsight was of little use to Semple now. "I can only repeat, my lord, that I came here in all innocence. I admit that I had agreed to assist my sister in finding a suitable individual to work with her on her expansion plans, but—"

Anubis abruptly stopped relishing the latest beef morsel and cut her off. "Let's just suppose for a moment that you'd actually come here with an open invitation and all of the correct documentation and diplomatic credentials. The matter of your attempting to coerce one of our subjects—a subject that we own and hold in thrall—to come back with you to the realm of your sister would pose a serious problem within itself."

Semple wasn't sure where he was going with all this, so she decided to play dumb. "I don't understand, my lord."

"If you recruited your fantasy artist here in Necropolis, you would be effectively depriving us of a piece of our personal property. You would be nothing more than a thief."

Semple immediately adopted an attitude of injured outrage. "My lord, I am not a thief."

"No? Everything and everyone in the city of Necropolis and the surrounding territories and protectorates constitutes our personal and inalienable property. How could the removal of an individual be anything but theft against our person?"

"That was not my intention, my lord."

"Didn't they used to say that the road to Hell was paved with good intentions? As one who has attempted to organize her very own minor Hell, you are probably well aware of the axiom."

At this point, Semple could do nothing to stop her control from slipping. How dare this mutation-mutt cast aspersions on her creation? "My Hell is more than minor, my lord."

Anubis's stare turned decidedly walleyed. "Is it?"

Semple was reminded how Zipporah the primary concubine had warned her not to argue or contradict Anubis. Anubis's remark about her "very minor Hell" had driven the instruction clear out of her mind. Anubis repeated the question, his voice a threatening snarl. "Is it?"

Semple quickly backpedaled. "The word might be 'modest,' my lord. Or perhaps 'boutique'?"

Anubis snapped back impatiently. "Minor? Modest? Boutique? Does it really matter? Is it anything like Necropolis?"

Now Semple could answer with heartfelt truthfulness. "No, my lord. That is very true. It's absolutely nothing like Necropolis."

"In its size?"

"No, my lord."

"In its grandeur?"

"No, my lord."

"In the complexity of its design?"

"No, my lord."

"Then it hardly really matters, does it? It's an inferior construct and we have no reason to discuss it any further."

Semple was sorely tempted to snap back that Necropolis was also the worst totalitarian mess since Albania gave up communism, but she restrained herself and spread her hands in courtly surrender.

"A poor thing but mine own, my lord."

Anubis looked as though he were about to respond unfavorably even to this conciliatory gesture, but right then the figure in the robe slid briefly forward, out from the shadows, and whispered something to its lord and master. Anubis beamed and nodded. "Very good point. In fact, an excellent point."

The figure in the robe faded back to the shadows, leaving Semple none the wiser about who or what it might be. She had momentarily glimpsed a pair of glinting eyes, but all else remained concealed beneath the cowl. Anubis looked sideways at Semple. "Our dream warden points out that, even leaving aside your intended theft of our property, the fact that your sister intends to expand her environment may in itself create a problem."

Now Semple really was at a loss, and had in no way to act to seem dumb. For a start, what the hell was a dream warden? "A problem, my lord?"

"Our dream warden suggests that this expansion may be a prelude to your sister's attempting to achieve some manner of godhead. As all thinking entities should be well aware, *we* are the only accredited god in this quadrant of the Afterlife."

Semple straightened her back. It was time to stand up to this pompous lunatic and his goddamned dream warden. She adopted the demented formality that seemed to be the only way to deal with Anubis. "I believe, my lord, being much more fully acquainted with my sister and her intentions than your dream warden, I am in a far better position to assure you that nothing could be further from her mind. She simply maintains an environment for the comfort and protection of those from the lifeside who arrive here seeking a traditionally fundamental Christian heaven. Of course, if my word is insufficient, you can always take the matter up with my sister."

Semple felt quite pleased with herself. She had refuted the dream warden without being directly confrontational and argumentative. Better still, Anubis seemed to be buying it. He was at least chowing down on yet another wafer of sirloin and thinking about it. Unfortunately, the dream warden moved forward for another shot. After more whispering, Anubis smiled again. "Our dream warden now points out that these discussions regarding the aspirations or otherwise of your sister in the matter of deification are largely academic. You're unlikely to be seeing your sister at any time in the predictable future."

Semple didn't like the sound of this. She also didn't like the way Anubis was smiling. "Why should that be, my lord?"

"Because, our dream warden quite rightly informs us you yourself are now also a piece of our property."

Semple's confidence plummeted. "How does your Dream Warden deduce that, my lord?"

Anubis made a gesture indicating the answer was simplicity itself. "You came to our realm uninvited and without any prior understanding as to your status during the duration of your visit. You requested no letters of transit or any other kind of contractual preliminaries. You requested no audience and presented no credentials. You didn't even come to us craving right of sanctuary or metaphysical asylum. Had you done any of these things, the situation might have been different. As it is—"

Semple clutched at any passing straw. "Suppose I were to petition for sanctuary right now?"

Anubis frowned and glanced at the Dream Warden. The cowl moved slightly as the Dream Warden shook his or her hidden head. Anubis turned back to Semple. "No, we are advised that you've been here far too long. The petition could not be made with acceptable sincerity. Maybe if you'd come to us immediately on your arrival something might have been worked out; instead, you chose to haunt low bars and get yourself arrested and nearly sold into slavery. It's much too late now, Semple McPherson. You're here and you're ours."

He paused as though considering some new point that he had only just thought of, but then shook his head as though dismissing it. "The only question that remains is, *what do we do with you?*"

Jim floated in an ocean of blue electricity. His body lay limp. He checked all of his available senses, and the consensus appeared to be that he was floating. He wasn't going anywhere. He simply *was* and that was about it, in a blue limbo surrounded by crackling static. The situation bothered him. The thing about limbo was you never knew how long you were going to be there. Jim did realize, however, that he had engaged in violent confrontation with a bunch of aliens on their own turf, and that he had been shot with a ray gun for his pains. "I guess I should have taken the medical exam. I probably would have been better off in the long run."

Thinking out loud at least reassured him that some kind of external universe existed in this new fine mess in which he found himself. He hadn't become a prisoner of his own mind; the flashing static wasn't merely the firing of his own synapses. Thinking out loud also got him an immediate answer.

"You *should* have taken the medical exam, *shouldn't* you?" The voice was greatly blue-muffled, but he thought it might have been the voice of the doctor alien. It definitely wasn't Bogart.

"So how long are you going to keep me here?"

Jim was suddenly on a soft padded floor, with a crisscross, nonslip texture. He was starting to realize that if you asked the UFO a question, you had a good chance of receiving an answer, even if it was nothing like the one you were expecting. After checking that he was still intact after the scuffle, that no parts of his body or mind were missing or mysteriously changed, he sat up very carefully, watchful for any fresh surprises. He was sure the extraterrestrials had by no means finished with him yet.

The interior of the chamber in which he found himself was a creation of irregular ovoids. Jim seemed to be in a domed half-ovoid blister or bubble, like an egg cut lengthwise and placed down on the flat cut, creating an ovoid floor about twenty-five feet across at its widest point. Two flat ovoid slabs of some plastic or rubberlike substance were apparently supposed to serve as benches. A much larger slab of the same stuff seemed to be an approximation of a bed. High in the upper dome, a collection of small ovoids floated in eccentric orbit around each other, not unlike the mobiles that had enjoyed a brief vogue on lifeside Earth, except that, where Earth mobiles had used wires and balance beams, this decorative arrangement had no visible means of support.

Even the door or entry port was yet another ovoid, conforming to the curve of the wall at the narrow end of the chamber, though it came with no visible handle, lock, or other external means of operation. Jim got to his feet and decided to conduct an experiment. He walked to the door, placed his hands flat against it, and pushed, gently at first and then applying increasing pressure. No matter how hard he pushed, it neither yielded nor budged. Maybe it wasn't a door at all, just a decorative panel set in the wall. If that was the case, though, how did anyone get in and out?

Jim didn't want to entertain the thought that he was actually sealed in this place, walled up like some futurist heretic. Instead, he took a step back and spoke to what he still thought of as the door. "Open, please?"

Nothing. He tried once more, instructing rather than asking. "Open the door, please."

Again the result was negative, but Jim couldn't help smiling at what he was doing. "Open the pod bay door, please, HAL."

He didn't really expect a result, and the door didn't disappoint him. Jim turned away from it and sat down on the ovoid bed to take stock of this new situation. The flat surface yielded just the way a mattress would; at least some consideration had been given to the most basic of his creature comforts. Then again, he was still lacking an ovoid minibar or cocktail cabinet. Creature comfort had its limits.

"Could I get another martini in here?" No dice.

Jim was so focused on wondering what the next alien move might be that the true nature of the room escaped him for quite some time. When it did, though, realization dropped on him like a load of futuristic glass bricks. "Jesus H. Christ, it's the fucking *Jetsons*."

The aliens had locked him up in a Cadillac construct of 1950s science fiction. What he was coming to think of as his prison was nothing more than a set from one of the better, big-budget, atomic baroque space operas: *Forbidden Planet* or *This Island Earth*. It had to be either a created illusion or a controlled hallucination. He could scarcely believe that actual aliens would subscribe to some retro–Captain Video school of interior design. The obvious scenario was that it had been custom-tailored for him, based on information gleaned directly from his own mind; either he was on the receiving end of another variation of alien rat-maze behaviorist testing, or they were dementedly attempting to put him at his ease.

"I wish this place had a goddamned window."

Jim all but jumped out of his skin when a large section of wall simply melted away to reveal the black grandeur of the interplanetary starfields in all their celestial glory, with the planet Saturn and its rings dominating the foreground.

"Damn!"

The vision was so extraordinary that a moment of fear stunned him. The flying saucer was disintegrating. It had been struck by a meteor, blown up by a photon torpedo. Then he realized that he was viewing the raw vacuum of space through a clear viewing port, oval, but as large as the picture window in a suburban split-level.

"Sweet Mary Mother of God."

Jim's first glimpse of space from space filled him with a holy awe so total that it rivaled even his earliest acid trips. Tears came to his eyes. It was terrible in its magnificence. The sky was a deeper black than he had ever experienced or imagined. With no atmosphere to act as a distorting filter, the constellations blazed in unwinking brilliance. One of the Saturn's moons—maybe Titan, Jim didn't know for sure—was breaking across the giant ringed planet's horizon. He didn't care if the whole thing was real or illusion, and he didn't care what the aliens had in store for him. Whatever they might do, it would be worth it to have seen this.

"Fucking unbelievable."

All through his life on Earth he had harbored three great irrational regrets. He'd never seen the young Elvis Presley performing live, he was unable to fly like Superman, and he'd never looked into the deep vastness of space. One down and two impossibilities to go. If he hadn't already been dead, he would probably have been able to die happy. Jim was so transfixed by the infinite beyond the port that he totally failed to hear the ovoid door slide open.

"Hello, Jim." The first voice was blond, breathless, and afraid of its own power.

"Good evening, Jim." The second voice was cool, lazily aloof, with a hint of contempt.

Jim quickly turned and was confronted by a spectacle in its own way as wondrous as the view beyond the ovoid picture window.

"I am Epiphany."

"And I am Devora."

"Were you admiring the stars, Jim?"

"Now it's time for you to admire us."

Jim knew this couldn't be anything but an elaborate illusion, but in that first moment, he really didn't care. The 50s sci-fi tableau was now complete. The two women were Wally Wood creations straight from the cover of an EC space comic. Each was at least as tall as he was, perhaps taller, statuesque, each a warrior showgirl in a form-fitting fantasy space suit and transparent bubble helmet with articulated hose running to a tiny finned air tank on her back. Epiphany was as blond as she sounded, and her suit was silver accented by a pale shade of the same blue as the room. Devora was a brunette with honey high-yellow skin, her suit was midnight metalflake with crimson pinstriping. Jim was almost as impressed with the suits as he was with the women. They were fetish feats of bizarre body-shop engineering. The women's torsos were clad in what looked to be highly polished plastic or fiberglass, with the kind of multicoat, hand-rubbed finish usually saved for top-of-the-line hot rods. Rigidly molded and contoured to the bodies beneath, the detailing went right down to loving re-creations of navels and nipples. Epiphany's and Devora's Las Vegas legs were encased in long thigh-length boots with absurdly high heels, their arms sheathed in long evening gloves that came to well above their elbows. Both gloves and boots matched the color of the body units. Their thighs and upper arms, on the other hand, were quite bare, something that, in any real exposure to the vacuum of space, would immediately cause explosive decompression.

Jim knew, however, that these outfits would never be exposed to anything beyond him and this egg-shaped blue room. They had been crafted for his seduction and his seduction alone. He also knew that Epiphany and Devora, these equal and opposite Queens of the Galaxy, nasty and nice, good and evil, were the gift wrapping on some chill alien agenda that, if it had to be so seriously camouflaged, probably would have repulsed him if he'd been forced to witness its unvarnished reality. On the other hand, if the aliens had the decency to run an erotic con on him, he might as well go along with the gag, as long as the gift wrapping held up. He certainly had very little to lose. And so, when Epiphany moved toward him with a demure yet lascivious smile, Devora just one step behind her, Jim returned the smile. When their smiles broadened and their hands went to the throat fastenings of their bubble helmets, he stood his ground. It was only then that he noticed how, although Epiphany was unarmed, Devora wore an unusually phallic art deco ray gun in a low-slung, tied-down, speed-draw gunfighter holster.

"Do the handmaidens have to stay?"

Anubis turned. He'd been absorbed in picking at a tray of crackers and tiny chips of dried fish. It seemed that Anubis did eat constantly. Maybe it was the dog in him, or perhaps the parents of the mortal child had done something really terrible to him like repeatedly locking him in closets without supper, lunch, or breakfast. As in the Throne Room, a pair of near-naked handmaidens carried the trays of goodies, following the God-King as he moved from one part of the bedroom to another, while two more stood flanking the silk acreage of the dog-god's bed, waiting on his pleasure.

Anubis regarded Semple disdainfully. "Of course they have to stay; we don't know when we might require them."

"And the guards, too?"

"The guards always stay. For all we know, you might be planning an attempt on our life."

Semple observed that, even in the semi-privacy of his bedroom, Anubis continued to use the royal "We." The son of a bitch must have been a seriously abused child. Why else would he require such constant reinforcement of his self-esteem? Semple knew that she and Aimee had their problems, but not even the sum of their collective hang-ups could approach Anubis and his monstrous dysfunction.

"As this is our first time together, I might respond better to you if we had a little more privacy?"

The fingers that held the latest cracker halted halfway to the dog-god's mouth. "Our intention is to fuck you, you stupid woman, not consummate some passionate romance. You will respond just as we want you to respond or you'll find this interlude will have a very unpleasant aftermath. Besides, we might decide to have one of the handmaidens join us at some point in the proceedings if we're so inclined."

Semple caught the two handmaidens beside the bed exchanging weary glances behind Anubis's back. It was good to see some spark of resistance surviving in this absurd autocracy. She wished she could slip them some sign of sisterly solidarity, but Anubis was looking straight at her. Anubis's decision of what to do with Semple couldn't have been more predictable if he'd been wholly dog instead of just dog from the neck up. After an unpleasantly rambling debate with himself regarding Semple's ultimate fate, complete with a couple of lengthy and loathsomely perverse digressions, Anubis had suddenly declared that he was bored and wished to leave the Throne Room and retire to his private suite. He had risen petulantly and the Nubian guards had fallen in, swiftly and silently, on either side of him. With a curt gesture that Semple should follow, he had walked quickly to a concealed door behind the right leg of the giant statue. The Dream Warden had attempted to tag along, but Anubis had turned in the doorway and shaken his head. "We won't be needing you right now. We suggest you busy yourself with that matter we discussed earlier."

The Dream Warden seemed about to protest, but at a sign from Anubis, the Nubians closed the door on him. Anubis had glanced at Semple and smiled nastily. "The Dream Warden is not happy. We had halfway promised you to him, but then we changed our mind and decided, for the moment, to keep you for ourself. You should feel honored. Our whims are not always so charitable."

"I am honored, my lord."

Anubis's eyes flashed with amusement. "Learning submission, are you, Semple McPherson?"

No, dogbreath, I'm just a poor girl doing her level best to survive in an untenable situation.

"I'm attempting to please, my lord."

"You wouldn't have preferred the Dream Warden?"

She smiled nicely. "How could anything be preferable to being noticed by you, my lord?"

Anubis had then switched position like a spoiled child. "Are you saying that you have something against our Dream Warden? That you're maybe too good for him?"

Semple sighed inwardly. Don't you ever give it a rest, Benji? "How can I say, my lord? All I've seen is a figure in a robe."

"And you don't want to see what's beneath that robe, believe us. It's disgusting."

Semple couldn't let this pass. She decided the highest level of reproach that she could risk would be to pout prettily. "And you were going to give me to him, my lord?"

"But we didn't, did we? If we were you, we'd be thinking about original ways in which we could express our gratitude."

Anubis's private suite ran to some twenty rooms, each of which apparently came with its own complement of handmaidens and Nubian guards. Anubis, however, showed no inclination to treat Semple to a tour of his private turf. Instead he marched straight for what turned out to be the master bedroom, although the very word "bedroom" was hardly adequate. The place was the size of a small ballroom and the bed could have accommodated ten or more, and probably had. The color scheme was a bruised midnight purple that Anubis probably thought was decadent and erotic, but struck Semple as simply nightshade poisonous. Multiple mirrors were arranged in such a way that, from almost any point in the room, it was possible to see infinitely repeating images of oneself. A flickering, flashing, almost psychedelic lighting pattern confused and flattered these reflections, created moving pools of deep shadow and complex refraction patterns, while industrial-strength incense censers belched clouds of perfumed smoke. The mirrors had momentarily taken Semple by surprise. She hadn't thought of Anubis as so overtly narcissistic, but it made sense. The dog-god's boudoir was a place of smoke and mirrors, darkness and deception, and pretty much what she'd expected of her host and putative owner.

A large pyramid-shaped television set was placed so it could be easily observed from the bed. Anubis's first move on entering the bedroom was to go straight to it and turn it on. Semple moved slightly so she could see the triangular picture. On the screen, a parade of naked women with fixed smiles desperately swayed and jiggled down a narrow catwalk. It had to be *Fat Ari's Slave Shopping Club*—unless, of course, Fat Ari had competition. Before Semple could observe any more of the show, Anubis switched the channel. The screen now showed the God-King himself engaged in athletic, canine-style coitus with a moaning blonde, while a second, red-haired woman with a freckled back lay beside them, assisting him and his primary companion in any way she could. Was Anubis so far gone that he had to have sex to the accompaniment of a visual record of a previous triumph?

Anubis waved his hand abstractedly in Semple's direction. "Remove your garments."

Yeah, and peel me a grape, you son of a bitch. You could at least look interested. Hiding her contempt, she engaged a neutral smile. "Anything you say, my lord."

Stripping in a place where the bulk of the population went topless was hardly a big thing. She certainly didn't feel like treating Anubis to any kind of bump-and-grind routine and, anyway, he seemed more interested in his homemade porno tapes. On the triangular screen, the moaning blonde was either enjoying the orgasm of her life or creating an Oscar-winning simulation. Her pièce de résistance was to run up a near-perfect vocal scale in high C, only to blow the effect by going flat on the highest top note. With all the aloof elegance she could muster, Semple sighed discreetly to regain the dog-god's attention and let the hawk-wing cape drop from her shoulders. A single tug loosened the wraparound skirt and it joined the cape on the floor at her feet.

"My lord?"

Anubis inspected her nudity and nodded with what she interpreted as grudging approval. At the same time he let his own kilt fall to the floor and Semple could hardly believe what she was seeing. It reminded her of the ancient adage of a baby's arm holding an apple in its fist, except it was a deep mahogany, gnarled like the trunk of a vine, with long twisting veins standing out in clear relief. At first she thought that it must have been a put-on, an elaborate showboat codpiece, a strapped-on construct of wishful thinking. Only when it started to move did she realized that this was wishful thinking made fantasy flesh. Anubis again eyeballed her nudity, then looked down at himself and grinned like a proud Doberman. "Does it frighten you?"

Had Semple been terrified out of her mind, she would never have admitted it. Since he so plainly intended to fuck her, she did have a certain trepidation about being able to accommodate the thing without too much physical modification to her own body, but she had quickly buried that, approaching the experience with a kind of academic curiosity. Conducting herself as a connoisseur of the extremes in experience was infinitely better than tearing her hair and rolling her eyes like a degraded slave.

She deliberately arched an eyebrow. "Your . . . manhood is truly magnificent, my lord. I have never seen anything like it."

Anubis smiled smugly. "I very much doubt that you have."

Anubis beckoned to her, and Semple steeled herself with deliberately dark thoughts. Hold on, Fido. Semple McPherson's day will come. She was now bent on not only escaping from Necropolis, but also putting the hurt on Anubis before she went. She didn't particularly care how she hurt him—physically, emotionally, materially, spiritually, it was neither here nor there. She just wanted to hurt him where it hurt.

The desire intensified as the dog-god crooked an imperious finger. "Come here and kneel in front of me."

She had assumed that he'd be content to simply stick it in her and have done with it. She now realized she was expected to fondle and play with the monstrosity. It was becoming clearer and clearer that, in Necropolis, on all levels, absolutely nothing came easy.

Jim groaned and closed his eyes. He didn't want it ever to stop. He didn't care that it was all alien illusion. He didn't care what the aliens might be doing to him in reality. Reality had never been this good to him. He could cruise all the way to infinity locked in this custom fantasy. Epiphany's thighs gripped him, encircled him, held him fast, while a hundred hands with a thousand fingers seemed to move over his body, and even caress his very nervous system.

"Epiphany, don't stop."

Her voice breathed inside his head. "Don't worry, baby. I won't stop until you beg me."

It was only moments earlier that Epiphany's hands, the same hands that were now driving Jim to the edge of insanity, had gone seductively to the silver ring fastening of her bubble space helmet.

"I'm going to have fun with you, Jim Morrison."

One turn had detached the helmet, a second turn had caused the hard shell torso section simply to disappear. Jim didn't know how she pulled the trick of the disappearing space suit, and she didn't give him any time to puzzle over it. She was standing in front of him in long boots, long gloves, and nothing else, demanding and getting his total attention. Slowly and suggestively she pulled off the gloves. "Oh yes, I'm going to have a great deal of fun with you, Jim Morrison. Do you think you can handle all the fun I'm going to have with you?"

It scarcely worried him when he noticed that Devora had made no attempt to divest herself of any part of her suit. Jim was now beyond caring. So Devora wanted to play the voyeur? So what? Wasn't Epiphany promising him the stars?

"Stars like you never imagined, baby."

Together they had sunk down onto the surface of the blue Jetson ovoid, and sensual delirium had immediately overtaken Jim. It was only as he went down for the last time that he saw that Devora had unholstered the phallic art deco ray gun and was applying a clear lubricant gel to the barrel. By then, it was far too late to do anything about it.

Semple groaned and closed her eyes. She wanted it to stop. She'd had it with the infinite reflections of herself, spread-eagled under the weight of the dog-headed god. She'd had enough of Anubis slamming into her with his absurd oversized penis. She was tired of his lapping her breasts with his rough dog tongue, and worst of all, she was tired of being expected to moan appreciative clichés to make the idiot feel omnipotent. "Oh my *lord,* it's so big, it hurts, it hurts so much, please, it feels like it's going to split me in half. *Oh, my lord!* It's hurting me, but don't stop, please don't stop . . . "

At first she had managed to hold gagging revulsion at bay by disengaging from her physicality, distancing herself first from what she was expected to do and then, as things progressed, from what was being done to her. From this point of view the cavernous purple bedroom with its drifting layers of scented smoke, the picture of the powerful and rapacious dog-headed creature crouched over the prone white body, positioning and repositioning it as it gasped and groaned beneath him, had a certain Pre-Raphaelite pornographic charm. Her undoing came when, in that state of detachment, she had perversely started to enjoy herself. The moment she gave in, she was reminded what a sick piece of slime Anubis really was; repulsion had elbowed its way in, detachment had taken a cab.

But then, just as she started to reached the limits of her tolerance, something new began to happen.

Something new began to happen. Jim's senses were already in serious disarray. Epiphany was somehow simultaneously all around him, under him, above him, and front of him, a Möbius continuation, the galaxy made rhythmic flesh. The blue ovoid room came and went. Forward and back, the two of them in sync to the erotic pulse-of-the-spheres. One moment the room, the next a state of free fall above the methane and ammonia atmosphere of Saturn. The rings arched over them and left them gasping in the vacuum, reality capriciously disengaged. The only constants were that Devora, still in her midnight-blue space suit, was always behind him, at the periphery of his distorted vision, and that some foreign object had penetrated his body. And yet, the intrusion in no way bothered him. Quite the contrary, it only added to the mind-thrashing fun he was already having with Epiphany. If his unexpected paramour's companion wanted to bugger him with the lubricated chrome of her ray gun, who was he to complain?

When the flash came from out of nowhere and almost blinded him, Jim was concerned that Devora, in some moment of cold alien excitement, had inadvertently—or maybe even deliberately (a little mantis in everyone)—pulled the trigger on the ray gun. He was still conscious enough to know that could mean trouble. Jim felt as if his spine were going to snap, his brain boil out through his eyes. He was hard-pressed to tell agony from ecstasy. Then, suddenly, he was in another place.

Semple felt as though her spine were going to snap, her brain boil out through her eyes. She was hard-pressed to tell agony from ecstasy. Then, suddenly, she was in another place, with another person, a man, indistinct but definitely a man. His hair was shoulder-length and dark, but his features kept shifting, like the indefinable face in an elusive dream. And they were together, with a power passing between them though neither of them knew why.

Jim was in the arms of the Queen of the Nile, black ringleted hair billowing around him, kohl-rimmed eyes gazed into his. She gripped him with a terrible urgency, as though she knew they had encountered each other in a transitory place that could only be the result of a glitch in the cosmic flow; in a nanosecond, he knew they would be parted. She pressed her mouth against his in simultaneous welcome and farewell. Then Jim was falling. Multiple orgasms of a kind that he had never experienced before were ripping through him. And he was once again falling.

Semple was screaming. Multiple orgasms were ripping through her. And he was screaming. And she was screaming.

4

The question of human edibility is a tricky one.

As Jim hit slimy water with a splash and sank, he had a fleeting glimpse of the UFO above him. It was already nothing more than a tight cluster of colored lights in the sky, zigzagging away on an erratic and illogical course and vanishing into a gray overcast, just like they did in all the sighting stories and blurry handheld camcorder tapes. For an instant, he was filled with a burning if illogical outrage. He'd been used like the proverbial one-night stand, the universal tramp. He didn't even qualify as an intergalactic whore: to the best of his knowledge, he'd received absolutely nothing in return for the bodily invasion except a residual burning in his rectum and the feeling that he had been victimized. As far as could tell, he'd been dropped from a chute in the underside of the saucer, dumped out like garbage, without so much as even the parting acknowledgment of metaphoric cab fare.

As he sank, his mouth, nose, and ears filled with slime, duck-weed, and swamp water, and resentment gave way to the urgent necessities of survival. Jim hit bottom, or at least hit mud. He floundered up again, stumbling, splashing, drenched, with his previous fury returning. Not only had he been discarded and disrespected by the fucking aliens, but something magical had been interrupted by his fall. He didn't even have a clear memory of what had happened. All he knew was that it had been important and now it was gone. A new and mysterious cake, not simply left out in the rain, but hit by a monsoon, the recipe irretrievable. A woman with dark Cleopatra hair hovered at the core of the fragmenting memory, but already he could no longer picture her. The drapes of perception were rapidly closing, like the falling curtains of dreamwaking.

Gasping, treading water, getting himself covered in mud, he discovered that the water in which he was struggling was actually only chest deep. At the same time he also heard a voice. "Over here, pal. There's a few square yards of dry land where I am. I don't know what good it'll do you, but you're welcome to join me."

The voice was not unlike that of a frog in an animated cartoon. A cockney frog, to boot, with vowels decidedly British, and the kind of epicene vocal droop affected by Mick Jagger in his speaking voice. The frog, if indeed it was a frog, sounded dense but trustworthy, and for want of a better offer, Jim waded laboriously in the direction of the voice.

"Say something else, will you? So I can get my bearings?"

"Tossed from a flying saucer, were you? Give you the treatment and then heave-ho you into the swamp, did they? Those fucking aliens have a lot of fucking nerve, I'm telling you."

Jim was now only up to his waist in water, pushing through the thick reed beds that flourished in the shallows. It was hard to see. The swamp was heavily shrouded in a gray drifting mist. The Anglo-frog seemed be leading him in the right direction, but he needed to keep it talking. "You get a lot of folks ejected from UFOs around here?"

The frog voice was blasé. "Happens all the time."

"All the time?"

"Maybe not all the time, but often enough to be noticeable. Local speculation has it that the aliens have this thing about the Jurassic. Maybe something to do with the Nemesis Asteroid."

Now Jim was totally confused. "The Jurassic?"

"That's right."

"You're saying this is the Jurassic?"

The frog voice croaked, perhaps to clear its throat. "Or a loving reconstruction of same."

Jim halted in his squelching tracks. "Get the fuck outta here."

"Surprised? Most folks are when they first fall out of the UFO."

"I'm in the Jurassic era?"

"You're in the Jurassic."

"I don't believe it."

"I'm afraid you're going to have to, my old son. Plus there's not very much you can do about it apart from trying to avoid being eaten. Bit of a difference in the old food chain back here. I can understand your confusion, though; it must be hard to go from Master of the Universe to a snack on legs."

As if in confirmation of the point, the mist temporarily parted and a huge form became visible in the distance. It stood well over fifty feet tall, with a long serpentine neck and tail, a hunched body like a small hill, and a mud-caked hide wrinkled green and brown, with markings not unlike jungle camouflage. It stood grazing on the top foliage of a medium-sized tree, and even its slightest movement caused twenty inches of oily swell to roll across the swamp, threatening Jim with inundation. Jim Morrison stood frozen by the sight of his first live dinosaur. Suddenly he wished he'd never been so rash as to call himself the Lizard King. In terms of monarchy, this beast had him. Jim wasn't sure if it was a brontosaurus or a diplodocus. He had always confused the two. The frog voice piped up helpfully. "I wouldn't worry about her too much, pal. Strictly herbivorous."

Jim became defensive. "I knew that."

"Sure you did."

At that moment, the creature raised its tiny head and never-ending neck to the sky and emitted a wailing but strangely harmonic cry, something between the call of the humpback whale and a mournful foghorn. It was immediately answered by similar calls from elsewhere in the swamp.

"They do like to sing of an evening."

Even though Jim was fairly certain that the frog voice—and the human archaeologists of his own time—were correct in believing that such dinosaurs were harmless, he stood and waited for the giant beast to finish its song before resuming his struggle to dry ground. He recalled that a raging bull was also technically a herbivore, and he certainly had no idea what kind of red rag it might take to raise the ire of a diplodocus.

"Makes you nervous, does she?"

"Anything a few thousand times my size makes me nervous."

Jim was now wading out of the swamp toward an area of coarse grass hummocks and tortured willows a few poor inches above the general water level. The mist was more patchy on this marginally higher ground, and off in the far distance he could see a dense plume of smoke rising from what he took to be an active volcano. He really did seem to be in some young Jurassic world. He looked around for the source of the frog voice, but could see nothing that qualified. "So where are you, friend?"

"I'm over here, aren't I?"

The voice was coming from a tall clump of vegetation that ran rampant between two willows. The plant or plants were like nothing that Jim had ever seen before. Three elongated, open top gourds stood together in the middle of a base of fleshy green and yellow leaves, and a long, whiplike tendril extended from the mouth of each gourd. Jim could still, however, see no sign of the frog or any other creature from which the voice might emanate.

"Why don't you show yourself?"

"You're looking straight at me. I don't know what else you expect me to do."

Jim noticed that, each time the voice spoke, the lower leaves of the plant rubbed against the gourds in exact time to the words. A look of incredulity came over Jim's face. "You're the plant?"

"Why shouldn't I be a plant?"

It was a reasonable question, and all Jim could do was shrug. "No reason, I guess. I just never met a plant that talked before. Also you sounded so much like a frog."

"It puts the real frogs at their ease before I eat them. It gives them the illusion they're dealing with one of their own."

"You eat frogs?"

"Never met a plant that ate meat before?"

Jim nodded. "Sure. I had a Venus's-flytrap when I was a kid, but—"

"Strictly small-time."

"Are you telling me you're a carnivorous plant?"

"You have a problem with that? A vegetarian or something? I have to tell you, vegetarianism looks very different from my perspective."

Jim took a step back. "I'm not a vegetarian."

"I'm glad to hear it."

Jim took another step back. "But how do I know you're not going to eat me?"

One of the tendrils made a gesture as though such a suggestion was close to insulting. "You really think I'd eat someone with whom I had just been talking?"

"You talk to the frogs before you eat them. You just told me that yourself."

"Yes, but you're not a frog, are you?"

147

"That's true."

"So come closer and tell me all about your adventures with the aliens."

Jim didn't move. "I think I'll just stay where I am for the moment."

The tendril stiffened as though offended. "You don't trust me?"

Jim drew himself up to his full height and adopted a cool pedantic tone. "I seem to recall that most carnivorous plants I ever heard about feed by luring their prey into reach, either by the enticement of scent or color or by some kind of sugar excretion."

"You think I'm trying to lure you to your doom with witty and urbane conversation?"

Jim nodded. "It's a possibility I have to consider. I mean, you can hardly blame me for being cautious, can you? I may not be a frog, but I'm just as edible. More so, in fact, considering I'm larger. You'd be happily digesting me for a week."

The plant sounded offended. "That does rather put me in the same class as tyrannosaurus rex."

"Believe me. If I saw a tyrannosaurus rex, I'd run like hell regardless of what it might say to me."

The tendril made a limp curling gesture; Jim would have sworn the plant was pouting. For such a rudimentary limb, it was able to manage a high degree of expression. "I have to tell you that your suspicion makes me very unhappy. Especially after I helped you find your way out of the swamp and onto dry land."

As guilt trips went, this was pretty effective. Jim almost felt compelled to approach the plant as a sign of trust. Before he could take the first step, though, another voice came from behind him. "Don't believe a word it's saying. That overgrown weed is a consummate con artist. It's been trying to get me for years."

The voice came from a small mammal, about the size of a raccoon, that sat on its hind legs on one of the tussocks of coarse swamp grass. The creature resembled a lumpy combination of hamster, prairie dog, and potbellied pig. Jim looked down at the little animal. "You really think he's going to eat me?"

The animal nodded. "If he gets half a chance. He's trying to sucker you in with that phony Brit accent. He wants everyone to feel sorry for him, but the truth is, he's like all the rest of us here, except the dinosaurs—another dead asshole one jump ahead of a bad reincarnation. I mean, take me, for example. My species doesn't even have a name. Nobody ever found so much as a fucking fossil's worth of us."

Jim pushed his hair out of his eyes and scratched the back of his neck. The mud was starting to dry and his skin itched. "I'm sorry."

The animal's expression was ruefully resigned. "Don't be. I wanted to be a giant sloth, but I miscalculated by a couple of million years and came out a distant ancestor. Sometimes I think I ought to let one of them eat me and start all over again, but then I think, fuck it, maybe I'll wait for the asteroid to wipe them all out. I'd definitely like to see that."

"The dinosaurs?"

"Who else?"

At this point, the carnivorous plant interrupted. "I'm sure you mammals have a lot to talk about, but—"

The odd little mammal looked bleakly at the plant. "You've had your shot, now *can it*," He turned back to Jim. "My suggestion is that you head for the big house."

"The big house?"

"The big old run-down mansion in the swamp, with the trees all around it and the Spanish moss. There's a rumor that Elvis lived there for a while before he moved on."

"There are people living there?"

"Sure there are people living there."

"What kind of people?"

"Buncha weirdos. Kind of people you'd expect to be living in a big old spooky mansion in a Jurassic swamp."

Jim didn't know if he really liked the sound of this. On the other hand, first impressions could deceive. Doc Holliday's little town had seemed pretty promising, until the Voodoo Mystères had shown up and Doc had eighty-sixed him. Perhaps an uninviting mansion might have compensatory depths. While Jim was considering the idea, the carnivorous plant tried to butt in again. "Listen, this is all very nice but—"

The small mammal snarled at him. "Why don't you just shut the fuck up. You know you ain't going to get your tendrils on either of us, so forget it." The mammal glanced up at Jim. "Unless you want to get eaten and use that as a way to get back to the Great Double Helix and start over? I actually wouldn't recommend it. I understand it takes him a day or so to digest something as big as you. Whether you'd be conscious or not is another matter. I can't speak from experience, but—"

Jim quickly cut him off. "The matter of digestion already came up."

The mammal glared at the plant. "Then that's that, isn't it?"

The plant's leaves blushed; its tendrils quivered and retracted into the gourds. The small mammal shrugged. "I guess we've heard the last of him for a while."

Jim had made up his mind. He would try to find this mansion in the swamp. From his standpoint it at least seemed like an even bet. The way his luck was running, it would probably be no cakewalk, but it might also provide a way out to a more convivial and civilized place. He needed time to ponder the encounter with the mysterious dark-haired woman, to work on salvaging his lost recall. Even though the memory was nothing but gossamer fragments, he was becoming increasingly convinced she was more than merely a random erotic hallucination. "So how do I find this old house? Preferably by a route that doesn't involve too much wading through dirty water."

"I'll take you and show you, if you like."

"You would?"

"Sure. Beats sitting around waiting to be a dinosaur's breakfast."

It had been more than a week, if such terms made sense anymore, and Semple had failed to send word back to her sister. To say the least, Aimee was far from pleased. On one level, she was actually concerned about Semple's well-being; it was hard to shake the fear that her sister's silence was the result of some mishap or accident. Although Semple was able to erect an impressive facade of bravado, and held in pretty high regard both her own beauty and her genius, she suffered from a lack of foresight that rendered her incapable of calculating the future effects of her actions. She was a total impulse victim, and her incurable habit of leaping without looking, just the way she had leapt the wind to Necropolis, had resulted in a history of trouble that had dogged her on the lifeside and in the time since their death and separation.

Recalling all the incidents caused by Semple's impulsiveness, though, was usually enough to transform worry to fury, and Aimee soon began convincing herself that nothing was wrong with Semple at all. She was merely off on some self-gratifying adventure, with Aimee and her mission long forgotten. Even Aimee's anxiety regarding Semple's health and safety wasn't without an ingredient of self-interest. They had never managed to discuss it, but both sisters were deeply obsessed by the question of what might happen should one of them be removed from this phase of the Afterlife, returned to the Great Double Helix, or suffer some other drastic fate. Whenever Aimee pondered the question, which had been often since Semple's departure, she thought of those surviving Siamese twins who, when their lifelong companions died, were left with no will to continue.

Aimee's dour mood may have had a second, more fundamental source. Semple's absence had deprived her of certain fringe excitements, a backwash of tingling resonance from her sibling's varied encounters, adventures, and random cruelties that served to satisfy latent appetites of her own. While she would never admit it, she had come to derive a sustaining enjoyment from these vicarious feelings and she longed to have them back in her life.

Semple's silence, however, was only one of Aimee's problems. Strange things had begun happening in her Heaven. Whether these incidents were somehow related to Semple's absence was hard to say. They had started soon after her sister's departure for Necropolis, but Aimee couldn't see any logical connection even though she was well aware that, in the hereafter, logic could be highly twisted. Of course, there had been strange occurrences in her Heaven before, but back then she had been able to blame them on Semple and her nasty pranks. With Semple gone, Aimee was left with no one to blame—and also no solid explanation for all the bizarre extranormal phenomena. At first, when it had just been merely a matter of lights in the sky and unaccountable frogs, Aimee had thought briefly that Semple might be trying to drive her mad by remote control. Then the escalation had started. The sea monster had cleaved its way across the lake, rapidly followed by an all-day plague of six-inch-tall cartoon rodents wearing shorts, who walked on their hind legs and ate everything that wasn't inside a locked cabinet. With that, Aimee was forced to abandon the long-range nuisance theory. Sea monsters and cartoon rats just weren't Semple's style.

The UFO that had risen majestically from behind the ice-cream mountains one singularly neurotic afternoon had been the most spectacularly disturbing incident to date. Although it hadn't actually done anything more than descend and hover over the lake, it had filled Aimee with a fear that, far from being in any position to enlarge and improve her Heaven, she was at risk of losing control of the place. The thing had simply hung there, dark blue and metallic, an inverted dish with a turret on top and three hemispheres below,

radiating a sense of unease and impending failure. Just to complicate matters, one of the white-faced monkeys from Golgotha had
appeared on the terrace unbidden, hopped up onto the flat stone
lintel of the balustrade, and then proceeded to make odd rhythmic
hand signals to the UFO. At the same time, a strange fleeting feeling had come over Aimee, as though her entire postmortem nervous system had been immersed in warm water. For the first time in
her life after death, Aimee found herself on the verge of despair.
She sobbed in a quiet, mournful voice, so low that not even the
white-faced monkey would be able to hear. "Semple, please phone
home."

"Semple, you have to get out of the pool right now."

But Semple didn't want to get out. She had managed to arrange
herself so that the most abused parts of her battered body were positioned exactly in the path of the bubble streams from the whirlpool,
and she didn't intend to move until she ceased to feel, both inter-
nally and externally, like she'd been trampled by a herd of wild ele-
phants. She also didn't want to talk to anyone. In the warm,
rose-scented water, she found it was almost possible to recapture the
sparse remains of the unique sexual hallucination that had gripped
her during that first time with Anubis, and the memory of the face-
less man who had figured in it. "Just leave me alone, will you?"

Zipporah's lips pursed. She clearly had no intention of leaving
Semple alone. "I'm serious, we only have two hours before we
leave."

"Isn't it enough that I have to fuck him until I can hardly walk? I
don't even *want* to see his miserable bomb go off."

Semple had hoped that the seraglio of Anubis would be a place of
idleness and overheated lethargy, a hothouse of women with time
on their hands and sex on their minds. Before she arrived there, she
had conjured a vision of scantily clad wives and concubines, lounging beside perfumed crystal fountains between marble pillars, draped
with gold and sheer silk, eating bonbons, watching TV, exchanging
razor-edged gossip, red in both tooth and claw. The reality turned
out to be a little different. Sure, the fountains and the marble were
there. Anubis missed no measure of architectural opulence. The
bonbons were served on silver dishes and satin and brocade cushions

made lying around and watching the many triangular television sets a far from arduous task. Superior cats slept, played, licked their paws, and stared from vantage points on the backs of sofas, revered as they had been in historical Egypt. The interaction of the women, however, transcended mere gossip, no matter how vicious. What went on in the seraglio was full-blown political intrigue, from elaborately planned character assassination to highly organized espionage and even the poisoning of rivals. With Anubis functionally crazy, always continually in the grip of some new tangential enthusiasm, the day-to-day running of the metropolis almost totally depended on influence, bribery, and corruption. Although the wives and concubines were supposed to have little or no contact with the outside world, all manner of petitioners from all castes and classes managed to find access routes to the God-King's women in the hope that they might use their influence on their lord and master.

The ultimate power broker and wielder of influence in this sequestered world was Zipporah, the Deneuvian primary concubine, who at this moment was berating Semple for lying too long in the comfort of the seraglio pool. "You have to be there. There's no discussion about it. Anyone who doesn't show will need an impossibly good excuse."

"I have a perfect excuse. The bastard has all but crippled me."

The expressions of the other women as they overheard this final retort registered not only shock but also the kind of covert satisfaction that came with watching a possible rival drop herself into deep trouble. Every inmate in the harem acted on the principle that each word they uttered would be overheard, recorded, and relayed to Anubis, and Semple could easily be digging her own grave by mouthing off. To call the God-King a bastard was a near certain fast track to the oubliette: the "forgetting place", a set of tiny cells in a damp subbasement so cramped that it was all but impossible to lie or stand. Concubines and courtiers could be confined without food, water, or even light in the oubliette, in some cases until they went mad, withered, died, or reached some other approximation of the terminal state.

As Anubis's current favorite, Semple did have a certain leeway regarding her behavior; the flavor of the moment could get away with a lot. But Semple was also coming to understand that Anubis's relationships with his women were exactly like his tastes in food. The God-King would obsess on a specific delicacy, gorge on it continuously for a period of time, but then abruptly tire of it and either go on to some new innovation or return to the tried and tested. Semple knew that her ability to get away with open blasphemy had a very limited shelf life.

Zipporah didn't seem as shocked as the other women, but she stared down at Semple from the side of the pool with a knowing and world-weary expression. Without saying a word, she made it abundantly clear that she had seen them come and go, and Semple should take care while she could. "That won't exactly qualify as a good excuse."

"And what would?"

Zipporah smiled coldly. "Sudden discorporation might just get you off the hook, my dear. Short of that, I can't think of very much else. Acting the spoiled brat because you're the temporary favorite certainly won't cut it. Remember this is only the master's second atom bomb, and he's very anxious about it. The scientists have all been threatened with slow extermination if it doesn't go off totally according to plan, and I doubt if any of us would fare very much better if we failed to show up for the great event."

The detonation of the second Necropolis nuclear device was Anubis's current obsession. Although, as far as Semple could glean from the seraglio scuttlebutt, the thing was little more than a small and very dirty bomb, not even up to Fat Man magnitude, the dog-god was so taken with the idea of letting off his very own man-made sun that he was designing an entire holy event around the explosion: a religious festival of the highest order, a full, dawn-to-dark day dedicated to the glory of his divine cleverness.

"You're not going to let me slide on this one, are you?"

Zipporah shook her head. "I doubt I'd let you slide even if I could. I want you out of that pool and into the dressing room in the next five minutes."

"You really don't like me, do you?"

Zipporah regarded Semple with a look that was, at the same time, both sharp and glassy. "No, I don't much like you, but that's hardly relevant. All that concerns me is that you're difficult, time-consuming, and potentially dangerous. When you finally get yourself into trouble, as you eventually will, you're quite likely to drop some of us in the excreta right along with you."

"You seem to have formed a very precise opinion of me in the short time that I've been here."

"You aren't the first to try to test the limits of her position."

"Is that what I'm doing?"

"Of course it is. And even though I don't particularly like you, I will give you one word of cautionary advice. Once the gloss of your novelty has worn off, you'll need all the friends you can get."

Semple nodded and reluctantly lowered her feet to find the bottom of the pool. She knew that in her own way Zipporah meant well, but Semple was resolved not to be a part of Anubis's harem long enough to find out what it was like to fall from favor. She climbed from the pool, waving away the handmaidens who were hastening toward her with a robe and towels. As she passed Zipporah, she communicated what she hoped was a certain measure of respect. "I'll watch the bomb go off and make nice. I'm not looking to clash with you."

Zipporah acknowledged this as something akin to an apology. "I appreciate that, if you mean it."

Semple pushed her wet hair out of her eyes. "Oh, I mean it. There's more to me than just overbearing self-indulgence."

With that she padded away to the dressing room, dripping water and trailing handmaidens, wondering all the way what kind of lunatic constructs and detonates atom bombs for his own personal amusement.

"So, as you can imagine, I was feeling pretty bad by the time that kid shot me dead back there in that bar in El Paso. I mean, a man's sunk damned low when he's riding with a crew of pistoleers who can turn up at a wedding, gun down the groom, the best man, the bride's father, and the priest, and then go on to rape the bride, the bride's mother, the matron of honor, the six bridesmaids, and a couple of nuns who just happened to be passing, and then have no remorse or any real excuse 'cept being in the fifth day of a week-long shitfaced mescal drunk."

Jim nodded. He was aware that the small Mammal with No Name hadn't had a chance to talk to anyone or anything but the carnivorous plant in a long time, and it didn't bother him if he wanted to prattle on. "I kinda know how you feel."

"Of course, those were hard days. 1869—"

Jim was amazed. "You've been in this swamp since 1869?"

"Sure have."

Jim blinked. "That's quite a sojourn."

"I had a lot of guilt."

"Even so, that means you've been here longer than Doc Holliday, and not had half as much fun, from what I can see."

"There aren't many who have as much fun as Doc."

"You know Doc?"

"Sure, I know Doc. We come from the same territory."

"I thought you got yourself shot in Texas. Doc was more around Arizona and Colorado."

"When I say territory, I'm talking more about time and ethos than the geography. Me and Doc were both good ol' boys who headed west after the War Between the States. There were hundreds of us on the move back then. Talk about an evil season. A lot of them who went out West were crazy as a shitbug to start with. Sick and insane with seeing too much death, and knowing fuck-all except kill or be killed. I mean, after Shiloh, Vicksburg, the Wilderness, and Pickett's bloody Charge, what did anyone expect? No one had ever seen a war like that, my friend. We faced miniballs that could rip off half your arm at close to a mile, canister that could blow away a platoon of men with one shot. The world had never witnessed such a mechanical fucking slaughter. The first fully organized carnage of the Industrial Revolution. They say boys went crazy in Vietnam, but I'm telling you, Vietnam wasn't dick compared with Chancellorsville. We lost as many in a bad afternoon as they did in all twelve years of Nam. After it was all over, and Bobby Lee surrendered at Appomattox Courthouse, we had homicidals and spooked-out psychotics wandering all over the Frontier for ten years or more. Some went after the Indians, like Custer and Sheridan, thinking a taste of genocide would lay the ghosts. Others, like the James boys and the Youngers, just went right on fighting the war—"

"And others went on a mescal jag, gunned down the groom and raped the bride and her bridesmaids and all of the rest?"

The mammal grinned and nodded. "You got it."

Jim and the Mammal with No Name were picking their way over the uncertain dry ground above the water level of the Jurassic bayous. While the mammal told its long and involved story, Jim was content to make the right responsive noises while gazing out at the new world in which he found himself. The worst of the mist had been burned off by a white sun that blazed in a mushroom-pink sky, and now he could see a great deal more of his new prehistoric environment. At the horizon, no less than three volcanoes belched smoke from a range of jagged, snaggletoothed mountains. Closer up, the place looked a lot like the Florida Everglades, though the plant life was further back down the evolutionary trail. The resemblance was, however, enough to remind Jim of all the trouble that had befallen him in Florida. Miami was where they'd arrested him for allegedly flashing his dick at the audience. The straight truth was, Jim couldn't remember whether he'd done it or not. He'd been drunk and tripping, flying at altitudes so high that, if asked to testify on oath, he couldn't have sworn in all honesty that he'd even been wearing pants, let alone deliberately unzipped them.

A dozen or more large herbivorous dinosaurs seemed content to loiter, partially submerged, grazing on trees and bushes, while other, smaller reptiles splashed in the shallows. To Jim's great relief, none of them showed anything but the most casual interest in him and the Mammal with No Name, and made no attempt to approach them. What bothered him more were the pterodactyls that circled lazily overhead. Although he suspected the flying lizards were meat eaters, the mammal assured him that they posed no threat. "Their eyesight's so rotten, they never go after anything smaller than a horse."

Jim didn't find this as reassuring as the mammal had intended. The little creature could well have been taking a speciescentric view of the situation. The pterosaurs might not have been able to see a furry little ground dweller, but Jim was considerably larger; a pterodactyl with decent vision might tag him as a tasty morsel. And so he scanned the sky to make sure none of the flapping leather-wings was drawing a bead on him, and felt a lot happier when their route took them under the shelter of spreading palms and conifers rather than along the exposed edge of open water.

Although the reptiles mercifully kept their distance and their own counsel, the same could not be said for the millions of insects that flourished in the Jurassic. Great dragonflies, with wings spanning eighteen inches or more, scared the hell out of Jim by buzzing him at eye level; only when they failed to follow through with anything worse was he able to relax. The clouds of mosquitos, gnats, and midges, on the other hand, took a great deal more getting used to. They dogged the steps of Jim and the mammal every step of the way. They didn't seem to bother the mammal, with its thick furry hide, but by the time the sun had reached its zenith they were making Jim miserable. One settled on his exposed left forearm and he squished it angrily. As he wiped away the smear of blood, he smiled grimly. "Steven Spielberg isn't going to reconstitute any DNA from you, you son of a bitch."

The blood made him take yet another look at the pterodactyls aloft, and when he did, he noticed something decidedly unusual. The sun was moving visibly across the sky. Jim glanced down at the small mammal. "How long are the days in this place?"

The mammal looked puzzled. "How long should they be? Same length as anywhere else. The Earth isn't spinning any quicker, far as I know."

Jim stopped and peered into the sun, shading his eyes and squinting like Clint Eastwood at high noon. "Then why is it I can see the sun moving?"

The mammal stopped in his tracks. "Uh-oh."

This was the third time that Jim had heard a warning "uh-oh" in much too narrow a time frame. Saladeen of the puffball Afro and jewel-encrusted teeth had uttered the first two, all too recently, when one of the Voodoo Mystères had appeared in the distance beyond Doc Holliday's town. Now Jim could only guess what was coming next. "Trouble?"

"We may have a slight problem with time."

Semple had known that Anubis's nuclear fireworks display was being promoted as a big deal, but the size of the deal exceeded all her expectations. The actual detonation, as it turned out, was billed as the culmination of a twenty-four-hour Divine Atom Bomb Festival, throughout which Anubis intended to bask in the full glory of his own ego. The test itself was to take place in the desert some miles outside the city, but prior to that the God-King, his court, harem, retainers, praetorian guard, and half the Army of Necropolis would travel to the test site in spectacular procession, followed by more or less the entire population of the city: a public holiday had been declared to allow them to marvel at the triumph of their glorious monarch. Anubis, as fond of food as he was, had ensured that the entire event would be lavishly catered, all the way from the wine and delicacies that would be available during the course of the procession, through the picnic that would precede the detonation, to the massive al fresco feast and bacchanal that would follow.

Before Zipporah outlined the itinerary of the Divine Atom Bomb Festival, Semple hadn't been aware that Necropolis was even surrounded by desert. Nor had she known that the environment extended so far that it would take a full two hours for Anubis to progress in beatific splendor to the city limits. She was accustomed to Afterlife environments that were as superficial as movie sets, all facade, illusion, and trompe l'oeil; a construction that encompassed two hundred square miles of downtown slums and suburbs took her completely by surprise. She disliked the dog-god no less, but she had to hand it to him for going all the way with his megalopolis. It was only when the procession actually got under way, and she saw both the slums and the suburbs for herself, that she finally grasped the extent of Anubis's obsession. Like Aimee's Heaven, much of the city was a scrapbook of its mad lord's favorite things.

As was only befitting His Godhead, Anubis along with his immediate retinue was to ride in a special parade vehicle the size of a Greyhound bus, of a design that combined elements of an art deco railcar, Cleopatra's royal barge, and a spacecraft from the Alex Raymond *Flash Gordon* comics. On the morning of the festival, as she and the other wives, concubines, and handmaidens walked through the huge and echoing hangar this preposterous craft shared with the God-King's fleet of dirigibles, the chatter of idle conversation dwindled to an awed silence. Either none of the other women had ever seen the monster before in all its gold-plated glory, or it had been specially constructed and decorated for the Divine Atom Bomb Festival.

Anubis himself, who would, of course, be the last to arrive and board the craft, was obviously to take pride of place, seated on a throne on a raised quarterdeck at the stern of the machine, attended by the ever-present Nubian guards and handmaidens wafting long-handled fans and bearing the obligatory trays of culinary delicacies. The members of the harem would ride in front of their lord and master in the well of the craft, to gaze up at him adoringly. The prow of the ship, shaped like the vulture head of the lesser god Horus, was occupied by another squad of guards, police in full dress uniform, armed with far more serious weapons than the spears and scimitars of the ceremonial Nubians. Their heavy machine guns were capable of unleashing instant destruction on any section of the crowd who might prove threatening, unruly, or impious.

The harem boarded the royal carriage by means of a mobile flight of steps. Semple observed that, as the women climbed aboard, the craft swayed slightly; and that it seemed to be floating six to eight feet above the ground, supported, as far as Semple could guess, by some Nikola Tesla system or perhaps an antigravity fantasy reminiscent of the vimanas of Gilgamesh. The more Semple saw of Necropolis, the more she became aware that the entire place was a galactic collage of fanciful minutiae. Semple had little time, though, to ponder the inner mechanics of Anubis's ceremonial craft. Zipporah quickly clapped her hands, indicating that the harem should assume its position. The armed guards on the prow, until now busy shooting covert glances at the diaphanously clad concubines, radiating random lust from behind the visors of their helmets, stiffened to attention. Anubis himself was coming.

The arrival of the dog-god constituted a mini-parade all by itself. Preceded by a formation of his Nubians carrying long gold-tipped lances, and followed by a gaggle of handmaidens, he rode to the craft in a litter borne by four strapping blond slaves. The Dream Warden walked beside the litter, and Semple groaned inwardly. She had half hoped their day out would be unencumbered by that potentially dangerous weirdo, but it was inevitable that the sinister robed figure should show up for the detonation of the Holy Bomb. As the dog-god climbed the steps, the women all adopted expressions of adoration. When he looked in Semple's direction she smiled radiantly but muttered under her breath, "At least you can make the stairs unaided, you psychotic son of a bitch."

When Anubis was finally seated on his elevated throne and his court was satisfactorily arrayed around him, the craft started forward with a slight lurch that had some of the women reaching for handholds. It nosed its way out of the hangar and into the hazy polluted sunshine of a Necropolis morning. As it traveled, the keel rose to a height of twelve feet above the surface of the raised highway the procession would follow all way to the test site. Anubis may have wanted his people to see and worship him, but he obviously didn't feel any need to let the common horde get too close.

The procession itself was perhaps a quarter of a mile long. First up was a squad of the city's rocketeer police mounted on big, smoke-belching Harley-Davidsons and World War II–Indians. The bike cops were followed by a massive sculpted bust of Anubis himself fashioned from reflective silvery material, borne on a float that moved under its own power. A human garnish of young women in Mylar bikinis and body paint was draped around the neck and shoulders of the bust, and crowded the plinth that supported it, beaming like beauty queens and strewing rose petals, coins, strings of good-luck beads, and other small trinkets over the heads of the organized multitude thronging the highway. The bust was followed by the first of four marching bands, short on tune but strong on cacophony. Comprised mainly of hammering copper-shell drums and big brass wind instruments, sousaphones and tubas, the bands produced a relentless metallic braying that seemed to set the tone for the entire holiday.

Semple had hardly expected that Anubis would forgo the chance to put on a display of military power. Whenever a hole presented itself in the order of the parade, Anubis had filled it with dress phalanxes from the various regiments of his army. The clatter of the hooves of his plumed and cloaked cavalry vied with the grinding roar of ornately gilded battle tanks. Neither the God-King himself nor anyone in the massed crowds seemed embarrassed that the style and weaponry of the Army of Necropolis should span some three thousand years, and Semple wondered if she was the only one to whom the parade looked like nothing more than a small boy showing off his toys. Even the air above the parade hadn't been neglected. Formations of biplanes and dirigibles moved lowly across the sky, while small solo aircraft left trails of hieroglyphics in colored smoke. Flags fluttered, banners waved, and huge tethered balloons, in the shape of eagles, vultures, dragons, and one bulbous inflatable ankh, floated overhead, an old-fashioned communist May Day procession in chaotic collision with Macy's Thanksgiving Parade.

The drawback of actually being in a parade was that, once the procession was on the move, anyone actually taking part in it had only a limited view of the proceedings. After a while, Semple, between smiling and looking as radiant as was expected of the God-King's current favorite, stopped craning her neck to see what was going on up ahead or back behind the ceremonial craft and started looking farther afield, at parts of the city that she had never seen before. At first it was very much what she had expected—large, bombastically imposing, Egyptian-style buildings, once magnificent, now run-down and in need of paint and maintenance—but as they moved farther out, the architecture started to change. The towering temples, commercial towers, and apartment blocks gave way to a seemingly endless sprawl of crudely constructed single-and two-story hovels, huddled together in what looked, from the elevation of the highway, to be insanitary and overcrowded neglect amid garbage, chaos, graffiti, and stands of wilted and apologetic palm trees.

This endless acreage of slums only deepened the puzzle for Semple. Why would anyone live here? What misery-prone spirit would leave the Great Double Helix to be ghettoized in such a depressing and degrading hereafter? The only conclusion was that Anubis had deliberately created the millions of souls it so obviously took to fill all this sorry real estate. Was he really so driven by the need for glory that he surrounded the place of his dreams with miles of wretchedness and underclass squalor? Semple wasn't attempting any moral judgment. She accepted that her own personal history left no room for condemnation of another's fantasy. What she totally failed to understand was what percentage Anubis gleaned from all the pointless work and organization.

"What the hell is going on?"

A huge dinosaur flashed past, sprinting backward at alarming speed. Only Jim and the Mammal with No Name seemed to remain in one spot. The rest of the world was in sudden and violent reverse motion. The sun whipped across the sky in entirely the wrong direction, so fast that the alternation of night and day was turned into the rapid beating of a huge black wing. The mammal, its eyes made eerie by the strobing sunlight, stared at Jim with metaphysical resignation. "I think we have a time fuckup."

"A time fuckup?"

"Right."

The mammal seemed to accept the situation as if it were eminently natural. Jim, on the other hand, had never experienced anything like it and didn't like it at all. "This happen often around here?"

"Not often, but it happens."

The sun was now traveling so fast that it was nothing more than a gray blur blending perfectly with an increasingly blurred landscape. The spectacle struck Jim as the visual equivalent of a deep and overwhelming depression. "Do these time fuckups always run backwards?"

"Only half the time."

"So what happens? We stand here like idiots until we're swallowed up by the Big Bang?"

The Mammal with No Name frowned. "I guess it would be more of an Ultimate Implosion than a Big Bang, seeing as how we're going backwards. Usually it doesn't get that far, though."

"It doesn't?"

The mammal shook his head. "Not usually. No."

"So what does happen . . . usually?"

"Usually someone puts a stop to it."

"Like who?"

Again the mammal shook his head, embarrassed at his lack of knowledge. "I don't know."

"You know *how* whoever it is stops it?"

"I'm afraid I don't."

"So what do you do when one of these happens?"

"I just keep my head down and wait."

"I guess you don't have any idea what causes these things."

"Not really. I suppose I could hazard a guess."

"Hazard away."

The mammal avoided Jim's eyes. "I'm not sure I like to."

Jim was starting to lose patience. After all the mammal's boasting about what a desperado he'd been back lifeside, his sudden passivity was decidedly irritating. Could it be a practical, small-animal caution was progressively eroding its former cowboy recklessness? "Why not?"

"You might take it personally."

"Are you saying that I might have something to do with it?"

The mammal answered reluctantly, "It's possible. You or the UFO. One or both of you may have caused a rupture."

Jim started to grow angry. "I didn't ask to come here."

"There you go. You *are* taking it personally."

Jim sighed. "No, I'm not. I'm just wondering what to do about it. Maybe if it was me that caused it, I could somehow stop it."

"Maybe."

"But you don't have any suggestions?"

"Not a one."

"Damn."

The world was now nothing more than a gray blur with twinkles and sparkles dancing in the middle distance and a faint blue line where the horizon used to be. Clearly something had to be done, but

Jim had no idea what, and the mammal was no help. Jim thought for a moment, if, indeed, moments truly existed in their current predicament, but all he could come up with was the one thing that had stood him in reasonable stead since his death. "When in doubt, do the obvious."

The mammal looked puzzled. "Say what?"

"I said, when in doubt, do the obvious."

"And what might that be?"

Jim couldn't help himself. "I'd have thought it was obvious."

The mammal looked offended. His eyes were doglike in their reproach. "Now you're fucking with me."

Jim felt bad. He was a sucker for reproachful eyes. "Yeah, I'm fucking with you. I shouldn't do that. You're not the one responsible."

The mammal nodded forgivingly. "That's okay."

"Let's try something."

"Try what?"

"Watch and learn."

Jim took a deep breath, inflating his lungs to their fullest. He had always managed to achieve things with his voice. He turned and faced the blue line of the horizon and bellowed with all his might, "HAVE THIS STOPPED!"

And it stopped. Time reverted to normal, leaving them in the dark of night. Stars twinkled overhead, things rustled in the reeds and tall grass; in the distance, a dinosaur was singing. The mammal looked up at Jim with undisguised admiration. "Wow."

"Pretty neat, huh? Pretty good?"

"I have to hand it to you."

"Except that it's now the middle of the night, and for all I know, we could be ten thousand years in the past."

The small mammal thought about this. "Would it really matter?"

Jim nodded. "It would matter to me."

"It would?"

"I'd be dead before I ever got born. I'd be a walking paradox."

The mammal's voice took on a tone of you-think-you-got-troubles. "I'm dead before I was born *and* my species doesn't have a name."

"So you really are a walking paradox."

"I guess I am."

"But that doesn't really help our current situation."

The mammal shrugged. "I guess it doesn't. I was just figuring, since you'd already found yourself washed up in the Jurassic, ten thousand years either way isn't going to make all that much difference."

Jim looked around but could see very little in the darkness. "Maybe I could work the same trick again."

He took a second deep breath. "NOW PUT US BACK WHERE WE WERE!"

Nothing happened except the dinosaurs paused in their song. The night remained impenetrable. Jim scowled. "Shit."

The Mammal was philosophical. "I guess you can't win them all."

"So it would seem."

"I wouldn't worry about it too much."

"I guess we don't get to go to the old mansion in the swamp after all."

The mammal frowned. "Why the fuck not?"

Jim looked at the mammal. He really could be pretty obtuse at times. "Because we don't know if it even exists in this time frame."

Now the mammal looked at Jim as though he were the one being obtuse. "It exists."

"It does? How do you know that?"

"You can see its lights."

Jim peered into the black of night. "Where?"

The mammal extended a paw. "There."

Now Jim saw it, a pinpoint of light way off in the distance. "Is that it?"

"That's it. The lights are always on at night."

"You're sure?"

"Sure I'm sure."

Jim sighed. He supposed living in the Jurassic without a name would make anyone slow. "Why the hell didn't you tell me that before I started all that yelling?"

"You didn't ask."

As the parade finally arrived at the area where the detonation would take place, Semple saw that as much trouble had gone into the planning, arrangement, and construction of the viewing area and picnic site as into the procession that had brought them there. Necropolis might be sinking into ruin and decay, but when it came to one of Anubis's pet obsessions, apparently no effort was considered excessive. Semple's first impression was that the design of the Divine Atom Bomb Festival was a fanciful attempt to marry a medieval tournament with a hippie rock festival of the late 1960s. Long lines of covered bleachers had been erected so the rich, powerful, and well connected could idle away the event in varying degrees of luxury, sheltered from the bright, iron-gray sky and the relentless desert sun.

Each section of these bleachers came with its own attendant clustering of tents, marquees, and pavilions, where food and wine were served and musicians serenaded the drinkers and diners. Blue smoke and a variety of cooking smells rose from al fresco barbecue kitchens, where sweating chefs basted the browning flanks of whole roasting steers or labored over broiling racks of smaller delicacies. Bunting tossed and fluttered in the afternoon breeze above open-air stages on which jugglers and illusionists, fire eaters, and escapologists performed, and dancing girls and young men displayed both their moves and their bodies. Flag-draped booths hawked all manner of mementos, from commemorative plates to souvenir dark glasses, all of which bore the black and gold mushroom cloud that was the Divine Atom Bomb Festival merchandising logo. For what seemed to Semple a highly unnecessary additional diversion, wild animals were displayed in cages, human criminals had their bodies bent out of shape by creatively crafted sets of mobile stocks, and here and there bottom-feeding slave dealers with wheezing, vapor-leaking portable steam computers were running fast-bargain, knockdown auctions of fetch-and-carry domestics, disposable body serfs, and low-grade sex objects.

It was, however, only the rich who got the goodies. All of these treats, diversions, and spectacles were exclusively lavished on the extended court of Anubis and the invited guests from the affluent elite. The city's rabble of poor were expected to devise their own protection from the sun and provide most of their own predetonation amusement on a large and increasingly dusty tract of open land, well in front of the facilities provided for the aristocracy. Here, despite considerable discomfort from heat and insects, the proles were hunkered down, waiting for the Holy Explosion. The lower classes had largely provided their own refreshments, although beer, soda, and junk food were being dispensed by pushcart vendors each with his own teakettle computer running the barcode scanners.

The most popular prebomb recreations for the proletariat seemed to be sex and gambling. As the procession passed through the area set aside for the poor, Semple had noticed couples unselfconsciously copulating on the open ground without any apparent shame. Men huddled around dice games, while professional card cutters spotted and isolated their marks. Larger groups gathered around pairs of fighting animals. Roosters, pit bulls, and small bipedal lizards snarled and slashed at their opponents while spectators yelled and cursed.

As Semple and a dark-complected concubine called Parsis looked down at a lizard fight just below the passing carriage, a question occurred to her. "If the barcode is the only means of exchange here, how do these people make their bets?"

Parsis looked at her as though she were the epitomic idiot outlander. "They swap markers, don't they?"

In another part of the well deck of the royal carriage, some of the handmaidens had spotted a threesome—two men and one woman, all having sex together. The sight had inspired an outbreak of smothered girlish giggles and whispered lewdnesses. Semple looked briefly in the direction of the mini-orgy and turned back to Parsis with a frown.

"What do you mean, markers?"

"Slips of papyrus with the bets scrawled on them. When the fight's over, they'll all troop off to one of the pushcart vendors and he'll settle up for them on his computer for a percentage of the action." Parsis pointed. "Look, there go some of them now."

A fight had just finished. One green lizard lay bloodily dead in a small temporary arena of banked dirt, and the owners of the badly mauled victor were placing it carefully in a wicker basket. A small crowd, moments earlier baying and catcalling at the combatants, were now marching as one to the nearest pushcart. The vendor was already waving away the people standing in line to buy soda and candy, anticipating his more lucrative wager settlement commission.

Semple shook her head. "I guess folks will always find a way to get a bet down."

Parsis half smiled. "You want to see them when our lord and master falls into Caligula mode and decides to stage the Games. That's when the plebs start getting their bets down in the worst possible way. At the end of a good long all-day session at the Games, you get nearly as many killings among the spectators as there are in the stadium."

Something in Parsis's tone made Semple look at her thoughtfully.

Semple had already noticed that Parsis was something of a kindred spirit; she didn't quite go with the flow inside the seraglio, tending instead to stand aloof from it, not making waves, doing what was expected of her but otherwise keeping to herself. "You don't exactly fall down and worship our lord and master, do you?"

Parsis eyed Semple warily. "Maybe I do and maybe I don't, but I sure as shit ain't going to court disaster by admitting anything out loud and in public."

Even this reply set her apart from the mainstream of the dog-god's women. Precious few of them, even versed as they were in advanced debauchery, would casually employ a phrase like "sure as shit." "Do you mind if I ask you a personal question?"

Parsis shrugged. "I don't know. It'd depend on the question."

"You weren't custom-created for this place, were you?"

Parsis stared at Semple as though she were about to take offense. "Hell, no, girl. Do I look like one of those?"

Semple quickly tried to reassure her. "Not in the least. That's why I was asking. I was wondering, if you're your own person and not one of the dog-god's fabrications, why do you continue to stay in this place?"

Parsis was still suspicious. "I could ask the same of you."

Semple glanced around to see that none of the others, particularly Zipporah, was paying any attention to their conversation. No one was. In fact, most of the rest were hanging over the rail looking for rutting couples among the masses of the poor. "I blundered in here by mistake and only just avoided getting branded and sold on the Fat Ari show. Believe me, the moment I see an opening, I'm out of here."

Parsis slowly nodded; for one moment, Semple wondered if she had made a terrible mistake by confiding her intentions to this woman. Parsis must have sensed this because she suddenly smiled. "Don't worry, honey. I ain't going to repeat what you just told me."

"I'm grateful for that."

"On the other hand, you'll have to be content if I tell you that I ain't looking for no way out just now."

"You like it here?"

Parsis gestured around at the opulence of the carriage. "It's easy enough." She stared significantly at Semple. "And I ain't his favorite, so I really don't have to have that much to do with the dogheaded son of a bitch. Besides, you should have seen what I was lifeside."

"What was that?"

Parsis grinned. "Baby, you really wouldn't want to know."

Before Semple could say anything, the carriage came to a stop with a slight lurch. Zipporah was suddenly bustling around, directing the women of the harem in the direction of the steps that were being moved alongside. "Everyone off as quickly as you can. Hurry it up. We don't want to keep our lord waiting to make his grand entrance."

The golden carriage had come to rest beside the royal pavilion and viewing box. In an area totally covered in lavish and exotic creations of canvas, brocade, and silk, the royal pavilion outdid all rivals by a power of ten. It consisted of a tall pyramidal structure of huge tapestry panels showing scenes from the supposed life of the god Anubis. In front of the pyramid itself was an elaborate construction of risers and platforms, made from gold-tinted Lucite and polished steel, at the apex of which stood the divine throne from which Anubis himself would watch the detonation. Its backdrop was a giant sun symbol with a mushroom cloud superimposed over it. Surrounding the dog-god's perch were smaller thrones and couches, arranged for the accommodation of the court and Anubis's favored guests. When they arrived, the intention was for the women to hurry off first, preceded only by the soldiers from the prow, and fan out at the base of the steps to form a human background for the ceremonial arrival of the God-King at his nuclear celebration. Things didn't quite go according to plan, however. As the women attempted to arrange themselves decoratively, they found they were immediately brushed to one side by sweating, unshaven men in rumpled clothes, booze on their breath, laden down with multimedia equipment and aiming bulky, shoulder-mounted TV cameras or big Speedgraphics at the top of the steps where Anubis would first appear. Apparently Necropolis was possessed of its own press corps and paparazzi. Who knew?

As Anubis stepped into sight, Semple realized that, until this moment, she had never seen the dog-god in public before. While the flashbulbs popped, TV cameras zoomed in, and his image was relayed to the half dozen triangular, billboard-sized screens dotted around the festival site, Anubis posed like the god he'd made himself. He squared his perfect shoulders, turned his head, regal from snout to ear, first to the left and then to the right, offering every lens all the conceivable variations of his divine profile. He concluded the display by flexing biceps, triceps, pectorals, and deltoids like a contestant in the Mr. Universe contest. For Semple, widely recognized as his current favorite, the display was embarrassing in the extreme.

When Anubis finally decided that his subjects had been allowed their fill of his static perfection, he started down the steps in studiedly unhurried majesty. This was the cue for the cameras to pull back and the wives, concubines, and handmaidens to move into shot, to bow low in supplication and gaze adoringly on the wondrousness of his being. Anubis even paused for a calculated moment, as though weighing whether the very ground was worthy to bear his amazing grace. Having taken this one short step of faith, Anubis halted for a reprise of the Charles Atlas routine, this time with the leading lights of his harem draped about him in hypnotized devotion. Semple, as the choreography dictated, hung on an upper arm with an exaggerated expression of swooning ecstasy, all the while wondering just how long dogboy could spin out this orgy of narcissism.

Fortunately, another of Anubis's driving passions distracted him relatively quickly. Whether it was the smell of exotic cooking coming from the elaborate field kitchens or merely the demands of his holy metabolism, his attention suddenly shifted from self-aggrandizement to food. He shook himself loose from his women and strode purposefully into the main area of the royal pavilion, directly behind the viewing boxes, where a buffet had been laid out of an extent, a sumptuousness, and a variety that verged on the insane. While chefs and courtiers alike watched anxiously, Anubis advanced along the heaped-up yardage of groaning board, sampling morsels at random, judging every bite against the high gourmet requirements of a god.

After considerable snuffling and lip smacking, the God-King finally rendered his verdict. He nodded curtly to his Lord Victualer, his High Butler, and Head Chef, and a whisper of relief spread through the pavilion. All was well, at least with the food; the culinary staff would live to slice, dice, and fricassee another day. Immediately a circulating army of waiters moved out en masse, bringing drinks and finger foods to the multitude. Anubis remained, content to feed himself directly from the buffet, beckoning to selected courtiers to join him. He started with the hooded Dream Warden and a procession of his techno-priests, subjecting each new arrival to what, from a distance, looked to be an intense and urgent interrogation.

Semple could only conclude that he was checking that the

countdown to the atomic blast was proceeding without a hitch. The situation suited Semple perfectly. As long as Anubis was fully occupied with his scientists and atomic advisors, he wouldn't be bothering his women. Semple imagined he would certainly demand sex once the bomb had been exploded, however it turned out. If the blast was a success, he would undoubtedly feel the need for carnal confirmation of his genius, and if it failed, he would require a violent venting of his rage. Semple didn't want to think that far ahead. In Necropolis life could only be lived moment by moment, and at that moment she was happy to be left alone.

She accepted a glass of a pale gold sparkling wine that tasted like overvoluptuous champagne: even though she normally had only the most meager interest in recreational eating, she couldn't resist sampling some of the hors d'oeuvres. She surprised herself by taking an immediate and almost gluttonous liking to some tiny, wood-skewered cubes of marinated and stir-fried meat in a peanut butter sauce. At first Semple had assumed it was pork, but even through the heavy flavor of the marinade, it somehow tasted sweeter and had a somewhat different texture. Almost without thinking, she ate a full six servings and then felt a little guilty at her self-indulgence. She wondered, slightly horrified, if the ways of Anubis were starting to rub off on her.

In addition to the food and drink, waiters were also making the rounds with baskets of dark-tinted visors and handing them out to the guests. Some, like Semple, simply held their visors, not wanting to wear them until they were needed to protect optic nerves from the first nuclear flash. Others, on the other hand, put theirs on, lending the gathering the air of an impromptu masked ball. One of the first to don a mask was Dr. Mengele, whom Semple had spotted across on the other side of the royal pavilion, and avoided to the extent of moving if he showed the slightest sign of coming in her direction. As a further reminder that the moment of detonation was coming, a fanfare of discordant trumpets, like those in the parade's marching bands, seemed to come out of nowhere, followed by a booming voice that brought all conversation to a stop. *"Zero minus sixty minutes and counting."*

Hiking through the swamp in darkness was far harder than it had been in daylight. The Mammal with No Name seemed to have good night vision, but Jim found himself constantly stepping onto what he thought was dry ground, but turned out to be viscous sucking mud from which he had to carefully extract himself without losing his boots; every so often a reed bed would part under his weight, plunging him hip-deep into rank, brackish water. Fortunately, after about an hour of this stop, slop, and go progress, a full bulbous moon had risen from behind the broken teeth of the volcanic mountain range and given him a visual fighting chance. With the rising of the moon came the dinosaur chorus, a keening, booming, atonal call-and-response that rang from one end of the swamp to the other as long necks, silhouetted against the skyshine and starfields, rose to their fullest stretch.

Jim scrabbled, gasping and winded, up a fairly dry slope, and sat gratefully down on a fallen trunk. The mammal stopped in front of him and looked him up and down. "What's the matter with you?"

"I'm not only dead, but I'm starting to realize that I'm seriously out of shape."

"It's not much farther to the house."

"Thank God for that."

The mammal was staring off into the distance, and Jim turned, following his gaze. The dry area, elevated well above water level, afforded a good nighttime view of the house and its surroundings. As far as Jim could tell, the structure stood on a similar raised area, surrounded by a grove of primal oak and plants that resembled giant celery, a half mile away across an expanse of iris, swamp grass, and black water. For the first time, Jim realized that the light he and the mammal were following was, in fact, a combination of five lighted windows, three down and two up, spilling their yellow radiance into the night and illuminating parts of the surrounding land and trees. There were figures moving around the outside of the place, and although Jim had no idea what kind of reception he might receive when he reached the place, he was at least reassured that someone was home.

Anubis had finished, for the moment, with the Dream Warden, and now the hooded figure was engaged in a conspiratorial head-to-head conversation with Mengele on the opposite side of the royal pavilion from Semple. That her two archenemies were consulting wouldn't have bothered her if they hadn't repeatedly glanced in her direction. Their covert glares were more than enough to make Semple uncomfortable. The tied-back tent flaps of an exit conveniently presented themselves to her right, and she turned and walked toward them. She didn't look back to see if Mengele and the Dream Warden were watching, but deliberately swayed her hips as she walked, in an obvious display of physical insolence. Let the bastards plot all they wanted. She was the dog-god's favorite for the time being, and she would do her level damnedest to see the pair of them brought down before she was through.

The exit she'd chosen led out into the open air, to a part of the exclusive royal enclosure right by the al fresco meat kitchens. She found herself amid the overpowering smell of roasting oxen, pigs, sheep, cattle, and other creatures that Semple didn't recognize, plus entire racks of ducks and chickens, slowly turned on automatic chain-driven spits above glowing beds of coals. More buffet tables had been set up beside the field kitchens and one of the first people that Semple saw there was Fat Ari, awesome in one of his tentlike costumes, helping himself to a whole leg of roast pork.

Semple's first reaction was to avoid the slave dealer just as she had avoided Mengele and the Dream Warden. She was about to reverse course and move off in the opposite direction when she thought, what the hell? She had nothing to fear from Fat Ari. Why not sashay past him, demonstrating what she'd become since she'd been removed from his clutches? Too few chances for fun presented themselves in this benighted city; why not grab a few rosebuds of payback while she might? She drew herself up to her full height and assumed the carriage of the acknowledged favorite of the God-King. She sauntered toward Fat Ari.

He recognized her right away. To Semple's mild surprise, Fat Ari showed absolutely no sign of resentment. He looked up from his pig-leg meat, nodded, and smiled with only a hint of regret. "Guess you lucked out, huh?"

Semple treated Fat Ari to a bright but slight favorite-concubine smile. "I guess I did."

Ari took a fresh bite out of his roast pork and continued to talk, generating a fine spray of spittle and fragments of flesh. "I would have sold you to some son of a bitch in the slums."

"I kind of gathered that."

"No hard feelings, though, right?"

"None on my part. Did Anubis ever pay you for me?"

Fat Ari swallowed what he was chewing. "Did he fuck. That psycho bastard never pays for anything he takes a fancy to. Claims it's his divine right to help himself."

A number of passersby overheard Fat Ari's heretical last statement and looked around in horror, but the slave dealer didn't seem to care. His position in the hierarchy must have been so well entrenched that he believed he had nothing to fear. At that moment the trumpet fanfare rang out again, and the same booming voice intoned the countdown. *"Zero minus thirty minutes and counting."*

Semple supposed she ought to be making her way back to her assigned seat in the royal box. It hardly made sense to antagonize Zipporah by showing up late for the bomb. Right at that moment, though, she would have been quite happy to stay and gossip with Fat Ari. With the possible exception of his table manners, Semple found that she was starting actually to take a liking to the man. He might have been an overbearing bully, without consideration for anything but his profit margins, but at least he was honest about what he was; he seemed free of the usual Necropolis delusions and affectations. Raising the leg of pork to his mouth, he treated Semple to a calculating look. "In fact, I figure you probably owe me one."

Semple planted a hand on her hip and raised a questioning eyebrow. "Oh yes? And how do you work that out?"

"If it hadn't been for me, you might still be rotting in the city jail."

"That's one way of looking at it, but I'm not sure it would be my way."

"So if I was to ask you to put a helpful word in the doghead's ear, you wouldn't be willing to do it for me?"

"That would depend on the word and how I was feeling at the time."

Fat Ari looked at Semple as though she were a major disappointment to him. "You're not forgetting where you came from, are you?"

Semple was about to tell Ari that he wouldn't believe where she came from, when she suddenly noticed that the crisp, slightly charred skin of his leg of pork was decorated with an indistinct but unmistakable tattoo, a faded scarlet heart above three hieroglyphs. Shock made her speak without thinking. "What the hell are you eating?"

Fat Ari looked at her as though she'd lost her mind. "Roast

teenager, gorgeous. That's the one redeeming feature of doghead's compulsory parties. There's always some human on the menu."

Suddenly Semple's mind flew back to her recent feast of marinated mystery meat. Why the hell hadn't she paid attention to Aimee back in Golgotha? *"I've also heard he encourages the practice of cannibalism."*

"I think I'm going to have to leave you here."

Jim looked at the mammal in amazement. "What are you talking about? I thought we were partners. I thought we were sticking together for the duration."

The final half mile to the old spooky mansion in the swamp had been the hardest part of Jim's whole Jurassic journey. He had to stop and rest four times, and it was during the last that the mammal made his startling announcement. Jim's immediate thought was that he'd done something to offend the creature. "Do we have a problem?"

The mammal shook his head. His eyes were sad. "No problem. But I smell something that makes me think I ought to make myself scarce."

Jim looked around in alarm. "Smell? What do you smell?"

"VC."

"VC?"

"Viet Cong."

Jim couldn't believe what he was hearing. "You smell Viet Cong in a Jurassic swamp?"

"There are groups of them all over this swamp. They seem to like it here."

"You're kidding me."

"I'm not. I figure either they've made a camp close to the house, or they've been hired on to guard the place."

Jim was at a loss for words. "Why would the Viet Cong want to live in a Jurassic swamp?"

The mammal gestured with his paw, the equivalent of a shrug for an animal with no noticeable shoulders. "You should know by now there's no accounting for what folks do in the Afterlife. I mean, look at me."

Jim thought about this. "If there's VC around, maybe I should get out of here, too."

"I doubt they'll bother you. They only mix it up with the ghost grunts."

"Are there U.S. soldiers here, too?"

The mammal nodded. "I've never seen them, but they leave their crap all over. Wherever they bivouac there's a mess of cigarette packs, Coke bottles, empty Spam cans, and used needles. Of course, they could be fabrications, set dressing for the VC. Or they could both be third-party creations."

Jim felt bemused. "Why in hell would anyone in their right mind want to reproduce the Vietnam War in among the dinosaurs?"

The small mammal's lip curled. "Like everyone here's in their right mind?"

Jim sighed. "Yeah, I guess you're right, but why are you so worried about them?"

"They might eat me. The story is, they look on my kind as a special delicacy."

Later, in retrospect, Semple was willing to accept that she may have overreacted to the sudden confrontation with cannibalism in Necropolis, but right then, in the shocking heat of that moment, revulsion boiled and overtook her reason. Fat Ari, however, was so engrossed in his disgusting snack that he failed to notice the expression of pure horror on Semple's face, and he continued to talk with his mouth full. "You should try the marinated infant in peanut sauce they're serving inside."

Semple's horror doubled. *Infant?* Bile rose in her throat; choking it back, she spun away from Fat Ari, who looked up and blinked. "What's the matter with you?"

She was too near gagging to answer. Fat Ari stared after her in confusion as she stumbled blindly across the royal enclosure with a fist pressed to her mouth. Her eyes watered and she had trouble forcing the unholy contents of her stomach to remain where they were. The Necropolis elite stared at her curiously as she staggered past, but no one spoke or tried to intercept her, and most turned back to what they had been doing, assuming that she was nothing more than an early emotional drunk. It was only when she approached one of the guarded entrances to the enclosure that anyone did anything to arrest her mindless flight. One of the huge Nubians, assigned to keep the common herd from mingling with the God-King and his aristocracy, lowered his spear as Semple approached, barring her way with its polished wood shaft. "You can't go out there, my lady."

Under more normal conditions, Semple might have been intimidated by the Nubian, seven feet tall and rocklike in his muscular perfection. Now the only thing that could replace Semple's unthinking horror was unseeing rage. Her voice came out somewhere between a sob and a scream. "I'm Semple McPherson and I can do exactly what I want. And right now I want out! I want away from all these fucking cannibals!"

At a loss, the Nubian decided the best thing was to repeat himself. "You really can't go out there, my lady."

"I'm the Lord Anubis's concubine. I'm his fucking favorite. Are you intending to stop me?"

The spear remained in place, but the Nubian shook his head. "I can't stop you from going out there. I will have to stop you, though, if you try to come back in. Admittance to the royal enclosure is strictly according to barcode. One may only enter the royal enclosure from outside if one's barcode is on the list. And obviously . . ."

He nodded in the direction of Semple's forehead. The goddamned barcode again. That thing was going to dog her every move until she was out of Necropolis entirely. But that was okay. Suddenly resolved, she snarled at the Nubian, "Remove that spear and let me pass."

The Nubian must have sensed that she was at the end of her tether, because he quickly returned the spear to it's upright parade position. "I can only warn you again: you will not be *readmitted*."

Semple managed to get her voice under control. "That's perfectly okay. I'm not coming back." She glanced a last single time at the royal enclosure. "I think I'd rather have my eyes burned out than come back in here."

The Nubian's face stiffened and he stood at rigid attention. Semple guessed he was less than comfortable around what he saw as a harem girl having a neurotic outburst and his only defense was to turn robot. "Don't say I didn't warn you."

"Don't worry, I won't."

She stepped past the Nubian and, as far as she was concerned, detached herself from the court of Anubis. At the same moment, the trumpets blared. "*Zero minus twenty minutes and counting.*"

✳

The mansion was close, and even in the moonlight Jim was able to make out some of its architectural details. Whoever designed the place had gone all the way with the Old South. A tall, porticoed, Gothic Graceland with flying buttresses and narrow conical turrets rose like a warning from its attendant grove of trees. Up close, the place was so threatening that Jim started wondering why he'd allowed himself to be talked into coming there. He was beginning to feel like Jonathan Harker approaching a Dixie Castle Dracula, and he wondered if the mammal was in fact some kind of elaborate serial prankster who, for his own mysterious satisfaction, took total strangers into the worst part of the swamp and then abruptly abandoned them. At first Jim had been saddened by the little creature's departure, but as he drew nearer to the mansion and saw its forbidding exterior more clearly, his mood rapidly soured and he became sorely pissed off. Even the yellow light spilling from the windows was cold and unwelcoming. Folks who chose to live in the darkest depths of this ancient swamp hardly seemed the kind who would embrace a passing stranger.

Jim caught his foot in a knot of submerged roots and nearly went sprawling again. He was about to start cursing when he heard a rustling in the reeds only a few yards away. Jim looked carefully around, but could see nothing. Then the rustling came again, and at once he knew it was being made by a human or animal uncomfortably close to him. He bent his knees and lowered himself, as silently as he could manage, until just his head remained above the water. The move didn't come a moment too soon. Almost immediately, dark figures broke through the undergrowth in front of him, wading purposefully through the swamp water, weapons held high, with easy precise movements that only come from absolute knowledge of the terrain. The worst part was, they were coming directly toward him.

As soon as Semple was outside the Nubian-guarded entryway to the royal enclosure, she found herself assaulted by the sounds and the smells of the masses. Out there in the poor people's area of the Divine Atom Bomb Festival—in what might have been called the cheap seats, had there been any seats—the stench was a physical presence. Unwashed bodies, the halitosis of a multitude, the urine-feces-vomit stink that wafted from the improvised latrines, and the sour-grease reek of bad junk food all conspired in olfactory assault. To make matters worse, Semple immediately found herself an instant curiosity about to be elevated to sideshow status. A ragged, swarthy, and very drunk man in a filthy kilt and bolero lurched up to her and attempted to grope her. "Bitch, if you wanna go slumming, you could do a lot fuckin' worse than go slumming with me." The man seemed to assume she was some courtier looking for rough-trade thrills out in the country of the proles.

Semple didn't bother to disabuse him; her intention was to simply sidestep and hurry on. But hurrying on presented something of a problem, since she had no idea where she was going. This made it difficult to carry off her usual air of command. She slipped past the man, who yelled after her, "Stuck-up whore! What's your fucking problem? Think you're too good for my kind?"

Semple, who was having enough problems with the human flesh in her digestive tract, tried to keep walking, but the man wasn't finished. "So what are you doing out here if you think you're so fucking good?" He started to follow her, yelling at her retreating back. "You get back here and talk to me! You fucks from the palace ain't no better than the rest of us!"

The man's tirade had the unfortunate effect of causing everyone within earshot to turn and look at her. At first these gawkers were merely curious. Up to that point, Semple had been too freaked to consider the impact she might cause, but with a hundred or more of the ragged, dull-eyed Necropolis poor staring at her, she suddenly realized just how sorely she stuck out, a painted and perfumed butterfly misplaced in a realm of deprived and disgruntled roaches and scorpions.

It didn't take long for simple curiosity to transmute into dull, lumpen anger, and the randomly loitering began to gather into a loose knot of resentful faces. Semple could almost hear their thoughts. What could they do with this strange apparition, this gratuitous visitor from a world that they could only imagine with envy? At first the crowd kept its distance, moving with her but staring with growing hostility. The first to break ranks and actually advance toward her was a full-breasted woman in cheap and disheveled holiday finery, who had come from rutting in the desert dirt with two well-developed young men while a third took instant photographs with a cheap plastic camera. The woman halted a couple of paces in front of Semple, barring her way. She dusted off her hands and slowly looked Semple up and down. "So what happened, lovey? The doghead throw you out of paradise?"

Semple was forced to stop, but she didn't think the woman's sneering question merited an answer. She looked around for an avenue of dignified retreat, but none presented itself. The ring of poor had closed and she was surrounded. Fear hovered on Semple's horizon of emotional options, but she knew that any hint and the mob would be on her in an instant. As far as she could assess the situation, the proles had decided she was Marie Antoinette and they wanted their cake. Emboldened, the woman took another step toward her. "What's your problem, girl? Think you're too good to talk to the likes of me? You're on our turf now and you're going to have to learn a new set of manners."

Semple treated the woman to a look of what she hoped was sufficiently withering contempt. "Are you suggesting you're going to teach *me*?"

The woman laughed and turned to the crowd of spectators. "You hear that? The bitch still thinks she's safe on the inside."

The woman was now close enough for Semple to smell the combination of booze, sweat, and the earthy body stink of recent sex. As the woman faced her again, Semple glared warningly into the smeared makeup of the gaudily painted face. "You'd be well advised not to start anything with me." In fact, she wasn't as confident as she sounded. This harlot from the slums had a mean scar over her left cheekbone, but Semple refused to be intimidated.

The woman's eyes glinted dangerously. "Well advised? You're telling me that I'd be well advised? You think some gang of Nubians is going to come running out and rescue you?"

Two other women had left the circle of watchers and were moving to join the first. Semple knew the situation was already on its way to becoming a class war flashpoint, and she was at a loss as to how to handle it when it turned ugly. To her dismay, the crunch came even sooner than she expected. The woman extended a dirty hand with chipped purple nails, trying to grab the jewel-encrusted gold collar from around Semple's neck. "So what about this thing? You may have a dozen of them, but, out here, that could keep a family for a year or more."

Semple jerked the collar out of reach. The piece didn't even belong to her. It was merely on loan from the seraglio strongroom. As a possession of Anubis, she had no personal property, but she couldn't expect the crowd to understand this. All she could do was maintain a bold front and hope for the best, and so she quickly snarled at the woman, "Keep your fucking bitch prole hands off me."

A voice shouted from the crowd, "Strip the stuck-up cow!"

Semple's lip curled. "You may find I'm not as easy to take as you imagine."

Another seconded the motion. "Yeah! Strip her naked!"

A ripple of laughter ran through the spectators, followed by another shout. "Six to four on Suchep the Whore."

Others picked up the phrase like a chant. "Six to four on Suchep the whore."

Semple assumed Suchep the whore was the woman in front of her still eyeing the gold collar.

"Six to four on Suchep the whore."

At the prospect of betting, men in the crowd were instantly galvanized. "I'll take a piece of that."

Some laughed at the double entendre, but the more serious gamblers eyed Semple with appraising eyes. The way Semple looked right then, in all her harem finery, straight from Anubis's parade, she couldn't imagine anyone giving six to four on her in a no-holds-barred, straight fight.

"Who'll give odds on the harem broad?"

"Four to one against."

"I'll double it if Suchep kills her."

The bookmaking faltered for a moment as the trumpets sounded and the voice boomed. *"Zero minus fifteen minutes and counting."*

Fifteen minutes was plenty of time. The mob's attention returned to the fight at hand. "I got twenty says the aristo ain't as soft as she looks."

Semple was amazed. They were starting to exchange markers, getting bets down on the dragout between Semple in the god's gold jewelry and Suchep with the big tits and purple nails. It was as if they were a pair of pit bulls or fighting lizards. Merely one more excuse for the movement of money. There was one consolation, though. A catfight might have been the last thing that Semple needed, but a crowd busy wagering wouldn't so easily turn into a ravening lynch mob. Unfortunately, the two other women now standing a little behind Suchep the whore missed this point. Their lupine grins and clenched fists suggested they were eager to help take Semple apart, and maybe share in the proceeds. Semple knew her first move should be to put them straight. "You two better keep out of this if you don't want to be blamed for screwing the odds."

The two women laughed as though Semple were bluffing, but then Suchep shot them each a warning look and they got the point. As the two retreated, she turned back to Semple. "So you think you can take me, do you?"

Semple smiled sweetly. "Don't be deceived by appearances."

The woman smiled. "I'm going to rip your prissy fucking face off."

Semple gestured to the scar on Suchep's cheek. "Where did you get that from? A pimp?"

That was enough for Suchep the Whore. She lunged once more for the collar around Semple's neck, and Semple jumped back again. This time, however, she came straight back, fully on the offensive, and punched her adversary hard in the face.

As the VC came at him, Jim's muscles locked in panic. He found he could neither run nor completely submerge himself in the brackish water. Long seconds passed before he managed to regain his control, and by that point it was altogether too late. The dozen of them were so close that he could see their flat, stern faces, clear proof of the Nietzschean axiom of the Afterlife: "That which killed them also made them stronger." He found he could make out the fine mechanical details of their AK-47s. He could even read the slogan, THE TRUTH IS OUT THERE, on the T-shirt one of them wore under his black pajamas. Nearby a dinosaur coughed and snuffled and the VC column silently halted, instantly alert. With weapons at the ready, they carefully scanned the surrounding area. At least one of them looked directly at Jim, making what seemed to be complete eye contact, and yet he showed absolutely no reaction. It was as if the guerrilla couldn't see him, as if he were somehow invisible to the man.

The dinosaur coughed and snuffled two more times and them started to move off, away from Jim and the Viet Cong. The swell created by its departure all but swamped Jim, his mouth and nose went under, and he rose spluttering, right in front of the VC with the TRUTH IS OUT THERE T-shirt. Again, the impossible happened. The man seemed to have no idea that Jim existed. He moved on past him as though he weren't there, only missing him by a matter of inches, and the rest of the column went right along with him. Jim got back to his feet, wiping the water out of his eyes, wondering what the hell had just happened. He knew well enough that weird shit could come to pass in the backwaters of the Afterlife, but this brief encounter was more than passing strange. Perhaps the VC's inability to see him had something to do with the time disturbances that had occurred earlier. If somehow the VC had been slightly in the past and Jim had been slightly in the future, it might just be possible that he could see them while they could not see him. He had to admit it was a pretty threadbare piece of reasoning, but it did cause him to wonder what would happen when he reached the mansion. Would anyone see him at all?

One thing Jim knew for sure was that he wouldn't learn anything by standing around, up to his waist in dirty water. He had no real option except to press on, so he once again dragged one boot and then the other out of the glutinous sucking mud and toward the yellow lights.

Suchep went sprawling, then pushed herself up on one elbow and put a hand to her nose. Blood was on her palm. It also ran down her upper lip and into her mouth. "You broke my fucking nose."

Semple wagged an index finger at her opponent. "Never judge a book, bitch."

Without warning, Suchep's legs flashed out in a scissors move, a sneak attempt to throw Semple to the ground, and Semple only eluded her in the nick of time. Semple's sideways retreat also gave the woman the chance to scramble back to her feet, and she came at Semple half crouched, hands reaching, fingers clawed. Semple knew in an instant that she had no chance of besting Suchep in a fair fight. She had neither her adversary's down-and-dirty skills nor her stomp-and-gouge reactions. Her only hope was to think of something tricky, and fast. If she couldn't fake out this incarnate piece of lewd aggression, she'd be toast.

The two women circled each other while the crowd bayed, teeth bared, faces stretched and ugly. Markers were changing hands at a furious rate now that Semple had unexpectedly drawn the first blood and the odds had radically shifted. The more money that went down, the more the crowd's natural bloodlust was amplified by personal financial involvement. "Go get her, baby! Kick her in the cunt! Rip her tits off. We're counting on you, Suchep!"

Suchep looked for an opening and Semple thought furiously. As the woman lunged, hoping to twist her talons into Semple's long hair, Semple again ducked out of the way; suddenly an idea occurred to her. Her hand went to the fastening on the jeweled collar and she yanked it free. She smiled nastily at the Suchep, holding the collar at arm's length. "You wanted this, didn't you? What was it you said? This thing could keep a family for a year or more? So why don't you come and get it? Take a chance on a year's pay."

Suchep frowned. Her blood and makeup were blending with the dust of the desert, which had been trampled fine by hundreds of feet, and sweat was washing the mix into dirty rivulets that snaked from brow to cheek. Suchep knew Semple was up to something, and was trying to figure out what. Semple sensed she had the upper hand, and she liked it. "So, are you going to come and get it?"

The woman lunged and Semple sidestepped, laughing. The confrontation was taking on the aspects of a bullfight. "Better still, why don't you run and fetch it like a dog?"

Semple tossed the collar so it landed a few yards from where the two of them were facing off. Suchep was transparent. She knew she shouldn't take her eyes off Semple, but she couldn't resist looking to see where the precious piece might be lying. She glanced around and Semple punished her by punching her hard in the side of the head, just below the ear. Suchep staggered but at least had the presence of mind to move closer to the collar. Unfortunately, this was exactly what Semple wanted. As she'd hoped, her throwing the collar had brought the two other women back into the picture. When the betting had started, they had wisely moved back to give room to the designated contenders. With the jeweled collar on the ground for the taking, the picture instantly changed. The pair were now eyeing the prize, wondering if it was worth interrupting the fight, and how they could beat the wrath of the crowd and make off with the treasure. Suchep also saw what was happening and, probably against her better judgment, jumped back and attempted to snatch up the collar.

Semple was on her in an instant, kicking her in the side as she bent over. Suchep grunted and rolled over in the dust, winded and hurting. Semple kicked her again, and again Suchep rolled, but this time she came up with the collar in her hand. Semple backed off, grinning. "So what are you going to do now? Fight me with one hand or let go of a fortune?"

It was in this moment that Semple overreached herself, though she didn't realize it until Suchep's left hand came up and shot a well-aimed cloud of dust into her face. In the instant that she was blinded, the trumpets brayed a new updated warning. *"Zero minus ten minutes and counting."* But Semple didn't hear them. Now she was the one taking the punishment. Suchep's experienced fists were pounding her chest and stomach. The woman had wrapped the collar around her right fist and was using it like a set of gold knuckles. Semple staggered back, giving ground in the face of the onslaught. She could taste blood in her mouth. The crowd was roaring and the odds were in motion again. A few moments earlier, when Semple had looked so good, a newcomer couldn't have hoped to get into the action at better than evens. Now it was anybody's guess. Semple took a stunning blow to the side of the head and, as her knees buckled, Suchep grabbed at her skirt and tugged. Before it pulled free, the skirt acted as a hobble around her legs, and Semple fell heavily. Even her blurred vision told her that Suchep was standing over her with a look of triumph on her face.

"Now I'm going to finish you, you stuck-up harem bitch."

The first gray streaks of a false dawn were beginning to show in the eastern sky as Jim moved gratefully up onto dry land. His boots squelched water and more trickled down the inside of his leather jeans. He was soaked to the skin, but since the night was as oppressively warm and humid as Orlando in high summer, it hardly mattered. A clean crisp shirt would have been turned into a damp dishrag in a matter of minutes, even without repeated immersion in the swamp. He was just pleased to be able to walk without having to drag every second step from seven inches of suction. The trees that surrounded the old spooky mansion were directly in front of him, but before he could reach them he had to struggle through a fringe of undergrowth where the water met land. Primitive mangrove and a tangle of some kind of organic barbed wire—with wicked two-inch and toxic-looking thorns—represented the worst and final obstacle. As he gingerly eased and squirmed his way through the flesh-threatening foliage, he rejoiced that he had never abandoned the Lizard King affectation of leather pants. He only regretted he didn't have the matching jacket. Although his legs came through unscathed, the thorns ripped his shirt and drew blood from long scratches to his hands, arms, chest, and back.

When he'd finally battled his way through these defenses, he found that, once under the trees, he was walking on a soft carpet of shaggy moss, growing lush on the mulch of fallen leaves and pine needles. More signs of humanity presented themselves. Over to Jim's right, the rusting remains of a huge automobile lay stranded without wheels like a beached whale, perhaps a Lincoln or a Pontiac or a Buick Rocket 88 that, in its heyday, must have been equal in magnificence to Long Time Bob Moore's Caddy. Most of the hulk's paneling was now nothing more than red, flaking rust, corroding away from the chassis, but here and there patches of faded pink paint were still visible. His first thought on seeing the remnants of a pink paint job was the mammal's remark that Elvis might once have occupied the house. The immobile hunk had surely rested there for sixty or seventy years; a fairly substantial conifer had grown up through the interior, punched through the sunroof, and continued to grow for another forty or fifty feet. Logic suggested it was some long time since Elvis could have graced this sector of the Afterlife, except this Jurassic was in such a state of time flux that logic could not easily apply.

His main objective was still the dark bulk of the mansion, but Jim made a detour to take a closer look at the remains of the car. Even the outside chance of an afterglow Elvis presence wasn't something one happened across too often. When he reached the dead two-door, he placed the flat of his hand on the pitted and discolored hood. Right then, worn out as he was, he could have used a strong jolt of Elvis magic, but the ruin of the car failed to deliver even the faintest residual slapback. More than a little disappointed, he turned his attention back to his primary target. One of the ground-floor lighted windows was on the side of the building directly facing him. An elaborate bay was surmounted by stone gargoyles with sculpted fangs and scales, holding up a heraldic relief, a coat of arms that bore the insignia of a key and an open hand with an eye in the palm. No detail seemed to have been spared in this homage to the intricate conventions of the Morticia Addams school of architecture.

Jim approached the lighted bay window with caution. He definitely wanted to see the inhabitants of the house before they saw him. He covered the last few yards to the house in a full crouch; then, with one hand on the carved stone of the sill, he slowly raised himself and looked inside. The spectacle that presented itself was hardly one of domestic tranquillity. The walls of the room were paneled in a dark walnut and hung with a half dozen paintings of grimly aristocratic men and women in flowing robes, posturing with dogs and falcons, against backgrounds of storm clouds and mountains. Aside from the paintings and the paneling, the room itself was dominated by a huge and magnificent fireplace, an edifice in black marble streaked by veins of yellow and green and with carved basilisks supporting a wide mantel. A log fire blazed in the grate, which might have invested the room with a modicum of hominess had it not been burning with bizarre blue-purple flames. Even more bizarre was the single figure standing motionless in the corner farthest from the fire. Jim couldn't tell whether it was a man, woman, or even a lifelike replica, since it was covered from head to foot in a swarm of moving, jostling live bees.

Jim let out a low whistle. "What the hell do we have here? Jean Cocteau meets Edgar Allan Poe?"

As if his low whistle had triggered it, a door just within Jim's field of vision opened and a woman came into the room. Jim instinctively ducked as the woman glanced in the direction of the window, even though he was convinced that, all other things being equal, she would be unable to see him lurking in the twilight beyond the light reflected in the window glass.

"Maybe Jean and Edgar meet Leopold Sacher-Masoch."

Although she wore no furs, the woman was unarguably Venus. She was dressed—encased—in a cat suit of scarlet leather, pulled skin-tight to accentuate her decidedly statuesque figure by sets of lacings that ran from armpit to ankle on either side of her body. The ensemble was completed by a matching pair of platform spikes that elevated her height to well over six feet, long cocktail gloves with similar lacing, and a voluminous chiffon bridal veil in the same color. Her hair was jet-black with a bluish sheen, styled to recall the coifs of Jane Russell and Wonder Woman. As she turned to face the window, Jim saw from her ghost-pale face, with somber eye shadow and imperious scarlet mouth, that innocence had long been displaced by hard-won experience.

Jim stared mesmerized as the woman glanced once at the motionless, bee-covered figure and then walked to the fireplace and halted, looking down into the flames. He was sure that somewhere, somehow, he had seen her before, either lifeside or in the hereafter, but he was unable to dredge time, place, or circumstance from his fragmented recall. His first thought was of the strange and hazily recalled woman in the hallucination during his alien sex encounter, but no, it couldn't be her. He knew instinctively that she had been fundamentally different.

The woman inside the room contemplated the fire for a few moments, then straightened her shoulders and turned. Jim was just able to catch the expression of weary sadness that preceded this visible hardening of her resolve. She moved with the air of a woman following orders. In the exact center of the room, she positioned herself facing the fire and stood very erect. Her hands moved in a series of ritually complex motions. The air in front of her shimmered and then a dark circular walnut table suddenly appeared out of nowhere. The table was a pretty neat trick on its own, even without the simultaneous materialization of a number of objects arranged on its surface in what looked like a symbolic pattern. All the kinetic materialization Jim had ever managed was a less than reliable ability to pluck the odd, usually stale cigarette out of thin air, and that didn't always work. The woman in red leather was clearly a past mistress in the art of raising objects from nowhere.

The stuff on the table struck even Jim as a little strange, although hardly out of character with what he'd seen of the place so far. A long rapier, resting on a needle point and with ornate hilt, bisected the table. To one side of it lay a coiled cat-o'-nine-tails, with a Lucite handle, made from translucent optical fibers and with a tiny glowing sphere at the end of each individual lash. A branding iron in the shape of a curlicued letter S reposed on the other side of the sword, along with three square-headed iron nails at least nine inches long, a cell phone, and a clamplike device constructed from solid chrome. Jim had no idea of the purpose of this last object, except a suspicion that it was intended to cause some manner of protracted pain, likely as not to human male genitals. An earthenware jug of the kind that traditionally contained corn liquor was set slightly apart from the other items. The woman considered these objects for a few moments, then picked up the whip and flicked it experimentally, spreading the plastic thongs. As the scourge swished in the air, the tiny spheres glowed brighter, but the effect didn't seem to please the woman. She recoiled the whip and returned it to the table. Now she picked up the sword, and as with the whip, she swung it testingly. The cold steel seemed more to her liking, and with the sword still in her right hand, she reached for the cell phone, at the same time glancing toward the door through which she had entered. Jim could hear her clearly as she spoke into the phone. "Inform Morrison that the Lady Semple has readied herself for his attendance."

Jim twitched. Morrison? Was she talking to him? He quickly looked around, but no sign indicated his presence had been detected. He turned back to the window and saw that a third figure had come into the room. This one Jim recognized instantly. It was him. Out of shape, with half a beard, a flabby beer gut hanging over the concha belt of his leather jeans, and the ravages of depravity and dissolution clearly showing, it was unmistakably an older version of himself.

The older Morrison halted beside the table and stood looking down at the floor. The woman in red put down the cell phone and flexed the blade of the rapier into a tempered steel arc. "So you haven't changed your mind?"

The two so clearly knew each other that Jim, outside the window, wondered if his foggy recognition of the woman was some kind of displaced front-end memory at work. Inside the room, the older Morrison raised his head and met the woman's gaze. "No, I haven't changed my mind."

"There's still time."

"I know that."

"But you're determined to challenge my cruelty?"

"Do I really have any other choice? We've come too far to turn back now."

The woman shrugged slightly. "Then you'd better remove your shirt."

The older Morrison was wearing an embroidered Mexican wedding shirt and, as he slowly stripped it off, any doubts that Jim might have had that this temporally advanced version of himself drank too much and got virtually no exercise were put to rest by the sight of his bare torso and fish-belly flesh. The woman in red again flexed the sword. "Then you know what to do, don't you?"

The older Morrison sighed with almost overwhelming world-weariness and reached for the jug. As far as Jim could gather, the upcoming ceremony was now so routine it was approaching a tedious normality. "Yes, I know what to do."

The woman flicked the sword, creating an impatient staccato whoosh. "Then you don't need a drink first. Just do it."

The older Morrison put down the jug and moved to face the fireplace. He placed his hands well apart on the mantel, his arms all but fully extended. He leaned forward slightly so his pants legs wouldn't be scorched by the flames. In that position, the mantel came to just below his chin. He moved his feet slightly apart as though starting to brace himself. His head was lowered; he might have been staring down at the flames, or perhaps his eyes were closed. Jim couldn't quite see. The woman put the sword down on the table again, then picked up the branding iron and examined it, turning it over in her gloved hands. "My first thought was that at last it was time for me to brand you."

The older Morrison's shoulders tensed. "So brand me. You, if anyone, should know enough to follow your instinct."

Two Viet Cong appeared in the doorway and stood silently watching. One was wearing a THE TRUTH IS OUT THERE T-shirt; Jim could only assume it was the same Charlie he had seen in the swamp, unless X-Files shirts were a trend among the Jurassic VC. Either the woman was ignoring the two guerrillas or she was unable to see them. She returned the branding iron to the table. "But then I changed my mind. I decided branding was a little too, shall we say, final. It would constitute a fresh benchmark in our relationship."

"Avoid fresh benchmarks at all costs."

The woman picked up the sword again. "Are you being funny?"

"As funny as it's possible to be in this position."

"Then that settles it."

Jim on the outside and the VC on the inside watched as the older Morrison turned his head slightly. "Settles what?"

"I'm going to carve my initials on you."

"You've done that before."

The woman extended the point of the blade so it was not quite touching the skin of Morrison's back. "So it's no benchmark."

The older Morrison's flesh crawled visibly as though anticipating the slicing kiss of cold steel. Perhaps he wasn't quite as jaded as he first seemed. He sighed, either in sadness or surrender. "That's true."

For a moment the woman sounded almost as wistful. "It's sad, really. The mark of the last time is all but healed. You can only see the faintest white shadow of a scar."

"Maybe you didn't cut it deep enough or write it big enough."

Her voice hardened. "Then this time it'll be written large, you son of a bitch. Are you ready?"

The older Morrison lowered his head. "Yes, I'm ready."

The woman in red took a deep breath. "Close your eyes. Don't look at me until I'm finished, and don't make any noise."

With a swift, deft movement, she traced an arching curve with the rapier point all the way from slightly below one shoulder to slightly below the other. Blood immediately welled through the lacerated skin, holding the shape of the mark for a moment and then trickling downward. The older Morrison bit his lip but, as instructed, made no sound. Outside the window Jim felt his own spine tingle. Without faltering, the woman in red reversed the path of the blade and brought it diagonally across the small of the older Morrison's back. Then the blade curved back once more, just above the waistband of his jeans, and she finished with a small circular flourish. It was the mark of Zorro in reverse, all in a single complex stroke.

The second initial started with a firm downstroke, but Jim would not see it finished. As the woman in red completed the first stroke, a hand fell on Jim's shoulder, creating an ice-blue plasma flash of time distortion. Doc Holliday's bloodshot, heavy-lidded eyes were looking into his. His face was arranged in the deceptively mild half-smile of his diamond foppishness, and when he spoke, it was with the drawl of gentlemanly decadence. "This is really not a good place for you to be, my young friend. Really not a good place at all."

"Zero minus five minutes and counting. All spectators must now be in their places and protective eyewear should be ready."

With only five minutes to go before the detonation, the onlookers were torn. Obviously they didn't want to miss the end of the catfight, but their God-King's atom bomb was calling; the outcome of the confrontation between Semple the Concubine and Suchep the Whore had looked like a foregone conclusion from the moment that Suchep had stooped down and picked up the rock. Now she stood astride Semple in primitive triumph, naked but for the tatters of her skirt, body smeared with dirt, blood, and sweat, the golden collar wrapped around her wrist like a trophy, and the rock raised above her head in both hands, ready to bring it down to crush Semple's skull and send her back to the Great Double Helix by the most direct route. Semple could do nothing. She was dizzy and her strength was gone. When Suchep had looked around for a suitable rock with which to administer the coup de grâce, Semple had seen her opening, but her legs had refused to work. Now all she could do was close her eyes, accept the inevitable, and hope that any pain would be over in an instant. Acceptance wasn't that easy, however. A part of her was still seething, resenting that she had come so far only to fail so ignominiously. When she finally returned from the pods, she doubted that she could ever face Aimee again. That is, if Aimee even existed in whatever sector of the hereafter Semple eventually emerged. Only time would tell what might happen if one of them died a second time.

"Zero minus four minutes and counting. Protective eyewear should now be in place."

At the blare of the trumpets, Suchep, rock still poised, hesitated for a split second. The crowd was now yelling, goading her to finish Semple so they could settle their bets before the bomb went off. In that instant, Semple saw the last possible chance of a reprieve and took it. With an effort she would later consider superhuman, she simply kicked straight up. Her shin hit Suchep hard and squarely in the crotch. The woman gasped and staggered, and the rock dropped from her hands. One victory was all Semple needed. The magical, last-ditch burst of energy extended itself long enough for her to quickly twist and trip her off-balance opponent. Now the crowd was really torn. The catfight had taken a new lease on life, but the main event would go off in three minutes and a diminishing number of seconds.

Semple crawled to where Suchep lay face down in the dirt. She was attempting to push herself up on her arms, but she appeared even more exhausted than Semple. Semple grabbed her by the hair and jerked her head backward so Suchep was staring straight into her face. "So you thought you were going bash my head in with a rock, did you?"

The tables had turned so suddenly that Suchep seemed to be having trouble grasping what had happened. "I—"

Semple slammed the woman's confused face hard back into the dirt and then raised it again. "Thought you were going to score points with the boys by killing me, did you?"

This time Suchep didn't even attempt to answer. She seemed almost as resigned to her fate as Semple had been a few moments earlier, and Semple took a perverse delight in ramming her face once more into the dirt. When Semple jerked her head up again, Suchep's nose was again bleeding. "My name is Semple McPherson, sweetheart. You'd best remember that. You made a serious mistake when you tagged me as some fragile harem pet."

To emphasize her point, Semple twisted her fingers viciously in Suchep's hair. "I could kill you right now if I wanted to."

Because of her bloody nose, Suchep's breath was coming in short harsh grunts. "No, please . . . don't . . . "

"Are you begging me?"

"Don't . . . kill me . . . I . . . "

"Zero minus three minutes and counting."

Even though she was enjoying hurting this bitch who had tried to put the hurt on her, Semple realized she had to finish Suchep or let her go. She toyed with the idea of making a theatrical appeal to the crowd for a thumbs up or thumbs down, but decided they hardly merited that much respect or display. Also, she wasn't in the mood for murder. To remain angry with this woman for long enough to beat her to death seemed a misuse of energies. Semple leaned forward and breathed into Suchep's ear. "Just let me hear you beg."

Suchep's bruised mouth twisted. "Okay, okay, I'm begging."

Semple had to give the woman credit for managing to retain a shred of defiance in her tone, even while begging for her life. She lowered the woman's head slightly. "If I let go of you, you'll just lay there, okay? No tricks? No double-cross?"

"I swear . . . "

"The damned bomb's going to go off any minute."

Suchep groaned. "No tricks. I swear."

Semple let go of Suchep's hair, straightened up, and got wearily to her feet. True to her word, Suchep lay face down on the ground, not moving. Semple unwound the collar from the woman's wrist. "I fear you're going to spend the next year on your back, earning your living the old-fashioned way."

Semple faced the crowd as the victor, but the crowd had no time for applause. Self-interest was their only concern as they jostled to cash in their markers before the explosion. Even though many of them had made money off her at long odds, no one thought so much as to offer her a blanket with which to cover herself. Both she and the fight were history.

"Zero minus two minutes and counting. All monitor and bunker crews must be in place. All loose objects must be secured."

Semple slowly turned, totally at a loss for what to do. She was beat up, dressed only in a thong bikini, and on the lam. The remnants of her skirt lay in the dust where Suchep had ripped it off her. She gathered up the tatters, wrapping them quickly around her waist as a makeshift kilt. Most of the crowd had started to move back. With the detonation so close at hand, the air of festivity had wilted, giving way to an anxious anticipation. The majority finally seemed to have grasped that Anubis's atom bomb might be no more efficient than anything else in Necropolis. For all any of them knew, it could just as easily set fire to the atmosphere as go off as planned.

"Zero minus ninety seconds and counting."

Semple noticed the protective visor she had been given in the royal enclosure was on the ground where she'd dropped it at the start of the fight. She quickly picked it up and put it on. After she'd run from Anubis and battered Suchep bloody, she saw absolutely no point in being blinded by the nuclear flash. She also looped the collar around her neck. Maybe next time around it could buy her some luck instead of provoking trouble.

"Zero minus seventy-five seconds and counting."

Semple knew she must have presented a decidedly odd figure in her improvised loincloth, wild disheveled hair, and black plastic visor, wearing a gold collar that was worth a small fortune, but this was no time to worry about how she looked. Almost all of the crowd had now donned various forms of what the countdown voice had called protective eyewear, investing them with a strange zombie uniformity that reminded Semple of the audiences at one of the those 3D movies back in the lifeside 1950s. The atomic explosion obviously represented something beyond mere B-movie special effects, though. The act of putting on their souvenir visors and sunglasses seemed to have helped convince the crowd that the bomb constituted more of a threat than they had previously imagined. A low-level mass apprehension was creating a general retreat toward the barriers around the royal enclosure, and a line of Nubians—with spears tipped with functional steel instead of ceremonial gold—had moved out of the enclosure to reinforce the wood and canvas barricades against a sudden nervous rush by the lower orders. The Nubians were soon augmented by rocketeer police in full riot drag, who emerged from the enclosures at a dead run. Like so much else in Necropolis, the Divine Atom Bomb Festival was now threatening to turn ugly in its final seconds.

"Zero minus sixty seconds and counting. The subclass will prepare to prostrate itself."

Semple wondered if now, by default, she qualified as one of the sub-class, but she had no intention of kneeling or otherwise humbling herself. Much against both her will and her good taste, she had found herself on her knees in front of the dog-god more times than she cared to dwell upon. As far as she was concerned, that had ceased for good when she'd fled the royal pavilion.

"Zero minus fifty seconds and counting."

Even Suchep had managed to get to her hands and knees and was crawling after the rest of the crowd. Semple, who had so far refused to retreat, now found herself close to the front ranks of the spectators.

"Zero minus forty seconds and counting."

She could feel the fear that was permeating the mob, but there was no way she was going to give in to it. To move away from the bomb was to also move toward Anubis, and that was out of the question.

"Zero minus thirty seconds and counting. The subclass will now prostrate itself."

To Semple's amazement, the majority of the crowd was dropping to its knees.

"Twenty-nine . . . twenty-eight."

She had expected the Necropolis underclass to be more rebellious. Even in the mire of dog-god religious repression and poverty, she could hardly believe that a strata of old-time anarchy or drunken bolshevism hadn't evolved. It looked as though the majority were lacking even the balls of a whore like Suchep.

"Twenty-seven . . . twenty-six . . . "

The invisible trumpets now maintained a constant scream under the hectoring voice. *"Twenty-five . . . twenty-four . . . at twenty seconds all knees will be bowed, all souls will grovel before the might of Anubis."*

The voice had taken on a chanting, liturgical measure. Anubis or maybe his Dream Warden seemed to have decided that the big bang would take place in an atmosphere of worshipful devotion.

"*Twenty . . .*"

The crowd was on the ground.

"*Nineteen . . .*"

Semple was one of the very last to remain standing.

"*Eighteen . . .*"

"Fuck this."

"*Seventeen . . . sixteen . . .*"

With the crowd all prone, Semple had a clear and perfect view of the chrome obelisk, at the very tip of which lurked Anubis's sacred nuke.

"*Fifteen. All praise be to the mighty Lord Anubis.*"

A celestial choir intoned a rising atonal cadence and the low rumble of a Bach organ was mixed in with the trumpets.

"*Fourteen . . . thirteen . . . twelve . . .*"

Semple was finding it all too much. Rather than stand around, knee-deep in prostrate proles, she decided she needed to be positive, to go boldy against the flow of this Necropolis lunacy, to counter it with some lunacy of her own.

"*Eleven. Laud and magnify the Lord Anubis and his mighty weapon.*"

She started to walk toward the obelisk, carefully picking her way through the mass of huddled grovelers.

"*Ten . . . nine . . . eight . . . seven . . .*"

She was nearing the front of the crowd. She started to hurry. She wanted to be alone with the bomb.

"*Six . . . five . . . four . . .*"

She stopped dead at three. She was a very long way from the obelisk, but at least she was clear of the crowd. She stood upright and spread her arms. The Divine Atom Bomb could take her if it dared, and damn the gamma rays.

"*Two . . . one . . .*"

In the first nanosecond, it was nothing more than a point of infinitely bright light.

"*Ignition!*"

But this grew into a ball of cosmic fire, as though a piece of the sun had been touched off at ground zero, so impossibly, searingly bright that, even from behind the visor, Semple could feel her retina commencing to burn. Beyond the realm of visible light, she could also feel the lashing waves of radiation ripping and jackhammering at every cell of her body. Her very molecular structure seemed to be at risk; her skeleton was clearly visible, glowing with a dull red fire, beneath flesh rendered translucent by the nativity of this new sun. At any moment she felt she would melt away, blasted back to Great Double Helix by the awesome solar wind—and, right then, Semple didn't care. The chips could fall where they might. And she was surprised to find the experience was far from unpleasant. The intensity of the screaming protons, neutrons, and electrons that howled through her transcended by quantum factors any experience she had ever known. It was worth everything that had gone before and anything that might come later. Semple was seized by a mind-bending awe at the infinity of this bliss.

"Oh! No! Yes! Oh no! I don't believe this! I can't *conceive* this!"

And then the heat and blast hit.

Aimee McPherson let out a small shriek. For an instant she had been blinded by clear white light, and nothing like that had ever happened to her on this side of the veil. Migraine? Brain tumor? Surely such things were impossible here in her perfect Heaven. In that instant of questioning, she knew instinctively that it was a print-through from Semple. As if in confirmation, her body was suddenly racked by a surge of feeling that doubled her over and forced a gasping groan from her lips. "Oh my . . . "

She was about to appeal to God, but by now she was so far on the outs with the Almighty that she couldn't bring herself, even in this extremity, to utter his name.

"Oh my."

The nuns who were accompanying her on her walk on the terrace quickly gathered around, the cartoon bluebirds milled anxiously in the air, and a small winged Pegasus whinnied nervously. A novice stood beside her, wanting to put a comforting arm around her, but was too paralyzed by reverence to do so. "Are you all right, Mother Aimee?"

The sensation coursing through her body wasn't exactly unpleasant, but she wasn't about to admit that to the nuns. "Of course, I'm fine . . . except I'm wondering what in the hereafter my sister is up to."

⁎

Jim all but jumped out of his skin. Doc Holliday was the very last person he'd expected to see in the Jurassic, although later he'd realize that Doc was more than capable of being in any time or place he wanted to be, and on occasion in more than one place at a time. "What—"

Doc put an amused forefinger to his lips. "For mercy's sake, be quiet, boy. They'll hear you inside."

Jim dropped his voice to a whisper. "What the hell are you doing here?"

Doc was dressed for traveling. His boots were caked with mud and his long duster coat was stained with algae from the swamp. His pale face had a three-day growth of stubble and he appeared cumulatively hungover. He regarded Jim bleakly. "I'm getting you out of an entire mess of shit that, as of now, you're not even aware you're heading into."

Bewilderment seemed to be Jim's only option. "Mess of shit? What are you talking about?"

Doc indicated the deviant tableau in the room beyond the window. "That guy getting his back carved by the fire, that's you, only older, am I right?"

Jim nodded. "It sure looks like me."

Doc was becoming impatient. "It's you. Take my word for it."

"Is it really me, or is it another me?"

Doc pushed back his hat and looked sourly at Jim. "Don't get cute with me, boy."

"I was just asking."

"It's you. Accept it."

"And who's the woman doing the carving?"

"That's Semple McPherson."

Jim couldn't help but smile. "Are you telling me the initials were S and M?"

"You don't know her?"

"I don't think so."

"So you haven't met her yet?"

"Not that I can remember, and I think I'd remember her."

Doc thought about this. "Then I guess you'll meet her later. Or maybe you won't. Your alternate paths of destiny seemed to be busy tangling themselves in a highly untidy manner."

"So what's all this shit I'm about to get into?"

"I thought you might have learned better by now, but I guess you haven't."

"Learned better about what?"

"That it's a terribly bad idea to be meeting face-to-face with an older version of yourself. Most times, the results are messy for the bystanders and *apocalyptically* ugly for the two directly involved."

"Are you saying we ought to get out of here?"

"Right now, boy. With all the haste at our command."

"How are we going to do that? Dematerialize or something?"

Doc sighed. "You're getting a mite fancy, aren't you? We're getting out of here by boat. I've got one hidden under the trees. A motorboat of some power."

"A motorboat?"

"That's what I said. You have some problem with boats? You don't get seasick or anything unseemly like that, do you?"

Jim shook his head. "It's just that there are Viet Cong all over the place."

Doc frowned. "You're not telling me they can see you? You're not telling me that, are you?"

"No, they can't see me. I was just wondering if they could maybe see you."

Doc's face hardened. "Are you trying to insult me?"

Jim quickly changed the subject. He wasn't sure he and Doc were speaking in the same tongue and he decided it might be wise to stick to simple topics. "So shall we head for this motorboat of yours?"

Doc nodded. He and Jim straightened up and moved silently away from the window. Jim was about to turn for one final look back at the strange scene inside the room, but Doc shook his head. "It'd be best if you didn't."

"Pillar of salt?"

"Maybe worse."

The two men walked carefully through the grove of prehistoric trees, watchful for VC or anything else that might jeopardize their departure. As they were passing the rusting hulk of the car, Jim glanced questioningly at Doc. "Here's one thing I don't quite understand."

"What's that, my friend?"

"Why are you doing all this? Why are helping me like this?"

Doc was surprised by the question. "I figured after what you did for me, I owed you the courtesy of at least one favor. When one of the Mammals with No Name told me you were headed on out here to this godforsaken pile on your own, with no idea that the Old Jim was here already, I decided I'd better follow you and make sure you didn't get yourself blended or warped."

One confusion seemed to be progressively layering on the last. "After I did what for you? What did I do for you?"

Doc raised his eyebrows as though he still couldn't quite believe Jim didn't know what he was talking about. "When someone saves Doc Holliday from a room full of aura-tweaking Selenites, I generally consider I owe that man a personal debt of gratitude."

"I saved your ass from a bunch of aura-tweaking Selenites?"

Doc grinned. "Indeed you did. I thought I was pod-bound before you came gallantly walking into that misbegotten gin mill with a blaster in your hand."

Jim sighed. Once again, the world in which he found himself was shedding its resemblance to reality so rapidly, it was making his head spin. "Are you sure about all this?"

"It's hardly something a gentleman makes an error about."

"As far as I'm concerned, the last time I saw you, you were throwing me out of town."

Now it was Doc's turned to be confused. "How is it I have no recollection of that?"

Jim shrugged. "Like you've been telling me. Time and memory can get weird on you."

"So what do *you* think happened?"

"We were in this town you seemed to own. You came out of Sun Yat's opium den, then went into the cantina. When you came out, you told me to leave town."

Doc nodded. "That sounds like me. What happened next?"

"I protested some, and then Long Time Robert Moore offered me a ride . . . "

Doc seemed not to recognize the name. "Long Robert who?"

"An old blues guy with an alien connection."

Doc considered this. "Curiouser and curiouser, as Dr. Dodgson used to say."

"It's too late to worry about it."

"So what did I do when you protested?"

"You very pointedly showed me the Gun That Belonged to Elvis."

In almost a reprise of the night in question, Doc allowed his duster coat to fall open. The selfsame weapon nestled in a well-oiled shoulder holster. "This one?"

Jim nodded. "That's the one."

"At least something's consistent. So what was it you did to awaken my ire all the way back in Sun Yat's Palace of Mirrors?"

"It wasn't exactly what I did . . . "

"It hardly ever is, in retrospect."

"These three Voodoo Mystères came burning into town in a ball of fire and—"

Before Jim could finish, Doc's face darkened. He suffered a brief coughing fit, and when he was over it, his flamboyant and slightly inebriated tone dropped away. "Are you telling me the truth, boy? Voodoo Mystères are no joking matter."

Jim was losing his own patience. "Of course I'm telling the truth. There were three of them, Danbhalah La Flambeau, Dr. Hypodermic, and Baron Tonnerre—"

"Jesus wept, boy. Are you crazy? Don't say their fucking names out loud. We don't need that trio showing up. The Mystères have a nasty habit of coming if called." Doc halted and looked around as though he expected the unholy three to instantly appear out of nowhere. "Dr. Hypodermic visits this place enough, anyway. I half expected to cross his path on the way here." He scanned the horizon. "In fact, I still wouldn't be surprise to see one of his hearses rolling across the swamp."

Jim was now progressing from mystified to perturbed. "I really don't understand."

"No, you probably don't."

"Dr. Hypodermic rides a hearse?"

"He enjoys all manner of transportation. Although the old Rolls-Royce is among his favorites."

Doc paused for a moment, but when nothing happened, he took Jim by the arm. "Let's get to the goddamned boat. I have a nautical bottle stashed."

The boat turned out to be a solidly constructed heavyweight powerboat from the 1930s, with beautifully maintained and varnished timbers, tied up to a small dilapidated jetty. Doc went ahead to climb aboard first. He steadied the slight rocking of the craft as

Jim followed close behind. Jim was about to step into the boat when a sudden flare of light appeared silently, low in the western sky, as though reflected from someplace beyond the horizon, a white-through-red pulsation, accompanied by a strange twinge of unease. With the Voodoo Mystères still on his mind, Jim looked quickly at Doc, who was attempting to start the boat's engine.

"What was that?"

Doc turned the key in the ignition and the boat roared into life. He didn't seem unduly bothered. "It looked like a nuclear explosion in another quadrant."

"A nuclear explosion?"

"It's nothing to bother us."

Jim wasn't so sure. "A *nuclear* explosion?"

"There's no knowing what some folks will get up to."

"Is it my imagination, or are things getting out of hand?"

"My young friend, things have always been out of hand. It's just that, now the Afterlife is so goddamned crowded, we tend to notice it more." Doc gestured to the boat's mooring rope. "Cast off that line, will you?"

Jim did as he was told and then settled into the seat next to Doc. As soon as they were under way and heading out into the open water of the swamp, Doc brought out his nautical bottle of bourbon, took a pull on it, and handed it to Jim. "Have a drink, young Morrison. I think we got you out of there not a moment too soon. I shudder to think what might have come to pass if you and yourself had come face-to-face."

Jim gratefully accepted the bottle. "There is one other thing that's still puzzling me."

Doc adjusted the boat's course to avoid coming too close to a group of foraging diplodocuses. "What's that?"

"What was the story on the guy covered in bees?"

Doc blinked as though the story were stupidly obvious. "He's a guy covered in bees. What else? A lot of people keep one around."

"Why?"

Doc looked at Jim as if he were a total moron. "For the honey, of course."

5

Ħe don't say nothing.

Semple found herself spinning, half flying, feet lifted from the ground, tossed about in a violent, superheated vortex of dust, debris, and contorted figures; figures that were once human but now nothing more than radiating, dull red skeletons beneath smokelike flesh that barely retained its humanoid shape. Semple was probably screaming, but it was impossible to tell. No single voice, even her own, could rise above the howling cacophony that shrieked across the complete audio spectrum like the seismic howl of a world in cataclysm. Even the sliver of rationality that remained at the deepest core of her identity was filled with a bitter, all-consuming rage. "You really managed to do it this time, didn't you, you deranged fuck?"

The only thing that could have satisfied that tiny, articulate part of herself would have been learning that Anubis had so overdone his atom bomb test that he himself was now suffering in the same red-mist agony. She prayed, with a fervor worthy of Aimee in her stride, that his royal enclosure, with its cloth-of-gold hangings, its tasteless statues, simpering courtiers, and cannibal snacks, was being shredded in the radioactive maelstrom, that the towers of his despicable city would also soon be melting and burning.

At the same time, Semple's fury at Anubis was only a momentary distraction from her concern about what might actually be happening to her, and what lay on the other side of the burning nuclear hurricane. The all-consuming power with which it ripped at the very fabric of Necropolis surely had to presage a fate infinitely worse than just a return to the Great Double Helix. Semple's fear was that she was plunging through an event window that, for all practical purposes, would amount to a death beyond death, perhaps even to the long-rumored outer reaches of Limbo.

"Whatever nightmare I'm going into, I just hope you're going with me, you dogheaded bastard."

And yet there was no nightmare awaiting Semple, who merely tumbled anticlimactically to the burning sand as a rude, almost insultingly mundane afterflurry of earth tremor and hot wind sent her sprawling on her hands and knees. The storm of heat and dust and noise was over leaving her with ringing ears, a feeling of having been both flayed and roasted alive, but otherwise intact. The gold collar had become so hot that it was painful to touch; she tore it off and flung it angrily away from her. Moments earlier, it had been a priceless prize. Now it was worthless and irrelevant.

"Damn you and everything connected with you!"

The impossible had occurred; she had survived the atomic assault and if, right there and then, she could have expunged all trace of Anubis and his loathsome domain from her memory and consciousness, she would have done it. The mess that his grandiose folly had created was all around her. Red-ocher dust hung in the air, mingling with the smoke from dozens of small fires, cutting visibility to just a matter of yards. The once-garish flags and banners that had previously fluttered triumphant now flapped weakly in the last eddies of the explosion like burned and mutilated bats. What had once been a crowd was now a scattered profusion of bodies, like dry fallen leaves in the wake of a gale. They lay amid damaged, upturned pushcarts, buckled seats, and tangles of scorched draperies ripped from the viewing stands, and crawled from beneath other wreckage too blackened and twisted to be recognizable. Some almost immediately started sitting up, looking around, eyes glazed with uncomprehending shock, amazed as Semple that they were still in one piece. Others even tried to pick themselves up and rise unsteadily to their feet. Although their clothes were in tatters or ripped away entirely and they were caked with a combination of desert dust and a fine green-black atomic soot, most of those who were already moving looked to be only superficially the worse for the A-bomb trauma. On the other hand, there were quite a number who weren't moving at all. Next to her a motionless figure lay face down, apparently not breathing, so begrimed that Semple was unable to tell whether it was a man or a woman.

Suddenly the figure started to twitch. Its body was wrenched by an arrhythmic series of spasms. It let out a wrenching groan and slowly began to curl into a fetal ball. Something strange and unpleasant began to happen to its skin. At first Semple thought it was merely the coating of dust flaking off and causing a tracery of hairline cracks to spread rapidly across its torso and back; it was only after a moment, to her horror, that she realized the unfortunate's actual skin was cracking. Worse still, as the fissures widened, a thick and stinking liquid, the brown color of organic decay, began to ooze from within. As Semple watched, both mesmerized and nauseated, the entire body began wetly to disintegrate. What had once been living flesh melted in loathsome ropes and skeins of goo, away from a brittle ivory-yellow skeleton. Despite its obvious viscosity, this body slime quickly soaked into the sand until all that remained was a dark and foully septic oil slick surrounding a collapsing skeleton.

Semple's first instinct was to get away from this hideousness. She crab-scrabbled backward, putting as much distance as she could between herself and the sickening remains. After gaining a swift two or three yards, she angled her legs under her and sprang to her feet. Without thinking exactly where she might go, she turned and looked for a route of escape, only to find the same process of accelerated decomposition had more bodies in its disgusting grip. They jerked and contorted as they melted like vampires in the sun, creating a tableau like something from an especially lurid and gruesome fifteenth century painting, with a stench like that of a charnel house.

Not everyone, though, was coming apart. At least for the moment the ones on their feet seemed okay; cut, bruised, and battered, maybe, but definitely in one piece and with their bodily fluids just where they ought to be. Like Semple, they stared at what was happening to their erstwhile companions at the Divine Atom Bomb Festival with horrified revulsion. Had they been spared this hideous fate, or was the same thing about to happen to them? Semple looked down at herself. She was inconveniently naked, but otherwise she seemed intact. What had happened? How could it be that some turned to liquefying mulch and others didn't? Was it a matter of mind-set? Or were the ones oozing on the ground merely reproduction crowd fillers, while those who remained unaffected were true entities from the lifeside?

Just as Semple was gaining confidence, the first of the standing figures began to melt, quickly followed by a second and a third. Flesh streamed down their bodies like wax cascading down a blowtorched candle. Semple was suddenly and frighteningly certain she could feel something happening inside her own body. It was like a bizarre and disturbing tingle from what she could only describe as the place where flesh clung to bones. Her response was to shout in loud, angry defiance.

"No!"

She would not let herself go like that. She would not allow herself to be reduced to a skull, a rib cage, and a stain. She would hold her body together with the last measure of willpower she could muster. She concentrated, totally focused on locking in the integrity of her physical self, attempting to exert control over each cell, each engineered structure of bone and sinew, each circuital continuation of her nervous system, and each and every vein and artery down to the narrowest microcapillary. On the lifeside, such complete awareness and command of one's being would have been beyond anyone but the most advanced shaman; in the Afterlife, however, where so much of a person was a deliberate material construct, it was mercifully much easier, although the effort still involved an exhausting expenditure of energy.

On every side, survivors were divided into those who could halt the disintegration and those who couldn't. Some continued to melt, while others, as far as Semple could tell from the intense frowns on their begrimed faces, appeared to be doing the same as she. Within a matter of just two or three minutes, it was all over. Those who failed to hold themselves intact were gone. Only the strong maintained their shape. The last skeleton collapsed into the last putrid puddle on the sand, and then there were no more meltings. The whittled-down survivors peered around at each other, almost reluctant to believe that they were safe, afraid to jinx their comparative good fortune.

In the next few minutes, however, new troubles emerged. New and very different figures appeared in the lingering remains of the dust storm, not wandering dazedly, but moving with purpose and precision. Phalanxes of Anubis's guards, both Nubians armed with spears and regular Necropolis rocketeer police with flack jackets over torn and singed dress uniforms, and carrying far more formidable full-auto riot guns, advanced through the dust and debris.

Semple's stomach clenched. If these cops and Nubians were on their feet, disciplined and organized, the atomic explosion, far from razing Necropolis as she had hoped, must have done little more than muss the hair of those within the royal enclosure. She wondered if Anubis, his harem, or any of his court had fallen victim to the hideous flesh-melt. She passionately hoped that the dog-god was now nothing more than a canine skull, an oily skid mark, but she knew in her heart he wasn't. Anubis might be one of the most demented psychotics since Ivan the Terrible, but she couldn't pretend he didn't have the chops to survive. The real question was, what the hell did the cops and the Nubians think they were doing? The obvious assumption was that they had arrived to provide what aid and comfort they could to those who had survived the Divine Atom Bomb, but Semple somehow doubted that. Aid and comfort were simply not the God-King's style.

This was dramatically reinforced when a survivor, still confused from the effort of saving himself from the meltdown, stumbled blindly into a Nubian, who promptly ran him through with his gold-tipped spear. Nearby survivors reeled back in terror.

"What the fuck did you do that for?"

Outrage outweighed judgment among one knot of men who had witnessed the stabbing. They started angrily toward the line of mixed authority. "Are you bastards out of your fucking minds?"

No less than three riot guns roared into life, and the knot of bystanders was cut down in its tracks. For a moment, survivors stood stunned. What had they done? What was the slaughter all about? Why had these men, who they thought were the spearhead of some relief effort, suddenly turned on them? Then self-preservation took over. Whatever the reasons, the only hope of escaping was to run.

Semple had some ideas of her own, but she didn't stick around to test them. Her instinctive suspicion was that Anubis had gone completely insane after the nuclear malfunction, and ordered all those who had witnessed the debacle to be put to the sword or the machine gun. His technician-priests had almost certainly been executed already. To avoid her own extermination she scattered along with the rest, running swift zigzags as gunfire crashed out behind her and the wounded began screaming. For a few moments Semple sought cover to catch her breath, sheltering from the wild bursts of random shooting behind a solid copper boiler from the computer of a burned-out pushcart. Then the Nubians struck up a rhythmic vocal cadence, stamping their feet and calling the moves as they massed in a curved horns-of-the-bull formation. Once their blood was sufficiently up, they lowered their spears and advanced on the fleeing remains of the crowd at a measured lope. The atomic test site was about to become another kind of killing field.

Semple knew she wouldn't stay hidden for long. The mass of Nubians were sweeping forward, gathering speed, systematically impaling everything in their path, lifting bodies high on their spears while the rocket-man cops gunned down any stragglers that they might have missed. Semple broke cover and started to run, unpleasantly certain that the only possible escape led directly out into the desert, straight toward where the mushroom cloud stood tall and mockingly proud, gray-white and tinged with pink, surrounded by an aura of tiny glowing subparticles.

Doc Holliday waved a proprietary hand across the landscape. The Jurassic swamp was now far behind them, the sun was up, and the dinosaurs and weird scenes in the old mansion were diminishing in substance like the black gossamer of a fading nightmare. "Behold the Great River, my boy. Some will tell you that this is the genuine River Styx, the Central Transit of the True Hereafter. And who knows? Maybe they're right. You've never happened to find yourself on the Great River before, have you?"

Doc had decided that Jim needed to rest up after his trek through the swamp, and he had taken the helm of the boat while Jim lazed on the seat cushions in the stern of the launch, drinking and reflecting on how Doc cut something of an incongruous maritime figure, even in the context of this putative River Styx. His filthy, swamp-stained duster coat had been discarded, and he stood behind the wooden wheel in his slouch hat, ruffled shirt, and brocade vest, the skirt of his long gunman's frock coat whipping in the morning slipstream, as though he'd been displaced from another movie entirely. The elegant motor launch, with its varnished timbers and brass hardware, made a brisk twenty knots, its bow slicing a perfect V wave in the untroubled surface of the water as Doc carefully maintained a course a little to the left of the river's exact center. Jim took a drink, silently conceding that the legendary pistoleer could maintain a polished dandy's assurance and a stoned killer's certainty, no matter what the situation. He shook his head in answer to Doc's question.

"I can't remember being on the river, but then again, I still don't remember too much about too much. For all I know, I could have been running up and down this stretch of Styx like a full-time pirate."

Jim was growing a little irritated with the mess that was his memory. It had been bad enough when he'd been traveling alone, avoiding man-eating plants or fending off alien proctologists. Now that he seemed, for the present, to be running with Doc Holliday, he was forced to play novice to Doc's all-knowing mentor. It made for an irksome inequality in their relationship.

"They don't have too many pirates in this stretch of Styx. They mainly stay downstream, in the delta beyond the swamps, where the pickings are riper. This bit of the Great River is mainly for relaxing and admiring."

At least Jim was starting to feel alcohol-relaxed, which made Doc's geography lesson a little more palatable. He'd discovered that Doc had an entire marine cocktail cabinet in the form of a roomy ice chest stuffed with chilled beverages. With a tall green condensation-wet liter of Chinese Tiger beer augmenting his original bourbon, Jim was also doing his fair share of admiring. As Richard Nixon might have said, it certainly was a Great River, a great blue-gray-green, planet-scale artery of slow-flowing water, worthy of landscape paintings in styles from Rousseau to Turner. It flowed broad and smooth, with darker, moss-green rainforest overhanging each spacious bank, combining all the best features of the Mississippi, the Amazon, the Mekong, and the Zambezi. Somewhere inland, in the deep jungle, distant drums beat with a hollow and languorous baritone sensuality. Not drums of warfare or conflict, not the kind of drums that brought a man out in a cold sweat when they stopped, these were the drums of a slow ecstatic ritual in the name of some benignly sexual earth goddess who could make her followers understand that the Afterlife, far from being a shadowy projection of the mortality that had gone before, was actually a stripping of limitations, a removal of blinders and restraints.

The distant drums may have provided the sound, but what was left of Jim's poetic instincts told him that the river itself pulsed like a mighty hidden heart, from which all surrounding life emanated. It was the energy source of the monkeys who howled in the forest canopies and the thousands of parrots that would suddenly take to the air in brilliant multicolored clouds. It was the yellow light in the eyes of the black panther that slipped along a hunting trail, just yards in from the riverbank; it was what moved the cranes and kingfishers that darted in the shallows while hippos wallowed in the deeper waters. That so much vibrant life could exist in a place beyond death had Jim totally convinced that the Great River was more than just the creation of some master illusionist. If it hadn't been for recent events, Jim would have found the situation primally idyllic. Unfortunately, drink as he might, he couldn't altogether shake the impact of all the recent nightshade images. They might fade with the coming of the sun, but they refused to depart completely.

"It was kinda weird back there, Doc. One strange gold mine, that old house."

Doc didn't turn or take his eyes off the river. "I long ago gave up making judgments about what's weird and what isn't."

"It seems like it's going to be the way I end up, though."

"Beer-fat and sexually twisted ain't what you call ending up. It's nothing but one more piss stop on that lonesome highway."

Jim took a swig of beer and chased it with a little whiskey. "That's how I ended up on the lifeside. Fat and crazy in Paris. Except I was shooting dope instead of having some broad carve the mark of Zorro on my back with a sword. Of course, I died that time around."

"So you've done that one already. You won't be dying again. Only one per customer. That's the rule of the universe. Unless you count the reincarnies."

"Now time just keeps going out of joint on me."

Doc's shrugged, indicating that worse things could come to pass. "Do you miss it?"

"Paris or being fat?"

"Shooting dope."

Jim shook his head. "Come to think of it, not in the least. I guess, if you die of something, it maybe cures the craving."

"There's still plenty of heroin here in these afterdays. A lot of those coming across in recent times seem unable to resist the temptation to reconstitute themselves as junkies. I can't tell whether it's a new kind of self-abasement or just old habits dying hard."

Jim smiled wryly. "I did try it a couple of times after I got here."

Doc turned and looked at him. "One of the things you do remember?"

"Not the where or when, but certainly the doing."

"Not the same?"

"Some of the same seduction, but it didn't have that way about it."

"That way about it? That's a goddamned tame description, even for a self-proclaimed ex-poet."

Jim cringed slightly. "It didn't have that big jolt; that moment when Sister Morphine makes her promise of absolute and perfect peace, and it becomes the central core of all one's motivation. I guess, without the risk of death, a lot of the appeal goes out of it."

Doc nodded. Now Jim was at least trying to be articulate. "So you went back to drinking?"

Jim looked at the bottle in his hand. "I guess I did."

Doc laughed and beckoned to Jim. "Why don't you stop drinking and take the helm for a spell so I can do some kicking back and gazing at the scenery?"

With a certain unsteadiness on Jim's part, the two men switched positions and roles. Doc issued instructions as he settled himself in the stern. "Just keep her steady and don't try anything fancy. All the caveats about drunk driving also apply to boats."

Jim straightened his shoulders and gripped the wheel, attempting to act the part of the responsible helmsman. Doc rummaged in the ice chest. "All we had in my day was laudanum and opium."

"Wasn't that enough?"

"I kinda thought so, and so did a lot of other folks, from what I observed. In the golden days, it got so there was an opium den behind just about every laundry and chop suey joint from one end of the Santa Fe Trail to the other. And the shit they had back then, my boy, you wouldn't have believed it. We had Shanghai black tar so powerful that even Curly Bill Broscius and Wes Hardin were seeing visions of the Golden Buddha. Although Curly Bill, who was a fool at the best of times, would usually have to go and try to shoot out the goddamned moon, braying like an ass and claiming the Buddha made him do it."

"Is it true that Wes Hardin shot a man for snoring?"

"That's how the story goes. But I wasn't there, so I could hardly say for sure. I do know that Mr. Hardin was so all-out sociopathic that he'd kill his fellow man without even the courtesy of an excuse. A less oft-told tale is the one about how he carved a whore to dog meat for laughing at the size of his less-than-magnificent penis. She was a Hungarian harlot who called herself Magda, generous of mouth and thigh, but a little short on diplomacy when it came to what she found funny. That such a notorious desperado should be

211

hung like a hamster was just too much for her, and I fear her amusement cost her dear."

"You were there for that one?"

"Indeed I was, Jim Morrison, indeed I was. And an unpleasantly bloody business it was, too. I found myself tempted to call the son of a bitch out on the matter. I liked Magda, but sadly I didn't like the odds. Mr. John Wesley Hardin was pure, true, and deadly, and he had an arrangement with a backshooter who went by the name of Nathan Charlie Christmas to give him an extra edge if confronted by the likes of me. I feared he would have bested me, so poor Magda went unavenged. Such is too often the way with whores, particularly on the frontier. I believe Mr. Clint Eastwood made a film about a similar incident."

"The Mammal with No Name told stories like that."

"He most probably would. His name was Billy Blue Perkins and he had a mean and violent reputation, all through New Mexico and well across the border, for being a nasty homicidal drunk. I never met the man lifeside that I recall, but I saw a wanted poster for him once after he and his jolly saucy crew had raped and killed some nuns at a wedding party. Funny thing, he kinda looked similar to how he looks now. Kinda weasely of face, if you know what I mean."

"He's real remorseful now. Seems to want to be eaten by a pterodactyl."

Doc tilted his head knowingly and looked mildly contemptuous. "Not remorseful enough to let himself go all the way and be eaten, though."

Jim had to think about this for a few minutes. Doc was emerging as a high absolutist when it came to matters of guilt and morality. "Either regret nothing or go all the way and take the beating?"

Doc nodded. "That's always been my opinion, sir. For what small measure it may be worth."

Jim wasn't sure how much he agreed with Doc, but he was already a little too drunk to ponder the point. Instead, he changed the subject. "So who's this Semple McPherson I'm going to find myself shacked up with in my relative future?"

Doc raised an amused eyebrow. "Curious?"

"Wouldn't you be?"

"Maybe."

"You know her?"

"Maybe."

"But you're not going to tell me?"

"I think it's something you need to find out for yourself."

"It's seems I'm predestined to meet her, though."

"Who the fuck knows? I'd be the last one to claim that it's all written and unchangeable. Your timeline seems so fucked up I wouldn't bet bookmaker odds on anything."

Jim frowned. He was about to start worrying like a terrier at the paradoxical bone of the distortions of time and fate; but then a pleasure boat, a veritable palace in white and gold, hove into view, way ahead upriver, but coming toward them. Jim adjusted the wheel to give the larger boat a wider birth. Doc nodded his approval at the maneuver. "Stay out of her wake, boy. I don't want to get so rocked I spill my drink."

He coughed three or four times. Jim couldn't figure why Doc clung to his rotting lungs. "Are you ever going to do something about that TB?"

Doc shook his head. "I doubt it. It's like a trademark."

As the pleasure boat came closer, Jim marveled at its strange and luxuriously complex design, somewhere between a sculpted iceberg and a floating wedding cake, and far larger than he had first imagined when he'd seen it in the distance. It loomed over the launch like a small ocean liner, but like no ocean liner Jim had ever seen. Parts of it had the appearance of being constructed from custom-fabricated, translucent gemstone crystals, purposely and chemically grown but seemingly too huge to be plausible, especially with their heavy overlay of gold filigree and their surreal engineering. From out of nowhere, the phrase "crystal ship" jumped into Jim's mind, and reverberated in the wreckage of his memory. Where the hell had he heard that before? He glanced around to Doc. "That thing scarcely seems possible. Like it shouldn't exist, even here."

Doc nodded gravely. "I'll allow you don't see too many of those. In fact, I wasn't even aware he did boats. He usually sticks to dry land projects."

"Who does?"

"Phibes."

Doc nodded to the bigger craft, now almost level with them. His expression was one of weary disdain. "Yonder monster of overelaboration is a product of the excessively celebrated Runcible Phibes."

Jim frowned. "Should I know about Phibes?"

Doc pushed back his hat. It was the teacher/pupil routine again.

"Runcible Phibes is the leading light of the post-logical school. Some say post-logicalism is the first truly indigenous art movement of the hereafter, but I fear I am not one of them."

"Does it really float? Or run on wheels on the river bottom like those Pirates of the Caribbean boats at Disneyland?"

Doc snorted. "I've never yet laid eyes on Disneyland, boy. I was seventy years dead when that damned place opened."

"I wasn't thinking."

"I wouldn't worry about it. I suspect I didn't miss much. A good friend told me once, and I totally trust his judgment, that Disneyland put him in mind of what Hitler would have wanted the world to be after he'd killed everyone he didn't like."

Jim nodded. "That's definitely one way of looking at it."

The mushroom cloud grew in Semple's perception until it overwhelmed all else in the landscape. It seemed to be drawing her to it. Somehow its elemental force had managed to infiltrate her consciousness, as though it wanted to force her to join it, or at least to abase herself before it. It seemed to be talking to her, telling her it was the only symbol that remained for her, the Pillar of Cloud in the wildness, the Great Tree of Evil Fruit. She had almost called it the Tree of Life, but there was no way that the word "life" could ever be appropriate for this towering blossom of fundamental destruction, or the accursed place and equally accursed mind that had brought it into being. The only mercy was that, in running to it, she had left the Nubians way behind. Where most of the pursued had milled around and attempted to double back, to circle toward the city, Semple had carried on as straight and as fast as she could, directly into the desert. The ones who had tried to return to Necropolis had been sent bloodily to another place. The curve of the Nubian formation had surrounded them, the horns of the bull had closed, the golden spears went to work, and the victims took their leave of Anubis's desert, to the pods with a final scream. As far as Semple could observe, she and the rearing atomic cloud were all that remained.

She looked back a number of times, just to make sure all pursuit had ceased, before she felt safe enough to stop running and attempt to catch her breath. It was only when she finally stopped that she realized just how winded she was. She leaned forward, hands on knees, eyes closed, bent double, gasping, with the circulation pounding in her head. Her legs were shaking and threatening to give out on her. For one fearful moment, she wondered if this heralded the onset of another bout of the melting horror, but her body managed to struggle back to normality and she slowly straightened up. For a brief time, this fear of the melting had pushed the influence of the atomic cloud out of her mind. As she reopened her eyes, she half hoped that it might have gone, borne away on some desert wind, but the mushroom of poison vapor was still in front of her, showing no sign of dissipating or even losing its shape. Indeed, the mighty fungoid head, atop its roughly cylindrical trunk, appeared to be expanding still, growing between her and the sun, so that a dark shadow advanced across the blast-blown desert directly toward her. A new impulse suddenly entered her mind. She no longer had to go to the cloud. All she had to do was to wait for the shadow to come to her.

As far as she could tell, the outer edge of the cloud-cast shadow was maybe seventy yards from her, but it was moving quickly closer. It seemed to cover the desert at something well in excess of walking pace, and the seventy yards quickly dwindled to fifty, thirty, twenty-five, and the nearer it came, the more her strength ebbed, leaving her without the will to resist or flee. As it moved inexorably closer to the immediate ground on which she stood, she began to feel almost transparent, as though her very being were ebbing. What was this? Some bizarre new unknown ending? With the shadow just a few feet from her, she felt as though she could no longer breathe; her motor functions spun out of control, she was hot and then cold, her thoughts became randomized, without thread or pattern. She was scattering. She hardly knew who she was, even had doubts as to *what* she was. And then the shadow touched her and she became a part of the blackness that hid the sun. As a conscious being, Semple ceased.

Doc shaded his eyes and looked more closely at the passing pleasure boat. "I see they have their own shipboard entertainment."

A dancer was performing for a small audience on the quarterdeck of the great white and gold river palace. All but naked, she turned, undulated, and pranced, legs lifted high in mock classic symbolic poses that looked to Jim privately like bullshit, having engaged in some similar bullshit himself back in the days of yore. The dancer's arms dipped and waved, trailing a long chiffon scarf. Jim grinned at Doc. "Isadora Duncan disciple?"

"It could be the divine Isadora herself."

"You think so?"

Doc squinted from beneath his hat, looking more closely at the dancer. "It's too far to tell for sure, but it looks like her. If I just had binoculars powerful enough that I could see her mole, I'd know . . . "

"You know her?"

"Isadora took a fancy to me once, way back down the road. I recall we spent a memorable three nights in a hot-sheet, yab-yum motel out on one of the caravan routes."

"You're kidding me."

"As a gentleman, I surely can't elaborate. It did seem, though, even back then, the manner of her death hadn't done anything to put her off her taste for flowing scarves."

"Isadora Duncan, huh?"

"Watch your course there, boy."

They had passed the bigger ship now, but while Jim's attention had been fixed on the dancer, he had allowed the launch to drift uncomfortably close to its backwash. He quickly adjusted the wheel and then took a final look at the dwindling form of the near-nude dancer. He grinned at Doc. "Three nights, huh?"

Doc pulled down his hat so his eyes were hidden. "Maybe, in some time yet to come, my boy, you'll take this Semple McPherson to the same place. If you find yourself doing that, ask for a hostess called Shen Wu. She really likes her work."

Jim didn't smile. The idea of this woman who might be in his future filled him with both unrequited curiosity and a strange unease. He turned back to steering a straight course and did his best not to think about her. He knew that kind of obsessive thinking about something he could do nothing about was a guaranteed shortcut to neurosis.

While Jim was trying not to think about the mysterious Semple McPherson, Doc drank in the shade of his hat brim. Each in his own way was too absorbed to notice another, smaller appearance on the river. A hundred yards astern of the launch, the black upper lens housing of a submarine's periscope broke the surface and peered unblinkingly in its direction.

※

"A woman is a better conductor of heat than steel."

"What?"

"Aluminum is a better conductor of heat than steel."

"I have to be dreaming."

"A shaman is a letter seductor to cheat and steal."

"Oh no, I must be dreaming."

But how could she be dreaming when she never slept? Semple had not constituted herself for sleep when she had separated from Aimee. At times, her spirit might wander; not exactly as lonely as a cloud, but equally ethereal. She knew, however, that this wasn't one of those times.

"A hymen is abetting the reaction to beat and feel."

"Stop this now!"

Semple seemed to be somewhere underwater, deep water; somewhere in the depths of a deep body of water, and the repeating, distorting, irritating voice had a deep, sewer-pipe, bubbling sound that bounced and came back at her like the ping pulses of sonar. "A dolmen is—"

"I said, *stop*."

The repeating irritating voice changed. It suddenly sounded resentful, querulous. "But I go with the hallucination."

"I'm trying to rid myself of the hallucination."

Exotic, multicolored warm-water fishes swam all around her; above her head, a large object, perhaps a submarine or an aquatic reptile, moved purposefully between her and the rippling dapple-green light that had to be the surface of the water. Semple had known at once this was a hallucination. If the atomic cloud had actually somehow returned her to a primal sea of origin and rebirth, some unknown parallel of the Great Double Helix, she knew she'd be accepting it with a lot more resignation. In fact, all she wanted was to fight. She wanted to kick out and swim to the surface and scream in fury at whatever fate had precipitated her into this fine new mess. Moreover, if this were the Helix, she wouldn't be so goddamned thirsty. Despite being entirely immersed, she was parched, her tongue swollen, her lips threatening to crack. She knew that to slake the thirst, all she had to do was open her mouth, but something told her with that first drink she would also drown, and be swept away to the Great Double Helix.

But how could she drown if she had no body? The realizations and revelations were coming thick and fast. In a flash she knew that the raging, illogical underwater thirst was the only corporeal aspect to this entire new episode. She looked down, or rather, she *perceived* down and saw . . . *nothing,* no legs to kick, no arms to power herself upward, no body to move. She seemed to be nothing more than a bubble of consciousness; and her consciousness had no buoyancy. All the time she remained submerged and without physical form, she seemed to be sinking deeper, until the light from above became a vestigial thing. The fish took partners, touched fins, and waltzed in these newly plumbed depths, their own luminescence providing passing mirror-ball highlights in their watery ballroom. She might have stopped to admire this circling aquarial tableau had she not been so consumed with fury; and yet the angrier she became, the faster she sank. "What the hell is going on here? Is this supposed to be some kind of torture? If so, what the fuck did I do? Whoever's doing this, at least have the balls to show your goddamned self!"

This outburst finally took her all the way to the bottom, where she bounced leadenly on surprisingly hard and resilient mud, and then came to rest, an angry and misshapen balloon, like those toxic orange ones made from that plastic ooze from a tube that hucksters used to sell to kids at fairgrounds. Dark, submarine plants undulated around her with the current; she lay, helpless and immobile, like one more piece of discarded jetsam on the bottom of this unholy sea. Surely this wasn't her final fate? Was she condemned to remain there, unable to do anything but gather silt and watch the fish dance?

"Oh no, I must be dreaming."

But how could she be dreaming when she never slept? Semple had not constituted herself for sleep when she had separated from Aimee. At times, her spirit might wander . . .

At the very moment her repeating thoughts began to circle back on themselves, the water miraculously started to fade. The hallucination must have completed its cycle. Her surroundings were increasing insubstantial, and she could feel her body gradually reasserting itself. The sensation was one of rising, going up through the darkness to the light. She was pleased that she wasn't going to be imprisoned, disembodied, in a sagging, orange plastic sac, but the experience reminded her a little too much of her and Aimee's death, and that did a lot to temper her relief. This time she was confronted with a new set of illusions, hallucinations, call them what she might. The first arrived in the twilight zone of her ascent. He was a tall, impossibly angular, and scarcely human figure in what looked like a cross between black undertaker's weeds and white tie and tails. The outfit was completed by a tall stovepipe hat, and the face under that hat was nothing more than a naked skull with glowing coal-ruby eyes. When this bizarre figure moved, it generated flashes of blue electricity. Semple knew she should have been afraid, but somehow she wasn't—even when the deaths-head face peered into hers so close that she could smell the neglected freezer reek of his breath, and hissed. "Where is Jim Morrison?"

The question made no sense to Semple. "I don't know any Jim Morrison."

"I am Dr. Hypodermic and I am looking for Jim Morrison."

"I just told you, I don't know any Jim Morrison."

The naked skull laughed. "You will, my dear, you will." And with that, it faded away. Body first, then face, ruby eyes remaining long after the rest of it had gone.

She rose on her own for a while longer, until she thought she spotted another figure; but this one remained in the shadows, showing no desire to approach her. For an instant she thought it might be the hooded form of Anubis's Dream Warden, but she couldn't be sure. If it was, could he be the author of whatever was happening to her? She had no time to think about it, though. Now angry, nasal, trailer-trash voices were shouting in the gathering nothingness, as though from a great distance, and the things they were saying did not bode well for whatever was next to come.

"Behold the naked harlot."

"The naked harlot is a trap for the ungodly."

"The naked harlot is set here as a trap for those who might linger wistfully on the sins of the flesh."

The ugliness of the tone was one Semple knew well from her life on Earth. She was surfacing among the viciously righteous.

"We must cast her from us."

Aimee's people, not hers.

"Let her be driven out and eaten by dogs."

The frying pan was once again tilting into the fire.

"Stone the whore!"

"In the name of the Lord, stone the whore!"

"So are we there yet?"

Jim and Doc had now been drinking for what Jim subjectively

conceived of as the entire long afternoon. He was well past his initial elation at being reunited with Holliday and at being rescued from the Jurassic. Bourbon shots with beer chasers had put Jim into a disgruntled discontent. His past was as fragmented as a surrealist quilt and his future looked to promise little more than prolonged degeneration and perversity. Like every drunk knew but usually forgot, introspection and booze never mixed well.

"So how soon do we get where we're going?"

Doc had declined to answer Jim's first Bart Simpson challenge, recognizing it as mere alcoholic petulance. When Jim asked a second time, Doc stared at him coldly; he, too, was reflective and grumpy from his own share of onboard drinking. "If you're going to get fractious and start whining before you've even finished your first bottle, I might start to surmise that maybe it wasn't such a bright idea for me to haul your sorry ass out of the mire back there."

Jim's face hardened. "I thought you did it because you owed me."

Doc's expression didn't change, except for his left eye, which took on a dangerous glint. "I didn't have to volunteer to pay the debt quite so freely, though, did I?"

Jim hadn't drunk so much that he failed to realize he was drawing close to the line. He was being unreasonable, and maybe a little ill-mannered, and a half-drunk Doc Holliday was hardly the kind of man with whom one copped attitudes. Jim shrugged. "I'm sorry. I guess I'm just kinda wondering how long we're going be on the river."

"You ought to know by now, kid. All time is relative."

The boat journey, which Jim was starting to view as an extended and now largely unwanted Disneyland ride, was getting tired. He'd already seen plenty of water in the swamp, and he was more than ready for some hot nights, and at least the illusion of being in a big city. His outlandish encounter with the alien creations Epiphany and Devora was far enough behind him to start him thinking about women. Images of women in the sexual abstract, long legs, flashing eyes, ruby lips, swaying hips, curly pubic hair, high-heeled shoes, cries and whispers, and revealing, although not yet specified, costumes—all flickered beckoningly at the peripheries of his mind, eager to lead him to the edge of that old-fashioned temptation and the urge to be elsewhere. He couldn't believe that Doc, from what he knew of him, wasn't feeling the same way, too.

It didn't help that the river had taken a decided turn for the depressing. The broccoli-colored jungle had been left far behind; now they were traveling in a corrupted Arizona, between tall, hollowly echoing cliffs of unhealthy sponge-yellow sandstone. In the shallows the water ran so thick with that silt that it gave these margins the look of diseased urine. Most of the animal life seemed to have gone, except for the buzzards and ravens that constantly circled overhead and, in the few patches of comparatively clear water, the swift outline of large, sinister fish. Here and there, on the river bottom, Jim could make out what looked to be masses of large orange spheres, angry and misshapen balloons, like those toxic orange ones made from that plastic ooze-in-a-tube that hucksters used to sell to kids at fairgrounds. Jim could only suppose they were egg sacs, laid, or maybe spawned, by some toadlike river life he had no desire to meet, undesirable and very large.

Jim's overall impression was that the higher they moved on the river, the less benign its aspect. As if to make this perfectly clear, a galley straight out of *Ben Hur* had labored past them a little earlier, complete with sweating, groaning slaves, whip-wielding overseers, a relentless and muscular drummer, an aroma of shit and misery, and an obese, toga-clad Nero figure lounging on the quarterdeck with body-slaves peeling grapes for him. Where in its first, jungle-fringed reaches the Styx had been close to idyllic, it was now turning blighted and grim. Doc had stared at the wretched fantasy trireme as it creaked past, but had not felt moved to comment. Both he and Jim were lapsing into long bouts of silence.

For Jim, real confirmation of the downhill slide arrived when the launch passed the huge tail fin of a downed B-52, sticking up from a roughly cylindrical tangle of submerged and rusting wreckage. The huge jet appeared to have crashed, long ago, halfway up the cliff wall and then dropped, smashing down in what must have been a spectacular impact at the water's edge. What Jim couldn't figure was how any pilot would have been able to pull off such a maneuver. The old nuclear bomber would have needed the performance vectors of a UFO to make it down into a canyon that, at its narrowest point, was only slightly wider than the plane's wingspan. The presence of a B-52, though, was enough of an uncomfortable memory, straight out of Vietnam, to make Jim lose any remaining enthusiasm for aimlessly rolling on the river.

Even the weather was taking a turn for the negative. In the shadowy places, where the sandstone walls rose to a hundred feet or more, the river grew chilly and a dank veil of cheap Bela Lugosi fog shrouded the water. What little sky was visible had darkened from blue to an implacable slate gray, and then became increasingly obscured by ominous near-black clouds.

"Are those rain clouds?"

"Smoke."

"Smoke?"

"Smoke from Gehenna."

Jim straightened up. "Gehenna?" He rose from the seat cushions in the stern of the launch and lurched toward the bow. "I have to see this."

Doc was taking his turn at the helm, making him once again irritable. "It's quite a sight, I promise you that."

Jim looked up at the dark clouds overhead. "It is smoke."

"That's what I told you."

"How soon till we see Gehenna itself?"

"You want to take the wheel for a spell?"

Jim nodded. He knew it was the least he could do if he wanted to get back into Holliday's good graces. "Sure."

The two men changed places and Doc sagged back into the cushions, reaching for a drink. "Just take us around the curve nice and easy, and for fuck's sake don't go running us into an oil rig or something else up there in the mist."

"Oil rigs?"

"I don't know. They look like oil rigs. Big metallic shit, planted on legs on the middle of the river. God only knows what folks do on 'em." Doc scowled. "All I know is we don't want to be stuck anywhere in the immediate vicinity of that smoking garbage dump they call Gehenna. Hell no. That's something we can absolutely do without. You read me?"

"I read you."

"And while you're at it, try not to hit any mines."

"Mines?"

Doc ignored Jim's expression of surprise and concern. "You sure you're not too drunk to be doing that?"

Jim quickly shook his head. He wanted to know about the mines. "There are mines on the Styx?"

Doc made a dismissive gesture. "On this stretch? No. Not too many, and most of them are back down near the swamps and on into the delta. Leftovers from the Barbiturate Wars. But you do see one bobbing past every now and again. Let me know it you spot one."

Jim took a deep breath. "Don't worry. I will."

The prospect of mines proved to be a highly sobering one. Jim was suddenly seeing single again, taking deep gulps of river air and giving all his attention to the navigation of the launch. It never ceased to amaze him how, since his death, some things had become so much easier. It was possible, if need be, to come out of the effect of intoxicants almost with a snap of the fingers. Of course, other things had grown nearly impossible. The writing of poetry was a case in point; Jim had reached the stage of wondering if his loss of creativity was caused, in some part, by the equal loss of any need to hedge his bets against death. Did other artists lose interest, on this side of the veil, in what had previously been the driving force in their lives? It hardly seemed so. Whoever had conjured a B-52 into the bottom of a canyon had to be up for some conceptual rock and roll sculpture pranking. And then there was this Phibes, with his seagoing wedding cake. Maybe Jim would have to fess up and admit he'd simply blown himself out back lifeside.

Blown out or not, self-deluded or not, this wasn't the time to be thinking about it. Following the curve of the river was a little harder than Doc Holliday had made it seem. High formidable cliffs loomed on either side of the narrowest channel they had yet encountered. The Styx had carved deep into the landscape, producing cliff walls with high curved overhangs, and ran fast and choppy, creating small white wavelets as it went into each tight turn. The launch, although powerful, had to run hard to make headway against the stream and repeatedly bucked the flow. Jim had to use both hands to maintain control of the wheel and keep the craft on a straight course. Any serious deviation would have been treated by the river as an invitation to hurl the boat into the rock face and smash its deep varnished panels into matchwood.

"You all right up there, Jim lad?"

"Shipshape and Bristol fashion, Skipper."

"You just keep it that way."

"She needs a firm hand now and again."

"Don't they all, kid."

"You say Gehenna's just around the bend."

223

"You just focus on the firm hand, boy. You'll see Gehenna in all its gory glory soon enough."

"Stone the whore!"

At first Semple was blind. The only information she was receiving was aural and tactile. She knew she had returned to her familiar body, which was of some comfort, but this was offset by the indignity of being stretched out on her back, totally without clothes, on hard stony dirt, staring straight up into a blindingly bright sun in a dangerously clear sky. She was covered by a fine layer of dust that even packed her nose, mouth, and ears, as though, in temporal reality, she had been lying there for quite some time. She also sensed that a number of people were standing over her. Presumably the ones who were talking about stoning the whore. It was possible that she wasn't the whore in question, but she wasn't holding out too much hope. Luck had hardly been with her on this adventure. Pain shot through the muscles of her arm as she raised a hand to shield her eyes from the sun. She really had been lying there a long time. As her vision gradually returned, she could make out dark shapes leaning into her field of vision, peering down at her through the sundogs and colored retinal burn. They *were* talking about her.

"I say get her on her feet and whip her out to the badlands."

"Stoning her would be quicker."

"She's right. We can't waste any time today. The Patriarch is in a foul temper. He wants to make twenty miles by nightfall."

One voice had a particularly snide and insinuating tone. "Maybe he'll change his mind when he gets a look at her. A good punishment could be just the thing to improve his mood."

As Semple's eyes grew more accustomed to the light, the darker shapes began to assume form. Now she was looking up into a circle of faces that were as coarse, malformed, and ignorant as any that could be found in any part of even the darkest backwoods of Arkansas or Mississippi. Narrow, suspicious eyes peered down at her from under low brows and lumpy foreheads. A hand came toward her, but she ducked away from it with a snarl. "You won't touch me if you know what's good for you."

The hand jerked back. Just as on Earth, Semple thought, trash was trash and you had to show it who was boss. Despite all of her disorientation and naked vulnerability, she had to take the offensive. Whatever might happen to her here, it could hardly be worse than what she had been subjected to at the hands of Anubis, Fat Ari, Mengele, and the rest. She was heartily sick of being shoehorned into a whimpering victim role. This time, she'd be damned if she was going to take it lying down, literally or otherwise. She snarled again and the circle around her backed off. The snarling routine seemed to be working, so she tried it a third time, with even more feeling, using it as a cover while she rolled over to get her hands and knees under so she could spring to her feet with a quick leap. As soon as she was on two legs, she dropped into a simian defensive crouch. She knew she probably made a scary enough sight to begin with, and she hoped that behaving like a feral thing might spook them entirely. If these fools believed she was some kind of desert djinni, some banshee she-devil, let them. Just as long as they stayed good and terrified, they'd be much less likely to start reaching for the rocks they'd seemed so gung-ho to start hurling a few moments earlier.

She turned slowly; snorting through her nose with what she hoped was sufficiently demonic ferocity. It certainly seemed to be working. The circle around her retreated another couple of paces. She continued to turn, acting every inch the cornered succubus, carefully observing all the while. The small crowd was completely composed of women, although, a short distance away, a number of men and a flock of scrawny, black-faced sheep stood staring; dealing with she-demons was women's work. The women in question were possibly the ugliest and most depressing collection of broads she had ever encountered. Perhaps she could somehow turn this to her advantage. If these horrors were a representative sample of local womanhood, the men might well be drawn to their sheep; given the look of the men, the sheep were the ones truly getting the shitty end of the deal. And Semple knew whereof she spoke. The camp meetings they had run when she and Aimee were alive and one, starting out on the rocky road to fame and fortune in the evangelism racket, had attracted more than their fair share of the benightedly repugnant. This bunch clearly thought of themselves as the Children of Israel in a wilderness straight out of the *Classics Illustrated* Book of Exodus, but to her they resembled nothing more than a bunch of Ozark inbreds without even the benefit of dilapidated Ford trucks. She had managed their kind before; if they didn't immediately turn violent, she could manage them again.

The women came in all shapes and sizes, from eating disorder blubber to rawboned and desiccated. They were all dressed in cheap, coarse, Old Testament homespun, but their faces made them look like Elvis's educationally challenged cousins on his daddy's side: sour, mean, and ignorant, with built-up heads of resentment that stretched back so many generations it was encoded in their DNA. One who was a little braver than the rest, a tall streak of sour vinegar, turned and faced her companions. "I say stone her now. Before she can put a hex on the lot of us."

Semple laughed nastily. "You're all double-hexed already. You'll have boils all over your bodies within the hour."

She hoped this would put the fear into them. It seemed to work on some, who stopped glaring at her and began nervously peering inside the loose caftans, in search of latent blemishes. The tall woman, however, was not one of these. Semple had miscalculated. The threat only made her more determined. "How many times do I have to tell you? Stone the abomination, whatever it is!"

The tall woman appeared to possess a certain natural authority; after only a few seconds of hesitation, a majority of the others were bending down, reaching for rocks, pleased that someone was doing their thinking for them, and that the thinking involved direct and easy action. They started moving back, widening the circle so they wouldn't hit each other when the boulders commenced to fly. This wasn't going Semple's way. Trying somehow to crack this reality, Semple looked around wildly, but she knew it was impossible. Dull, fearful, and brutish they might be, but there were too many women gathered in this place for her to erase them with her mind. They didn't even need the sheep's help to keep this bit of stinking desert intact. She didn't want to believe she was going to be stoned back to the Great Double Helix by a bunch of primitive hick herdspersons, but it sure looked that way. If worse came to worst, was there any way to avoid the pain? She had to find an answer, and soon. The women were already winding up to throw. But then, miraculously, the cavalry charged to the rescue. There came an impossibly deep and booming voice: "AND WHAT IN THE NAME OF THE LORD IS GOING ON HERE?"

The voice resonated with fundamentalist and wholly phony electronic bass reverb. A new player had entered the auditorium. The women dropped their rocks, panic-stricken. As one they raised their right arms and signed an invisible circle in the air, hands arranged with index and middle finger extended, much in the same manner as a Pope blessing the multitude. Later Semple would find out that this was the so-called Sign of the Eternal Continuation, with which the followers of the Patriarch were expected to pay tribute to their leader. In other parts, she would also learn, it was known as the Universal Sign of the Donut. This new player was close to seven feet tall, with wild white hair, flowing robes, the beard of a prophet, and a carved wooden staff in his right hand. He'd had the good grace not to make himself look exactly like Charlton Heston, but he wasn't far off. Semple knew this had to be the Patriarch. Before she'd agreed to go on Aimee's fool's errand, she'd been aware that some damn silly demented Moses was on the loose in the wilds, pretending to look for the Promised Land with a bunch of retard followers. She heard he staged orgies just so he could get his kicks smiting the sinners. If this wasn't he, it had to be another exactly like him.

The Patriarch acknowledged the women's salute with a curt motion of the staff and repeated his demand. "I ASKED YOU, WHAT IS GOING ON HERE?"

The women avoided his eyes; not even the tall one managed to muster the courage to answer, so Semple, deciding she really had nothing to lose, placed both hands on her hips and adopted a pose of nude, if dusty, defiance. "This bunch of weary, sheep-cuckolded hags was trying to get up the nerve to stone me to death."

The Patriarch slowly looked her up and down. Although he maintained a pose of righteous outrage, Semple saw something else in his eyes that was far from righteous and all too familiar. The son of a bitch was as horny as the next guy. Maybe hornier. As Patriarch, he was probably above seeking the comfort of sheep. Catching on, she posed like a cheap pinup. "You must be this Moses character I've been hearing about."

"INDEED I AM MOSES, THE PROPHET OF THE LORD THY GOD, AND WHAT MANNER OF NAKED ABOMINATION ARE YOU?" Without waiting for an answer, Moses waved an arm in the direction of the now-silent women. "BRING LINEN TO COVER THIS THING!"

A short, fat woman hurried away and quickly returned with a rough, homespun caftan like the ones she and the others were wearing. She seemed frightened to approach Semple; only when Moses glared at her did she dare to step forward, eyes averted, to hand the garment over. Semple snatched it from her, as though impatient with all the fear and hesitation. It was probably the ugliest piece of apparel that Semple had ever been expected to wear, and before putting it on, she inspected it slowly and carefully. Although the same dun color as the desert, it seemed reasonably clean and free of lice, so finally she slipped it over her head and turned around as though modeling the thing for Moses. "Is that better? You'd rather have me clothed and shapeless?"

Moses seemed a little unnerved by Semple's pirouette, but covered himself by roaring even louder, "I ASKED YOU WHAT YOU ARE AND WHERE YOU COME FROM!"

Semple was determined not to be intimidated by Moses' crude bombast. She'd heard enough voice-amplification tricks in the court of Anubis not to be blown away by this fool's bass boost and slap-back echo. She stood her ground and inspected the Patriarch with an expression that verged on insolence. "Is this how you treat an unfortunate traveler who has fallen to misfortune in the wilderness?"

Clearly Moses wasn't accustomed to being addressed in this manner. Most of his followers were probably too dumb and brainwashed to speak unless spoken to directly. "I DEMAND TO KNOW WHAT YOU ARE AND WHERE YOU COME FROM!"

"You think you might lower the volume a little? I really find it very hard to conduct any kind of conversation under these circumstances. And while we're at it, if someone doesn't offer me some water, I'm liable to die of thirst and dehydration before you find out anything about me at all. I always assumed the giving of water, even to a stranger, was common courtesy among all desert peoples, no matter how primitive."

This gave Moses the easy out of barking another order. "FETCH HER WATER!"

Semple now knew she had the measure of this biblical blowhard. He didn't want to see her stoned any more than she did. At least not until he'd had a chance to get her on her own and see if she was up for a little patriarchal bodily tribute. And yet he seemed uncertain how to pull if off with all the women, plus the men and the sheep, watching his every move. Don't worry, Moses my boy, she thought. I'll give you any help you need. Just get me away from these potential rock throwers.

This time a different woman waddled quickly off to do the Patriarch's bidding. When she returned with an earthenware pitcher, she, too, shied away from eye contact. The water tasted brackish, but it was cool and wet, and just what Semple's parched throat gasped for. She drank slowly and with care, however. She was well aware that drinking too much, too fast under these conditions could cause all manner of physical problems, and she wasn't about to take any chances. She also suspected that, among the Moses Family, water was strictly rationed. If so, another way by which she might assert her separateness and superiority over this badland trash presented itself. When she'd finished drinking, she poured the rest of the contents of the pitcher slowly and deliberately over her head. As she'd expected, the women let out a collective gasp at her cavalier attitude to what, for them, was a precious fluid. She ignored their response and handed the container back to the woman with a satisfied sigh. "God, that was good."

Moses immediately rounded on her with a bellow. "YOU TAKE THE LORD'S NAME IN VAIN?"

Semple looked at Moses as though she were starting to lose patience. "Will you get off it? I know exactly what you are. And I'm not impressed by all your bellowing and bluster."

For a moment, she thought she might have overplayed her hand. Moses looked around at his followers as though he were going to give the order to let the stoning begin all over again, but instead he merely waved an angry arm. "DON'T YOU PEOPLE HAVE WORK TO DO? GET ABOUT YOUR ALLOTTED TASKS AND STOP STANDING AROUND GAPING. THERE'S NOTHING MORE TO SEE HERE."

Semple nodded to herself. Good thinking, pal. Send the common herd back to their business so we can get down to ours. As the crowd of women reluctantly moved away, he turned back to Semple. "NOW WILL YOU TELL ME WHO AND WHAT YOU ARE?"

At the sound of his voice, many of the followers stopped in their tracks and stared at the exchange. Some of the sheep bleated uneasily and Semple sighed. "It really might be an idea to lower the volume a bit. It doesn't impress me and makes it hard to retain our privacy."

For an instant Moses looked as though he were about to strike her down with his staff. Lust and the need to maintain authority stood conflicted. Then lust won out and he lowered the staff, at the same time killing the echo and reverb. He took a deep breath. It seemed he'd been playing the Wrath of God for so long that normal conversation was hard for him. "So what are you?"

Semple half smiled, restrainedly coquettish. "All you needed to do was ask me nicely."

His anger started to boil again. "Who are you and what are you doing in my desert?"

"I'm just an unfortunate refugee from cannibalism and fornication."

Moses blinked. "Are you serious?"

"I just escaped from of the city of Necropolis. You know about Necropolis?"

"Of course I know about Necropolis."

"And its dog-god Anubis?"

"May his name be cursed." The response was an unthinking reaction. Moses was intrigued. Semple moved a little closer to the Patriarch, as though she wanted to confide in him. She was aware that the women were still covertly watching. "Anubis just let off one of his dirty little atom bombs, except this one was a bit bigger and more complicated than I suspect he anticipated. I'm surprised you didn't see the flash or feel the shock."

Moses' face stiffened. "We saw the flash *and* felt the shock. The goats panicked and the herdsmen have only just finished rounding them up."

Semple smiled knowingly and gestured to the tribe. "That must have been a hard one to explain to the faithful. They don't look like they're quite up to the concept of nuclear technology."

"I told them it was Lucifer spawning demons from the lightning."

Semple laughed and nodded. "I guess that's close enough."

"You're one of Anubis's constructs?"

"I'm nobody's construct, pal. I was only in Necropolis because, out of the goodness of my heart, I went there on an errand for my sister."

Moses looked at her sharply. "SISTER?"

Unintentionally, he had put the echo and reverb on at full power. Semple clapped her hands over her ears. "Don't do that!"

Moses cut them off. "I'm sorry. It's a habit. What about your sister?"

Semple realized she might have said too much. "Nothing, she's just a sister."

Moses' eyes narrowed and he shot her a sly, sideways look. "You're not Aimee Semple McPherson, are you?"

Now it was Semple's turn to take a deep breath. "I'm Semple McPherson. Aimee and I separated a while ago. I guess you could say we used to be in the same racket as you."

Moses frowned, then stared speculatively a Semple. "I think we'd better take this conversation to my tent. It's a little too public out here. I have to keep up my image in front of the rubes."

Semple kept her face expressionless. His guard was down now and he was revealing himself for the con artist he really was. This faux Moses could talk about rubes, but she had him as hooked as any carny mark on the midway.

His first sight of Gehenna was enough to make Jim wish that he was drunk again. Even before visual contact, the stench that wafted down the river, the stink of punishment and pain, of violated bodies, ozone, sulfuric acid and ammonia, hot blood and decaying flesh, burning hair and unidentifiable toxic pollution, was an olfactory cocktail that boded the worst kind of ill. With it came an amalgam of noise that was equally daunting: massed voices cried and lamented in a seamless howl of screams, shouting, and psychotic laughter. The human wailing was accompanied by a counterpoint of growls and barking that had to come from the throats of things so evil they could hardly qualify as animal. Underpinning it all was the deep rumble and straining grind of unholy massed machinery. And yet the sound and smell were only mild precursors of the full visual spectacle. Hieronymous Bosch was made real with a brutality that leapt quantum measures beyond any mere painting's imagined nastiness. Those who dwelled there had come to suffer in a manner unimaginable even to one with Jim's deviant background.

In a massive, smoke-filled crevasse carved out of the living sandstone like an axe wound in the rock made by some god or spectacular giant, creaking and straining mechanisms of suffering labored at their infinitely repeated tasks. While flames belched from fissures in the rocks, pistons rose and fell and steam leaked from huge driving engines. Revolving cam shafts and greased axles turned cogs of wood and brass and long spiral worm gears that, in their turn, caused lacerating steel blades to rise and fall and huge hammers to drive iron nails into writhing flesh. Countless victims were bound, strapped, and secured to gallows, gibbets, and structures so bizarre in the contortions they inflicted on the human frame that Jim was unable to give names to them. Long, slow-rolling conveyor belts moved the damned from one automated theater of cruelty to the next, in endless cycles of relentless automation. Huge cauldrons steamed and bubbled at a slow simmer, each filled to the brim with a foul stew on the surface of which bobbed the shrieking, sobbing heads of submerged humans. Others were crushed, over and over, by huge stone rollers, while more were continuously flogged with lashes as long as the leather traces of teamster wagons.

Although the mechanical structures presented the impression that Gehenna was a dark clockwork universe of meaningless repeating torture, it had no real precision about it. Its mechanisms strained and shuddered; elbows in its maze of pipework leaked steam and dripped boiling water and oil. Its nooks and crannies were thronged with masses of wailing humanity being subjected to less systemized acts of fiendishness. Jim watched while what was left of a man, flesh all but stripped from his bones, was dragged along a dripping, reeking catwalk over one of the cauldrons. A barbed fishhook pierced his rib cage, and the rope attached to the hook was dragged behind a blood-spattered golf cart being driven by a pair of grinning demons. Other victims were enmeshed in tumbleweed tangles of rusty razor wire, while guffawing reptile things, and other strange creatures that looked to be entirely composed of leather, laughed at their agonizingly futile efforts to free themselves.

High on the sides of the crevasse, shackled work gangs of naked, filthy men and women labored, quarrying with picks and shovels, balancing on impossibly narrow ledges or perched on rickety scaffolding, actually attempting to enlarge the valley of pain by the strain of their muscles and the sweat of their brows, while other demons and reptile creatures encouraged them with long black bullwhips. At regular intervals, a worker would lose his or her footing, slip, and fall. Either the unfortunate would be saved by those linked to him on the particular chain gang, or else all would be dragged down, plunging to the rocks and fires below, to the great merriment and amusement of the demons and reptiles in charge.

Gehenna even seemed to have developed it own unique flora and fauna. Amid the machinery and instruments of pain, huge misshapen fungoid growths reared corpse-white and unhealthy, as large as trees. Other things Jim didn't recognize, like damaged mutant eggs with traceries of poisonous green and purple veins dappling their shells, grew out of the charred black soil between the flame gushers and fire pits, ranging in size from just a few inches to six or seven feet at their widest diameter. Huge rats and scrawny, red-eyed dogs made their own contribution to the misery of the valley's human denizens, as was to be expected in such a nightmare landscape, like the crows, ravens, and vultures that circled overhead and settled to peck at the miserable undying carrion. The presence of the demons, reptile men, and leather creatures also conformed to a certain hellishly medieval logic. What Jim didn't understand were the impossible bird-headed women, the bat-winged toads, the hogs with fangs and flippers, or the animated slime that constantly shaped and reshaped itself. They all seemed to have been included as nothing more than horrific additional background.

Once he had taken in enough of Gehenna, Jim turned and looked at Doc. Jaded as he might be, he still felt sickened by the entire wretched panorama of this hideous garden of delights. It bore too uncomfortable a resemblance to one of his old earthside nightmares. "Jesus Christ, talk about the horror and the horror."

Doc smiled sourly. "You can't go up the river without meeting it in one shape or form. Ask Ol' Joe Conrad . . . or poor Marlon Brando."

"Every one of those dumb suffering bastards could leave if they wanted to. Right?"

"That kinda depends. If they're only set dressing, they haven't got a prayer; strictly speaking, though, nobody does anything they don't subconsciously want to do. Those who went there by choice stay there by choice."

Jim shook his head. "Too much old-time religion at an early age can just eat some folks all up."

Doc himself was also staring into the Valley of Gehenna that was now mercifully starting to retreat astern. "A little Bible is a dangerous thing."

"Guilt and the need for punishment."

Doc agreed with a sigh. "Fortunately neither you nor I, my friend, are burdened by either."

No sooner had Doc spoken than three dark shapes detached themselves from a black-rusted wrought-iron pier that jutted out into the river at one point at the water's edge. Doc frowned uneasily and gestured to Jim. "Now, what the hell do we have here?"

Jim squinted in the direction that Doc was pointing. "I don't know, but I don't like the look of them. I also don't like it that they seem to be coming after us."

Doc turned in his seat and reached under his coat. "Better open the throttle all the way, boy. I don't like the look of this, either."

Jim didn't comment or argue. He just did as he was instructed. The Gun That Belonged to Elvis was in Doc's right hand, and the older man was clearly not treating this as any joke, coincidence, or false alarm. Under the full power of its twin diesels, the launch surged ahead, but in the reaches of the Styx that flowed past Gehenna, the current was fast and not going their way. Jim glanced back. The slipstream that came with the increased speed whipped his hair across his face. He took a hand from the wheel and pushed it out of his eyes. The black shapes were gaining on them. Jim could now make out that their pursuers were small, hunched, ring-tailed gargoyles riding Jet Skis, two to each craft. Presumably the one in front was doing the driving, but the function of the passenger had yet to reveal itself. That revelation, however, wasn't long in coming. The rear gargoyle riding the Jet Ski that was closest to them started swinging a steel grappling hook at the end of a long line. Clearly the intention was to intercept and board the launch. Jim, still holding the throttle wide open and zigzagging as best he could to make things hard for the gargoyle cowboy swinging the hook, glanced back at Doc. "What do those things want?"

"My guess is they're recruiters looking for new meat for the mill."

"I thought everyone was there by choice."

"Supposedly, but I guess the locals aren't above dragging in the odd unsuspecting and weary traveler for a little extra amusement. In these parts, nothing is written in stone."

The gargoyle's most recent cast had only missed the stern of the boat by a matter of a foot or so, and Jim spun the wheel so they looped and dipped across the full width of the river. "I'm sure as shit not going to Gehenna."

"I'm with you there, kid. Hold her steady for a minute so I can do something about this."

While Jim watched the river, and held the launch on as straight and steady a course as he could manage. Doc took careful aim with the Gun That Belonged to Elvis, but the boat was still bouncing enough to make shooting at a moving target highly problematic. Then Jim heard one explosion, followed immediately by a second and third. Jim looked back and the three Jet Skis had vanished. All that remained was some scattered flotsam and smoke on the water. Jim grinned. "You're one motherfucker of a shot, Doc Holliday."

Jim had expected Doc to look at least mildly pleased with himself, but the gunfighter's face was troubled. "Normally I wouldn't argue with you about that, but the truth is I never fired a single round."

"What are saying? What happened to those things?"

"Something else blew them up. Something under the water. I had nothing to do with it."

Aimee McPherson had not emerged from her locked and barred sanctuary for the equivalent of a full three days. After two more inexplicable fainting fits, she was convinced that her nuns and even some of the seraphim and angels were looking at her with increasingly less guarded speculation. She was certain they were secretly discussing whether or not their leader, Divine Mother, and virtual Godhead might be beginning to lose control of her powers and even her grasp on reality.

In the beginning it had been concern and anger over Semple's refusal to communicate. Next had come the unexplainable intrusions: the cartoon rodents, the sea monster, and the UFO. After that, matters had turned inward, attacking her directly. First a growing pain in her stomach, and an increasing shortness of breath. These had been followed by headaches and double vision; finally there were the fits. The first attack had come out on the terrace, in the open, while walking with her nuns. She had staggered and reeled, hurting and disorientated, with agonizingly white light blazing in her head. The second of these fits, mercifully, had come in private with none of the nuns looking on. That time, the white light was replaced by a terrifying sense of drowning that had left her gasping for air like a goldfish that had flopped from its bowl.

The third had been the worst of all. She had been going over the daily records with three of the senior accounting nuns when she found herself in the grip of what she could only describe—and she wasn't even accustomed to using such terms—as a violent, all-convulsing, grand mal orgasm. While the stunned nuns looked on, Aimee had jerked to her feet, tottered a few quivering steps, and fallen to her knees. She had then proceeded to roll on her back, twitching and contorting, mouth open, eyes screwed shut, pelvis arching upward, all the while gasping, snarling, screaming, calling on God and Jesus, talking in tongues, and finally repeating the two phrases, "Fuck me, you bastard! Fuck me until I die!" over and over like some unholy obscene mantra. After that she had passed out cold for an indeterminate time, only to awaken and find a gathering of a half dozen of the sisterhood making preparations for a full-scale exorcism.

Doing her best to cover her fear and confusion, she had jumped to her feet and attempted a stammering explanation that it had been nothing more than a spiritual visitation. The nuns clearly hadn't believed a word of it and exchanged significant glances as she'd fled to the sanctuary of her private quarters, certain that what she had experienced was some ghastly print-through of her sister having sex. She should never have trusted Semple in the first place. Now she knew for sure that her sister was using the mission on which she'd been dispatched as an excuse to conduct some pornographic libertine's grand tour.

Although the fits had been the worst of it, they were by no means the only signs that all was not well in her Heaven. It actually seemed as though the structure were starting to fall apart. Initially it had been only a matter of angels shedding the odd feather, or one or two bluebirds lying feet up, cartoon-dead on the terrace that overlooked the lake. Then two of the Scotch pines on the headland on the far side of the water had succumbed to some mysterious and uninvited tree disease and now stood leafless, sere and dead. The indigo of the water itself and the ultramarine of the sky faded at regular intervals to drab shades of somber gray. The wind seemed always to be blowing from Golgotha, making Heaven fetid with the reek of crucifixion. The once-immaculate grass that ran down to the edge of the lake was now patchy, unkempt. Dark unhealthy mold was growing on parts of the temple on the promontory; the diaphanous virgins had all but stopped dancing and spent most of their time on their hands and knees shooting craps.

The intrusions had also come back. After the UFO, there had been something of a lull as Aimee merely suffered. Then disturbingly abstract cloud formations started drifting across the once-idyllic vista; in the middle of one dour afternoon, a massed formation of black, 1930s-style, three-engined bombing planes, carrying sinister death's-head insignia on their wings and fuselages, had growled overhead and disappeared beyond the same heliotrope ice-cream mountains whence the flying saucer had come.

With the fits and the bombers, Aimee had reached a kind of breaking point. She had to get away from it all, go into seclusion until she could find a way to reimpose some measure of normality. The chamber in which Aimee had isolated herself was a perfect gray cube, oppressively small and punitively bare, with just a straw sleeping pallet on the hard stone floor, a knotted scourge hanging from a nail driven into the wall, and an overhead light so intense that it made relaxation impossible. It had been designed as a place for self-mortification and introspection, but neither of these seemed to be doing Aimee any good. She had spent the first day alternating between flagellation and lamentation, but even with her bared back bloody from repeated self-thrashings with the scourge no relief came. No insight or enlightenment, no peace of mind or redemption, just an ongoing fury at Semple. Where was her sister? What was she doing?

On the second day, in an attempt to answer that question, Aimee had conjured a television in the hope of picking up some ether-born image of her sister, but even that refused to come out right. She had hoped for a modest Sony Trinitron, but what materialized was a dubious piece of highly deviant equipment with exposed circuitry, a weird triangular screen, and no remote. No matter how many times she sent it back and tried again, it always returned the same. Finally, in exasperation, she turned it on, hoping it would do the trick. Even in that, the thing failed her. She found she had no way to tune it or even surf the channels. All it seemed able to do was flip through an endless sequence of random soundless images at rock video speed—an atomic explosion; a parade of some kind; giant ants in the process of destroying a gas station; some lewd TV show with naked young men and women being paraded down a catwalk; a black and white Philip Morris cigarette commercial; grainy sadomasochistic porno; an unshaven man in leather pants and a dirty shirt struggling through a swamp in the company of a small mammal; the same man with an older individual on a boat on a river; what appeared to be the interior of some potentate's harem; a scene from *Bewitched* featuring Agnes Moorehead as Endora; giant black men armed with gold spears attacking a crowd in a cloud of dust; a public hanging; black-faced sheep wandering in the desert and drinking at a water hole.

Then, after much more of the same, and to Aimee's total shock and horror, the headlong MTV imagery halted and held on a lingering long shot of Semple. Aimee had been hoping to catch a glimpse of Semple, but this was hardly the glimpse that she needed. Her sister was spread-eagled on a bed, in what looked to be a large and very well appointed tent, locked in a furious, passionate coupling beneath a tall man with an almost perfect body and the face of a 1950s movie actor. Suddenly sound cut in, deafeningly loud in the confines of the bare cell. "Fuck me, you bastard! Fuck me until I die!" over and over in lewd and rhythmic repetition. Aimee recognized them as the selfsame obscenities she herself had mouthed during her seizure; she bit deep into her lip, drawing blood but saying nothing. She only began to scream when Semple, pausing between eager pelvic trusts, looked directly at whatever served as a camera and winked lasciviously at Aimee. "Hi, sis. Wish you were here!"

"Do you have a cigarette?"

Semple lay back heavy-eyed, her breathing slowly returning to normal. How long would it be until she could once again have sex just for amusement? She was getting more than a little weary of being forced into positions where she could only save her ass by giving it up to the local number-one bull goose freak. First Anubis, now this seven-foot streak of Old Testament self-indulgence. To be strictly truthful, though, she had to admit that having sex with the self-created Moses was hardly a chore. He had been appreciative and seemed at least marginally to care if his partner had a good time.

Obviously, leading this tribe of disgruntled Bible Belters around the desert had afforded him little in the way of protracted romance, and when he'd first taken Semple to his tent and watched her wash the worst of the desert dust from her body, he had become positively cross-eyed with lust. Not that she had given him a chance to go any other way. She had stood flagrantly naked in the large porcelain bowl that he had thoughtfully provided, using water so freely that the parched tribe outside would have been scandalized to witness the display. At the same time she had recounted, in very matter-of-fact terms, an edited version of her encounters with Anubis, culminating in her escape from Necropolis. The contrast between her precise narrative and the sensually slow and suggestive way she moved his borrowed washcloth over her bare skin, paying particularly loving attention to her breasts, buttocks, and inner thighs, had robbed Moses of all biblical reason. Before she had even had a chance to dry herself off, he had picked her up bodily and carried her to his large and highly comfortable traveling bed, laying her atop the silk sheets, fur rugs, and embroidered cushions.

Forty-five very relative minutes later, Semple found herself satiated, probably bruised, and fighting off a major craving for nicotine. About the only thing that spoiled this otherwise satisfactory picture was an irrational impression that somehow Aimee had been watching her and Moses fucking. It was a feeling like the old days, when the two of them had been one, and Semple had brought home sailors or cowboys; Aimee had pretended to vacate the body, but got her kicks just the same. Moses lay flat on his back, eyes closed, his chest rising and falling, a smile of patriarchal satisfaction playing at the corners of his mouth. When she asked him for a cigarette, he opened his eyes and he smiled. "Under the prevailing criteria, cigarettes won't be invented for another five thousand years."

"Are you telling me you don't have any? This tent hardly conforms to any five-thousand-year-old criteria."

And indeed it didn't. Compared to the wretchedness endured by the faithful outside, the interior of their leader's tent was chock-full of goodies from the nineteenth and twentieth centuries. The atmosphere was chill, as though cooled by a hidden and silent air conditioner. Books and magazines littered small folding tables, a portable refrigerator and a water fountain stood in one corner of the rectangular bedouin structure, while Moorish hangings and Persian rugs provided a surprisingly decorative touch. Semple could only wonder which of the poor ignorant bastards outside had the unenviable task of toting all this stuff across the desert when the tribe traveled. Semple also noticed that there were an inordinate number of clocks and other timepieces scattered around the place, from hourglasses to ultramodern digital space chronometers, but she was too burned out to start conjecturing on Moses' time fetish.

Moses had leaned over and was rummaging among a collection of stuff on a bedside table. When he found what he was looking for, it turned out to be a pack of Lucky Strikes with the pre–World War II vintage red and green pack. He shook one loose, tapped it on his thumbnail, and put it between her lips. Her mouth twisted into deliberate tough-gal angles around the unfiltered cigarette. "So light me."

Semple knew the only way to deal with the likes of this Moses was to give as good as she got, if not better. She had, of course, come across plenty like him before. All those traveling preachers in the old days had been just the same. In public they'd preach hellfire, damnation, family and moral purity, but back at the hotel, they'd want nothing more than to drink prohibition needle gin and do the eagle rock all night long with two or three or more professional sinners or amateur enthusiasts; and, being natural performers, with a performer's need to please the crowd, they could usually muster as much style and grace as this Moses. After a little more rummaging, he came up with a book of matches with a shocking pink cover that bore the inscription BABY DOLL LOUNGE. This little artifact was something else Semple tucked away in her memory for future consideration.

She took a grateful drag on the cigarette and looked around the tent. "You live pretty well here."

Moses eased himself up on one elbow and surveyed the tent and its contents and furnishings with a look of smug proprietary pride. "Believe me, it's not all gravy being a prophet of the Lord. I figure I deserve a few home comforts."

"Doesn't that cause a problem with the flock? Don't they ever come in here and start to wonder what's wrong with this picture? You've got more than enough creature comforts stacked up in here to start a major mutiny among even those lamebrains."

Moses laughed. "They don't come in here."

Semple looked at him in surprise. "They don't come in here."

"They all think I keep the Ark of the Covenant in here and they'll go blind if they so much as peek inside."

"So you've got them snowed."

Moses winked. "In drifts up to their dirty necks. When they have to pack the shit to carry it, I insist they keep their eyes tightly closed."

Semple again peered around the tent. "And do you have the Ark of the Covenant in here?"

"I used to. Unfortunately, there was a bit of a freakout at the last Golden Calf orgy and the Ten Commandments got broken."

"What happened?"

"That drunken tubercular son of a bitch Doc Holliday took a shot at me. I'm lucky he didn't nail me; he used a gold bullet and the

Gun That Belonged to Elvis, and he could have done me some real damage."

"So what did you do?"

"I let loose the plasma on them. Probably blasted the pair of them all the way back to the Great Double Helix."

"The pair of them? Who's the other one?"

Moses scowled. "Holliday and that Morrison."

Synchronicity booted Semple hard. "Morrison?"

"Jim Morrison, that drunk singer from the sixties. Why do you ask?"

Semple covered her surprise as best she could. "No reason. The name just came up recently."

"Of course, this asshole probably wasn't the original Jim Morrison, the real Morrison. There's plenty of them running around pretending to be Jim Morrison, Jimi Hendrix, or Jerry Garcia, trying to pick up women."

Moses' hand was now cupping her breast, and she could feel a second-time excitement building in him. She would have liked to point out that he wasn't doing so badly in the celeb impersonation department himself, but she restrained herself. Arch observations at this stage might place too much of a strain on her already pretty threadbare luck. Moses was now licking her ear. The first time had been fun, a relief after all the tension that had gone before. She was reluctant to humor him a second time, but she knew she'd have to go along. She slid a hand down to his already stiffening cock and began to stroke it gently. Maybe she could excuse herself with just some creative masturbation. She put her mouth close to his ear. "It feels like you haven't done this for a while."

"It's been some time."

"The tribe doesn't have the odd good-looking Daisy Mae among its number that you can bring in here for your amusement? You ever think of blindfolding them, so they supposedly couldn't see the Ark?"

Moses rapidly stiffened under her hands and his words were punctuated by short gasps of pleasure. "That's what I used to do, but afterwards they had to go. I couldn't have them talking to the others."

Semple's hand halted in midcaress. What the hell did that mean? He "couldn't have them talking to the others"? Was he implying that . . . ? The thought made a sickening kind of sense: patriarch doubling as pseudo, netherworld serial killer.

Moses sounded aggrieved. "Why did you stop? I was enjoying that."

This time Semple didn't hold back. She said exactly what was on her mind. If she was going to the Great Double Helix, it might be the best thing. In this incarnation, she seemed to be cursed to encounter nothing but barbarous psychopaths. "Will you be getting rid of me once you're done with me?"

"A submarine boat. I guess it couldn't have been anything else."

Jim half smiled at Doc's antiquated turn of phrase. "In our time we just called them submarines, or even subs."

Doc shrugged. "So I'm stuck in Jules Verne. The fact remains, it must have been something of the kind that took out those things on Jet Skis."

Jim frowned. He had slowed the launch to a cruising speed once the danger of pursuit had passed, and now he stared thoughtfully at the debris and smoke still visible astern. "If it was a submarine that took out those things chasing us, it must have been blockading Gehenna."

Doc didn't seem to buy this idea. "Why in hell should anyone be blockading Gehenna?"

"How should I know? That's what I'm saying. It doesn't make any sense. The only other alternative is that someone down there likes us and is cruising around under the surface to make absolutely sure we get where we're going. And since I don't have a clear idea myself where we're going and I can't remember having any friends, lovers, or benefactors who own submarines, I find myself left at something of a loss. You know what I'm saying? This is one of those conundrums that can invite a mess o' speculation."

Doc picked up the bottle that had been set aside during the emergency. He seemed considerably less concerned than Jim. "The one thing I've learned during my long sojourn in these places is that speculation rarely yields a profit. Or a prophet, for that matter."

Jim wasn't sure what to make of Doc's attitude. Either he'd been dead so long that possible futures didn't worry him, or he knew something Jim didn't know and wasn't about to tell. "You're not confused or disturbed?"

Doc hesitated for a few moments before answering. "I try never to get disturbed, but I will admit that I'll be a whole lot happier when we make it up to the tunnel."

Moses got up from the bed, went to the wet bar on the other side of the tent, and slowly prepared two rum and Cokes. He seemed amused at Semple's concern. "Of course I won't get rid of you. You're not like those cretins outside. You're not one of them. I can do what I like with those hicks. I mean, they belong to me. Either I made them or they came here from the pods of their own free will, and only remain on the understanding that they're mine, body and soul, chattels to do with as I please. The difference between them and the sheep and goats is so marginal it hardly signifies. Sometimes I sacrifice a sheep and sometimes I sacrifice a young woman. Why do you have a problem with that?"

Even though the subject under discussion was her own immediate fate, Semple couldn't help but be amused by the rum and Coke being poured into the two rapidly frosting sapphire-blue glasses. It was a detail so far from the Old Testament desert outside the tent that its absurdity was almost charming. She also couldn't help but admire the magnificence of the body Moses had created for himself. Naked, the face was considerably enhanced by a muscular symmetry straight out of Michelangelo. "I'm still wondering if I'm going to be tomorrow's sacrifice."

Moses handed Semple her drink and continued his stream of self-justification. "And what's so wrong with a human sacrifice? Didn't God instruct Abraham to kill him a son?"

If Semple hadn't been so aware of the potential jeopardy she could be in, she might almost have laughed at the prophetic gravity with which Moses spouted his nonsense. "Don't bullshit me, Prophet of the Lord. The bit about 'killing God a son' is from Bob Dylan, not the Bible. And, anyway, God called off the sacrifice. It was only a loyalty test. Read Genesis 22. It takes up most of the chapter."

"You know your Bible."

Now Semple was starting to grow angry despite her fear. "Of course I know my fucking Bible. I'm one-half of Aimee Semple McPherson, aren't I?"

Moses turned and treated her to a searching stare. "Back in this place where you and your sister dwell, you've never been tempted to abuse your creations?"

Semple thought of Aimee's Place of Skulls and her own torture chambers. She didn't want to admit the existence of either to Moses, but to deny it would be pure hypocrisy. She decided to avoid the question. "When it's a woman you've just had sex with that you're sacrificing, it seems a little too like the way of the praying mantis."

Moses assumed a superior smile. "With the mantis, it's the female who kills after sex."

The smile irritated Semple. "Okay, so how about ritual serial killing? Isn't there a touch of the Norman Bates about it?"

"I don't keep my mother in the root cellar. And besides, I don't think poor Norman ever had sex with any of his victims."

"He still killed them."

"But I'm not killing these girls. Get real. They're all dead already, aren't they? We're all dead already. At worst, I'm just sending them back to the Great Double Helix, and in that I could well be doing them a favor. Maybe after another spell in the pods, their choice of reality might be a little more intelligent. Ignorance may be the choice of the stupid, but if the stupid are ever capable of learning anything, it must surely be that ignorance is a steep path to climb, with nothing to break the fall and deadly sharp rocks at the bottom."

"Very poetic."

"It's expected of me. It goes with the gig."

"It's a gig I know well. My sister and I helped write the book on twentieth century evangelism. It's a damn shame we didn't live long enough to get on TV. Could have made a fortune. Maybe even opened an amusement park."

"Tell me more about yourself and your sister."

Despite Moses' assurances that he wasn't about to do away with her, Semple remained wary. "We were once one and now we are two. What else do you need to know?"

"I recall that you said something about going to Necropolis on an errand for your sister."

Semple looked thoughtfully at Moses. Up to this point, she'd had him pretty much pegged in the same paranoid megalomaniac bracket as Anubis. Maybe she would have to revise her first impression. This one at least paid attention and remembered. "Necropolis was only the starting point. Unfortunately, I became enmeshed in the dubious practices of Anubis that culminated in the business with the atom bomb."

"And now you're enmeshed with me?"

Semple pulled a swath of silk sheet around her nakedness. "Is that how you see it?"

"I'm not sure how I see it until I know more about this mission you were on for your sister."

Semple held her gaze steady. Was Moses starting to reveal why he was keeping her alive and being implausibly pleasant? What imaginable thing could he think he might gain from her and Aimee? "It was an errand, not a mission."

"Mission or errand, you seem a little reluctant to tell me about it."

"Only because it's a family matter and I know my sister doesn't like the world to know her business."

"Even people in that world who might be able to render her a positive service?"

Now Moses was looking straight into Semple's eyes. She wished she could look away, but she knew it would be tantamount to giving him the game. "You believe you could render my sister a service?" She moved slightly so the silk sheet was stretched tightly across her breasts. "My sister Aimee is not in the least like me, you know? I'm what you might call the worldly one."

"I have it on good authority that your sister needs help with the expansion of her Heaven."

"Good authority?"

"There have been rumors."

Semple cursed inwardly. "Rumors are not always good authority." It had to be those damned nuns of Aimee's. Semple always knew they couldn't be trusted. "And even if my sister did need help to expand her Heaven, do you seriously believe you're in a position to offer such help?"

Moses looked smug. "Perhaps."

"And what form might this help take?"

Moses gestured to the desert beyond the confines of the tent. "I have a following, and certain powers of creation."

For Semple, the conversation was taking a decidedly strange turn, but she did not want Moses to suspect her confusion. When Aimee had first come to her with her request for a poet, Semple had actually thought of him, before dismissing him as a prospect. The stories she'd heard about this supposed Moses in the wilderness had made him sound a little too unstable. Now, with a more intimate knowledge of him, she knew for a fact that he was demented, but if using Aimee as a bargaining chip helped extricate her from her current predicament, her gain would have to be Aimee's loss. It was at that moment that a thought hit her. She had been cudgeling her brains as to what Moses might want with Aimee, and then suddenly the answer had presented itself. Her eyes opened wide and she grinned knowingly, full into Moses' face. "You want Aimee's Heaven as a Promised Land, don't you?"

Later, when she told the story, Semple would freely admit that one of the things she had liked about Moses was, when his objectives were spotted or revealed, he didn't bother to try to smokescreen his way out. Moses had grinned right back at her. "And that's why I'm keeping you alive. So you can tell me where to find it."

And Semple had her bargaining chip. Only it came with a new set of problems. The first and most pressing of these was, it didn't free her from Moses and his crew. In fact, it bound her more tightly to them. The second was that, if the truth were told, and she prayed it never would be, she didn't have a clue, after all the twisting and turning that she had gone through, how to get back to where Aimee waited with her wretched nuns and her equally wretched bluebirds.

The sky was now nothing more than a jagged, distant band of gray-blue, framed by the impossibly tall black glass cliffs. In this new stretch of the Great River, any semblance of similarity to life and Earth had been totally abandoned. The cliffs gleamed with a sinister sheen from the torrents and waterfalls that cascaded down them, and the razor edges on their acute, irregular angles looked sharp enough to cut a man's flesh from his bones. The water the launch now traversed was a deep purple, whipped to a lighter magenta foam by the headlong speed of the current. Scattered flakes of burgundy snow swirled in a spiraling conflict of breezes, even though the chill in the air was still above freezing. Jim had little chance to observe these new surroundings, however. He had to spend all his time fighting the wheel to stay on course and avoiding the outcrops of dagger-like glass shards that projected through the surface of the roiling torrent, and Jim didn't like it. In fact, he'd so had it with this stretch of river that his dislike boiled to a head when he had to wrestle the launch around to avoid tearing out a portion of the vessel's side on one of the of jutting glass spear points. "This is getting dangerous."

Doc lolled in the stern, unworried and unconcerned. "Don't sweat it, Jimbo. We'll be okay."

"Are you for real, or just blithely self-destructive?"

"I'm telling you, nothing's going to happen to us."

"Why do I have the feeling you know something that you're not telling me?"

"Maybe because you're paranoid?"

"Or maybe because you're not telling me something."

Doc straightened in his seat and his eyes glinted with a first hint of warning. "Do I detect a touch of rancor in your tone?"

Maybe Jim was getting a little too used to Doc, and he certainly spoke without weighing the consequences. "Damn right you do. I'm sick of traveling blind up this goddamned river. I want to know exactly where we're heading. Why does the destination have to be a fucking secret?"

"Like I told you earlier, I'm not the fucking tour guide. We'll be there soon enough and you can see for yourself."

"And what's this tunnel you mentioned?"

"Like I said, you'll see for yourself."

Jim's fury boiled over. "Fuck you, Doc Holliday!"

Doc laughed. "You've got a lot of balls when you get mad, young Morrison. There aren't many who've stood as close as you are to me, with me armed and them not, and uttered the words, 'Fuck you, Doc Holiday.' "

Jim took a deep breath. "Yeah, well, maybe I'm the one that's blindly self-destructive."

"What exactly has come over you, sport?"

Jim waved an all-encompassing arm at the river and its black glass cliffs. "Just fucking look at it. The farther we go up river, the worse it gets. The jungle was okay, but then there were the sandstone cliffs and the downed B-52 and all the other junk, then Gehenna, and now this. So what comes next, Doc? I'm feeling distinctly without a paddle. What are we sailing into now? Man-eating sharks? Giant squid? Or do we just plunge over Niagara Falls?"

Doc regarded Jim from behind an expression of blank neutrality. "This stretch leads directly to the tunnel."

"So that's the next surprise."

"You'll see the tunnel mouth in about five minutes or so."

Jim could not resist pouting. "All time being relative?"

"The tunnel mouth can be quite a sight if you've never seen it before."

Jim's lip curled. "In five minutes?"

"Give or take."

In fact, what Jim saw, and in considerably less than five minutes, was a cluster of slender towers like spindly bones that rose higher even than the glass cliffs. Jim looked quickly back at Doc. "I thought you said we were coming to a tunnel."

"The mouth of the tunnel is cited as one of the wonders of the underworld."

"It looks more like a fucking cathedral."

"A fucking cathedral? Perhaps not the most appropriate simile. The entrance to the tunnel does tend to overwhelm and intimidate, though. It's always reminded me of Gaudi's Church of the Holy Family in Barcelona, only on a much grander scale—"

Jim interrupted him. He hadn't asked for a lecture and suspected that Doc was trying to screw him into the ground with pompous overinformation. "When were you ever in Barcelona?"

"It was one of my few hauntings. I was taken there by a freshly deceased Spanish anarchist. It was during their Civil War. He wanted to show me the communists fighting the anarchists and how a revolution could mindlessly tear itself apart."

Jim would have continued the conversation, but a sudden buffeting of waves forced him to turn his attention back to the launch's helm. He very quickly saw, however, that Doc was absolutely right. As more of the strange and imposing structure that housed the mouth of the tunnel was visible, it became evident that the resemblance to a cathedral was mainly the effect of the towers; holy had been replaced by an organically mutant distortion more akin to the work of movie monster maker Kurt Geiger. In its twists and turns of pillar, buttress, and crenellation, the tunnel mouth was unlike anything that Jim had ever seen, save perhaps in his human nightmares. And even those merely reptilian environments of Freudian horror were humble in comparison. The architecture that now confronted him seemed to draw on all the phobias of the bicameral mind.

Soon the fine details began to be revealed. Within the grand sweep of the structure lurked carvings from every conceivable myth and demonology. Screaming Incan feathered serpents jostled Notre

Dame gargoyles for pride of place. Thunderbirds and dragons rampantly intertwined with banshees and monsters of the northern deeps. Ghouls and vampires formed ranks with night stalkers of the African veldt, chupacabra, and Chinese saber-toothed lions. And in the center of it all was a massive multiple inscription. Huge characters, letterforms, ideographs, and hieroglyphics had been carved in an area of smooth polished glass the size of a tennis court. Like some vast Rosetta stone, the same inscription was repeated over and over in more than a hundred languages, from Armenian to Zulu, with Latin, Swahili, and Basque at various points in between. Jim knew enough Spanish for that translation to send chills into him, but it was only when he found the English version, engraved in an elegant Roman serif face, that his blood truly turned cold.

ABANDON ALL HOPE, YOU WHO ENTER!

He turned to Doc with a scream. "You brought me here?"

"It's hardly what you think it is."

"You brought me *here*?"

"You're operating under a serious misapprehension."

"Did somebody pay you to do this, or was this your own whimsical idea?" Jim took his hands from the wheel. "I'll tell you one thing. I'm not driving myself into your tunnel. If you want to play Charon the Shadow Boatman, you get up here and do it yourself."

Jim let go of the helm, and the boat yawed out of control. Doc was on his feet, reaching for the wheel. "You have it all wrong, my friend. My only thought was, where better to raise figurative hell than in Hell itself?"

The movement of Moses and his tribe proved to be no simple affair. This walking asylum of the neo–Children of Israel proved to be not only more of a multitude than Semple had previously expected, but a multitude possessed of an all-but-intractable inertia. The men, women, and sheep who had responded so negatively to her arrival turned out to be only a small section of the whole. She had been so speedily whisked away to the air-conditioned tent of the Patriarch that she'd had no chance to observe the rest of this hapless and misguided army of faithful. When she was finally able to grok the dusty and disorganized fullness of what Moses had wrought for himself, she could only wonder once again why so many in the Afterlife felt compelled to do things on such a grand but logistically impossible scale.

As far as she could estimate, Moses' ragged battalions numbered between two thousand and three thousand souls who might loosely be described as human, plus maybe three times that many sheep, goats, mules, asses, and camels. To get the humans packed up and on their feet was sufficient problem on its own, laden down as they were with goods, chattels, offspring, and the responsibility of motivating the livestock. Just as it seemed that one section of the tribe was ready to get under way and labor out into the desert, sheep would scatter or lose themselves, pots, water skins, or pieces of bedding would go missing, or a child would wander off and have to be located by its weeping mother. The packing of Moses' tent and belongings proved to be a daunting task. It took seven men a full two hours to disassemble, crate, and load all the stuff the Patriarch considered vital to his comfort onto the backs of mules and some of the stronger men and women. The task was, of course, severely hampered by the fact that those actually breaking down the tent were required to keep their eyes tightly shut throughout and work by touch alone, lest they set eyes on the nonexistent Ark of the Covenant.

While the Children of Israel readied themselves to move out, Moses prowled the length and breadth of the confusion, bellowing, abusing, and berating in a voice so artificially amplified and enhanced that he sounded, for all the world, like Elvis Presley recording "Heartbreak Hotel" in the big RCA echo chamber. Despite Moses' vocal force, Semple observed that he had little effect on the humans and actually frightened many of the animals into even worse panic and disorder. Whole flocks of sheep would scatter at his very approach, and the sound of his voice, for some bizarre reason, appeared to have a violently aphrodisiac effect on some of the camels. Moses only had to bellow within their earshot and certain male camels would commence furiously humping their nearest companion regardless of gender. Needless to say, these outbreaks of dromedarian passion played their own part in the slowdown of the proceedings.

While all around her stumbled, Semple simply waited, and for once in her life she was quite content to let it be that way. The longer it took for the tribe to get moving, the longer it would be before Moses figured out that her directions to Aimee's Heaven were pure deceitful fiction. The deal they'd struck had been a simple one. She would show the way to Aimee's Heaven; Moses would prevent the tribe, who were still quite convinced that she was some previously unseen variety of desert she-devil, from stoning her to death. Moses, however, didn't seem to have too great a grasp of travel in the Afterlife. He clung to the erroneous belief that the geography of the hereafter was actual rather than deceptively symbolic, and if Semple ever did decide to take him back to Aimee, it would be a matter of using the brutish mass energy of the tribe to precipitate the two of them into a wind-walk mode, after which she would endeavor to find Heaven by pure homing instinct. Aside from providing the raw energy, the tribe had no part in any of it. Once she and Moses were gone, this gathering of benighted trailer trash would be left to fend for themselves and figure their own salvation. To paraphrase Woody Guthrie, with whom she'd once spent a memorable night under the stars of a Tarzana orange grove, so long, it's been lousy to know you. In the meantime, she'd let the Patriarch and his flock meander around the desert for a bit while she considered the situation and looked for an out. She hoped this time around the out would be less drastic than a nuclear explosion.

When Moses had demanded she tell him what course to set for the first leg of the supposed long march to the Promised Land, she had scanned the horizon for a while, finally selecting a broken-looking volcanic mountain. "There."

Moses had squinted into the bright distance. "Where?"

"That mountain that looks like a cat on its back. Head directly for that. When we get there, I'll give you another bearing."

Moses had looked at her doubtfully, but camels were nearby and he kept his voice low. "Are you certain?"

Semple had put on an aggrieved face. "Of course I'm certain. It's where I come from, isn't it?"

"You know the consequences if you're giving me a bum steer."

"You think I'm stupid?"

"Just reminding you."

"Then please don't. This isn't easy and I don't navigate well under pressure. Just head for that mountain."

Semple may have pointed the way, but that still didn't mean the tribe came any closer to getting itself on the move. After a further half hour, it was beginning to look to Semple as though the Children of Israel were never going to move at all. Then the vanguard, which consisted of some hundred or so black-faced sheep and an escort of swarthy herders, actually began to head slowly out of what had been the campsite and into the open desert. Walking point, in front of both men and beasts, was a gnarled old ram with china eyes and curling yellow misshapen horns. Semple wondered what he might have been in a previous life.

Ultimately the entire tribe was on the move. Semple had to admit that they did have a certain slow, unkempt grandeur; their sheer size seemed to consume the desert physically as they made their way across it. Lumpen and ignorant they might be, hag-ridden by superstition and further confused by the arbitrary and often contradictory teachings of Moses, she nevertheless had to concede that they had a determination that bordered on awesome. They toted their babies and lifted their bales; hauled their carts and shepherded their sheep; raised the desert dust with the slow, measuredly resigned slap of their sandals; all with a dull, unquestioning, and infinitely patient optimism that, someday, in some way, the Promised Land would arrive as promised, the milk and honey would flow, and all their trials, Lord, would finally be over. And all the time, relentlessly plodding, one hoof in front of the other, the ram with the malformed horns led them. It made Semple almost sad to know that their beliefs were so cruelly unfounded.

Semple had actually expected Moses himself to be leading the migration. At the very least, being up front kept one out of the worst of the dust. She was mildly surprised when it turned out that he took a position a dozen or more ranks from the front, in the very center of the column. It made a kind of military sense, giving him a considerable shield of cannon fodder should the column be attacked. What she couldn't imagine was what or who might attack such a large mass of people in a desert that was apparently devoid of all other life.

After a while, however, Semple found that she had to start revising her ideas. Maybe the dry, blistering terrain of scrub, thorn, and dirty sand wasn't as devoid as she had initially imagined. The first indication was a wrecked gas station. The place looked as though it had been ripped apart by one or more huge mechanical grapples, and very recently, too, if the freshness of the breaks in the wood was any guide. When she first spotted the fallen Exxon sign, the shattered pumps, the flattened and compacted Coke machine, Semple had looked quickly at Moses. She was about to say something, but from the look of him, leaning lightly on his staff and gazing straight ahead, she knew instinctively that for him the place didn't exist. She turned to see if any of the others were aware of the destroyed facility, but their faces were as blank as ever and they, too, seemed completely oblivious to it. Semple was the only one seeing it; and she decided, until she could figure out what was going on, it was best to keep her mouth shut.

The next oddity proved to be a drive-in movie theater, long abandoned, slowly ground down by wind and sand. A lopsided marquee showed that its last presentation had been a double feature of *Ocean's Eleven* and *A Hole in the Head*. A large hole had been punched in the center of the otherwise intact screen, as though something fantastic had not taken kindly to the work of Frank Sinatra. Once again, Moses and his people showed no sign of being aware of it, just as they didn't, about a half hour later, see the overturned Packard sedan. The automobile lay on its side, bodywork ripped as though by some huge gouging tool, possibly the same entity that had totaled the gas station. Like the gas station, the destruction of the car looked to be a fairly recent event. Its paint was unblemished, the raw metal of its wounds still bright and uncorroded.

Semple plodded on, pondering this discrepancy in perception, even toying with a vague hope that she was leading them into some kind of reality shift in which she might vanish herself, never to see Moses or his wretched congregation again. Stranger things did occur in the netherworld and she sure as shit was due for some kind of break. It was just as she was allowing herself this faint hope of a paranormal escape window when the ram halted in its tracks.

The ram with the malformed horns stopped and stood looking around uneasily. The next moment the earth trembled with a set of measured, even shocks, about two seconds apart. The tribe stopped dead, a common fear falling on each and every one. The Children of Israel stood, eyes wide, not daring to speak. Babies and sheep alike quieted themselves. And then the air was split by a raucous, grating scream, distant but still deafening.

"Ggggaaaawwwwwwwwwrrrrrrrrr!"

A corresponding murmur of pure terror ran through the crowd. At first it was just a whisper, but it rapidly rose to a crescendo of panic. "The Beast! The Beast! The Beast is come! God save us, the Beast is come!"

Semple looked at Moses and saw, to her consternation, that he was as mortally afraid as the humblest goatherd.

6

Ḧell hath no road maps.

T he mouth of the tunnel itself was sneeringly anthropomorphic, a vast misshapen maw like a twisted grin of sculpted triumph, with the half-lowered spikes of a giant steel portcullis substituting for jagged predator fangs. Jim, however, was too far gone. He sat slumped in the stern of the launch, drinking so hard and fast that the movement of the bottle to his mouth had taken on a steady rhythm. Not even the booze, though, could stop his mind from screaming. It was just his body that was in collapse. Had there been a moon, his brain would have upped and bayed at it. As it was, his simian mind gnawed at the wire of its cage, and its reptilian base consciousness tried desperately to recall the chameleon trick of changing color in the face of danger. Not withstanding everything that had been said, done, hallucinated, and imaged, he was finally going to Hell after all. The only thing that kept him from total whimpering surrender was a burning anger at the manner in which he'd come to this place. He'd been conned and deceived; worse than that, by a man he admired and had believed was becoming his friend.

Of course, while alive, he had resolutely disbelieved in the horror of the biblical Hell. Aside from being a stance that he couldn't credibly take, it had always seemed too cruelly and logistically unsound. What possible purpose was there in torturing sinners for their minor human imperfections, their petty foibles and failures? The Hell of the fundamentalists seemed so irrationally all-consuming. Why was the kid who masturbated to his old man's back issues of *Playboy* plunged into the same lake of burning lava as Adolf Hitler, Pol Pot, or Vlad Tepes? And if one was to experience anything for a period as vast as eternity, surely one would eventually adapt? The lake of fire could hardly remain a punishment. After the initial shock, wouldn't the nerve endings burn out and turn it into nothing more than an environment, and a pretty ridiculous environment at that? Jim's philosophy toward Hell had been one part Descartes; one part *Lost in Space*. It didn't compute, therefore it couldn't be.

In common, though, with everyone else who had lived through the spiritual battering of a basic Judeo-Christian upbringing, the tiny voice from the unassailable infant compartment in his consciousness would remind him, whenever it got the chance, that Hell was real and Jim Morrison was damned to go there. Jim had thought that voice had been stilled forever after the night in Paris, in the old-fashioned bathtub with the claw-and-ball feet, in the slowly cooling water with the three grams of China white running chaotic and deadly wild in his bloodstream and the disposable syringe lying where he dropped it on the blue and white mosaic tile floor. Even amid the garbage dump that now passed for his memory, the first thought, when he'd discovered himself on the other side of the overdose, in a pod in the Great Double Helix, still remained bright, clear, and intact. The priest, Popes, prophets, and conservative politicians had got it all wrong. The Afterlife was a million times more psychedelically complex than the imaginings of Saint John the Divine. He'd been right and they'd been wrong. You could not petition the Lord with prayer. And yet, as he approached the gates of Hell, the voice was back and shrieking like a toddler deprived of its Ritalin:

"Told you so! Told you so!"

It had all seemed so clean and clear, so much more as it ought to be. Admittedly, he hadn't up to this point, done anything too productive in the netherworld. His only excuse was that he had felt the right to a vacation after the shit he'd been through in the last few years of his life. Too many people had seemed bent on laying the hopes, fears, and psychoses of the 1960s squarely on his shoulders. Up until Charlie Manson and his riot girls had happened along, hadn't he been the dark side personified? Sure, after he'd died, he'd ambled and rambled, fought with the hopeless Dionysians, and generally gone on drinking and carousing and losing his memory, maybe more than once, for all he knew. Was he supposed to have been scoring points of some kind instead of frittering away his time?

Or was all that had happened since his death merely a sadistic prologue, a vicious lull before the full-blown shitstorm of God-fear could crash back on him as it apparently had when he read that legendary inscription. LASCIATE OGNI SPERANZA VOI CH'ENTRATE! Now the small voice had grown so large it drowned out all other thoughts. Doc Holliday, Long Time Robert Moore, and all the others who had eased him down the path to perdition were nothing but a conspiracy of illusions. Abandon all hope, Jim Morrison, you're en route to the unthinkable.

"Told you so! Told you so!"

The tide that was physically floating him to the unthinkable ran fast and straight, between arching walls of masonry like a set for *The Phantom of the Opera*. Had Jim not been so far gone, he might have noticed how his entering the Domain of the Damned through a replica of the Parisian sewer system wasn't without a certain irony. For some reason, presumably to make turning back much more difficult, the River Styx had reversed its direction and was now flowing headlong to whatever awaited. Doc had even turned off the launch's motor, allowing it to run free with the rapid current. The air in the tunnel smelled musty and ancient, almost like a tomb. He also thought he heard echoes of mass moaning, but it was too indistinct for a certain identification. When he thought he saw lights up ahead, he quickly looked to see how much whiskey remained in the bottle. A bare two inches. "Might as well meet the devil as drunk as a skunk."

Jim attempted to finish what was left in one fell gulp, but managed only to choke on it. "Shit, can't I do anything right."

Doc, standing at the wheel, glanced around. "You know something?"

Jim angrily shook his head. "I'm definitely not talking to you."

"Still believe I'm luring you into the pit of Hades?"

"Aren't you?"

Doc coughed wetly and shook his head. "You wouldn't believe me if I told you."

Jim's lip curled. "You're not the tour guide and I'm going to have to see for myself?"

Doc's expression turned bleak. "I'll have you know, sir, you're starting to try my patience."

Jim hefted the bottle angrily. "You want to know how I feel right now?"

"You'd like to eat my children if I had any?"

"You've fucking got it."

"In about two and half minutes, you'll be begging my forgiveness."

Up ahead, the light at the end of the tunnel was growing increasingly bright. Jim glanced at it, and then back at Doc. "You think so?"

Doc adjusted the wheel so the launch didn't run into the green, algae-slick wall of the tunnel. "I know so."

"You're pretty fucking sure of yourself."

Doc's voice graveled out. "That's why I'm the doctor."

Jim had no answer to this. Doc thoughtfully scratched the back of his neck. "You remind me a lot of my old running buddy, Louie Celine."

"What's that supposed to mean?"

"Except you don't appear to be the fascist type."

"I'm glad to hear it."

"Of course, his long day's journey ended with the night. You want to keep the party going well past dawn. To the end of the night, so to speak."

"What's that supposed to mean?"

"I don't think there's time for an explanation."

And indeed there wasn't. Within moments, the launch slipped out of the tunnel into something that was not quite daylight, but Jim would have been hard-pressed to pinpoint the difference. Certainly the spectacle that presented itself was nothing like Jim had imagined. It had none of the trappings he'd visualized in his tunnel fugue of funk and fear. No burning lakes of crimson fire, no tortured souls, no horned demons. He had entered the tunnel expecting Gehenna to the fourteenth power and now he was leaving it with Doc laughing at him. "Here it is, boy, although what it *really* is we can never be too sure. Some say it is and some say it isn't."

"You're telling me this is Hell?"

"That's what the majority claim, although the majority, of course, have a vested interest in the tourist trade. Me, I never like to commit myself. I've always had a sneaking suspicion that the place was fabricated."

What the launch was now cruising into looked for all the world like a small port, possibly in the eastern Mediterranean, around the romantic end of the fifteenth century, the time of merchant princes and pirate kings. The light was a little weird, admittedly, coming as it did in great blue-tinged curtains of luminance through a series of fissures in a basalt ceiling too high and cloud-shrouded for clear observation. This one concession to the subterranean situation, however, didn't seem to deter the large numbers of apparently untortured folk who made the docking area a bustling place of commerce and transit.

Although Jim and Doc had encountered no other boats in the tunnel, traffic in and around the port was intense. A large number of small craft, from every conceivable period, were moored at the wooden jetties and stone piers. Taxi boats like Venetian funeral gondolas, with tasseled black canopies of watered silk and top-heavy superstructures of ebony inlaid with jet, were poled in and around the stationary craft by caped gondoliers, while a magnificent Mississippi-style paddle-wheel riverboat was majestically emerging from a tunnel similar to the one the launch had just left.

"Not exactly what you'd expected, huh?"

Jim ruefully shook his head. "Not exactly."

"Wondering how to start begging my forgiveness?"

"I thought . . . "

"I never believed someone like you would revert so easily."

"When I read that damned inscription, I . . . "

"But now you're sorry?"

Jim nodded ruefully. "I should have waited and seen."

"But conditioning goes deep?"

"I really am sorry."

"But you just find it hard to say?"

"I usually try to avoid being put in that position."

Doc suddenly laughed. "Don't worry about it, my boy. I'm through rubbing your nose in it. I've never like admitting I was wrong, myself. In fact, back when, truth be told, I shot the odd man rather than admit being in error."

"I'm glad you didn't shoot me."

Doc looked at Jim in silence for a long moment. "Do you know how close you came?"

"I think so."

"Remember that in the future."

Doc guided the launch into a vacant mooring at one of the granite block piers. He deftly threaded a painter through an iron ring and tied it off, then he turned and looked at Jim. "So? Are we going to Hell? Shall we see what the town has to offer?"

Jim looked up at the waterfront beyond the jetty, crowded with people in transit. "Are we just going to abandon the launch?"

"You looking to go back down the river anytime soon?"

Jim shook his head. "I think I'm done with the river for the time being."

Doc picked up his filthy duster coat, but then let it drop again as though it were too far gone to be worth bothering with. "So leave the boat. Someone else will make use of it. Easy come, easy go."

As they climbed the stone steps up to the wharf, Jim wondered what Doc meant by the last remark, but it didn't seem the time to ask. As soon as they reached the top of the steps, they became part of the crowd and were quickly carried along with it. None of those arriving in Hell looked particularly worried about it and those leaving didn't appear at all desperate, so Jim, in that moment, decided to put the last of his fears behind him, as well as any curiosity about the origins of the launch and, like Doc had said, see what the town had to offer.

To say that the mob that thronged the waterfront was eclectic could be considered a magnificent understatement. They came in all shapes and sizes, ages and dispositions, from all eras and cultures, and of every sex, multiples and none. A few could not even be specifically termed human. Three Aztec jaguar gods wrangled in an unrecognizable language that seemed to consist of grunts and trilling whistles with a pair of leather creatures similar to those that Jim had seen in Gehenna. Jim looked a little askance at the leather things, wondering at their hellish function. Gehenna had given him a fairly accurate grasp of what their sense of fun was likely to be. A suspension bridge troll and a crusader in full, if rusted, chain-mail armor, having carelessly shouldered each other in the press, halted to curse and abuse each other, and looked likely to fall to fighting. More general and widespread curses were also aimed at a trio of lizard men from the Planet Mongo, so shitfaced drunk they needed to hold each other up, who repeatedly lurched into people while trailing a bile-colored stink of gin vomit and brimstone in their wake.

Once away from the water and the immediate vicinity of boats and piers, the majority of the two-way traffic was centered on a bank of descending escalators fashioned from copper, steel, and dark bronze that seemed to plunge to infinity, flanked by two huge carved angels of death with wings that extended to form the roof of the shaft. As far as Jim could see, these moving staircases were the only way in and out of the cavernous docking area. Jim assumed this was where Doc was heading, and so was surprised when Holliday veered off, going in the direction of a stone colonnade over to their left that housed a number of booths doing a brisk business, if the lines forming in front of them were any indication.

"First thing we have to do is get in line and sell our souls."

Jim blinked. "Sell our souls? Who in Hell would want to buy *our* souls?"

Doc shrugged as though it were the most natural thing in the underworld. "It's the way it works in this Hell. You make your mark and supposedly sell your soul and then they load you up with a bag of the local currency to spend on drink or drugs or women, or gamble away at the tables, or generally dispose of on whatever might be to your own particular taste and downfall."

Jim's eyebrows rose in surprise. "That's all there is to it?"

"Soul-selling is the foundation of the local economy. You got to admit it's no weirder than a lot of other monetary systems. Ask John Maynard Keynes."

Jim made a "whatever" gesture and followed Doc to the nearest of the lines. "Still, there's a slightly ominous ring to selling one's soul."

Doc looked back at Jim, starting to lose patience gain. "Shit, Morrison, will you once and for all put *'ominous'* out of your vocabulary? You're in Hell, sport. What else can they do to you? Send you to Peoria?"

When their turn finally came, a clerk in pince-nez, business suit, bow tie, and high starched collar, straight out of the counting rooms of Kafka's castle, stood in the teller's cage of a Victorian banking house, ready to supervise the transaction. He pushed two moist clay tablets, covered in sparrow-scratched cuneiform, in front of the two men. "Make your mark, we'll bake them later."

Jim look doubtfully at the wet surface of the clay. "Shouldn't we read these things before we sign them? I've signed a lot of dumb contracts in my time and regretted it later."

The clerk sniffed and looked at Jim over his half lenses. "You read ancient Sumerian, I suppose?"

"No."

"So?"

Jim sighed, reached for the stylus, and made his mark. Once the mark was committed, the clerk hefted two large leather bags onto the counter and pushed one to Jim and the other to Doc. "Move along now, there's others waiting."

As soon as they were away from the clerk's booth, Jim opened his bag and peered inside. At first it seemed as though the pouch were filled with large gold coins, like Mexican double eagles or Spanish doubloons. The moment Jim reached in to pull one out, though, he knew different. The coin was merely gold plastic. "We've been had. It's just plastic."

Doc wasn't in the least worried. "They work just as well."

"Hell ran out of gold?"

"Gold got too damned heavy to tote around."

Jim had to admit there was a certain practicality to the idea. "I guess that makes sense."

Doc was scanning the crowd. "The first thing we need is a Virgil."

"A Virgil?"

"It was the poet Virgil who led Dante Alighieri through the levels and circles of Hell."

Jim scowled. "Even I knew that."

"So these days, now that torture has apparently given way to tourism, the tour guides all pretend they're Virgil."

Doc indicated a group of old men in soft gray robes waiting, scanning the faces of the crowd moving to the up escalators. "Virgils."

"Why do we need a guide? I though you knew your way around Hell."

Doc shook his head. "These days, Hell has a nasty habit of shifting its geography when you're least expecting it. The Virgils are among the few who can keep track of all the twists and inversions, and certainly the only ones plying for hire. Indeed, it's how they make their humble nut in the underworld. It's good to have one, at least until you get to the general area where you want to be."

"So folks work for a living in Hell?"

Doc laughed. "Did you imagine Hell would be anything but a sink of terminal capitalism and wage slavery?"

As he spoke, he beckoned to one of the old men. "Ho, Virgil, attend us if you'd be so kind."

The Virgil bowed and hurried toward them. Doc fished in his pouch and pulled out two of the plastic coins. He formally returned the Virgil's bow and held out the coins. "*Onorate l'altissimo poeta.* Honor the greatest poet."

The Virgil took the coins and pocketed them. "The poet accepts the honor and will lead you where you may."

Doc nodded. "Then, like Orpheus, shall we start by descending?"

They were about to move to the head of the escalators when a commotion near the water caused them to pause. A craft, seemingly unusual for even the entrance to Hell, had appeared in the boat basin and the crowd on the wharves was pressing forward to gawk. A massive baroque submarine had surfaced, right beside the Mississippi paddle boat. The black iron monster had a definitely nineteenth century air about it, despite the fact that, in the nineteenth century, submarines were little more than a fantasy. Its cast Birmingham platework was decorated to the extreme, sporting fanciful scallops, rolling cornices, bas relief dolphins, and Neptune with his trident as a figurehead. A line of steel spikes along its dorsal ridge were also ornate, but looked as if they could rip the bottom out of most surface craft. Jim quickly glanced at Doc. "Could this be our benefactor from the river by Gehenna?"

"I fear it might be."

"You fear?"

Doc nodded. "That's what I said."

Jim studied the craft. "It looks like Captain Nemo's *Nautilus*."

Doc shook his head. "That's not Nemo."

As Doc spoke, a hatch in the conning tower opened and no less than the Voodoo Mystère Guede Docteur Piqures—Dr. Hypodermic himself—climbed out with the angular movements of a spider in evening dress. Doc took Jim and the Virgil urgently by the arm. "I think it would be a very good idea if we got out of here as swiftly and unobtrusively as possible."

"GGGGAAAAWWWWWWWRRRRRRRRRR!"

Semple had been certain that the Beast, the one the whole damn tribe was screaming about, was at least going to be the Great Beast of Revelations, the mighty usher of the End Times, with the traditional seven heads, each with ten horns, the feet of a bear, and the mouth of a lion, as biblically advertised. Instead, the massive figure that loomed over the horizon was something out of a whole other cultural ethos. How in creation had the great green, mountain-sized superstar and post-atomic Japanese monster movie icon found his way to this place of barren biblical hokum? Perhaps it was merely that, when you're green and the size of a mountain, you can pretty much go where you want. Maybe the phrase "post-atomic" should have given

Semple something of a clue, but right at that moment the analytical part of Semple's mind was in temporary shutdown and she stood, mouth open with an expression the British describe as gobsmacked.

"Godz . . . !"

"GGGGAAAAWWWWWWWWRRRRRRRRR!"

The ground shook repeatedly as the King of the Monsters advanced ponderously toward the faux Children of Israel. At first, it had only been possible to see his head and shoulders above the line of the horizon, but the rest of him came rapidly into sight, his potbelly, foundation legs, and finally his mighty four-toed feet, each of the latter kicking a dust storm with every impacted step, but nothing in comparison with the billowing clouds raised by the angry sweeps of his impossibly massive tail.

"Boy, do you look mad."

Semple didn't figure how or why, but somehow she knew instinctively, by some third, fourth, or even fifth sight, that to utter the King of the Monsters' name in English could not only cause him extreme and maybe litigious vexation, but also create other malevolent resonances all over the Afterlife. That was why she had cut off her instinctive utterance in midsyllable. He looked angry enough already, with his eyes burning red and his feathery dorsal wattles erect and quivering. Semple quickly racked her brains for the acceptable Japanese nomenclature. Gojiro?

Wasn't that what they called him?

The Tribe of Moses weren't worrying what the advancing monster was called. They seemed to know that he was bad news by any name and immediately scattered in every direction, running for their lives. Men ran and women ran, sheep and goats stampeded, and camels made themselves scarce at a galloping thirty to forty knots. Only Semple remained where she was. Although Semple was far from sure if she was simply stunned or other more perverse forces were at work, her refusal to move made about as much sense as everyone else's flight. It is virtually impossible for a human, or even a camel, fleet-footed from fear, to outrun a being with a stride of five hundred yards. As if to demonstrate the point, within another three stomping paces one great foot had crashed down, flattening some twenty of the faithful and a few dozen livestock. A second seismic stomp crushed twice as many humans as well as assorted sheep and goats. Leaning slightly forward, the mighty Gojiro now brought his tail into play and, with a resounding slap, sent a good twenty percent of Moses' remaining followers wind-winging their involuntary way to the Great Double Helix.

"GGGGAAAAWWWWWWWWWRRRRRRRRR!"

Semple had lost sight of Moses shortly after Gojiro had first appeared, and when she looked around she could see no sign of him. She was a little surprised that he had run with the rest. She imagined that he would have at least made a brief attempt to stand his ground and vibe down the living green mountain. The Patriarch had proved a chickenshit. This strip of stinking desert might be a tract of low-rent wilderness, but after all it was his very own self-created turf, wasn't it? Unless, of course, she had been wrong all the way down the line. Now that she thought about it, she'd only been assuming. He'd never actually said how and why he and his people were there. For all she knew, Moses and his mob might be interlopers on the bad end of a netherworld reconstruct of Monster Island. As to why she was standing her own ground, Semple couldn't quite say. She had no territorial imperative, and she certainly had no intention of vibing Gojiro down. Later, thinking back over her behavior, she could only remember a firm but irrational certainty that the megasaur intended her no harm.

Even in hindsight, this idea was hardly backed by the evidence. Gojiro clearly intended absolute harm to every human in the vicinity, and was bent on quite literally stamping them out. Even as Semple attempted to understand her lack of action, he was, to this very end, performing a quick flatfooted dance, a four-four combination with a hop-skip at the end and a whack with the tail on the off beat, and that was all anyone wrote for half of Moses' followers. The accompanying earth tremors were Richter-scale-worthy. As the survivors became more widely scattered, Gojiro changed his tactics. He stopped dancing and began taking long, deliberate, hopscotch strides, like a child methodically killing a colony of ants. Every few steps he would pause to mop up small groups that had managed to elude his feet with a burst of incandescent electric-blue breath. Again Semple wondered what Moses and his crew could have done to so anger the King of the Monsters. If his movies were to be believed, he was rarely so vindictive with anything but high-tension power cables and Tokyo subway trains.

"GGGGAAAAWWWWWWWWWRRRRRRRRR!"

Except for a handful of the fleetest of foot, most of Moses' tribe were now history. For all practical purposes, Semple stood alone.

Gojiro had his back to her, busily uprooting a small clump of date palms in which one of the largest group of survivors had fruitlessly attempted to conceal itself. She seemed to be the only one in whom the Monster King had no apparent interest; could it be that some new reality distortion had come into being and he actually couldn't see her? A swift blast of nuclear halitosis dispatched the last of the desperate fugitives among the ripped-up palms, and then Gojiro started to turn. He stared directly at where Semple was standing, and one look at the glint in his enormous red eyes collapsed her invisibility theory once and for all.

For almost ten seconds, the giant reptile did nothing but stand absolutely still and frown thoughtfully at her, furrowing his great scaly brow. Then he seemed to make up his mind about something and began to move toward her—but now his movements were completely different. He lumbered forward with all the care that something of his size could muster. He seemed to be taking great pains to not shake the earth or spook her in any other way. Not that he was very successful. As he came closer, the ground beneath her feet still bounced and vibrated so thoroughly that she was forced to spread her feet in a surfing pose to remain standing. At first it seemed as though the great reptile were going to reach down and scoop her up in one of its massive hands, like Fay Wray or Jessica Lange, depending on which version of King Kong one favored. Proportionally, Gojiro's hands were rather dainty, particularly when compared to his behemoth feet, but each was still the size of a railroad flatcar, and the idea of being scooped into one of them held little or no appeal.

Gojiro leaned forward, but neither of his hands moved in her direction. Instead he just bent forward so his huge head was only twenty feet from the ground, close enough for her to smell the ozone tang of his lizard breath and hear the deep rumblings of his bodily functions. As his face came toward her, the monster snuffled slightly. Even his slight exhalation was more than enough to send a small dust cloud spiraling at Semple, forcing her to shield her eyes with her hands. "Holy shit, pal! Watch it, will you? You almost blinded me."

Gojiro straightened up slightly and took a half step back. Although it was hard to read his expression, Semple could have sworn he looked regretful, even apologetic. The motion, however, was almost enough to send her stumbling. This time, though, she didn't complain. The King of the Monsters seemed to be intrigued with her; he had neither stomped her to pulp nor vaporized her with his Roentgen breath, and she deemed it unwise to place any undue stress on her apparent good fortune. She contented herself with merely muttering under her breath, "Anubis and Moses were one thing, big boy, but if *you* expect me to fuck you, you'd better forget it."

The monster lowered his head farther, peering closely at her. He closed one eye for a better look as though he had trouble focusing at what, for him, was such a short distance. Even a giant reptile looking at her in this way made Semple feel uncomfortably on display and she reflexively smoothed the folds of her rough caftan. "If I'd known you were going to stop by, I would have thrown on something a bit more presentable. Unfortunately, you find me somewhat lacking a wardrobe."

The great red eye came closer. It had a vertical iris like the eye of a bird, and in it she could see her own distorted reflection. "I have to tell you, in some cultures, staring like that is considered highly ill-mannered. You're Japanese. You ought to know about that kind of thing."

No sooner had she spoken, however, than something bizarre began to happen to Semple. It felt as thought her essential soul-force were being drawn out of her body and pulled toward the huge red eye. Semple swallowed hard. "Oh my God, now what?"

Jim, Doc, and their hired Virgil rode down the endless escalator. Their final glimpse of the boat basin had been of Dr. Hypodermic stepping down from the hull of his submarine and walking across the surface of the water, leaving wisps of steam and blue crackles of energy while the crowds on the piers and jetties fearfully backed off to give him plenty of space. The Virgil noticed the way that both men had stared nervously at the black figure in the stovepipe hat and he'd looked at them with deferential curiosity. "You have a problem with the renowned Doctor H?"

Jim glanced sharply at the Virgil. "You know him?"

The Virgil made a slight bow. "Everyone in Hell knows Doctor H, but I'm glad to say that I've had no personal contact or involvement with him. I do know, though, that if he wants to find you, he will. And if that's the case, although I've contracted to be your guide, I will immediately flee if Hypodermic so much as approaches either of you."

Doc nodded. "I understand the limits of your loyalty, *altissimo poeta.*"

"You are a man of infinite grace and subtlety, Doc Holliday."

"Thank you, *altissimo poeta.*"

Jim looked sideways at Doc. "Is it more likely to be you or me that Hypodermic seems to be shadowing?"

Doc looked hard at Jim. "I don't know, my friend. What's your best impression?"

"You seemed to be on pretty good terms with him back at that town of yours with the cantina and the opium den."

"On *good* terms? With *him*? I never did hear of anyone exactly being on *good* terms with Dr. Hypodermic."

"You went into the cantina without too much hesitation and talked to all three of them. I was the one that had to leave town."

"All three of them?"

"All three of them. The awesome trio, the three voodoo Mystères—Queen Danbhalah La Flambeau, Baron Tonnerre, and Dr. Hypodermic."

The Virgil glanced uncomfortably at Jim and then turned to Doc. "Your young friend tosses these names around unwisely."

Doc sighed. "Indeed he does, *altissimo poeta,* indeed he does. He's one of those devil-may-care junko partners who won't be told. You probably know the kind. If he wasn't also paranoid, and occasionally halfway resourceful, he would have found himself consigned to some unimaginable place a long time ago." He turned back to Jim. "It's unfortunate that I have no recollection of this alleged meeting with the Mystères."

"That's not to say it didn't happen or that it isn't going to happen."

"Indeed it isn't. I'm just saying I have no recollection."

"It's the only recollection I do have. I don't remember ever seeing a Mystère before that."

"But there's a great deal you don't remember. The dark Doctor H is the ruling spirit of narcotics and those addicted to them. You could well have had dealings with him and be quite incapable of remembering."

Jim scowled. "Give me a break, Doc. You aren't exactly a stranger to narcotics. Why do I have to take the rap for this one?"

Doc's face took on one of his dangerously good-humored expressions. "Therein lies the conundrum, my boy. Either or both, or maybe neither and it's all a coincidence. One way to find out would be to go our separate ways and see which one Dr. Hypodermic follows."

"Is that what you want?"

Doc thought about this. "You're kind of amusing to have around . . ."

Jim glanced back, but the escalator had been steadily descending its sloping shaft for some time and no clue was yielded as to what now might be happening in the dock area. About the only thing Jim could say for sure was that Dr. Hypodermic was not coming after them down the moving stairs. The Virgil looked impassively at Jim. "Doctor H has more ways of observing your movements than simply following you. But I imagine you're probably aware of that."

Jim shook his head. "No, I wasn't."

The Virgil gestured to the large, four-sheet advertising posters that lined the escalator shaft, held in place by ornate brass frames and protected by Plexiglas. Not only was Hell militantly capitalist, it was also inundated by advertising. Jim noticed for the first time that regularly placed graphic representations of Dr. Hypodermic lurked among the standard hard-sell images—the square-jawed cowboys and bikini babes, the nurturing moms and the adorable cuddly critters. Although the picture of the Mystère was the same in every case—a grinning death's-head and a skeletal hand holding up a small dark green bottle with an ornate nineteenth century label—the banner slogan came in a selection of languages that ranged from Japanese to Hittite. Jim looked around for one in English and, when he found it, it was predictably oblique.

THE DOCTOR IS SO IN.

Jim turned to the Virgil. "Are you saying he can watch us via the damned posters?"

The Virgil nodded. "The Mystères are very sophisticated in their uses of imagery."

Jim shook his head. More shit in hell than dreamed of in your philosophy, Jim boy. He turned to Doc. "So, do you want us to split up or what? If you do, I'll go back and get me a Virgil of my own."

The Virgil quickly intervened. "That will not be necessary, young sir. I can easily summon one to come to us."

Jim ignored the old man in the robe, staring intently at Doc. "Do you want us to split up?"

Doc half-smiled. "Do you?"

"No, I don't. I feel better with you around, but if you're afraid of some Voodoo god of dope fiends . . . "

Doc's voice was quiet. "Anyone in their right mind is afraid of Dr. Hypodermic. He can take you places you really don't want to go."

"So it's a parting of the ways?"

"I didn't say that."

"So what are you saying?"

Doc suddenly grinned. "I'm saying calm down, young Morrison. We stay partnered until the Mystère tips his hand."

"And then?"

Doc's grin widened. "And then, like the good Virgil, I'll decide what's best for Doc Holliday."

Even though the elevator had seemed endless when they first boarded it, the bottom was now in sight.

As the vertical iris of Gojiro's giant eye closed behind Semple with a moist butterfly whisper, the red light filling the King of the Monster's head faded. She was now not only inside what she could only assume was the creature's brain, but in a darkness that was more total than anything that she had previously experienced. Oddly, though, she was still completely unworried. She knew she should have been experiencing some combination of fear and fury, but the odd serenity that had been with her ever since the green beast had first appeared abided and endured. She was certain that the darkness was only a temporary condition, and in a minute or so, as far as she was able to estimate time, she was proved absolutely correct. A soft algal glow started to suffuse her vision, and she found that she was in a perfectly cubical room with soft padded walls covered by bottle-green leather or plastic. She didn't want to look too closely lest she discover that the leather or plastic wasn't leather or plastic, but some material far more disturbing.

By a stroke of what could only be pure Dada, a tall, free-standing mirror had been placed near the center of the cube's floor. Semple decided it might be best if she took a look at what she had become now that she had apparently entered the brain of the beast. The first sight of her new self came as nothing short of a sharp shock. "What the hell's been done to me? I've become a goddamned cartoon character."

Not that her reaction was entirely negative. If she'd wanted to become a cartoon character, she could have done a lot worse. Her hair was a blue-black mane and her skin ivory white. Her figure was idealized and considerably slimmer and more curvaceous than it was in reality. Her legs seemed to go on forever, accentuated by the thigh-high scarlet platform boots on which she now found herself teetering. The costume was completed by a pair of highly revealing hot pants made from the same reflective plastic, a matching brassiere/breastplate, and a dark wraparound visor that hid her eyes. Her hair had been reinvented. It was still as black as it had ever been, but now it rose to a height of ten or twelve inches above her head and danced in place like the flames of some unholy fire. He face had been stylized to a simple elongated oval, with a pair of perfect velvet lips and a vestigial nose that was little more than a pair of cutesy nostrils. She had, however, acquired a beauty spot just below her right eye that she had never had before. She had also inherited a weapon of some kind: a baroque and highly phallic *Flash Gordon* blaster pistol in an equally baroque holster, strapped to her right thigh.

"And how long am I supposed play the part of some two-dimensional piece of animation?"

When there was no answer, she decided she might as well check out how the new body moved. Her first tentative step proved that she was more than merely two-dimensional. This body had a strange consistency somewhere between illusion and reality. As she twirled experimentally in front of the mirror, the motion reminded her of a computer simulation, of a flat drawing translated into a solid object by digital enhancement. For a while, the narcissistic study of her new corporate condition kept Semple fully occupied. On balance, she wasn't too displeased with what had happened to her, although a certain feeling of incompleteness made her a little uneasy. She could no longer feel her heartbeat, or the blood coursing through her veins. She missed the tiny snaps, pulses, and unfoldings that made a human believe she was functioning. She might have been put out or even angry at this except that her emotional responses seemed to have undergone a similar reductive simplification, as though she'd been stuffed to the gills with *animé* Prozac. The old, fully fleshed Semple might have threatened her reflection in the mirror; the cartoon Semple just regarded it with mild puzzlement.

"The question has to be asked. What's the purpose of this transformation? If I'm like this because I'm supposed to save the universe from a lot of cartoon monsters or something, I can't say I'm too happy about it. This costume looks like it was designed for an audience and I'd really like a little early warning who that audience might be, and what they might want of me. In case anyone's forgotten, I'm still supposed to be finding Aimee her damned creator-poet to help her get her Heaven together."

And, as in any other well-regulated fantasy, the simple question only had to be asked to receive a response. A plain oak door with inset rectangular panels appeared in the soft wall. Semple walked toward it, hips swaying, attempting to master the motion of the platform boots. "I suppose I have once more to quest into the unknown?"

The lower end of the escalator ultimately unloaded its human and semi-human cargo out onto a wide circular concourse of blue light and moving figures, as though Grand Central Station had been converted into a vast ballroom discotheque. The only missing element was the music, and that was almost compensated for by the rhythmic throb of the huge engines that presumably powered the escalators. Even the beat of the engine, however, was enough to add a certain coordinated homogeneity to the movements of the mass of people who passed through and conducted their business there. The motif and predominant transaction of the concourse, over and above the simple logistics of getting to and from the escalators, seemed to be casual sexual encounter. For Jim, this made a certain sense. By simple law of averages, sex would be on the minds of a large percentage of those both leaving or entering Hell. Jim was well aware that, since the dawn of man, travel and sex had been indivisibly interconnected. Any new location offered new promises and possibilities; in Hell, this would logically go a few stages deeper. New arrivals like himself could carnally confirm that their worst fears were unjustified, and those about to leave could be tempted to one final fling before heading elsewhere. This was not to mention the ones who simply waxed lascivious from the boredom of schedules and connections. Looking around at the considerable numbers who purposefully cruised the concourse, Jim imagined that those who still clung to their illusions of transgression and retribution could take comfort that these determined sinners seemed doomed to repeat the carnal cause of their original fall.

Rent boys strolled by, flaunting every style of allure from Axl Rose to Lord Alfred Douglas, including a number who might have amused Caligula. The women spanned an even greater bandwidth of fetish and fascination made flesh. In togas and bikinis and Marlene Dietrich tuxedos and the harnesses of harlots of the Marquis de Sade, they prowled and pouted and vied for the attention of the carriage trade. Hips swayed, asses posed pert, long legs stepped high, breasts made themselves known, while mouths and hands spoke the universal languages of allure and come-on. Perfumes piqued appetites, cosmetics enhanced and enticed, and nudity reduced matters to essential basics. For those with more cultured and jaded tastes, lace partially concealed, silks whispered down the twilight places of memory, and polished leather and burnished chrome promised precise brutalities. Over and above the women and boys, the androgynes, the hermaphrodites, and the totally unidentifiable made their unique and peculiar pitches. Jim wondered and frankly stared at the circling parade with all the awe of a yokel. He was astonished that so much temptation could be crowded into just one geographical space, and at how all of it could be consummated by the hour in the hot-sheet hotels that ringed the concourse behind electric signs over darkly modest doorways.

"This is definitely what I've been missing."

An Oriental woman in saffron latex and rhinestones with straight black hair that reached well below her waist smiled at him. A painted and powdered young man with blond curls like an epicene Harpo Marx eyed the crotch of Jim's leathers and ran his tongue slowly over his upper lip. An older woman paused en route to the up escalators to give Jim an appraising inspection, as though she believed that he might be one of the ones available for sale. A mugwump vibrated its multiple udders at him and each one became tipped with a tiny telltale pearl of milky fluid. Belly dancers writhed, double-jointed mutations demonstrated lewd flexibilities, and a tall Valkyrie with a spiked copper brassiere, buckled-on broadsword, and a thick Teutonic accent whispered huskily to Jim as she passed, "Mine namen ist Zena und you look so good to me I'd fuck you twice for free."

The words were delivered as a poorly scanned rhyming couplet; Jim was tempted to follow and investigate the reality of the offer. The Virgil must have overheard, though, and he shook his head at Jim. "It would be counterproductive to pause for pleasure at this early a juncture, young sir. I can assure you the offers that will come deeper in the labyrinth will be at the very least equal to any you'd find here."

Jim was momentarily disappointed to be hurried past such a welter of delight, but he soon realized that the Virgil was only reiterating Smokey Robinson's adage about the advisability of shopping around. He was aware that, even though Dr. Hypodermic might be on his trail, he was actually starting to feel good. He was back in the rough-and-tumble trade of imperfect humanity, and that in itself was starting to make him feel more human. He was also reaping the psychological benefit of being desired by something other than an alien simulation. It didn't matter whether that desire was based on his good looks or his new bag of plastic gold. He hadn't been desired since the Moses orgy, and at that ill-fated gathering desire had been a highly debased coinage. This was not to say that desire was any more pure and genuine in the concourse of Hell, but at least it wasn't so mindlessly drugged, and it certainly made him feel once again a part of the great erotic dance of humanity. He straightened his shoulders, hooked his thumbs in his belt, and began to walk with a new spring in his slouch, letting himself be admired by any who cared to.

He turned to Doc to gloat about his newfound attitude, only to discover the gunfighter deep in conversation with the Virgil on how this present Hell had come to be, more taken by the old poet's theorizing than the imperious beckoning of an importunate kitten-with-a-whip who had taken a shine to him.

"So you're saying that Hell really succumbed to its own essential paradox?"

The Virgil glanced briefly at the sex kitten and then nodded. "If it was designed to be the ultimate in infinite horror and suffering, what was there left with which to threaten those already incarcerated within? It ultimately failed from the illogic of its dynamic."

"So after ten thousand years they gave up and turned it into a tourist attraction, *altissimo poeta?*"

The Virgil smiled as if he considered Doc an apt pupil, though he may have just been looking to enlarge his tip by some applied flattery. "It's certainly a very plausible way of looking at what has come to pass. Those of us who have made our homes here find that it's better to regard Hell as an entity rather than a place. That which cannot adapt must surely perish."

273

Jim caught on to the end of the discussion. "So Hell, just like everything else, is subject to entropy?"

As he spoke, Jim caught sight of something that stopped him in his tracks. Even among the wide diversity of the women who thronged the concourse, this one was strange. Not human, but certainly not anything else. She was more like a comic book character, brought up from the printed page in gleaming scarlet and somehow rendered three-dimensional. To make matters even less believable, she seemed to be floating about a foot or so above the ground, oddly insubstantial, more like a hologram or a ghost than a solid form. This wasn't the full extent of Jim's shock, however. Though her face and figure had undergone considerable graphic alteration, he instantly recognized the image on whom the strange figure was based. He let out an amazed gasp. "Semple McPherson."

As Jim gasped, Doc looked around. "What?"

And, in the moment that Doc turned, the figure vanished.

Jim was at a loss. "She was right here . . . "

"Where?"

"She was right here, but now she's gone."

"I think you'd be well advised to get that lady off your mind, my boy. At least for the moment."

"I wasn't even thinking about her. She just appeared out of nowhere and then vanished again."

The Virgil attempted to communicate his own lack of concern to Jim. "Many apparitions come and go in this place. They should be no cause for either concern or speculation. It is gone now and will not return."

Jim's face was set. "No disrespect, *altissimo poeta*. But I think I'll be seeing this one again. Doc and I already had one sneak peek at the future and she was right there, in a starring role."

Clearly the mind of the King of the Monsters was so underemployed that it could accommodate guests, strangers, even those who were some part of both. Apparently some had even gone so far as to set up their own virtual world in between the system tracks of the big beast's consciousness. One thing Semple didn't understand was why the vista in front of her looked as much like Japanese *animé* as she did. She knew Gojiro was an icon of the Setting Sun, but she wasn't certain that was the full explanation. All she knew was that she had to venture into this new land, unless she intended to hide in Gojiro's eye forever, and she could only hope she would learn more about it as she went. Her first step through the door and into this strange, hand-drawn world had been an unfortunate one. A glitch in reality of some kind had occurred in the instant that she crossed the threshold. She had briefly experienced a sudden falling sensation. A momentary chasm of open-air vertigo had yawned beneath her, causing a stomach-wrenching illusion of being in two worlds at once. Part of her was entering the cartoon world that lay beyond the door, but some other sector of her perception was in an echoing place of blue light and moving figures, a huge ballroom filled with insinuating whispers between the throbs of powerful machinery. For the nanosecond she existed in this blue world, a young man in black leather pants and a white shirt, with curly dark hair and intense eyes, had stared at her in amazement; in the same instant, she knew that he was the one from that strange erotic experience all that subjective time ago in the bed of Anubis.

When, by whatever means, the vision winked out, the portal closed, and the glimpse was terminated, Semple was more than a little disappointed. The blue ballroom had seemed considerably more lively and interesting than the environment that now confronted her, the young man more interesting still. She knew she could do nothing to recall the glimpse, though, and in a short time she began to doubt that it had ever happened. The new world awaited her and she knew that she had no choice but to leave through the doorway to the soft room and press on. The opening of the door had hardly presented her with any multitude of choices. In front of her, a seamless white bridge of an indeterminate cartoon material arched over an impossibly wide mountain gorge, the sides of which seemed to be composed of massive hexagonal rock crystals drawn in the same style as herself. The artist behind this creation must have been a painstaking obsessive, always combining three or maybe four interlocking concepts, layer imposed on layer, where one might have sufficed. Not content with the creation of the towering crystal mountains, he or she had then embarked on the monumental task of integrating them with a form of organic honeycomb architecture that infiltrated large expanses of translucent cliff face with structures that Semple could only think of as a futuristic pueblo.

At the bottom of the gorge, a foaming cartoon river rushed down to an unknown destination in a series of mist-shrouded cataracts. In the air above the plunging water, free-floating and irregular structures, complex motherships of metal and plastic, floated in defiance of gravity, huge projection video screens circling their undersides like giant TV billboards. On them, doll-like oriental models and slogans in Japanese characters promoted unguessable consumer products and unfathomable political philosophies. In order to see this world at any closer proximity, Semple had first to cross the bridge. The bridge was a single, elegantly arching span, plainly intended for a pedestrian like herself and yet without guardrails or balustrade, lacking protection of any kind. It appeared to be a challenge she had to take before she could go on. Normally Semple was less than enthusiastic about heights. On Earth she and Aimee had never been inclined to look down, and much of the fear had irrationally continued into their afterlives. Under different circumstances Semple would have thought long and hard about crossing such a bridge, and probably refused to do it, citing her unaccustomed platform boots as the reason. In what she was coming to think of as the cartoon haze in her mind, though, she hardly thought of the drop, wondering only if, should she fall, it would be strictly according to Isaac Newton at thirty-two feet per second squared or more in the survivable cartoon manner of Wile E. Coyote, who could always stagger away from the worst of falls.

As she stepped out onto the bridge with only the slightest wobble of her ankles, the Hokusai waves and decorative groves of cypress and pine looked to be more than a mile below her; and, in her animation tranquillity, she found that, by the time she was halfway across the span, the sheer quantity of naked air below her was becoming a trifle daunting. By the time she reached the far side of the span, it was with a definite sense of relief.

All the while she'd been crossing the bridge, Semple had somewhat naively assumed, although for no good or logical reason, that she was the only inhabitant of the place. Her half-formed and barely explored idea had been that this odd graphic world inside the brain of the King of the Monsters had been expressly created for her sole amusement. Thus she was taken somewhat by surprise when the three tiny women greeted her.

"Welcome, Semple McPherson. He awaits you in the dome."

The little women were eighteen inches tall and totally identical.

Their doll-geisha faces were exactly the same, as were their pink-and-blue-flowered kimonos. Semple could only think they had to be cousins to the tiny girls who sang to Mothra in the monster movies. "How did you know my name?"

"He told us to expect you and to give you directions."

"He?"

"He knows everyone's name. He even marks the fall of sparrows."

That there appeared to be yet another all-powerful "he" in this place triggered alarms even in her dulled cartoon condition. "He told you to give me directions to where?"

The little women looked at her as though they were too polite to show just how obtuse they thought her. "To the dome, of course."

"The dome?"

"Where he waits."

"Of course."

"You will go to the dome?"

"I don't know. I mean, who the hell is *he*?"

"He said to tell you that you would know him when you saw him."

The little women were so humorlessly earnest that Semple could only counter with sarcasm. "And that I'd love him when I knew him?"

"He said nothing to that effect. Just that you would know him."

Semple was liking this less and less. "In other words, he told you not to tell me his name?"

"We only repeat what he tells us."

Semple had already decided she didn't really want to go to this dome. The fact that the mysterious "he" didn't want to reveal his identity up front and the distinct suggestion that they may have met before hardened her resistance. "Actually, I don't think so."

The little women looked distressed and confused. "We beg your pardon?"

"I said I don't think so. I don't think I'll be going to your dome."

The little women looked at her as though what she said was making absolutely no sense. "But you have to go to the dome. He desires it. Besides, there is really no other place to go."

From the get-go Semple had suspected that she might have very little choice in the matter. "What you're telling me is that it's the dome or nothing?"

The little women smiled sweetly. "We would never do anything to infringe on your free will, but . . . "

"But the answer is yes?"

The little women at least had the decency to cast their eyes downward. "Yes."

"I've recently been through a couple of singularly unpleasant experiences."

"We're sorry."

"So if this turns out to be another one, I promise I will come back and beat the three of you to miniature bloody pulp."

The little women beamed. "We understand perfectly."

Semple nodded grimly. "Okay, so are you going to point the way?"

"We'll do better than that. We will take you there. Please follow us."

Semple had wondered if, when they moved, the tiny girls would move in unison, and found it oddly satisfying when they did.

"Are you still thinking about that McPherson woman?"

Jim shook his head. "No, I was actually wondering where we might be going. Where the hell *are* we going, Doc?"

Doc pointed ahead, and Jim noticed for the first time a reflection of red and blue neon at the far end of the broad stone passageway down which they were walking.

"The *altissimo poeta* here is taking us to this joint I know where they just might make us welcome and I can find myself a poker game worthy of my talents."

He hadn't given the matter much thought, but Jim was a little surprised that Doc was headed for something as mundane as a card game. He had somehow thought the goal of his first entry into Hell would have had some more lofty objective. Doc, on the other hand, seemed convinced no loftier objective existed. "We're in Hell, boy. What better and more challenging place to ply the noble trade? Did you think that, just because we'd become traveling companions, I was going to renounce my vocation? You're starting to sound like a wife."

The last thing Jim wanted was a confrontation with Doc, particularly over a matter that was so plainly dear to his heart. He quickly backed down. "I was only wondering what I was going to do. I've never had the single-mindedness to win at games of chance."

Doc nodded as though acknowledging Jim's retreat. "Don't worry about it, my boy. Our goal is a place of many wonders and temptations. I'm confident you'll find something to your liking."

"You're telling me I should wait and see?"

"At least this time you can be assured that the wait won't be long."

"There is just one point, though."

Doc, who was walking ahead, looked back at Jim. "And what might that be?"

"Don't you think a casino might be the first place that Dr. Hypodermic might look for the both of us?"

Doc's eyes turned bleak. "If the Doctor is looking for both or either of us, sport, he already knows where we are and where we're going. I thought the Virgil made that clear to you back at the elevators."

Since leaving the elevator concourse, the Virgil had led them down a series of dark and winding medieval stairways into what appeared to be one of the older parts of Hell. Some of these tunnels were so ancient that hanging stalactites had overgrown much of the arching masonry of the roof. The walls were covered by such a thick patina of limestone that it concealed most of the bas relief carvings with which they were decorated, but since these were of human faces twisted into the distortions of unimaginable torment, Jim felt that time's overlay was a distinct improvement. He looked questioningly at the Virgil. "So what was this place used for when Hell was really Hell, *altissimo poeta?*"

"It was the sector reserved for suicides."

Jim laughed. "And they turned it into a casino?"

"It seems somehow appropriate, don't you think?"

From the outside, the mysterious dome looked to have been constructed with more than a modicum of good taste. For Semple, this was at least an initial encouragement. She had followed the three tiny women away from the bridge and along a white stone path that curved between carefully manicured banks of flowering shrubs. After about a hundred paces, it crossed a small fast-flowing stream where rainbow trout and huge antique carp ran in the shallows, and kingfishers and dragonflies hovered in wait for their prey. Every detail seemed calculated to invoke a mood of harmony and peace, but Semple couldn't help but wonder. Should she take everything at face value, or was she was being suckered into some kind of trap? Surprisingly, she found herself leaning to the former, something she put down to her new set of cartoon emotional responses and their constant drift to a state of naive wonderment. As she crossed the stream, she had to restrain herself from remarking how groovy it all was.

"What the hell is happening to me?"

The only jarring note was the box privet maze that had been planted at a distance from the path on the far bank of the stream. Something about it awoke the old mistrustful Semple. The leaves were too damned green, the interior too dark and forbidding, and she didn't like the look of the hard-eyed gulls that circled the spiral of hedges, as though those who couldn't find their way out might be left in there to die. Even this wasn't enough, though, for her to build a full head of belligerent trepidation. She found herself blithely dismissing the maze. None of her concern. It was the dome she was going to, wasn't it?

The dome itself was in no way threatening. It nestled, as unobtrusively as a seventy-foot brilliant white hemisphere could nestle, in a low depression between decorative outcroppings of yellow-veined rocks. To further ensure that it didn't muscle out the rest of the landscape with its geometric perfection, it was partially hidden by exotic conifers, shaped on the large scale but with the elegant contortions of bonsai.

The three tiny women, in a single singsong voice, directed Semple's attention to the path's end at a low entranceway like a giant mail slot in the base of the dome. "You go in there."

"You don't come in with me?"

"We never enter the dome except when invited."

"And this time you weren't invited?"

"We were only instructed to meet you at the bridge."

"And you only do as you're instructed?"

"Of course."

"Instructed by *him?*

"Who else?"

Semple nodded. "Right." Even in her dumbed-down condition, she had the distinct feeling that she might be walking into another Anubian harem horror. Unfortunately, she lacked any other real alternative.

Now that she was closer, Semple could see that the wide, low entrance sported triple doors of cartoon black glass with dramatically drawn highlights. She left the three tiny women standing on the path and moved briskly toward the doors. She hardly expected them to be locked against her after he had gone to so much trouble to get her there, but she wouldn't have been surprised at some kind of entry ritual, if only as a show of strength. To her mild surprise, the doors simply slid open at her approach as though controlled by some concealed sensor. She stepped through and immediately found herself in an airlock or antechamber, with a second set of doors preventing her from going any farther. As the outer doors closed behind her, bright ultraviolet light streamed down from overhead luminous panels. This took Semple somewhat by surprise. Was this supposed to be some kind of sterilization process? If it was, it didn't augur well for her first meeting with *him*. To maintain a Howard Hughes phobia of germs after one's death required an incredibly enduring paranoia.

Semple had no sooner reached this conclusion than something happened that forced her to radically revise her thinking. Her entire body started to rearrange itself under the UV light. The cartoon physicality began to morph and fill out, returning herself to her natural form. The sudden transformation wasn't in any way painful, but it left her with a queasy, light-headed feeling, and rapidly fading double vision. The skin-tight comic book clothing proved less than comfortable, now that her human flesh was squeezed into it. Before she had any chance to take stock of this unexpected state, however, an inner door opened and she knew she was expected to go on through. She noted as she stepped through the door that the ray gun was still strapped to her thigh. She wasn't sure if it would be of any practical use, but it had a comfortable heft to it; she wished she'd had something similar during her first encounters with Anubis and Moses. She also observed, glancing at her reflection in the glass of one sliding door, that she had retained the beauty spot from her cartoon face.

The great circular interior of the dome was so sparsely furnished that its occupier, the mysterious "he," appeared to be doing little more than squatting in the manner of the most squalid of young single males. Half-unpacked boxes littered the floor, and the large leather couch, the apparent focal point of the space, was surrounded by drifts of papers, beer cans, and discarded Japanese food containers. Only one side was free of debris, and that was where a monolith of black electronic components squatted with LEDs blinking, flanked by a black refrigerator and a microwave oven. The couch looked directly at a large seventy-millimeter projection TV screen, some twelve feet across and letterbox in format, mounted above a powerful complex of speakers. The screen so dominated the space that it looked to Semple as though the entire dome must have been devised for snacking and TV watching. A movie was playing as Semple entered; Frank Sinatra, Cary Grant, and Sophia Loren in *The Pride and the Passion*. The only other permanent feature, apart from the small sun-sphere that floated high in the apex, supplying an approximation of outdoor light, was a small cross-shaped swimming pool off to one side of the screen. A cross-shaped pool was a little weird by most standards, but by far the most startling object among the dome's assorted contents was the goat, who stood amid a scattered pile of hay just inside the door to the UV chamber, contentedly chewing. Semple instantly recognized it as the gnarled old ram with china eyes and curling yellow misshapen horns who had led Moses' tribe through the wilderness, and perhaps, since he was now here and seemingly at home, to Gojiro and their destruction.

"What the hell are you doing here?"

The goat looked up, but didn't stop chewing. "I've taken up residence here, haven't I?"

Semple had never heard the goat speak before and was surprised by its lilting Welsh accent. "I didn't know you could speak."

"I never spoke around Moses and his bunch. In fact, look you, the only time I said anything was when Moses took it into his head that I'd be a handsome item on the sacrificial altar, and then I had to put him straight. I never did approve of going willingly into that dark night, you know?"

Semple cut him off, suspecting that once he got started, he might go on chatting ad infinitum. "So Gojiro didn't get you?"

The goat regarded her with its mismatched eyes. "Gojiro? No, he didn't 'get' me, as you put it. The Big Green and I are chums."

"So you're the *him* the tiny women were talking about?"

The goat look surprised. "What on earth makes you think I'm *him*?"

"You're the only one here."

The goat nodded in the direction of the pool. "He's there. It's his meditation time."

Semple found herself at something of a loss. "He's in the pool?"

"Lying on the bottom, contemplating the infinite cosmos. You can take a look if you like. He won't mind."

Semple moved toward the pool. On the screen, hundreds of Spanish extras costumed for the Napoleonic Wars were hauling the huge siege cannon up a mountain while Sinatra and Grant watched with worried expressions. She reached the edge and peered down. A young man lay on the white-tiled bottom of the geometric pool, eyes closed, arms outstretched, mirroring the shape of the cross. He was white and handsome, with a soft blond beard that had never felt a razor. His long and equally blond hair waved slightly with the motion of the water. Semple glanced back at the goat. "This is him?"

"That's him."

"Does he know I'm here?"

"Who knows what he knows?"

Semple tried tentatively to get his attention. "Excuse me, but the three tiny women told me I should—"

The goat interrupted. "There isn't much point in talking to him when he's like that."

"How long does he stay like that?"

"It's hard to say. Usually not that long. He has a lot of movies to watch."

No sooner had the goat spoken than the figure in the pool opened its eyes and rose rapidly to the surface. Semple took a surprised step back. "Jesus Christ!"

His face broke the surface and he spoke. "You have it in one."

Semple couldn't bring herself to believe that this was the one-time Messiah. Although his eyes were deep-set and he did work them in a way that seemed to lend him a certain mystic significance, he lacked the aura she'd expect in anyone claiming to be God's own offspring. For the moment, however, she thought it best to go along with the charade. "Does that mean I have to revise 'he' to 'He' with a capital 'H'?"

The self-proclaimed Jesus was now treading water like any normal man. He might be able to lie on the bottom of the pool with his eyes closed, but it seemed as though he wasn't much at walking on the surface. He pushed his wet hair out of his eyes and grinned at Semple. "That might be nice."

He paddled to the edge of the pool and started to climb out. "You're very good-looking for one of Moses' bunch."

Semple was outraged. "I am *not* one of 'Moses' bunch.' I sincerely hope you don't imagine I have any connection to that inbred trash except by force of circumstances."

Jesus apparently failed to notice that he'd caused the least offense. "That's where Gojiro found you, wasn't it?"

"I was unwillingly passing through."

Jesus was now out of the pool and standing naked in front of her without a trace of self-consciousness. "Passing through, huh? So why don't you pass me a towel?"

As she stiffly handed him the towel, she noticed that this Jesus was a near-perfect physical specimen, but the same could have been said for Anubis or Moses, and Semple resolved to treat it as nothing more than a skin-deep phenomenon. Jesus paused in his vigorous toweling off and waved a hand in the direction of the couch. "Could you switch channels? I don't think I can take much more of *The Pride and the Passion*."

Semple was a little surprised. Not standing on formality was one thing, but this was offhand to the point of rudeness. "You mean me?"

The goat snorted. "He doesn't mean me. You can't work a remote with hooves."

Semple was about to snap back at the goat with a crushing retort, but decided that maybe it was a little early in the game to be throwing her weight around. Instead, she went looking in the vast depths of the central couch for the remote. Sure enough, in one of its bottomless corners lay something black with color-coded buttons, only slightly smaller than a laptop computer. Semple decided this had to be the Remote of Jesus. She picked it up and glanced at the goat. "Which button do I push?"

The ram had moved from his pile of straw and was now grazing on a cardboard packing case. He spoke with his mouth full. "It doesn't really matter. He's almost completely unselective in his viewing."

Semple hit a button at random, and *The Pride and the Passion* was replaced by a segment of *Zombies of the Stratosphere* in which a young Leonard Nimoy appeared as a zombie. As she adjusted the remote, Jesus flipped the towel over his shoulder and walked, still naked, to the fridge. "Brew?"

Semple shook her head. "Not right now."

The goat looked up from his destruction of the packing case. "You could bring me one while you're up."

Jesus handed Semple a ring-pull can of Rattlesnake beer, chilled from the fridge, and Semple opened it and passed it to the goat. Jesus gestured in his direction. "You've met Mr. Thomas, I see."

"I didn't know that was his name."

"He was once a famous poet, but after he drank himself to death, in a bar called the White Horse in Greenwich Village, he was so racked with guilt that he came to the Afterlife as a ram." This Jesus seemed freely to indulge an oblivious and gratuitous petty cruelty that Semple hardly found becoming in even a wannabe Messiah. Mr. Thomas stopped lapping and stared balefully at Jesus. "I'll have you know I enjoy being a goat. We goats can eat just about everything and we also get to fuck a great deal. As you well know."

This last remark caused Semple to look covertly from Jesus to Mr. Thomas and back again. Were these two an item? And if they were, why had she been invited here? Before she could say anything, though, Jesus glanced at the screen and shook his head. It seemed that *Zombies of the Stratosphere* didn't meet with his approval. "Try something else, would you?"

Semple hit another key on the huge remote. *Zombies of the Stratosphere* was replaced by Eva Bartok in *The Gamma People*. Jesus shook his head. "I don't think so."

Semple tried again. What the fuck was going on here? She hadn't come here to change the channels for him. *The Gamma People* were history. Now they had *Journey to the Seventh Planet*. Jesus didn't seem to like this any better.

"No."

Semple punched buttons, surfing a whole selection of drive-in fodder, while Jesus stood unselfconciously naked, beer in hand, staring critically at the screen. She whispered a low aside to the goat. "I though you said he was unselective."

"Except when he's just come up from the bottom of the pool."

Next up, *The Curse of the Doll People*?

"No."

A trailer for *Invasion of the Star Creatures*?

Jesus merely shuddered.

Atom Age Vampire?

"No."

The Town That Feared Sundown?

"No."

Track of the Moonbeast?

"No."

Yog?

"No."

Revenge of the Creature?

"No."

Alien Contamination?

Jesus shook his head.

Flying Disc Men from Mars?

"No."

At *Death Race 2000*, Jesus hesitated. For a moment he seemed tempted, but then he changed his mind. "Maybe not."

Panther Girl of the Congo?

"Definitely not."

"Listen—"

Jesus seemed unaware that Semple hardly shared his enthusiasm for locating the perfect ambient movie moment, and was oblivious to her growing irritation. "Try a different combination; we seem to be locked in some psychotronic sector."

Semple held out the remote. "Why don't you try? I'm clearly hopeless at this."

Jesus took the remote. With a swift and skillful dexterity, he entered a long combination of keystrokes. The screen flashed and there was a grainy black and white Irving Klaw one-reeler of the great Betty Page, near-naked in stockings and shoes, with manacles on her wrists. What was unusual, and had Semple riveted, was that this particular one-reeler also had a man in the frame. In fact, Betty was on her knees giving him enthusiastic head, cupping his balls with her chained hands, while he reclined on a couch strangely like the one right there in the dome. Semple had been certain that Betty, whom she once met briefly in Florida, had never in her life done hardcore. It had to be a morphed simulation of some kind. Semple glanced quickly at Jesus. "If it was vintage porno you wanted . . . " Then she stopped in midsentence. "Wait a minute."

The camera had panned up to the ecstatic face of the man, and she instantly recognized him. It was that same long-haired young man again, the one who had featured in her orgasm vision with Anubis, and again during the strange brief flash while stepping into the *animé* world. Who the hell was he, and what did he want? She turned to see if she might get this or maybe some other answers out of Jesus, but she found that Jesus was gone. He was still nude, and still standing there as a physical entity, but his mind was somewhere up there on the screen with Betty and her mysterious paramour.

"What the fuck is going on here?"

Although it coincided with Semple's question, Jesus's gesture was in no way a reply. He made a slow pass with his right hand. The lights dimmed and the volume of the moaning, gasping audio rose. He started to move backward toward the couch, never once taking his eyes off the images on the screen. Semple's irritation escalated to anger. "Can you hear a damned word I'm saying?"

Without looking away from the screen, Jesus sank into the couch, pulled his legs up, and slowly curled into a fetal positon. Then, as though motivated from deep within a dream, he began to masturbate. Semple was outraged. "This is getting absurd."

A Welsh accent came from the other side of the room as Mr. Thomas looked up from the packing case he had all but demolished. "Did you know that goats discovered coffee?"

A white tuxedo and a clean dress shirt over his trademark leather jeans and boots, a black bow tie hanging unknotted around his neck, a scotch on the rocks in one hand, and a cigarette in the other; Jim felt ready for anything. He was cleaned, shaved, modestly cologned, and now leaned against the bar and surveyed the *salon privée* and decided that, maybe, with a couple more scotches inside him, he might actually be ready to face down Dr. Hypodermic and whatever that entity might have in store for him. When it came to gambling in Hell, Doc Holliday had to be given full credit for finding his way to the glittering diamond heart of the matter. The *salon privée* was clearly an anthology of the best of every *belle epoch* in classic high rolling. A Sean Connery–era James Bond commanded the baccarat shoe and seemed to be winning with heroic consistency, while, facing him across the table, an overfed epicure in a burgundy velvet smoking jacket, who greatly resembled Orson Welles, chain-smoked Cuban Perfectos and looked exceedingly unhappy about the situation. As they'd entered the large, ornately furnished room, Doc had whispered discreetly to Jim, "That could well be Le Chiffre sitting over there. Or a ringer, who'll do, for all practical purposes. I'd seriously advise against doing anything to ruffle or disoblige him. In

fact, it would probably be a good idea if you didn't even bring yourself to his attention."

"Watch out for the carpet beater?"

"You've got the right idea."

At another table, four Regency bucks played hazard. They were
going heavy on the port and the claret and their brittle badinage
was growing a little slurred, and Jim noticed that two of them were
probably well on their way to taking it to the terrace. In contrast,
the five Fu Manchu mandarins playing fan-tan at a nearby table did
so in absolute silence, letting the click of the tiles do their talking
for them, with a nuance of clack that could vary from smug to angry.

When Doc had pointed out the lights at the end of what Jim now
thought of as the Sewer of Suicides, he had expected just a single
casino, some kind of smoky western-movie gambling den with
hunched degenerates losing the price of their souls to dealers in
striped vests and eyeshades, while hostesses in fishnets hustled blow
jobs and red-eye to the unshaven, whiskey-breath carriage trade. Jim
quickly discovered he had set his sights mournfully low. Instead of a
lone gambling joint, he found himself walking down an entire plaza
of well-appointed casinos, fascias hewn from the living rock, much
in the manner of the desert city of Petra, each with its own complex
riot of animated neon. The lights he'd seen up ahead weren't just
from a single source but from a diffusion of many. What confronted
Jim when the tunnel opened out was a complete subterranean strip:
Vegas, Reno, or Monte Carlo consigned to the rocky bowels of the
hereafter. In some respects it could almost be viewed as a refinement
of a much older concept of Hell. Instead of lakes of fire and brimstone, souls could find themselves doomed to draw to an inside
straight through all eternity, not unlike the sex-locked denizens of
the elevator concourse. Not that Jim was thinking this way when
the Sewer of Suicides first opened out onto this cavernous boulevard
of honky-tonk angels, five-card stud, and broken dreams. He just
looked around in surprise and bad-boy delight. "This is really fucking something."

The Virgil had looked at him with a hint of reproach in his expression. "Did you really think I'd steer you to some funky clip joint,
my young master?"

Jim had half expected Doc to go straight into the first establishment in line, which went by the name the Atomico and sported an

elaborate nuclear explosion in garish red-orange and yellow as its electrical come-on. Jim had even started to move toward the entrance before Doc had shaken his head. "Not that one, my boy. I have a reputation to maintain."

"Isn't one casino much like another?"

"To a drinker, maybe, but certainly not to a gambler. All this tourist mill has to offer is slots, Wayne Newton music, and seven-deck blackjack to discourage the counters. Not that anyone who goes in there is going to be able to count beyond the sum total of their fingers and toes."

As if in practical confirmation of Doc's summation of the Atomico, a squad of casino security, in silver radiation suit uniforms, forcibly ejected three sweating, Day-Glo-pink, very drunk pigmen. The pigmen, hominids but hairless, with snouts, curly tails, and perky little ears, existed in some numbers throughout the length and breadth of the Afterlife. No one really knew where the pigmen originated or for what purpose they had been designed, but some humans claimed that they were the leavings of an unholy Cold War genetic experiment. Others simply theorized that they were kept around to make everyone else look good.

Doc also declined to enter Glitter Gulch, the Alhambra, the Shalimar Sporting Club, the Four Aces, and the inevitable Flamingo and Golden Nugget. He was setting a course for the far end of the street, where a magnificent flight of steps led to what could only be Hell's grand casino. So grand, in fact, that it didn't even need to display its name. Where the others were purely gaudy, this last place made its point with dignity and fine architecture. Flames danced from cressets flanking the stairs, and the porticoed entrance was guarded by men dressed in the uniform of Napoleonic lancers. As they drew nearer, Doc nodded approvingly. "That's the place we need, my friend. I've always found money flows cleaner and more smoothly in surroundings of quiet elegance than amid gaudy trash."

Jim had looked down at his tattered shirt and general filth and then at Doc's equally disheveled appearance. Although Doc had left his filthy duster coat in the launch, his boots were scuffed, his frock coat was dusty and stained, and neither of them had shaved in days. "They're not going to let us in there like this, are they? We look like a couple of bums."

Doc stared at Jim disappointedly. "Oh, ye of little faith, do you think there's a gaming room anywhere that's going to refuse admission to Doc Holliday?"

Jim shrugged. "Sure, they might let you in, but what about me? I don't have any gambler's rep."

Doc sighed. "Have some trust, will you? You're with me."

And, as it turned out, being with Doc was all that it needed. Two of the Napoleonic lancers looked stonily askance at Doc and Jim as they first approached, but then Doc gave then a strange high sign with his index and pinky fingers raised and they seem perfectly content with that. The maître d' had raced up to the pair the very moment they set foot inside the door, and for an instant Jim had thought that they were going to be thrown•out after all; but the maître d's only concern was to rectify their condition of grime and travel stain without delay. After receiving tips from both Doc and Jim, the Virgil had taken his leave of them, telling them he would be in the Virgil's lounge if they needed him to go elsewhere. With that business attended to, the two travelers had been whisked into an elevator and taken to a lavishly appointed basement locker room with mirrors, marble showers, a half dozen highly attentive valets, and three barbers' chairs with no waiting. Clean shirts had to be purchased, but a black satin frock coat for Doc and white tux for Jim came with the compliments of the house, as did cocktails on demand. At the end of the process, Jim had regarded himself in multiple mirrors and been highly satisfied with the result. As a final touch, he'd bought himself a pair of Ray•Ban Wayfarers at the casino gift shop. Prices in Hell seemed to be extraordinarily cheap.

They had been left to make their own entrance into the casino. Jim had been all ready to follow the curving, velvet-carpeted stairs down to the main room, where a guitar player who looked a lot like Long Time Robert Moore, only in a white suit and now supposedly blind, was playing blues with a trio whose sound was far too casino-genteel for Jim's more raucous taste. Once again, though, Doc had steered him in a different direction. "Stick with me, my boy. The main room's strictly for amateurs."

Jim was tempted to remind Doc that he *was* an amateur, but decided to follow the flow. How many times did a man penetrate the *salon privée* of the best casino in Hell? The initial impression had been luxuriously pleasing. The cigar smoke was exclusive and harmonized with the most expensive of perfumes and that indefinable bouquet of seasoned money. Players sat with piles of plaques in front of them, some almost as large as dinner slates and plainly worth a fortune, while Van Goghs, Toulouse-Lautrecs, and Picassos looked down from the walls. On the lifeside it would have been called old money; here Jim thought of it as dead money. In his rock star days Jim had now and then found himself in similar places but always as an interloper or a sideshow. To enter as the companion of Doc Holliday, on the other hand, seemed to guarantee him instant acceptance.

Doc immediately handed over the bag containing the entire take from the sale of his soul for a croupier to convert into plaques and chips. Doc, it seemed, was going for broke. For the moment, meanwhile, Jim was left with precious little to do. In the *salon privée*, if you didn't play, you could be little else but a silent spectator, and Jim had never found card games a spectator sport. The bar, whose booze certainly tasted top-shelf, filled his time for a while, and when its novelty wore off there were always the women to observe. One could never divorce money and sexual tension, and the women in the *salon privée* were of a unique standard of predatory beauty. Unfortunately, their attention was on the players, not any kibitzer in the twilight, no matter how romantically he might sip his scotch. One, however, did seem to be paying Jim a certain amount of attention. She had jet-black hair, cut in a severe geometric fringe low across her eyebrows, and was wearing a 1950s-style sheath dress in dark aquamarine. Jim didn't recognize her, although she did in many ways remind him of . . . what was her name? The great underground lingerie and bondage model? Jim was certain he'd never seen the woman before, but the covert glances she kept slipping in his direction, which seemed to be a combination of desire and anxiety, were hardly the kind to be directed at a perfect stranger, no matter how perfect that stranger might be.

The reason the woman's glances were so covert was immediately apparent. She was with a tall, narrow-shouldered, impeccably correct character in full white tie and tails, who went all the way to the wearing of white kid gloves to handle his cards. It took Jim no time at all to peg him as an aristocratic sadist from the old Heidelberg school, right down to the dueling scars on his cheek, the monocle screwed into his left eye, and the way his hair was shaved high above his ears. Heidelberg was losing badly at twenty-one and when he rose to resupply himself with chips, the woman quickly scribbled a note on a drink napkin with a slim silver pencil. She handed the napkin to a waiter and nodded in Jim's direction. Sure enough, the waiter, without being too obvious about it, brought the note quickly to Jim. The handwriting was flamboyant and urgent, with the characters formed large and with decorative curves. The content, on the other hand, hardly made any sense at all, unless Jim's memory was even more damaged than he had so far assumed.

My darling,
I beg you, for tonight, pretend that you don't know me. The man that I am with would do terrible things to me if he discovered that we knew each other. It would be ten times worse if he should ever see that film! Even though, for my safety, we must act as strangers, don't think I have forgotten that earthshaking night and all the awful and wonderful things you did with the DEVICE!
Forever your slave and admirer,
Amber.

Jim read the note twice and then looked in this Amber's direction. Heidelberg had now returned, and she studiously avoided his eyes. Either another time-shift was going down, or he was in a lot of trouble. How the fuck could he forget a night with that woman? and what the hell was the *device*? Since he obviously wasn't about to go and risk Heidelberg's wrath by speaking to her, he folded the note carefully in half and slipped it into the pocket of his tuxedo.

It was only moments after doing this that he saw someone he actually did know and recognize. Through the door, maple-syrup shoulders above a second skin of emerald sequins, had come Donna Anna Maria Isabella Conchita Theresa Garcia (but you can call me Lola). She noted the presence of Doc, who was warming his poker skills before he went to the big show with four black-tie rubes, one of whom resembled the Duke of Windsor, the abdicated English king, and another the perfect likeness of Nazi foreign minister Joachim von Ribbentrop. Having checked out Doc, Lola turned and headed straight to the bar. Although she was diametrically different from the *Viva Zapata!* bandita Jim had encountered in Doc's forgotten town, it was definitely her.

Unfortunately, she didn't seem to know or recognize him. He smiled a friendly greeting, but was met by a blank stare as she passed him to take the tequila sunrise that the bartender had started mixing the moment she'd walked into the room. Surprised, but putting it down to the same time problem that seemed to be affecting Doc, Jim broadened his smile. "We have met, but perhaps you don't remember."

This time, her response was an expression of unbreakable Andean ice. "We have never met."

"Donna Anna Maria Isabella Conchita Theresa Garcia, but you can call me Lola?"

Lola took a deep breath and then lowered her voice. "I'm not supposed to speak to you."

Jim was mystified. "What is this?"

"Doc doesn't remember the last time we met and I'm not supposed to, either, but I like you, Jim Morrison, so I'll take a chance on breaking the rules. I seriously advise you to get out of here as quickly as you can. Take your Virgil and go."

"Out of the casino?"

"Out of Hell itself."

Jesus' free hand moved to the remote, apparently of its own accord. The Irving Klaw porn had ended without too much denouement and was suddenly replaced by *Zorro's Secret Legion*, a Republic serial that, in its whip work and leather costumes, ran with a distinct S&M undertow that was probably lost on the ten-year-olds for whom it was intended. Or was it? This Jesus didn't look like a ten-year-old, but he did tend to behave that way, and he was continuing to jerk himself off while staring unblinkingly at the screen. Semple looked from screen to couch and finally at Mr. Thomas, the goat. "What do you mean, goats invented coffee?"

Mr. Thomas finished munching on a piece of cardboard. "The way I heard it, sometime around the thirteenth century an Ethiopian goatherd called Kaldi noticed that his animals were getting high as kites on the red berries of a particular wild shrub. Being of an inquiring mind and curious disposition, this Kaldi tried the berries himself. When he, too, not only got high as a kite but also remained awake for fifty-seven hours straight, Kaldi knew he was on to something. Of course, being Islamic, Kaldi's first thought was that the said berries would be a way to stay awake and remain at one's religious devotions longer than would have been previously possible. After chewing the berries, he decided this was a bit too much of a jolt. Soon he hit on the idea of stewing the berries in boiling water and drinking the resulting liquid. As you've probably guessed by now, the red berries were wild coffee beans and—"

Semple rather rudely interrupted the anecdote. "Is everyone around here totally crazy?"

The goat looked at her both surprised and a little offended. "Not really. Not when you consider that we're living in the brain of an entirely fictional, massively oversized Mesozoic dinosaur."

"One's jerking off to an old Zorro serial and the other's telling me how coffee was invented?"

"Strictly speaking, we're not even in the brain itself. We actually occupy a tumor on that brain."

Semple was horrified. "A tumor?"

"What do you think this dome really is?"

"Is it malignant?"

"Not for us."

"I meant for Gojiro."

The goat tore off another piece of packing case and started munching. In that he seemed to need to talk with his mouth full, a conversation with Mr. Thomas was not unlike ones she'd had with Anubis. "That's something of an academic point. The Big Green has one motherfucker of a post-nuclear metabolism and I'd imagine it's going to take a good uninterrupted ten thousand years for a tumor to hurt him."

Semple was still uneasy. "I'm not sure I want to be in a tumor."

"After a while, you don't even think about it. What are you doing here, by the way?"

Semple blinked at the goat. "You're asking me that?"

"You walked in here of your own accord."

"I hardly knew what I was doing. I just followed the directions of the three tiny women."

"You always do what tiny women tell you?"

"Only when I don't have a better idea."

"You came in like the mote in Godz's eye, right?"

"As far as I can tell. But you know what happened. You were there when Moses' tribe got stomped."

The goat avoided her eyes. "I have a bit of a problem with that."

Semple frowned. "Either you were there or you weren't."

"It's one of those cat's-cradle time problems. Some of the time I seem to have been the lead goat for Moses and his stinking followers, sometimes I'm the companion of someone who may or may not be Jesus Christ and who thinks I may or may not be the reincarnation of Dylan Thomas."

Semple glanced at the still-masturbating Jesus. "Can't he hear you? He might not like his Jesushood being questioned."

Mr. Thomas shook his head. "He's totally in the zone. TV has that effect on him."

An unpleasant thought struck Semple. "I'm not here to entertain you, am I?

"Not specifically, but if you were to offer, I'd be most pleased to—"

Semple cut him off. "Let's leave that for a while. My sex life has been far too complicated of late. I really don't feel inclined to go interspecies right now. I couldn't take on a goat no matter how glowing his possible literary antecedents."

Mr. Thomas chewed cardboard, apparently considering the rejection. "That's a pity. 'After the first death, there is no more.' "

"It really isn't anything personal. I'm very fond of *Under Milk Wood.*"

"That wasn't from *Under Milk Wood.*"

"I'm sorry."

"It's from something else."

"Oh." Semple covered her gaffe by looking around the dome. "How about, 'it was spring, moonless night in the small town, starless and bible-black . . . ' "

The goat was mollified. "That's better."

The episode of *Zorro's Secret Legion* had concluded in a seeming sudden-death cliff-hanger. Jesus' hand twitched and a new movie was on the screen, Audie Murphy in *Bullet for a Badman,* picking up the story midway through the action. "I'm starting to feel that maybe the best thing I could do would be to get out of here. The possibilities seem a little limited."

The goat swallowed. "Unfortunately that may be difficult."

Semple's eyes narrowed. "What are you telling me?"

Mr. Thomas scratched himself with his left hind leg. "You came in animation mode, am I right?"

Semple answered cautiously, unsure of what was coming next. "Yes. That's where I got this gun and the ridiculous costume."

"But then, on the way in, you passed under the lights?"

"Right."

"And you changed back to normal?"

"That's right. I did. Apart from the beauty spot."

"Then that's it. You can't go back out again. Not in human form. No humans in Toon Town."

"What would happen to me if I did?"

"It's hard to explain, but very nasty."

"So how do I change back to a toon?"

"You can't."

"Why not?"

Mr. Thomas nodded in the direction of the prone and masturbating Jesus. "He's forgotten how to do it."

"Are you telling me I'm a prisoner of that bastard faux Jesus?"

"Does he really look like a captor?"

Semple touched the ray gun that was still strapped to her leg. "Maybe this might get his attention?"

"I really wouldn't try firing that thing."

"Why not?"

"There are two likely outcomes, look you. Either it wouldn't work at all, or it would explode and blow your arm off."

"How do I know you're not lying?"

The goat looked a little sheepish. "You don't, but I really wouldn't recommend testing the point."

Semple and Mr. Thomas seemed to have reached an impasse. Jesus eighty-sixed Audie Murphy and replaced him with Charlton Heston playing Michelangelo in *The Agony and the Ecstasy*. "He was very creative once. Before the TV got him."

"Creative?"

"He built most of the stuff outside."

"No kidding." Suddenly Semple was thinking. An idea had arrived on the half shell.

The goat hadn't noticed, however. "In fact, it was him who saw the potential of the Big Green's brain in the first place. He even figured out how he could get inside here and make Godz do what he wanted him to do."

Now two ideas were simmering side by side. "He can control Gojiro?"

"If someone could turn off the TV and get his attention."

"So why don't you turn off the TV and get his attention?"

"I already told you, didn't I? My hooves can't work the remote."

✳

Heads turned and even the fops stopped their banter. The Duke of Windsor folded his hand despite the fact he was holding three sevens and had yet to make the change. It wasn't so much the man as the aura that entered with him. Jim could only imagine that Dracula might have a made a similar entrance. The tall man in the powder blue, narrow-lapel sharkskin suit, goatee beard, and porkpie hat looked nothing like the legendary count. In fact, he was an almost perfect double for Ike Turner; although Jim knew immediately that it wasn't Ike—Jim had played ballrooms with Ike and Tina and, although Ike could be mean, even he didn't spread the kind of malignancy, like a sulfurous miasma, that was rapidly filling the *salon privée*. Lola was now noticeably nervous. "Go. Get out of here and stop being an idiot. You're completely out of your depth here."

Jim stubbornly shook his head. "I'm not running. I'm sick of having no fucking control over my destiny."

Lola looked at him in way that made Jim glad he was already dead. "It's not just your destiny, you moron. You could blow it for the rest of us.

Jim was going to continue to protest, but the Ike Turner doppelgänger turned his head in Jim's direction. The scotch had yet to slow Jim to the point of not being fast enough to avoid the evil eyes, but even the close pass he experienced was enough to send a glacial chill through his nervous system. In the instant, he knew that Lola was right. He had no clue what was going down in the private salon, and he certainly had no place there. "Okay, I'm going. But how will I hook up with Doc again?"

Lola fluttered her hands as though willing him away. She just wanted him gone. "Don't worry about it. You'll find each other."

Jim moved as unobtrusively to the door as he could and quietly slipped through it. Out on the main staircase, he glanced at the nearest Napoleonic guard. "Some weird look-alike show back in that gold mine."

The guard nodded stiffly. "It's that time of the night, sir. Can I call you your Virgil?"

Jim shook his head. "No, thank you. I think I can find my own way."

"Whatever you say, sir."

Jim hurried on down the stairs, only to find himself confronted by yet another bizarre spectacle. Sid Vicious was coming through the casino's revolving doors, swaying slightly, with a woman in a wedding dress who wasn't Nancy on his arm. Just to make the picture a tad more off kilter, Vicious was wearing an outfit virtually identical to Jim's—white tux, leather jeans, and engineer boots—except that Sid was lacking a shirt, and his trademark padlock and chain dangled on his scarred and scrawny chest. He immediately spotted Jim and his face twisted into a somnambulent sneer. "The Doctor's looking for you. And he's got some wicked gear."

"Holliday or Hypodermic?"

"Which one do you think, you fucking hippie?"

Semple knew that she was trying Mr. Thomas's patience, but she didn't care. An awesome payback and an end to her adventure were almost within her grasp. "When Godz gets going, it's usually bad news for the nearest city. Am I right?"

Mr. Thomas wagged his wisp of a tail uncomfortably. "He eats it."

Semple hesitated, trying not to look too eager, but wholly failing. "So what would it take to get the Big Green to eat the a city like, say . . . Necropolis?"

"You want to see Necropolis eaten?"

"Just a hypothetical question."

Mr. Thomas didn't believe her. "You've got your reasons to see him eat Necropolis."

"You have a problem with that?"

Jesus was still prone on the couch, but at least he'd stopped masturbating. Seemingly the Sistine Chapel didn't turn him on. Mr. Thomas shook his head. "No problem at all. I've seen TV from Necropolis. The place would seem infinitely suited as a snack for the Big Green."

"So what would get him to head in that direction?"

"Not much at all, if they've got the makings of nuclear weapons there."

"He likes nuclear weapons?"

"He *loves* nuclear weapons."

"The ones Anubis has are pretty small and pretty dirty."

"He likes the small and dirty best of all. It was a nasty, dirty little bomb that thawed him out of the Arctic ice, don't forget."

"So it's just a question of getting him started?"

On the screen, Michelangelo was complaining to the Pope about how he hadn't been paid, but apparently doing little for Jesus, who jumped to an episode of *The Newlywed Game*. Mr. Thomas paused before he answered. "Only Jesus can do that."

Semple looked hard at the goat. "The TV has to be turned off."

"I really wouldn't advise doing that."

"It would be for his own good."

The goat looked at her knowingly, calling her bluff. "You're not interested in his good. You just want to see Godz eat Necropolis."

"Okay, I admit it."

"Turning off the TV just like that might traumatize him."

Semple treated Mr. Thomas to her hardest stare of authority. "Are you going to stop me?"

Mr. Thomas seemed undecided. "I've a handy pair of horns, don't I?"

"You want to spend the rest of your days shut up in a tumor with a terminal couch potato?"

Mr. Thomas thought about this. "You do have a point there."

"So you won't stop me?"

"I'm still not happy about you shutting down the telly."

Semple knew she had the goat cornered. "But you won't try and stop me?"

"I suppose not."

Semple walked to the couch and took the remote from Jesus' close-to-lifeless hand.

Jim was about to step into the revolving door when a worried-looking man pushed in front of him, elbowing him out of the way. Such rudeness hardly seemed in keeping with the ambience of the grand casino, but Jim could only suppose that the individual had his reasons. It took about forty seconds for those reasons to become abundantly clear. As Jim disengaged from the doors, the man had already reached the bottom of the steps. He halted and let out a soul-wrenching sob. "I've lost it all. She'll never forgive me."

With these words, he pulled a small chrome-plated revolver from his jacket, pointed it at his right temple, and pulled the trigger. The gun went off and a spurt of gray-pink brains was propelled almost to the other side of the wide flight of steps. Two Napoleonic guards hurried forward as the man's body shimmered and vanished, taking its corporal leave for the pods of the Great Double Helix. The squirt of brain remained, though, and one of the guards quickly called for a cleaner.

"Brilliant. Blew his brains out just like that. Never thought I'd get to see it." Jim turned. Sid Vicious was standing behind him. The punk had apparently followed him back out of the casino just in time to catch the incident.

Jim shrugged. "I guess it goes with the territory. This was once the section of Hell reserved for suicides."

"You believe all that fucking bollocks?"

"A man has to believe something."

"That's the trouble with you fucking hippies. Always looking for shit to believe in." Vicious laughed nastily and gestured to Jim with his right hand. " 'Ere, Morrison, catch."

He tossed a small silver ball to Jim, a sphere with a circumference little larger than a quarter. Without thinking, Jim caught it one-handed. The sphere immediately started to glow and sparkle, an electric shock ran up his right arm, and his surroundings began to glow and distort. He tried to drop the sphere, but it clung to the palm of his hand. The experience wasn't at all unpleasant, except that Jim instinctively knew the sphere's intention. He was caught. The sphere was going to absorb him and take him someplace, he didn't know where or how. About the only thing he knew for sure was that Sid Vicious had only been a pawn in this game. He had merely delivered the snare. The identity of the real hunter was something he didn't want to think about.

7

Can you say Relief?

The dome tilted violently and tiny loose objects rolled across the floor. Jesus appeared not to notice as he operated the remote, making adjustments to Gojiro's forward direction with the rapt concentration of a twelve-year-old playing an advanced video game. The couch had now become his command chair, and he was totally locked into the task of guiding the huge creature to Necropolis. The dome lurched again and Semple grabbed for a handhold. Mr. Thomas simply braced his legs. He seemed quite adept at rolling with the motion, although Semple suspected that it was easier to handle the jolting effect of the giant reptile's walk when you had four legs instead of just two. And, of course, on the lifeside, Dylan Thomas had been a highly adept drunk. Hadn't he walked from the White Horse Tavern to the Chelsea Hotel with hardly a liver on the night that he died?

Jesus had surprised Semple by taking quite readily to the suggestion that he power up Gojiro to destroy Necropolis. After some initial blinking incomprehension, a brief tantrum, and then a quick dip in the cross-shaped pool, he had adopted her plan with comparative alacrity. He seemed relieved to have someone else to suggest a course of action. He had certainly exhibited no moral qualms about setting the monster in motion with the deliberate goal of eating an entire city. In fact, the only objections had come from the goat. "You're supposed to be the Prince of Peace, boyo. Or had you forgotten that?"

Jesus had brushed the reminder aside. "I've been meaning to drive that fucking Anubis out of the temple for a long time."

301

Semple didn't want any geographical confusion. "Actually, he doesn't have a temple, just a huge overbearing palace."

"Same difference. I come not bearing garlands but with a sword."

Mr. Thomas had snorted. "That's not even the correct biblical quotation."

Jesus had glared at him. "Those fucking gospel writers never got my shit right. They screwed up all the best bits."

The goat gave him a look of cool disbelief as it coped with the next sway of the floor and Jesus went back to his remote. "I seem to have forgotten how to stop the dome from rolling each time he takes a step."

"Go into DOS and try Esc-control-alt-F12."

Jesus keyed the suggested sequence and immediately the swaying was reduced from the wild tilting of a yacht in a cyclone to little more than a rhythmic ripple. Jesus grinned at Mr. Thomas. "You remembered."

"So would you if you hadn't taken up residence on *Gilligan's Island*."

"What would I do without you?"

"Sometimes I wonder."

It had taken Jesus a few minutes to recover from the soporific effect of TV grip. He had keyed the wrong commands, and, as far as Semple could read the repercussions in the dome, he more than once set Gojiro reeling and staggering like a drunken mountain. In short order, however, helped by his own recovering faculties and a series of scathing reprimands from Mr. Thomas, Jesus regained his grip and put the great beast on line for travel and ultimate assault. Even the dome itself was altered by the process. The TV screen that Jesus had previously watched with such obsessive languor enlarged to a 180-degree wraparound format that appeared to offer all of the monster's forward vision plus considerable peripherals. When it was first up, the image was shaky and unstable, subject to snow, flare-out, and solarization. It needed a couple of passes at the remote before he managed to bring it under control and activate a kind of Stedicam effect, which eventually got him, Semple, and Mr. Thomas a panoramic view of the swiftly passing desert as Gojiro jogged toward his target at a speed in excess of one hundred miles an hour.

Semple may have made the first crucial intervention when she'd taken the remote from Jesus and cut the electronic umbilical, but once the King of the Monsters was set on his lumbering way to Necropolis,

Semple was relegated to little more than a spectator's role. The scene inside the dome was, to say the least, a strange one. Mr. Thomas stood foursquare in front of the screen, acting as forward spotter. Jesus sat in the center of the couch, the large remote on one knee, also staring at the screen like the commander on his bridge. Semple, in her scanty red superheroine costume and platform shoes, stood behind the couch that had now become Jesus' command chair. Fortunately, Jesus was no longer naked. He had at least bothered to slip on Nike sneakers, a purple linen toga, and a totally unnecessary pair of Erwin Rommel goggles, pushed back on his forehead, before he put Gojiro into operational mode. To Semple's mind, they were a highly unlikely trio to be in apparent charge of a massive reptile primed and looking for a fight.

"Do you have to steer him?"

Jesus shook his head. "No, he smells enriched uranium. He'll go straight for it. Radiation is, quite literally, in the Big Green's blood."

Jesus was leaning back on the couch in a woodenly confident pose of overstated authority that he could have learned only from William Shatner. Trying to look every inch the commander of the massive instrument of destruction that Gojiro had now become, he was now the absolute diametric contrast to the prone and priapic figure that he'd been such a short time before.

"How long will it be before we see Necropolis?"

Jesus gave a half shrug, as though it hardly mattered. "Fifteen, maybe twenty minutes. Certainly no more."

Semple wondered how Jesus might react if she introduced him to her second idea over the course of the short journey to the target. He certainly seemed to be in a new mood for adventure; maybe it would be okay to deliver the second hit of the one-two combination.

"I have a sibling."

Jesus nodded, keeping his new, hawklike Starfleet concentration on the forward screen. "That's very interesting."

"She has a need to make the acquaintance of someone like you."

"It's said the whole of humanity needs to make my acquaintance."

Semple ignored this messianic ego flourish and began to describe Aimee, her Heaven, and her predicament in terms that were glowing if not necessarily accurate, using every chance at her disposal to stroke and flatter. She must have made some impression, for at the end of her recital he actually looked in her direction. "You're saying that she needs a man to run her Heaven for her?"

"You could be her savior."

The goat rolled his eyes; Semple was overdoing it. Jesus, on the other hand, basked in the appeal of the idea. It seemed that, where his supposed messianic qualities were concerned, flattery could get one just about anywhere. He stroked his beard and smiled. "And which of you would I be expected to have sex with? You or your sibling?"

Semple decided she didn't like this Captain Kirk version of Jesus any better than the comatose masturbator, but he might be exactly what she needed to inflict on Aimee. He could well turn her sister's Heaven into a living Hell. She quickly played along with the gag, although she was starting to suspect, if only on instinct, that Jesus was probably impotent where women were concerned. "Perhaps the two of us will have to fight over you."

This must have really caught his imagination, because he looked around sharply. "That could be the most interesting part."

Semple kept her fixed smile, but now she knew for sure; this was the one she wanted to dispatch to Aimee. Jesus, though, was having second thoughts. "I don't know if I should travel from here. The Big Green might need me."

This stopped even Semple's fixed smile in its tracks. "Need you? Why should he need you? You don't do anything but watch TV inside a tumor."

Jesus turned on the couch and looked at her with a nastiness she hadn't previously observed. "Well, it sure as shit beats dragging a cross through the streets of Jerusalem, doesn't it? How would you like to get crowned with thorns, scourged, and crucified? You want to spend your time schlepping up loaves and fishes for thousands of the great unwashed, start doing miracles at parties when the booze runs out, and have to ride around the desert on a recalcitrant stinking donkey? Or maybe you'd rather have me go through that shit all over again? Are you one of those miserable traditionalists?"

Semple had no diplomatic answer to any of this, and Jesus might have railed on much longer had not something on the forward screen caught his attention. The air on the horizon had become a smudge of dirt and pollution. "We'll have to discuss this later. That's Necropolis up ahead."

Jim was strung out, a million molecules stretching to near-infinity, playing host to a traffic of vibrations that manifested itself in the form of screaming, unimaginable, and totally unendurable pain. Pain defined his entire being. The receptors in his brain howled and hurt for things they couldn't have. An interlocking helix revolved around him at sickening speed, blazing with colors unconfined to the limitations of the visible spectrum. He felt like he was going through an even more hideous death than his last one, but he knew this wasn't the comparatively ordered interface between life and death, this was something far more complicated and far more awful, and that Dr. Hypodermic was deliberately doing it to him. His only recourse was to wail in his agony and helplessness. "How much more do you want from me? I fucking *died* for you the last time, didn't I?"

In response, a voice hissed in his ear, a voice with the faintest trace of a French Caribbean accent. "My *petit ami*, Sid Vicious told me you were running away from me."

"I wasn't running—"

"So what were you doing?"

"I just didn't want to get involved again."

The red eyes of Dr. Hypodermic glowed like twin sources of malignant energy in the deep black space beyond the interlocking helix. "Involved?"

The helices increased their dizzying speed. Nameless blind larvae of things too iniquitous to contemplate snuffled at Jim's stretched and strung-out molecules and Jim groaned. "Just make this pain stop."

The disembodied eyes were pitiless and the voice ignored his plea. "Jim Morrison doesn't want to get involved?"

"I don't even know that I'm really Jim Morrison."

"You know exactly who you are, and besides, *mon fils*, would it really matter? You made the addict's compact, whoever you might be. I never forget one of my own."

Jim was suffering to the point where he'd agree to anything. "Okay, okay, I don't deny it. I'm yours. I'm a fucking thrall. I belong to you. I'll never try to get away again. Just make the pain stop."

"Look on this as a negative reinforcement, a remembrance of anguish past."

Jim wondered if abject pleading might do any good. "Please, in all mercy, make the pain stop."

It didn't. "Now you know what Hell used to be like when Lucifer was running the show." Explosions of blazing orange-yellow lava rocketed through the helix spirals, creating trajectories of fire. Suddenly Jim's agony grew exponentially worse, and Dr. Hypodermic chuckled. The sound was blood-chilling. "Where's it written that death would separate us, *mon brave?*"

"There was nothing ever written."

"Wasn't the accord of addiction ratified in blood?"

"I told you already. I give up. I'm yours, anything you want. You don't have to torture me to make your point. I'm not fucking resisting."

"And I am not making a point, *mon ami.*"

"So what's this all about? You already said it was a negative reinforcement. Is this Limbo?"

"Not Limbo, just a reprise of the pain before the gift of relief."

And suddenly the pain was not only gone but hardly a memory. Jim free-floated fetal, curled naked, in the surrounding safety and warm liquid protection of a perfect womb, a dark star child whom no one could touch and only one could approach. The Caribbean hiss of the Doctor was his complete lullaby, the only one he needed or cared about. Hypodermic laughed again. "And now the gift of relief before the return of the pain."

Mr. Thomas glanced back at Jesus. "Dirigible with fighter escort at eleven o'clock."

The tallest towers of Necropolis were now visible on the horizon, as were one large black dot and three smaller ones in the air above the city. Jesus laughed. The prospect of the attack on Necropolis had raised his energy levels to a point where he was close to manic, and the messianic adrenaline seemed to be pumping double-time. "They always send up the air defenses first. It's the standard opening move. Anubis is looking for a chess game."

Semple was still standing slightly behind Jesus' command chair. "Are those planes going to be a problem?"

Jesus grinned and shook his head. "The last time he went after Tokyo, they sent F16s against him. All they managed to do was make him angrier." He glanced at the goat. "What do you think those things are, Mr. Thomas?"

"One Zeppelin heavy gunship and three fighters. Two Fokkers and a Sopwith Camel, as far as I can tell. Either he's confusing Godz with King Kong or he's going for a World War 1 motif."

Jesus grinned. "This is going to be a November turkey shoot."

He hit the remote and to Semple's surprise she found herself looking at a split-screen triptych. The center panel was the forward view as before, but on either side were two medium-shot side views of Gojiro moving across the desert. "How do you do that?"

"It's the second and third unit."

This piece of illogical tech was more than Semple cared to delve into, so she remained silent. If Gojiro traveled with his own movie crew, she really didn't want to know the how or why. She was content to watch as he loped across the desert. As the three elderly planes homed in on him, the King of the Monsters made no attempt to attack or evade them. Either he or Jesus, whoever was really in control, held the same course, going straight for the city. The Zeppelin cruised at an altitude roughly equivalent to Gojiro's eye level. Jesus noted this and nodded knowingly. "Whoever's in command of the thing thinks he can come in head-on, make a half turn, and open up with a broadside. He doesn't have a clue what he's dealing with."

"They're very confident of themselves in Necropolis. Particularly the officer corps. I think it comes from a regular diet of roast baby."

Mr. Thomas glanced at the two of them. "The commander could be a woman."

Semple shook her head. "Not in Necropolis."

The three fighters were adopting a different tactic. They were climbing, gaining height for a formation power-dive attack. Gojiro seemed to see the planes for the first time and slowed his pace. His giant brow furrowed and he stopped completely, letting out a slow, tentative growl.

"Ggggrrraaapph."

The three fighters reached their operational ceiling and went into a slow turn.

Jesus' eyes gleamed. "Here they come. They do think he's bloody King Kong."

The fighters dived, gathering speed as they dropped. Gojiro looked up; in the dome, the leading plane increasingly filled the forward screen section. Despite herself, Semple ducked and Jesus and Mr. Thomas exchanged smiles. The next moment, Gojiro took a deep breath and exhaled violently. The leading biplane was enveloped by his electric-blue, radioactive breath. The plane instantly burst into flames and spun out burning. The monster continued to breathe out, hosing down the other two fighters so they also burned and fell. Jesus let out a whoop.

"Yes!"

Semple's eyes narrowed. To her mind, the way Jesus exulted in the thrill of the kill was a little close to unhealthy—something to note for future reference. The Zeppelin had now started to turn, though whether to bring its guns to bear or simply to get the hell out of there was unclear. This time, Gojiro chose not to use his radioactive breath. He charged forward, tail waving, and grabbed for the dirigible like a child reaching for a toy balloon. The airship managed to elude his reaching hands with a sudden and desperate surge of speed, but hardly had the maneuverability to do it a second time. The King of the Monsters grabbed and twisted the length of the fuselage very much like a man tearing apart a baguette of French bread. The aluminum skeleton that gave the airship its rigidity buckled and snapped, the fabric skin ripped, but then a spark must have been struck, for a hydrogen fireball suddenly exploded right in Gojiro's hand. The monster hurled the blazing Zeppelin away from him with an angry shriek of pain.

"GGGGAAAAARRRK!"

The dome swayed dangerously. Jesus lurched sideways on the couch, Semple grabbed for it to stop herself from falling, and even Mr. Thomas staggered. Jesus' hands flew deftly over the keypad of the remote and the environment quickly righted itself. The supposed messiah grinned. "Now he's good and mad. There'll be no stopping him after that."

Mr. Thomas peered up at the screen. "Mad or not, they look like they're going to have another try at slowing him down. There's more aircraft coming up."

"How many?"

"Five."

"What kind?"

The goat squinted at the forward section of the screen. "They look like Sabre Jets to me, or maybe MIG-15s. Certainly Korean War vintage."

"So now we're getting a bit more serious."

The handful of jets came at Gojiro low and fast, racing across the flat desert in a perfect V formation, presumably hoping that, by staying low, they would avoid the worst of his radioactive halitosis. A thousand yards from the target, the lead plane lifted and fired a pair of wing-mounted rockets. This second attack rocked Gojiro, worse even than the exploding Zeppelin. Again he was hurt and the dome reeled as he roared in pain.

"GGGGRRRRAAAAARRRGGGHHH!"

Mr. Thomas voiced a concerned warning. "I think the Big Green's sustained a chest wound."

"Is it bad?"

"I don't think so."

Even though red blood ran down his chest, contrasting sharply with the green of his wrinkled hide, the great reptile didn't appear to be weakened in any way. He seized the lead jet by the tail and, using it like a club, smashed down the next two in the formation. The fourth jet managed to loose its rockets, but the pilot must have panicked, because they flashed past wide, leaving white vapor trails. Gojiro turned and loosed his destructive breath at this and also the fifth and final jet as they screamed past him at head height. As two explosions created billows of black smoke, Jesus again grinned like a fiend. "He can be real fast when he wants to be."

The dome was bounced around again as Gojiro performed an impromptu victory dance and Jesus laughed out loud. "I think that's all they wrote."

Mr. Thomas shook his head. "There's something else coming at us."

Jesus' face straightened. "What?"

"It looks like a Flying Wing."

Jesus looked puzzled. "What can they hope to achieve by that?"

"We may have a cultural reference going down here."

Jesus' puzzlement deepened. "Cultural reference?"

"Remember the George Pal version of *War of the Worlds?*"

"Of course."

"In the movie, the Flying Wing was used to drop the atom bomb on the invading Martians."

"You think Anubis would use an atom bomb on us? We're already real close to the city suburbs. He'd kill a lot of his own people."

Semple supplied the answer to this. "That wouldn't bother Anubis at all. Can Gojiro survive a nuclear attack?"

Mr. Thomas looked deeply unhappy. "I very much doubt it."

Jesus was also worried. "In the movie, the Martians neutralized the bomb with their energy shields."

Semple didn't like the sound of this. "Do we have energy shields?"

Jesus looked up angrily. "What do you think? We're in a fucking giant dinosaur, not a starship."

The womb burst wetly and Jim found himself crawling across the overgrown, stone-flagged floor of a ruined temple. Tropical rain fell in leaden sheets, and he was immediately soaked to the skin. Miniature rivers followed the cracks and irregularities in the paving, with tiny torrents washing down the accumulated debris of leaves and twigs. Beyond the broken walls, napalm exploded, and the jungle burned despite the downpour. Helicopters clattered overhead and a stream of tracer cut through the smoke and steam of combat. Silhouetted against the explosions, a huge smiling Buddha had half its face blown away. The skeletal figure of a man in ragged olive drab squatted in the flame-shadows with his back to one of the broken walls. An M16 and a steel helmet were beside him and his poncho was pulled forward over his head to shelter him from the rain. Leaning forward with rapt concentration, under cover of the tented poncho, he was cooking up three white paramedic morphine pills in a blackened spoon over the flame of a candle in a K-ration can. A disposable syringe was clamped between his teeth. When he saw Jim crawling toward him, he fixed him with a hollow-eyed stare. "You stay the fuck away from me, okay? Fuck this up and I'll cut you in half. It's the last of my dope."

Before Jim could say anything, Dr. Hypodermic came out from behind the Buddha, impossibly tall, impossibly thin, and totally out of place in his black stovepipe Abe Lincoln hat. Blue sparks clicked from his patent leather shoes and some kind of enveloping energy field stopped the rain from touching him. The junkie grunt looked up from under his poncho as though he weren't in the least surprised to see the Voodoo Mystère. His voice had been threatening when he'd spoken to Jim, but now it turned into a complaining whine. "Look at the Buddha, man. They blew his fucking brains out."

Dr. Hypodermic gestured soothingly with white-gloved hands. "I'm sure the Buddha will be able to handle it."

The grunt shook his head as he drew the morphine solution up into the syringe through a ball of dirty cotton wool. "The motherfuckers didn't have to blow a hole in his head. There was no need for that."

Dr. Hypodermic's death's-head grin broadened as the junkie grunt tied off and went looking for a vein. "In half a minute, you won't be worrying about it."

Jim pushed his wet hair out of his eyes. He couldn't imagine what game Hypodermic was playing with him, but he didn't like it, and his own tone was very close to the junkie grunt's whine. "You wouldn't like to tell me why you've brought me here, would you?"

A burst of small-arms fire erupted in the nearby jungle, but Hypodermic didn't even look around. "I thought the two of you should get acquainted. You both died of the same cause in the exact same second."

"He OD'd?"

Dr. Hypodermic nodded. "Chuck here OD'd in the middle of a firefight."

Another burst of gunfire sent Jim scrambling and rolling for the cover of a pile of wet rubble. Chuck, the junkie grunt, had pushed back his poncho. He'd found a vein, eased in the needle, and was now lovingly raising a little blood into the syringe. Jim cautiously raised his head. "He doesn't look like he wants to be acquainted with anyone."

"Chuck doesn't want anything except what he's got right now. That's what happens when you make the end unthinkable and refuse to permit the reality of death. Chuck here's been going around and around in the same five-and-a-half-minute cycle, shooting the same three morphine pills since the bullet ripped the top of his head off. He's built himself a closed loop. Hell as an eternally revolving door in the worst place he ever experienced."

"I though you said he OD'd?"

"The dope killed him, but before he even had time to fall over, a slug from a VC AK-47 lifted his scalp."

"Isn't what killed him kind of academic?"

"A sequence of events is a sequence of events. What he doesn't know is that the damaged Buddha is an analog for his own head wound."

Chuck pulled the needle out of his arm and looked blearily at Dr. Hypodermic. "I ain't going anyplace and that's a fact. Never leave the temple. That's the key to everything. Never leave the temple."

A grenade exploded somewhere on the other side of the Buddha. Jim pressed himself closer to the wall. "Is this supposed to be some kind of object lesson?"

Dr. Hypodermic shook his head. "It's just part of the tour."

"The tour?"

"We have big things planned for you, Jim Morrison. Shall we move on? Or maybe you want to stay here with Chuck? I'm sure we can set you up with a needle and a spoon and a poncho to keep the rain off. It's a blissfully simple existence."

Jim was having enough trouble keeping up with the shifts and surprises Dr. Hypodermic seemed to be springing on him. His mind felt seared from the previous plunge into discorporal pain. He sighed and leaned against the wall, letting the rain stream down his face. "Of course I don't want to stay here. It's a bliss I can very well do without."

"Perhaps you'd like to go back to your Parisian bathtub?"

Jim shook his head. "You'll do what you like, whatever I say."

Dr. Hypodermic nodded. "*C'est vrai.*"

Jim smiled bitterly. "So you've got me. I give up. Roll me on to the next horror."

"It's gaining altitude."

"It could actually be a bombing run."

Semple was frightened, but she was also furious. She hadn't allowed herself a full-blown tantrum in a very long time, but one was definitely boiling beneath the surface. "This is too fucking much. I swear. It just can't happen to me. I've already been fucked up by one of Anubis's nuclear weapons. It can't happen twice. It just isn't possible."

Mr. Thomas was hardly the master of diplomacy. "It's starting to look all too possible."

Jesus leered at her. "It brought me to you, didn't it?"

"And that was such a treat, wasn't it? I got to watch you masturbate and talk to the goat."

Mr. Thomas turned. He was clearly offended. "And what's so bloody terrible about talking to the goat, may I ask?"

Jesus picked up the thread. "And what's so bad about watching me masturbate? I've known women who were quite turned on by it."

Semple looked at the two of them in furious bewilderment. "What's with you two? How the fuck can you talk like that when one of Anubis's psychotic flyboys is maybe going to drop an A-bomb on us?"

Jesus shrugged. "I'm Jesus Christ. Nothing can hurt me."

Mr. Thomas also didn't seem that concerned. "And I was tired of being a goat."

"What about Gojiro? Anybody think about what happens to him?"

Jesus acknowledged this with a look of less-than-sincere sadness. "It will be a loss."

Mr. Thomas nodded in agreement. "It will be a loss."

Semple clenched her fists in frustrated fury. She would have punched Jesus, but she couldn't see how it would do her any good. She also couldn't see the point of screaming, but that didn't stop her. "But what about me? I don't want to be blown up by an atom bomb!"

Mr. Thomas was staring at the screen again. "A small object has just detached itself from the Flying Wing."

"What is this place?"

"It's one of the points where life and death interface."

Jim and Hypodermic were standing together on a high ledge above a huge tunnellike cavern that seemed to stretch to infinity in either direction. The air was chill with a smell of mold and cold fungi, and Jim found himself shivering helplessly. His shirt was still soaked from the downpour in the Vietnam hallucination. The cavern was a dim, gloomy, twilit place, lit only by a faint white light in the far distance. It wasn't the physical surroundings that held Jim's attention, though. The flat floor of the cavern was consistently inclined so it formed a long continuous slope, like a never-ending ramp, and up this ramp trudged an endlessly moving tide of humanity. Heads shaved, every last one of them dressed identically in a shapeless gray coverall, they moved ever upward in a slow and weary lockstep, no military precision, but in rough ranks and rows, backs bent, shoulders drooped forward so their arms hung with a loose simian swing. They didn't pause or even glance around at their surroundings, and their faces were made uniform by dour hopelessness. They didn't speak, even to complain one to another, but the cavern was nonetheless filled with a perpetual, drawn-out, sighing whisper of absolute despair.

Dr. Hypodermic fixed Jim with a ruby laser gaze. "You hear that?

"What is it?"

"The breath of the dead."

"And who are all these people?"

"A particular subsection of the recently deceased."

"Subsection?"

The skull face displayed a singularly impatient contempt. "The regiments of the righteous, the drug-free, the ones who gratuitously ignored their imaginations and allowed their lives to be punctuated by TV commercials every eight minutes. The Great Double Helix can be a hard concept to grasp after a life of Diet Sprite, *Touched by an Angel*, the missionary position, and some corporate Insect King lunching on your slave-employee ass. These are the ones who did what they were told and just said no to everything that might have redeemed their miserable lives."

"And where do they think they're going?"

"They don't have a clue. The only idea they have is to walk toward the light. That's all they've ever heard. When dead, walk to the light. These ones will go to any white light that presents itself."

"Will they ever make it to the pods?"

"Most will. When they finally manage to work it out. The recruiters will get some of them, though."

"The recruiters?"

Hypodermic allowed himself a dry-bone, demigod laugh. "How do you think they keep Gehenna, Stalingrad, and Necropolis filled? Show them an Electric Xmas Tree Angel and they will follow you to the racks and the heated tongs of perdition."

"How come I never saw this place?"

"You were one of my *garçons*. I spared you from this stage of things."

"You mean I was too stoned to notice?"

"I mean you were always doomed to the fast track and the early conclusion."

Semple watched transfixed as a dark speck dropped from the underside of the Flying Wing. It was so tiny that it could easily be mistaken for a fault in the screen's image or a floating trick of the eye. That something so insignificant could pose such a terminal threat was all but inconceivable, but Semple was unfortunately all too able to conceive it. As she watched it fall, slowly at first, but rapidly gaining speed, she felt her body start to stiffen. Her legs felt weak and when she put a hand on the back of the couch to steady herself, her nails dug into the leather upholstery, red on black, causing deep creases. For a micromoment, she found herself fascinated by her own hand. Very soon it would be gone, never to be seen again. Her mind, even her soul, if she had such a thing, might continue, but this flesh was about to be vaporized, her body, her hair, her internal organs all gone, and the absurd comic book costume along with them.

She looked back at the screen and the bomb had grown larger. The second and third units showed that Gojiro had come to a complete stop and was sitting back on his tail staring up at it. As the bomb came silently down, one of the great reptile's hands flashed out and, in a more-than-reptilian turn of speed, he caught the bomb. Semple, turning on her platform shoes, cringed from the screen, knowing that this move would have to detonate the nuclear device. After five seconds of nothing, she opened her eyes, scarcely daring to look. When she did look, she incredulously had to raise her superheroine visor, unable to believe what she was seeing. Gojiro sat, tossing the bomb up and down on the palm of his massive hand, not unlike George Raft with his trademark silver dollar. Quickly, she bit back a scream. "Is the damned lizard out of his mind?"

Mr. Thomas took the question literally. "He's a lizard, so it's a little hard to tell, isn't it?"

Semple turned on Jesus. "Can't you make him throw it away or get rid of it somehow?"

Jesus shrugged. "He's running the show right now."

"Does he even know what it is?"

Mr. Thomas nodded. "Oh, I think so."

And with that, Gojiro tossed the atom bomb somewhat higher, caught it in his mouth, and swallowed it with a gargantuan gulp, much the way a particular kind of extrovert human might toss a peanut into his mouth, or a chocolate-covered Whopper. Semple stood stunned. "I don't believe it."

"Oh yes, he swallowed it."

"What the hell happens now?"

"I guess we'll find out."

For approximately five seconds, Gojiro sat perfectly still. His eyes closed and the enormous hawser muscles in his neck worked convulsively. Mr. Thomas stroked his beard with a front hoof. "He looks like a pachuco who swallowed a full half pint of tequila on a bet."

"Gggggggrrrrrrrwwwwwzzzzzz."

Gojiro let out a long rasping wheeze that reverberated through the dome like a ripple in its very fabric and caused Semple to grab again for the couch. At the end of the breath, a perfect smoke ring of brightly glowing vapor floated from his mouth.

"Krrrkkk."

Semple's legs felt weak. "I see it, but I hardly believe it."

Mr. Thomas seemed equally awed and even Jesus was unable to remain totally blasé. "So it seems the Big Green's digestive track can neutralize nuclear fission."

Semple sank down on one of the arms of the couch. "I can't handle this and stand up at the same time."

Jesus, on the other hand, done with being impressed by the King of the Monsters' gastric prowess, wanted to get back to the wanton destruction of the city. "I imagine we can assume that Anubis has nothing else to throw at us."

He keyed commands into the remote, but Gojiro remained sitting. Jesus frowned. "He refuses to move."

"He's just put away one hell of a snack. Perhaps he doesn't feel too good."

"We can't just sit out here in the desert doing fuck-all. There's Necropolis to tear down."

Mr. Thomas looked at Jesus as though he secretly considered him an idiot. "After digesting an atomic blast, he may not be too hungry."

Jesus worked the monitor again. At first it seemed as though Gojiro absolutely wasn't going to move. Then the monster belched.

"Bbbbbrap."

Very slowly, he lumbered to his feet. He looked around for a few moments as though confused and possibly disoriented. Sniffing the air, he appeared to make up his mind. Falteringly at first, but quickly gathering speed and momentum, he started in the direction of Necropolis.

Jesus laughed out loud. "I guess the suburbs go first."

The totality of the darkness was only punctuated by the struck blue sparks that told Jim Dr. Hypodermic was still with him. All was silent except for his own breathing and the occasional reverberating rattlesnake buzz and hiss that also confirmed Hypodermic was near. Obviously the Doctor's tour was still in progress, but Jim had no clue where they might be or even why the Mystère had brought him to this place, which seemed to be devoid of absolutely everything except their own presence. Then the light appeared. At first it was nothing more than a point, a lone and errant flame-yellow star, but as it grew in the sky, Jim could see that it was actually one point of light surrounded by a strange flattened halo. It took Jim some time to realize that what he was really seeing was a light moving across water. It was the ripples in the halo that gave it away and his whole perspective suddenly changed. He grasped that he was standing on some dry-land vantage point, overlooking a vast black unseeable sea.

In the moment the visual revelation came, Jim also heard distant music drifting like smoke across the water. Male-voice Wagnerian singing, unaccompanied but pitched to Nordic perfection in a minor key, robust but at the same time mournful. He had to wait a while longer as it drifted closer to see the source of the light and the singing. A Viking longship with dragon prow, most of its deck consumed by flames, floated silently past, followed by a second boat with a black sail and a crew of dark warriors who, with swords uplifted, sang the lament.

Jim turned to where he imagined Dr. Hypodermic to be standing. "The nine-forty-seven to Valhalla?"

"You're beginning to learn, *mon frère*."

Semple was gratified that the very first thing that Gojiro attacked was the same elevated highway the procession had taken on its ceremonial way to the Divine Atom Bomb Festival. His first move was to remove most of the traffic with wide sweeps of his tail. The smaller vehicles went flying with hardly a second glance from the Big Green, but then a Necropolis city omnibus attracted his attention. He picked up the double-decker in both hands and flattened it end to end, like a small boy crushing a cardboard box. He destroyed a couple of large semi trucks the same way, but then the tanks started rolling down the highway toward him. The gold-plated armor of Anubis's crack elite came in with pennants flying and guns blazing. The peppering the tanks gave him with their cannons and heavy machine guns did Gojiro no actual bodily harm, but nonetheless irritated him intensely. Rather than deal with them piecemeal and have to tolerate the gadfly pinpricks of their firepower, he seized the two sides of the highway in his flatcar hands and began to pull up the roadbed, ripping it loose from its supporting pillars. He then proceeded to roll it up, like a crusty old carpet so reinforced with filth and chewing gum that it just had to go. The tanks tried to reverse away from him, but Gojiro could roll up highway faster than they could retreat, and they were crushed inside the curl of steel and concrete like the filling in a jelly roll.

Within the tumor in the monster's brain, Semple watched the multiple images in awe and wonderment. "How strong is he? Are there no limits to what he can do?"

Outside the dome, blue and blinding electricity crackled as banks of synapses went into reptilian overdrive. The industrial-strength dinosaur brain-lightning was visible though the fabric of the dome/tumor, which was now translucent. Mr. Thomas looked up at Semple in the eerie flickering light. "Almost no limits on this scale. Especially when his dander's up. The Big Green has a wicked temper."

Semple glanced around anxiously. "Are we safe in here?"

Jesus laughed and gestured to the images. "A lot safer than in that building."

When the roll of highway became an untidy spiral bale more than half his own considerable height, Gojiro appeared to decide that the logistics were too taxing and transferred his rage to punching the tensile integrity out of a twenty-story high-rise. Semple had never imagined that the buildings in Necropolis were particularly well made, but she hardly expected that a couple of right and left jabs to the middle floors were all it required to reduce the structure to a pillar of dust and rubble. From Semple's point of view, the only unfortunate part of the King of the Monsters' attack was the considerable number of wretched underclass shacks that were crushed underfoot each time he made a move. Although she had personally not fared well at the hands of the Necropolis poor, she didn't really believe that they deserved to be trampled by a living mountain. On the other hand, it wasn't something she was going to waste too much time or regret over. What with all the pollution, oppression, poverty, and cannibalism, for many it was probably a merciful release.

She also couldn't quite see why the great lizard was so content to hang around in the suburbs, crushing shacks, rolling up roads, and knocking down modest buildings. "Is there any way to get him to move on to downtown? I want to see him total the palace and the TV studios."

Jesus looked at her with one of his hand-rubbingly wolfish smiles. "Impatient for some payback?"

"Damn right I'm impatient."

He looked down at the remote. "Then let's see what we can do."

Jim tilted the pipe to the right, about thirty degrees from the vertical, and the impossibly beautiful Asian woman applied the blue and yellow flame of the small lamp to the ball of purest tar-black Shanghai opium that nestled inside. Jim was beginning to get used to the near-seamless shifts of reality. He had quickly realized that his only safe course was to go where the Mystère took him, accept each new situation on its face value, and not struggle or kick or ask too many damn fool questions. Certainly the current environment was very easy to accept. Hanging chimes sang soft and lazy harmonics in the slight, sweet-scented breeze created by gliding fans. Candles flickered in sevens, tens, and dozens, positioned before dark mirrors and behind the diffusion of parchment screens or the refraction of the cracked leaded glass of hexagonal Tiffany shades that split light into unimagined spectra and cast soft auras of protection over all those safely gathered within.

Jim drew long and steadily on the ivory pipe and, although the tiny carved dragons didn't actually move, the eighteen-inch tube all but had a life of its own as the living smoke insinuated the receptors of his brain, formally bowing with mandarin manners and welcoming itself as an old and valued friend before it moved on to enfold him in its perfect velvet detachment and gently lead him beyond the reach of hurt or destiny. When they had first arrived at the Palace of Mirrors, Dr. Hypodermic had told him, "Don't get too accustomed to this place. It's only an interlude, a rest stop before the tour continues." He now saw the reason for the warning.

The other dragons, however—the ones on the slit silk skirt of the impossibly beautiful Asian woman's vibrantly tight cheongsam—did move. They came animatedly alive as she replaced the long pipe in its ornate holder and got respectfully to her feet from the opium den version of the Hefner bunny dip that she had assumed while ministering to his needs. "Are you content for now?"

Jim smiled blissfully, sinking back into the fully reclined seat. Hypodermic had told him not to get too accustomed to the place, but Jim was already wishing for the interlude never to end. "I don't think it would be possible to be any more content."

Like the cabin attendant of some divine airline, the woman moved on to the next passenger—or client? customer? trick? Jim watched the sway of her hips and the exquisite sheen of her perfect legs. He appreciated the small reflections from the garment and the way it stretched taut as she leaned forward to address the intoxicant needs of the racked and inert figure in the recliner across the aisle. He appreciated the contours of her ass in a way that was almost completely lacking in active desire. Such was the relationship between the drug and the sex drive. Even the spurs of the flesh to that which was ultimately pleasurable were blunted to a glorious objectivity. As she held the lamp to the new pipe, the flame triggered a rainbow of hallucinations, equal in their perfection to the wafting curves of the woman's hypnotic body. The true glory was that Jim didn't have to do a damn thing about it. All he needed was simply to relax down into the magical wonder of it all, where the dreams were waiting to claim him. With time at least temporarily negated under the opium spell, he didn't need to worry that Hypodermic would wake him and insist that they continue the tour of the Mystère. He didn't even have to worry about the fact that the figure in the next recliner looked a great deal like Doc Holliday.

An inset window came up in the top right corner of the forward screen. Jesus smiled. To Semple's mind, he was becoming altogether too pleased with himself as the trashing of Necropolis progressed. "I think you'll like this."

Gojiro was now wading knee deep in the city's business district, wrecking imposing corporate structures left and right. A hapless Zeppelin swung into the King of the Monsters' field of vision and was instantly incinerated by a burst of blue breath. Its hydrogen exploded like a giant phallic firecracker. Boom! Gojiro trundled on. All around him, pillars of red fire and oily black smoke marked where entire city blocks were burning, ignited by electrical sparks and the gas tanks of recklessly hurled vehicles. Gushers of steam erupted as progressive sections of the computer network blew its boilers. Jesus looked round at Semple and Mr. Thomas "Don't you just love to see a city on fire, trapped in its own death throes?"

The great creature's newest objective appeared to be a squat and singularly ugly double-triangle pyramid festooned with tall steel broadcast antennae and satellite uplink dishes. Semple peered at the screen. "The TV center?"

Jesus nodded. "Watch the inset."

At that moment all the window showed was random, cathode-stream snow, but then the snow cleared and Semple found that, of all the TV shows on all the TV channels in the Afterlife, she was watching *Fat Ari's Slave Shopping Club*. Semple blinked. "How the hell did that get there?"

"Watch and learn."

In black and white so crude and grainy that it was almost an insult to the viewer, and with all the production quality of a snuff movie, the painted and powdered naked women Fat Ari treated as the merchandise paraded down the catwalk, smiling into the camera with painfully phony, frightened allure, and leaning forward so the potential customers on the other end of the process could clearly read the barcodes on their foreheads.

Mr. Thomas chewed a chunk of plastic packing material and snuffled through his nose. "There but for the grace of someone . . . "

Semple looked at the goat in surprise.

"You know about me and Fat Ari?"

"Even a goat has his sources."

Jesus glanced up from running the remote. "If you'd made it to the catwalk, I certainly would have put in a bid for you."

"Am I supposed to take that as a compliment?"

Jesus shrugged. "I would have thought so."

Mr. Thomas looked around for something else to eat. "Of course, you didn't have a barcode . . . "

"How the hell do you guys know all this?"

Jesus looked down at the remote as though he suddenly had something very important to do, and Mr. Thomas simply avoided her eyes. Semple, oblivious for the moment to what Gojiro might be doing outside, planted her superhero gauntlets on her hips and looked disgustedly at Jesus and the goat. "Are you telling me that you two used to sit up here and watch Necropolis TV for *fun?*"

Mr. Thomas nodded, looking a little shamefaced. "It can be one of the more entertaining channels for the warped of taste."

"And did you buy any slaves?"

Mr. Thomas nodded at Jesus. "He tried it a couple of times."

"And where are they now?"

"Unfortunately there was a bit of a screwup with the animation process when they entered the Big Green's brain."

Semple shook her head. "I can hardly believe you even watched this crap, let alone actually tried to buy people."

Jesus finally contributed to the discussion by gesturing to the screen. "I somehow don't think we'll be doing it anymore."

In the inset window, one of the slaves had looked up at the roof of the studio and started screaming in tight close-up. On the larger screen, Gojiro was ripping loose one of the triangular sides of the TV center. Suddenly, his forward vision was peering down into the studio where *Fat Ari's Slave Shopping Club* was going out live. As slaves and technicians alike scattered for their lives, a huge green hand entered the black and white picture and ripped up the catwalk. A lone cameraman was sticking it out to the end, more concerned with preserving potentially historic images than his own continued continuity. Apart from the cameraman, the only individual who had stood his ground was Fat Ari himself. In fact, he actually advanced on the King of the Monsters as though completely unaware that the thing he faced was many thousands of times his own size. He stomped down the stairs from the control room, his irate tented bulk quivering with the same fury that Semple had faced when he discovered her lack of barcode.

"Do you know what you're doing to me, you fucking mutant iguana?"

Gojiro stopped and Gojiro blinked, and then Gojiro lifted a mighty foot and brought it down with Richter-scale force, crushing Fat Ari, the intrepid camera operator, the rest of the set for *Fat Ari's Slave Shopping Club*, and anyone else who might have remained in the vicinity. For an instant, Semple felt a twinge. Fat Ari was advanced cannibal pimp scum and definitely deserved to be flattened, but at least he had departed with class. Then she steeled her attitude.

"One down and some more to go." She looked down at Jesus. "On to the palace?"

Jesus nodded, seemingly aware that Semple had taken charge, but having no immediate quarrel with the situation. "That won't be a problem."

Jim had entered an opium dream of unmatched extravagance, extravagance on a par with those visions of paradise Hasan-e Sabbāh, the Old Man of Mountains, had offered his razor boy and blade maiden hashasheens to keep them killing and putting the fear of Allah and Hasan into the politicians of the twelfth century. Jim's vision was a dark and smoky mirror viewed through drapes of burnished golden chiffon, which was probably in keeping with his character and disposition and with the fact that, as far as he knew, he was still somewhere in the loose confines of Hell. The vision was also colored by its origins with Dr. Hypodermic, for Hypodermic was not the kind of furnish marble pools, fleecy skies, and pliant handmaidens in any Morrison illusion of perfection. Hypodermic would never bring Jim to any Beverly Hills consumer lotus land of whiteboy vices and Wonderbread sins. If Jim had indeed achieved his Xanadu, it would have to be a stately pleasure dome of night and mysterious mist, as far, far down in Coleridge's caverns measureless to man as it was possible to go. It would hug the crags and surf and romantic chasms of ice and fire, where Alph the sacred river seethed at the apex of its ceaseless turmoil and crashed into the kraken depths of the great and sunless inward sea.

His Xanadu was a savage place and holy, both brutal and enchanted. A beast within a city, rampaging at its heart. Above the ring of Fenders and dulcimers, Bechtstein grand music loud and long, and the crash of dancing timpani and rocks, the voices of women soared as they wailed for their doomed and demon lovers amid a perfect chaos and a tranquillity of disorder that even Jim himself had never been quite able to visualize. The stillness of his dope-fiend vision was the peace in the ultimate eye of the hurricane. Why had he never thought of that before, made it his objective? The magic of the pipe had brought it all into such clear focus and sharp perspective. Previously he had only closed his eyes in holy dread and ridden upon the storm with his cold silver-ringed fingers locked into the mane of the nightmare. Around him, all was a spiral of magnificent fury. Fountains gushed scarlet flame and reptiles slithered about their business of corruption and seduction, but at the center of it all, he had finally found the strength and stability of the truly and fantastically free, free to waste an infinity of time if he so desired. Free to regard his right foot for a millennium if he so desired. To reinforce this bold discovery, his own face came toward him, with a woman, *the* woman, dark curls and pale, ready to reveal, repeating that it was true, it was all true, voice muffled but becoming clear, through the mirage of the ion-charged mist of Avalon, and no one cried, "Beware! Beware!" at his flashing eyes and floating hair or wove a circle around him thrice because he on honeydew had fed and drunk the milk of—

"Okay. Enough, *mon ami.* You're slipping into borrowed poetry. Time to wake and move."

And Xanadu was gone and Jim was out of the dream and into a place of ice and freezing cold. "Fuck you, Hypodermic! I was just starting to enjoy myself."

Semple had never seen the exterior of the palace before. Always before she had been on the inside scheming to get out; now she was on the outside scheming to destroy. From above, from the perspective of Gojiro looking down, the layout was that of an ankh enclosed within a pentagram, with tall steel and glass obelisks positioned at each of the intersecting points of the five-pointed star, and an ornamental reflecting lake in the upper teardrop of the ankh. In the design of the sweeping ground plan, Anubis had made sure his architect-priests had covered every symbolic base, but Semple knew it was going to take a great deal more than symbolism, no matter how perfectly crafted, to save the dog-god from reptile apocalypse.

Already the streets around the palace and even the palace gardens themselves were thronged with people fleeing the advancing monster. From the height of Gojiro, they formed ant-scurry patterns in and around the fake Egyptian, building-block structures. Then shots from nearer the ground started coming in on the auxiliary screens. (Again Semple wondered how the hell this was achieved.) The single-minded fear in the faces said it all. No heroics or civilized niceties like women or children first. Just run like hell and the devil take those who faltered. It was every man for himself. In a classic low-budget horror movie panic, children and senior citizens were trampled underfoot. Jesus laughed uproariously as a fat woman dropped the jewel box she'd been hugging to her ample breast. She hesitated, tempted to stoop to retrieve scattered gold and baubles. A man slammed into her and she staggered. Her black Cleopatra wig flew off. The jewelry might have been debatable, but the wig was nonnegotiable. She bent to grab for it, four more people cannoned into her, and she went down in the stampede. In the moment that the wig went flying, a pig-pink shaved head was revealed and Semple wondered if the woman and the guard who had given her barcode problems back in the city jail could be one and the same. It seemed too much of a long-shot coincidence, unless, by some strange and unknown process, the close-ups were somehow being geared to her personal payback.

At that point, whoever or whatever was directing the live coverage of Gojiro against Necropolis grew tired of close-ups of the human panic and switched back to the monster onslaught against the local real estate. As Gojiro snapped off the first obelisk he encountered and, using what was left of it as a makeshift mace, began reducing a considerable portion of the palace to random debris, the God-King's air force decided to mount a last-ditch kamikaze defense. After the attack of the Flying Wing and the revelation that Gojiro was quite capable of swallowing a small nuclear device with no detrimental effects beyond a little flatulence and irritability, Semple would have given up and used all her remaining aircraft to get as far away from the Big Green as possible. She was well aware, though, that Anubis's thought processes were very different from her own, and she could well imagine the dogheaded boy holed up in some deep palace bunker screaming for final death-or-glory stands by whatever was left of his armed forces. When the ill-assorted squadron came in low over the ankh in the pentagram, she was hardly surprised, and equally unmoved, as Gojiro, starting with the P51 Mustang that was leading the attack, used the obelisk to bat them out of the sky with all the ease and unconcern of a major leaguer playing amateurs. The last stand failed to so much as lay a suicidal glove on him.

After that, there was no more resistance, and the King of the Monsters fell to a routinely systematic demolition of Anubis's palace, up one wing and down the next, like an automatic and highly inevitable wrecking machine. Semple was almost tempted to become bored, but then she spotted the cluster of tiny figures standing on a flat roof near the high point of the ankh. She looked quickly at Jesus. "Can you zoom in on something?"

"Where?"

"There."

"There?"

"That's right."

He played with the remote and a new inset appeared. This time it was an overhead color shot, but not from Gojiro's POV. (How the fuck *was* this being done?)

"There he is!"

And there he was. Canine head swiveling anxiously, Anubis, God-King of Necropolis, stood surrounded by harem, courtiers, and guards, both ceremonial Nubian and the more practical rocketeers with their automatic weapons, who looked equally perturbed by their situation.

Mr. Thomas shook his head in puzzlement. "What does he think he's going to achieve by waiting around up there?"

"Maybe he's hoping to be airlifted out."

"You think he's got any planes left?"

Jesus studied the screen. "Never underestimate a deity when it comes to self-preservation."

Gojiro didn't seem to have noticed Anubis and his court or their ongoing attempt to save themselves. He was too busy on the other side of the palace complex playing the saurian bulldozer. Semple looked at the screen more closely. "People I know are down there."

It took the goat to state the obvious. "Hardly surprising, considering you were one of his concubines."

"There's Zipporah, and Parsis, and that bloody Dream Warden."

Mr. Thomas snorted. "If Anubis had half a brain, he'd simply wind-walk out of there."

Jesus shook his head, as though he totally understood the underlying psychology of Anubis. And quite possibly he did. "He won't. He's enjoyed being a god for too long. For him, starting over somewhere else would be unthinkable. He couldn't face rebuilding his power and his environment. To re-create the entire city all over again would be close to unthinkable."

"He isn't going to have too much city left after the Big Green gets through with it."

"He not only has to escape but be seen to escape, at least by what he thinks of as his loyal followers. Kind of like Hitler at the end of World War II, getting away to Argentina in the U-boat."

Mr. Thomas belched. "Nasty little shit, that Hitler. A vegetarian, used to fart all the time. Also he didn't drink. Never trust a man who doesn't drink or eat meat."

"Aren't you a vegetarian?"

"I'm a goat. I eat anything. Barbed wire, nails, you name it."

"I take it back."

"You know the weirdest thing about Hitler?"

"Aside from the mustache?"

"The bastard was a lazy son of a bitch. Never got out of bed before noon, and would sit up all night watching movies."

Semple smiled. "Just like some others we could mention." She paused and frowned. "But how could you have known Adolf Hitler? The time frames don't compute."

Mr. Thomas looked a little shamefaced. "It was on this side. After the boyo had laid low for a couple of decades, Der Führer decided he'd have another stab at Götterdämmerung and I, for my sins— quite literally for my sins—got a gig as a regimental goat in the Nibelungen Division of the Afterlife. Of course, I deserted once the Barbiturate Wars got started."

Jesus ignored the entire exchange, even the passing reference to himself. "It's like I was saying, if Anubis can pull off a spectacular last-minute escape, at least he'd be able to play the god in exile, and sit around conspiring and planning acts of revenge and terrorism against his supposed enemies."

"What would be the point of that?"

"To his mind, he'd be maintaining an accepted and traditional continuation. He'd still be able to consider himself a god, albeit a god fallen on hard times. In fact, he might quite enjoy the situation. It would give him infinite scope for self-pity and acts of paranoid violence."

"I'd be very upset if he were to get away."

Jesus glanced at Semple. "You don't forgive easily, do you?"

"I don't usually forgive at all. I'm the dark half of the deal, don't forget. Let Aimee run around granting dispensations and forgiving trespasses." She looked at the screen, where Gojiro was still ignoring Anubis and his entourage of refugees. He appeared fixated on one particular section of palace near the lower left point of the pentagram. Not content with reducing it to rubble, he was actually digging in the rubble he'd created with his huge hands, delving into foundations and subbasements, like a dog after a deep-buried bone, tossing bits of debris over his shoulder like Henry VIII eating chicken. Semple pointed angrily. "What's his problem? Why doesn't he notice Anubis and his crew and do something really unpleasant to them?"

Gojiro unearthed what looked uncommonly like a large chunk of a cyclotron. Scrutinized it for about twenty seconds, licked it, and then pitched it away. Jesus turned to Semple. "Where did Anubis keep his weapons-grade uranium?"

Semple looked at him blankly. "How the hell should I know? Concubines weren't party to that kind of information."

"But was it someplace in the palace?"

"Yeah, I guess so. There was supposed to be this bit that no one was allowed into, with guards and steel doors and big chrome Tesla things that sparked and flashed. Anubis and the Dream Warden were always in and out of there. Sometimes girls were sent in for the scientists. At least, that was the story. I wasn't around long enough to find out for sure."

"That's it, then."

"That's what, then?"

"He's going after the U-248."

Semple shook her head. "I don't understand."

"Pigs go rooting for truffles. The Big Green goes for super-enriched uranium. It's his favorite delicacy."

"Fuck the great green overgrown retard and his favorite delicacies. Can't you do anything to distract him? I want that bastard Anubis chewed up and spat out."

Mr. Thomas stared at Semple as if to bring her back to earth. People who lived in brain tumors didn't throw rocks at the Big Green when he was on a roll. "There's no stopping him when he's digging for uranium."

But, as the goat spoke, Gojiro hit paydirt. He dragged up what must have been, on any human scale, a safe the size of a large room, raised it to his mouth, and squeezed it like Popeye opening a can of spinach. Something gray and metallic squirted into his mouth. After swallowing, he sat back on his haunches with a satisfied gloat on his face. Almost immediately, all hell broke loose in the dome. The screens instantly degenerated into distorted acid-trip light shows. A distended arterial system appeared in the fabric of the structure, pulsing green-death radiance. A high-frequency shriek forced Jesus and Semple to cover their ears and almost sent Mr. Thomas into convulsions, unable as he was to do likewise with his hooves. The disruption seemed to last for around a hundred seconds and then subsided. Afterward, Mr. Thomas looked decidedly sick. "I hate it when he eats fissionable material. I swear that's what gives him tumors."

Semple, on the other hand, was immediately back to taking care of business. So the goat thought she was pushy. She hadn't come all this way to be bilked out of watching Anubis get his. She rounded on Jesus. "So now that he's had his fun, let's get him moving again."

Jesus shook his head. "I don't think so."

Semple was uncomprehending. "What do you mean, you don't think so?"

"I fear our jolly green buddy is going to be a bit sluggish for a while."

"Sluggish?"

Mr. Thomas, who had regained some of his equilibrium, explained. "His usual pattern is to go to sleep for a while after a snack of uranium. Especially enriched uranium."

"He can't go to sleep now."

Jesus shrugged. "There's not much we can do about it."

The picture was now back intact on the auxiliary screens and it showed a King of the Monsters who was definitely looking smug and somnolent. Semple, on the other hand, was close to throwing a temper tantrum. "Can't you give him some kind of shock?"

Again Jesus shook his head. "Nothing so he'd notice."

"But look at the screen!" Semple pointed at two large passenger-carrying autogiros that were running low and fast straight for where Anubis and his entourage were waiting. The large, bulbous planes, with their big, forward-mounted radial engines, huge rotors, short stubby wings, red and silver livery, and art deco fuselage styling, had to be Anubis's ace in the hole—his ticket to ride. Semple's voice modulated toward the high C of an anguished wail. "That dog-headed fuck is going to get away! After everything, the bastard is going to escape!"

Jim's breath steamed with each exhalation as he looked around at the ice cavern. The opium spell was irrevocably broken and he was cold to the point of shivering. All around, twisted glacial shapes loomed over him, as though some great cascade had been instantly frozen, only to crack under its own internal stresses and then re-freeze again, leaving gaping crevasses and bottomless fissures, straining without motion against the forces of some great internalized kinetic agony. Wasn't one of the moons of Neptune like that? So unstable that it constantly blew itself apart, but so cold that it was immediately returned to a sphere of sunless ice? Dr. Hypodermic sat some twelve or fourteen feet above where Jim was standing, angular arachnid legs formally crossed and smoking a long thin cheroot, the smoke from which drifted on an almost horizontal plane in the sub-zero air. While he sat and smoked, frost formed white on his shoulders and the crown of his stovepipe hat. "This is what used to be the very core of hell. Where Lucifer sat entombed in ice after his great bust-up with God."

Jim turned. "I don't see him."

"I'm telling you how it was then, man. Not how it is now."

"So where's Lucifer now?"

"Quite likely playing cards in the casino with Doc Holliday."

"Doc play cards with the devil?"

"Doc has always been a student of challenging all possible limitations."

"But gambling with Satan?"

"Something of a tradition, n'est-ce pas?"

Jim nodded. "I guess so. Except that I thought I saw Doc in the opium den."

"How many places can Doc be at once? Let me count the ways." Hypodermic produced a leather cigar case with silver fittings. "You want one of these?"

Jim nodded. "Why not?"

The Doctor tossed Jim a cheroot. He caught it deftly and with equal dexterity conjured a flame at the tip of his thumb and lit it. The smoke tasted good and he was pleased that he had accomplished everything so neatly in front of the Mystère. The Mystère, meanwhile, gestured around the ice cavern like a real estate broker hustling a client. "This place could be your fortress of solitude."

Jim looked up quizzically. "Are you suggesting that I sign on as Superman?"

"It's one way to go."

"What is this? Some kind of sequence of temptations?"

"Not exactly."

"So what is this all about?"

"It's simple. You were a star, then you were a drunk, then you were a junkie, and that made you mine. Now I have to figure out what to do with you."

"And you're trying different contexts on for size?"

"You got it, *mon ami*."

Gojiro's eyes slowly closed and the forward screen blacked out. The second-unit images showed that the two autogiros were taking a circular course, giving the monster the widest possible berth before making the final approach to pick up Anubis and his people. Semple was bedside herself. She stood with Mr. Thomas, in her ludicrous superheroine outfit, all but beating her gloved fists on the screens in angry frustration as the autogiros slowly made their turn. "I can't believe this is happening."

Mr. Thomas's eyes were large and phlegmatic. "It's the luck of the draw, girl."

"I don't need fucking platitudes."

"You can't win them all."

"I can't win any of them."

Jesus put the useless remote aside and leaned back in the couch. He, too, seemed to accept the escape of Anubis as inevitable. "Self-pity is very unbecoming."

"Fuck unbecoming. You two didn't have to sleep with the dog-headed psychopath."

Mr. Thomas waggled his horns. "And for that we are profoundly grateful."

"You also didn't nearly get blown apart by his bloody atom bomb."

Jesus looked offended. "It brought you to us, didn't it?"

"You said that before."

"But it's still true, isn't it?"

"And, like I asked you before, what good has that done me? I'm decked out in this absurd fucking outfit, and—"

Mr. Thomas looked up at her. "I rather like the costume."

"Then *you* fucking wear it. It looks dumb. It leaves me half naked. It's uncomfortable. It constricts and cuts in all the wrong places and these boots were certainly not made for walking."

As Semple railed against fate, Jesus, and Mr. Thomas, a mighty snore echoed through the dome. For Semple, this was the last straw. "The damned thing's gone to sleep."

Jesus yawned in sympathy. "I'm afraid so."

"If you were any kind of real messiah, you'd do something. You wouldn't just sit here in a tumor with a goat and cross-shaped pool. Jesus Christ? If you saw a real fucking cross, you'd run a mile. Three Romans with nails and no one would see you for dust."

"Rudeness and insults are even more unattractive than self-pity."

Semple swung around, fists clenched. This time, she was more than ready to punch out the phony Christ. Maybe a black eye and a bloody nose would do something for his calm self-satisfaction. As she turned, however, the forward screen suddenly came to life again. "What's happening?"

"He seems to have woken up."

The autogiros were now just a hundred yards from the roof where Anubis and the courtiers and concubines were waiting, moving slowly in for the pick-up.

Mr. Thomas was the first to grasp what was going on. "It's the autogiros. The Big Green hates aircraft."

The dome trembled and Jesus grabbed for the remote, at the same time looking reproachfully at Semple. "I'll do what I can, but you really don't deserve this after what you said to me."

Gojiro stumbled ponderously to his feet and lurched toward the two aircraft. The autogiros immediately took evasive action, swinging away from Anubis's rooftop refuge, but in two mighty strides the irritated monster had them within his grasp. He grabbed the nearest of the pair just behind the cockpit, literally ripping the plane out of the air and crushing it between his three-fingered hands. The pilot of the second aircraft, seeing what had happened to his partner's machine, immediately threw his into a climbing turn, desperately trying to make both height and distance and get himself out of reach of the reptile's clutches. Unfortunately, the Necropolis version of the autogiro was neither fast enough nor maneuverable enough to do what was required of it. A green hand flashed up and seized it firmly by the tapering tail. The pilot's last forlorn option was simply to open the throttle as wide as he could and hope he could tear himself free by sheer raw horsepower. This theory actually worked, up to a point. The engine screamed as it revved beyond all safety limits, but instead of pulling free from the monster's grip, it simply tore itself loose, destroying the autogiro in the process. The detached engine's momentum carried it on and up for an instant, but then it flipped over and began to spiral crazily to the rubble below. The body of the plane remained firmly in Gojiro's left hand. A crewman plunged through the gaping hole in the fuselage, and Gojiro glanced down as the body fluttered to earth like a twisting leaf. A mere falling human could hardly hold his attention for very long, though, and with a terminal gesture of finality he mashed the second auto-giro with a thunderous clap of his hands.

Semple watched with bated breath, her previous anger forgotten, and even Jesus and Mr. Thomas were leaning in, rooting for the big guy. "Okay, now go for the people. Go for the people on the roof."

As though for Semple's benefit, one of the mysterious second units closed on the potential targets on the roof. To Semple's undying delight, the God-King of Necropolis appeared on the verge of a very ugly panic. He paced and he raved and was obviously wishing that he could order violence done to someone he could hold responsible. Sadly, from Anubis's point of view, the only entity responsible for his current predicament was green and vastly unassailable. Gojiro, on the other hand, continued to be completely unaware of Anubis's existence.

"Get him, you great idiot."

Of course the King of the Monsters couldn't hear her, so she flashed around on Jesus. "Isn't there any way you can direct his attention?"

Jesus fumbled with the remote, shaking his head. "He doesn't seem to be interested."

Semple's fury rolled back in again. "Then *make* him interested, damn it."

Jesus attempted a few halfhearted commands but to no avail. "He doesn't want to know."

"How can the damn thing be so fucking useless?"

"Wait a minute." Mr. Thomas nodded to the screen showing the close-up of Anubis. Anubis was issuing orders to his rocketeer guards. Although the dome was not blessed with sync sound, his intention was obvious. He had clearly decided that the monster might, in fact, not be as unassailable as it appeared. The rocketeers moved to the edge of the roof and formed a double line. As one, they raised their weapons. Each jacked a round and switched to full auto. Semple could hardly contain her excitement. "Will you look at him? That half-witted maniac thinks he can hurt Gojiro with machine guns."

＊

Jim should have expected the graveyard. The disembodied pain, the opium den, the frozen heart of hell—why not a fucking graveyard? By this point, he wouldn't have been surprised to suddenly find himself a womb-entombed fetus. Jim could, as yet, see no pattern in what Dr. Hypodermic was doing to him or doing with him. He didn't believe the bullshit about finding him a context. Perhaps he was being sucked into some deeply convoluted Afterlife version of addiction, but he couldn't even see a pattern that might lead to that. All he could see was that the graveyard was elaborately Catholic; white marble angels clutched their brows and wept while seeking the support of broken pillars. Porticoed family mausoleums reared like baroquely munchkin cathedrals, and flat-topped sepulchers lay sprawled so large they would do justice to a Transylvanian count. Depressed and depending willows and sinisterly contorted pines drooped over an acreage of crosses and headstones so closely packed that the avenues between them resembled the narrow streets of a dark miniature city; along them blue vaporous tumbles of wraith-fire danced and flared. Overhead, ten thousand almost unflickering stars shone down from a cold velvet sky, mirrored on the ground by ten thousand flickering candles, which dripped wax on almost very available flat surface.

Dr. Hypodermic gestured in a proprietorial manner. "You like the candles."

Jim showed no emotion. "It's like the lighters at the end of a Grateful Dead concert."

"My cousin, Le Baron Samedi, spends a lot of time in places like this."

"This isn't a real place, though, is it?"

"It's largely symbolic."

The two of them drifted rather than walked through the graveyard, almost becoming an extension of the wafting wraith-fire. Jim wondered if this was how it felt to be a ghost. If it was, maybe he should try it sometime. "I hope this isn't my funeral. I've already been buried."

"This isn't your funeral."

"So whose funeral is it?"

"Here it is now."

A funeral procession carrying more candles, and dressed in scarlet robes, moved down one of the broader avenues between the tombs, making for a small vacant plot with a freshly dug grave. Two Shakespearean sextons leaned on their spades and tried to look unobtrusive. A white, child-sized coffin was borne on the shoulders of four black-clad pallbearers. Jim looked hard at Hypodermic. "I asked whose funeral it is."

The Doctor's eyes glowed eerily. "Does it really signify?"

"It looks like a child."

"It's a dwarf who was bitten by a poisonous spider."

"Can they see us?"

"They can see you, kind of."

"What do you mean, kind of?"

"They think you're the Gatekeeper of the Underworld. If you stick around, they'll offer you the traditional libation. A few shots of that stuff and you can really wail."

"Why is it I have the notion that this graveyard libation can quickly become one bad motherfucker of a habit?"

Hypodermic smiled as wryly as is possible for a naked skull. "Because you know me too well."

"I'm starting to remember."

Jim noticed the woman who led the mourners was carrying a gold chalice. He was all but tempted to check out the libation. "But I'm not the Gatekeeper of the Underworld."

Dr. Hypodermic brushed tiny diamond particles like lint from one black sleeve. Where the hell had they come from? Tiny stardust from the largely symbolic sky? "The gig could be yours if you wanted it. If you got a taste for the stuff, you might really enjoy it."

"But I don't want it."

"The gig or the libation?"

"Neither."

The woman with the chalice was coming straight toward Jim. Hypodermic treated him to one of his most penetrating stares. "You sure you don't want to try it?"

Jim shook his head. "Not even for a dwarf who's been bitten by a poisonous spider."

"I thought you were always ready for a new stimulant."

Jim continued to shake his head. "I've got enough confusion going for me."

"Are you turning soft on me?"

"You can't dare me to drink it. I'm past that."

"You're not afraid of me anymore, are you?"

"All that stuff about finding me a context was bullshit, wasn't it?"

Dr. Hypodermic's eyes flickered from red to yellow and back again. "I asked you first."

"Am I still afraid of you?"

"Right."

"No, I don't think I am."

"You're only afraid when you're running away from me?"

"Right."

"Then we'll have to do something about that, won't we?"

With an illusionist's flourish of white gloves, Dr. Hypodermic snapped his fingers and Jim found himself in a brightly lit padded cell.

The rocketeers opened fire and Semple had to give them credit for acting with heroic panache while engaging in what they must have known to be a suicidally impossible action. They had formed two firing lines, the front kneeling, the rear standing, and on their God-King's command they started blasting. Even the ceremonial Nubians sought to get in on the act, taking short runs across the flat roof and gamely hurling their spears at the great beast. The spears, unfortunately, all fell short, and although the small-arms fire hit the target, it did Gojiro no harm whatsoever. All it achieved was to get his angry attention. Semple shook her head in disbelief. "I wouldn't have thought even Anubis could combine that degree of arrogance and stupidity."

Gojiro also looked as though he couldn't quite believe the audacity of these human survivors. The first bursts of automatic fire hit him in the side as he sat digesting his meal of U-248. His eyes opened; he blinked three times and turned his huge head. The next burst hit him square in the face, dislodging flakes of loose skin, like dinner-plate-sized dandruff. At first he'd only been mildly interested; now he was exceedingly pissed. He flexed his shoulders at the effrontery and rose majestically to his feet.

"GGGGGGGGGRRRROOOOOOOAAAAARW!"

Again, Semple had to give the rocketeers points for blind

courage. Even in the face of Gojiro, drawn up to his full height and mad as hell, they didn't break and run. They held their orderly ranks and went right on firing. This was absolutely too much for Gojiro. He took two fast steps and, like a man who, wishing to make a dramatic point in the grip of a temper tantrum, furiously clears a shelf of ornaments with a single sweep of his arm, the reptile sent the two lines of Anubis's masked police flying clean off the roof and out into empty air. At the same time, in the background, unnoticed by anyone—even Semple—the Dream Warden quietly vanished, leaving only a rapidly collapsing gray robe. Unable to resist the hopeless flourish, a Nubian guard hurled one last spear. With the range less than a quarter of what it had been previously, the crazy Nubian actually managed to lodge his spear in Gojiro's left eye. It hung there for a couple of seconds before the monster blinked it away and then reached out for the unfortunate man. With an impossibly delicate neatness for one so vast, Gojiro lifted the Nubian between thumb and index finger and brought him up to eye level, turned the Nubian over twice, and then closed his fingers, squashing him to a red smear.

With the rocketeers taken out and the Nubian borne aloft to his messy fate, Anubis appeared to grasp, for the first time, that the game was up. A window appeared on the dome's screen that showed the God-King in tight close-up. With nothing left between his holy personage and the wrath of Gojiro, his eyes widened in shock and his tongue lolled out. He seemed to be saying something, but Semple couldn't hear the dog's final words. "Why the fuck don't we have sound in here?"

Anubis, still staring transfixed at Gojiro, began slowly to back away across the roof to where the near-hysterical remnants of his harem were huddled together waiting for the end. After half a dozen paces, he managed to break the paralyzing eye contact and turned and fled, pushing his way into the group of concubines and actually holding one of them, a pouty, full-breasted teenager Semple had known as Nephra, in front of him as a human shield. Semple was instantly outraged. "Will you look at that shameless son of a bitch hiding among the women? He can't even go out with fucking dignity. He's got to know there's no way the body of one nubile babe, no matter how big her tits, is going to save him. Why can't he accept that he's pod-bound and exit with a bit of class?"

Mr. Thomas sniffed. He wasn't taking the fate of Anubis quite as personally as Semple. "A lot of leaders have tried to get away among the women. Britain's Charles II tried it, so did Bonnie Prince Charlie, and Jeff Davis after the Civil War."

"But he knows he can't escape."

In one respect, Semple was wrong. Whether it was actually Nephra's ample breasts or not was unclear, but when Anubis grabbed her, Gojiro did actually pause. Although he could have crushed Anubis and the women of the harem in one fell handslap, he hesitated. Inside the dome, lizard-brain fireworks were visible as synapses processed the dilemma. Could it be that the big reptile held the dogheaded king's cowardice in as much contempt as Semple? He hardly seemed capable of such finesse, and yet there he was, standing and waiting, wondering what to do next. Semple, too, was at something of a loss. She had no personal animosity against the women. When Anubis had appeared on the rooftop, she had assumed that they would share the same fate as the other innocent victims of the razing of Necropolis—regrettable, but too damned bad. Now that Gojiro was displaying this unexpected streak of dinosaur chivalry, she saw that she was going to have to revise her ideas.

"Has he ever behaved like this before?"

Jesus shook his head. "It's extremely peculiar. He never used to be a respecter of gender."

Gojiro's next move was even more peculiar. He extended a clawed index finger and pointed at Anubis. It was the simplest of gestures, but its effect on the God-King was electrifying. His dog jaw dropped; he hurled Nephra from him. Gojiro continued to point at Anubis as he ran to the edge of the roof. Now it was Anubis's turn to hesitate. He was plainly teetering in both mind and body, unable to decide whether to jump or to wait for the Big Green to tender his fate. Semple had no doubt what she wanted him to do. "Jump, you bastard! Do the decent thing and end it now."

But Anubis didn't jump. Clearly, terminating his own incarnation was not a part of his nature under any circumstances. Gojiro, however, had an idea of his own about how the wretched creature should meet his fate. The monster pressed his lips together and very gently blew. The radioactive breath came in a narrow stream, but it was enough. Anubis was engulfed in flame. His entire body was burning like a torch as he lurched over the edge of the roof and fell. Arms and legs outstretched, he spun as he dropped, leaving a spiral of smoke while plummeting to the ruins below. He struck the ground on an incline of rubble beside an upended block of masonry with a tangle of steel projecting from its broken end. As sharp steel penetrated his burning body, a final hiccup of flame vaporized all that remained of Anubis.

Semple was silent for a moment. "So I guess that's the end of that."

Mr. Thomas asked the obvious question. "And how does it feel?"

Semple didn't immediately answer and Jesus cut in. "The most divine of emotions is that of revenge well executed."

"I'm not so sure about that."

"What do you mean?"

"To tell the truth, it doesn't feel as good as it ought to."

"You wanted him to suffer more? It was a long fall and he was on fire all the way down. He definitely crashed and burned."

Semple frowned. "It's not that. It's just that what's done is done, and I guess it's over and that's kind of hard to accept."

The goat gave a superior sniff. "They say some people are never satisfied."

Semple bridled. "I didn't say that I wasn't satisfied—"

"I'd also point out that it isn't exactly over. The women are still there. Didn't they used to be your co-workers?"

"What do you think he's going to do to them?"

"I suspect that's exactly what he's thinking about now."

Gojiro stood staring at the trembling group of women. Semple shuddered. "I wouldn't like to be in their position."

Jesus raised an eyebrow. "Do you really care?"

"They've got to be scared out of their minds."

"But do you really care?"

Semple turned angrily on them. "I don't know. I'm safe in here, so it's all fucking hypothetical, isn't it?"

Gojiro turned and began to walk away. The women of the harem, up to this point huddled together, started to spread out as if they couldn't quite believe their unexpected deliverance. After a half dozen paces, though, Gojiro halted and looked back. The women also froze.

"Is he going to kill them after all?"

The thought may well have crossed the King of the Monsters' mind. Certainly, inside the dome, Semple, Jesus, and the goat were treated to another brief synaptic fireworks display, but then the second-unit screens showed him turning again and moving on.

"He let the women go."

"I guess he's still into this new knight-in-shining-armor mode."

"Yeah, but where's he going now?"

The forward view on the screen was an extreme long shot, the replication of Gojiro's distant gaze, fixed somewhere beyond the city limits, not only in a direction in which Semple had never been during her sojourn in the city, but directly into a totally surprising and highly colorful purple and magenta sunset.

Mr. Thomas looked worried. "Where did that fucking sunset come from?"

Jesus spread his hands. "Don't look at me, I didn't conjure it. Besides, the colors are just a result of crap in the air. It's probably the dust he kicked up smashing down all those buildings."

Mr. Thomas looked even more worried. "I think he deliberately made the sunset himself."

Jesus shrugged. "He always gets a bit weird after he's whacked a city."

"He never made a sunset before."

"You can't say he doesn't have a sense of theater. We've always known that."

Mr. Thomas refused to let the matter drop. "I think he made the sunset to walk off into."

"So he wants to impress the girls on the roof. So what?"

"So I think after he's walked off into the sunset, he'll go right on walking all the way to the polar ice cap."

Jesus went white. "You're not serious."

Under stress, Mr. Thomas's accent had become extremely Welsh. "Of course I'm bloody serious, boyo. That's why I'm looking so worried."

Semple interrupted. "Would someone like to tell me what's going on here? Why should he be walking off to the polar ice cap?"

"If he's walking off to the polar ice cap, it means he's going to go to sleep for a couple thousand years and we're in a lot of trouble."

"I didn't even know there was a polar ice cap in the Afterlife."

"If there isn't, he'll make one."

"And we're in serious trouble."

Semple was perplexed. "I don't understand. What's the problem?"

"If he goes to sleep, we're prisoners in here for the next two millennia or more. No light, no heat, no power, no TV. We'd go insane."

Semple looked at Jesus and the goat as though they were total idiots. "But that's crazy. With the three of us, we ought to be able to raise the kinetic energy to wind-walk out of here."

Jesus and Mr. Thomas exchanged glances. "Will you tell her or shall I?"

"I tried to explain it to her earlier."

"We can't get out of here."

"Why not?"

Jesus shifted uncomfortably on the couch and put the remote to one side. Gojiro was now jogging steadily across the landscape with an ominous sense of purpose. "It's the bit between the tumor and the eye. Remember the way you came in?"

Semple nodded. "Of course I remember. It wasn't that long ago, even though it might seem like it."

"In order to make it through there, we have to put ourselves in animation mode."

"Mr. Thomas already told me that."

"Well, we can't do it anymore. The equipment broke and we couldn't fix it."

Semple turned sternly to the goat. "I though you said he'd forgotten how to do it. You didn't mention equipment."

"I was giving you the simplified version."

Jesus arched an eyebrow. "And probably trying to make me look bad at the same time. He does that, you know?"

"But it's true that we can't get out of here?"

"Absolutely. One hundred percent."

Semple thought about this for a long while. "My sibling Aimee and her nuns may be able to get us out of this."

Mr. Thomas treated her to a long and slightly suspicious sideways look. "They could?"

"I think so."

"How?"

"Either of you know the gold telephone trick?"

341

8

Round and round and round we spun.

A gold telephone materialized out of nowhere on the balustrade of the terrace, right next to a dead cartoon bluebird. For fifteen seconds, it did absolutely nothing, and then, exactly on the sixteenth second, it rang. Aimee was so taken by surprise that she didn't immediately answer it. No less than four of the double-time European-style rings went by before she finally picked it up and tentatively put it to her ear.

"Hello."

All around her, Heaven had continued to deteriorate. The sky was now a perpetual slate gray. The once-lush lawns were sere, brown, and dead. The trees had lost nearly all of their leaves. The lake had turned oily and polluted and every day more dead fish floated amid the greasy green scum on its surface. Increasing numbers of cracks and structural faults had appeared in the once-pristine buildings and window glass constantly and mysteriously shattered. Strange and sinister Santa Ana–style winds came in from the mountains and whipped up vortices of garbage and dead leaves, and threatening black smoke rose from beyond the same mountains from invisible fires that never ceased burning. To add the final insult to this catalogue of environmental injuries, the young women who had once danced by the temple on the Maxfield Parrish headland now spent their time consuming a diet of vodka, recreational amphetamines, and quaaludes, and coupling in wanton lesbianism.

"Who is this? It's a very bad connection."

Aimee had dispatched squads of nuns to do something about these girls flaunting their depravity right under her nose, but the young women were clever. Whenever the nuns were spotted, they simply ran off into the hazy mid-distance over which Aimee now had little or no control, a less-than-stable area into which the nuns were loath to follow them. As soon as the nuns gave up the chase, the young women would reappear and, once again, start disporting themselves, large as life and twice as obscene. Since the establishment of her Heaven, Aimee had never ordered the crucifixion of a woman, but in the case of these dirty and insolent little bitch perverts she would have happily made a precedent-setting exception—had she been able to catch them. Unfortunately, they proved totally uncatchable.

"Semple? Is that you? You sound so far away."

Her own physical condition was on an exact par with the state of affairs in Heaven. She was plagued with respiratory problems and stomach pains, and in the last few days, each time she brushed the golden tresses of which she had always been so inordinately proud, she found the bristles of the hairbrush filled with alarming quantities of dead hair.

"You'll have to speak up. I'm having a lot of difficulty hearing you."

Perhaps the worst of the slings and arrows to which she had become heir since Semple's departure was the awareness that her nuns were moving ever closer to a state of mutiny. Even as she tried to make sense of the mysterious phone call, half a dozen of them stood in a watchful, conspiratorial group whispering among themselves, eavesdropping, their expressions not unlike those of a pack of carrion scavengers waiting for the prey to die. If it hadn't been for her ability to keep conjuring Prozac, she would have given up and returned to the pods long since.

"What are you trying to tell me? You're bringing someone to do what?"

The nuns were edging nearer. The arrival of the gold phone was an occurrence so out of the ordinary, they weren't able to contain their red-nosed curiosity.

"You're bringing Him? Are you serious? Him? I'm telling you, Semple, things are not good here. I don't have the reserves or the energy to put up with any of your nonsense. If this is some joke, it's in extremely poor taste and—"

Aimee was suddenly paying such undivided attention to what her sibling was saying at the other end of the crackling phone line that, for the first time in what seemed like an age, she had momentarily forgotten the decaying world around her, the resentful plotting nuns, and even her deteriorating health.

"Yes, yes, I realize you can't say whether he's authentic or not. Right at this moment, even a low-rent replica would help matters a great deal. Just as long as he has some kind of power. He's been living *where?*"

Now Aimee really couldn't believe what she was hearing.

"Just tell me this isn't one of your elaborate hoaxes. Just please tell me that."

She knew credulity might be the product of a truly desperate hope. She wanted to believe Semple so badly. "You want us to wind-walk you in?"

Maybe her sister really was on the level.

"Yes, yes, I think we can do that. In fact, I'm certain we can do that."

What made her inclined to believe Semple was that she could already feel energy flowing into her. Even through the phone, even at an incredible distance, contact with Semple was reconstituting her strength. The possibility would very soon have to be faced that she and Semple might well be indivisible—that the bad fueled the good, that the light was only possible because of the darkness. Except that Semple sounded as though she were suffering no diminishment in her powers as a result of their separation. In fact, she sounded healthy and dangerously energetic.

"I'll have to put the phone down and talk to the nuns about it. I won't hang up. I'll just put it down and go and talk to them. Hold on. Don't go away."

As Aimee's energy increased, her Heaven began brightening before her eyes. The gray of the sky was slowly transformed to a faltering azure. The dead bluebird beside the phone twitched a leg, flexed the claws of one foot, stirred, then sat up. It staggered groggily to its feet and attempted a hoarse whistle. Aimee walked purposefully to the surly crew of nuns, who were looking around at these sudden changes in some surprise. Best to hit them when they were off balance.

"I need you women to do something for me right now. I want you to quickly form a circle." They looked at her as though she were mad, but her rekindled air of authority was enough to move them. To speed them along, she clapped her hands like an impatient gym teacher. "Come along, hurry up. Everyone link hands and concentrate. My sister Semple's is returning with a very important visitor and we have to locate her and wind-walk her in."

One of the nuns, a malcontent barracks-room lawyer of a girl who had started out in Doc Holliday's whorehouse and had once been called Trixie, but had changed her name to Bernadette when she took her vows and donned the habit, seemed about to make some kind of protest. Bernadette was a potential leader of mutineers if Aimee had ever seen one, and Aimee quickly cut her off. "There's no time for any discussion. Just do it, please."

To Aimee's relief, Bernadette shut her mouth and grumpily took hold of the hands of the nuns on either side of her. "Just stay like that. I'm going to tell Semple that we're ready."

As she hurried back to the gold telephone, a miraculous rainbow appeared above the mountains. The maidens on the headland stopped their carnal cavorting and stared at it in sheepish awe. Aimee picked up the phone. "Very well. We're ready."

She was actually daring to hope that things might really work out for the best.

Jim was in a padded cell. Had he said something about a womb-entombed fetus? This was close. And not only was he in the padded cell, but his arms were pinned by a straitjacket, and they kept turning the lights on and off for random irregular periods, presumably in some totalitarian attempt at full-scale psychological disorientation. The second time they tried it, Jim had furiously yelled at them, "Don't try the KGB shit on me. It won't work. I took too much acid way back when."

And yet, during the periods of darkness, Jim could clearly see a single red glowing eye peering through the peephole in the door. Jim had assumed that he'd been tossed into this illusion of stained quilt walls and catatonic boredom because of Dr. Hypodermic's fit of pique after Jim had announced he no longer feared him. That didn't explain, however, why the red eye fixed him like a laser in the darkness.

"You didn't tell me you were bringing a goat."

Mr. Thomas's expression became chilly and offended. "You have something against goats, madame?"

Although everyone was trying to pretend otherwise, the McPherson sisters' reconciliation was decidedly odd. Semple, Jesus, and Mr.

Thomas had materialized in a fairly conventional shimmer in the center of the circle of nuns. Jesus, who was quickly revealed to have both an act and agenda of his own, immediately bowed low to Aimee. "I know it's you I have to thank for sending these good nuns to the rescue, Mother Superior."

Aimee had looked a little flustered. "I'm not the Mother Superior, my Lord. I'm—"

"But you are infinitely superior. I can see that at first glance."

In fact, it was the nuns who were exchanging glances, and, as Semple saw it, with good reason. Semple hadn't often witnessed flattery that so bordered on toadying. Jesus had also managed to make some fairly drastic and theatrical transformations in himself during the period of the wind-walk. While Semple had come through still in her tired superheroine costume and Mr. Thomas, too, was exactly as he'd been when they'd left the tumor, Jesus had somehow replaced the Nikes, goggles, and purple toga with a dazzling white robe, complete with a gold tie belt and matching sandals, and a realistic bleeding heart on its breast. He'd even organized himself a garish multicolored halo, straight out of a Russian Orthodox icon. Semple considered this overdoing the accessories, but Jesus appeared to be in overdoing-it mode. Back lifeside, arrant fawners had buttered up Aimee with a lickspittle abandon, but they paled in comparison to the blarney job that Jesus was giving out. The faux messiah was laying it on with a trowel, and, worse than that, Aimee was lapping it up. In fact, she was so carried away by the Christ-charm that she acted decidedly offhand with the other two arrivals. First she put Mr. Thomas's nose out of joint by treating him like a mere domestic animal; then she'd moved on to Semple, looking her up and down and inquiring with a scathing edge, "What is it that you're wearing, my dear? Isn't it a bit extreme, even for you?"

Semple scowled and slowly surveyed Heaven. Despite the recent general upswing, the signs of decay were still very much in evidence. "Since I appear to have pulled your chestnuts out of the fire, sister dear, I'd really recommend being a little pleasant to me by way of gratitude." She nodded in the direction of Jesus. "You have no idea what I've been through to bring him here."

Aimee arched an eyebrow. "I may have more idea than you imagine."

Semple shook her head. "No, dear. You may think you do, but believe me, you really don't know even a fraction of it." She gestured to Mr. Thomas. "And if you ever speak to him disrespectfully again, you'll have me to reckon with. He has powerful literary credentials."

Aimee stared at the goat and the goat stared right back at her. "She's absolutely right. I have powerful literary credentials."

Jesus quickly stepped in, seeking to gloss over the building sibling confrontation. "Come, now, girls, let's not have a petty squabble. Not when the two of you have just been reunited."

Both Aimee and Semple turned and, as one, looked daggers at him. "Let's get one thing straight before we go any further. Whatever happens while you're here, don't ever try to get between us."

"Our quarrels may be a lot of things, but they are never petty."

The nuns glanced covertly from face to face as an embarrassed silence ensued. It might have gone on for a great deal longer had not Jesus proved that, in his determination to insinuate himself into Aimee's Heaven, he'd assumed the emotional skin of a rhinoceros. He stepped up next to Aimee and took her by the arm. "If you're not too tired from assisting us in the wind-walk, perhaps you'd like to give me the fifty-cent tour."

Knowing him better, Semple would never have bought this act, but Aimee immediately melted. "Of course, my Lord, I'd be honored. The sooner you see what the problems are, the sooner we can get started putting them right."

Jesus smiled. "I can't wait to be working with you."

Over Aimee's head, he shot Semple a don't-screw-things-up warning, and then he and Aimee walked away along the terrace, trailing bemused nuns behind them. Both Semple and Mr. Thomas decided to forgo the grand tour and remained right where they were. The goat thoughtfully watched the others depart. "I don't trust those nuns."

Semple nodded in agreement. "The sight of Jesus has temporarily confused them, but if she doesn't play this really carefully, they'll be at her throat pretty damn soon. At least, that's my reading of it."

Mr. Thomas nodded. "I think your reading is right on the money, girl."

Semple went to the edge of the terrace and looked out across the lake. "I never did like this place. In fact, I think I'll head out to my own happy hunting ground."

Mr. Thomas examined one of his hooves. "Might there be something to drink in your hunting ground? A liquid trifle to enhance the happiness?"

Semple grinned. "Believe me, pal. I have a lot to drink in my little kingdom."

"Enter bearing whiskey? That's an unusual one even for you, isn't it?"

Dr. Hypodermic came through the door of the padded cell carrying a bottle with no label that was filled with a dark amber liquid. "It's not whiskey, it's hundred-proof rum."

"That makes sense."

"I thought you might be in need of a drink."

"Damn right I'm in need of a drink."

Dr. Hypodermic leaned over Jim and began to unbuckle the straitjacket. Although Jim was pleased to see the bottle of booze, he made it clear to the Mystère that he was more than marginally pissed off. "You want to tell me something?"

Hypodermic pulled off the straitjacket. "What's that?"

Jim flexed his cramped arms and shoulders. "What's this padded cell routine all about? More negative reinforcement?"

The Doctor pulled the stopper from the bottle, took a hit, and then offered the bottle to Jim. "Here, drink this, *mon ami*. It'll put you in a better mood."

Jim went on massaging his shoulders and stretching his back. "I'd be in a lot better mood if I hadn't been stuffed in a fucking straitjacket. Do you intend explaining what that was all about?"

Hypodermic held the bottle under Jim's nose. "Just drink."

Jim took the bottle. The bouquet of the rum was highly seductive, but he hesitated before drinking. "This isn't going to whisk me off to some brand-new Zen hallucination, is it?"

"It's nothing more exotic than straight booze."

Jim shrugged, not quite believing Hypodermic, but knowing he had little alternative. He put the neck of the bottle to this lips and discovered, as the raw fiery liquor hit his throat, that his skepticism was well founded. With an electric click and a blinding ultrawhite flash, the padded cell vanished. For a few seconds Jim was blinded by colorful retinal floaters, but as they faded he saw that he and Hypodermic were sitting, if not at the same midnight Crossroads where Long Time Robert Moore had started him on his encounter with the aliens, certainly at one that was very similar. The surrounding fields were covered by so many crop markings, they resembled graffiti in a barrio. By way of an extra nose-thumbing reminder, three Adamski saucers cruised silently across the sky in a triangular formation.

Jim looked long and hard at Dr. Hypodermic. "I can't trust a word you say, can I?"

The Doctor grinned broadly. "Absolutely not."

Semple opened the liquor cabinet for Mr. Thomas. "Help yourself."

"That's the problem. I can't help myself. The hooves, you know. That's partially why I had myself reincarnated as a goat in the first place. So I couldn't pour the sauce for myself, if you see what I mean."

Semple looked surprised. "I don't usually act as bartender in my own domain."

Mr. Thomas looked unhappy. "Then we have an impasse?"

"Not really." Semple picked up a small bell from a side table and shook it so it tinkled musically. Almost immediately a butler entered. "You rang, my lady?"

"Indeed I did, Igor. We need drinks to be poured."

"Yes, my lady." Igor glanced at Mr. Thomas. "A gin and tonic, I would assume, sir?"

"How did you know that?"

"It was self-evident, sir."

"Was it really?"

Igor was already putting ice in the glass. "Oh yes, sir."

The goat blinked. Although Igor was not a hunchback in the strict Frankenstein tradition, he fit the bill in most other ways. Round-shouldered in his black tailcoat, he was little more than four feet tall, and his full enigmatic lips and big sad goldfish eyes prompted comparisons with Peter Lorre. He handed Semple a cognac and Mr. Thomas his gin. "Will that be all, lady and sir?"

Mr. Thomas thought about this. "Now that you mention it, I am a little peckish."

Igor nodded. "I will attend to it straightaway."

He left the room, but returned in a matter of seconds with a snack plate of lettuce, thistles, and two copies of *Vogue*. The goat looked at it delightedly. "That's wonderful, Igor, my friend, exactly what I wanted. You could have read my mind."

Igor bowed modestly. "I did, sir."

Mr. Thomas frowned. "I'm not sure how I feel about that."

"Don't worry, sir. I never pry."

As Igor backed out of the room bowing, Mr. Thomas looked up from his plate and glass. "Is he for real?"

Semple nodded. "Oh yes, I didn't make him. He just turned up one day looking for a job as a domestic and he's been with me ever since."

"He does what he does from choice?"

"He's just a natural seeker after servitude. He's very good, although now and then he deliberately fucks up. It's a sign that he wants me to give him a sound ceremonial thrashing. That's the basic trade-off."

"And he's a telepath?"

"I wouldn't worry about that too much. When one assumes a role of authority, one has to get used to the fact that no secrets can be kept from the servants."

When Semple had returned to her sanctuary with Mr. Thomas, her first objective had been gratefully to strip off the absurd comic book costume and take a lengthy shower to wash away the accumulated depravity of the outside world. While she accomplished this, she left Mr. Thomas to his own devices in a luxury suite of rooms that had been designed to generate an atmosphere of opulent Renaissance splendor. When she returned, dressed in a robe originally designed by Gianni Versace for Lucrezia Borgia, she moved in full lady-of-the-manor mode. With a drink in her hand, she gratefully sank to a soft reclining couch littered with silk and velvet cushions. "Do you know how good it is to simply relax? I believe I've had an overdose of deserts, dinosaurs, and dogheaded gods."

Unfortunately, this period of relaxation proved only the briefest respite. No sooner had she and the goat settled down to an idleness of alcohol and small talk than alarms went off all over her domain and the noisy footfalls of leather guards slapped down the corridors. The doors of the renaissance suite burst open, and four of the rubber guards hurried inside, weapons at the ready. The leader of the quartet bowed to Semple and addressed her with wheezing breathlessness. "We have detected the approach of an unannounced and unauthorized intruder, my lady."

Semple seemed doomed to live in interesting times. Both she and Mr. Thomas got to their feet, looking around nervously. "Where exactly is this intruder supposed to arrive?"

"Right here in these rooms, my lady."

Now Semple was really nervous. She had made a number of enemies in her recent travels, and although she hadn't thought of it
before, she supposed there was always the possibility that one or
more of them might have followed her there. It suddenly occurred
to her that she hadn't seen the Dream Warden die on the rooftop in
Necropolis. She urgently gave her orders to the guards. "Be ready to
shoot on sight."

The four rubber guards nodded, stiffened, and raised their blasters.

"If some son of a bitch has come here to make trouble, he'll be
blasted to Limbo. I'm really not in the mood for this."

No sooner were the words out Semple's mouth than a shimmer
appeared in the exact center of the room. Quickly a materializing
figure formed inside the shimmer. It was only when the shape stabilized that Semple recognized it and shouted to the guards, "Hold
your fire! Hold your fire! It's Aimee, goddamn it!"

The shimmer faded and Aimee stood in the middle of the room,
worried and distraught. Despite her obvious distress, Semple instantly vented all of her shock and surprise on her sister. "Why the
fuck couldn't you call first? You never come here unannounced."

"I never come here at all."

"All the more reason to call. My guards almost burned you
down."

"I didn't want the nuns to know where I was going."

Mr. Thomas lapped his gin again now that the danger had passed.
"You're having trouble with your nuns?"

Aimee glared at the goat as though he had no place to be asking
her questions. Semple angrily intercepted the look. "Don't treat Mr.
Thomas like that. He's a good friend."

"But he came with him, with that . . . that . . . " Aimee was at a
loss for a suitably apt description.

Semple filled in for her. "Jesus?"

"He isn't the real Christ."

"We knew he wasn't the genuine article. I told you that up front."

"But you didn't tell me what he really was."

"What do you mean, what he really was?"

"Women have started vanishing."

"Vanishing?"

"First it was three of the dancers on the headland. I didn't really
miss them, but now some of my nuns have disappeared . . . "

Aimee was talking as though Jesus had already been in her

Heaven for a number of days, but Semple didn't comment on this. She was accustomed to time passing at different rates in the two neighboring environments. It always evened itself out in the end. "I don't actually see what the problem is. So you've mislaid some nuns and dancing girls? Surely you can replace them."

"That's not the point."

"So what is the point?"

"I think your phony Jesus has something to do with it."

"I thought you and him were getting on like a house on fire."

Aimee looked a little shamefaced, enough to make Semple wonder just how much of the house had been on fire. "We were getting along very well, but I couldn't be with him every hour of the day. There were lengths of time that couldn't be accounted for."

"And you think he was creeping around disappearing your women?"

"That's what the nuns think and they're blaming me for it."

While the two women had been talking, Mr. Thomas had started edging toward the door. Semple noticed this out of the corner of her eye and snapped at him, "Where the fuck do you think you're going?"

The goat did his best to present a picture of innocence. "I thought I'd go and talk to Igor. You two obviously have family business to discuss."

"You stay exactly where you are. Don't so much as move a hoof or I'll turn my guards loose on you."

Mr. Thomas looked decidedly unhappy. "I don't see what use I can be."

"You lived with him for fuck knows how long, didn't you?"

"Yes, but . . . "

"But what?"

"I mean, this is the Afterlife, isn't it? What does it matter if he's a serial . . . "

Both Aimee and Semple were stunned. "He's a serial killer?"

The goat was defensive. "Yes, but I mean, they don't actually die, do they? They either go back to the pods, or else it hardly matters because you can just make another one. It's really very minor compared to what happens in some places."

Aimee could hardly believe what she was hearing, and Semple had to remind herself what a sheltered life her sibling lived. "That's not the point. The nuns don't like it, and if I don't do something about him, I'm going to have a full-scale mutiny on my hands."

Semple peered curiously at Mr. Thomas. "How long have you known he had these kinds of . . . tastes?"

Mr. Thomas hung his head. "I guess I always suspected. Some of the things he said and the porno he liked to watch. It wasn't until the problems with the girls from Fat Ari that I knew for sure."

"The girls from Fat Ari weren't lost in transit?"

Mr. Thomas shamefully shook his head. "The truth became a little twisted in the telling."

"So why the hell didn't you warm me later, when you knew we were coming here?"

Now the goat felt that he was on firmer ground. "It wasn't my place to drop a dime on him. And besides, we were boxed in. We had to get out of the Big Green's brain."

"I thought you were my friend."

"I am your friend. I just didn't think about it. I didn't know you had a problem with serial . . . "

Aimee butted in. "Why don't you use the word 'murderer'? That's what he is, isn't it? A damned murderer?"

Semple ignored Aimee's outburst and thought carefully. So Jesus had turned out to be a highly unpleasant kind of pervert. If all things were equal, she really ought to leave her sister to deal with it as best she could. In the Nietzschean long run, solving the problem herself would only serve to make Aimee stronger. Unfortunately, things were never that equal; blood was blood and genes were genes, and Semple simply couldn't just leave her only sister at the mercy of rebel nuns and a phony run-amok Jesus Christ. The question also remained unresolved as to what might happen to the other sibling if one went to the pods. "We're going to have to sort this fool out, aren't we?"

Aimee nodded. "We are."

Semple sighed. The cliché "No peace for the wicked" seemed to be working overtime. "Let me put on something more suitable, and we'll be on our way. Do you think I should bring some of my guards?"

Aimee frowned. "That seems a bit drastic, doesn't it?"

Mr. Thomas now felt it was safe to make a helpful interjection. "Do the nuns have access to weapons?"

Aimee looked at him as if he were crazy. "What would nuns want with weapons?"

"You never can tell with nuns."

Aimee was shaking her head. "Armed nuns? That's absurd."

Mr. Thomas nodded. "I'm glad it's not my problem."

Semple turned angrily on him. "Who says it's not your problem?"

"You can't hold me responsible for what that idiot Jesus gets up to."

"I hold you responsible enough to take you with us."

Mr. Thomas sighed. "Me? You're taking *me* back to that ridiculous trailer-park Heaven?"

"That's right, *you*."

Jim took another drink. This time nothing happened. He turned back to Hypodermic. "Just what the fuck is with you? Why fucking pick on me? Or is it a thing you gods have, that you just like to mindfuck humans?"

"I suppose you think it makes us feel superior?"

"The idea did cross my mind."

"Believe me, we don't have to make any moves to feel superior. You humans can do it all by yourselves. Your kind can really surpass any species or culture in the field of aberrant self-destructive stupidity."

Jim was growing very tired of the Doctor and his attitude. Only the knowledge of how the Mystère was able to hurt him stopped him from coming right out and saying so. "So what have we come back here for? Are you planning to give me back to the aliens?"

"I don't believe the aliens want you."

This finally pushed Jim over the line. He was on his feet facing Hypodermic, who sat, bent-legged, arms impossibly folded, with his back to a Crossroads sign written in a script that Jim didn't recognize. Every so often, a blue spark would jump from his body. "What the fuck is your problem? I mean, okay, so I was a dope fiend at the end of my life on Earth, and according to you that makes my ass somehow belong to you. So you take me on this totally pointless trek from hallucination to hallucination, and I get hurt, then I get high, then I get frozen and scared and dumped down in Vietnam for five minutes, and at no point do you bother to explain to me what the fuck the purpose of all this is, except maybe to convince me that you're a hundred times better than me, and all the time I'm wondering what the hell is in any of this for either of us? I mean, I hope you're getting your kicks from all this, because I'm sure as hell not.

All I know is that I'm back at the fucking Crossroads, and as far as I'm concerned, this is where I came in."

"Have you quite finished?"

Jim shook his head. "No, but it'll do for now."

"You know that I could send you back to the Great Double Helix or even to Limbo?"

"Yeah, of course I know that. But you probably will anyway."

"You're getting exceedingly brave for a human."

"You ever hear the expression 'Thus far and no further'?"

"And if I said further and you said no?"

Jim glanced up as another triangular formation of UFOs crossed the sky. "I know as well as you do that there's nothing I can do about it." He looked back, directly into Hypodermic's red glowing eyes. "But that's what I'm asking you, isn't it? Why the fuck should you want to make me go further? What percentage is there in it for either of us? The only thing you prove is that you can make a drunk and an ex-junkie do what you want. There's no big trick in that."

"Did anyone ever tell you you had a destiny?"

Jim's expression became wary and suspicious. "No, not recently."

"Maybe that's something you should ponder on."

"What are you trying to tell me? That you're preparing me for some kind of destiny?"

"You wouldn't believe that?"

"It'd be hard."

"Some things we keep secret even from ourselves."

Jim wasn't letting Hypodermic get away with that piece of obliqueness. "Wait one minute . . . " But then he was distracted by a sudden shimmer of light some fifty yards down the road. "Now what the hell is that?"

Hypodermic lazily looked around. "Probably one more fool wanting to sell his soul so he can play the damned guitar like Keith Richards. He's hoping to find Legba, le Maître Ka-Fu, the Master of the Crossroads, but tonight he's only going to find disappointment."

But the figure appearing out of the spinning shimmer was not carrying a guitar. Nothing so mundane. She was nine feet tall, not including her massive headdress of spun gold and ostrich plumes, and she wore a floor-length robe tailored from sheets of frozen flame. Danbhala La Flambeau had arrived at the Crossroads, and now Jim had two Mystères to contend with instead of just one.

"Ça va, le bon Docteur Piqures?"

Dr. Hypodermic didn't exactly seem pleased to see his statuesque female counterpart. "We're talking English here."

La Flambeau drifted toward them. Her feet didn't touch the surface of the road. "Are you still torturing that poor boy, Hypodermic?"

"The more I try to reason with him, the more recalcitrant he does become."

Jim glared at the Doctor. "When did you try reasoning with me, you son of a bitch?"

Hypodermic appealed to La Flambeau. "You see what I mean? Now he calls me a son of a bitch."

"And what did you expect? The boy had to develop a backbone sooner or later."

If Jim had been angry before, now he was furious. "Are you telling me this has been no more than some kind of bullshit boot-camp character-building exercise?"

La Flambeau smiled knowingly. "You didn't really expect to drift through the entire Afterlife getting worthless drunk and telling everyone how you lost your memory and didn't know which side was up, did you?"

Jim, having already faced Hypodermic, saw no reason to back down to La Flambeau, even though she did seem as formidable and direct as the Doctor was sinister and devious. "But I did lose my memory. There's still a fuck of a lot of it missing."

"But you didn't lose your anger and your passion, did you?"

"I assumed a lot of that stuff was left behind on Earth."

Now Hypodermic started in on him again. Two against one at the Crossroads. "That's mainly because you died like a wretched defeated hophead."

Jim didn't like the odds at all and he reacted without thinking. "And whose fault was that?"

Both La Flambeau and Hypodermic looked at him sharply. "Yes, whose fault *was* that?"

Jim realized what he'd said, and all he could do was shrug. "Yeah, I guess I'm the only one who can take the bottom-line rap for that."

La Flambeau nodded. "That, at least, is progress."

"Progress toward what?"

"Progress to the kind of attitude you are going to need when you get where you're going."

"Where I'm going? There's some kind of destination to all this?"

"Oh, indeed there is, Jim Morrison."

Jim had fallen into these kinds of traps before. This new line of the Mystères' was starting to sound like a close neighbor of Doc Holliday's doctrine of wait and see. "And is anyone going to tell me what it might be? Or do I have to go on twisting in the wind?"

La Flambeau looked at Hypodermic. "Shall I tell him or will you?"

Hypodermic's jaw clicked. "You tell him. I've spent enough time with him not to want to give him the satisfaction."

La Flambeau smiled at Jim. "The Doctor is famous for his charm both in this world and the last."

Jim nodded. "I've already observed."

"It's time for you to move on, Jim Morrison, and learn some new lessons. It's time for you to visit the Island of the Gods."

Jim took a step back. "Wait a minute—"

"There's no time left to wait."

"I thought time was strictly relative."

"That doesn't mean we have it to waste."

"I've always tried to steer clear of the gods."

"We do tend to limit the choices of humans."

"I've heard things can happen to men who get too close to gods."

"Things worse even than death?"

"That's what I heard."

"So you admit there may be worse things than death?"

"Is this all a subtle way of telling me that I'm going to go whether I like it or not?"

Hypodermic's eyes glowed like heated coals. "It's also a subtle way of telling you to be careful. On the Island of the Gods, some are not as patient and tolerant as we are."

The sky of Heaven had turned a chill, early morning bleak, and the nuns wading in the water were shivering despite their green rubber thigh boots as they floated the blue-white, wet body toward the others who were waiting on the lakeshore. As they reached the shallows, more nuns got down into the water, soaking the long hems and flowing sleeves of their black habits. Very gently they lifted the corpse that had once been a woman from the water, over the lily pads, and laid it on the grass at the margin the lake. A cartoon deer came into sight from out of a grove of pines, saw what was happening, and turned tail and fled. It was plainly no place for Bambis or bluebirds. The nun Bernadette, who had been leading the search party, detached herself from the shocked group around the body, stripped off her rubber waders, and walked to where Aimee, Semple, and Mr. Thomas were waiting, flanked by a half dozen of Semple's rubber guards. "It's her. It's Mary-Theresa. She's been strangled and mutilated."

Bernadette didn't have to say anything else. Her expression told it all. The slaying was without question the handiwork of the now-vanished Jesus, and she, and presumably at least a majority of the other nuns, held both Aimee and Semple, who had brought him there, directly responsible. The nuns weren't going to accept the excuse that Mary-Theresa hadn't really died but only temporarily returned to the Great Double Helix. The suffering that had been inflicted on her before she'd discorporated was more than enough to leave her scarred for her next three or four incarnations, and the nuns wanted payback. If they couldn't get Jesus himself, the two sisters would be the next best thing.

"He has to be found."

"I've got nuns looking for him all over, but there's a distinct chance that he's already out of here."

Semple and Aimee exchanged glances. The situation appeared increasingly sticky. Semple knew that all Aimee wanted to do was cut loose and rage all over her, but she wasn't about to do it while the nuns were watching. Under the constant scrutiny, they had to maintain a united front and pray that Jesus was still around and would be caught. Semple walked past Bernadette to where the body was lying on the grass. The nuns around it glared at her with open hostility, but so far they didn't seem to feel ready to make any kind of overt move, although one of them did snarl out of the corner of her mouth, "Why don't you get away from her? You're not wanted here."

Semple glanced down at the corpse and then fixed the nun with a glacial glare. "Believe me, I don't want to be here, either."

It only took one long look to satisfy Semple that everything Bernadette had said was true. She turned her back on the angry nuns and returned to where Aimee was standing. "She's right. It's just like the other one."

The body of Mary-Theresa wasn't the first of Jesus' victims to be discovered. Just four hours before, the body of one of the dancing girls from the headland had been found in the rosebushes below the terrace, bearing identical marks of violent abuse. It was clearly the worst crisis in the history of Aimee's Heaven, and try as she might, Semple couldn't shake a certain measure of guilt. She was the one who had set the whole nightmare train of events in motion. Back in Gojiro's brain tumor, it seemed like a fine prank to inflict a lunatic on her sister, but now that the prank had turned into a serial killer rampage, she knew she didn't have a moral leg to stand on. She supposed she could claim that at the time she'd had no idea of the extent of his lunacy, but she knew that plea would fail to cut much ice with either Aimee or the nuns.

Bernadette, who was rapidly emerging as the undisputed leader and primary spokeswoman of Heaven's nuns, may have had squads searching all over the environment for the homicidal messiah, and even bluebirds recruited to act as scouts and spotters, but Semple had grave doubts about whether they were going to find him. Had she been him, she would have had her nasty fun and then been gone like a cool breeze. On the other hand, she was aware that she was making the cardinal error of equating his thought processes with her own. It was something she should long since have learned never to do. Psychos didn't think like her or anyone else. They heard the voice of the Almighty, Sam the Dog, or the TV set in their head, and acted accordingly. Given that, it was extremely possible Jesus was still around. Such was this last straw she clutched at, but without much expectation that it would keep her afloat. Thus, when the shout went up, the tally-ho that the quarry had been sighted, Semple was among the most surprised of all.

Jesus was initially spotted by a bluebird. He was skulking and muddy, on the far side of the headland where no one ever went, because, as a piece of coherent reality, it wasn't properly finished. Following the bluebird's directions, the nuns gathered, and armed with rakes, hoes, shovels, and other gardening implements pressed into service as weapons, they went to intercept him in a crew only slightly more disciplined than a lynch mob. Semple sent her rubber guards with them, with instructions that they should restrain or deflect the nuns should they decide to discorporate Jesus on the spot. Semple wasn't altogether sure, though, that the rubber guards would actually be able to pull it off. They hadn't fared too well in the transfer from her domain to Heaven, and were looking saggy and a little strained around the seams.

Needless to say, neither Semple, Aimee, nor Mr. Thomas went with the nuns. If the search did indeed end with Jesus swinging from a stately oak, the necktie party could all too easily be expanded to include the three of them. The two sisters and the goat waited on the terrace; for the next twenty-five minutes, they listened to the shouts and the coordinating whistles as the hunters closed in.

Jesus was bruised and bloody when he was finally dragged to Aimee. He hadn't actually been lynched, but beyond that the sisters had shown precious little mercy. His white robe was torn and filthy, his sandals were gone, and he had wisely lost the halo. For one so beat up, he showed amazingly little remorse or repentance. They brought him to the bottom of the steps that led up to the terrace, so Aimee was at least able to pass judgment while looking down at the man. For the moment, the nuns were still respecting her authority. Jesus, however, showed nothing but contempt for the ad hoc proceedings. He seemed unable to grasp that his life was at stake. His first move of defiance was to shake himself free of the nuns who were holding his arms, and angrily protest to Aimee. "Do you have no control over these maniac women?"

Semple had to admit that her sister rose to the occasion with an inspired magnificence. Despite all the tension that had gone before, she drew herself up to her full height and regarded Jesus with a demeanor of judicial frost. "From where I'm standing, I can only see one maniac."

Jesus' two hands indicated his injuries and disheveled clothes. "You can see what these mad bitches have done to me."

"They are understandably angry."

"And what right do they have to be angry?"

"Do you deny that you attacked and mutilated at least two of their number?"

"Why should I deny it? I was invited here to help you expand your environment and I presumed that I had all of its facilities at my disposal."

Bernadette glared at him, fists and teeth clenched. "Including women to murder and mutilate according to your sick whim?"

Jesus ignored her and continued to address his remarks to Aimee. "These women I'm supposed to have attacked. What were they? Surely nothing more than property. Why should a few of them disappearing present any kind of problem? I'm entitled to my fun, aren't I?"

This produced a noisy and dangerous outburst from the women. Unlike Semple, they hadn't heard this glib argument before. They hadn't known Anubis. Jesus was nunhandled and jostled, and Semple's rubber guards moved quickly to protect him. Aimee held up her hand for silence. When the tumult finally subsided, Jesus looked around angrily. "I'm not saying another word until I get a lawyer."

Aimee looked at him as though he were insane. "A lawyer?"

"That's right, a lawyer."

"You think there are lawyers in Heaven?"

He pointed to Semple. "What about her?"

Semple looked outraged. "No McPherson has *ever* been a lawyer. Preachers and horse thieves, maybe, but never a *lawyer*."

A superior smile spread across Jesus' face. "This trial can hardly continue if I can't have adequate representation."

Bernadette shouted angrily, "You can speak for yourself, can't you?"

Now it was Aimee's turn to look superior. "And who said this was a trial?"

Jesus' smile faded. "So what is it, then?"

"I merely wanted to hear what you had to say before I passed sentence."

"You can't sentence me. I'm Jesus Christ and this is supposed to be Heaven. You've got a major jurisdictional problem on your hands. I'm the Son of God, damn it." He turned and looked at the nuns. "I mean, all of you, you're all supposed to be brides of Christ, aren't you? So, if that's the case, you all belong to me and you shouldn't be creating this nonsense."

Bernadette and the other nuns could hardly credit what they were hearing. "We don't belong to you, you son of a bitch." They gestured to Aimee. "We don't even belong to her."

Jesus abruptly changed tack. He became the affable, placating used-car salesman. "Okay, okay. I tell you what. Let's look at this another way. I admit that I messed up the women. It was a mistake. I confess. I shouldn't have done it. I thought they were part of the facilities and I thought I was mutilating them in good faith, but that was an error. If anyone's got a problem with me mutilating women, I'm sorry. Different strokes and all the rest of it. It's probably a result of all the TV I've watched. But why don't we just leave it at that? I'll get the fuck out of here and I'll promise to stop telling people that I'm Jesus Christ and we'll forget the whole thing. I mean, think about it. What's the point of sending me back to the pods? I'll be just the same when I get out. Maybe even worse."

When Jesus finished, an incredulous silence settled. Then a lone nun spoke in a quiet voice. "Crucify him."

The refrain was taken up and grew louder. "Crucify him!"

"Crucify him!"

"Crucify him!"

Bernadette held up a hand and the shouting subsided. "We should do worse than crucify him. We should peel his skin off in strips."

The idea gained an immediate constituency. "And then cut up his flesh in even smaller pieces."

"And barbecue each piece as he's forced to watch."

Semple determinedly shook her head. "No barbecue. No cannibalism."

The traditionalists began shouting again. "Crucify him!"

"Crucify him!"

"Crucify him!"

"Crucify him!"

Aimee was determined to have the last word; ever the traditionalist herself, she decided to stick with the tried and tested. "Behold the man! He shall be crucified."

The crowd broke into wild applause. Jesus couldn't believe what he was hearing. "Wait a minute . . . "

Aimee looked at Bernadette. For once, they were in complete accord. "Is there a fresh cross?"

"There is."

"Nails?"

"All we need. It only takes three."

"Just wait a minute . . . "

"Then take him to Golgotha and make it so."

As Jesus was dragged away kicking and screaming, Aimee turned on Semple. "Now it's your turn."

"What do you mean, it's my turn?"

"You brought that monster here, didn't you?"

"I told you he wasn't any real Jesus Christ, and you were more than happy to go along with the gag."

Now that they were alone, Aimee was almost hyperventilating. "Is that what you thought it was? A gag? Just one of your accursed pranks? Do you know what you've done to me? Bernadette and her nuns will be at my throat the moment they've finished with your damned Jesus."

Semple hadn't realized just how tightly wrapped her sister really was. "I didn't know he was a serial killer, goddamn it."

"That's your trouble, isn't it? You never do know, do you?"

"Are you aware what I went through just to get him for you?"

"From the feedback I got, it looked like you were whoring your way across the Afterlife, and finding that creature was nothing more than an afterthought."

Now Semple was losing her temper. "Yeah? Is that what you think?"

Aimee was turning red in the face, an effect that verged on the grotesque with her pale complexion and golden hair. "You don't give a damn about me, do you?

Semple smiled nastily. "Why would I? As you keep telling me, I'm no good. I'm the whore, aren't I? I'm the evil twin."

Semple realized she shouldn't have smiled. Aimee lost all control and began to vibrate; she was building up a head of destructive force that, when it reached a crucial peak, she would launch at Semple, blasting her to kingdom come. "Don't start vibrating like that; you'll hurt someone."

Aimee's voice became powerfully strange; Semple would have suspected demonic possession if she hadn't known better. "Do you know how much I hate you?"

Semple raised a defensive vibration of her own. The two sisters were now close to violent conflict. "Of course I know how much you hate me. That's why we separated. I really wouldn't try to do anything to me, though. You'd have a lot of trouble surviving without me; you saw how things fell apart when I was away from here."

Logic made no dent in Aimee's fury. "And do you know how much, above everything, I hate knowing I have to keep you around?"

The sound of hammer blows came from away in Golgotha and Jesus started screaming. Semple half turned, momentarily distracted. Her guard dropped, and in the nano-instant Aimee struck.

Jim stepped ashore on the Island of the Gods to the sound of drums. Drums were beating all over the tropical island, and complex cross-rhythms pulsed through the warm, sweet, slightly sticky air. He was already accustomed to having everything accompanied by a hollow and echoing throb, like a universal and collective heartbeat. Drums had hammered on the trireme, keeping the rowers to their designated stroke. The drummer on the galley sat central and elevated, sternward on the well deck, behind and above the tiers of oarsmen, pounding his mallets into the hard hide heads of his twin kettle-drums with massive repetitive strokes of his tree-trunk arms. The drummer in his loincloth and oiled torso, and the tall broadshouldered female overseer in studded leather who wielded the whip, could almost have been brother and sister. With the woman standing well over seven feet tall and the drummer possessed of muscles beyond the wildest steroid dreams of any human bodybuilder, they seemed to be some midpoint hybrid of man and god, like the legendary Hercules or the Titans.

The trireme was longer, sleeker, and of tighter trim than the other galley that Jim had seen plowing up the Great River, but it still used bench-chained prisoners for propulsion. On his arrival Jim had wondered why the Voodoo gods didn't use zombies to provide the manpower for the galley. He had pointed this out to Danbhala La Flambeau, who had shaken her head as if to suggest that Jim had watched too many cheap horror movies. "Zombies were ruined by George Romero, boy. These are Obeah submissives who love every minute of it."

Jim's major surprise had been, of course, that he, Dr. Hypodermic, and Danbhala La Flambeau hadn't simply wind-walked directly to the island, but had set down in this galley, which was, as far as Jim could estimate, lying some ten miles off the night-shrouded coast. They had jaunted from the Crossroads to the boat by the same kind of instant special shift that Hypodermic had employed to take him to Vietnam, the padded cell, and all the rest of the locations that they had visited, and he couldn't understand why the boat was needed as an intermediate stopover. When he asked about this, he'd received another impatient reply. "This is the transit point, the Ship of Agoueh. Everyone has to come in this way. We can't just have people floating directly to the Island of the Gods. If we allowed that, we'd go the way of Hell and be reduced to nothing more than a tourist park."

Not that finding himself at sea bothered Jim unduly. He actually welcomed the time aboard to acclimate to the idea that he was entering a whole new phase of his Afterlife. He was able to lean on the rail of the quarterdeck where the gods took their ease, while dolphins, orcas, and undulating manta rays lazily shadowed the boat, marlins jumped in the mid-distance, and families of sea monkeys danced in the purple troughs of the gentle swell of what, to Jim's mind, couldn't be anything but Byron's wine-dark sea. He did note, however, that he was yet again traveling across the Afterlife by water and he wondered, as he stared at the approaching island, whether there was any symbolic or mystical significance to the fact that so many of his recent journeys were by made by way of river, sewer, swamp, or ocean.

The appearance of the island itself revealed very little, just a dark mass in the soft deceptive night with the red lava glow of a volcano at one end of the landmass. Jim looked a little dubiously at the volcano. He'd seen quite enough hot angry mountains lately and he hoped they weren't becoming another recurrent motif. He couldn't raise much enthusiasm for an Afterlife spent slowly sailing past volcanoes. He did suppose, however, that the Island of the Gods couldn't really exist without one. Presumably some of the inhabitants actually needed to live inside it. But the red lava glow wasn't the only illumination on the island. A thousand points of light, either moving or static, indicated that the Island of the Gods was anything but underpopulated. They winked and twinkled like tiny gems, instilling the place with the needed quality of magic, even from a distance.

Another advantage to the brief interval on the boat had been the attendants. The tall, slender, coffee-colored Amazons looked as if they came from the same basic gene pool as the drummer and the woman with the whip, and they seemed to have the sole purpose of keeping the passengers satisfied. They served him rum-based fruit drinks that came complete with slices of pineapple and small paper umbrellas. One had even offered to give him a rubdown with herbs and hot oil. Jim had been sorely tempted, but he'd shot a covert glance across the quarterdeck to where the three Mystères were deep in earnest conversation in a bizarre and lilting Creole patois. In addition to the Doctor and Danbhala La Flambeau, the Baron Tonnerre was also aboard the Ship of Agoueh. Indeed, he had been waiting in one of his elaborate, bemedaled uniforms when they'd arrived on board. The original trio was again complete, and Jim decided that maybe a massage was too frivolous for an occasion invested with such gravity, even if no one was about to tell him why. He passed up the hot oil and herb rubdown and settled for a succession of the powerful rum drinks. As a result, when the trireme shipped its oars and moored at the pier, and Jim finally descended the gangplank, he was more than three parts drunk and walking a little unsteadily.

Mercifully, Jim found he wasn't required to walk very far. An open car with a landau top was waiting. It was unlike any car Jim had ever encountered, dwarfing any automobile he'd seen in either dream or life. The hood alone must have been thirty feet long and the tonnage of chrome outweighed that of even the most fancifully customized semi, and that wasn't to mention the gold trim. From knowledge acquired from his long-lost hot-rod home boys back in the metalflake sixties California of Big Daddy Ed Roth and Rat Fink, Jim knew that the lustrous pearlized finish could only have been achieved by a minimum of twenty-nine hand-rubbed coats of lacquer, platinum dust, and exotic fish scales. It was truly the cherry paint job of the gods. The machine might once have been a 1930s movie-star Duesenberg, but it had been stretched, enlarged, extended, and so elaborately curved and curliqued that it was scarcely recognizable. Jim wondered who might create and customize these mobile palaces for the ancient African gods. Did they dream them up themselves and just make them real in a flash of kinetic magic? Or were there somewhere, perhaps in sweating caves under the volcano, holy and secret chop shops where car-culture Leonardos pushed the envelopes of their talent, working with dedication and diligence for their exalted masters?

As Jim and the Mystères left the pier and approached the supercar, a chauffeur opened the door for them. He wore the uniform of the Baron Tonnerre's crack honor guard, and seemed to be yet another part human, part demigod kin of the trireme's drummer, mistress-overseer, and attendants. Two more similarly uniformed outriders waited a little way in front of the car astride two of the largest Harley-Davidsons in creation.

From this first impression, Jim could only assume that the Voodoo pantheon did everything in massive and highly flamboyant style. This was immediately confirmed as the huge car and its outriders moved forward along the crushed-shell gravel road that led away from the harbor. Screened by stands of cypress, groves of palms, and luxurious banks of rhododendron and fire dragon, sprawling and elaborately fanciful mansions were set back from road, some lit flamboyantly like Graceland on a Tennessee summer night, others remaining masked and dark with strange flames sporadically showing at mullioned windows. In parks and gardens that were at one and the same time both wild but carefully tended, fountains sang and sparkled, and fires burned in braziers atop tall stone beacons. Big cats prowled; peacocks strutted; on one opulent lawn a herd of decorative white rhinos grazed on the greensward and cropped the shubbery. While most of these palaces and mansions favored a basic European billionaire luxury from the school of high Beverly Hills or Colombian narco lord, the open supercar twice passed the formidable, thorn-thicket outer walls of much more traditional Royal Zulu kraals from the time of Cetshwayo. He also spotted no less than four domed and minaretted quasi-mosques, a number of brick beehive structures, but with the bricks fashioned from solid gold and silver, outsized opals, and squared-off blocks of emerald and diamond. He even saw one exact reproduction of the White House, and another of the Alhambra.

When he was first told that he was going to the Island of the Gods, Jim had naively expected to find some across-the-board melting pot of religions and denominations, a place where Baal, Quetzacoatl, Crom, and the Lord Krishna all dwelled discreetly, cheek-by-jowl, like some ecumenical Olympus. In this, he discovered he had been extremely and hopelessly wrong. The Island of the Gods proved to be highly segregated, the exclusive turf of the basic Afro-Creole pantheon along with a few related and kindred spirits.

The big Duesenberg went on climbing higher and higher into the island uplands that culminated in the crater of the volcano. After a while, this started to give Jim pause. Although he was insulated by the quantities of god-rum he had consumed on the Ship of Agoueh, the idea did occur to him that, in the name of sundry gods, more than one white boy had been taken up to a volcano never to return. For a while he contemplated jumping out of the car and making a run for it; he decided against this, however, even though the open supercar was actually proceeding up the white shell road at a very stately pace. He'd noticed quite soon in the ride that, although each god was deity of the manor in his or her own enclave, the highways and byways of the island were heavily patrolled by Baron Tonnerre's red-uniformed troopers with their peaked caps, gold lightning-flash badges, and inscrutable sunglasses even at night. Presumably their mission was to deter and eject interlopers, trespassers, and the uninvited. Even if he did manage to make a break, Jim figured he'd probably last about twenty minutes loose on his own in the tropical paradise, a very strange stranger in a very strange land.

As the crater neared, Jim increasingly worried he might be earmarked for a dive into the magma; then, to his relief, the car turned off and headed toward a projecting headland where two massive carved megaliths supported an even bigger capstone. This upper stone was shaped like an eagle with its wings extended, and the closer Jim came to this towering structure, the more he realized that he was in the presence of something incredibly old, maybe older than humanity itself. This atmosphere of the impossibly ancient begged the hallowed question of whether the gods had been around before man had crawled from the swamp, or if it had taken humanity to validate their existence. Like most right-thinking individuals, Jim had always been of the latter opinion, but the closer the supercar came to the megastructure, the less certain he became.

The white road terminated a quarter of a mile from the megaliths themselves. Beyond where the road ended, a paved walk had been laid that described a huge spiral almost the same quarter mile in diameter. The car halted and the chauffeur climbed out and opened the door for the passengers to alight. The Mystères indicated that Jim should get out first. He glanced at Danbhala La Flambeau as he stepped down from the car. "And what happens now?"

She gestured to the ancient curving flagged pavement. "You walk the spiral while we wait for the others to come."

Semple was nothing more than a mass of fragments, down with the atoms, only held in the loose amalgamation of a meteor shower by the attraction of a simple internal gravity. The single mercy was that she felt no pain. In fact, she felt hardly anything, as though she didn't have enough singular integrity to experience any of the usual mental or physical sensations. An anger at Aimee for doing what she'd done seethed somewhere in the backwash of her previous consciousness. An unfocused fear drifted along with the knowledge she was free-falling into a total unknown, without the power to stop or even slow her headlong progress. Even when she'd died, she'd had Aimee with her as part of the composite. Now she was totally alone—more than alone, if the truth were to be told. Many familiar parts of her mind on which she had always depended were now absent, leaving her ill-equipped to deal with the shocks the future undoubtedly had in store. As far as she could tell, she was in Limbo. She had enough memory left to recall that Limbo was a place rarely mentioned in the Afterlife, the ultimate distant nothing to which a soul could be consigned to loiter in the absolute end of the void until it perhaps chanced randomly to drift in the direction of the Great Double Helix. It was probably fortunate that she didn't have enough emotional makeup left to feel the rush of terror the prospect of Limbo usually inspired. All Semple could really do was dispassionately observe her surroundings, make of them what she could, and wait to see what would happen next.

Beneath her was a micro-world where shiny billiard-ball protons and neutrons circled majestically around clumped spheroid nuclei, and electrons sparked and flashed in spectacular displays of red, blue, and yellow primal fireworks. A small shard of her being was able to appreciate the beauty of it all. She had always imagined that the subatomic world would be a black empty space and an appreciative fraction of what remained of her mind was surprised at the jostling density of this new environment, but it also reminded her that this might not be a real subatomic environment, merely a personal interpretation of the completely unknowable.

As she drifted farther, she began to see that the animated complexity of spheres and lightning had a finite limit. At something like a curved, if not clearly defined, horizon, the bouncing, oscillating atoms and the flashing electrons ended in a seething margin of quantum foam, and beyond that was a seemingly endless black nothing, empty but for a tiny, multicolored, glowing helix. Semple knew this was the Great Double Helix, but so far away it was reduced to the insignificance of a distant nebula. Aimee's anger had pushed her unimaginably deep into the unknown. How long would she drift helplessly before she reached a point where the pods might draw her in, and set her on the laborious uphill path to a fresh incorporation? If she got lucky and even reached the distant Double Helix, enough of her sanity might not remain for her to be worth a new persona or a new incarnation. It was lucky she didn't have too much capacity for forward-looking fear; otherwise she might have started screaming right there and then, embarking on the lurch into dementia with no further ado.

She had assumed that the long wearisome drift into the void would be one of uniform, uneventful tedium. But then the flames appeared, directly in her path at the edge of the void, and she had to revise that idea.

Danbhala La Flambeau had called to Jim as he started along the path of the spiral. "Whatever happens, don't stop until you reach the center. It's vitally important that you don't stop under any circumstances."

Jim had almost stopped right there and then. His first reaction was to get the hell out, and fast. Unfortunately, there was nowhere to get the hell out to, so Jim continued along the curve of the ancient paving at a reserved saunter. If he couldn't escape, he was probably best advised to do like Danbhala La Flambeau had told him. On the other hand, he saw no sense in rushing to whatever awaited him when he'd finished traveling this series of ever-decreasing circles.

As Jim completed his first half circle and the path led him past and away from the standing stones, the other gods started to arrive. Some arrived in custom variations of the giant limousine that had brought Jim to the standing stones—Cadillacs and Rolls-Royces, Mercedes and Hirondels, a Cord and even an enormous Packard Patrician. Others came by more outlandish means. Marie-Louise, a frail and incredibly old woman in a mantilla and black lace shawl, drove up in an ornate open phaeton, with skeleton driver and footmen and drawn by six black horses, all wearing plumes as though for a funeral. Sarazine Jambe and Clairmesine Clairmeille both appeared in entities of pulsing, revolving light like the one that had, all that time ago, brought La Flambeau, Hypodermic, and Tonnerre to Doc Holliday's township. The frighteningly beautiful Erzulie-Severine-Belle-Femme insinuated her presence into the area in something similar, a scintillating, undulating, and sinuously dancing aura of perfumed sexuality made glowing, dancing energy. The military form of Ogou Baba, dressed in the white cloak and spiked helmet of a Mamluk, with a gold saber hanging from his belt, rode up on a stamping, snorting, black-as-night stallion. Captain Debas thundered in, kicking up gravel, on an antique Norton motorcycle.

Jim had never seen these new gods before, but their names seemed to reverberate in his head: Kadia Bossou, Baron Le Croix, Mam'zelle Charlotte, Erzulie Taureau, Zantahi Medeh, Ou-An Ille, Gougonne Dan Leh, Man Inan, An We-Zo, Zaou Pemba, Ti Jean Pied-Cheche, Papa Houng'to. One by one, and then in increasing numbers, they gathered around the outer perimeter of the spiral. Every single one of them would have been enough on his or her own to strike terror in the bravest of mortals; en masse, they were formidable to the point of overkill. Towering figures, in robes and headdresses, uniforms or the alluring near-nudity of Erzulie-Severine-Belle-Femme. Some weren't even in any approximation of human form. Erzulie Taureau was a massive Babylonian bull with gilded horns and garlands of orchids, Adahi Loko was a similarly exotic elephant, and Baron Azagon was nothing more than a living flame. As they crowded and jostled for position, auras collided and sectors of energy sparked shorts of power, headdresses bobbed and weaved, and the saber of Ogou Baba became entangled in the flowing train of Mam'zelle Charlotte, while his stallion plunged and pranced, nervous in such a vibrant crowd. The only god who was given absolute space to go and do where and what she liked was the venerable Marie-Louise.

The spectacle was such that Jim would have stopped and stared openmouthed, but Danbhala La Flambeau had told him not to stop for any reason, and he wasn't about to buck that program now that the gods had arrived. Jim went right on walking. La Flambeau hadn't told him not to look, and as he walked he took in every detail of this sight that few, if any, mortal humans had ever witnessed. Maybe, if he came through all this intact, he really would return to his poetry. The gathering was so close to impossible that it just had to be recorded. At the same time, though, Jim could feel that something was happening to him. Cultures as far apart as the Anastazi in New Mexico and the Druids in England had employed the power of the spiral in their religious and ecstatic ceremonies and rituals. The belief had been that to walk the spiral was, in many ways, an intoxication similar to ingesting yage, peyote, or psilocybin, and as Jim progressed along the endless circular path to the center, he started to subscribe very strongly to that arcane belief. At first it was hard to tell if anything was really amiss, whether he might be entering an altered state. To spot a hallucination is hard in a place where reality at its most normal is an almost hallucinatory condition.

By the third circuit, however, Jim was well aware that the gods had started to lurch and flow one into another, and even the ground beneath his feet was taking on some unique tactile wave patterns. Jim was getting strangely high, flying without benefit of wings, but it certainly wasn't an unpleasant experience. He could hear the soaring tone of a distant Jimi Hendrix guitar echoing out from some other place on the mountain, and it occurred to him to question why Jimi, the Voodoo Child, wasn't there at the gathering. He certainly deserved his place. Maybe he was elsewhere on the island, maybe the echoing guitar was real. Jim recalled their obscenely drunken nights at Steve Paul's Scene in New York City and the last time the two had seen each other at the troubled British open-air rock festival on the Isle of Wight, just human weeks before the two of them had died. "If you're here, man, get on down and help me out."

Jim wasn't joking. His legs were becoming increasingly rubbery and he was having some difficulty staying on the curving path. The inclination to lurch off to the left was increasingly powerful, but La Flambeau held him to making every effort to stay the course. No help came, however. Quite the reverse. The gods seemed to believe that Jim was the key to something and each had something to say to him. They talked at him in a way that made the words throb physically in his head, drowning out the sound of the guitar.

"We used to be the link between the world of the living and the realm of the dead."

"But no longer."

"Humans now come through in numbers that increase out of all proportion."

Jim could feel the gods' eyes boring into him.

"The humans push us farther and farther from our ancient domains, until all we have left is this island."

"Humans die and humans die and they go on dying."

Jim was starting to feel that the Voodoo gods held him personally responsible for their troubles. He wanted to turn and protest, but still he kept walking.

"The numbers of them expand and expand again. All the time, more and more humans crowd into what was once our world."

As he rounded the curve that brought him to the point where he was moving back toward the megaliths, he clearly saw the red eyes of Dr. Hypodermic among all of the others. "It surely can't be that bad."

Hypodermic's eyes glowed angrily in the darkness. "It's worse than bad."

"But you can't hold me responsible. I didn't want to die. I would happily have gone on living, well into the twenty-first century."

"You humans have no respect for the unique properties of this Afterlife. You stab it with knives in the heart of the dawn. You shatter the patterns of harmony. You pay no respect to those who were here before. You waste its pure base energy in the shaping of diseased environments, built from false memories and evil dreams. You rip and you plunder, trampling underfoot the magical potential of the true treasures."

In the background, the Hendrix guitar wailed a sustained note of raw bleak grief.

"You have all but doomed your own lifeside world and you seek to do the same to ours."

The painfully beautiful face of Erzulie-Severine-Belle-Femme, surrounded by a halo of black diamond flame, floated into Jim's increasingly psychedelic field of vision. Jim suddenly found himself aching for the god-woman, unable to stand her expression of sad reproach. "For us, the fruitfulness of humanity is the curse of extinction. We gods, spirits, and demons are an endangered species. Do you want to see us gone from this place?"

Jim kept walking. Unbidden tears ran down his face. All he wanted was for Erzulie-Severine-Belle-Femme to enfold him in her arms and tell him that he was forgiven, but still he managed to keep on walking. He knew if he stopped, everything would fail. "Of course not. You're the gods."

The face of Erzulie-Severine-Belle-Femme was replaced by that of the incalculably ancient Marie-Louise. "Then you will do anything that we ask of you?"

The trip was becoming desperate. "Of course I will. You already know that. Just tell me what I'm supposed to do."

"You don't have to be told. You will know."

Jim could feel his sanity slipping, but he kept on walking. "You keep telling me that."

The bright black eyes in the shrunken wrinkled face penetrated clear into Jim's soul. "That is the first thing we require of you. You must make the leap of faith. The blind leap of faith."

Jim shook his head. The center of the circle was very close. "I've been leaping blind all my days. I was the fucking Lizard King!"

Marie-Louis smiled as though Jim had finally stated the obvious. "That's why you were selected."

The curving path ended in a flat, circular, blood-red stone, engraved with the Sword of La Place, dividing it into the equal and opposite halves, pethro and rada, the alive and the dead, the good and the evil, while the symbols of the joukoujou veves extended all around the circumference. Without knowing why, only that it needed to be done, Jim deliberately placed one foot on either side of the sword. Then he turned and screamed to the gods, "So what do I do now?"

"Face the stones."

Jim slowly did what he was told and saw the stars. Between the stones, exactly framed by the two uprights and the lintel they supported, a geometric arrangement of nine stars blazed unwinkingly, only visible from the exact center of the spiral.

"Okay, I see the stars. It still doesn't tell me what I do now."

"When the other one arrives, it will begin."

The flames reached out, encircling and enclosing, encompassing all the fragments that had once been Semple McPherson. The flames warmed them . . . no, more than warmed, they were being heated, moving them together, fusing one piece to the next, solidifying their integrity. Inert molecules once more moved. Old connections started to re-form, and sundered synapses began exchanging tentative sparks of data. Semple—and once more she could just about think of herself as Semple—knew an armature of being was somehow being reconstituted. She wasn't functional enough to hope, but something was definitely happening, right in Limbo, where *nothing* should be happening. At the same time as this perception came to her, she was also aware of another presence beside her own, a presence that seemed to have come with the flames and the warmth. It might have been the flames themselves, but there was more to it than that. The presence radiated a comforting, if implacable strength, a strength Semple had no desire to go against, but a strength that, at that moment, was slowly and surely restoring her soul.

"What are you?"

"I am Danbhala La Flambeau and I have come to bring you out of here."

"I don't understand. My sister, my other half, blasted me into Limbo. It's over for me."

"Your sister made an angry error. Your course is not yet run."

"My course?"

"I am Danbhala La Flambeau and I have come to bring you out of Limbo and back to the familiar Paths of the Dead."

The lightning came right out of the formation of stars, and the crash of thunder that went with it all but deafened Jim. At the same time, the flash when the lightning struck the spiral completely, if temporarily, blinded him. He cringed away from the violent blue-white electrical explosion but still didn't step out of the blood-red central circle, and his feet remained planted on either side of the Sword of La Place. Why was it that the gods had to work with so many explosions and in so many sudden furious rushes? Jim didn't need to be any further dazzled or impressed. He was convinced. He would have yelled through the ringing in his ears, but he knew it was pointless. The gods would do what the gods had to do, without outside consultation and regardless of little things like whether one insignificant human went blind, deaf, or crazy. These sons of bitches were jerking him around the way their Greek counterparts had jerked around poor fucking Oedipus.

"If I'm so fucking insignificant, why do you feel the need to fuck with me so much?"

Even when his vision started to clear, he could see little on the other side of the spiral except an ion-shattered mist. It was only as it started to dissipate that he saw the figure of the woman. She stood swaying and then stumbled slightly. Jim couldn't believe that she'd come with the lightning. "Semple?"

The gods had finally brought them together? For a purpose that only the gods knew? He was about to step out of the circle and go to her, but then the presence of Danbhala La Flambeau was everywhere in the spiral, authoritative and urgent. "Stay where you are! Let her come to the center! Don't go to her or you'll lose her!"

Jim froze. His instincts told him to go with his humanity and run to her, but the compulsion to obey La Flambeau couldn't be fought.

"Semple, it's me, it's Jim Morrison. We met in space and again in Hell. Follow the path. Quickly. Come to where I am. Just follow the path. You can make it."

Semple looked around, shaky and disorientated, but Jim could only suppose that she, too, was picking up the urgency from Danbhala La Flambeau. She quickly pulled herself together and started to walk along the flagstones of the spiral. After a half dozen paces, she stumbled, but regained her grip and began walking again.

"Just follow the path. If you start to feel weird, don't worry about it. Shut everything else out and just keep right on walking until you get to me."

Semple's voice faltered. "All these people, these things, what are they?"

"They're the Voodoo pantheon."

"The Voodoo . . . ?"

"Don't even think about it. Just walk, okay?"

"I'm doing my best."

Haltingly at first, but rapidly gaining strength, Semple made the circuits of the spiral, laboriously coming closer to Jim.

"I think I'm starting to hallucinate."

"Just try to ignore it. Concentrate on walking."

The revolutions Semple walked were growing smaller and smaller. It hardly seemed that she was walking toward Jim. She was now just going around and around him.

"Why don't I just step across to you?"

Jim quickly shook his head. "No way. Don't even think about it. That would trigger a disaster."

"What's going on here?"

"That's the great mystery."

"I don't understand any of this."

"That makes you part of a very exclusive club."

"How can you make jokes?"

"It stops me from clutching my head and screaming."

Semple came around the final curve, staggering and half falling toward Jim. Jim moved to catch her and bring her into the central circle. In the instant that they touched, however, a light came out of nowhere. Before either Jim or Semple had a chance to react, the two of them were enclosed in a needle of light that lanced straight up to the sky, and they rose right up with it.

9

In room 1009 . . .

Jim awoke in pain to a vicious morning after in the enclosed TV twilight of a cheap hotel room. The TV set opposite the bed dated back to the early fifties, an antique black and white model with the exposed picture tube mounted above a flat rectangular cabinet that contained the circuitry. The station it had been tuned to had gone off the air, and an electronic snowstorm spattered the screen, providing the only light in the room. The low white noise that accompanied it was the only sound. Jim's first emotion was a need to kill the TV. If he'd had a gun at hand, he would have put a bullet through the damned thing right there and then and screw the fact that the report might split his suffering skull. The hotel room looked like the kind where a man should have a gun, perhaps a black Colt .45 automatic, under the pillow or in the drawer of the bedside table. The cheaply framed painting above the bed—a rearing rattlesnake on black velvet—said it all. He was in some knocked-off Jim Thompson scenario with a meat-cleaver headache and no clue as to how he came to be there. His monumental motherfucker of an alcohol hangover was further complicated by the fact that Jim, as far as he could reconstruct the pieces of the puzzle, had just awakened from a highly realized nightmare filled with primal figures from some Jungian black museum. He couldn't recall the details, but he had the distinct impression that the primal figures were urging him to take some action—action both difficult and dangerous. He groaned; all this thinking was causing a shattering agony to lance through his head. "No more, okay? I don't have the strength yet to crawl from this bed and start looking for clues."

But he knew he would, even before he reached into the drawer of the nightstand to see if there really was a gun in there. Instead of a gun, he discovered a mirror, about seven by seven inches, with a single-sided razor blade, a section of red and white plastic drinking straw, and an almost immodest quantity of leftover cocaine. Idly and still mainly asleep, he licked his right index finger so some of the white powder would cling to it when he dabbed it on the mirror. When he put his powdered finger in his mouth and rubbed the coke onto his upper gum, he felt an immediate tingle. It was good shit. "Must have been some kind of party here last night."

Other inanimate telltales of a wild revelry: a bottle of Old Crow with about two inches left in it; two glasses, one with scarlet lipstick smears; an ice bucket with about a half inch of chill water in the bottom; a brimming-over ashtray in which half the butts also bore lipstick traces. A woman had obviously been there. Where the hell was she now?

The ashtray reminded Jim that he wanted a cigarette. Moving his bleary focus a little farther afield, he spotted a crumpled but half-full pack of unfiltered, king-sized Pall Malls. It lay on the floor where it must have been dropped, next to the remnants of a torn slip and a pair of laddered nylon stockings. Clearly he and the woman had done more than just smoke, drink, and snort cocaine. As if he needed further confirmation of debauchery, there were dozens of Polaroid pictures scattered over the floor at the foot of the bed. On the flat top of the dressing table was the big early-model Land camera that must have been spitting prints all night. Jim reached down and picked up one of the nearest pictures. The grainy black and white image was unmistakable: Semple McPherson in a cheesecake standing pose. She was positioned for maximum provocation, in bra, panties, high heels, and black nylons held up by a garter belt, leaning forward to maximize her cleavage, one foot up on a chair, *Blue Angel* style, revealing a seductive expanse of white thigh. Her eyes stared directly into the camera, made vampire-strange by the reflection of the flash off the back of the retina. Jim reached instinctively to take a hit from what was left in the bottle of Old Crow before he picked up another of the instant prints.

The next image was again of Semple, this time topless, on all fours on the bed. Despite his headache, he leaned forward and gathered up a bunch of the Polaroids. As he rifled through them, they told a clear, if not quite consecutive story, almost an explicit photo strip cartoon, and proved, beyond any shadow of a doubt, that Semple McPherson was absolutely devoid of erotic inhibition. He found himself looking at Semple McPherson bending over, presenting a symmetrical and almost perfect ass to the camera; Semple McPherson in only heels and stockings, legs spread and ecstatically caressing herself for full pornographic impact; Semple McPherson wearing just one stocking, hands tied with the other and gagged with a scarf, struggling against the makeshift bonds; and Semple McPherson, tongue extended, licking what Jim could only assume were his own testicles. He let out a low whistle, pain temporarily forgotten. "Go, girl! I must have been holding the camera at arm's length to get that one."

He flipped over more of the cardlike prints and found that he also figured in a good percentage of them. He could only assume that in these cases, Semple had been operating the camera. He appeared exhibitionistically masturbating, eyes closed, hair hanging down, half covering an expression of divine suffering; he appeared, shot from above, kneeling on the hotel carpet kissing Semple's shoes; another arm's-length shot revealed him suckling one of her breasts. Another sequence of pictures were of the two of them coupling in variations of an embrace so energetically passionate that it was, at times, hard to tell what limbs or areas of flesh belonged to whom. Jim wasn't clear how these last pictures could have been taken. Either the camera was set to a time delay, or at some point a third party had been in the room. Another showed Semple half dressed, curled up in an armchair that was not now present in the hotel room, pointing the Land camera at the lens of whatever camera had taken this picture. Where had the second camera come from? While wondering about these logistics, Jim scooped up another selection of prints. At some time during the proceedings, they had become really adventurous. Both Jim and Semple were pictured near-naked in the hotel corridor and even in the elevator, obviously high on the potential risk of discovery.

Jim slowly put down the Polaroids. They were a visual record of a sexual romp that was the complete antithesis of any quick drunken tussle that might later be consumed by a whiskey blackout. This encounter had been of a duration, variety, and escalation that should have remained in his memory. "So why the fuck can't I remember it?"

The plaintive cry jogged loose the realization: the Jungian dream hadn't been a dream at all. Pieces began to link themselves together into the full picture. He had been in the casino; Lola had warned him to leave; then he'd been hijacked by Dr. Hypodermic and run through a tour of illusion that had culminated in an unclear sequence of noise and spiral disturbance, of an island of strange gods and violent light. It was possible that what had gone down between him and Semple was simply another illusion, and yet, as far as he knew, you couldn't take Polaroids of a hallucination. Unless, of course, what he was going through now was the illusion . . .

"Hold it!"

Jim put the brakes on this train. He slowly and carefully lit another cigarette, hoping that the familiar and comfortable action would slow his racing thoughts. To deal with the truckload of paradox and confusion, he needed more than the last inch of Old Crow. He needed coffee. He needed a Bloody Mary. He needed room service. He needed to find out where this funky hotel was located. He reached for the old black bakelite rotary phone, but before he could pick it up, it let out an earsplitting jangle. Jim jerked and stared in horror at the thing as though it were the living cousin of the rattlesnake on black velvet. He took a long drag on the Pall Mall to calm his nerves and picked up the heavy black handset. "Hello?"

"Jim?"

"I think so."

"What's the matter with you?"

"Who is this?"

"It's me, for chrissakes."

"Semple?"

"Who the fuck else would it be? Is there something wrong?"

"I'm very hungover."

"I'm not surprised."

"Could I ask you what might sound like a strange question?"

"I would have thought, after living on bourbon, depravity, and room service for almost a week, you could pretty much ask me anything. We even sent out for a pair of instant cameras."

"Where am I?"

Semple glanced over her shoulder, peering around the hotel lobby through the glass of the old folding-door phone booth. Two hookers and a junkie, waiting for the pay phone, were shooting her hostile looks. Why the fuck had Morrison taken it into his head to hole up in the sleaziest hotel in all of Hell? The junkie was plainly jonesing out; the hookers had their own urgent telephonic needs. She wasn't about to indulge Jim if he was in the throws of some lunatic fugue. "We're in Hell, you idiot. Where do you think we are?"

"In Hell?"

"In room 807 of the Mephisto Hotel in the Third Circle, just down the street from the Grand Elevator Concourse. Is that precise enough for you?"

"Does the name Danbhala La Flambeau mean anything to you?"

"Of course it does. She's stopped by three times to see how we were doing."

"And has anything strange happened to you recently?"

"I woke up earlier with a tattoo I never had before. A rattlesnake on my left shoulder that I never would have chosen for myself. Does that qualify?"

"I guess so."

She could hear the confusion in his voice. She knew Jim had a few missing parts that caused him to meander in and out of reality, but this was hardly the time to be losing control. She would have thought that, after the way they had been pushing the one-on-one envelope, he would have been solidly centered and fully focused. Semple had always believed that the phrases "fucking one's brain out" was highly inaccurate. Excessive sex tended to make her sharper, more perceptive, and highly energized.

"Listen, my love, whatever's going on with you, just can it, okay? We've got a problem and there's no time for any cosmic wandering. You do know you're dead, don't you?"

Now Jim sounded impatient. "Of course I know I'm dead."

"Just checking."

The junkie was now peering through the glass of the phone booth. At any moment he was going to start banging on the door. "Listen carefully, Jim. This is important. We've got a problem."

"What problem?"

"Doc's in trouble."

"Doc Holliday?"

"What other Doc do you know?"

"There's a Dr. Hypodermic."

"I don't think he'd ever need your help."

Jim had obviously forgotten that Danbhala La Flambeau had taken the time to fill Semple in on everything that had gone before with Jim and the gods—or that she'd gone on to tell them that they could amuse themselves in any way they liked until Doc surfaced but, at that point, their mission would begin in earnest.

"Doc's in room 1009, in a poker game that's now well into its seventh day."

"Doc wouldn't welcome us dragging him out of a game."

"He's in there with some deeply dangerous people. They've started playing for really weird stuff, bits of each other's being, hearts, minds, and souls. He's got to get out of there. He needs some kind of intervention so he can walk away while he's still intact."

Jim sounded a great deal less vague, like he was rising to the challenge. "And the game is right here in the Mephisto?"

"Like I said, room 1009."

"So I'll throw some clothes on and get up there."

"I want to come with you."

"Is that a good idea?"

"Good idea or not, I don't want us getting separated right now."

"Suit yourself."

By now the junkie was pressing his face to the dirty glass of the phone booth and tapping on the door. "Listen, Jim, I've got to go. I'll give you ten minutes to get yourself together and then I'll meet you by the elevator."

As Semple stepped out of the booth, the junkie all but knocked her aside, barging past her, sweating and snarling. "You holding a fucking telethon in there?" The hookers also gave her dirty looks, but she ignored them. For the ten minutes she was allowing Jim to get himself dressed and in motion, she went into the coffee shop and bought a donut and a cup of greasy metallic coffee. The Mephisto was not noted for its cuisine, which Semple suspected had a lot to do with the quality of the clientele. In the steam and grease atmosphere, enclosed by sweating plastic panels and under merciless overbright, overhead neon, unshaven and conspiratorial men in long overcoats, anarchists perhaps, or Bolsheviks, huddled in groups of three or four at dirty tables, drinking soup and black tea while apparently plotting strange insurrections among the dead. Young women in shapeless clothing, pale as the corpses they had left behind on Earth, sat by themselves, shutting out the world with paperback anthologies of Emily Dickinson and the works of Virginia Woolf. Junkies and other addicts twitched furtively and tried not to contemplate the possible horrors of the immediate future. Cold-looking street women and lipstick boys sipped coffee while they rested their psyches and their feet. Semple took her coffee to a table occupied by a solitary woman in a simple cape and leotard, and the most elaborate pair of boots Semple had ever seen. Between foot and thigh, each boot must had over two dozen tiny buckles holding it fastened.

"Do you mind if I sit here?"

The woman shook her head. "Of course not."

Semple seated herself and picked up the donut. It was forty-eight hours stale. "That's really an amazing pair of boots."

The woman's expression was entirely neutral. Her skin was coffee-colored and she had a small red caste mark in the exact center of her forehead. "Many people tell me that."

At the end of the allotted ten minutes, Semple got up and, leaving a third of the aging donut and half of the cup of deadly coffee, walked out of the coffee shop and headed for the elevators. The woman in the buckle boots watched her as she made her exit and then continued to stare after her through the steamed-up glass of the window.

Semple was right, Jim noted as he closed the door behind him. It *was* room 807. In the time since Semple had phoned, a great deal had come back to him—most of the events on the Island of the Gods, up to the point where the light had come down and whisked them away. To his deep chagrin, however, the recent days of what Semple had described as "bourbon, depravity, and room service" were still a total and frustrating blank. Still worrying about his less-than-complete memory, Jim started down the corridor just in time to cross paths with a large brown rat with a pink naked tail that slipped out of a door marked STAFF ONLY. The rat looked up at Jim as though he had a full and equal right to be in the corridor. "Hey, Morrison, you know Doc's on the tenth floor and he's not doing too well." The rat had a thick Irish brogue.

Jim nodded. "I heard already. I'm going up there right now."

"If you need any help, just whistle. Doc's an old pal o' mine."

"I'll keep that in mind, but how did you know my name?"

The rat shook his head. "Jayzus, you think I'm an eejit or something? Don't I know Jim Morrison when I see him?"

After the third floor, Semple was the only passenger in the elevator, and when the doors opened on the eighth, Jim was standing waiting. Semple beckoned him in. "Come on. We might as well go straight up to ten."

As he stepped into the elevator, she noticed a strange expression on his face. When the doors closed, Jim suddenly pulled her to him. His hands traveled over her intimately. "Most of the last week just came back to me. I guess it was the elevator that triggered it."

The suddenness of it all took her breath away. Her arms went around him, and she kissed him, wide-mouthed and deep. Her legs felt weak with a sudden flow of desire. With his left hand he raised her skirt, stroking the backs of her thighs, whispering in her ear. "Now that I can remember, I want to experience you in the present. I want to live those Polaroids all over again."

"Two floors hardly gives us time."

Jim sighed ruefully. "I know that."

"You're just going to have to wait."

The elevator doors opened. Semple took Jim by the hand. "Let's go and see about Doc."

They stepped out into the tenth-floor corridor, and were immediately confronted by two men walking toward them. One was an elderly transvestite in a bottle-green, satin cocktail dress that was a harmonic disaster with his sallow, heavy-jowled complexion and pet pug face. It also didn't help that he hadn't shaved in two days and one of his false eyelashes was missing. He was walking clumsily bow-legged in high-heeled pumps, while counting a large number of plastic gold coins into a patent leather purse. The other man was tall with the tentatively obsequious look of a longtime companion and flunky. When all of the coins were safely stowed in the bag, the transvestite glanced at his companion with a grin of unpleasant self-congratulation. "I think we got out of there just in time."

"You know they were letting you win, Edgar."

The transvestite looked around testily. "Of course they were letting me win. You think I'm a fool? They always let me win. Even here, they're still afraid of me."

As Jim and Semple passed the pair, Jim quickly leaned close and whispered, "Do you know who they are?"

Semple shook her head. "No, should I?"

"It's J. Edgar Hoover and Clyde Tolson."

"Here in Hell?"

"Can you think of a better place for them?"

Jim stopped walking and half turned. His face was angry and set. "I really ought to do something about that bastard."

Semple frowned. "Like what?"

"Like punch him clear out to the pods, like payback for all the good people he fucked and fucked over."

"We ought to be focusing on getting Doc out of the poker game."

Hoover and Tolson were waiting for the elevator. Hoover glanced at Jim with an expression of routine contempt. Jim clenched his fists. "It'd give me a fuck of a lot of satisfaction to know I'd put J. Edgar Hoover's lights out."

"There's got to be worse than him running around the Afterlife."

"Not many."

"We really don't have the time. We have to concentrate on Doc. That's what Danbhala La Flambeau said."

The five-card stud was cutthroat and Doc Holliday was running on pills and fear. His lungs felt raw from too many cigars; he suspected they might be bleeding again. The various kinds of dope he'd taken were clashing with the alcohol; he was developing an epic headache from staring at the cards. His frock coat was hanging over the back of his chair, long since shucked off, sweat soaked the armpits of his evening shirt, and the lace ruffles were wilting. The game had been going on for longer than he could remember, and he knew he was in well over his head. This in itself was no big thing. He'd been in a hundred previous games—more if you counted lifeside—in which the waters had threatened to close over him. What made this one different was that Lucifer seemed to be playing for keeps. In the old days, the Prince of Darkness would have been looking for souls to come into the pot: these days, since souls no longer signified, he was into pieces of minds and memory when the chips were really down. Already one player, a bizarro in a silver suit who called himself the Saber-Toothed Kid, was lying in the back room alternately catatonic and whimpering, having anted up the connections to a selection of synapses on a marker to Lucifer when he'd been cleaned out of ready cash chasing a busted flush. No one seriously expected the Saber-Toothed Kid to recover, although the question of what to do with him when the game was over had yet to be resolved. Doc had toyed with the idea of maybe selling the Kid as a warm body to Hoover and Tolson, but had kept it to himself. It was likely others might join the bizarro before the conclusion finally came to pass.

Not that Doc was, as yet, reduced to such dire straits as parting with segments of his brain as collateral. He still had a reasonable poke of coin remaining, but he knew the vise was tightening. The amateurs and thrill-seekers had long since been whittled away; the ones who only wanted to tell the story of how they'd been there, lost their rolls, and departed. Hoover had left with Tolson, his nonplaying boyfriend, in tow—and a considerable winning poke, as was always his wont. That left just five of them at the table, and the game appeared destined to go to the death. What Doc had to do was ensure that the annihilation in question was someone's other than his own, and this was where the fear came in. For the past few hours, he had been doing little more than holding his own. Each time his turn to deal came around, Lucifer would clamp a mechanic's grip on the deck and spin out cards from the top, bottom, or middle, only able to cheat so overtly to the professional eye because he knew no one would have the stones to call him on it, in his own game, right there in Hell.

Lucifer was formidable in any form, but his current Ike Turner persona—processed Beatle wig and pencil mustache, ruffled disco shirt, diamond sleeve garters, open to the navel and revealing a weight of neck gold sufficient to carry him for at least three rounds of betting—gave him an ass-tightening edge. Anyone going up against him would be left in no doubt that they were finally down with the baddest in town. If anyone could match Lucifer, menace for menace, it was the inscrutable Kali, who sat directly to Lucifer's left. Topless, as the Hindu goddess of death always appeared in statues and religious prints, with fully exposed blue-black breasts and ruby nipples, but with her extra arms retracted at the request of the other players, Kali had so far been playing an incredibly tight, no-lose/no-win game, never going after any of the big rich pots. When Hoover had left, however, Kali had removed her crown of skulls, and Doc wondered if this was a sign that she was about to get serious.

Richard Nixon always played seriously, not to say deviously, but he only ever seemed to go in big-time when he was sure of his cards. So far, as revealed by the call, Nixon had yet to bluff in a major way, but with his shifting eyes, sweat beading his upper lip, and the five o'clock shadow moving toward eight or nine, it was almost impossible to guess what he was thinking. Like Kali, he had been tailgating the game most of the time, sweeping up the smaller pots to keep himself solvent but avoiding any protracted showdown with Doc or Lucifer. Doc had few worries about the final player. He was a stone-faced North Korean, a former secret policeman who had been reassigned from torturer to victim in Kim Il Sung's second-to-last purge. By all accounts, he had held out through over three weeks of physical and psychological horror before being slowly garroted by some of his former subordinates. Although a master of the implacable bluff, the secret policeman was essentially out of his league in present company, and Doc suspected he would be the next to go. His stack was already running grievously low, but Doc didn't expect him to depart easily. Dour communist tenacity might well force him to risk his entire nervous system before he was closed out and forced to join the Saber-Toothed Kid babbling mindlessly in the adjoining room.

With the Korean eliminated, Doc would be the next logical target. Lucifer and Kali would never go after each other while humans remained to be skinned and sliced. Both were extramortals and their kind tended to engage in their one-on-one combat away from the mere human witnesses. It was always possible that they would go after Nixon next, but Doc considered this unlikely. The disgraced ex-president was a professional survivor; Doc, on the other hand, survived despite himself. Doc's reckless potential for self-destruction was well-known. Nixon, should he lose all his money, would simply bow out, maybe even demanding the courtesy car fare traditionally due the tapped. Doc would just smile coolly and toss his entire brain into the middle with little more than a second thought. Lesser mortals might have asked him why he simply didn't rise from the table and walk away. Doc would only have shrugged. "It's no recreation if a man doesn't play for blood and sanity."

The deal passed to Lucifer once more. He tapped the deck and stood up, moving to the small wet bar to pour himself a drink. On this particular night, Lucifer was drinking turquoise science-fiction concoctions from the surface of which a heavy vapor flowed. As he moved from his chair, he glanced back at the others. "Can I get anyone else a drink while I'm up?"

Kali ignored him; she imbibed nothing except the occasional nasal pinch of a dark red powder taken from an ornate enamel and silver snuffbox with a red scorpion inlaid on the lid. Doc had a nasty feeling that the powder was dried blood of some kind, but the blood of what he neither cared to know nor speculate. In response to Lucifer's offer, the secret policeman nodded curtly. "Whiskey." Which, for some unknown reason, actually meant vodka. Nixon turned the prow of his ski-jump nose in Lucifer's direction and smiled his wan smile. "I'll have a scotch and soda, my friend, if it's not too much trouble."

Doc stood up. "It's okay, I'll pour my own."

The last thing Doc wanted was for Lucifer to pour him a drink. He wouldn't have put it past the Dark Disco Prince to slip him a Mickey Finn, mind-numbing or worse; although it would have had to have been a pretty damned powerful Mickey to numb Doc's mind, considering his mighty tolerance for most drugs known to this world and the last. As Doc moved to the bar, he took a discreet pull on his pocket flask of laudanum to calm himself. The very last thing he needed was to perform a blood-hacking coughing fit for this opposition. He figured he still had a couple of hours to go before he would face the combined wiles and chicanery of Kali and Lucifer working in tandem. He knew he would be best advised to just go on walking, out of the game, out of the room, maybe out of the Mephisto Hotel, and perhaps out of Hell itself. He knew, though, that his pride wouldn't allow it. Even if it destroyed him, no one would ever be able to say that Doc Holliday ran from a challenge, even if the challenge came from the Devil himself. He would not, however, have minded in the least if some deus ex machina had come along and interrupted the game. Where was Big-Nosed Kate to burn down the saloon?

A guard had been posted outside room 1009, a sumo wrestler in a voluminous yellow plaid suit that could only have come from the personal tailor of Nathan Detroit. As Jim and Semple approached the door, he simply shook his head. Jim and Semple halted. "No?"

The sumo wrestler again shook his head. "Not a prayer."

"No one goes in?"

"No one. Boss's orders."

Semple was wondering whether the best tactic would be to bluster, bribe, or seduce their way past the guard. "So who's the boss?"

The guard looked at her as though her naïveté quite surpassed his understanding. "This is Hell, missy. Who the fuck do you think is the boss?"

"We need to see Doc Holliday."

"If he's in there at all, he'll be coming out one of these days. You can see him then."

"We got a call."

The sumo wrestler shook his head for a third time. It seemed to be his sole mannerism. "Nobody called out from in there."

Semple, with great presence of mind, produced a bag of the Hell coinage. "Doc needs more money. We were supposed to bring it to him." Semple had decided that, of her three possible options, bribery was the only practical solution. The guard seemed unbluffable; seduction was too complicated, not to mention distasteful; it would have to come down to greasing through on a cash gratuity. She hefted the bag so the coins clinked one against the other. "I have the cash right here."

The sumo wrestler's eyes fixed on the bag, validating Semple's judgment. Who said Hell was without corruption? "Why don't you give that to me and I'll take it in to him?"

Now it was Semple's turn to shake her head. "I really don't think so."

"You don't trust me to give it to him?"

Jim decided it was his turn to play at least a supporting role in this exercise. "It's not that she doesn't trust you, it's just that she has her orders. She has to bring him the bag personally, otherwise it's her ass."

The guard's eyes moved from Jim's face to Semple's ass. Maybe seduction might have been a better shot, but it was too late now to change trains. Semple tilted the bag and let a coin drop into the palm of her hand. The guard's attention moved up again to where she was showing him the money. She let a second coin drop, them a third and a fourth. On five, the guard's expression changed. He almost looked understanding. "Listen, I don't want to see old Doc strapped for cash in a big game like this one."

Jim smiled. "I'm sure old Doc will be very grateful."

Semple quickly slipped half a dozen plastic coins to the sumo wrestler. Before opening the door to 1009 and easing them through, he treated them to a hard look and a quick instruction. "You've got five minutes and then I want you back out here. Don't be making no noise or upsetting anyone, okay? Or your ass is mine."

With that, he swung the door open.

The interior of the room was filled with an old-fashioned fug of to-bacco smoke, so thick that it glowed in the areas where the light hit it. Doc and Lucifer were smoking cigars, and a hard-faced Oriental held a Turkish cigarette in a steel holder. A good many of the face-less kibitzers lined around the dark periphery of the room also had cigarettes, cigars, and cheroots burning. All focus was on the game in progress, and what light there was came from the lamp directly over the green baize poker table with the cracked, nicotine-stained Tiffany shade. It illuminated the white cards, the hands of the play-ers, and maybe their shirt cuffs, and all the paraphernalia they had laid out on the table in front of them. As Jim and Semple entered, Lucifer was dealing a hand, and neither he nor any of the players looked up. Lucifer flipped a black ace to Doc and Jim hoped that his hole card wasn't either of the red eights. Or maybe in Hell a dead man's hand didn't matter.

As quietly as they could, Jim and Semple merged with the spec-tators. They were inside, and if the guard outside was as good as his word, they had five minutes to figure a way to get Doc out of there. Jim spotted the small bar and decided that it was as good a spot as any to set up a vantage point—and a shot of something would cer-tainly help him think on his feet. It was only as, with Semple right behind him, he eased toward the booze that he spotted Nixon as one of the players. In the same instant, Nixon saw him and frowned slightly, as though not quite recognizing him. Suddenly Jim knew he wasn't going to keep his mouth shut, despite what the guard outside might have told him. He stepped forward into the light and glared at Nixon. "You may well frown, you son of a bitch."

Semple grabbed him by the arm. "Jim!"

Jim shook his head. He wasn't going be silenced or deflected. "I may have let Hoover slide, but I'm going to have my say with this bastard."

Doc looked up and recognized Jim. "Hello there, young Morrison."

"Hi, Doc."

Lucifer looked at Doc. "You know this guy?"

Doc nodded. "Sure, I know this guy. It's Jim Morrison. A little confused and headstrong, but basically he's all right."

Two large men in back of Lucifer moved forward. They looked to be at least kissing cousins to the sumo wrestler outside, with very much the same taste in clothes. They waited on Lucifer for the word to remove Jim and Semple. Lucifer frowned at Doc and pointed to Semple. "And the broad?"

"Semple McPherson."

"As in Aimee Semple McPherson?"

Doc nodded again. "The very same—at least, half of her. She's going to be the love of young Morrison's life."

Semple started to protest. "Who says I'm going to be the love of his life?"

Everyone ignored her. Lucifer was studying Jim. "And what do you want here, Jim Morrison?"

"I came here to get Doc out of this game . . . "

Lucifer shook his head. "Doc can't leave this game. He's still ahead. It'd be more than his reputation is worth."

Jim gestured to Nixon. " . . . but now that I find *him* here, I may have to change my plans."

Lucifer raised an eyebrow. "You have a beef with Tricky Dick?"

"My whole generation has a beef with Tricky Dick."

Nixon's face twisted into a familiar sour scowl. "Are we here to play poker or listen to this hippie bum run off at the mouth?"

Lucifer smoothed his pencil mustache while he considered the situation. Kali and the Korean carefully placed their hands flat on the table. Their faces showed no easily read expression, but later Jim would swear that Kali was amused. Finally Lucifer made up his mind. "Let him say his piece. We've got free speech here in Hell."

Nixon looked outraged. "I'm sorry. I really have to protest. Since when was there free speech in Hell? I never heard that. Where is that written? Particularly for long-haired troublemakers who come barging into a private card game."

Lucifer grinned, apparently enjoying baiting the onetime president. "There's been free speech in Hell since I said there was free speech in Hell. And besides, my boys are probably going to beat the shit out of him afterward for his temerity."

Nixon quickly picked up on the nearest available red-herring detail. "Extreme. That's the word. On the lifeside, I was forced to deal with these kinds of extremists all through my career."

"You mean like your goddamned enemies list?"

"I did what was needed to protect the national security and the office of the president."

"You had Groucho fucking Marx on your list."

Doc leaned back in his chair and stared up at the ceiling. "Groucho has already moved to the higher level. One of the fastest move-ups on record. Nearly as fast as Einstein."

"He advocated my assassination."

"He said you were the only dope worth shooting."

"Is that your problem, young man? You didn't like the way I treated Groucho Marx?"

Jim leaned angrily forward. "Yeah, I didn't like the way you treated Groucho Marx, or the Black Panthers, or John Lennon, or the people of Cambodia, or the fact that you let tens of thousand of poor bastards like me go on dying and getting maimed so you could look good in the history books."

"I presume you're talking about Southeast Asia?"

"Can't you even say Vietnam, you bastard?"

"That war is history."

"I recently visited a kid called Chuck who's still living it over and over."

"You can hardly blame me if some unfortunates are unable to move on."

"I'm not talking about blame. I'd just like to see you sharing a piece of their suffering instead of sitting here playing fat-cat five-card stud with Lucifer."

The entire room was silent as Nixon looked coldly back at Jim. "And how exactly do you intend to do that? I would remind you that I more than earned my place here."

"I can believe that."

"So this is just hot air, isn't it, Morrison? There's really nothing you can do."

Jim looked around the table. Everyone seemed to be waiting to hear his response. "Maybe, maybe not." He looked at Doc "Do you still have that piece of Elvis Presley's former property?"

Doc nodded. "I certainly do."

"Could I take a look at it?"

Doc nodded again. "I don't see why not."

Nixon shook his head as though he considered Jim completely out of his mind. "Elvis Presley? My God, he was another one. A drugged-out, pill-swallowing maniac." He turned to Kali and the Korean. "I met him, you know. He was completely insane. He actually tried to hug me, just like that crazy coon Sammy Davis."

Kali spoke for the fist time. Her voice was a steely purr of death and seduction. "You had your photograph taken with him, though, didn't you?"

Nixon gestured impatiently. "It was that fool Haldeman. He thought it would raise my standing with the country's youth. But let me make it perfectly clear, I was against it. I was against the whole thing. I kid you not."

Lucifer lit a fresh cigar. "Elvis was what he was, but the blue lights were there when he was born. No blue lights in Yorba Linda, Dick. That's why you're here and he moved on a long time ago, just like Groucho and Einstein."

Nixon was about to respond to Lucifer when Doc casually pulled the Gun That Belonged to Elvis from where his coat was draped over the chair and handed it to Jim. At the sight of the pistol, the entire room froze. The Korean's hand started to edge toward a bulge under his own uniform coat, and Kali's extra arms rematerialized. Lucifer merely exhaled, a stream of blue smoke aimed directly at Jim. "And what do you intend to do with that?"

Nixon was now sweating profusely, his eyes fixed on the gun. "You're being ridiculous, Morrison. You can't kill me. I'm already dead, damn it."

"Like Doc once told me, a golden bullet from the Gun That Belonged to Elvis might not kill you, but it'll sure fuck you up."

Lucifer seemed highly amused by the situation. He gestured to Jim with his cigar. "You know what would happen if you fired that thing in here?"

Jim smiled wryly. He was starting to like Lucifer, although he knew that liking the Devil was no reason to underestimate him. "No pun intended, but I figure all hell would break loose."

"And there will also be hell to pay."

"I don't have any beef with you."

"I know that."

Jim turned to Kali and the Korean. "I also have no problem with either of you."

Lucifer took another drag on his cigar. "I still can't allow you to put a bullet in Dick here."

"You can't stop me from pulling the trigger."

"I can make you wish that you hadn't."

"Suppose I were to take his money?"

"You want to rob Lucifer's poker game? You've got a lot of gall, kid."

"I don't want to rob you, or Kali, or the Korean gentleman."

Nixon looked at Lucifer. "You're going to let this happen?"

Lucifer nodded. "You're on your own from here on out."

"I thought we had a deal."

"We had a deal when you were alive to make you president, and you've got a deal now to rebuild your place in history, but I sure as shit don't recall guaranteeing to protect you from any hothead who wants to rip off your poker stake."

Jim pointed the Gun That Belonged to Elvis at Nixon's head. "Fork over the cash, you sorry son of a bitch."

After a short reluctant pause, Nixon pushed the coins across the table. Jim gestured with the gun. "And the rest."

"What rest?"

"Are you telling me you don't have a little slush fund stashed away?"

With sullen reluctance, Nixon reached under his blue suit coat, pulled out a small leather bag, and tossed it on the table. "You'll pay for this. You know that, don't you?"

Jim's lip curled. "Sure, I don't doubt it. I'll be looking over my shoulder for the rest of my days." He gestured to Doc. "You're coming with us, right?"

Doc smiled. "I don't have much choice, do I?"

Jim shook his head and Doc looked around at the other players. "I hate to leave you all while I'm still ahead, but I've always made a point of never arguing with a man with a gun."

"That was a pretty spectacular diversion."

"Actually a lot of it was strictly personal. I didn't know Nixon

394

was going to be there. Did he really make a deal with Lucifer to be president?"

"More deals are made with Lucifer than you might ever suspect."

"Did you ever make one?"

Doc coughed. "Believe me, if I'd cut a deal with the devil, I'd be a lot better off than I am now."

Jim, Doc, and Semple rode down in the elevator. The two men seemed pumped, almost as if they were enjoying this adventure, but Semple wasn't quite able to share their excitement. "Having made your big grandstand play, have either of you considered what we're going to do next?"

Doc looked at Jim. "You don't have a plan?"

"What do you mean, a plan? This has all been played strictly by ear."

"Are you telling me you don't have a way out of here set up?"

Jim started to look angry. "Wait a damned minute—"

Semple interrupted before Jim and Doc could embark on some absurd male argument. "All Danbhala La Flambeau told us was to get you out of that suicidal poker game."

"La Flambeau? Where the fuck did she come into all this?"

As briefly as she could, Semple explained her and Jim's encounters with the Voodoo gods and what had transpired on the island. When she'd finished, Doc slowly shook his head. "I can't leave you alone for a moment, can I?"

Jim was still looking marginally belligerent. "Listen, if Hypodermic gives me the full softening-up treatment, and then La Flambeau and Marie-Louise say jump, I just ask how high."

Doc's mouth slowly opened. "*Marie-Louise* is involved in this?"

Jim nodded. Doc shook his head. "Do you know how deep you've got us in?" He sighed. "And do you know how long I've waited to get back in a poker game with Lucifer? And now I'm almost certainly persona non grata in all the casinos of Hell."

Semple never could figure men's lack of logic, and she certainly couldn't believe that Doc was complaining about being rescued. "You would have come out of the game a brainless cabbage and you know it."

"That's hardly the point."

Before Doc could explain what the point actually was, the elevator doors opened and the three of them stepped out.

Aimee could hear the breakaway nuns chanting somewhere behind the large cloister. Bernadette's voice rose above the general chorus in a strange wailing counterpoint. The language was one that Aimee didn't recognize. A weird glossalia, a unison speaking-in-tongues, as though some dangerous spirit were upon them. Aimee knew that they had to be psyching themselves up, building up a head of righteous rage before they finally came to finish her. The handful of sisters and angels who had remained loyal looked on as she knelt in the Sacristy. She pretended to be praying, but all she was really doing was sobbing to herself.

"Oh my God, Semple, what have I done? If you were here, you'd know what to do. Except you're not here. You're fragmented in Limbo and very soon they're going to come for me. They're going to come for me and take me to Golgotha. I didn't mean to do what I did. I was just angry. You can't blame me for being angry, after all the terrible things that happened. I'd make it just like it was before if I knew how, but I don't. Since I destroyed you, I haven't been able to make anything."

Aimee would have prayed, had there been any point, and had there been anyone to listen to her prayers, but she knew there was no one. God had deserted her—or had never existed in the first place—and Jesus, after the briefest of honeymoons, had turned out to be a homicidal pervert. Never, either in life or Afterlife, had she felt so powerless and alone. As she knelt and sobbed, one of the loyal nuns tentatively approached her. "Sister Aimee?"

Aimee took a deep breath and got exhaustedly to her feet. "What is it, my dear?"

"Do Bernadette and her women intend to hurt us?"

Aimee didn't answer right away. She knew that if Bernadette and her mutineers could break into the area of Heaven where she and the loyalists were holed up, they would almost certainly drag all of them out and crucify them. Bernadette had started calling herself the Hammer of God, and anyone who adopted such a title was unlikely to be interested in any kind of truce or accommodation. Whether the few nuns that had remained loyal needed to know the worst was a moot point. Aimee didn't want to deceive them, but at the same time, if they knew how hopeless their situation was, they, too, would probably desert her. Aimee closed her eyes and took a deep breath. "I really don't think they mean us any good. They are very angry women."

"It wasn't your fault that Jesus did what he did."

"They don't seem to see it that way."

Another nun joined the first one. "If there was a way for us to get some weapons, perhaps we could drive them off. Show them we mean business."

Nuns talking about weapons came as something of a surprise to Aimee. "But this is Heaven. We never had a need for weapons."

Now a third nun came into the discussion. "We heard that Bernadette and her people have a lot of weapons. We heard that she managed to conjure them."

Perhaps the idea of these nuns wanting weapons wasn't so far-fetched as it seemed. They might have taken holy orders, but, prior to that at least three of them had flat-backed it in Doc Holliday's disgusting brothel. Perhaps they still had a fighting core at the center of their being. The trouble was Aimee had no experience in conjuring things like weapons. In fact, since she'd destroyed Semple, she was finding it nearly impossible to hold Heaven itself together. Large circular Swiss-cheese holes had appeared in some of the buildings, giving the landscape the air of a surrealist painting.

"Couldn't you conjure us some weapons? Maybe some light machine guns? We wouldn't want to hurt anyone, just scare them off."

Aimee looked at the nuns with an expression of terminal sadness. "I don't know if I'm able to do anything like that. I have no experience. I've always been a pacifist."

"What about Semple? Maybe she could help us."

Aimee hadn't exactly explained to the nuns and angels what had become of Semple. All they knew was that she'd left after Jesus was crucified. They certainly didn't know that Aimee had blasted her into Limbo, and she wasn't about to reveal that now. Aside from the fact that it would blow her image as the Princess of Peace and the helpless victim of Bernadette and her renegades, some of the loyalists might start asking why she couldn't set up a similar vibration and blow Bernadette and her cohorts way into the back of beyond. "I don't think Semple's going to be coming back here for a very long time. She feels very guilty about bringing the false Jesus here."

One of the angels rustled his wings. "Maybe if we went to Semple's domain? She could have weapons there. And there are those strange guards that she invented. Perhaps they might protect us."

Aimee was about to explain why retreating to Semple's horrible environment was out of the question, but then it occurred to her that the angel might actually have had an inspired idea.

As Jim, Doc, and Semple emerged from the elevator, the woman in the elaborate buckled boots was coming out of the coffee shop. Semple nodded to her but received only a blank stare in response. The two men were still debating the best way to get out of Hell, and neither of them noticed the woman at all as they headed for the revolving doors of the Mephisto Hotel's main entrance. The entrance led out into a broad tunnel that in turn would take them to the concourse at the foot of the elevators. Directly outside the doors, a small knot of Virgils were plying for hire. Jim glanced at Doc. "Do you think we should get one?"

Doc thought about this. "I don't know Hell well enough to get around without some sort of guide, but it's taking a chance. Word could go straight back to Lucifer."

Semple looked around cautiously. "You think Lucifer will be coming after us?"

"Indeed I do. Kali, too, for that matter. Young Morrison here may not have actually taken their money, but he did rob the game, and that's something neither of them can allow to be seen to happen."

"So it's really just my ass that's on the line?"

Doc shook his head. "I fear Lucifer and Kali don't go in for such precise apportionment of blame. We were all there, we all left together—we're all tarred with the same brush."

"So it wouldn't help if we separated?"

Doc half-smiled. "A noble thought, my boy, but it wouldn't do any good." He glanced slyly at Semple. "Besides, I thought you two were in the throes of lewd acquaintance."

Jim glanced at Semple and then turned back to Doc. "What's the point in getting acquainted if I'll only end up dragging her down with me?"

Semple stiffened. "Listen, darling, before you start trying to do any far, far better thing, let me decide when and where I want to be dragged down."

Before the subject of Jim taking the rap could continue, a Virgil came up to them and bowed with studied if importunate courtesy. "Lady and gentlemen, you seem a little lost. Can I be of any service?"

Before either Jim or Doc could respond, Semple took the bull by the horns. "We have to find the fastest way out of here without anyone knowing about it."

"We Virgils act only in the strictest confidence."

"Yeah, right. Of course." Jim didn't exactly seem convinced.

The Virgil looked almost offended. "No, no, young sir. I assure you. We could hardly function if our discretion was held in any doubt. This is Hell, after all. Many who need a guide do not want their purpose or destination made public."

Jim looked inquiringly at Doc. "Do we trust him?"

"I think we have to. I don't have a clue where we should go."

He faced the Virgil. "So, *altissimo poeta*, do you think you can get us out of the city without being seen or intercepted?"

"That may well be up to you, young sir."

Jim stared at the Virgil with deep suspicion. "And what is that supposed to mean, *altissimo poeta*?"

The Virgil's face was a mask of formality, impossible to read. "The ancient ways, the ones that are seldom used any longer, these are the paths to take if you need to leave here undetected."

Doc's eyes narrowed. "Are you suggesting we ride the Dragon, *altissimo poeta*?"

Bernadette and her renegades had stopped chanting, and Aimee knew she had to assume they were on their way to the Sacristy. She looked around at the assembled nuns and angels. "I think it's time we joined hands. I hate to abandon the Heaven we've all worked so hard to create, but the angel here does have the only practical suggestion. We must seek refuge in Semple's domain."

What Aimee wasn't admitting to her small band of followers was that she wasn't at all sure Semple's domain was still actually there. It might have imploded when she'd blown Semple into Limbo. If the little group wind-walked to a place that wasn't there, they would find themselves randomly consigned to absolutely anywhere. They could easily end up, either individually or as a group, in a place that was completely uninhabitable, airless, burning hot or freezing cold, or filled with ravening predators. Despite this, Aimee had already conceded that it would probably be better than crucifixion and whatever Bernadette, in her new role as the Hammer of God, might decide to inflict on them before they were actually nailed to their respective crosses. Aimee suspected that Bernadette was entertaining dreams of inquisition and auto-da-fé. To return to the pods was one thing; prolonged torture was entirely another.

The group linked hands and the energy began to flow. Although they were only eight in number and were badly depleted by recent events, Aimee knew they should be able to raise the power to lift out of there. She focused all her concentration on what she remembered from her single visit to Semple's territory, and hoped against hope that a destination would still exist when they arrived. As they waited to dematerialize, any question of turning back or revising the plan was eliminated. Bernadette's rebels began battering on the Sacristy's carved oak door. The door was formidable, but it would only be a matter of time before they broke it down.

The attack came out of nowhere. One moment Semple, Doc, Jim, and the Virgil had been walking quietly through one of the larger passages in the maze of dank subterranean avenues that made up the greater part of Hell's Third Circle. This fairly deserted thoroughfare of cobbles, paths, and dripping stones—a habitat for grotesque creeping things and misshapen growths of fungi—was an ideal place for an ambush, but they were being reasonably vigilant, and certainly not loitering. The next moment Semple let out a low gurgle and was suddenly dragged backward. The section of passage through which they were traveling wasn't particularly well lighted, with only ancient, hissing Jack-the-Ripper gaslights every thirty feet, and it took Jim and Doc a couple of seconds to grasp exactly what had happened. A dark figure had slipped out of a doorway, tossed a knotted white scarf around Semple's neck, and dragged her backward, strangling her. Jim, who was nearest to Semple, had already returned the Gun That Belonged to Elvis to Doc, but even if he'd still had the piece, it wouldn't have done him very much good. The black-clad attacker was not only throttling Semple, but using her as a shield while he did so. Doc pulled the gun, but from where he was standing, Jim and the Virgil stood in the way of a clear shot.

Jim saw that he was Semple's only chance. Without thinking, he lunged forward, fists swinging. More by luck than judgment, he connected with the dark shape and heard a muttered curse. He punched twice more and connected again. The attacker let go of one end of the scarf and pushed Semple hard into Jim. As Semple dropped to her knees, coughing and choking, Jim stepped around her and lashed out with his foot, attempting to trip the assassin as he turned to flee. Jim had never exactly been a brawler, but some kind of street-fighting good fortune seemed to be with him there in the Third Circle. His kick swept the attacker's feet out from under him and he fell heavily on the cobblestones. Jim dropped on top of him, pinning his arms. The attacker still had his legs free, however, and attempted to break loose from Jim by bucking and kicking. In two paces, though, Doc was by Jim's side, pistol in hand, pointing it at the attacker's head.

"Keep still, you son of a bitch, or I'll put a gold .45 slug clear through your damned brain."

At least the assassin had enough common sense to know a fait accompli when he saw one and he stopped struggling. As Jim pushed himself off, he was surprised to find his hands making contact with a full breast and a narrow waist. "Holy shit, it's a woman!"

Doc pushed him out of the way. Now that they were able to see a little better, Jim's tactile discovery was a little more obvious. It was indeed a woman—a very good-looking young woman—dressed in a black cape and a kind of one-piece ninja leotard. Her face was hidden behind a black bandanna, and she was wearing an extremely elaborate pair of boots with dozens of tiny buckles. As Jim straightened up, Doc leaned down and pulled away the bandanna. The face that was revealed had dark coffee-colored skin, large angry eyes and a red caste mark exactly in the middle of the forehead. Doc whistled under his breath. "A thugette."

"A what?"

"A thugette, one of Kali's killer virgins. The distaff version of the thugee."

"You mean like in *Stranglers of Bombay?*"

Doc nodded. "Right, if you must equate everything with some low-budget movie to get a handle on it. They kill for the goddess with the knotted scarf."

The Virgil was helping a coughing Semple, who, despite the obvious discomfort of a nearly crushed windpipe, moved quickly to where Doc and Jim were standing over the prone assassin. Picking up the knotted scarf on the way, she took one look at the buckled boots and went whiter than she already was. "Goddamn it. I saw that homicidal bitch in the coffee shop at the Mephisto. We sat at the same table. I even spoke to her."

Doc glanced up and down the street. "She must have been one of Kali's minders, waiting for her mistress to get out of Lucifer's poker game. I guess she's been following us ever since we left the hotel."

Semple frowned. "The question is, what do we do with her now? We can't let her go and report back."

She glanced significantly at the gun in Doc's hand, but Doc shook his head. "I can't shoot a woman in cold blood."

Semple glared at him. "Why the fuck not? She tried to waste me, didn't she?"

Suddenly the women spasmed briefly, gasped out a choking gurgle, stiffened, and then went limp. Doc quickly knelt down beside her and felt the side of her neck for a pulse. "She's solved the problem for us."

"She's left for the pods?"

"Or wherever her kind go. She must have had a cyanide tooth."

By this point, the Virgil had also joined them and he looked very unhappy. "Good sirs and lady, did I overhear you correctly? Is it Lucifer and Kali from whom you flee?"

Doc nodded grimly. "I fear it is, *altissimo poeta*."

"Then I must respectfully terminate our agreement. I am a Virgil and it is implicitly understood that I leave at the first sign of danger." He gestured to the thugette's inert body. "And that is a more than contractually adequate first sign."

Doc gestured with the Gun That Belonged to Elvis. "I'm sorry, *altissimo poeta*, but we are going to have to impose on you over and above the terms of any implied agreement. You will lead us to the start of the Dragon Ride, or I will, with the greatest regret, send you after this young woman here."

The Virgil looked at Jim and Semple, but they gave him no sign that they were in anything but total agreement with Doc. "I must protest this, good sir. I will lead you, but this is no way to treat a Virgil."

Doc lowered the pistol to his side, but didn't return it to its holster. "Your protest is noted, *altissimo poeta*."

※

"What are you doing here?"

"I'm the only one left, aren't I?"

The very last thing Mr. Thomas needed was the sudden appearance of Aimee McPherson, five nuns, and two angels right in the Louis XVI Suite of Semple's domain. Since Aimee had totaled her sister, the environment had been shaken by what he could only think of as a series of violent earth tremors, bringing down plaster and mosaic tiles from the ceilings, shaking objects from shelves, causing paintings and artworks to come crashing down, and creating jagged structural cracks in the floors and walls. He knew the earth tremors weren't truly seismic disturbances. They were a symptom that Semple, as the Afterlife knew her, was history, and her environment would progressively collapse as her residual energy dissipated and ebbed away to chaos and entropy. What would become of him when that happened was highly debatable. In the aftermath of Aimee's trashing of Semple, he had managed to slip away and windwalk back to the domain under his own power. That, unfortunately, was about as far as he was able to make it unaided, and without help he wasn't going any farther.

Right then, though, Mr. Thomas hadn't been thinking too much about the future. While Semple's real estate remained more or less real, he had resolved to get drunk and stay drunk. To this end he had formed an alliance with Igor, who had discovered that the wine cellar and liquor cache had remained pretty much intact through the upheavals. The only unfortunate part was that Igor showed absolutely no inclination to leave. His fealty to Semple was such that he wanted nothing more than to go down with the sinking illusion. Mr. Thomas hoped that, as the place started to come more unglued, the Peter Lorre–looking butler might reexamine his devotion to a woman who was long gone; perhaps the two of them would join forces and attempt to get away. In the meantime, the goat had resolved to let the martinis flow and face the hangover when it came.

In Mr. Thomas's opinion, Aimee McPherson, with her crew of nuns and angels, pretty much qualified as an early and unwanted hangover. He couldn't imagine why they should come bursting in, but he knew he was going have to deal with it, and since Igor seemed to have pulled a vanishing act, he was going to have to deal with it on his own. His first tactic was to go for open hostility. He might be a little unsteady on his four legs, on account of how recently he'd forsworn glasses and taken to drinking his martinis from a galvanized bucket, but he had a full head of resentment to use as fuel. He planted himself squarely in front of the blond McPherson sister and looked her up and down with as much Welsh contempt as he could muster. "So what's the big idea, toots? You come here with a team to loot out your sister's domain before it falls apart?"

One of the nuns advanced angrily on him. "How dare you talk to our Holy Shepherdess like that? You can't address the Lady Aimee as 'toots.' "

Aimee motioned the nuns back. "Leave him be. He's probably upset."

Mr. Thomas nodded. "Damn right I'm upset. And I'm also shit-faced drunk. Ever since I fell in with you McPherson sisters, it's been nothing but trouble, but right now we're not talking about me. You still haven't explained why you're here."

"We came here looking for a sanctuary."

"A sanctuary? Don't make me laugh. There's no sanctuary here. The place is on the verge of coming apart. You might as well look for refuge in the House of Usher."

"The other nuns—"

"Turned on you, did they, now?"

Aimee was still spent from the wind-walk out of Heaven, coming as it did on top of the huge amount of energy she had expended on Semple. Explaining herself to a goat was more unnecessary effort than she really cared to squander. "The militant one, Bernadette, she's started calling herself the Hammer of God."

"So you thought you'd hide here from her and her gang?"

"We didn't know what else to do."

"Didn't occur to you that this might be the first place she'd come looking?"

"It was the only thing we could do."

"So now I'm going to wind up sharing whatever nails this Hammer of God wants to drive into you and yours?"

Aimee started to get angry. "Don't you think of anything but your own miserable self?"

Mr. Thomas drew back his goat lips in a mirthless sneer. "Lately, I seem to be all I've got."

A sudden wheezing sound behind him told Mr. Thomas he was no longer facing Aimee and her nuns and angels alone. Three of Semple's rubber guards tottered slowly into the reproduction of Versailles, moving like a trio of Frankenstein monsters in a cheap Universal horror movie, and breathing like Darth Vader. Since Semple's departure the rubber guards had become increasing slow and cumbersome, but it seemed that they could still make an entrance. Ignoring Mr. Thomas, they lumbered toward Aimee and her people, with the leader issuing his formal challenge in a voice like a slowed-down phonograph record. "You-are-unauthorized-intruders. You-will-remain-exactly-where-you-are-or-we-will-open-fire."

The rubber guards may have been slow, but they still had their weapons, and these were pointed directly at Aimee, the nuns, and the angels. Aimee looked quickly at Mr. Thomas. "Can't you call them off or something?"

Mr. Thomas shook his head. "Even if I wanted to, I couldn't do that."

"What do you mean?"

"Now that Semple's no longer with us, the only person they respond to is Igor and he's hiding somewhere."

Aimee's nuns were looking increasingly confused. "What does he mean, now that Semple's gone?"

Aimee rounded on her angrily. "Shut up, you stupid bitch. This isn't the time."

Mr. Thomas laughed drunkenly. "You mean you haven't told them what you did to your poor little sister?"

Aimee turned and snarled at the goat, "If I had a weapon . . . "

"But you don't, do you, Aimee?"

Before Aimee could formulate a comeback, the rubber guard leader started with the second phase of his warning. "You-are-unauthorized-intruders. You-have-twenty-relative-seconds-to-remove-yourselves-from-this-environment-or-suffer-the-consequences."

Aimee looked distraughtly from the rubber guard to Mr. Thomas and back again. "Can't you get Igor and make him call them off?"

The goat shook his head. "Not unless Igor wants to be got. I fear it may be the pods for you, Holy Shepherdess."

"Is the Dragon Ride what I think it is?"

The Virgil avoided Jim's eyes. He, Jim, Semple, and Doc were hurrying along a dim, narrow, rarely used passageway, another thoroughfare in Hell where the stalactites had completely taken over the ceiling and moss and algae grew on the damp walls. The Virgil was clearly more concerned about Doc Holliday, who still had the Gun That Belonged to Elvis hidden at his side, than he was with Jim's questions. "It is one of the oldest and least used ways out of here."

"And it'll supply the energy to move us?"

The Virgil nodded. "It will do that."

"But there are problems?"

"There are certain . . . " The Virgil glanced uneasily at Doc, as though worried he might shoot him should he deliver any bad news.

Doc attempted to allay the Virgil's fear. "Certain what, *altissimo poeta?*"

"What you might call . . . side effects, good sir. I have never personally ridden the Dragon, so I cannot speak from experience, but I have it on good authority that one needs to concentrate very hard on one's destination, and, even then, certain distracting illusions may present themselves."

Jim didn't like the sound of this. "Distracting illusions?"

"As I said, I have never taken the Dragon Ride, young sir. Indeed, it is only the Virgils and a few others who even know of its existence."

Semple cut straight to the heart of the matter. "But it will get us out of Hell?"

"It will do that, madame."

"Then that's all we need to know for the moment."

It wasn't quite enough for Jim. "If we have to focus on a destination, it might be an idea to have some destination in mind. Simply wanting to get out of Hell covers a whole mess of territory, and I, for one, have been shuttling between fires and frying pans a bit too much recently."

Semple wasn't in the least fazed by the question. "The obvious answer would be for us to all go to my domain."

Doc sniffed. "All back to your place?"

"You have a problem with that?"

Doc shook his head. "No problem. I was just wondering if you still had a place to go back to. How do you know it's still intact, after your sister blew you off into Limbo?"

"It's there. I built it and I can still sense it. It's a bit battered around the edges, but it's still there. You can trust me on that."

Doc looked a trifle squint-eyed, as though trusting Semple's feeling was hardly the guarantee he wanted. "I'm supposed to kick off on the Dragon Ride on the say-so of a woman I've only just met?"

Jim quickly intervened. "Give her a break, Doc. I'll take her word for it. I think maybe I love this woman."

Now Semple was looking squint-eyed. "You think *maybe* you love me? After spending days and days having every kind of sex known to man, woman, god, or beast, you think *maybe* you love me?"

Before Jim could come up with an answer, Virgil interrupted. "Sirs, madame, could we please move along? I know I have to accomplish this task, but I'd prefer to discharge it as quickly as possible."

With the precision timing of extremely bad luck, Jim could hear running footsteps way down the tunnel, just as the Virgil finished speaking.

Three factors that Mr. Thomas would later consider dubiously serendipitous were all that saved Aimee and her angels from a summary dispatch to the Great Double Helix. The first was the slow-down in the rubber guards' responses since Semple had departed. The guards' twenty-second deadline extended itself to well over two minutes; then, just before even that ran out, the second factor staggered into the room in the form of Igor. Igor hadn't been drinking his martinis from a bucket, but he was nonetheless just as far in the bag as Mr. Thomas, so drunk that he found it difficult to grasp what was happening.

"What the hell is going on here?"

"I think you turned up just in time to see the firing squad in action."

Just then, Mr. Thomas didn't particularly care what happened. He still had a major grudge against Aimee for what she had done to Semple, whom he considered not only a friend but also a drinking companion. If the rubber guards wanted to execute her and her ridiculous cohorts, so be it. At least he'd be left in peace. It was only as the rubber guards raised their guns and trained them on Aimee and her cowering followers that Igor blinked twice and finally made sense of the situation. "Wait a minute."

The rubber guards ground to a stop without firing their weapons. Mr. Thomas looked blearily at Igor. "Why did you stop them?"

"I can't have the guards shooting the mistress's sister. That would never do."

"But she's the reason your precious mistress isn't here anymore."

Igor swayed. "Blood is thicker than water."

"What's that supposed to mean?"

Igor shook his head as though trying to clear it. "I'm not quite sure."

Mr. Thomas turned and faced Igor. "Listen to me, okay?"

Igor nodded, but looked exceedingly vacant. "Okay."

"These people are only here because a bunch of armed rebel nuns is after them."

Now that Igor was very drunk, his resemblance to Peter Lorre, in both appearance and voice, was quite uncanny. "Armed rebel nuns?"

"That's right."

The rubber guards stood poised, as though waiting for a fresh set of instructions. Mr. Thomas moved confidingly toward Igor. "I have much more experience in this sort of thing."

Igor frowned. "What sort of thing?"

"Acting decisively when very drunk."

"When I'm drunk, I can't feel the noise inside other people's minds. That's why a lot of telepaths are alcoholics. They can't take the constant noise."

Mr. Thomas was being very patient with Igor. He could see that Aimee, the nuns, and the angels were rapidly getting over their fear of the rubber guards. Aimee even took a tentative step forward, but this was enough to set the guards in motion again. "Do-not-move. Remain-where-you-are-while-we-await-our-orders."

Aimee couldn't believe that the very continuance of her existence was in the hands of a goat and a semi-dwarf, both mindlessly gin-drunk. She tried a direct appeal. "Igor—"

Mr. Thomas shook his head warningly. "Don't listen to her, Igor."

Igor was now totally confused. "What should I do, Mr. Thomas?"

"I think you should order the guards to shoot them, Igor. Then, when the really mean and nasty nuns break in, we can claim that we're on their side. Otherwise we'll end up crucified right along with this lot."

"I don't want to be crucified, Mr. Thomas."

"Of course you don't, bach, so give the order to fire."

But before Igor could give the order to fire, the third factor that saved Aimee came into play. A loud crash in another section of the environment was followed by a shock and a bang as though a grenade or a charge of explosive had gone off. The rubber guards were galvanized into slow-motion action by this new intrusion, which they saw as more pressingly dangerous than the intrusion of Aimee and her group.

"Emergency-emergency! Armed intruders in the Moorish colonnade! All-guards-respond! Armed intruders in the Moorish colonnade! All-guards-respond! All-guards-respond!"

This call to the guards appeared to countermand all previous programmed imperatives. Aimee and her people were forgotten as more formidable interlopers threatened. As the three rubber guards trundled from the Louis XVI Suite, Aimee smiled nastily. "So, goat, Igor left it too late, didn't he? Now we sink or swim together."

The pursuers emerged from the tunnel that Jim, Semple, and the Virgil had just left and immediately opened fire. As the first bullets ricocheted from the stone of the carved Dragon, all ducked for cover. The Virgil looked anxiously at Jim. "I can't be expected to involve myself in this."

Jim was busy ducking bullets; he was hardly able to pay attention to their guide and his troubles. "I don't much want to be involved in it myself."

"But this is your problem, not mine."

A fragment of lead or stone all but parted Jim's hair. "Can you get yourself out of here?"

"I'd be more than happy to."

Jim quickly reached inside his coat and pulled out the bag of coins he had taken from Richard Nixon. He tossed it in the Virgil's direction. The Virgil deftly caught the bag, hefted it to feel the weight, and treated Jim to a brief formal smile. "I thank you for your generosity, young sir. And now I must bid you farewell. I'm sorry I can't stay to observe the outcome of this."

The Virgil made a complex pass with his right hand and instantly vanished. Jim blinked and glanced at Doc. "How the fuck did he manage that?"

Doc was crouched behind the Dragon's other extended foreleg. He shook his head. "Don't ask me, boy. I guess the Virgils have their secrets."

With the Gun That Belonged to Elvis in his hand, Doc was taking aim at the shadowy figures and muzzle flashes on the other side of the cavern. He fired three fast shots that exploded where they hit in highly destructive puffs of ghost plasma. A scream indicated that at least one of his projectiles had hit its mark, but Doc's return fire also triggered another intense volley from the hidden pursuers. Jim ducked lower, seeking every inch of cover. "I wish we had that trick."

Doc fired again. "Unfortunately, we don't. Our only hope is to get ourselves into the Dragon's mouth and away. Can you and Miss McPherson make it in there if I give you covering fire?"

"We don't have any other choice, do we?"

"Not that I can see."

"What about you? We only have the one weapon."

Doc allowed himself a deadly grin. "Don't worry about me, boy. If I can't hold these clowns at bay, I don't deserve to make it at all."

"Surely they'll just follow us inside."

"I'm hoping, once we're inside, we'll be able to wind our way out almost immediately."

"I sure as shit hope so, too."

"Are you ready?"

Jim glanced at Semple to confirm she knew what the plan was. She nodded tensely and Jim looked back at Doc. "We're ready."

"Then go for it!"

As Doc laid down a positive fusillade of fire and the dim cavern was lit up by more flashes of plasma, Jim and Semple scrambled for the open archway formed by the mouth of the huge Dragon statue, bullets kicking up fragments of stone around their feet. The moment they were inside the dark sculpted maw, they turned to see if Doc was going to make it. With the same nonchalant lack of concern for his own safety that had made him a legend in the Old West, Doc rose to his feet. Two of the pursuers broke cover, a zoot-suited vato armed with a sacred Thompson gun and a thugee in dirty robes with a nineteenth century Martini carbine. Both ran toward Doc. Apparently they assumed that Doc was surrendering. They learned their mistake as Doc, still without hurrying himself, took aim and reduced them to dissipating plasma with just two shots. The disappearance of their two companions gave sufficient pause to the other pursuers that he was able to stroll calmly after Jim and Semple and into the mouth of the Dragon. As he approached them, he looked extremely pleased with himself. "Shall we get on with getting out of here?"

When the vato and the thugee came out into the open, it was the first time that Semple, Doc, or Jim had seen the people who had been following them. Until that moment Jim had been entertaining a paranoid flight of fantasy that the footsteps were nothing more than an audio illusion sent to drive the three of them crazy, and that maybe the Virgil was also in on the deal, leading them around and around in circles until they finally cracked. Real or not, the audible footfalls of the pursuers had dogged them, through tunnels and passageways, all the way into what had to be one of the most ancient sectors of Hell, an area that was dark, derelict, all but deserted, and largely forgotten by a population now occupied with well-lit tourist attractions. Unfortunately, the sector hadn't been forgotten by the relentlessly following footsteps.

The Virgil had done his best to shake the unseen posse by making use of every twist, turn, and doubling-back corkscrew he could dredge up from his encyclopedic memory of Hell's geographic backwaters. They had used tunnels so small that even Semple had to duck her head to pass through them. They had rounded hairpins, climbed and descended narrow spiral staircases, and crossed fragile bridges over abyssal chasms with red molten lava flowing in their depths. On several occasions the sound of the pursuit had faded to nothing, but no sooner had Doc, Jim, and Semple breathed a collective sigh of relief than the advancing echoes had started up again and they were forced to hurry on.

The long trek through Hell's labyrinth ended in a high, rough-hewn cavern where, in its ancient but unweathered glory, stood a massively heraldic, couchant Dragon, carved from living rock aeons earlier by some unknown demon sculptor. Beyond its gasping, stone-fanged mouth lay the mysterious power source that would, according to fable, transport them out of Hell and, within reason, take them anywhere they wanted to go. Unfortunately, when they had reached the cavern, their pursers had finally caught up with them and the firefight had ensued.

Even once they were inside the mouth of the dragon, the mystery of the Dragon Ride itself was far from revealed. They found themselves in the darkness of yet another tunnel. The only light came from a dull red glow deep in the interior. Nothing about this place encouraged either Jim or Semple to press on into the gloomy unknown, but they knew they had to. The crew sent after them by Lucifer and Kali was not going to call off the chase just because Doc had gunned down two of their number. If anything, it would probably make them even more vengeful. While Jim and Semple initially stood and stared, attempting to make sense of their new surroundings, Doc moved purposefully forward. "Come on, young lovers, we're not out of the woods yet."

"It's seems like we're going in deeper and deeper." Semple fell into step beside him while Jim hurriedly brought up the rear. Doc glanced back, but there was no sign of the pursuers—not yet.

"I think we have to operate on the principle that it's going to get pretty damned dark before the dawn comes."

"Or maybe we're just whistling past the graveyard?"

Doc treated Jim to a bleak look. "Just don't whistle, okay? I wouldn't want to listen to it."

As they moved quickly down the tunnel, the red light grew brighter; along with it came an intense sense of foreboding. The end of the tunnel brought no end to the apprehension. When it opened out onto a high ledge above a vast lake of liquid fire, Jim and Semple both stopped in their tracks, though they knew their pursuers had to be only minutes behind them.

"How the fuck is any of this going to help us get out of here?"

Doc pointed to something far along the ledge. "I think that may be the answer."

"What?"

"That."

Semple peered into the distance, shading her eyes against the glare from the burning lake. "Are you talking about that bridge?"

"You see anything else that could work?"

"But that bridge isn't complete; it looks like they never finished it. It only goes halfway across the lake."

"And we have to cross it."

Semple halted and planted her hands on her hips. "Are you out of your mind, Doc Holliday? What happens when the bridge stops?"

"We keep on going."

"And fall into the lake of fire?"

"Hopefully we go on and up and out. The end of the tangible bridge being the jumping point for the wind-walk."

"*Hopefully?*"

Jim pushed his hair out of his eyes. The heat from the burning lake was causing him to break out in a sweat. "We just have to take it on trust. Doc's right, there's no other way."

But Semple was digging in. Jim hadn't known her that long, and most of that knowledge was carnal, but he was already starting to recognize her capacity for resolute stubbornness. She was quite prepared to face down Doc Holliday if need be. "I bow to the fact that you've been around the Afterlife far longer than either me or Jim, but I've crossed a few bridges in my time and I'm pretty well versed in their symbolic content. I have to assume that a bridge that only goes halfway is exactly what it claims to be, a dead end. With the accent on *dead*."

Doc gave her a hard look. "I wouldn't spend too long bowing to my experience. I can hear the bad guys coming down the tunnel."

With no other alternative, they scrambled along the ledge toward the elegant stone arch of the ambiguous half bridge. Semple shook her head even as she ran. "I still think we're doing the wrong thing."

They were almost to the bridge when the pursuers came out of the tunnel. Bullets peppered the rock walls above the ledge, but none came close enough to be a threat. The posse was shooting on the run, more as matter of brute psychology than out of any serious intent to do harm. In no time they would catch up with Jim, Semple, and Doc, and the fugitives would be in the bag. Doc didn't even bother to fire back. In four more paces, he was on the bridge. Jim was immediately behind him. For a moment Semple balked, then two more shots hit the rock wall and she started forward again. "Damn you both. This is insane."

"You want to fall into the clutches of Kali?"

"I don't want to fall into the burning lake."

"Trust that you won't fall."

"I can't just walk off into empty air like Daffy Duck."

Jim and Doc held out their hands. "We'll do it together."

Semple grasped their hands. With Jim and Doc on the outside, and her in the middle, the three of them stepped into nothingness, with only the lake of fire beneath them. In the last second, Doc laughed out loud. "Entering the Dragon Ride—if the damn thing exists!"

10

Ḧow easy to survive?

What has happened to my creation?"

Anger and alarm were Semple's first response as she grew to human form out of the rolling swirls of orange Day-Glo mist in which she, Doc Holliday, and Jim Morrison had made their vaporous, billowing reentry from the Dragon Ride. She sprang to her feet before Jim and Doc were even fully formed and looked around furiously at the ruins of her onetime kingdom, as yet unaware that she was jaybird-naked. "I thought there'd be damage, but never anything like this."

Jim was now also fully formed and he, too, had come through without a stitch of clothing. Doc, on the other hand, was clothed and correct—except, mysteriously, for his boots, each now on the wrong foot. As he irritatably tugged his left boot from his right foot, he glanced at the nude and bemused Jim. "Were you two having sex in the middle of all that?"

Jim looked at Doc and blinked sheepishly. "What makes you say that?"

"I heard some sounds just as we were being transformed into fog."

Semple turned and glared at Doc. "Then you should have been minding your own business, shouldn't you?" Her clothes were now assembling around her out of thin air. Not the red dress she had worn in Hell, but a midnight-blue, semi-military ensemble with a pencil skirt, padded shoulders, and epaulets that matched her current belligerent mood. Now that she was back home, Semple seemed to be building up a head of rage at everything around her. Jim's time-honored leather jeans and loose shirt also appeared; only the white tuxedo jacket he'd been given at the casino had vanished along the way. The three of them had arrived in the same mosque-like chamber with the high-domed ceiling, black marble floor, and ruby glass where Semple had once amused herself by torturing her prisoners and slaves.

In some ways, it was an apt reentry point, although right at that moment Semple was too angry to see it as such. Her blood was boiling at the ravages to which her glorious construct had been subjected. The marble was cracked and shattered, and part of the dome had fallen in, littering the already-damaged floor with rubble, smashed mosaics, and broken beams. The air was filled with dust, smoke, and the stench of cordite, indicating that some of the damage had been caused by indoor explosions since Semple's departure. The gaping hole in the dome now let in an eerie, green-death light that had never been any part of her original design. Breathing hard, she repeated her question as though expecting someone or something to provide her with an answer. "What have they done to my beautiful home?"

The sounds of automatic weapons fire and a muffled explosion from another part of the environment supplied an answer of a sort. Doc finished switching his boots and warily eased to his feet, at the same time drawing the Gun That Belonged to Elvis from its shoulder holster. "They still seem to be going at it."

Semple kicked angrily at the rubble and turned to face the two men. "It's fucking Aimee."

Doc frowned. "Your sister did all this?"

"She did some of it when she blew me into Limbo, but I think the rest of it's the work of Bernadette and her rebel nuns. I'll lay Vegas odds that the inevitable uprising has risen, and this is collateral damage."

Jim and Doc looked at her with unhappy frowns. "Rebel nuns?"

"Uprising?"

"Collateral damage?"

"Don't we even get a chance to recover from the Dragon Ride?"

The Dragon Ride, although a close relative of the more familiar wind-walking, had been an arduous and exhausting experience. The violent psychic buffeting and energy shifts, the nightmare apparitions and hallucinations, all left Jim's and Doc's minds feeling folded, spindled, and mutilated. Semple might have complained of being equally ripped and crumpled, except that she was running on the adrenaline rush of a foul fury. Partway through the nerve-wrenching experience, Jim had wondered if perhaps some joker of yore, with an arcane, Hell-spawned sense of humor, had deliberately arranged for the ancient escape route to be as harrowing as possible, passing as it did though the death-stinking, blood-soaked interior of the Pyramid of the Moon, the hideous fetid lair of the Great Decapitator of the Moche, and through interstellar space, amid death rays, particle beams, and bad science fiction as Battlestar Galactica fought off an attack by the Cylons under Count Baltar.

Jim looked from Doc to Semple as another burst of gunfire rattled the here and now. "I don't know about you two, but I'd be willing to move on someplace else." Semple stared at him grimly but said nothing. Jim grimaced and shook his head. He knew she was upset, but the facts had to be faced. "I hate to say this, babe, but this place is trashed beyond repair and I really don't see how it can do us or anyone else any good to get involved in some feminist jihad."

To underline his point, a faint tremor shook the ground, but Semple could only snarl. "They wrecked my fucking place. I want to see someone suffer for what's happened to it."

The clap of a distant grenade going off made Doc shake his head. "It can be kinda hard to extract payback when you're outnumbered and outgunned."

Jim immediately backed him up. He felt sorry for Semple, but the shooting was coming closer. "He's right, girl. Our best bet is to get the fuck out of here."

Semple, however, was ready to make a stand. "And how the hell do we do that? After that damned Dragon Ride, none of us has an iota of energy left. We couldn't so much as levitate across the room."

She had a serious point, but Jim was starting to lose patience. "So what do you suggest we do?"

Before Semple could answer, something moved in the shadows by the fallen Moorish archway. A young woman stepped around a curved panel from the fallen dome. Her head was shaved cue-ball smooth, and she wore a red robe with a strange gold insignia of a clawhammer and three nails on the breast. This had to be the new uniform of Bernadette and her mutineers; the red of the habit was most likely symbolic of the blood spilled by the serial killer Jesus, while the meaning of the hammer and nails was pretty much self-evident. A little incongruously, the nun-militant wore paratroopers' heavy-duty lace-up jump boots, and bandoleers of ammunition across her chest. She also held a late-twentieth-century machine gun trained on the three of them. The rebel nun seemed in no way intimidated by the sudden appearance of Semple, Jim, and Doc. The muzzle of the weapon didn't waver as she moved through the arch and into the chamber.

"The three of you stay right where you are."

A second concussion grenade exploded and the nearest rubber guard folded and collapsed, a thick, dark blue liquid flowing from a rent in its hide and oozing thickly across the floor of the corridor. Plaster drifted down from the ceiling and small fires burned amid the debris of previous explosions. Red-clad nuns advanced down the corridor in fast zigzag rushes, firing bursts from their MAC-10s and AK-47s. Even with the help of Semple's strange, soft-shelled robot guards, it was clear to Mr. Thomas that Aimee and her handful of loyalists were fighting a losing battle. They were steadily being pushed back, room by room, corridor by corridor, staircase by staircase. The rebels, in their new red habits and freshly shaved heads, were taking casualties, but it hardly mattered. Clearly these red sisters were happy to go to the pods in the righteous cause of Bernadette, the Hammer of God, their leader and inspiration. If it came to a battle of attrition, Aimee's little band simply lacked the numbers to win. The hopeless course was set for their last stand. Run out of her Heaven and forced to take refuge in the despised domain of her destroyed sibling, her options were scant: it was either go down fighting or give herself up for crucifixion.

Mr. Thomas had no desire to make Thomas the Goat's last stand, but from where he stood at the far end of the burning corridor, as far from the fighting as he could get, he wasn't holding out that much hope. His eyes were burning and watering from the smoke, and precious little retreat remained. He was starting to resign himself to taking on a new incarnation. He could only tell himself that maybe he'd gone as far as he could go in goat form; perhaps it was time for a change. As far has he could see, his one hope to remain in this reality was somehow to separate himself so the mutineers wouldn't associate him with Aimee. He needed to make himself look like an innocent victim, or maybe even a helpless hostage. Could he get himself some kind of Lamb of God gig with the new regime, and lie around all day being fed beer and glossy magazines by bald, red-robed nuns? It was a long shot. He knew "Goat of God" didn't exactly have the same ring to it.

Another grenade went off and started a flurry of commotion among the defenders. Mr. Thomas couldn't quite see what was happening through all the smoke and dust until the dirty white rag was waved aloft tied to a piece of broken lath. That message was unmistakable. Aimee McPherson had given up the fight. The towel had been thrown in. Mr. Thomas knew it wasn't a flag of truce. It had to be unconditional surrender. As far as he was concerned, the only question that remained was whether or not a goat could be crucified.

"It would seem we have a Mexican standoff."

Despite the machine pistol the red-robed nun had pointed at Doc, a lot of her militancy dropped away when she found herself staring down the barrel of the Gun That Belonged to Elvis. The legendary pistol had magically appeared in Doc's right hand, trained at her head. At the sight of her confusion, Doc laughed. "I wouldn't be too upset, my dear. Drunk and sober, I've been doing this kind of thing for a very, very long time. It's no disgrace to be faced down by Doc Holliday." He inclined his head and looked more closely at the young woman. "Don't I know you?"

The rebel nun looked sheepish. "Yeah, Doc. You know me. You'd probably recognize me straightaway if it wasn't for the haircut."

Doc frowned. "You're . . . "

"I'm Aura-Lee. I used to work at . . . "

Doc smiled. He didn't need to be told any more. "Right."

"Until I renounced the sins of the flesh—"

"The sins of the flesh? Aren't we getting a little overbearingly Victorian? From what I recall, you used to quite enjoy your work."

"I only enjoyed it because I didn't know any better. Bernadette told us—"

"Bernadette? Who the hell is Bernadette?

"Bernadette is the Hammer of God."

Doc was starting to look as though he didn't have time for this. "What the fuck kind of title is the Hammer of God?"

"You knew her as Trixie."

"Trixie? She's behind all this? That troublemaking bitch is call-

418

ing herself 'Bernadette the Hammer of God'? I always had her pegged as whorehouse lawyer, but I didn't think she'd go as far as to infect you all with bloody Jesus."

Aura-Lee looked exceedingly unhappy. "I always liked you, Doc. You always treated me on the up and up, but you have to be careful what you say about Bernadette. Very soon, she's going to be deciding your fate."

Doc's eyes narrowed dangerously. "A lot of people have been convinced they could decide Doc Holliday's fate."

"Please be careful. She'll be here very soon."

A cherub, scarcely taller than Mr. Thomas, clad in a red diaper with little fleecy wings growing out of his back, clambered over a pile of rubble. Mr. Thomas might have laughed at the spectacle except for the big chrome .44 Magnum the cherub had gripped in his chubby fist, and the intimation that, small as he might be, he knew how to use it. When he saw Mr. Thomas, he stopped in his tracks and brought the gun up. "Feel lucky, punk? I suggest you raise your hands, nice and easy, now."

Mr. Thomas didn't like having guns pointed at him, especially by fat little cherubs with implausible baby voices pretending they were Clint Eastwood. It took him a moment to find his own voice, and when he did, it rasped from smoke and apprehension. "I can't raise my hands up. All I have is hooves."

"So raise your hooves."

"I can't do that. If I did, I'd fall over. I'm a bloody quadruped, you moron."

The cherub brandished the Magnum in Mr. Thomas's face. "Don't you call me a moron."

Mr. Thomas instantly realized that insulting anyone holding the most powerful handgun in the world, even if that someone was only three feet tall, was a moronic act. "Listen, kid, I'm sorry. I'm suffering from a lot of stress, you see?"

The cherub stuck to the basics. "Quadruped or not, you're my prisoner."

"That's the problem, isn't it? All this has nothing whatsoever to do with me. I'm an innocent bystander, aren't I? A noncombatant, look you. I'm not even supposed to be here."

"You'll have to tell that to Bernadette. As far as I'm concerned, you're a prisoner."

The cherub turned. Bernadette and her red nuns were coming down the corridor. The cherub gestured to Bernadette. "There's another one over here, Mighty Hammer."

As Bernadette came through the arch and into the chamber, followed by her armed cohorts and bound prisoners, one of whom was a loudly protesting goat, Doc and Aura-Lee continued to stand with their guns mutually trained on each other. Doc knew that the arrival of the main body of the insurgents totally changed the dynamics of the confrontation, and the new odds were definitely not in his favor. Doc wasn't about to admit this, though, or even acknowledge it in word or deed. Two dozen guns might have been pointed at him, but he was quite prepared to bluff to the last. Jim and Semple, being completely unarmed, knew they had little choice but to go wherever Doc's lead might take them. Semple had no illusions of receiving any mercy at the hands of Bernadette.

As Jim pretty much expected, Doc started his game with an openly reckless lack of concern. He looked past Aura-Lee and called out cheerfully to Bernadette, "How are you doing, Trixie? Aura-Lee tells me you're calling yourself the Hammer of God these days. Do you really think God needs a hammer?"

Bernadette colored and cast about for an angry retort, but Doc pressed blithely on. "Is that Donna I see there with her head all shaved and toting that M-16? And Lisa and Linda and Matilida, and Charlotte at the back there trying to hide her face? Seems to me we've got ourselves a real reunion, all my whores who went holy."

Bernadette finally found her voice.

"What the hell are you doing here, John Holliday?"

"*John* Holliday, is it? You can't call me Doc anymore? After all the good times we spent together, way back whenever it was?"

Bernadette flushed all the way to the top of her shaved head. The other ranks were looking to her for guidance, but even with a multitude of guns at her back it wasn't easy to confront Doc Holliday's glib and perverse charm. "*Good times.* You can talk about *good times* after all the awful things you forced us to do?"

"Isn't your memory getting a little distorted here, Trixie, my darling? I don't recall anyone being forced to do anything."

"I asked you what you were doing here, Doc."

"Doing here? Why, Trixie, I'm hardly doing anything here. I just happened to stop by on my way out of Hell with my good friends Jim Morrison and Semple McPherson."

At the mention of Semple's name, Aimee immediately let out a wail. "Semple, do something, for God's sake. She's going to crucify us."

An angel clapped a hand over Aimee's mouth, cutting off her cries. Semple didn't move; she was too focused on the interchange between Doc and Bernadette. Bernadette took a step closer to Doc. "Maybe you should have stayed in Hell."

As Bernadette spoke, the environment shook once more, this time violently, and with a deep and primally disturbing sub-bass rumble that threatened to liquefy the brain of everyone present. As the shaking escalated to a bouncing side-to-side motion, a number of people were thrown to the ground, and wide fissures appeared in the floor. An angel fluttered his wings, attempting to maintain his balance, and a red nun dropped her Uzi, causing it to discharge and accidentally waste two of her comrades. As Jim braced his legs, struggling to stay on his feet, he saw a way to back Doc's play. Capitalizing on the fact that victorious euphoria was rapidly being replaced by a superstitious dread, he shouted so all the nuns could hear, "It doesn't look like God's too pleased with what you've been up to."

The shaking subsided slightly and Semple took this as her cue to step up beside Doc and face Bernadette. She took a more practical tack. "As the creator of this place, I think I should warn you that it's about to come completely apart."

Even Bernadette put her theocratic power play to one side in the face of the emergency. "What do we do?"

"My best bet would be to pool our resources and wind-walk the fuck out of here before we're all toast."

Semple's expression was bleak. "With our resources, the only place we're going is Heaven."

Jim had never seen Aimee's Heaven in its overtime Walt Disney glory, and the damage and decay only caused him to wonder why anyone in their right mind would ever have wanted to live there. Most of the buildings were now burned-out, smoke-scarred ruins. The great lawn was plowed up by shell craters, and a World War II vintage Nazi Tiger tank, crudely painted a garish scarlet, stood abandoned on Aimee's favorite terrace overlooking the lake, where it had apparently been shelling the bejesus out of the Great Cloister with its turret-mounted eighty-eight. Shells and mortars had shattered the trees on the headland where virgins once danced, and reduced the Maxfield Parrish temple to a pile of rubble. Dead bluebirds littered the ground, where they'd expired with beaks agape and feet in the air. Weird mutated Bambis lurked in the ruins, five-legged and two-headed, Siamese twins and ones who looked perfectly normal except for foam at the edges of their nostrils and a distant rabid stare. The lake itself was now nothing more than a gray-green expanse of dead, polluted water with the flotsam of conflict floating on its oily surface, while over everything lowered a threatening sky the color of elderly mold.

As Jim got to his feet after falling heavily out of the end of the wind-walk, he looked round in total disbelief. "What the fuck *is* this place, some kind of physical representation of clinical depression?" He glanced at one of Bernadette's angels who had emerged right beside him. "*This* is what you were fighting over?"

Just to complicate matters even further, the mass wind-walk from Semple's imploding environment had turned out to be a major disaster. Jim had been one of the lucky ones. He'd only materialized in Heaven a couple of feet off the ground and suffered nothing worse than a mildly bruising fall. A half dozen of Bernadette's nuns had been so tightly bunched up when they made their exit that they had merged in transit into a hideous composite of limbs, heads, and tattered pieces of bloody garment protruding from a shapeless mass of amorphous flesh like a joint nightmare of Francis Bacon and John Carpenter. Doc had emerged close to this abhorrent mess of human meat and was staring at it with grim revulsion. The heads and mouths that remained on the outside of the quivering mound of tissue started to scream in unison. "Finish us! Finish us!"

Doc turned and beckoned quickly to Bernadette. "Are you going to get your people to destroy that thing or do I have to shoot it myself?"

"Shoot it?" Bernadette looked groggy and was having difficulty grasping what was going on. She might even have been regretting her grab for power.

Doc glared angrily at her. "Yes, shoot it. Or blow it up with a grenade. Put the poor bastards out of their misery one way or another."

The screaming went on. "Finish us! Finish us!"

Bernadette was close to panic. "I can't waste my own people."

Doc's voice was tinged with contempt. "It goes with the territory. Put up or shut up."

Bernadette held out a hand and a nun gave her a German stick grenade. Doc tried to shout a warning as she pulled out the pin. "Let the rest of us get fucking clear first!"

But he was too late. She'd already tossed the potato masher into the screaming flesh.

A large number of nuns and angels ran straight for the lake to wash away the gore. Among them was Semple, who had a clot of brain tissue lodged in her hair, but most came to a halt before they reached the water's edge. Already spooked by the wind-walk and the subsequent vile disaster and explosion, the sight of a huge white letterbox-format screen, more than seventy feet across, rising majestically from the waters of the lake had the majority of them down on their knees, praying for their souls and sanity. The screen continued to rise until it was floating ten feet above the surface, with no visible means of support. It was hardly a biblical apparition, neither a leviathan nor a burning bush. Either of those might have been more understandable to the nuns. At least they would have been congruent with their religious zeal. Something so techno-geometric filled them with more irrational dread than the sight of Jonah's whale, a pillar of fire, or the Archangel Gabriel playing a Miles Davis composition on his trumpet.

Jim was probably one of the first to realize what it was: a big Diamond Vision projection TV screen of the kind that had come into use at big-time stadium rock concerts a few years after his death. Certainly, along with Doc and Semple, he was one of the few who didn't go into a paroxysm of Pentecostal confusion when the first image appeared on the screen. To Jim's relief, it wasn't some rerun of a middle-aged Mick Jagger in concert, but a logo sequence of a woman's arm brandishing a gleaming sword, rising slowly from a crystal-clear, pristine lake that put Aimee's stagnant body of water to shame. The arm was accompanied by a written legend in veve-Voodoo characters. After holding for about twenty seconds, it was replaced by three huge and formidable close-ups of Dr. Hypodermic, Danbhala La Flambeau, and Baron Tonnerre. They peered from the screen as though, via some two-way system, they were seeing the inhabitants of Heaven just as the inhabitants were seeing them.

After carefully inspecting whatever image they were viewing, Hypodermic glanced at La Flambeau. "It's all going according to plan, wouldn't you say?"

Although Jim well knew that gods were impossibly hard to read, they seemed inordinately pleased at the ravages that Aimee's Heaven had so far suffered. Doc glanced at Jim. "What do you think they're doing this for?"

La Flambeau leaned forward as though searching for something. Finally she spotted what she sought, smiled, and pointed. "There you are, Jim Morrison. And Doc Holliday, too. Where's the McPherson girl?"

"She's washing her hair. She got somebody's brains in it."

La Flambeau glanced at the male gods on either side of her and then looked down at Jim and Doc. "The Doctor and the Baron don't particularly want to admit it, but we all feel that all three of you have done an excellent job."

Jim and Doc looked at each other in surprise. "We have?"

"Indeed you have. This place is now a shambles and no new religion is going to start up here."

Doc raised a dangerous eyebrow. "And that's what we've been doing? Putting down self-appointed deities?"

Jim was thinking. "What I don't understand is why you should need us to do the dirty work. I mean, you're gods—you're all-powerful. You could have taken out Anubis with a deftly aimed thunderbolt anytime you wanted."

The Baron scowled. Jim had never heard him speak in English before and his voice rolled out like thunder on the mountain. "We're gods, little man. We have more important considerations to absorb our time and our energy. We're too ancient to get our own hands dirty. And why should we, when we can manipulate the human dead to do it for us?"

La Flambeau smiled indulgently. "The McPherson girl set in motion a chain of events that caused Gojiro to destroy both Moses and Anubis. And then these women crucified the one who wanted to be Jesus. And now you appear to have neutralized the absurd Aimee and this equally ridiculous Bernadette who calls herself the Hammer of God."

Unfortunately, Bernadette chose that moment to demonstrate that she wasn't quite as neutralized as La Flambeau might have assumed. She stood up in eighteen inches of dirty water, where she'd been washing the blood from her hands and face, and stared truculently at the big screen. "Listen, you trio of abominations. I am a servant of the One True God—"

Doc attempted to head her off. "Trixie, my dear, I advise you to table this defiant little speech of yours. You can't even start to comprehend the kind of power you're going up against."

Bernadette glanced back at Doc but decided to ignore him. Once again she faced the screen. "I am the servant of God and nothing you demons can do will deflect me from my purpose." She gestured to Doc and Jim. "I have the protection of faith around me, and if I decide to crucify these agents of Lucifer that you send against me, there's nothing you can do to stop me."

Some of the red nuns seemed encouraged enough to start retrieving their guns. Jim feared that defeat was about be snatched from the jaws of victory, and he shouted at the Mystères, "I know you don't like to get your hands dirty, but why the fuck don't you zap her right now and save us all a whole lot of trouble?"

The smile with which La Flambeau responded to Jim was nothing short of patronizing. "I wouldn't worry about her too much, *mes petits*. She is an alarmingly stupid human being and very soon she is actually going to meet her One True God."

When she heard a sound behind her, Semple spun around and grabbed for the machine pistol, spraying water from her wet hair like a dog coming in from the rain. Only the sound of a familiar voice stopped her from firing blind. "Semple, it's all right, it's only me."

Semple had been bent over what might well have been the last functioning sink in Heaven, washing the brains out of her hair with some of Heaven's remaining hot water. Realizing she wasn't going to get properly clean in the chaos by the lake, she had hunted through rubble-strewn rooms to find this final intact bathroom. By way of a precaution, she had picked up a red nun's machine pistol that had been dropped in the confusion, and she didn't lower it as she pushed her hair out of her eyes and regarded Aimee with slit-eyed distrust. Her sibling stood in the doorway of the bathroom in a filthy robe. "Please Semple. . . . "

Semple's lip curled. "Please Semple, what? Maybe I should just shoot you right there where you're standing."

"I know I did a bad thing, but . . . "

"You know I've literally been to Hell and back since you saw me last?"

A hairline crack snaked across the ceiling. Both Aimee and Semple looked up at it. "If someone doesn't stabilize this place, we're going to be in an empty void without even a place to stand."

"This Jim of yours, he could help pull Heaven back together?"

"Jim? Are you out of your mind? He's not the Heaven-building type. He hates bluebirds."

"He'd do it for you, wouldn't he?"

"Maybe for a while, but in the end he'd get bored and want to move on."

"Could he at least help to stabilize it?"

Semple sighed and lowered the gun. "I suppose he might, but it wouldn't stop there, would it? I know you, Aimee. You always have to push it. You always have to have that little bit more."

"If this place falls apart, I'll be finished."

"You'll survive, Aimee."

"Will I? You've seen what happened when we were separated."

"If Jim wants to leave, I'm going with him."

"You'd choose a man over your sister? You'd just leave me to waste away and vanish?"

Semple turned; she couldn't face her sister. "Shit, Aimee, don't the guilt trips ever stop?"

Jim was becoming more than a little concerned about the deteriorating condition of the environment. It had been a mess when they had arrived; now it was becoming messier by the minute. Jagged orange-white lightning crashed between huge thunderheads that were rapidly moving in from beyond the mountains. The lake moved with bizarre and chaotic ripples, and huge bubbles broke the surface. The great screen still hung over it, but the images of the Mystères were continuously distorted. The ground under Jim's feet quivered, while on the headland a small but growing wind vortex whirled dirt, dead leaves, and the limp, lifeless corpses of bluebirds into the air. In the middle of it all, Bernadette was attempting to rally her nuns and angels. Jim yelled to Doc, "By the looks of it, we've got some apocalyptic trouble coming hard down on us."

A sudden sinkhole, some twenty feet wide, opened in the terrace, right under the scarlet Tiger tank. The machine crashed down into it and its gas tank exploded, shooting flame, black smoke, and chunks of hot metal into the air. Doc coughed blood into his hankerchief and shook his head. "And I fear this is the bona fide end of the world. At least for this cosmic neck of the cosmic woods."

In confirmation of just how bona fide the end of the world really was, a great light like something from the Book of Revelation blossomed in the sky. A nun began screaming, "It's God, I see God!"

Doc stared at the sky with a resigned and quizzical expression. "Either that or a thermonuclear airburst was just added to our catalogue of woe."

A section of corridor ceiling crashed down behind Aimee and Semple, and the two of them broke into a run. A crystal chandelier was dripping liquid glass like melting ice. The vibration was now worse than the worst earthquake Semple had ever experienced in lifeside Los Angeles or San Francisco. She was still carrying the gun she'd found, but she had little idea as to what she was going to do next. Her single impulse was to get out into the open before the entire structure collapsed and buried them. She imagined that if one was buried alive it could take an agonizing time to expire and that wasn't the way she wanted to return to the pods, fighting for breath as dirt filled her mouth, nose, and lungs, and chunks of masonry crushed her bones. Her only thought was to get back to Jim and Doc, and if relying on the two men was the best she could come up with, she knew she was tactically tapped out.

The building shook again and a huge chunk of plaster smashed into the floor directly in front of them. Aimee stumbled over a fallen beam and would have gone down if Semple hadn't grabbed her by the arm. "Just keep moving, okay? Just keep moving."

Aime clung to Semple, her grip like a vice. "Semple, promise me."

"Promise you what?"

"Promise you won't let me just disappear into nothing."

The white light became approximately spherical and touched down between the lake and the terrace, if "touched down" was the right phrase. Bit by bit it began to diminish until it was no longer so hard on the eyes, and a figure became visible at its center. Jim wondered if perhaps one of the Mystères had relented and decided to rescue them after all. Hypodermic, La Flambeau, and Tonnerre were still up on the screen, but the chance remained that some other Voodoo god had taken pity on them. If he was really lucky, maybe it was the beautiful Erzulie-Severine-Belle-Femme, or at least Ogou Baba or the venerable Marie-Louise.

The glare of the sphere not only diminished, but flattened to the ground, became two-dimensional, and spread rapidly outward, running across what had once been Aimee's prize lawn, hugging the contours in a perfect geometric ring of bright energy. Many of the nuns fled as it came toward them, but since Doc was standing his ground, Jim did the same, and as the arc of energy went past and through him he felt nothing but a slight electric tingle. He looked to Doc for some kind of comment, but Doc was staring intently at the figure that stood in the epicenter of the power ring.

The figure was certainly not one of the Voodoo gods Jim had previously seen, and totally lacked any trace of their characteristic flamboyance. In many respects, it resembled a Carthusian monk, in its full-length gray robe. The cowl was pulled up and forward over the being's face, so it was fully hidden from Jim. As the ring of light reached what seemed to be some outer perimeter and faded to nothing, the figure slowly turned and raised a hand in greeting to the three Mystères on the screen, who, in turn, bowed with infinite courtesy. The exchange was so mutually respectful that Jim could only assume the salutations were between entities who were acknowledged equals. With the niceties of formal protocol observed, the robed figure shifted its attention to what was going on around it, and actually spoke. To Jim's complete surprise, the figure's voice had the carefully trained and modulated tones of an English Shakespearean actor. "Would someone like to explain what exactly is going on here?"

Jim looked at Doc and Doc looked at Jim, and all of the nuns looked at each other. Since the question had not been specifically directed at anyone in particular, everyone seemed to be wondering who ought to answer and waiting for someone else to step into the breach. For a moment it looked as though Doc was going to make the move. He drew himself up to his full height and coughed once, but before he could utter a word, Semple and Aimee appeared on the terrace. Semple looked more angry and distraught than Jim had ever seen her. She also had a gun in her hand, a small, light-caliber machine pistol that must have been dropped by one of the red nuns. At first sight of the robed figure, she didn't hesitate. She lifted the pistol and fired a withering, full-auto burst straight at it.

When Semple saw Anubis's onetime Dream Warden standing on the scorched earth between the terrace and the lake, all thought and reason left her. She lifted the gun and squeezed the trigger. She didn't even know if the pistol would fire at all. It might even have been out of ammunition and completely useless. It actually came as a total surprise when the thing roared and bucked in her hand, spraying out the entire contents of the clip in what seemed like little more than a second. She was equally surprised when the burst of fire had no effect whatsoever on its target. With a move so leisurely it could only have been a time distortion, the Dream Warden raised a hand, and a curved, shimmering, bullet-stopping energy field appeared in front of his body. Furious at the ineffectual pointlessness of her reaction, Semple hurled the gun petulantly to the ground, anticipating hideous retribution at any moment. Her third surprise was when the Dream Warden, instead of blasting her to horrible perdition, merely sounded a little disappointed. "Now, is that any way for old acquaintances to greet each other?"

"*Acquaintances?*"

"We were both at the court of Anubis."

"You were the fucking heart of darkness, the evil behind the throne . . . "

The Dream Warden sounded quite pleased with himself. "I can pull together rather a good show when I put my mind to it."

"A *show* . . . ?"

"Couldn't you tell I was feeding his madness? I like to think that you and I, with a little help from Gojiro, did a reasonably efficient job of getting rid of him and his wretched kingdom."

Semple almost pleaded. "*Who* are you?"

The Dream Warden sighed. "Oh dear, I suppose it was a mistake to arrive in the Dream Warden drag, but I do rather like the way it stops people from wanting me to do things for them."

The Dream Warden unbelted the robe and let it fall to the ground at his feet, and Semple found herself facing a cultivatedly distinguished middle-aged man who greatly resembled the actor Christopher Plummer. He was dressed in an immaculate double-breasted white linen Savile Row suit with every crease as sharp as a knife. An aquamarine shirt with a matching Windsor-knotted tie gave a roguish, almost mobster aspect to the ensemble, although this was offset by a slight femininity of posture. Semple wasn't sure if he was actually homosexual or merely arrogantly English. A white Persian cat that must have been hidden in the sleeve of the Dream Warden robe scrambled up onto his shoulder and sat staring at Semple with blue eyes that nearly matched the shirt and tie.

Although this revelation was more than enough to convince Semple that she was in the presence of an entity of great importance and power, she was still without a clue as to who this might be. Jim was looking around curiously; even Aimee herself was totally mystified. The only one who appeared to suspect was Doc, who had an amused smile on his face. It took Mr. Thomas, emerging from where he'd been hiding behind a marble copy of Michelangelo's David, to effect a less-than-conventional introduction.

"Don't you gaggle of fucking idiots know who this is? It's Him, isn't it? Yahweh, the Lord God Jehovah, and all of the other Thousand Names. It's bloody God himself, look you."

The voice of a nun came from somewhere at the back of the crowd. "I told you it was God."

God made a self-depreciating gesture. "I used to be Allah as well, but we had to subdivide around the twelfth century. The crusades were making us schizophrenic."

A number of nuns were already on their knees, and angels and cherubs were starting to gaze with all the adoration that was expected of them. Aimee, on the other hand, wasn't buying so soon. "You're really God? Not just another of Semple's malicious pranks?"

God sighed. "What did you expect? George Burns?"

"There's been a lot of unfortunate confusion here lately."

"Surely you don't want me to prove it to you? I don't have to walk on the lake or anything, do I?" He noticed Doc Holliday at a distance and nodded with genteel courtesy. "How are you, Dr. Holliday?"

"I'm feeling pretty well, my Lord. How about your good self?"

"I fear I may be looking at a few problems here."

Aimee stared at Doc. All the color had drained from her face. "He *is* God."

Doc gestured in the affirmative. "The Lord of Hosts and none other."

God looked amusedly resentful. "So, Aimee McPherson, you need Doc Holliday to confirm my identity?"

Not only did Aimee's color return, but she was rapidly developing the expression of a near-psychotic. "Damn right, I need Doc Holliday to confirm your identity. The last one had a halo and called himself Jesus, but then he turned out to be Ted Bundy. How I am I supposed to tell? When did you ever make thyself beknown to me? When was I granted the revelation? When did I ever see even one of your faces? I've devoted my entire life and hereafter to lauding and magnifying your name, and what have you given me in return? Nothing. Zip. Nada. Zilch. Not a sign, not a rainbow that I didn't have to make myself. Not so much as a phone call. You couldn't even pick up a gold phone and tell me, 'Keep up the good work, Sister Aimee'? Oh no. That would have been too much effort. And now you're surprised I don't immediately recognize you and fall on my face when you show up in your fancy handmade ice-cream suit and your four-hundred-dollar blow-dry haircut. Well, I'm sorry, my Lord, but adoration is supposed to be a two-way street."

God gestured to Doc. "You see what I mean? They all expect something from me."

Doc demurred. "Fortunately, I have such a bad reputation, few are disappointed at the way I treat them."

The Persian cat smiled at Jim. "He's very good at talking to everyone at once."

"I don't know how He does it."

"Well, He's God, isn't He?"

"It all sounds like babble to me."

"That's because you have a poet's sensibility. Mr. Thomas hears much the same thing. The others all think they're having a one-on-one with their Creator."

"What are they all talking about?"

"Most of the nuns are just behaving like fans, gushing compliments and making themselves ridiculous. A few want favors, dispensations, or forgiveness for their sins. The Aimee half of the McPherson sisters has totally lost it, and she's berating him as though he were an unfaithful lover. The hooker called Trixie, who turned herself into Bernadette, is boasting about all the sinners she's sent to the pods on his behalf, and he and Doc are discussing the finer points of single-malt scotch."

"That's a pretty neat trick."

"I think he'd rather dispense with the rest and just be talking to Doc."

"And what's Semple doing?"

"She's keeping quiet. She seems a little bemused."

"I'm sorry, Aimee, but you have fallen for the same self-delusion as hundreds of thousands before you. You humans constantly operate under the assumption that I, God, give a rat's ass about the petty comings and going of a species of big-brained, overdeveloped, and rather violent monkeys. It's just plain absurd. Some of you start praying to me when you lose your bloody car keys. Okay, a prayer is a prayer, and I don't mind fending off the odd holocaust or arranging a cancer remission if it's in a good cause, but *car keys*? Football games? Lotto? The two-thirty at Aqueduct? Give me a break. It's nothing more than theological junk mail. All it makes me do is want to put as much distance between myself and humanity as I can. Yes, bad things do happen to good people. And no, Aimee, there is no Santa Claus. It's a cruel and random universe, full of black holes and entropy, where all manner of terrible things happen, deserved or not. And contrary to popular opinion, I didn't make it, either in a week or two billion years, so you can't blame me when shit comes to pass. Poor little crippled children are a DNA freakout, not a result of any malice on my part. Ebola was a result of you morons cutting down the rainforest, not my divine bloody judgment. I only added a few of the finishing touches—orchids, woodpeckers, and, to my eternal shame, you nasty humans. Believe me, as far as the rest goes, the math is far too complicated. The universe was originally put together by a consortium of forces that I can only just understand and you couldn't even begin to take my word for. Have you any idea what the numbers for the Theory of Everything look like? They make quantum mechanics look like two plus two."

"But it says in the Bible—"

"I'm God, so please don't quote the Bible to me. That's another of the great fallacies. I didn't write that ridiculous book. You think I have nothing better to do with my time than sit around writing inane dietary laws, accounts of primitive battles, and long, boring lists of who begat whom? There's a Gideon Bible in every hotel room only because MKULTRA put microchips under the gold leaf on the cover. The hippies who used to use the pages to roll joints with when they ran out of skins had the right idea. The damned Bible was cobbled together by a bunch of ancient, too-long-in-the-sun psychopaths sitting in caves in the stinking desert, finished up by a conspiracy of patriarchal prehistoric sheep herders who wanted to believe that, somewhere in the sky, there was some Great Shepherd who would take care of them the way they took care of their blasted sheep and goats. And don't look at me like that, Mr. Thomas. I have nothing against goats; in fact, I number them among my more likable creations. It's the shepherds I have the quarrel with. I mean, they only had to see a bloody bush catch fire and they were off and running. Do you know just how stupid the original Moses was? It took the fool forty years to get across the bloody Sinai. T. E. Lawrence did it on a camel in less than a week and he took time off to kill one of his boyfriends on the way by dropping him in quicksand."

Aimee was floundering. She would have liked to believe that this so-called God was some preposterous impostor, but she knew in her heart that she was talking to the real deal and her heart was plunging to the sub-basement. Just to make matters worse, each time she opened her mouth, it sounded like the blurt of an imbecile. "You mean Lawrence of Arabia?"

God nodded. "The very same. I thought O'Toole played him very nicely."

"But what about Jesus? Didn't you send him to save us all from original sin?"

"That's what he told you, wasn't it? Actually, I just wanted to get him to leave home. The kid was a pain to be around."

"But the Jesus that was here—"

"That homicidal idiot. I don't know if he was the genuine article or not. It's been so long, I've actually lost track. Either way, that boy was a born troublemaker. I take it you crucified him yet again? It's usually the best thing for him. It gets him out of the way for a while. The only trouble is, he comes back twice as nasty. He was actually quite well-meaning the first couple of times around. But then the power started to get to him. Loaves and fishes weren't good enough. Oh dear me, no. First he got into starting wars and pogroms; now the latest fad seems to be old movies and serial killing."

"But he might have really been your son?"

"Who can tell these days, with so many impostors coming out of the pods? Either way, he's certainly better off crucified."

The Persian cat continued to look at Jim. "You see what I mean about multiple conversations?"

Jim nodded. "I'm beginning to get the picture."

"Aren't you glad you're well out of it?"

"I surely am."

"Now, listen, Trixie . . . "

"I'm not Trixie anymore. I'm Bernadette."

God gestured impatiently. "Yes, yes, I know all about that. You fancy yourself as Bernadette, the Hammer of God. Well, I'm sorry, lovey, I'm God and I have absolutely no need of a hammer. I have no desire to hammer in either the evening or the morning, and if I did, I'd go to the ironmongers and buy one."

"But I—"

"Please don't interrupt."

"But I was—"

"I said, don't interrupt. As it is, I'm not particularly pleased with you, and if you keep interrupting, I may have to do something judgmental. Don't you think I've had to deal with your kind before? It's really all about sex, isn't it. Sex and more bloody sex. That's all you overblown chimps seem to have on your minds. I know what those machine guns and phallic blasted missiles are all about. I've seen hundreds like you before, and you never fail to annoy me. I blame it all on that absurd prude Saint Paul. The repressed Syrian tentmaker fouled everything up. The man was completely obsessed with sex. He couldn't stand the very thought of it. Hated women more than he probably hated himself. Started all those fish-smell jokes. I never encountered such a rancid mind in anyone who managed to get himself canonized. And, believe me, there were some foully rancid saints. And then there were all the bloody Popes that came after him, and those repulsive fools Ferdinand and Isabella, not only putting up the money to find America when it wasn't lost in the first place, but also forking over the cash for the disgusting Inquisition so people could be branded with hot irons and have their eyeballs gouged out and be hanged and burned alive, and all in my name. I'm God, damn it! I absolutely don't care what people do in the privacy of their bedrooms, or even out in the street, for that matter, as long as they don't annoy the horses. I think Tennessee said it best when he had Blanche Dubois deliver the line, "I'm never disgusted by anything human as long as it isn't unkind or violent," or words to that effect, I don't remember it all that well. My recent trouble with Marlon has quite put the exact text of *Streetcar* out of my mind. Unfortunately, most of what your kind do is very unkind and ultraviolent. Do you really think that, if I wanted human beings to be celibate, I would have given them genitals and the urge to use them in the first place?"

He halted in his holy tirade and looked hard at Bernadette. "You're not taking any of this in, are you?"

"I'm trying to."

God sniffed. "I'm not sure you're trying hard enough."

"I'm still a little confused."

"Yes, and you'll probably stay confused for all of eternity, so I suggest you go away, think about it, and stop bothering me."

He clapped his hands once and Bernadette/Trixie vanished into thin air. God then turned and looked at Jim.

✳

"And what about you, Morrison? You don't have much to say for yourself?"

"I didn't think there was much point in adding to the babble."

"That's right—you used to be a poet, didn't you? I'm glad you still have the magical hearing, even if you refuse to do anything with it."

"There's also the small matter that I never really believed in you."

God laughed. "And now you feel a little sheepish, with me standing here in all my glory?"

Jim spread his hands and half-smiled. "Something like that."

"What was that line? 'You cannot petition the Lord with prayer'?"

"That's what I wrote."

God smiled. "And never was a truer line written. Do you know how irksome it can be getting prayed at all the time? I was just telling Aimee McPherson all about it."

"I had teenage fans when I was a rock star."

"Then you do have a vague idea. Is something else bothering you?"

Jim hesitated. "There is one thing that's puzzling me."

"And what's that?"

"I thought you claimed you were the only God. 'Thou shalt have no other gods before me,' and all of that stuff." Jim gestured to the screen in the middle of the lake. "And yet you seem to have no trouble getting along with those guys."

God grinned slyly. "That's because I lied."

Jim was amazed. "You lied?"

"You think God doesn't lie?"

"I kind of assumed you were perfect."

God blinked. Now it was his turn to be surprised. "If deception was an imperfection, Shakespeare would have been a tax collector. You, if anyone, ought to know that."

436

"So why the big deal about being the one and only? It kind of set things up for a whole mess of intolerance."

God shrugged. "Maybe. But as I was just attempting to explain to the truly confused Trixie, humans hardly need an excuse to torture, slaughter, and generally victimize each other. It's a thing with us gods. You either join a pantheon or you avoid complications by putting it around that you're the one true deity. I couldn't really handle a pantheon. I believe I'm what sociologists call unclubable."

God turned his attention from Jim, looked around at everyone present, and raised an authoritarian hand.

"If you'll be so kind as to simmer down for a moment, I have a few general remarks that I'd like to address to all of you."

God waited and the babble slowly died away in Jim's head. Then God took a deep breath. "Thank you."

He paused to scan the faces that were now giving him their undivided, and, in some cases, very apprehensive attention. "As you've all probably gathered by now, I'm not overly enamored of the human race. When the Cro-Magnons started in slaughtering Neanderthals, I pretty much knew that, as a species, you were well off the rails already. I wanted to flood you all out, but I allowed that wretched Noah to talk me into letting him build his ark because he promised to save the giraffes and the rhinoceroses. A little later, I seriously believed that the aliens where going to nuke you all to extinction, but all they did was fry Sodom and Gomorrah, which I guess only tends to confirm how wrong I can be when it comes to humanity. I didn't much like the Roman Empire; the Dark Ages were a mess; I suppose the Renaissance was okay, but then the Industrial Revolution started the whole fossil fuel greenhouse thing going and I knew it would only be a matter of time before you turned it all over to the roaches. What you might call the last straw, the thing that really pissed me off, was that *Time* cover story. There it was, white out of black—GOD IS DEAD—in damned great letters, and I decided to give up on the whole pack of you. If you chose to think I was dead, so be it. I was history. You had a gang of oily evangelists to address your needs to worship, and I was about to take a cab."

At this last statement, Aimee colored beet-red. God treated her to a raised eyebrow and then continued. "In fact, I was very tempted to destroy the whole planet: fire, pestilence, plagues of frogs, every volcano going off at once. The entire apocalyptic works. I was even toying with the idea of making the sun go nova, or at least dropping a large asteroid in the Pacific Ocean. About the only thing that stopped me is that I'm still inordinately fond of giraffes and rhinos—and also cats and whales, harp seals, dolphins, bears, and penguins—so I refrained. Why should they vanish without a trace just because you bipedal bastards are unable to behave yourselves? Oh yes, I know you built some very nice cathedrals, and I really liked Marilyn Monroe and fettuccine alfredo. But they were, in turn, canceled out by your concentration camps, *Queen for a Day*, and man-made neurotoxins. In some respects, I suppose I only have myself to blame. Right back at the beginning, I should have made the entire Earth fireproof. If you'd never discovered fire, your kind would have remained a bunch of monkeys standing up to peer over the tall grass. My only excuse is that I didn't imagine you would be cunning enough to go from rubbing two sticks together to a thermonuclear weapons capability in little more than the flutter of a cosmic eyelash."

God paused to pet the white Persian cat, who was growing restless. "Thus, right or wrong, I decided against wiping you all out, and resolved instead simply to wash my hands of the great majority of you. For some time now, I've been happily going about my business with no inclination to worry about the human race. Your prayers all went into the shredder and, for the first time in about fourteen thousand years, I was without a care. Then, unfortunately, a deputation of my peers and colleagues came to me to appeal to my better nature."

God gestured to the Mystères on the big screen. "These good Voodoo people of the Island, plus also Wotan, Krishna, Isis, the White Goddess Sofia, Oogachaka, Crom, Head 58, the Lord Bacchus, Snireth-Ko the Dreamer, and even the Buddha—although he seemed a lot more preoccupied with his next earthly incarnation—all prevailed on my good graces to help them try to find a solution to the human problem. Wotan was talking about a *final* solution, but having decided once not to wipe you all out, I didn't think it was good policy to go back on my word. Also, the old boy is a little addled from all the drinking in Valhalla and he couldn't really grasp how decimating your numbers on the lifeside would hardly have helped what was really bothering them."

Again God paused. He lifted the cat down from his shoulder and placed it on the ground beside him. It rubbed against his leg and then looked up at him. "You know we're supposed to be at the meeting with Stephen Hawking? The one about trying to encourage dark matter to do something useful?"

God glanced down at the cat. "Professor Hawking has a very flexible appreciation of time. He won't mind if I'm a little late. Besides, I still have a few more choice remarks to deliver."

He looked back to the small multitude in the ruins of Heaven. "Since my friend here informs me that I'm late for my next meeting, I'll give you all the *Reader's Digest* version. In a nutshell, we gods are angry. Not being content with gratuitously overpopulating your lifeside planet to the point where it will be almost completely uninhabitable by a week from Thursday, you are streaming into the Afterlife in such numbers that the infrastructure cannot possibly support you all. The Great Double Helix is currently groaning under the weight of all the extra pods and shorting out its primary circuits. That's why we couldn't allow Wotan to go ahead with his Day of Ragnarok extermination plan. The influx of the dead would be so massive it'd red-line the macroboard, the Helix would unravel, and that would be the Fat Lady's aria for just about everything. We'd be left with another bloody singularity, then Big Bang II, and that is much too expensive a price for mankind's inability to control its numbers. Do I make myself clear so far?"

Some of the nuns nodded. Others simply avoided God's eyes.

"It was thus resolved that, as unpalatable as it might be, a deal would have to be struck with Yog-Sothoth the Unspeakable to begin to filter the human dead into a rented and previously underused section of his Black Dimension. Obviously it will not be too pleasant until those who first arrive make a few adaptations, but it will at least relieve the strain. And let's face it; if you people will voluntarily elect to go to Gehenna, you'll pretty much adapt to anything. The only stumbling block to this contingency plan was the energy drain created by the complex environments set up by some of you humans, and the quasi-divine status that was being claimed by some of the rulers of these environments. This directly challenged our own godhood and our ability to negotiate with Yog-Sothoth, who is a devious devil at the best of times. Without a negotiated settlement, the end result could be interdimensional territorial warfare, and all because of you damned irresponsible monkeys and your ridiculous birth rate. And if I ask you what an interdimensional conflict means, don't nod your heads like a flock of bloody silly sheep, because you absolutely don't have a clue and never will have."

He paused once more and gestured to Jim, Doc, and Semple. "Fortunately, some of the worst of these phony gods have now been neutralized. We have to thank Semple McPherson, Jim Morrison, and Doc Holliday for their help, albeit unwitting, in neutralizing Anubis, the phony Moses, Aimee McPherson, and the recently departed Trixie, and also alerting Lucifer and Kali to their greater responsibilities, and perhaps even convincing the aliens that they should start minding their own business and stop writing obscenities in the waving fields of grain. In other sectors, we have also arranged, via similar agents, the downfall of three fake Hitlers, one ersatz Haile Selassie, a faux Hammurabis, two Alexander the Greats, a completely implausible Ivan the Terrible, and a gang of very nasty Essenes."

Jim shook his head in bewilderment. "So we're actually secret agents of God, are we? Even though it was a secret from us as well and we didn't have a clue what we were doing?"

God smiled. "It can hardly be news that I move in mysterious ways."

Jim shrugged. "I can live with the idea of being a divine secret agent."

"And you can be justifiably proud of yourself." God indicated that a small round of applause might be in order, and most obliged, although Aimee didn't join in.

Quite the reverse, in fact. Aimee still looked a lot like the betrayed inamorata. "So, my Lord. Now that you've conspired with my sibling and these two notorious drunks to destroy the Heaven I took so many pains to create in your honor, what am I supposed to do?"

"You can do whatever you want, Aimee. I've stabilized the place so it won't decay any further. If you want, you can bring back the Bambis and bluebirds and start a nice secular little Afterlife theme park along the lines of Disneyland. Anything you like, just as long as it has absolutely nothing to do with religion."

"But I've devoted the whole of my life to religion."

"And you've done very nicely out of it, but now you're at the end of that particular road. You will have to try something else. I repeat, though, no religion, or terrible things will happen to you. Remember Ezekiel 25:17? I can still do that kind of stuff." He turned away from Aimee. "Any more questions?"

Jim stretched his back. He suddenly felt very tired. "Does this mean our jobs are at an end? I mean me, Doc, and Semple?"

"Not only that, but, as I already said, you have the gratitude of the gods, and that's no small thing."

"So we can go where we like? No more secret missions?"

"You can go where you like, dear boy. Honky-tonking with Doc Holliday, or, if you're looking for adventure, you might rejoin the Dionysian heroes, who I understand are planning a fresh assault on the Apollonians. Or, if total depravity is your craving, you could head out to Hatheg-Kla and howl and dance with the Great Ones. The choice is yours, although I did understand that you and Semple had started something."

Doc had a much more simple and direct question. "But how do we get out of here?"

God laughed. "Now, that is a piece of cake."

With an extended index finger, he described a circle on the ground and then took three paces back as a portal, rather like a giant manhole, opened in the earth. "With enough power to take you anywhere of your choosing, anyplace you are able to imagine."

And with that, God picked up his cat and rose vertically into the air. He went straight up for about twenty feet and then moved horizontally across the lake toward the screen and, by some process of complex morphing, was absorbed into it. As God entered the picture, Hypodermic offered him a cheroot and, when God gratefully accepted it, also lit it for him. "Hawking?"

God nodded. "Hawking. Even he can't be kept waiting forever."

When the four very different gods walked away into the final fade, the background was suddenly visible. They were walking away down a road constructed from yellow brick.

"Sometimes I think Hawking's smarter than any of us."

"But he's human."

"Weird, isn't it?"

As they diminished in size and their voices faded, the big screen sank slowly and majestically into the lake. A nun looked nervously at Doc. "Was that really God?"

Doc burst into wheezing laughter. "Sure thing, Sister. That was God, all right. No impostor could put on an act like that. The suit!

The cat? The accent? The whole bit? Oh yes, sweetheart, you have just met with the Almighty."

Doc was already peering down into the portal, staring at the shimmer of rainbow colors that seemed to descend for infinity. He had assumed that Semple and Jim were right behind him and was surprised when he looked back to see them still some distance away, in what, from the tenseness of their body language, looked to be a confrontational discussion. Aimee stood a few paces off, staring at the two of them. Without hearing what was being said, Doc instantly grasped the dynamic of the situation. Semple was the object in a tug of war and obligation between Jim and her sister. Bearing in mind how the two sisters had once been one, Doc could see that the conflict was virtually inevitable. He was tempted to go and join them, but decided it was a less-than-wise move. He couldn't recall ever being thanked for intervening in a domestic dispute. Doc was also aware, though, that time was pressing. Most of the nuns had already checked out, some so disconcerted by the way things had panned out that they'd ripped off their habits and were stepping off into the portal clad in nothing more than bras and panties, ensuring themselves a provocative entrance when they arrived at wherever they had selected to go.

Doc decided that all he could do was attempt from a distance to force a resolution to what looked uncomfortably like an emotional impasse. "Not wishing to interrupt you young people, but I think we ought to make up our minds where we're going to go and go there. This thing isn't going to stay open and energized forever."

Jim turned in his direction and shouted, "Hold on there a minute, Doc."

"We don't have much more than a minute. We have to go while the portal's still hot."

Jim exchanged more words with Semple and then hurried to where Doc was standing. "There's a problem."

"Haven't we had enough problems?"

"This one's a little different. Semple wants to stay here."

Although Doc had already guessed this was the situation, he still looked around at the ruins of Heaven in feigned mystification. "Why the fuck should anyone want to stay here? There isn't even a bar."

"While the shit was going down—before God showed up—her sister extracted a promise from her to stay and help her fix up the place."

"That's ridiculous. She can't hold Semple to that. God already stabilized the basics, and Aimee knows she can't rebuild her Heaven the way it was. God's going to drop the wrath on her from a great height if she does."

"Semple gave her word. She feels obligated to stick around until Aimee's back on her feet."

"Then you don't have a problem, boy. You and I will head out to Hatheg-Kla, and she can join us when she's discharged her supposed obligation."

"I'm afraid it isn't as easy as that."

"The business of the two of them just being one?"

"How did you know?"

"It wasn't hard to figure."

"Semple says Aimee all but came unglued while she was away."

"And she's afraid to be ever separated again?"

"That's about it."

"So it's more of a permanent arrangement than just helping her get back on her feet."

Jim nodded unhappily. "That is how it looks. I want Semple, but no way can I stay in this place for the duration."

"If you shack up with Semple, with her sister as a third wheel, I give the romance three weeks, tops."

"Aren't you always telling me time's relative?"

"It isn't relative where relatives are concerned."

"So what the fuck do I do, Doc?"

Doc slowly sighed. "I never found there was any percentage in giving advice to the lovelorn, but you do at least know one of the possible futures for the two of you."

"The old house in the swamp?"

"What else?"

"I should tell Semple about that. Maybe it would stop her from making me feel like a bastard for not wanting to stay."

Doc gave him a warning look. "That kind of vision shouldn't be talked about, sport. It tempts destiny too directly."

Jim and Doc both looked in the direction of Semple and Aimee. They were now in close discussion; Semple's shoulders sagged as though she were close to resignation or defeat. "I'm going to tell her about the old house."

Doc put a firm hand on Jim's arm. "I really wouldn't do that, Jim. It could set up all manner of destructive resonances."

Jim's expression was one of disbelieving suspicion. "What are you saying? That it's like telling your birthday wish?"

"No, but if it helps you understand the concept, you can think of it that way. Anyway, she seems to be coming to you."

Semple was walking quickly away from Aimee to where Jim and Doc were waiting. As she came close, it was clear that she was close to tears. Aimee was following more slowly, some distance behind her sister. Doc moved quickly to head her off and give Jim and Semple some privacy.

Semple faced Jim with a look of total desolation. "I have to stay with her. She's just had all the supports kicked out from under her. God was her whole life, don't forget. She could fade away to nothing."

Jim shook his head impatiently. "Can't you see she's conning you?"

"I know that, but I'm frightened. I . . . "

"What?"

"This time, I could be the one who fades."

"You won't, believe me."

Semple looked more conflicted than Jim had ever seen her. He gestured around at the wrecked environment. "You don't belong in this fucked-up place. You should be in Hatheg-Kla, with me. And all the other wild places."

"No, Jim, it's you that belongs in Hatheg-Kla. I have to be with Aimee."

"Are you saying you won't even come and join me?"

Semple suddenly clung to Jim. She held him for a moment and then stepped back. "Just go, Jim. Go with Doc right now. It's hopeless. I know you'd stay with me if I begged you, but in the long run you couldn't hack it. Aimee would drive you crazy. You'd get to hate me."

"For fuck's sake, woman. Forget about Aimee and come with me."

"Just go, Jim. I made a promise."

Jim hesitated for an Afterlife minute, then he turned, as though his brain had given up on the anguish of the choice and only the need to escape was driving him. That and a strange glimpse of the future. "So I'll be seeing you."

"I don't think so . . . "

Jim's suddenly smiled. In that instant he trusted the vision of the old house as much as he trusted anything. "Oh yes, you will."

"What makes you say that?"

"For once, I know something you don't know."

Before Semple could respond, Jim turned and walked to the portal. "Okay, Doc."

Semple called after Jim as Doc dropped into the portal and dematerialized. "What do you mean, you know something I don't know?"

Jim stepped into the portal himself. "You'll see."

Epilogue

On Blue Bayou . . .

Jim leaned on the porch rail with a twenty-four-ounce bottle of Ivory Coast Mamba Beer in one hand and a skinny Jamaican cheroot in the other, watching the sun sink behind the volcanoes and the sky turn bruised-fruit purple. Semple didn't mind Jim smoking cigarettes in the house; that was a given. But she claimed the cheroots stunk up the place and that Dr. Hypodermic only brought them to piss her off. Both the cheroots and the West African beer came courtesy of Dr. Hypodermic. He always brought a couple boxes of one and a case of the other on his regular visits, along with the rather large parcel of extremely assorted chemicals. Dr. Hypodermic might have tortured Jim once, but now, as a retired agent of the gods, Morrison found himself incredibly well treated. Hypodermic seemed to know when Jim was running low on supplies and would appear well before the situation threatened to become desperate. The only fly in this otherwise impeccable ointment was that Hypodermic and Semple just didn't get along. Whenever the great and ancient jet-black Rolls-Royce hearse would appear away across the swamp, driving on the surface of the water, swaying slightly on its shimmering private force field, Semple would retreat to the attic of the spooky old house to work on her dark abstract oil paintings and refuse to come out until after the Mystère had departed, which was usually after a couple of relative days of intense narcotic excess.

Jim wasn't exactly sure what lay at the root of the enmity between the two of them, but knew it had something to do with the fading and ultimate negation of Aimee. Although it had been Danbhala La Flambeau who had brought the freaked- and stressed-out Semple to Jim at the house in the Jurassic swamp, it was Hypodermic who had been there when Aimee had finally passed to nothing. He had been around during the demise of the "good" sister and must have seen things that made Semple uncomfortable around him. Semple had never really explained to Jim what exactly went down between her and Aimee that had left her as the lone survivor. He knew in broad terms that, once they were left alone in the wreckage of Heaven, a strange process of transfer had been set in motion: Semple became stronger while Aimee weakened, becoming progressively more ineffectual and transparent. Neither sibling was able to reverse or arrest what was happening to them, and Aimee had apparently gone into almost monstrous bouts of furious recriminations that only served to speed things along. What Jim didn't know, and was one of Semple's most veiled and shadowy secrets, was how Aimee had actually departed. All he knew was that it had been highly traumatic, if the state of shock in which La Flambeau had brought Semple to him was any indication.

Semple's powers of recovery were such that she had recuperated in surprisingly short order; to all outward appearances, she had returned to her old perverse, hedonistic, and curious self. The only detectable scar that remained surrounded Aimee's passing. No matter how Jim might coax her, when the night grew blue-black late and the brontosauruses sang their low winding trills off among the conifers and giant celery, the subject was strictly taboo. The closest she had ever come to discussing the matter was one night when, after consuming a number of orange and yellow pills washed down by half a bottle of fine cognac, she had smiled enigmatically. "Aimee is no more, my love. She didn't flex, and thus she broke. And when she broke, it all came to me. Ezekiel 25:17 included."

Prior to Semple's unexpected arrival, Jim had spent a long time, unshaven and rootless, on the run with a gun on his hip, wilding with Doc Holliday in all the environments that countenanced that kind of behavior. Eventually, though, he decided it was time to settle someplace and attempt to pull his poetry back together. Doc reminded him constantly that the dead had all the time in the world, but ultimately Jim felt he was compelled to go back to his avowed vocation, if he was to reclaim even a few shreds of his self-respect and not lose himself in the easy out of the drunken spaghetti-western yahoo.

Once Jim settled to it, the writing had been exciting, but after a few hundred pages, mainly concerned with the pantheon he had encountered on the Island of the Gods, it grew too weird to be workable. When he tried a course correction, he went to the other extreme and found that all he could produce was rhyming couplets so mawkish they would have sickened a greeting card hack. He'd attempted to bail himself out with William S. Burroughs cutups, Scrabble tiles, a planchette, all the way to automatic writing, hoping he'd make a little headway even if it had to be by means of chaos, random chance, and spirit intervention.

The wrestling match with his muse had been so thoroughly interrupted by Semple's arrival that his writing was again put aside as first he helped her, as best he could, regain her strength and equilibrium, and then, with that accomplished, they enjoyed a prolonged and at times quite spectacular honeymoon of depravity that found the two of them raving and rampaging through the echoing rooms of the house in the Jurassic swamp. After this frantic period of red-in-tooth-and-claw renewal, they had settled into a comfortably routine relationship that was both sheltered and secure, if perhaps a little isolated. Not that Jim and Semple lacked for diversion; over and above what they could provide for themselves when motivated by lust, devilment, or ingenuity, Doc Holliday visited on a fairly regular basis, usually crossing the swamp from the Great River in a borrowed launch or speedboat. When Doc didn't come in person, he wrote long, rambling, and very Victorian letters in a scratchy and curliqued dope-fiend hand. These missives always arrived by bizarre means that Jim assumed was a part of Doc's correspondence shtick. Often it would be an Aztec runner, with beaded apron, feathers in his braided hair, and oiled body, who would hand the familiar pale parchment envelope to either Jim or Semple without a word and then immediately turn and start jogging back along one of the less soggy trails across the swamp. On other occasions, the improvised mailman was a humanoid amphibian, a gill man who looked like a close cousin of the Creature from the Black Lagoon, and who, unlike the taciturn Aztec, expected to be invited in for a while and tipped with cans of sardines, anchovies, or tongol tuna before he swam off. The oddest and most memorable of these deliveries from Doc was brought by a trained eagle with a small leather pouch chained to its left leg. While Jim had removed the letter from the pouch, the eagle had eyed the Mammal with No Name as though the reincarnated western outlaw might make an acceptable snack to speed him on his way.

The Mammal with No Name had moved into the mansion and made himself at home in a compact little nook adjacent to the wine cellar, even before Semple had arrived. He obviously considered Jim's dark residence an ideal protection against pterodactyls and other Jurassic predators, and Jim, from his side of the arrangement, was actually glad of the company. The accumulation of what Jim later referred to as his and Semple's own private Addams Family had not stopped with the Mammal with No Name. In the wake of Jim and Semple's exhaustive and exhausting honeymoon, Mr. Thomas had arrived, looking much the worse for alcoholic wear and obviously hoping to be adopted for at least long enough to recover from his latest epic debauch. He had even offered to assist Jim with his poetry in an attempt to sweeten the bargain. In fact, no bargaining had really been necessary. Although Semple wasn't terribly fond of the Mammal with No Name, being less than keen on his interminable tall violent tales of the Old West and finding it hard to forgive him for his nun-raping past, she was overjoyed to see the goat, whom she considered a trusted comrade in arms from the fall of Necropolis. Jim, while not being as intimate with the goat as Semple, had no objection to someone who had perhaps once been an illustrious poet becoming a permanent fixture under his roof.

For a while, after they had left Aimee's derelict Heaven, Mr. Thomas had tagged along with Jim and Doc, but his physical limitations, and his habit of drinking the worst bathtub gin by the bucketful, had made it hard for him to keep up with the fast and furious, pistoleer ways of the other two. He had dropped off the wildman bandwagon and elected to become the town drunk in a strange little settlement where almost all the inhabitants had reincarnated themselves, either by accident or design, as deliberately eccentric animals.

The final arrival had been Igor. Semple's longtime butler had appeared a couple of relative months after Mr. Thomas had shown up at the house. He had apparently made it all the way from Aimee's failed Heaven under his own steam, with little help and no sense of the shortest route between two points. The trek through the Jurassic swamp had all but finished him, and he had fallen onto the porch and collapsed, one early dragonfly morning, filthy with slime and waxy and insubstantial from exhaustion and fever. As with the goat, Semple had greeted Igor as an old and trusted companion and retainer. He, too, was nursed back to servile health, and joined what was now becoming Jim and Semple's little colony in the swamp.

Once again, Jim had no objections. A butler was a largely beneficial addition. Now Jim had someone who seemed more than pleased to bring him drinks when he was too idle to get up and make them for himself; plus he was freed from doing almost any chores around the place. About the only peripheral drawback was that Jim, now living the life of the idly pampered, had started to put on weight, much as he had done on the lifeside, and a nascent beer gut was already starting to protrude over the concho belt of his leather pants.

As the sun made its last curtain call, shooting majestic rays through the valleys between the volcanic peaks, Jim continued to lean on the front porch rail. He took a swig of beer and dragged on the cheroot. The cheroots were rum-soaked and mildly opiated and produced a very slight hallucinogenic buzz. As often when stoned, Jim's mind wandered to the odd paradox that, sooner or later, a younger version of himself would come slopping through the mud and water, attracted by the light of the house, to creep and peer in the windows, just in time to watch Semple carve her initials on his back with the rapier. So far, his and Semple's lovemaking had only infrequently drawn blood, and certainly no sharp steel objects had yet been employed on the endless quest for higher and more esoteric planes of fun. So maybe it would be some time before the young Jim came tiptoeing by.

Out in the depths of the swamps, the diplodocuses and the other long-necked herbivores were starting into their sunset chorus, and a big carnivore, maybe a T-rex, was baying in triumph after an evening kill. By the rusting Buick, Mr. Thomas and the Mammal with No Name were taking turns drinking mint juleps from a plastic bucket while, overhead, pteradons were circling for one last snack while they still had the light. Jim knew that when darkness fell, the flying saucers would commence their nightly display. Of late, the UFOs of the night had been big and bright, close to a continuous traffic pattern. Paradoxically, however, no abductions had occurred, unless of course the aliens were now targeting some of the smaller dinosaurs for microchip implants and rectal probes. When, on one occasion, Jim had speculated about how it was that he hadn't been abducted a second time, Semple's answer had been simple, to-the-point, and not especially complimentary. "They've had you once already, and besides, you're a self-involved idiot who still insists on wearing foul-smelling leather jeans after all these relative years. What would any fastidious E.T. want with you?"

Jim had mixed feelings about alien abduction. He knew he would be exceedingly reluctant to go through the process again, but on the other hand the encounter with Epiphany and Devora—even though he still believed them pure illusion—had been one of the most memorable sexual thrill rides of his entire continuance, and had, after all, in its own strange way, brought him to Semple. Now and again he fantasized about somehow reuniting with the two space beauties and organizing a foursome with himself and Semple. He suspected that Epiphany and Devora were so formidably exotic that Semple might well have agreed to it, but he could hardly see how that kind of negotiation could be conducted with the big-headed little aliens.

As these thoughts passed idly through Jim's very slightly fogged brain, Semple herself came out onto the porch. "You never tire of watching the sunsets, do you?"

Jim smiled and nodded. "I guess it's a legacy from living so long in LA. The worse the pollution, the more awesome the sunset."

"Bloody red sun of fantastic LA?"

"That's about it."

Semple was wearing a long, black, almost transparent peignoir over a leather bustier, sheer black stockings, and five-inch Lucite heels, and Jim knew that in this instance it wasn't for his benefit. "Igor?"

"He was getting fractious and required a little attention."

"And where is he now?"

"Probably curled up in a fetal ball in some dark corner of the attic, nursing his cuts and welts and fondling himself while he relives his memories, detail by painful detail."

Jim had long since ceased to allow the psycho-erotic content of Semple's relationship with the diminutive butler to upset or bother him. "So he'll be in a fine mood tomorrow?"

Semple smiled. "Bright and early and more anxious to please than we've seen him in a long time. We might even get breakfast in bed."

Jim sighed and shook his head. "Is the way we exist weird or is it weird?"

Semple moved beside him. "You know as well as I do that none of the old lifeside criteria apply here. Here in the swamp it's just us. We set the standards. Whatever we do has to be normal because we are all there are."

The first of the UFOs moved across the sky; a cluster of the small, skittering red spheres that Jim always thought of as the jokers. Mr. Thomas and the Mammal with No Name both looked up and then glanced at Jim. Mr. Thomas's speech was slurred from the mint juleps. "Here they come again."

The dancing red spheres were followed by a pair of Adamski saucers, close together, line abreast with under-apron searchlights raking the swamp. Semple took hold of Jim's hand. "The Bee Man is coming."

"He is? How do you know that?"

"I can feel it."

"When?"

"Soon."

"You think it will be like the last time?"

Semple squeezed his hand harder. "It might be even more extreme. Plus we'll have the honey."

Jim turned and looked at Semple. "Is this love?"

Semple laughed. "Maybe."

Two large triangular spacecraft swung over the house. Semple's hair began to stand up on her head, and Jim could feel his own doing the same. "For all we know, its an eternal cosmic punishment," she continued, "but it doesn't seem so bad. Or maybe it's just another fake-out by the gods. Who the fuck knows for sure?" She moved close to Jim and kissed him. "And does it really matter? We're here, we're dead, and, by and large, we get along. What more can a human being hope for in eternity?"

A third triangular UFO swung low over the house, hurrying to catch up with the others.

GAYLORD F